What ʿĪsā Ibn Hishām Told Us

Volume Two

Letter from the General Editor

The Library of Arabic Literature series offers Arabic editions and English translations of key works of classical and pre-modern Arabic literature. Books in the series are edited and translated by distinguished scholars of Arabic and Islamic studies and are published in parallel-text format with Arabic and English on facing pages. These titles are also made available as English-only paperbacks. The Library of Arabic Literature includes texts from the pre-Islamic era to the cusp of the modern period, and encompasses a wide range of genres, including poetry, poetics, fiction, religion, philosophy, law, science, history, and historiography.

Supported by a grant from the New York University Abu Dhabi Institute, and established in partnership with NYU Press, the Library of Arabic Literature produces authoritative Arabic editions and modern, lucid English translations, with the goal of introducing the Arabic literary heritage to a general audience of readers, as well as to scholars and students.

Philip F. Kennedy
General Editor, Library of Arabic Literature

حديث عيسى بن هشام

أو

فترة من الزمن

المجلّد الثاني

محمد إبراهيم المويلحي

LIBRARY OF
المكتبة
ARABIC
العربية
LITERATURE

What ʿĪsā Ibn Hishām Told Us

or

A Period of Time

Volume Two

Muḥammad al-Muwayliḥī

Edited and translated by

Roger Allen

Volume editor

Philip Kennedy

NEW YORK UNIVERSITY PRESS

New York and London

NEW YORK UNIVERSITY PRESS
New York and London

Library of Congress Cataloging-in-Publication Data

Muwaylihi, Muhammad.
What 'Isa ibn Hisham told us, or, A period of time / Muhammad
al-Muwaylihi ; edited and translated by Roger Allen.
volumes cm -- (Library of Arabic literature)
In English and Arabic.
ISBN 978-1-4798-6225-2 (cl : alk. paper) -- ISBN 978-1-4798-1590-6
(e-book) -- ISBN 978-1-4798-7495-8 (e-book)
I. Allen, Roger, 1942- editor, translator. II. Muwaylihi, Muhammad.
Hadith 'Isa ibn Hisham. III. Muwaylihi, Muhammad. Hadith 'Isa ibn Hisham.
English. IV. Title. V. Title: Period of time.
PJ7850.U9H313 2015
892.7'35--dc23
2014044218

New York University Press books are printed on acid-free paper,
and their binding materials are chosen for strength and durability.

Series design by Titus Nemeth.

Typeset in Tasmeem, using DecoType Naskh and Emiri.

Typesetting and digitization by Stuart Brown.

Manufactured in the United States of America
c 10 9 8 7 6 5 4 3 2 1

Table of Contents

حـديث عيسى بن هشـام

المجلّد الثاني

What ʿĪsā Ibn Hishām Told Us

Volume Two

قال عيسى بن هشام: ولقد أعجب الباشا ما رآه في تلك المجامع والمشاهد، وخبره في تلك المجالس والمعاهد، لما احتوته من أسباب العظة والاعتبار، ممّا يغني عن طول التجربة والاختبار، وصادفت من نفسه ارتياحاً، ومن صدره انشراحا، وذهب عنه بفضلها ما كان يجده من مضاضة النائبات، وما كان يقاسيه من غضاضة المصيبات، فانقلب التقطيب بشرا، انقلاب العسر يسرا، كذلك من اختبر أحوال سواه هان عليه ما اشتد من بلواهوكان منذ خرجت به من مجلس العلماء إلى أن انتهينا من مجلس الأمراء، يلح في الاستزادة، ويلح في طلب الإفادة، فقلت له: لم يبق أمامنا من المجالس والمنتديات إلا ما اشتملت عليه الأزبكية من المخجلات المنديات، وما تضمنته من الموبقات والمنكرات، والمقامرات والمسكرات، وهو ما أرتفع بك عن ملابسته، وأنأى بك عن ملامسته، وأنا أجلك أن أسلك بك مسالك التهمة، وأحلك محال الريبة والشبهة، وأنفس بقدرك أن أهبط بك مهابط الشك والظنة، وأربأ بسنك ومقامك أن تخالط تلك الزمر، وأن تغوص في تلك الغمر، فتنحو بالضرورة منحاهم، وتقفو بحكم الصورة مسعاهم، وتحمل نفسك الشريفة ما لم تتعوده من مثل ما يعملون، وشروى ما يفعلون. ١،٢٦

فقال لي: تقول ذلك وقد آتيتني من دروس الحكمة العالية، والفلسفة السامية، ما أزدري معه عذل العاذلين، وأستخف به لوم الجاهلين، ولا يضير النفس الشريفة الطاهرة أن تجاور النفس الدنيئة الفاجرة، والمريض لا يعدي المريض، ولا تذهب رائحة الدفر برائحة الطيب، ورؤية النقيصة والرذيلة تزيد النفس الفاضلة تمكنًا من الفضيلة، وبالفاسد يعرف الصحيح، ولا تعلو قيمة الحسن إلا بمقابلته بالقبيح: ٢،٢٦

وبضدّها تتميّز الأشياء

ومن اشتغل بالأخلاق ولم يخبر بنفسه أخبارها، ويسبر أغوارها، فهو يرجم بالظنون، كالمتكهن بما يكون، أو كمن يرسم على الخيال، أو يصور على غير مثال –

Miṣbāḥ al-sharq 80, November 9, 1899[1]

ʿĪsā ibn Hishām said: The Pāshā had been amazed by what he had seen in these gatherings and meeting places and what he had learned in the sessions involved. They had offered object lessons and counsel that could dispense with the need for lengthy experience. They had offered him some relief and relaxation, and as a result his sufferings at the cruel hand of fate and destiny had dissipated. Frowns had turned into smiles, and difficulties had now become that much easier. So it happens that those people who have experienced hardships find adversity that much less of a burden. Ever since we had moved from the gathering of religious scholars to that of princes, he had kept asking for more of the same and insisting that he gain more knowledge. I told him that the only meeting places and clubs left for us to try were the scandalous clubs in the Ezbekiyyah, with all their varieties of filth, corruption, lechery, and drunkenness. "I've too high a regard for you," I said, "to bring into contact with such things; I should keep you far away. I have too much respect for you to lead you down paths that would see accusations leveled against you and raise doubts about your probity. I value your status too much to drag you down to such dubious haunts; my concern for your age and status will not permit me to let you mix with such people and dive into such a fetid pond. You will of necessity follow their lead and copy their ways. Your noble self will have to endure the kind of things they do, things the like of which you've never experienced. And they are evil indeed!" 26.1

"How can you say such things?" he replied, "when you've provided me with a whole variety of scholarship and philosophy that has enabled me to scorn the reproaches and criticisms of ignorant fools? A pure and noble soul will never suffer harm from being close to an evil and corrupt one. One patient rarely infects another; a foul stench can rarely dispel the odor of perfume. A close look at sin and vice only serves to strengthen the virtuous soul's adherence to virtue. The genuine is defined by what is corrupt, and the value of what is good is only enhanced through contact with what is evil. 26.2

Things are defined by their opposites.[2]

"Anyone who decides to study ethics without conducting research for himself or probing their depths can only indulge in conjectures, like someone trying to foretell what will happen, an artist using the imagination, or a

ذلك من فضل ما علمتني مما علمت رشدا - ولقد كان من أدب الحكام في أيام دولتنا، ورفعة صولتنا أن يغيروا من هيئاتهم، ويستروا من سماتهم، ويبدلوا أزياءهم المعروفة بأزياء لهم غير مألوفة، فينسابوا في مجتمعات العامة أوقات فراغهم لمسامراتهم، وساعات خلوهم لمحاضراتهم ليقفوا على جلية الأمور بالعيان والأثر، لا بالسمع والخبر فلم يكن امتزاجهم بالعامة مما يحط من قدرهم، ويخل بنهيهم وأمرهم، على أنني قد لبست من البعث بعد الموت جلبابا أتخذه بيني وبين الناس سترًا وحجابا، فهلمّ فاسلك بي هذي المذاهب، وادخل بي تلك المسارب، فإني أجد من نفسي توقًا إلى إدامة الاطلاع على مخبوء الأخلاق ومكنون الطباع.

قال عيسى بن هشام: فوافقته على عزمه، ونزلت على حكمه، وقصدت به قصد تلك الروضة الغناء، والجنة الزهراء، فلمّا وصلنا إلى بابها، ووقفنا تلقاء دولابها، وضعت فيه أجرة العبور، كما يوضع النذر في صندوق النذور، ثمّ درت فيه دورتي، ودار الباشا دورته، فكاد يهيج حرج الدولاب سورته، وقال: هل كتب على الداخل في هذا البستان، أن يدور في ساقيته دورة الثيران، فقلت له: شاع التخوين بين الناس في جميع الأشياء، وأفرطوا في التحفظ من بعضهم فاخترعوا مثل هذه الآلة الصمّاء، فهي تعدّ في كل دورة ما ينقده الداخل من الأجرة، فلا يضيع منه مثقال ذرة. ٣،٢٦

ولمّا تخللنا خلال مسالكها، وجلسنا على أريكة من أرائكها، أعجب الباشا حسن المكان وازدهاه، وتملكه الابتهاج وتولاه، وقال: ما شاء الله لا قوة إلا بالله، من صاحب هذه من كبراء البلد، فقلت: هي ملك كل واحد وليس يملكها أحد، جعلتها الحكومة من المنافع العامة، لنزهة الخاصة والعامة، فيتمتع الناس بهذه النزهة المفيدة، بتلك الأجرة الزهيدة.

قال عيسى بن هشام: ثمّ طفنا في أنحاء الحديقة، نتنزه بين أشجارها الوريقة، وأزهارها الأنيقة، والباشا يتأمل ويعجب، ويشاهد محاسنها ويطرب: ٤،٢٦

painter without a model. The appreciation of all this I owe to the good advice you've been giving me. In the time of our regime, it was considered appropriate for governors and senior officials to change their appearance, disguise themselves, and substitute unfamiliar attire for their usual uniform. They could then mix with people during their leisure time and hours of relaxation and chat with them. That way, officials could find out for themselves what social conditions were really like, rather than having to rely purely on reports and word of mouth. Such contact with the common people did nothing to affect their prestige or detract from their authority. In my own case, following my resurrection from the dead I've donned a garment which has placed a veil between me and the common people. So come on, take me to these places. I find that I'm eager to continue my research on the secret aspects of people's morality."

ʿĪsā ibn Hishām said: So I went along with his decision and complied with his request. I took him to the luxuriant and fragrant park in the Ezbekiyyah. When we reached the gate, we stopped at the turnstile where I put in the admission fee; it was just like putting votive offerings into a donation box. I took my turn in it and so did the Pāshā. Suppressing his anger he asked me why people entering these gardens were expected to go round in circles like an ox at a waterwheel. I replied that these days people distrusted each other and were excessively concerned about safety, so they had invented inanimate machines like this; it counted what the entrants paid at every turn, and so not a grain of dust was lost. We started strolling along the paths and then sat down on a bench. The Pāshā was overwhelmed by the sheer beauty of the place and expressed his delight. "God alone possesses power and might!" he exclaimed. "Which grandee owns this place?" "It belongs to everyone," I replied, "no one person owns it. The government has turned it into a public facility, so all kinds of people can take a stroll. Everyone can enjoy this park by paying a very small fee." **26.3**

ʿĪsā ibn Hishām said: We started walking around the various parts of the garden, looking at the leafy trees, luxuriant branches, and pretty flowers. The Pāshā kept looking at everything in amazement, utterly thrilled by what he was seeing: **26.4**

أرض إذا جردت في حسنها
فكرك دلتك على الصانع

وبعد أن نظر الباشا ذات اليمين وذات الشمال، التفت إليّ فقال:

الباشا ما لنا لا نرى هذا المكان مزدحماً بالناس يتفيأون ظلاله، ويشاهدون جمال مناظره وبديع صنعه؟ ما دامت الحكومة قد أباحته لكل داخل كما تقول، وكأنّ الأمر على العكس، فإني لا أرى فيه غير هؤلاء الأجانب في أزيائهم بأبنائهم ونسائهم، وكأنما الحكومة قد جعلته وقفاً عليهم دون سواهم، فإننا منذ دخولنا وتجوالنا فيه لم نشاهد من المصريين غيرنا.

٥،٢٦ عيسى بن هشام ليس الذنب في ذلك على الحكومة، وإنما اعتاد المصريون أن لا يلتفتوا إلا قليلا إلى اللذات الأدبية من ترويح النفس بالمناظر المبهجة والمرائي الشائقة، وتنزيه النظر ورياضة الفكر في مطالعة كتاب الكائنات ومحاسن المخلوقات، فترى الواحد منهم قد حبس نفسه في دائرة الوجود على الماديات فيكاد يمر عليه الدهر الطويل دون أن ينظر نظرة في النجوم، ودون أن يلتفت التفاتة إلى ما بين يديه مما تنبت الأرض من أشكال الأشجار وألوان الأزهار، على أنها ببديع جمالها، ولسان حالها:

تصيح بمن يمرّ أما تراني
فتفهم حكمة الصنع العجيب؟

الباشا أحسنت، ولكن قل لي: كيف لم يدرك المصريون نعمة هذه المشاهدة، ولذة هذه المطالعة، وكيف وصل إليها الأجانب دونهم؟

٦،٢٦ عيسى بن هشام قد عوّد الأجانب أنفسهم على ذلك حتى أصبح طبيعة من طبائعهم، وحتى عدّوا ممارسته فنّاً وعلماً من العلوم اللازمة للحضارة والعمران، وسرى ذلك في دمائهم يتوارثه الأبناء عن الآباء، فترى الطفل الصغير منهم أوّل ما يشب ويدرج يقتطف الزهور، ويجمع الرياحين من حديقة المنزل لتكون في يده أحسن ما يقابل به أهله من الإتحاف، ولقد تأصّل فيهم ذلك الشعور الجليل، ونما هذا

A spot that reveals the Creator to you
when you disclose your thoughts on its beauty.[3]

The Pāshā looked left and right and then asked me:

Pāshā Why isn't this place thronged with people? Why aren't they taking advantage of the shade and looking at the beautiful views and marvelous design? As long as the government has opened it up to everyone, as you've just told me, why does it look exactly the opposite? The only people I can see are those foreigners over there wearing their distinctive clothes with their wives and children by their side? Has the government reserved this place for Westerners to the exclusion of other people? Since we entered and started walking around, we're the only Egyptians I've seen.

ʿĪsā It's not the government's fault. It's just that Egyptians have grown accustomed to paying minimal attention to cultural pleasures, to seeking solace by looking at lovely views and spectacular sights, and to gaining insight and mental stimulation from reading books about nature and the beauties of creation. You find that Egyptians have put themselves into some kind of prison and confined their thoughts about the universe entirely to material things. An entire lifetime may pass by without them looking up at the stars in the sky or observing the variety of trees and flowers that the earth produces before their very eyes, so beautiful and eloquent that: 26.5

You shout at passersby: "Do you not see me?
For then you will understand the logic of amazing creation."[4]

Pāshā Excellent! But tell me, how is it that Egyptians don't appreciate such a blessing, the sheer delight of such contemplation? Why have foreigners achieved that, and not Egyptians?

ʿĪsā Foreigners are now accustomed to appreciating such things, so much so that it's part of their nature. They have come to regard such practice as one of the arts and sciences necessary for civilized society and culture. It flows in their bloodstream, and sons inherit it from their fathers. For example, a young child of theirs will pick flowers and gather scented plants from the house garden into a posy in his hand; for his family that will be the best possible present he could bring them. These noble feelings and lovely sentiments are now deep-seated in Western society; from natural truths they've moved on 26.6

الإحساس الجميل، فارتقى من الحقائق الطبيعية إلى الصور والنقوش الصناعية حتى إنك لترى الواحد منهم يبذل في رسم زهرة من الزهور أو مثال قطعة من الشفق، أو صورة راع من الرعاة، أو حيوان من الحيوانات ما تساوي قيمته ألوف الألوف ممّا تساويه قيمة الأصل الطبيعي

٧،٢٦ وقلّما تدخل دار ميسور منهم إلا وتجد جدرانها مزدانة بأنواع الصور وأشكال الرسوم ممّا يحاكي الكائنات الطبيعية، فلا يفوت صاحب الدار في داخلها ما ينظر من جمال المناظر خارجاً عنهاولقد جرّهم ذلك إلى الولوع بمشاهدة الآثار القديمة وشدة التنافس في اقتنائها، والتغالي في التحفظ عليها والضن بها، فكم رأينا من قطعة من الخنجر أو غيره تزدريها الأعين بيننا ولا يعبأ بها المصري فيطرحها في كناسة منزله، ولا تزال كذلك حتى يلتقطها الأجنبي فتصير عنده في قيمة درة التاج أو واسطة العقد، وكم رأينا من السياحين من يتكبدون مشاق الأسفار، ويتحملون أهوال البحار، ويصبرون على متاعب القفار مع إنفاق الألوف المؤلفة من الدراهم والدينار لمشاهدة بعض الآثار، وما عفا من الرسوم في هذه الديار، ونرى المصري ساكن القاهرة يولد ويشب، ويكتهل ويشيخ، ويهرم ويموت، ولم ير من الأهرام القائمة في جواره غير صورتها المرسومة على الورق، وربما لا يرى ذلك أيضاً.

٨،٢٦ الباشا تالله إنّ ذا لمن العجب، ولوكان الأمر يجري على القياس لكان المصريون أسبق الأمم إلى التمتع بلذة المشاهدة في بدائع المصنوعات، ومحاسن الكائنات للطافة شيمهم، ورقة طباعهم، وسرعة التأثير في نفوسهم، ولما ميّزهم الله به من حسن الإقليم واعتدال الجو وصفاء السماء، وفيض الماء، وجودة التربة، وخصب الأرض، ولانحصار موارد أرزاقهم، واقتصار أسباب معائشهم على الفلح والحرث والزرع والحصد وكل من رأى الإقليم المصري زبرجدة خضراء في وسط رمال الصحراء حسد أهله على التحلي بهذه الفريدة من عقد الطبيعة، وغبطهم على تمتع نواظرهم باجتلاء هذه المناظر التي تجلي البصر، وتثلج الفؤاد، وتنعش القلب، وترقق حواشي النفس، وتلطف من تشويش الفكر، وتخفف من بلابل الصدر، فتصفو الروح

to drawings and man-made pictures. You'll see someone busy painting a picture of a flower, a twilight scene, a shepherd, or an animal. The value of those images is thousands of thousand times more than their original in nature.

You'll rarely enter a wealthy person's home without finding the walls decorated with paintings and designs on panels portraying nature scenes. In that way the house owner is never deprived inside his house of the beautiful vistas outside. This in turn has led them to develop a great passion for looking at ancient relics and a fierce competition to acquire them. They go to excessive lengths to keep them exclusively for themselves. How often have we seen pieces of dagger or other objects that we despise? Egyptians in general ignore them; they even put them out along with their domestic rubbish. That's the way it continues until foreigners start collecting them; at which point they become worth as much as a precious jewel in a crown or a solitary pearl in a necklace. How often have we noticed tourists putting up with all the hardships of travel, the terrors of the sea and dangers of the desert, spending thousands of dirhams and dinars in the process, and all that so that they can look at some ruins and remains in this part of the world. Meanwhile, Egyptians living in Cairo, where they grow up, pass through middle and old age, and finally become old and senile, never even set eyes on the Pyramids which are right next to them. If they do, it's only because of the picture on postage stamps! Often they'll not even see that. 26.7

PĀSHĀ Goodness me, how amazing! If things worked in proportion, Egyptians would be in the very forefront of nations when it comes to enjoying the feeling of pleasure through contemplation of the wonders of creation and the beauties of mankind. They've an amiable disposition and a gentle character, and their hearts are rapidly touched and affected by emotion. God has favored them with a pleasant climate, temperate weather, clear skies, an abundance of water, and fertile soil. Their means of earning a living wage are limited to farming—ploughing, planting, and harvesting. Anyone who regards the area of Egypt as a green chrysolite amid the Sahara sands has to envy its people the fact that it's decorated with such a jewel from nature's necklace, and that the people can enjoy the contemplation of this wondrous spectacle that can clear the vision, gladden the heart, and nourish the spirit. In so doing, it can soothe their worries and anxieties and calm their souls. Then the soul can flit from the trammels of the lower world to a link with the rope to the 26.8

فتخفف من قيود العالم السفلي إلى الاتصال بحبل من العالم العلوي، فترتاح هنيهة ممّا تقاسيه في مصارعة الحياة من ضروب العلل والأسقام، وتفر برهة من وجوه الأكدار والآلام إلى «وجه ربك ذي الجلال والإكرام».

٩،٢٦ واعلم وهذه لفظة طالما أفادني تكرارها على لسانك فاسمح لي بها مرة من لساني وما أعلمك إلا عن خبرة وتجريب – أنّ الفرق بين الإنسان والحيوان ليس هو في الخلق، ففي الخلق ما يشبهه ولا في النطق ففي الحيوان ما ينطق، ولا في ذكاء القريحة ففي الهوام والطيور ما يفوقه ذكاء ويعلوه حزماً وتدبيراً، ولكن ما هو يمتاز بإدراك حقيقة الوجود بالإمعان والمشاهدة، وطول الفكرة في مخلوقات الله للاهتداء إلى معرفة خالقها، وتلك هي سعادته ولذته الروحانية التي تفضله مزيتها على سائر الحيوان، وهي أشرف اللذات وأصفاها وأفضلها وأبقاها، وإنّ أقرب ما يتقرب به العبد إلى الله زلفى وأرفع ما يعبد به الصانع القديم تعالى وجهه من أنواع العبادات أن يتأمل في حسن صنعه وبدائع خلقه، ولا يقف على مقدار هذه المزية الروحانية إلا من تجرّد مثلي يوماً من عالم الأجسام والفناء إلى عالم الأرواح والبقاء، وما ينبئك مثل خبير.

ولو كانت الأمور تجري على القياس أيضاً لاشتغل المصريون بهذه المشاهدة الأدبية إن لم يكن من باب الإحساس والشعور، فمن باب تقليد الغربيين والعمل على نمطهم لما رأيته في مختلف أحوالهم من الولع بتقليد الأجنبي في شكله وزيه ومعيشته وحركته وسكونه، ولكن لعل هناك من خفي الأسباب ما حرمهم من اطراد ذلك التقليد.

١٠،٢٦ عيسى بن هشام لم يكن هناك مانع، وإنما استحب المصريون الانكماش فسرى فيهم في كل أحوالهم المادية حتى تناول أحوالهم الأدبية، وهم على ما تراهم من تقليد الأجنبي لا يقلدونه إلا في الخفيف الساقط والدنيء السافل ممّا يكون وراءه ما يهيج أسباب الملاذ الشهوانية والبهرجة الكاذبة، والزخرفة المموهة، وممّا لا تأتي نتيجته إلا بسقم الجسم، وسقم المال، وما عدا ذلك من الأمور المدنية النافعة، فمجهول

upper world. There for a while they can find some respite from life's relentless struggle and varieties of sickness and disease, escaping for a short while from sorrows and miseries in order to come "face to face with your Lord, the possessor of honor and veneration."[5]

You should realize—and I've often benefited myself from an expression that you've used, so please allow me to use it this once, as what I'm saying to you now is based purely on good will and experience—that the difference between humans and animals is not limited just to their nature, for some things in their nature are similar; nor to the ability to speak, as some animals can speak; nor to cleverness, since some of the earth's vermin and birds can surpass mankind's prudence and organizational ability in that too. No! The quality which distinguishes humanity from all other animals is its awareness of the true nature of existence through close study and its prolonged contemplation of God's creatures so that it can be guided to a knowledge of their Creator. This is the spiritual happiness and pleasure which distinguishes mankind from other creatures. It's the noblest, purest, the most excellent, and most lasting of all pleasures. The closest a worshiper can come to God in terms of flattery, the most sublime mode of devotion that he can show to the Creator—may His visage be exalted!—is through contemplation of the sheer beauty and wonders of His creation. Only those who one day find themselves, like me, removed from the corporeal, ephemeral world to the spiritual, eternal one can fully grasp the true value of these spiritual pleasures. Only someone who has experienced it can tell you. 26.9

Furthermore, if things worked in proportion, Egyptians would be involved with these cultural scenarios, if not for the pleasant sensations involved, then at least as a consequence of the way they imitate Western people and copy their habits in different situations—posture, clothes, way of life, gestures, and repose. But then, perhaps there's some underlying reason that prevents them from extending their imitation into this sphere as well.

ʿĪsā There's nothing to stop them. It's just that Egyptians are too introverted, not only in material concerns but cultural ones as well. As you can tell, they imitate foreigners, but only in trivial and undesirable ways that incite lusts, false ostentation, and phony tinsel—the kinds of thing that only result in bodily disease and wasted money. But, when it comes to beneficial aspects of civilization, they're not merely ignorant of them, but they even disparage 26.10

عندهم بل هو مرذول لديهم، وأقول لك بالإجمال إنّ مثل المصري في إقباله على المدنية الغربية كمثل المنخل يحفظ الغث التافه ويفرط في الثمين النافع.

قال عيسى بن هشام: وما زال الحديث دائرًا بيننا على هذا الأسلوب وأنا مقيم بين طربين لا أدري أيهما أوقع في النفس وآخذ بمجامع القلب طرب السمع من كلام صاحبي، والفرح بما وصل إليه من علو الفكر، وسمو المدركة، وأدب النفس، وكرم الطبع أم طرب البصر من منظر الروض وقد وشحته الشمس بوشاحها بين الأصيل والطفل، فتذكرت قول أحد الخلان في وصف ذلك الروض الأريج والمنظر البهيج: ١١،٢٦

لمنظر روض الأزبكية بهجة
تقود قلوب الناظرين إلى الطرب
إذا جئته وقت الأصيل رأيته
زمردة خضراء في خاتم ذهب

ثمّ تمشينا حتى وصلنا إلى المغارة المصنوعة فيه فرأينا صنعاً جميلاً وشكلا أنيقاً، وأخذت الباشا هزة الطرب بخرير الماء، فأخذ كل منا مجلسه على كراسي فيها أعدت للزائرين وما كاد يلتفت الباشا لفتة حتى ارتد إليّ بسرعة وقال: ألا ترى أنّ هؤلاء الجالسين من المصريين؟ فالتفت فإذا هم كما قال، وإذا بهم ثلاثة يتجاذبون الحديث فأصغينا إلى حديثهم من زاويتنا فتبيّن لنا منه أنّ أحدهم من عمد الأرياف، والثاني من تجار الثغور، والثالث من أهل البطالة والخلاعة وسمعنا العمدة يقول للخليع في مجرى كلامه: ١٢،٢٦

العمدة وأين إذن ما دخلنا الحديقة لأجله؟ وهل كان جل قصدك أن نجلس هنا في كثافة الأشجار ورطوبة الهواء، ووخامة الماء؟ وما أجد فرقًا بين هذا المنظر وبين منظر ذلك المستنقع الذي خلفته خلف بلدتنا، ولعمري إنّ الإوز الذي يسبح فيه هناك أضعاف أضعاف هذا الإوز الذي يسبح أمامنا، وما لنا ولهذه الأشجار

them. In summary one may say that the way Egyptians have adopted the habits of Western civilization is analogous to a sieve that retains all the worthless waste and lets through the useful things with any value.

ʿĪsā ibn Hishām said: As our conversation proceeded in this fashion, I found myself delighted on two accounts; I wasn't sure which of the two was the more powerful emotion: my delight in listening to my colleague and realizing with joy how far he'd progressed in his thinking, appreciation, and psychological state; or my own delight as I looked at the gardens bathed in the late afternoon sunlight. I recalled the lines written by a colleague to describe this lovely park and its gorgeous vistas: **26.11**

The Ezbekiyyah Gardens possess a beauty
that delights the hearts of observers.
Should you come there before sunset,
you see a green emerald in a golden ring.[6]

We continued walking till we reached the artificial grotto in a section of the garden. We observed its beautiful shape and exquisite craftsmanship. As water gushed from clefts, the Pāshā was overjoyed, and we decided to sit down on some chairs placed there for visitors. No sooner had he looked round than he turned back to me quickly and asked: "Aren't those three people sitting over there Egyptians?" I turned round and looked. He was right. They were busy talking to each other, so we listened from our seats to what they were saying. From their conversation, we gathered that one of them was a country *ʿumdah,*[7] the second was a port merchant, and the third a dissolute playboy. We picked up the conversation the ʿUmdah was having with the Playboy: **26.12**

ʿUmdah So where's the thing we came to these gardens for? Did you really mean for us to sit here under these trees, with all this humidity and polluted water? I can't see any difference between the view here and the swamp I left behind in my village. By my life, the ducks swimming in the swamp there are far more numerous than the ones swimming around in front of us here. What's the point of these useless trees that don't bear any fruit or help relieve

العقيمة التي لا تسمن ولا تغني من جوع، فهلمّ فأطعمنا أنت من ذلك الثمر الشهي واللحم الطري كما وعدتنا.

الخليع مهلاً، فإنّ هذا لا يفوتك وما كنت أظنّ أنّ الأمر وصل بالحديقة إلى هذا الخراب إلا عندما سألت أحد المارين من خدمها الآن فعلمت منه أنّ الحكومة لخلوّ يدها من الأشغال لم تجد أمامها شيئاً في خدمة الوطن إلا التضييق على هذه الحديقة تضييق المصلحين عليها، فرأت أنّ إصلاحها لا يتم إلا بمنع ذوات البرقع والقناع من دخولها، ولا أقول إلا قول الجرائد في التأفف من أعمال الحكومة ﴿حَسْبُنَا اللَّهُ وَنِعْمَ الْوَكِيلُ﴾. ١٣،٢٦

التاجر وعلى هذا فقد ذهبت تلك الأيام التي كانت فيها الحديقة بهجة للناظرين، ومرتعاً للغزلان، وملعباً للغيد الحسان، ومنهلاً عذباً لطلاب الراح، وقصاد الملاح، وطالما دخلت هنا وحيداً فخرجت وقد اقتنصت من آرامها مثنى وثلاث ورباع.

العمدة يعلم الله أنّ القاهرة أصبحت على هذا الحال مما لا يصح فيها الإقامة إلا مسافة قضاء الحاجة والرجوع من الفور إلى البلدويا ليت الأمر كان قاصراً على الحديقة في حرماني هذه المرة من حظ النفس، فإني سهرت أمس مع فلان الموظف في الديوان الفلاني لأنزهه وأبسطه كعادتي في إنجاز حاجتي فسحبني قاتله الله إلى أماكن شتى من أماكن الأزبكية يهوى التردد عليها، فلم أجد في جميعها ما يوافق هواي كما تعلم، وخرجت من السهرة مصدع الرأس من الخمر خالي الجيب من القمار، وما اكتفى الخبيث بنفسه، بل دار حول أصحابه يجمعهم حولي، وأنا القائم بنفقتهم، وكلما رأى مني انحرافاً عن أحد منهم قال لي هذا فلان وله اليد الطولى في قضاء الحاجات.

التاجر ولِمَ هذا الإنفاق وهذا الانقياد وحاجتك لم تكن إلا عند شخص واحد. ١٤،٢٦

العمدة يحق لك أن تعترض فقد أخلاك الله وأراحك من متاعبنا، فإنّ أشغال التجارة في المدن لا تقتضي ما تقتضيه أشغال الفلاحة في الأرياف من وجوب

your hunger! Come on, feed us some of that luscious fruit and fresh game you promised us!

PLAYBOY Steady on! You won't miss a thing. I didn't realize that these gardens would have been reduced to such a state of desolation. But then I've just asked a servant who happened to be passing by. I've learned that the government apparently has nothing else to do; the only way it can find to serve the people is by restricting access to these gardens as reformers demand. Such reforms involve preventing girls with veils and shawls from entering the gardens. With that in mind, I can only quote the newspapers' phrase when grumbling about government action: «We count on God, and good is the trustee!»[8] **26.13**

MERCHANT In that case, gone are the days when this garden used to be a delight for the observer, a promenade for beauties, a playground for gorgeous maidens, and a sweet resort for those in quest of wine and beauty. I've often come in here by myself and have never left without ensnaring two, three or four hundred lovely little antelopes.

'UMDAH God knows, nowadays Cairo's turned into a place where you should only stay long enough to complete your business and then head back immediately to your hometown. If only things were restricted to these gardens; on this visit I'm feeling totally deprived. I spent last night in the company of X the government employee in such-and-such office. My plan was to take him around and give him a good time as usual so that I could achieve my purpose. But—curse him!—he dragged me to any number of places in the Ezbekiyyah that he likes to frequent, but, as you know, I didn't find anything I liked in a single one of them. I came out with an aching head from the wine and empty pockets from the gambling. This wretch wasn't content to involve himself alone, but dragged his friends in as well, all of whom clustered around me. I had to pay for everything. Every time he noticed me turning away from one of them, he told me that the person was Y, someone who was able to deal with my needs.

MERCHANT But why did you spend so much and go along with his scheme, when you only needed one person? **26.14**

'UMDAH You've every right to object. God has relieved you from the irksome problems we face. Your commercial business in the cities doesn't require the kind of fawning, dissimulation, compliance, and cautious strategizing that

المداراة والمواراة والمراعاة وقراءة العواقب، فإنّ كلمة واحدة من موظف صغير تكفي لتعطيل عمل كبير، وما يدريك أنّ من تزدريه العين وتحتقره النفس ممّن تراهم الليلة في الأزبكية ربما أصبح عندنا غداً حاكماً في المحكمة أو المديرية.

الخليع إذا كانت الليلة الماضية قد انقضت على غير هواك فلنا عنها عوض من ليلتنا هذه.

العمدة أنصدقك في وجود العوض وأنت لم تصدق في ما دعوتنا إليه في هذه الحديقة؟

الخليع صدقني فإني ما كنت أعلم بما أصاب الحديقة من أمر الحكومة، لأنني كنت مقيماً في حلوان مدة طويلة وجئت وأنا أحسبها على ما كانت عليهعلى أني والحمد لله قد رتبت لنا الآن سهرة تفوق في الحسن كل سهرة مضت، ولا تحسبني في ارتياد الملاهي مثل صديقك أمس فإني عثرت على من دلّني في هذه الأيام على بيضة خدر من بيت فلان باشا، فهلمّ بنا نخرج وعليّ أن أبذل جهدي، وأسعى بما في وسعي في استمالتها إلى مقابلتي هذه الليلة كاتماً عنها أمركما، ومتى وافتني في المكان الذي أعينه لها أرسلت إليكما من يحضركما إلينا فتدخلا على حين غفلة فلا تستطيع منكما اختفاء، وحينئذ يدور بنا المجلس دورة الأنس والسرور، ثمّ لا أكتمكما أنّ ما معي في هذه الليلة من الدراهم لا يكفي لإتمام معدّات هذا المجلس، وبودّي لو أذهب إلى البيت فأحضر ما يلزم على أنني أخشى إذا ذهبت إليه أنّ من فيه يمنعني عن الرجوع إليكما.

العمدة لا عليك فمعي من الدراهم ما يكفي وزيادة

قال عيسى بن هشام: وعلى هذا أخذ الواحد منهم بيد الآخر وقاموا يجرون أذيال ١٥،٢٦
الفسق والفجور، والباشا بجانبي يسمع ويتأمّل، تارة يضحك، وتارة يحوقل، ثمّ قمنا على الأثر

agriculture does in the provinces. A single word from a junior official can often bring about the failure of a big transaction. How are you to know that the person you disregard and ignore in the Ezbekiyyah one night will not turn out the very next morning to be a judge in court or provincial offices?

PLAYBOY If things last night weren't to your liking, then we'll make amends tonight.

'UMDAH Are we supposed to believe your story about amends when you weren't telling us the truth in inviting us to these gardens!

PLAYBOY Believe me! I'd no idea of the effect government regulations have had on these gardens. I've been spending a lot of time in Ḥulwān and came here assuming it was the way it used to be. But—God be thanked!—I've arranged a little soirée that will surpass all previous occasions. When it comes to frequenting night clubs, don't assume I'm like your friend of yesterday. I've come across someone who has shown me how to get to a cloistered maiden in B Pāshā's house. Come on, let's leave now! I'm going to have to make an effort to persuade her to receive me tonight. I'll keep you two a secret from her. Once she's arrived at the rendezvous of my choice, I'll send someone to bring the two of you. You can enter when she's not paying attention, so she won't be able to hide. Then we'll be able to sit and chat with her to our hearts' content. But I can't conceal from you both that the dirhams I have on me are not enough to make all the necessary preparations for this tête-à-tête. If I went home to get enough money, I'm afraid that my family would stop me from coming back.

'UMDAH Don't worry! I've got enough dirhams and more.

'Īsā ibn Hishām said: With that they grabbed each other by the hand and went off in search of debauchery and immoral pleasure. The Pāshā was sitting beside me, listening and thinking to himself; at times he was laughing, at others invoking God. We too stood up and followed them. **26.15**

مصباح الشرق ٨٧، ٤ يناير ١٩٠٠

١٫٢٧ قال عيسى بن هشام: وصل بنا الحديث في ذلك الروض العاطر إلى حديث الخليع والعمدة والتاجر وقد خرجوا منه ليدخلوا الفسوق من أبوابه ويأخذوا من للهو بأسبابه وكنت لم أزل أسير التردد والتحير في الانتخاب والتخير وانتقاء المجامع الحافلة والمجالس الآهلة متابعة للباشا في طلبها ابتغاء العبرة بها وإن هوت إلى دركات الانحطاط وقضت بالاختلاط بين الغوغاء والاخلاط فما وجدت أدنى إلى بلوغ الاربة وأجدى وأدعى إلى إصابة الغرض وأهدى من تأثر هذه الجماعة إلى منازل اللهو والخلاعه وقلت في نفسي فرصة والله آنت وصدفة حانت يجب دركها ولا ينبغي تركها لما آنسته في ذلك الخليع المحتال من النزوع إلى مواطن الغي والضلال حيث تستعر نيران الشهوات بين اللهاة واللهوات وهذا الخادع ابن بجدتها وناسج بردتها أعرف الناس بمواضعها وأهدى من القطا إلى مواقعها ثم أبنت للباشا ما ارتأيته وما اخترته ونويته. فرأى رأيي في اجتياز هذا السبيل والاهتداء بهذا الدليل.

٢٫٢٧ فتبعنا مسراهم من حيث نسمعهم ونراهم فسمعنا العمدة يقول: ما أحوجني لترييض البدن وتضييع الزمن إلى لعب دور بالبليار في الأبره أو النوبار فما أسرع ما صوب الخليع فكرته وحسن له بنيته وقال: ما ألطف هذا الاختيار فهلم وانتظراني في «الاوبرابار» ريثما أسعى لإنجاز وعدي وإيفاء عهدي لاستجماع أدوات اللهو واستتمام آلات الصفو ثم أعود إليكما وقد قمت بالخدمة على مقتضى الذمة فأجاباه بالامتثال وفارقاه عند ساحة التمثال.

فقلت للباشا قد علمنا الآن وجهتهم وعرفنا قبلتهم فقف بنا برهة أطرفك أسنى الطرف وأتحفك أبهى التحف فقال على م الوقوف؟ ولماذا؟ فأشرت إلى التمثال وقلت: لهذا فتأمل فيه هنيهة ثم وقف وقفة التبجيل والتعظيم وقال «سلام على ابراهيم» وقد أخذته هزة واضطراب وظهر عليه حزن واكتئاب ثم تنفس الصعداء وكاد يجهش بالبكاء فقلت له ما هذه الحالة المحزنة؟ أحنينًا إلى تلك الأزمنة وما انطوت عليه من حلوها ومرهاظ وما ذهب من خيرها وشرها بعد أن سلكت سبل

'Īsā ibn Hishām said: Our description of the perfumed gardens had reached the point of the discussion between the Playboy, 'Umdah, and Merchant. They had left it to indulge in some debauchery and lewd diversions. For my part I was still exercising caution in selecting crowded venues and places to visit, all in response to the Pāshā's request for object lessons from which to learn—even if that required us to descend into low haunts and mingle with the lowest levels of society. In order to achieve this goal and satisfy our question I could not imagine any more effective way than following this trio to notorious haunts. "This is a good opportunity," I told myself, "and a lucky chance that we should not miss." I had noticed that the crafty Playboy was a devotee of such nefarious places where entertainments and entertainers stoke the flames of passion. This particular con man was completely au fait with such venues; he knew where the best ones were and better than the sandgrouse how to get there.[10] I explained my plan to the Pāshā and told him what my intentions were. He agreed to go along with it. 27.1

We kept up with them so we could both see and hear them. We heard the 'Umdah say, "I really need to exercise my body and while away some time playing a round of billiards in the Opera Bar or New Bar." No one could have been quicker than the Playboy to satisfy his demand and fulfil his request. "What a splendid choice!" he said. "Come on and wait for me at the Opera Bar while I go and carry out the promise I've made; it'll be an occasion combining all pleasures into one and giving us total satisfaction. Once I've managed all that in accordance with my solemn pledge, I'll come back." With that they agreed to his plan and separated in the square with Ibrāhīm's statue. 27.2

"Now we know their plan," I told the Pāshā, "and where they're going. But stop for a moment and let me point out something to you that will be the greatest possible gift." "And what might that be?" he asked. I pointed at the statue of Ibrāhīm and said "That!" He stared at it for a moment and then stood to attention out of respect. "Hail to Ibrāhīm!" he said, quivering and shaking all over. He gave a bitter, sorrowful sigh and almost burst into tears. "Why so sad?" I asked him. "Are you nostalgic for times past with all their happy and bitter moments and the good and bad things that are long since past? Haven't

الهداية والرشاد؟ وبدت عليك تباشير الحكمة والسداد؟

٣،٢٧ فقال: كيف لا أبكي بكاء الحزين؟ أم كيف لا يظهر ذلك الحزن الدفين؟ وقد تمثل أمامي بطل مصر ورافع بنود النصر موقد نيران الوقائع وصاليها وغائص غمرات المعامع وجاليها؟:

في كل منبت شعرة من جسمه
أسد يمدّ إلى الفريسة مخلبا

مولاي وولي أمري ومنبت شرفي ومصدر فخري ومما أضرم ناري فما أستطيع أواري ولا أستطيع أواري وضع تمثاله في هذه البقعة وقد اشتهرت بسوء السمعه بؤساً لقوم بلغت بهم الغفلة إلى هذا الحد حتى جعلوا الهزل والدد تحت عنوان الرجولة والجد فقلت له: خفض عليك من همك ولومك فانما أنت ابن يومك وانظر إلى هذه البنية الايوانيه ذات الأرائك الخسروانيه فقال: أعظم به من بناء ولمن هو من الكبراء؟

٤،٢٧ فقلت: هو ملهى رفع اسماعيل قواعده وأقام دعائمه ومهد مقاعده فأحسن وضعه وأبدع صنعه:

ليس يدرى أصنع انس لجن
سكنوه أم صنع جن لانس

حتى أصبح بهجة النواظر ونزهة الخواطر بما يجمعه من أفانين الألاعيب وضروب الأعاجيب مما يؤخذ من أساطير الأولين وأقاصيص الغابرين يتمثل حاضراً للناظرين ليكون عبرة للمعتبرين وما يضمه من كل غادة حسناء فاتنة بالرقص مفتنة في الغناء على عادة الغربيين في ديارهم والعمل على آثارهم وقد بقي من بعده تتفق عليه الحكومة من اموال البلاد تسلية للنزلاء والقصاد وليس من وراء تشييده ووضعه سوى ان اثمه أكبر من نفعه

you now pursued different paths—those of maturity and common sense—and started to display symptoms of prudence and sound judgment?"

"How can I not shed tears of sorrow?" the Pāshā responded, "and express my profound grief when I see before me this hero of Egypt, someone who raised triumphal banners, kindled and burned fires of battle, and waded through the floods of tumultuous war and swept them clean: 27.3

In every pore of his body where a hair grew,
there was a lion extending its claws towards the prey.[11]

"My lord and master, source of my honor and prestige, kindling of my fire! I cannot dissemble. How can they have erected his statue in this place infamous for its dreadful reputation? Woe to a people whose indifference has brought them so low that frivolity and scrapping are now regarded as manly and serious."

"Calm down!" I told him, "Enough with your sorrows and censure. You're a creature of your own times. Just take a look at this columned building."

"It is indeed splendid," he said. "To which grandee does it belong?"

"It's a playhouse built by Ismāʿīl," I replied. "He was responsible for building its foundations and providing its seats. It was beautifully designed and constructed:[12] 27.4

No one can know: was it humans that built it for the jinn
to live in, or did the jinn construct it for humans?[13]

so much so that it has now become the cynosure of all eyes, the haven of delights, where all kinds of entertainment and wonders are assembled, plots taken from sagas of the ancients and tales of yore. Scenes are acted out before the audience and offer lessons for those who would learn. They offer gorgeous girls with all the allure of song and dance. All this imitates the way Western people do things in their countries and copies their traditions. The government has decided to spend people's money in this way in order to provide amusement for foreigners and tourists. The only logic involved in the building's construction seems to have been that its harm should be greater than its benefits."

ثم التفت الباشا إلى مجتمع الحاضرين ومزدحم الواردين والصادرين عند وصولنا إلى المكان المقصود والمنهل المورود والمعهد الموعود وقال: ما هذه الضوضاء العظيمه أمأتم ما أرى أم وليمه فقلت: بل هو المحل الذي نسعى إليه ووقع اتفاق أصحابنا عليه وهو مجتمع عام تتزاحم فيه الأقدام للسمر والمدام فاقتحمنا ذلك المجمع وتخيرنا مقاعد للسمع فإذا العمدة وآخر يلعبان البليار والتاجر وآخرون يلعبون القمار وإذا أربعة بجانبنا قد اشتد بينهم اللجاج واحتد الجدال والحجاج فظهر لنا من حديثهم أنهم يتألفون من سمسار وغني وصاحب قضية مع تبيع محام أجنبي ودونك ما سمعناه من مقالهم في منتهى جدالهم: ٥،٢٧

السمسار (للغني) لا نزاع في ان متابع الثروة قد قضيت بذهاب الأيام الماضية التي كان الإنسان يغتني فيها بكلمة ويثري بإشارة فيصبح أغنى الأغنياء بعد أن كان أفقر الفقراء ولقد وصل المصريون الآن إلى زمن كله عسر وضيق فليس من يهب الضياع ويقطع الاقطاع ويسدي الأموال ولقد بقي الغني منهم على حاله في خموله لا يستثمر ماله إلا بالرسائل التي احتكرها الأجانب بشركاتهم ولا يخفاك أن هذا المورد لا يكفي للانفاق على الاحتياجات المتجددة يوماً بعد يوم فهو ينفق من تلاده فيكون النقص مستمراً في ماله فان مضى إلى سبيله واقتسم أبناؤه ما بقي من ثروته لم يصب الواحد منهم إلا الكفاف وكن على يقين انه لا يمضي جيل واحد إلا وتندثر بيوت من بقي من الأغنياء واعلم أن البيت الذي يتدفق بالغنى الآن ويتكفل بالثروة ويفتح مغالق الكنوز ويقوم مقام القصور التي كان الإنسان يدخلها فقيراً فيخرج منها ليومه بل لساعته غنياً هو بيت البورصه. ٦،٢٧

الغني لا تذكر لي اسم البورصة وقد سمعنا في هذه الأيام عن فلان وفلان وفلان ما فيه عبرة للمعتبر ٧،٢٧

السمسار وأنا أرجو سعادتكم أن لا تستشهد بمن سميتهم فإن السبب في خسارتهم معلوم وليس هو من فعل البورصة ولكن من فعل أنفسهم بأنفسهم فإن الأول منهم كان يعتمد في المضاربة في بيعه وشرائه على ما تشير به عليه امرأة

When we reached the place where we were heading, our rendezvous point, the Pāshā looked at the crowds of people going in and out. "What's this colossal din about?" he asked. "Is this a funeral or a wedding?" "Neither," I replied. "It's the place we've been heading for, where we've agreed to meet our friends. It's a public meeting place where people crowd in order to spend the evening out and drink wine." With that we made our way inside and chose some seats so we could listen to the conversation. The 'Umdah was playing billiards with someone else, while the Merchant and others were playing cards. Alongside us four people had a row and started arguing and protesting. From their conversation it became clear that the group consisted of a stockbroker and a wealthy man, along with a plaintiff in a court case and a foreign lawyer's assistant. Here's part of the conversation that we heard as their arguments came to a close: 27.5

BROKER (*to the Rich Man*) There's no denying the fact that former patterns of wealth have vanished. The days of old are long gone when a man could become rich with a word or gesture and find himself thereby the richest of the rich after being considered the poorest of the poor. Egyptians now live in an era when everything is poverty and need; no one is handing out estates, granting feudal rights, and dispensing largesse. Wealthy people remain indifferent, only investing through notes on which foreigners with their companies have a monopoly. You're all too aware that such sources of revenue are not sufficient to meet needs that keep increasing day by day. As a result people have to spend part of their inherited property. The losses to a person's wealth never stop. If he continues this way and then tries to divide his property among his children, they each land up with just enough to live on and that's all. You can be sure that, before a single generation has passed, the wealthy's family homes that are left will vanish. But you should know that there is one place now that gushes with money and guarantees wealth. It can unlock treasure chests and take the place of those palaces where a person could enter in poverty, then emerge that very day, or rather that very hour, as a rich man. I'm referring to the Stock Market.[14] 27.6

RICH MAN Don't even mention the words "Stock Market." In just the last few days, I've heard what it did to X, Y, and Z. That's enough to give pause to any sensible person. 27.7

BROKER Please, Sir, don't use the cases of X, Y, and Z as examples. The reason why they lost is obvious enough; it's not the Stock Exchange's fault, but rather what they did for themselves. The first resorted to speculation in

سودانية وأخرى افرنكية تلك بودعها وهذه بورقها. وأما الثاني فإنه سمع رجلا مجذوبًا له اعتقاد فيه يصيح عليه في طريقه بقوله «اذهب عني يا زيد» وكان مترددًا بين البيع والشراء فتفاعل بالكلمة فأخذ بها فأدار المركبة إلى سمساره فأمره بأن يشتري له عشرين ألف قنطار فنصحه فلم ينتصح ومانعه فلم يمتنع فنزلت الأسعار وابتلع المغتر كلمة الشتم فاستفرغ زبدة أمواله. وأما الثالث فكان اعتماده على ما يستنتجه بنفسه من أقوال الجرائد وملاحظاتها وكلهم لم يأخذوا بالجد في العمل ولم يعملوا بنصيحة سماسرتهم الذين هم أدرى بالمضاربات وأعلم بوجوهها وأعرف بتقلباتها.

الغني أعلم أنه مهما برعت في الجدال وتفننت في إقامة البرهان فإني لا أعتبر مضاربة البورصة إلا مقامرة والمقامرة عين المخاطرة.

٨،٢٧ السمسار أما المخاطرة فهي مع الإنسان في كل حركة ومن حاول أن يحترس من الأخطار فلا يخرج من بيته على أنه فيه معرض للخطر أيضًا وإني مقنعك من نفسك : قلت لي الآن ان لديك من زراعتك ثلاثة آلاف قنطار من ستمائة فدان زرعتها قطنًا في هذه السنة وهذه القناطير مخزونة عندك تتربص لها صعود الأسعار غير مبال بما يلحقها من نقص الوزن وما يتهددها من الأخطار كالسرقة والحريق فإذا كنت تنتظر الزيادة والصعود في أثمان ثلاثة آلاف قنطار فما أولاك أن تنتظرها في أرباح ثلاثين ألفًا في الكونترانات وما اشتريت أرضًا وما أنفقت على حرث وما خشيت تلف زرع وما بذلت ماء وجهك رجاء ري وما دخلت في قضايا ومنازعات ومشاكل مع الجيران والحكام وما تخوفت الآفات سماوية كانت أو أرضية بل هو ربح عفوا صفوا ولا رأسمال له سوى أربعة حروف تخطها يدك في امضائك.

الغني مهما أقمت لي من الأدلة والبراهين فإني أجد نفسي غير مطمئنة إلى الدخول في هذا الباب

٩،٢٧ السمسار أنا لا أكلفك أمرًا عظيمًا ولكنني أدعوك إلى نفعك وما عليك إلا أن تجرب فتشتري الفين من الكونترانات فتضيفها إلى ثلاثة آلاف وتنتظر في الكل صعود الأسعار والضامن لك في الربح أن لا تخرج عن إشارتي ونصيحتي. وجملة القول

his buying and selling, relying on advice from one of two fortune-tellers: one a Sudanese woman using seashells, the other a European with bits of paper. The second one heard a lunatic whom he trusted yelling in the street "Go away, Zayd!" At that particular moment, he was wavering between buying and selling. Taking those words as an omen, he rushed in his carriage to the broker and told him to buy twenty thousand qanṭars. The broker tried to counsel against it, but he refused to accept the advice; all the broker's attempts to prevent a loss were rebuffed. Prices fell, and the idiot had to swallow his curses as he lost all his money. The third relied entirely on what the newspapers had to say. None of the three treated things seriously or took their brokers' advice. Those brokers are the people with the best information on speculation; they're the best informed about its ups and downs.

Rich Man You may have just given me an expert argument and skillful proof, but you should know that I can't regard speculation on the Stock Exchange as anything but a very risky venture.

Broker But man takes risks in everything he does. Anyone who tries to 27.8
protect himself from danger will never leave his house, even though it too can be exposed to risks. But let me try to convince you on the basis of your own situation. You've just told me that your yield this year is three thousand qanṭars from six hundred feddans of land. This year you've planted cotton, and the qanṭars are being stored in your house in anticipation of a rise in prices. You haven't taken into account the fact that cotton loses weight, nor the threat of other hazards such as theft or fire. If you were waiting with your three thousand qanṭars till prices rise, wouldn't it be better to wait for the profits from thirty thousand "contracts"? You wouldn't have to buy land, spend money on ploughing, or worry about crop damage and all the bother about irrigation. You'd never need to get embroiled in legal actions and disputes or problems with neighbors and government officials. You'd have no fears of disaster, whether earthly or heavenly. Instead it's all clear profit. The only capital involved is the four letters which you write as your signature.

Rich Man No matter how many arguments you advance, I'm still wary of getting involved in the matter.

Broker I'm not going to involve you in anything major; I'm only sug- 27.9
gesting something to your advantage. All you have to do is to experiment by purchasing two thousand contracts. You can add them to your own three thousand, and then wait for the rise in prices for all of it. As long as you accept

أن الفرق في سرعة الربح بين ما يشتغل به الناس من التجارة والزراعة والصناعة وبين أشغال البورصة كالفرق ما بين السفر على ظهور الجمال والطيران على جناح البخار أو ما بين الصعود على الدرج لطبقة عالية والصعود في المصعدة أو ما بين استنساخ الكتب وطبعها. وأنت المخير بعد ذلك في ما ترضاه لنفسك لنمو ثروتك.

الغني وكيف حال الأسعار اليوم؟

السمسار كما كانت بالأنس وهي فرصة للشراء.

الغني خذ لي الآن ألف قنطار.

١٠،٢٧ قال عيسى بن هاشم: وهنا تركنا العصفور قد وقع في الفخ وحولنا السمع إلى ما لا يزال دائرًا بين صاحب القضية وتبيع المحامي:

التبيع فإذا تبعت رأيي ووافقتني عليه فلا ترفع قضيتك إلى المحاكم الأهلية لأنها فضلا عما فيها من بطء التنفيذ في مثل هذه المسائل فإنها قلما تحكم على الحكومة وإن حكمت كانت الصعوبة في تنفيذ الحكم أما المحاكم المختلطة فإنها لا تخشى أن تحكم على الحكومة بجميع مصالحها والتنفيذ فيها أنفذ من لهم في الرمية كما أن المحاكم الأهلية لا تعرف قدر هذه القضية ومنزلتها من التاريخ ولا تهتدي إلى تقدير فوائدها الماضية من عهد من وضع يده عليها إلى الآن وأؤكد لك أنك لا تربح هذه القضية المهمة إلا إذا رفعتها إلى المحاكم المختلطة ولكن أسألك قبل كل شيء هل الشجرة مذكورة في الحجة باسمها التاريخي وهل نسبك مثبوت الاتصال بالواقف؟

صاحب القضية أما الشجرة فمذكورة في حجة الوقفية أنها على أرض سواد ومنصوص عنها أنها «شجرة العذراء» وأما نسبي فهو متصل بأحد عتقاء الواقف السلطان الظاهر بيبرس المستحقين في ذلك ولكن من لي بدخول القضية في المحاكم المختلطة؟ ومن لي بمحام أجنبي وقد علمت ما يلزم لهؤلاء المحامين الأجنبيين من المبالغ الجسيمة في مقدم أتعابهم؟

١١،٢٧ التبيع هون عليك الأمر فأما دخول القضية في المحاكم المختلطة فأمر سهل يكون

my advice, I can guarantee you a profit. To sum it all up, the difference in speedy profits between people who work on the one hand in commerce, agriculture, and industry, and on the other in the Stock Market is like the difference between traveling by camel and flying on the wings of steam, between climbing stairs to an upper story and taking the elevator, or between two copies of the same book, one handwritten, the other printed. This being so, it's up to you to choose as you please.

RICH MAN How are prices faring today?

BROKER Exactly as they were yesterday, a golden opportunity to buy.

RICH MAN Then take a thousand qanṭars.

ʿĪsā ibn Hishām said: With that, we left this sparrow who had just fallen into 27.10
the snare, and listened to the continuing conversation between the plaintiff and foreign lawyer's assistant:

ASSISTANT If you take my advice and agree with me, then don't bring your case before the Native Courts. Quite apart from the slow pace at which they function in situations like this, they rarely rule against the government; and even if they do, it's difficult to have the judgment imposed. The Mixed Courts, on the other hand, have no qualms about ruling against the government, using all their facilities in the process. Sentences are carried out quicker than a shot from a bow. In much the same way, the Native Court doesn't appreciate the importance of this case and its place in history, nor will it take into consideration the interest accrued from the time of seizure till now. I can assure you that you won't win this important case unless you take it to the Mixed Courts. But before anything else, tell me about the tree that's mentioned in the deed with its recognized historical name? Is your own descent traceable back to the endower?

PLAINTIFF It's mentioned in the endowment document as being on arable land and recorded as being "the Tree of the Virgin." My own descent can be traced back to a freedman of the endower, Sulṭān al-Ẓāhir Baybars, who had rights to it. But how can I bring the case before the Mixed Courts? How can I possibly afford a foreign lawyer when I'm well aware of the huge sums you have to pay them in advance fees?

ASSISTANT Don't worry about that! Bringing the case before the Mixed 27.11
Courts is easy: it's simply assigned to a foreigner. With regard to the foreign

بالتنازل عن القضية لأحد الأجانب وأما المحامي الأجنبي فأنا أتكفل لك بإقناع معلمي الذي اشتغل معه بقبول القضية من غير أن يكلفك دفع شيء من المقدم وغاية الأمر أنه يتفق معك على أن يكون له النصف في ما تأتي به القضية من مبالغ الربح وأما الأجنبي الذي تتنازل له عن القضية فهو تحت يدنا في مكتبنا لمثل هذه المسائل وما عليك الآن سوى النفقات والرسوم القضائية.

صاحب القضية لا بأس بما تقول ولكن البلاء أنه ليس عندي ما أستغني عنه من النقد لهذه النفقات ويعلم الله أني لو كنت واثقاً بكسب القضيّة لأقدمت على بيع الحصة التي أملكها في الربع ولكني أخشى أن أخسر القضية فتضيع عليّ أسباب معيشتي ومعيشة أولادي.

التبيع لو تعلم مهارة معلمي وماله من الشأن في المحاكم المختلطة ورفعة مقامه لدى الحكومة واتصاله بالقنصليات لاستخرت الله في بيع ما تملك ولنشطت إلى إقامة الدعوى.

صاحب القضية استخرت الله تعالى وأعجبني هذا الرأي.

التبيع إذن قد أذعنتني في الكلام مع معلمي وما عليك إلا أن تحضر لعقد الشروط غدا.

صاحب القضية امهلني حتى أجد من يشتري الحصة بالثمن المناسب.

التبيع أنت في سعة من الوقت إنما يجب أولا أن تبادر بإحضار الأوراق والمستندات للاطلاع عليها.

صاحب القضية بيني وبينك العقد في هذا المكان في مثل هذه الساعة.

قال عيسى بن هشام: فتركنا هذه السمكة وقد وقعت أيضاً في الشبكة بعد أن راعنا ١٢،٢٧
خطا العمدة في لعبته حتى أصابت الكرة وجه متفرنج متبرنط كان يلعب مع التاجر فاشتاط غضباً واحتدم غيظاً وقام عن اللعب يريد بالعمدة شرًا فحال التاجر بينهما والمتبرنط يدمدم ويطمطم والعمدة يجمجم ويغمغم فكان «وقف القبعة للعمامة» موقف الغراب للحمامة ثم أفضى توسط التاجر إلى فض ختام زجاجتين من «الشمبانيا»

lawyer, I'll guarantee I can persuade the lawyer with whom I work to accept the case without bothering about advance charges. All he'll request is half the amount of profit you get from the case. The foreigner to whom you'll submit the case is in our office ready and waiting to be made use of in cases like this. All you need do now is pay the costs and judicial fees.

PLAINTIFF That's all very well, but the problem is that I haven't any spare cash on hand to pay for such expenses. God knows, if I was confident of winning the case, I'd sell the portion of the property that I own. But I'm afraid I'll lose the case, in which case I and my children will lose our livelihood.

ASSISTANT If you knew how skilled my master was and realized what high standing he had in the Mixed Courts and how close were his contacts with the consuls of various countries, you'd be asking God for proper guidance in selling your part of the estate and making every effort to bring the case.

PLAINTIFF In which case I will indeed ask God for guidance. I like your plan.

ASSISTANT So then, you'll permit me to speak to my master. All you have to do is come tomorrow to settle the terms.

PLAINTIFF Give me some time to find someone to buy part of the estate for the appropriate price.

ASSISTANT You've plenty of time to do that. All we need for the moment is for you to bring the deeds and documents so that they can be perused.

PLAINTIFF We'll meet here at the same time.

ʿĪsā ibn Hishām said: At that, we left this fish as well to thrash around in the net. We were surprised to watch as the ʿUmdah played a billiards shot that hit a hatted foreigner who was playing with the Merchant right in the face. The man was absolutely furious and got out of his seat, hell-bent on doing the ʿUmdah an injury. The Merchant intervened between the two of them, with the hatted gentleman muttering and snarling, while the ʿUmdah kept stammering and mumbling. This was a genuine case of hat versus turban, or raven against **27.12**

في عقد الصلح على حساب العمدة وبعد ذلك طلب ملاعب العمدة منه أن يعود إلى إتمام اللعب فاستعفاه فلم يعفه فقام إلى اللعب مكرها ويده ترتعش وما كاد يرمي الثانية حتى أصاب جوخة البليار بصولجانه فخرقها فشقها عن آخرها فصاح الخادم بصاحب البار فجاء والخدم يتسابقون من حوله وقد التفت إليهم يؤنبهم كيف يسلمون البليار لهذا الأخرق فيخرقه ويشقه ثم وقف للعمدة يطلبه بثمن ما أتلف وتعويض ما عطل وقد قدر خسارته بخمسة عشر جنيهاً فأخرج العمدة كيسه وعدّ ما فيه فإذا هو لم يتجاوز الثلاثة عشر جنيهاً فأبى الرجل إلا ما قدره فتوسط التاجر والحاضرون في إرضائه بها فقبلها وحلف العمدة أن لا يعود لهذا النوع من اللعب وقال إن الا فعوان أسلم مَا من هاذ الصولجان.

قال عيسى بن هشام: وجلس العمدة بعد ذلك لا هم له إلا صرف همه بالشرب فما زال ١٣،٢٧
يطلب وصاحب البار يجود عليه حتى انتشى من العقار وانتهى صاحبه من القمار وقد قام منه يزعم أنه خسر فيه ثلاثة جنيهات ويظهر لصاحبه التأسف والتأفف فقال له: دعك بالله من هذا الأسف فالضائع ضائع ومصيبك على كل حال أخف من مصيبتي ثم ناوله كأساً وبينا هما يشربان إذا بالخليع قد عاد إليهما هاشاً باشاً فرحاً مرحاً يقول لهما:

الخليع أشرق أنسنا وسعدت ليلتنا وطاب وقتنا وأسأل الله تعالى أن يطيل ليلنا ويبعد نهارنا فقد تم مرادنا وهلم بنا.

العمدة ونحن نسأل الله أن يقصر ليلنا ويدني نهارنا فاقعد معنا نقصص عليك ما دهانا في غيابك ثم ما زالا يقصان عليه وهو يحملق فيهما حتى صار عرض يمينه طولا وقد تدلت شفته ولعبت أرنبة أنفه.

الخليع ويلي فأنا الملوم إذ تركتكما فوقع لكما ما وقع في غيابي ولكن قدر الله لكما ولطف بكما أما أنا فمصيبتي الآن أكبر وأعظم فماذا أقول وماذا أفعل وكيف أدفع وبماذا

dove. The Merchant's mediation ended up with two bottles of champagne being opened at the 'Umdah's expense as a way of resolving the issue. Now the 'Umdah's billiard partner insisted that he finish the game. The 'Umdah asked to be excused, but that was refused. He returned reluctantly to the table, his hand shaking as he did so. It was only two shots later that he hit the table cover with his cue and ripped it apart. The waiter yelled for the owner of the bar, and the other waiters hurried along behind him. The owner turned to them and scolded them for giving a billiard cue to such a clumsy idiot. "Now he's split the table and ruined it!" he told them. He then went over to the 'Umdah and demanded compensation for the damage he'd caused. He estimated the cost at fifteen pounds. The 'Umdah took out his purse and counted the contents; he only had thirteen pounds. The owner would only accept the full amount. The Merchant and several other people now interceded and asked him to accept the amount he had, and the owner finally agreed. The 'Umdah meanwhile vowed that he would never play that game again; playing with adders, he said, was safer than using a billiard cue.

'Īsā ibn Hishām said: The 'Umdah sat down, his only concern being to rid himself of his anxieties with drink. He kept asking, and the bar owner kept responding generously to his requests until he was drunk as a lord. Meanwhile the Merchant had finished his card game. He got up, claiming that he had lost three pounds, and made it clear to the 'Umdah how much he regretted what had happened. "For heaven's sake, stop feeling so sorry for yourself!" the 'Umdah told him. "At least the loser loses. Your misfortunes are not as bad as mine." He handed the Merchant a glass. While they were drinking, the Playboy came hurrying back all excited. He told them: 27.13

PLAYBOY It's time for our intimate little gathering. The night is blessed, the timing is right. Now I ask God to prolong this night for us and keep daylight far away. Our plans are complete. Let's go!

'UMDAH For our part, we ask God to shorten the night and bring daylight as soon as possible! Sit down, and we'll tell you what has happened to us while you were away.

As they both told him what had happened, he stared at them—right arm outstretched, lips drooping, and nostrils flared.

PLAYBOY Woe is me! I'm to blame for leaving you to get into this trouble in my absence. However, God has made provision and shown you His

أعتذر وقد أتممت الأمر واستحضرت المراد ومجلس الأنس في انتظاركما؟

التاجر الأمر أيسر مما تخشى فما يفوتنا الليلة ندركه الليلة الآتية.

الخليع هذا شيء لا يدرك في كل حين فهذه المرة بيضة الديك لبيضة الخدر وكيف يؤجل هذا المجلس وقد مضى قطع من الليل عظيم:

كيف الرجوع بها وحول قبابها
سمر الرماح يملن للاصغاء؟

فخلصاني ناشدتكما الله مما أنا فيه وانقذاني من هذه الورطة العظيمة.

التاجر وما وجه الخلاص وقد علمت الحال؟ ١٤،٢٧

العمدة تالله أن الحرمان من أنس هذا المجلس الذي وصفته لأعظم من كل ما نابنا ولوكان الوقت نهاراً لأسرعت بأخذ ما يلزم من البنك.

التاجر إذا كانت الرغبة انتهت بك إلى ذلك فالأمر يسير ومعي ما يكفي وأنا أقوم لك مقام البنك فكم تطلب ولأي ميعاد تكتب؟

الخليع هكذا الأصحاب تكون في وقت الشدة فحياك الله.

العمدة أعطني عشرين جنيهاً تكون معنا على سبيل الاحتياط.

التاجر هاك سبعة عشر جنيهاً تبلغ العشرين المطلوبة بالثلاثة التي خسرتها أمامك.

١٥،٢٧ قال عيسى بن هاشم: فما كان أسرع من الخليع أن استحضر الدواة والقرطاس وقدمهما إلى العمدة فرجاه أن يكتب الصك عنه ثم أمضاه وخرجوا والعمدة يجرر أذياله، ويحك قذاله، والباشا يفكر ويعجب، وينظر ويستغرب، ثم خرجنا في عقبهم لنرى كيف ينتهي الأمر بهم.

kindness. My problems on the other hand are much worse. What can I say or do? How can I pay? What excuse am I supposed to offer? I've arranged everything and managed to bring the object of our desire. The intimate soirée is waiting for us!

MERCHANT Things are much easier than you fear. What we miss tonight we can get tomorrow!

PLAYBOY Such things aren't always available. This particular occasion is totally unique for a secluded girl. How can I postpone our little gathering when it's well past midnight?

How can I return her, when around her domed mansions
there are brown spears poised attentively?[15]

I beg you both, please save me from the tricky situation I'm in.

MERCHANT You know the situation. What's the best solution? 27.14

'UMDAH By God, it would be terrible to be deprived of the intimate occasion that you've described, far worse in fact than any other misfortune we've suffered. If it were daytime, I'd hurry to the bank and get the cash we need.

MERCHANT Since you seem to be that keen, things are simple. I've got enough money on me now. I'll assume the bank's role for you. How much do you want, and what deadline can you set for repayment?

PLAYBOY Now that is true friendship indeed when circumstances are difficult! May God grant you a long life!

'UMDAH Just to be on the safe side, loan me twenty pounds.

MERCHANT Here's the balance, seventeen pounds. That's the twenty you're asking minus the three I lost here in front of you.

'Īsā ibn Hishām said: No one could have moved quicker than the Playboy in bringing inkwell and paper. He put it gleefully in front of the 'Umdah and asked him to fill out the check. Once he had signed it, the three of them left. The 'Umdah kept dragging the edge of his coat behind him and scratching his head. Meanwhile the Pāshā kept looking on in amazement and pondering. We followed them out to see how things would work out. 27.15

مصباح الشرق ٨٨، ١١ يناير ١٩٠٠

١،٢٨ قال عيسى بن هشام: فخرجنا والباشا يقول: ما هذا الذي نرى من أحوال هذا الورى كأن ناقعاً فقعهم في جابيه جمعت اخلاط الكبائر أو غاماً غمهم في خابيه وعت أمشاج الجرائر فإننا كلما خطونا خطوة رأينا من المكر والغش صنوفاً وأضرابا أو نجونا نجوة قرأنا من الخداع والنفاق فصولاً وأبواباً فما أتعس من يعاشرهم وما أنحس من يحيى فيهم وما أشقى من يجاورهم وما أسعد من يجافيهم واغوثاه من الإنسان في هذا الزمان فقلت له قدك بل وفي كل زمان

لن تستقيم أمور الناس في عصر
ولا استقامت فذا أمناً وذا رعبا
ولا يقوم على حق بنو زمن
من عهد آدم كانوا في الهوى شعبا

٢،٢٨ هكذا كان بنو آدم تأخر عهدهم أو تقادم فهم على ما هم فيه أبداً أمس واليوم وغدا وما عساك تقول في ذرية الشيخ آدم وحواء وقد قالت فيهم من قبلك ملائكة السماء ﴿أَتَجْعَلُ فِيهَا مَن يُفْسِدُ فِيهَا وَيَسْفِكُ الدِّمَاءَ﴾ وما عساك تذكر قوماً ترى أصغر صغير منهم وأحقر حقير فيهم يود لو افتدى بمنطقة البروج ومجرة الكواكب ما أسف من الدنايا وسفل من المطالب وما عساك تصف خلقاً أفضل ما في أعضائه أكبر سبب لشقاء الخلق وشقائه:

أفضل ما في النفس يغتالها
فنستعيذ الله من جنده

هذه المضغة التي بفيه ويقال أنها أفضل ما فيه لو نسجت مضغة على قدرها حماة العقارب حماك الله لحمتها ولعاب الأفاعي وسمام الأسلود أعاذك الله سداها وصبغتها لكانت مع ذلك أخف شرا ولكان هذا اللسان أشد منها ضرا وما عساك تنعت نوعا نعت الله واحداً منهم في القرآن الكريم بتسع صفات:

Miṣbāḥ al-sharq 88, January 11, 1900[16]

ʿĪsa ibn Hishām said: As we left, the Pāshā was saying: "What is going on with the things we see people doing? It's almost as though someone has soaked everyone in a jar containing a mixture of all the worst faults to be found in man or else dipped them in a pool full of the various categories of crime. With each step we take we seem to be encountering every conceivable type of fraud and deceit. Whenever we investigate something, we read whole chapters involving swindling and hypocrisy. Pity the poor devils who have to deal with them and live among them! How miserable their neighbours must be, and how delighted those who can elude them—so God help me against mankind in this era!" "Enough of such talk!" I replied, and quoted these lines to him: 28.1

In no age will people's affairs be in sound order,
nor have they ever been; here security, there alarm.
In no age do people uphold any right;
from Adam's time they were divided by caprice.[17]

Whether the era was backward or advanced, mankind was always this way; people now are exactly as they've always been, yesterday, today, and tomorrow. What can you possibly say about the descendants of Shaykh Adam and his wife Eve, when the angels have already had the following to say about them: «Do you put in it someone who will do mischief amongst them and will spill blood?»[18] How can you describe a society when, as you can see, utterly despicable and insignificant people aspire to be ransomed for the very zodiacal sphere and galaxy of stars? What despicable behaviour, what lewd desires! How can you characterize a created species when its most outstanding members are the chief cause of mankind's and their own distress? 28.2

The best things in the heart destroy it,
so we seek refuge in God from its army.[19]

"The morsel inside the man's mouth is the best thing in it," as the saying goes. If another identical morsel could be made with a scorpion sting as its meat—may God protect you!—and viper spittle as its pigment—may God shield you!—it would still be less harmful and pernicious when juxtaposed with this type of language. How can you describe a species, one of whom God Himself has described in a verse of the Qur'an with nine epithets:

﴿حَلَّافٍ مَّهِينٍ هَمَّازٍ مَّشَّاءٍ بِنَمِيمٍ مَّنَّاعٍ لِّلْخَيْرِ مُعْتَدٍ أَثِيمٍ عُتُلٍّ بَعْدَ ذَٰلِكَ زَنِيمٍ﴾

فأف لمصيرهم نهار وحندس
وجني رجال منهم ونساء
وليت وليداً مات ساعة وضعه
ولم يرتضع من أمه النفساء
يقول لها من قبل نطق لسانه
تفيدين بي أن تشكي وتائي

فإذا تأملت في أخلاط الأخلاق فلا تأس ولا تغضب وإذا مارست سجايا ٣،٢٨
الخلق فلا تدهش ولا تعجب وما يدريك أن ما رأيته من أخلاق هؤلاء النفر أهون حالا من أخلاق من علاهم من سادات البشر ولعل ما رأيته من طمع الغني ومكر السمسار وخداع التبيع وما شهدته من غش التاجر وغفلة العمدة واحتيال الخليع بما ينكشف من نياتهم وينجلي من طوياتهم هو دون ما تراه في كبراء الناس مخفي تحت حجب التكلف والتطبع مستوراً عن أعين الجلساء بأستار الموارَاة والتصنع وكلما اعتلى الإنسان درجة في المقام وخطا خطوة إلى الأمام تقنع لها بقناع وتلثم بلثام فتجد حقائق الخلائق مرسومة تحت صفائح الدهاء مضروحة تحت جنادل الرياء بل ربما كان المتجرد من خلق حميد وطبع مجيد أكبر متغال في التظاهر به ليشتهر فيه ويعرف عنه كان لي صاحب ثراء من لسانه غضنفراً رئبالا يحرس عرينا ويحمي أشبالا فكان يرهب الأكاسرة ويرعب القياصرة فإذا كشفت عن قلبه وحسرت عن لبه وجدته من الجبن نسيجة ترأم على سخلها وأمة تحنو على طفلها وأعرف آخر ضجت أحرف الفضيلة من وخزها بقلمه ولوكها في فمه وهو يخمش وجهه ويدمي جفونه إن سمع أن مختلساً اختلس دانقاً دونه وقد يتم هذا التصنع ويتمكن هذا التطبع فيملك المتصنع من وجهه ما يشتهي من أشكال الانفعالات المتناقضة وأوضاع العلامات المتعارضة فتكون دموعه طوع إرادته وابتسامته عند حاجته.

«An oath taker, despicable, a slanderer proceeding in his libel, a preventer of good, a transgressor and criminal, harsh as well and impure by birth»[20]?

So to blazes with their periods of day and night
    and their two sexes, men and women!
Would that a child died at the moment it was born
    and did not suckle from its mother in childbed!
It says to her before ever speech is granted:
    All you will get from me is sorrow and complaint![21]

As you contemplate different aspects of morality, don't despair or lose your temper. And as you experience people's various traits, don't act so amazed! Don't you realize that the moral integrity of the people you have been watching is by far preferable to that of their social superiors? Perhaps the things you've noticed—rich men's greed, brokers at their tricks, lawyers' assistants using all their wiles, the Merchant's treachery, the 'Umdah's ignorance, and the Playboy's crooked schemes—all of which clearly reveal their secret intentions and convictions—are actually significantly less pernicious than the things influential men and amirs keep under a veil of phony affectation, hidden from their colleagues' eyes behind walls of dissimulation? Every time someone is promoted a rank and takes a step forward, he enshrouds the process in a veil of secrecy. You'll find the truth about humanity recorded under pages of artful dissimulation and buried beneath cascades of hypocrisy. Indeed, people completely devoid of moral virtues and laudable qualities will be the ones who go to the greatest lengths of pretence in order to be known and recognized for them. I once had a friend who, on the basis of his talk, you would have assumed to be a raging lion guarding his lair and protecting his cubs, feared and respected by Caesars and Chosroes'. However, when you probed a little and penetrated his mind, you discovered that he was a complete coward, like a sheep leaning over its lambs or a wet nurse bending over her infant. I know another man who's made the letters of the word "virtue" shout, so often does he use his pen to prick with it and his mouth to spit it out. And yet, should he hear that someone has swindled a mere penny out of him, he scratches his face in anguish and gets sore eyelids from weeping. He's adept at using such fakery in his facial expressions to adopt a variety of different moods and symptoms; he can produce tears at will, and smiles when needed. **28.3**

قال رجل لآخر: ما أكثر ما تحول رقعة الشطرنج وتتقارب. قال له: تقلب وجه الإنسان أعجب وأعجب. وقد تبقى الصفات الذميمة. والأخلاق اللئيمة. مطوية عن النظر. محجوبة عن البصر. حتى يتاح لها كاشف من الحوادث فينزع عنها الفدام. ويحسر عنها اللثام. فيظهر الطبع السقيم. ويبين الخلق الدميم. ومن أصدق عوامل التبيين والبيان. لأخلاق الإنسان. «الخوف والحزن والغضب والسكر» وعامل السكر أمامنا فهلم بنا. نلحق بأصحابنا. ٤،٢٨

قال عيسى بن هشام: فأدركناهم وهم وقوف يتشاورون وسمعناهم وهم يتحاورون: ٥،٢٨

العمدة دعوني الآن من هذا كله فقد صاحت عصافير بطني لأنني من لقمة الصباح التي تناولتها مستعجلا ما دخل جوفي طعام إلى الآن فهيا بنا إلى السكة الجديدة نعطف على دكان العطفي لنأكل هناك فإن طعامه دسم وسمنه زبدة ولحمه سمين.

التاجر ما هذا العطفي؟ أين أنت من العجمي ورزه الذي يعد بالواحدة وأين أنت من كباب الفار بجانبه؟

الخليع ما هذا الخلط ونحن في الأزبكية وفيها ما تشتهي الأنفس وتلذ الأعين بين النوبار وسان جمس بار وأميركان بار واسبلندد بار وناهيك بهذه الأماكن ونظافتها وحسن خدمتها وعلو قدر الواردين عليها.

العمدة دعنا بالله من هذه الأماكن فإن طعامها لا يثمر ولا يغني من جوع خصوصاً وأنا على هذا الخلو وشدة الجوع.

الخليع وأنا على كل حال لا يمكنني أن أترك هذه الأماكن وأذهب إلى الأماكن التي تشيران إليها فإنني أخشى أن يراني أحد بها لما في ذلك من الحطة وخدش الشرف.

التاجر إذا كان الأمر كذلك فأنا على رأيك.

الخليع (للعمدة) لا مناص لك فضعيفان يغلبان قوياً فأدخل بنا النيوبار.

One person once said to another: "How often the chessboard changes in appearance, then comes together!" to which the other replied: "The changing aspects of people are even more remarkable." The sordid and depraved side of their moral character remains hidden from view until something happens to bring it to light. Then the seal is broken and the veil ripped away, revealing a foul and ugly disposition. In dealing with people's character the clarifying factors are fear, sorrow, anger, and drunkenness. The last of those, drunkenness, is right in front of us now, so let's catch up with our three companions. **28.4**

ʿĪsā ibn Hishām said: We caught up with them. They were engaged in conversation, and so we eavesdropped on them: **28.5**

ʿUMDAH I've had enough of this! The sparrows in my stomach are screaming! Apart for a morning snack, I haven't eaten a thing all day; and I ate that in a hurry. Let's go to the New Road.[22] We can go to al-ʿAṭfi's—there's plenty of good food to be had there, real butter and good fat meat.

MERCHANT What's this al-ʿAṭfī you're talking about? What about al-ʿAjamī's rice and kebab at al-Fār next door?

PLAYBOY Look, what's the point of all those places when we're in the Ezbekiyyah, with the New Bar, St. James Bar, American Bar, and Splendid Bar close by. They've everything to please the heart and delight the eye, not to mention cleanliness, good service, and the prestige of their customers.

ʿUMDAH No, forget about those places! Their food isn't rich enough. It won't be enough to assuage my hunger, especially when my stomach is so empty.

PLAYBOY Well, whatever the case may be, I can't possibly leave this area and accompany you to the places you've mentioned. I'm afraid people I know might see me there, and then I'd go right down in their estimation.

MERCHANT If that's the case, then I'm with you.

PLAYBOY (*to the ʿUmdah*) Well then, there's no question. Two weaks overrule a strong. Come on, let's go to the New Bar.

قال عيسى بن هشام: فدخلوا ودخلنا خلفهم وجلسوا وجلسنا على مقربة منهم وما خلع الخليع طربوشه ورداءه حتى نزع العمدة عمامته وعباءه وما طرق الخليع بيده على المائدة حتى صفق العمدة بكفيه يستدعيان الخادم فحضر ومعه قائمة الألوان فتناولها العمدة ونظر فيها ثم ناولها الخليع وقال: ترجم لي فأخذها الخليع وتأمل فيها ثم التفت إلى الخادم وقال له: وأين اللون الذي أكلت منه بالأمس فقد كان لذيذاً؟ وأخذ يسرد الألوان حتى ينتهي منها والعمدة لاه عنه والتاجر منصت إليه. ٦،٢٨

الخليع (للعمدة) ماذا تختار؟

العمدة أختار الشوربة ومن بعدها لحم الفرن.

التاجر وأنا أطلب كباباً ورزاً وقرعاً.

الخليع (للخادم) أعطني ما يفتح به الطعام ثم خلاصة اللحم ورزاً بفاكهة البحر ودجاجة بعش الغراب والكمأة وهليونا بالسمن.

العمدة ما هذه الأسماء؟

الخليع هذه مآكل خفيفة لا تقوى معدتي على هضم سواها.

التاجر كل ما يعجبك والبس ما يعجب الناس!

قال عيسى بن هشام: فيجيء الخادم أولاً للخليع بفاتحة الطعام وإذا هو زيتون وفجل وسمك ملح وزبدة فيتأمل العمدة فيها ثم يميل على قطعة الزبدة فيبتلعها ويقول ما هذا الخلط أزبدة وسمك فيطلب الخليع سواها وما يأتي الخادم بصحفة الشوربة للعمدة حتى يكون قد أتى على ما كان أمامه من الخبز ومال على نصيب الخليع فأكله. ٧،٢٨

العمدة (العمدة للخادم) وأين الخبز؟

فيأتيه الخادم بقطعة أخرى فيفتها في المرق حتى يفيض على المائدة وبعد أن يلتهم ذلك يطلب صحفة أخرى وخبزاً آخر فيأتي عليهما أيضاً ثم يطلب من الخادم اللون الثاني وفي أثناء ذلك يميل على أكل الخليع فيأخذ قطعة من الدجاجة ويضعها أمامه

ʿĪsā ibn Hishām said: They went inside, and we followed behind. They sat down, and we took seats nearby. The Playboy took off his tarboosh, and immediately the ʿUmdah removed his turban and cloak. When the former beat on the table with his hands to call the waiter, the ʿUmdah clapped with his. The waiter came up with the menu. The ʿUmdah grabbed it, took a look, and then handed it to the Playboy. "Translate for me!" the ʿUmdah asked. The Playboy took it and perused the contents. "Where's the item I had yesterday?" he asked the waiter. "It was delicious." The Playboy now proceeded to list the various choices until he reached the end. The ʿUmdah was paying no attention, but the Merchant listened carefully. **28.6**

Playboy (*to the ʿUmdah*) What would you like to order?

ʿUmdah Broth, and, to follow, grilled meat.

Merchant I'll have kebab, rice, and pumpkin.

Playboy (*to the waiter*) First I'll take the hors d'oeuvres, then a meat omelette, rice with seafood, chicken with mushrooms, truffles, and asparagus with butter.

ʿUmdah What are all those strange words?

Playboy They're light foods. My stomach can't digest any other kind.

Merchant As the saying goes, eat whatever you like, but wear clothes that please other people!

ʿĪsā ibn Hishām said: The waiter came back with the hors d'oeuvre for the Playboy: olives, radish, salted fish, and butter. The ʿUmdah took a look at them, leaned over towards the slice of butter and gulped it down. "What's this weird mixure?" he asked. "Butter with fish?" The Playboy asked for some more. But no sooner had the waiter reappeared with the bowl of broth than he discovered that the ʿUmdah had already eaten all the bread that had been put there for him. He leaned across to grab the Playboy's share and gobbled it down. **28.7**

ʿUmdah (*to the Waiter*) Where's the bread?

The waiter duly brought him another piece. The ʿUmdah dunked it in the bowl of broth until it spilled on to the table. He gobbled that down too and asked for another bowl and some more bread, both of which he downed quickly. He asked the waiter to bring something else. All the while, he kept

ويضع عليها السكين ليقطعها فتزوغ منه إلى الأرض فيتناولها بيده ويأكلها ثم يأخذ قطعة من عش الغراب فيقضم منها ثم يعيدها إلى صحفة الخليع ويقول له: ما هذا القشر؟ تطبخونه هنا وهو عندنا على الجسور يلعب به الصبيان؟

٨،٢٨ ثم يحضر الخادم بما طلب فيطلب منه خبزًا أيضاً فيزجر الخادم ويقول: ليس مخبز الرمالي هنا.

الخليع (للخادم) ما هذه السفاهة يا جورج؟ أليس كل شيء له ثمن ونحن بدرهمنا نطلب ما نريد؟

الخادم (للخليع) لا مؤاخذة فإن كلامي ليس موجهاً إليك.

الخليع إن لم يكن لي فإنه لصاحبي وصاحبي هذا أعز عليّ من نفسي.

العمدة دعه يأت لنا بالخبز ولا تشغل نفسك بما يقول.

التاجر (للخادم) اذهب إلى شغلك وأحضر لي أيضاً لوناً من الخضر.

العمدة وأحضر مع الخبز بصلا فقد ذهبت نفسي إليه.

الخليع كله يصح إلا أكل البصل فلا يخفاك أننا في أي مكان ونذهب إلى أي مكان ورائحة البصل لا تطاق.

ولما انتهى التاجر من أكل الأصناف التي طلبها بعد خلطها ببعضها نادى وطلب منه شيئاً من الحلوى أو الفاكهة.

العمدة إذا كان في الفاكهة رطب فأعطني منه.

الخليع وأنا أطلب موزًا وأناناس .

العمدة (مقهقهاً) ومن قال أنك لست من الناس.

الخليع (للخادم) هات زجاجة من النبيذ الأبيض أيضاً.

٩،٢٨ قال عيسى بن هشام: وفي أثناء ذهاب الخادم رأينا العمدة مال على صحفة الفاكهة فأخذ بيده خمس أصابع من الموز فوضعها في جيبه ولما انتهوا من الفاكهة والشرب

leaning over the Playboy's plate. He took a piece of chicken, put it down in front of him and tried to cut it with his knife. It fell on the floor. He got up from the table, picked it up in his hands, and ate it. He then took a piece of mushroom, nibbled at it, then put it back on the Playboy's plate. "What's this stuff?" he asked. "They may cook it here, but where I come from you can find it on dikes; children play with it."

The waiter came back with another bowl of broth. The 'Umdah asked for more bread. With that the waiter lost his temper. "My dear Sir," he said, "this isn't the Ramali bakery, you know!" 28.8

PLAYBOY (*to the Waiter*) What's that stupid talk for, George? Everything's got its price here, hasn't it? With our money we can ask for whatever we want.

WAITER (*to the Playboy*) Excuse me, Sir! My remarks weren't directed at you.

PLAYBOY If they weren't directed at me, they were at my friend here. He's worth more to me than my own self.

'UMDAH Let him go and get the bread. Don't bother yourself with what he's saying.

MERCHANT (*to the Waiter*) Get on with your job and bring me some vegetables as well.

'UMDAH (*to the Playboy*) And bring an onion along with the bread. I fancy one—

PLAYBOY You can do anything you like tonight except eat onions. Don't forget that from here we're going somewhere where the smell of onions won't fit!

Once the Merchant had mixed the various things he had asked for and eaten them all, he yelled out and asked for some dessert and fruit.

'UMDAH If you've any dates, bring me some.

PLAYBOY I'll have some bananas and pineapple.

'UMDAH (*guffawing*) Who ever said you weren't a man of the people!

PLAYBOY (*to the Waiter*) Bring a bottle of white wine too.

'Īsā ibn Hishām said: While the Waiter was away, we watched as the 'Umdah reached for the fruit bowl, grabbed a cluster of five bananas and put them in his 28.9

أحضر الخادم آنية من البلور الملون لغسل اليد فيهم العمدة بشرب ما في الإناء فيمنعه الخليع.

العمدة لماذا تمنعني عن الشرب من هذا الماء وقد شممت رائحة الزهر منه.

الخليع هذا يا سيدي ماء غسل أطراف اليد.

التاجر من عاش رأى.

العمدة (للخادم) الحساب.

التاجر القهوة.

الخليع الخلال.

الخادم يأتي بالقهوة والخلال وقائمة الحساب العمدة يتخلل بعود ونكش أذنه بعود آخر ثم يمسحه في المائدة ويقول للخليع: اقرأ بالله وقل لي كم علينا.

الخليع ثلاثون فرنكا.

العمدة ما هذا النهب والسلب؟ لو كنا ذهبنا إلى المكان الذي أشرت إليه ١٠،٢٨
قبل دخولنا لكنا ملأنا البطون وتمتعنا بالطعام الكثير مع الثمن القليل ولو كنت تذكرت أن عندي مما أحضرته معي من البلد برمة رز بحمام لكنا توجهنا إلى الأوتيل فإنها كانت تكفينا وزيادة ومع ذلك فإني أرى الخادم يريد أن يستغفلنا فأضاف على الحساب شيئاً ليختلسه وأنا لا أقبل الغفلة على نفسي ولا أدفع هذا الحساب فإني أكلت في محلات كثيرة مثل هذا المحل وظهر لي فيها اختلاس الخدم وأنا أكشف لكما هذا الغش فإنه يهون عليّ أن أنفق عشرة جنيهات في الهباء ولا أقبل أن أدفع قرشاً واحداً غشني فيه إنسان. ثم صك القدح بالقدح يستدعي الخادم فاهراق النبيذ على المائدة فحضر الخادم فعز عليه ما رأى.

الخليع (للخادم) هل في الحساب غلط؟

الخادم .. أي غلط فيه مع هذا البيان.

العمدة وأي بيان وأنت الكاتب له؟

pocket. Once they had all finished with the fruit and drink, the Waiter brought colored glass finger bowls to wash their hands. The ʿUmdah was about to drink from his, but the Playboy managed to stop him.

ʿUMDAH Why are you stopping me drinking that water? It smells like rose water.

PLAYBOY My dear fellow, it's for rinsing your fingertips.

MERCHANT Seeing is believing!

ʿUMDAH (*to the Waiter*) The check!

MERCHANT Coffee!

PLAYBOY And a toothpick!

The Waiter brought all this. The ʿUmdah used a toothpick on his teeth, then took another and used it to clean out his ear. He wiped it off on the tablecloth and turned to the Playboy.

ʿUMDAH How much do we owe?

PLAYBOY Thirty francs.

ʿUMDAH What's this? That's daylight robbery! If we'd gone to one of the 28.10
places I suggested before we came here, our stomachs would be full by now and we'd have had plenty of food for a moderate price. If I'd remembered that I've a pot of rice and pigeon that I brought up with me from my home town, we could have gone to the hotel. That would have been more than enough for all of us. This Waiter's obviously trying to make fools of us, so he's decided to overcharge us and keep the rest for himself. But I'm not the kind of person who'll tolerate such negligence. I'm not going to pay this bill. I've eaten in lots of places like this, and it's always obvious when the waiters are cheating. I'll show you both how we're being tricked. I don't mind wasting ten pounds on nothing at all, but I won't pay a single piastre for deceit of any kind.

With that, he clinked two glasses together to call the Waiter, and wine spilled all over the table. When the Waiter arrived, he was not at all happy at what he saw.

PLAYBOY (*to the Waiter*) Is there some mistake on the check?

WAITER How can there possibly be a mistake? Everything you ordered is clearly listed.

ʿUMDAH What an explanation! But you're the one who wrote the check.

الخادم أنا الكاتب له وأنت الآكل له.

العمدة وهل أكلنا ثلاثون صحناً حتى ندفع ثلاثون فرنكا؟

الخادم (للخليع) أرجوك أن تقنعه.

العمدة هل أنا جاهل حتى يقنعني؟

الخليع يقوم.

التاجر إلى أين؟

الخليع أراهم وضعوا في لوحة التلغرافات تلغرافاً جديداً فأريد أن أقرأه.

الخادم (للعمدة) أعطني الحساب ولا تعطلني عن الشغل. ١١،٢٨

العمدة يضع في الصحن عشرين فرنكا.

العمدة هاك حسابك ولا أعطي غير هذا.

الخادم ليس هنا محا المساومة في الطعام بعد أكله.

التاجر زده فرنكين.

الخادم لقد كان الأولى بكم أن تأكلوا في غير هذا المكان ما دمتم على هذه الصفات.

التاجر لا تغلط يا خواجا فإن حضرته يأكل في هذا المكان وفي أعظم منه ولكنه يحب الأمانة.

الخادم وهل أنا خائن؟ (ثم يتكلم باليونانية في حدته ويذهب مغضباً)

التاجر حقيقة أنه قليل الحياء.

العمدة وحياتك لا يأخذ مني غير هذا ولا أخاف من رطانته.

(ثم يعود الخادم مع صاحب المحل وقد عاد الخليع إلى مكانه.)

صاحب المحل ماذا جرى؟

العمدة خادمك يسرقنا ويشتمنا.

صاحب المحل هذا كلام لا يقال عن محلنا.

الخادم (للخليع) عهدي بك أنك تصاحب الظرفاء والمتمدنين من الناس فما ١٢،٢٨

WAITER I wrote it, and you ate it!

'UMDAH Did we eat thirty dishes to be charged thirty francs?

WAITER (*to the Playboy*) Please convince him, Sir!

'UMDAH Am I such a fool that he can convince me?

(*The Playboy now gets up to leave.*)

MERCHANT Where are we going now?

PLAYBOY I see they've put a new cable in the political cable sheet. I need to read it.

WAITER (*to the 'Umdah*) Pay me the full amount and stop keeping me from my work. 28.11

(*The 'Umdah puts twenty francs on the plate.*)

'UMDAH There's your check. I'm not going to pay any more.

WAITER This isn't a place where you haggle over the cost of food after you've eaten it.

MERCHANT Give him a couple more francs.

WAITER As long as this is the way you behave, you'd do better eating somewhere else.

MERCHANT Don't lose your temper, my good sir. This gentleman here eats in places like this and places even more important. But he likes people to be honest.

WAITER So I'm dishonest, am I?

(*He is so angry that he starts yelling in Greek, then goes away.*)

MERCHANT Modesty's obviously not his strong point!

'UMDAH By your life, I'm not afraid of him. What I've already paid is all he's going to get out of me.

The Waiter had now come back with the owner of the restaurant. The Playboy had also come back to his seat.

RESTAURANT OWNER What's going on here?

'UMDAH Your waiter here is overcharging us and being abusive.

RESTAURANT OWNER No one may say such things about our restaurant!

WAITER (*to the Playboy*) Up till now, I've only known you to keep company with charming, civilized people. What on earth are you doing bringing this shaykh to our restaurant tonight? His behavior's been criticized by 28.12

هذا الشيخ الذي جئتنا به الليلة وقد انتقده الحاضرون بأنه يبلع الزبدة. ويلف الخبز ويمد يده إلى صحن غيره ويعيد إليه فضلة ما يأكله. ويلوث المائدة بالمرق والنبيذ ويمسح يده في غطاء المائدة. ويكسر الكأس ويخفي الموز في جيوبه ويهم يشرب ماء الغسل وينكش أذنه بعود الخلال ويمسحه في المائدة. حتى أن من كان بجواره من المترددين على المحل قاموا اشمئزازاً واستكراهاً من رؤية هذه الأفاعيل القبيحة ولم يكتف بهذا كله حتى أخذ يغازل بعض السيدات ويغامزهن فقمن مستقبحات مستنكرات.

صاحب المحل حقاً إذا حضر عندنا شيخ مثل هذا مرة أخرى نفرت الناس وتعطل المحل

الخليع يغمز صاحب المحل.

الخليع لا تقل عليه شيخ فهو صاحب الرتبة الثانية مع لقب بك.

صاحب المحل لا تؤاخذ الخادم يا سعادة البك فهو خادمك والمحل محلك.

العمدة شكراً لك.

ثم يقول للخادم: يجب أن تعرف الناس وتتعلم حسن المعاملة من حضرة الخواجا.

ثم يلتفت إلى صاحب المحل ويقول: والله لولا معروفك لما أعطيت غير العشرين فرنكا ولكني أعطي الآن ما تطلبه. ١٣،٢٨

صاحب المحل (للخادم) أنظر ماذا يشرب حضراتهم وأحضر لنا دورا من المشروب.

ثم مال الخليع على العمدة يشير عليه بطلب دورين من عنده إكراماً لصاحب المحل فطلب ثم طلب ثم نقد صاحب المحل الحساب على أصله مضافاً عليه ثمن ما طلبه أخيراً وقام للخروج يتمايل ويتثاءب ويتمطى ويمسح عينيه بيده ويشكو للخليع هجوم النعاس عليه فيقول له: هذه عادة تكون بعد الأكل ولا يصرفها إلا قدحان من الكونياك فهيا بنا إلى بوديجا فخرجوا وخرجنا من ورائهم نستقصي بقية أنبائهم.

everyone in the restaurant. He's swallowed butter, wrapped up bread, reached over other people's plates and put the remains of what he has eaten back on them; he's stained the table with gravy and wine, wiped his hands on the tablecloth, broken his glass, pilfered bananas and put them in his pocket, almost drunk water from the finger bowl, cleaned his ear with a toothpick and then wiped it off on the tablecloth. Many of our regular customers sitting nearby have walked out in disgust at the mere sight of such appalling manners. And not content with all that, he has even been flirting with some of the women and making lewd gestures at them. They've all got up and left in disgust.

RESTAURANT OWNER Indeed, if a shaykh like this one comes here again, people will stay away and our restaurant will be put out of business.

PLAYBOY (*giving the Owner a wink*) Don't address this gentleman as "Shaykh"! He's attained the second grade of honor and is entitled to be addressed as "Bey."

RESTAURANT OWNER My dear Sir, please excuse the Waiter. He's always at your service, and the place is entirely at your disposal.

'UMDAH Thank you!

(*He then addresses the Waiter.*)

'UMDAH You need to find out about people and learn from the Owner how to treat them properly.

(*He then turns to the Restaurant Owner.*) 28.13

'UMDAH By God, but for your kindness, I would only have paid twenty francs. But now I'll pay the amount you ask.

RESTAURANT OWNER (*to the Waiter*) Find out what they are drinking and bring us a round.

The Playboy now leaned over to the 'Umdah and suggested that he ask for two rounds of drinks to honor the Owner. The 'Umdah asked for wine, then for more. Then he paid the restaurant Owner the original amount, to which was added the cost of the things he had just been asking for. The 'Umdah stood up to leave, swaying, stretching, and yawning; he kept wiping his eyes and complaining to the Playboy about feeling very tired. The latter replied that this was all quite normal when one was full; the only way to relieve the feeling was to have a couple of glasses of cognac. "Come with us," the Playboy said. "Let's go to the bodega." With that they left. We followed to find out what would happen to them next.

قال عيسى بن هشام: فأخذوا طريقهم وأخذناه وقصدوا قصدهم وقصدناه وفيما نحن نسير بين تفكير وتذكير وتصوير وتقدير اذ التفت الباشا الى ذلك النزل الكبير بل الخوانق أو السدير فرأى شموس الكهرباء مشرقة وينابيع الضياء متدفقة يلوح فيها زنجي الليل بقميص أبيض ويظهر فيها أديمه كالآبنوس المفضض وقد تناسقت عمدها تناسق الاشجار فأزهرت بالانوار مكان الأنوار وقام كل عمود منها كأنه عمود فجر يفجر ثغرة الدجنة أي فجر ورأى منثور المصابيح في ظلمة الحلك كأنها نجوم منثورة في قبة الفلك ورأى من تحتها صفوف الرجال وربات الحجال على أرائك متكئين وسرر متقابلين يرفرف عليهم النعيم وهم كالعقد النظيم رفرفة النسيم على النبت الجميم وسمع عزف آلات الطرب فوقف يسألني بين الدهشة والعجب: أتراه محتفلاً لأنس أم زفافاً في بيت عرس؟ انشق البيت عن غرفاته فانكشف للناظر ما في حجراته أم تراه ليلة مهرجان لرهط من الجان انسوا الى الانسان أنسة الدواجن من الحيوان فهجروا جوف الارض لظهرها وخرجوا من بطنها الى حجرها. ١،٢٩

فقلت له: نعم هؤلاء جن الارض وعفاريت الانس يطوون البر والبحر ويقطعون الحزن والوعر ويطيرون في السماء ويمشون على الماء ويخرقون الجبال وينسفون القلال ويجعلون الآكام وهادا ويبسطون الربى مهادا ويقلبون القفار بحارا ويحيلون البحار بخارا ويسمعون من بالمشرقين صوت من بالمغربين ومن بالمغربين صوت من بالمشرقين ويستنزلون لنظرك أقصى الكواكب ويعظمون كالجبل أصغر العناكب ويمدون الهواء ويذيبون الحصباء ويزنون الأضواء ويستحدثون الأنواء ويستشفون خبايا الأحشاء ويستكشفون خفايا الأعضاء. ٢،٢٩

فقال لي صاحبي: أنك لتصف جن سليمان في هذا الزمان فقلت له: هؤلاء كبراء الافرنج أرباب المدنية والحضارة الناظرون الينا من صياصي العظمة بعين الاستهانة والحقارة فان نظروا الينا من جهة العزة والمنعمة نظرونا بنظر العقاب فوق ٣،٢٩

Miṣbāḥ al-sharq 89, January 18, 1900[23]

'Īsā ibn Hishām said: They went on their way to the place which they had selected. As we followed behind them, we were lost in thought and assessing the situation. The Pāshā turned towards that great hotel, a veritable al-Khawarnak and al-Sadīr, and noticed the electric lights gleaming brightly like rising suns, so much so that darkest night shone in white raiment and its surface seemed like ebony embossed with silver. The street lamps resembled tree branches glowing with light rather than mere lamps. Each pillar seemed like a ray of dawn piercing the cavity of darkness—and what a piercing it was! In the pitch darkness the lights were like stars scattered throughout the dome of the firmament. Beneath these lights the Pāshā could see rows of men mingling freely with women. Favored by continuing good fortune and enveloped in a becoming opulence, they were sitting opposite each other and lounging on sofas, looking like an exquisite posy on a flowering branch caught by the rustle of the breeze. The sound of musical instruments could be heard. "Is this a reception for some sociable occasion?" the Pāshā asked me in amazement, "or a bridal procession? Has some house opened its rooms so that anyone can see what's inside? Or is it perhaps a festival night for a group of demons who are socializing with human beings like tame animals? They've forsaken the earth's interior for its surface, its belly for its lap." 29.1

"Yes," I replied, "these people are devils in human form. They traverse land and sea, cut through hard and rugged earth, and fly in the heavens. They can walk on water, penetrate through mountains, and pulverize mountain peaks, turning hills into lowlands, levelling mounds, making deserts into seas, and changing seas into steam. They make people in the East listen to sounds made by people in the West, and vice versa. They can bring down the remotest stars for you to see, magnify the tiniest spider into a mountain, freeze the air, melt stones, start gales, cure secret intestinal ailments, and discover unknown facts about the limbs." 29.2

My companion told me, "You're describing Solomon's jinn living in this era!"[24] "They're European officials," I replied, "steeped in civilized society. From their lofty perch they look down on us with utter contempt. From the perspective of power and prosperity, they regard us like an eagle perched on the peaks of Raḍwā and Thabīr staring down at desert grasshoppers and pool frogs. With regard to learning, it's like the great sage and teacher Alexander 29.3

شماريخ رضوى وثبير الى جنادب الرمل وضفادع الغدير وان نظروا الينا من طريق العلم نظرونا بنظر معلم الاسكندر حكيم الحكماء الى صبي يتهجى في العين والياء وان نظروا الينا من جهة الصناعة نظرونا بنظر فيدياس الى جرار أوكلاس وان نظروا الينا من باب الغنى نظرونا بنظر صاحب المفاتيح التي تنوء بالعصبة الى مجهود ينوء لقوت يومه تحت القربة وان نظروا الينا من حيث السجايا نظرونا بنظر رضوان الى الشيطان فقال لي الباشا: رويدك وهل هم في الحقيقة كما يزعمون فقلت: كلا بل هو قوم مدعون مباهتون مبتدعون قبح ما يعملون وساء ما يعملون أولئك هم سلاب الارزاق ونهاب الآفاق وقطاع الدهماء وقراصين الدأماء وسفاك الدماء أولئك هم الذين يخادعوننا بزبرجهم ويغشوننا بهرجهم ﴿سَحَرُوا أَعْيُنَ النَّاسِ وَاسْتَرْهَبُوهُمْ وَجَاءُوا بِسِحْرٍ عَظِيمٍ﴾.

وهم في اغترابهم هذا ينقسمون الى قسمين أهل السعة والبطالة والجدة والفراغ وهؤلاء هم مرضى السأم أرادوا بفرط غناهم وتفننهم في مدينتهم أن يمتازوا عن أبناء نوعهم فكان ذلك سبباً لتولد داء الضجر والملل فيهم فحطتهم القدرة الى الاستشفاء من ذلك برؤية الصخور ومعاشرة المنحطين عنهم درجات في المدنية في أكواخهم بل معاشرة الفهود والقردة في غاباتهم وأما القسم الثاني فهم أهل العلم والبحث الذين جعلوا علمهم آلة لسلب بلاد الناس ونزعها من أيديهم فهم يتحملون المشاق ويتعرضون للاخطار في أقاصي الارض وشواسع البلدان لمزاحمة الناس في أوطانهم وأرزاقهم واستعبادهم في ديارهم واسترقاقهم فقال الباشا انه لنبأ عظيم وخطب جسيم ولله الامر من قبل ومن بعد. ٤،٢٩

قال عيسى بن هشام وكنا قد اقتربنا من باب الحان فاذا الثلاثة جالسون حول الدنان فجلسنا بالقرب منهم لنحفظ الحديث عنهم: ٥،٢٩

الخليع البرنس هنا.

having to watch a boy spelling out his alphabet. In the sphere of arts and crafts, it's as though Pheidias the sculptor were placed alongside Euclas.[25] Concerning wealth, it would be like a man with a bunch of keys weighing down his waistband looking at a laborer wiping the sweat from his brow beneath a waterskin. Finally, if we investigate the finer qualities of mind, it would be like Riḍwān looking at the very Devil." "But wait a minute!" the Pāshā said. "Are they really the way they claim to be?" "Certainly not!" I replied. "They posture and show off, and keep bringing in innovations. Their activities are evil and their knowledge is pernicious. They're the people who rob others of their wages. They plunder territories, cross deserts and destroy common folk. They're the pirates of the high seas who make other people's blood flow. They're the ones who keep duping us with their finery and swamping us with their cheap trash. «They have bewitched people's eyes and terrified them; they have brought a mighty enchantment.»[26]

"When they travel abroad, they can be divided into two categories. The first consists of wealthy leisure classes with time to spare, people afflicted with the disease of boredom. They're so incredibly wealthy and so susceptible to the novelties of civilization that they're eager to separate themselves from their peers. As a result they're beset by the twin diseases of listlessness and boredom. The only way they can be cured is by staring at rocks and coming into contact with people in countries less civilized than their own, visiting their hovels and indeed rubbing shoulders with panthers and monkeys in their lairs. The second group consists of scholars who have used their knowledge to despoil countries and grab control of them. They can put up with hardships and be exposed to all kinds of danger in the earth's remotest corners and most distant lands, and all because people in their own homelands are so crowded and their salaries are so limited; everyone feels indentured and enslaved." The Pāshā told me that this was important information and a clear danger. The entire matter belonged to God alone. 29.4

ʿĪsā ibn Hishām said: By now we had reached the tavern. The three of them were lined up by the kegs. We sat down near them to record their conversation: 29.5

PLAYBOY   Is the Prince here?

العمدة (منزعجًا) هل يجيء هنا برنس وهل يليق بنا ان نجلس في مكان هو حاضره ولم دخلنا فقم بنا.

الخليع لا عليك وسترى كيف أفعل فلا تقوم الا وهو مصافحك ومجلسك.

العمدة لا تمزح ولا تهزأ فأين البرنسات منا؟

التاجر (للعمدة) صدقه. فإن لبعض البرنسات أخلاقًا لينة ترابية فيساوون أنفسهم بالناس في المعاملات والمجتمعات.

العمدة (للخليع) وما عساك تفعل هل لك معرفة به؟

الخليع نعم وكيف لا أعرفه ولي معه جلسة كل ليلة وكثيرًا ما أوصلته الى قصره؟

العمدة ما أكثر ما تبالغ.

الخليع لا مبالغة وهاك البرهان.

٦،٢٩ قال عيسى بن هشام فيقوم الخليع فيقصد مائدة عليها من الخمر والنقل أصناف وألوان فيميل الى واحد من الجالسين عليها وكان منشغلا بالشراب والنقل يد في الصحن ويد في الكأس ولقمة في الفم

الخليع أسعد الله أوقات مولاي دولة البرنس.

البرنس (مستبشرًا ضاحكًا) أهلا بصاحبنا أين انت؟ فقد طالت غيبتك علينا.

الخليع استغفر الله يا مولاي انا تحت الخدمة وعند الطلب وما منعني عن مجلسكم العالي الا هذان الصاحبان وأحدهما عمدة من عمد الارياف والآخر تاجر من تجار الثغور ولي معرفة سابقة بهما في بلادهما وهما لا يعرفان هذا البلد الا قليلا وكنت وعدتهما ان هما أتيا مصر أن أصحبهما.

أحد الحاضرين (مازحا) لا بل تسحبهما.

فيضحك البرنس ويقول: وهل هنا زريبة يا سيدي؟ فيقهقه الجميع ويقولون: الله در البرنس في هذه النكته!

ʿUMDAH (*astounded*) Do princes come here? Is it right for us to sit drinking somewhere in the same company as them? Why did we come here? Let's go!

PLAYBOY Don't worry! Just wait and see what I'm going to do. You won't be leaving here without the Prince shaking your hand and sitting with you.

ʿUMDAH Don't crack jokes at my expense. What business do we have with princes?

MERCHANT (*to the ʿUmdah*) You should believe him. Some princes are quite decent and down-to-earth people. They like to deal with people on equal terms in their various meeting places and transactions.

ʿUMDAH (*to the Playboy*) What do you plan to do? Do you know him already?

PLAYBOY Of course! Otherwise how could I get to sit with him every night? I often accompany him to his palace.

ʿUMDAH You're exaggerating!

PLAYBOY No, I'm not. And here's the proof for you!

ʿĪsā ibn Hishām said: The Playboy stood up and went over to a table piled high with various sorts of wine and dessert. He leaned over to one of the people seated there who was busying himself with the offerings; one hand was holding his plate, the other his glass, and his mouth was full. 29.6

PLAYBOY May God grant His Highness the Prince all felicity!

PRINCE (*laughing merrily*) Hello to you, my friend! Where have you been? We've missed you.

PLAYBOY Please forgive me, Your Highness. I've been performing a service and under obligation. What's kept me away is these two companions of mine: one's a provincial ʿumdah and the other's a port merchant. I've known them before in their own towns, but they're both unfamiliar with Cairo. I promised them both that, when they came to Cairo, I would accompany them.

ONE OF THE COMPANY (*cracking a joke*) Don't you mean "drag them"![27]

(*The Prince laughs, then says:*)

PRINCE Oh, is there a cattle pen around here?

(*Everybody laughs.*)

EVERYONE What a terrific joke the Prince has just made!

البرنس انا لم أتعلم التنكيت ولكن ذلك يصادفني في بعض الاوقات.

صاحب لآخر انظر يا أخي الى حدة لطافة البرنس وشدة رقته وضخامة ألفاظه.

الصاحب لصاحبه وأنت ما شاء الله ما أفصحك في تعبيرك واأبلغك في بيانك أتأخذ هذه الجمل عن الجرائد؟

البرنس (للخليع) تفضل أقعد. ٧،٢٩

الخليع وصاحباي؟

أحد الحاضرين يستريحان.

البرنس وهل هما من الاغنياء المعتبرين؟

الخليع العمدة يمتلك ألف فدان والتاجر في بلده أكبر خان وللعمدة عشرة وابورات للري والرتبة الثانية وللتاجر وابور للحليج ومعروض له على الرتبة الثالثة.

البرنس إإذا كان الامر كذلك فلماذا لم تدعهما للجلوس معنا.

الصاحب (لصاحبه) ما بقي علينا الا هذه المضايقة فأنا لا أطيق هذا المجلس بعد الآن فقم بنا.

الصاحب انتظر برهة حتى ياتي الدور المطلوب مع صحن بلح البحر الذي أوصى به البرنس.

٨،٢٩ ثم يعود الخليع الى صاحبيه ليجلس بهما في مجلس البرنس فيقوم العمدة له موقرًا مبجلا فيسقط فم السيجارة من يده على الرخام فينحني عليه العمدة يجمع شظاياه متأسفًا متأنفًا فيجره من يديه ويقول:

الخليع أتهتم بمثل هذا الشيء الحقير ولا تملك نفسك امام البرنس وهو يدعوك اليه؟

العمدة ليس اهتمامي به الا لكونه تذكارًا عندي من حضرة مأمور المركز كنت أهديته فرسًا فأهداني هذا الفم وهو عندي ثمين ولكن دعنا من هذا وقل لي أحقًا ان دولة البرنس يدعوني اليه وكيف عرفني وماذا قلت له عني؟

PRINCE I've never learned how to crack jokes, but once in a while something will strike me.

ONE OF THE COMPANY (*to another*) Do you see, my friend, how subtle and refined the Prince's wit is, and what lofty phrases he uses!

ANOTHER MEMBER (*to his colleague*) By God, you're also being very eloquent tonight! Did you get those phrases from the papers?

PRINCE (*to the Playboy*) Come and sit down. 29.7

PLAYBOY What about my two companions?

ONE OF THE COMPANY They're relaxing.

PRINCE Are they known to be rich?

PLAYBOY The 'Umdah owns a thousand feddans of land. The Merchant owns the biggest tavern in his town. The 'Umdah owns ten irrigation pumps and holds the second grade. The merchant owns a cotton mill, and is in line for the third grade.

PRINCE If that's the case, why not invite them to join us?

ONE OF THE COMPANY (*to another*) That's all the aggravation we need. I can't stand staying here any longer. Let's go!

THE OTHER MEMBER Wait a bit until they bring the round of drinks we've ordered and the bowl of mussels the Prince asked for earlier.

The Playboy went back to his companions to bring them over to the Prince's table. The 'Umdah got up to pay his respects, but, as he did so, dropped his cigarette holder on the marble floor. He bent down sadly to pick up the fragments, but the Playboy dragged him by the hand. 29.8

PLAYBOY Don't bother about such trifles now! Can't you control yourself when the Prince is inviting you over?

'UMDAH I'm only sorry because it was a memento I received as a present from the district's Municipal Superintendent when I presented him with a horse. That's why I valued it so highly. But let's leave that now. Tell me, has the Prince really invited me over? How did he even know me? What have you told him about me?

التاجر أي نعم قل لنا بالله كيف كان ذلك؟
الخليع قلت ما قلت فارسل حكيماً ولا توصه.
العمدة بالله ماذا ذكرت له عني فاني رأيته مسروراً يضحك كثيراً؟
الخليع أخبرته بقصتك مع سمسار القطن ونفوذ حيلتك فيه وهو الآن يحب أن يسمعها منك.
التاجر وعلى ذكر السمسار هل باع دولة البرنس قطنه أو هو ممن تأخروا في البيع؟
الخليع (للعمدة) تفضلوا بنا.

ولما صاروا امام البرنس مد العمدة يديه منحنياً ثم رفعهما الى رأسه فنظر اليه البرنس متبسماً وأشار بيده مسلماً وأومأ اليه أن يجلس فاستغفر ثم استغفر وأبى الجلوس حتى أجلسه الخليع فجلسوا.

البرنس (لاحد الحاضرين) ذكرني بالله غداً بتصوير الفرس الفلانية فان الدوك بروك أرسل اليّ من لوندره على يد صاحبه المستشار يطلب صورتها.
أحد الحاضرين الأحسن أن يؤخذ رسمها امامه بعد غد عند حضوره مع مفتش الري للغذاء الذي دعوتهما اليه.

العمدة يتأخر قليلا فتصيب رجل الكرسي اصبع التاجر فيقفز متضجراً ثم يجلس متململا

البرنس (للعمدة) ماذا تشرب يا شيخ يا بك؟
العمدة (واقفاً) العفو يا مولاي.
الخليع الامتثال خير من الادب.

البرنس يطلب دوراً ويطلب العمدة بعده دوراً آخرا باشارة الخليع.
ويأخذ الخليع علبة السجارات من امام البرنس ويعطي منها للعمدة وللتاجر فيتحاشى ٩،٢٩

MERCHANT Yes, do tell us how it happened!

PLAYBOY I said what I said. As the proverb puts it, "Send a wise man, but don't advise him."

'UMDAH What was said about me during the conversation? I saw him laughing a lot.

PLAYBOY I told him about the clever way you dealt with the cotton broker. Now he'd like to hear it from you in person.

MERCHANT Talking of brokers, has His Highness the Prince sold his cotton or is he one of the people holding back?

PLAYBOY (*to the 'Umdah*) Let's go!

When they reached the Prince's table, the 'Umdah extended his hand with a bow, then raised it to his head. The Prince smiled at him, gave him a greeting, and gestured to him to sit down. The 'Umdah declined and remained standing until the Playboy sat him down. With that everyone sat.

PRINCE (*to one of the company*) Remind me tomorrow about the picture of that horse. The Duke of Brook has written to me by way of his friend the Counselor asking me for a picture.

ONE OF THE COMPANY It would be better to have the picture taken in his presence the day after tomorrow when the Counselor comes with the Irrigation Inspector to the lunch to which you've invited them both.

The 'Umdah moved back a bit, and his chair leg hit the Merchant's toe. He leapt up angrily, but then sat down again, muttering to himself.

PRINCE (*to the 'Umdah*) What will you have to drink, my dear Shaykh, my dear Bey?

'UMDAH (*standing up*) If you'll excuse me, Your Highness, I won't have anything.

PLAYBOY In this case conformity takes precedence over good manners.

The Prince ordered a round of drinks, then at the Playboy's suggestion the 'Umdah did the same.

The Playboy reached for the cigarette box in front of the Prince and gave one to the 'Umdah and Merchant. The 'Umdah avoided lighting it in the Prince's presence, so he held it in his hand. Then a salesman came over and whispered something in the Prince's ear which made him guffaw. He told the **29.9**

العمدة اشعال السيجارة ويبقي في قبضته ثم يأتي أحد الباعة فيهمس في أذن ابرنس بكلام يقهقه منه ويأمر الخادم أن يعطيه كأساً فيشربه ويضرب العمدة كأساً بكأس يستدعي الخادم لاشعال سجارته ويطلب دوراً.

البرنس (للعمدة) كيف حال الزراعة عندكم وكم رمى الفدان من القطن.

العمدة رمى الفدان عندي ثمانية بأنفاس دولتكم.

التاجر نعم ان المحصول جيد ولكن الاثمان في هبوط وهل باع دولة البرنس أقطانه أم هي باقية الى الآن؟

البرنس (لاحد الحاضرين) أنا لا أدفع في الخنجر الذي رأيته ليوم أكثر من عشرين جنيهاً.

أحد الحاضرين واذا أصرّ صاحبه على الثلاثين.

البرنس (لآخر) أنا لم أزل متأسفاً على الكلب الذي مات والبيغاء الذي طار يا غلام علينا بدور آخر.

١٠،٢٩ ولما جاء الدور وتناول كل كأسه أخرج العمدة ذلك الموز من جيبه فمسح واحدة منها بمنديله وقدمها للبرنس وفرق البقية على الحاضرين فيجد أحدهم صوفاً متلبداً في موزته فيعافيها ويضعها على المائدة.

أحد الحاضرين (للعمدة) هل هذا الموز من عزبتكم ووهل تطعمونه بالصوف عندكم؟

العمدة كلا بل هم من الموز النوبار ولم يمكث في جيبي غير مسافة الطريق.

فيتأفف الخليع ويجمع الموز ويناوله الخادم فيسأله العمدة هل يجب أن نطلب شمبانيا فيصوب له رأيه.

العمدة (للخادم) أحضر لنا شمبانيا انكليزية.

أحد الحاضرين (لصاحبه) يظهر أنه رمى بعشرة.

الصاحب في العقاري.

Waiter to bring a glass for the salesman who drank it and left. The ʿUmdah then clinked two glasses together to bring the waiter over to light his cigarette and ordered another round of drinks.

PRINCE (*to the ʿUmdah*) What's the crop like in your area? How much cotton have you got per feddan?[28]

ʿUMDAH By your Highness's breath, I've been getting eight per feddan.

MERCHANT That's an excellent yield, but prices are falling. Has His Highness sold his cotton yet, or is he holding it back?

PRINCE (*to one of the company*) I'm not going to pay more than twenty pounds for that dagger I saw today.

MEMBER OF THE COMPANY What if the owner insists on thirty?

PRINCE (*to another member*) I'm still sorry about the dog that died and the parrot that flew away. Waiter, another round!

When the new round arrived and everyone had grabbed their glass, the **29.10**
ʿUmdah brought out the bananas from his pocket. He wiped one of them with his handkerchief and offered it to the Prince, then distributed the rest among the people present. One of them found some wool sticking to his banana, so he discarded it and left it on the table.

ONE OF THE COMPANY (*to the ʿUmdah*) Are these bananas from your farm land? Do you ripen them in wool where you come from?

ʿUMDAH No, my dear Sir, they're from the New Bar. They've only been in my pocket for long enough for us to walk here.

(*The Playboy is disgusted. He collects all the bananas and hands them to the waiter. The ʿUmdah asks whether they should order champagne. His offer is accepted.*)

ʿUMDAH (*to the waiter*) Bring us some English champagne!

ONE OF THE COMPANY (*to his companion*) It looks as though the ʿUmdah's crop has actually produced ten per feddan!

COMPANION Yes, in the real-estate bank!

أحد الحاضرين وما معنى انكليزية.

الصاحب يعني من جنس الجنيه.

وفي هذه الأثناء يعود البائع فيقوم البرنس ويخرج ثم يتسلل أصحابه من بعده واحداً بعد واحد ويميل العمدة على أطباق النقل فيستوعبها أكلا. ١١،٢٩

العمدة (للتاجر) كل من هذا قبل ان يعود البرنس فما ألذه ولكن ينقصنا الخبز.

الخليع البرنس ركب العربة وذهب.

التاجر ولكنني لم أره دفع شيئاً من الحساب.

العمدة لعل له هنا حساباً جارياً.

الخليع نسأل الخادم.

الخادم لم يدفع البرنس شيئاً.

الخليع وكم الحساب؟

الخادم سبعون فرنكا بما فيه ثمن الطعام.

العمدة أنا لا أصدق ان البرنس لم يدفع شيء طلبه وعلى فرض ذلك فلا بد ان يرجع فخذ الحساب منه عند رجوعه.

الخادم من عادته أنه اذا خرج على هذه الصورة فانه لا يعود في ليلته ومع ذلك فاني أقيد على البرنس قيمة ما تناوله فقط كما هي العادة أيضاً.

العمدة اذاكنت أدفع شيئاً فلا أدفع الا ثمن ما شربه البرنس وحده.

وفيما هم في هذا النزاع اذ دخل وكيل مديرية فنهض له العمدة ومد له يده والتفت الى الخادم. ١٢،٢٩

العمدة عليّ بتفصيل الحساب وقل لي كم شرب معي البرنس وكم أكل البرنس وكم شرب اصحاب البرنس وكم شربنا مع البرنس وكم شرب قبل مجيئنا البرنس هلم الحساب لأعطيك قيمته.

الخادم قلت يا سيدي انه سبعون فرنكا.

One of the Company What does "English" mean?

Companion From the same nation as the pound.

Meanwhile the salesman came back. The Prince got up at once and left. One by one the members of the company slinked out after him. The 'Umdah leaned over the leftovers from the dessert trays and helped himself. **29.11**

'Umdah (*to the Merchant*) Try some of this before the Prince comes back. It's delicious. But we don't have any bread.

Playboy The Prince got into his carriage and left.

Merchant I didn't see him pay any of the check.

'Umdah Maybe he has a standing account here.

Playboy Let's ask the waiter.

Waiter The Prince didn't pay anything.

Playboy How much is the check?

Waiter Including the food, seventy francs.

'Umdah I can't believe that His Highness would leave without paying his share of the bill. In that case, he must be coming back. Get the amount he owes from him when he comes back.

Waiter Whenever the Prince gets up and leaves like that, he usually won't be back that night. Even so, I'll add just the cost of what you've had to his account. That's normal as well.

'Umdah If I were going to pay for anything at all, it would only be for what his Highness the Prince had to drink.

While they were arguing in this fashion, a deputy governor entered. The 'Umdah got up to welcome him and offered him his hand. He then turned to the waiter: **29.12**

'Umdah Bring me a detailed bill listing exactly what his Highness the Prince had to drink and eat, how much the drinks cost for the Prince's companions, how much we drank with the Prince, and how much the Prince drank before we arrived. Bring me the check so that I can pay you the entire amount.

Waiter I've told you, Sir. It's seventy francs.

العمدة ينقد الخادم ثم يسأل الوكيل: .

العمدة (للوكيل) ماذا يشرب سعادة البك؟

الوكيل أشرب كأس كونياك.

العمدة لا والله لا تشرب الا شمبانيا كما شرب دولة البرنس.

الخليع (للعمدة) لماذا لم تعقد التعارف بيننا وبين سعادة البك كما هي العادة.

العمدة سعادته وكيل مديريتنا وحضرته. (مشيرًا الى الخليع) من ظرفاء مصر وحضرته (مشيرًا الى التاجر) والتاجر من اكابر التجار.

الخليع وكيف حال سعادة المدير فهو صاحبي وطالما قضينا معه ليالي سرور وأنس؟ ١٣،٢٩

العمدة (للوكيل) أظن ان سعادتكم اشتغلتم اليوم في لجنة الانتخابات.

الوكيل نعم وسيكون خيرًا ان شاء الله فطب نفسًا.

العمدة (للخادم) شمبانيا.

الوكيل يكفي فاني أريد أن أجلس برهة مع اخواننا القضاة ووكلاء النيابة الجالسين امامنا (ويشير اليهم).

الخليع لا تقم سعادتكم وانا أستدعيهم الى هنا فان فيهم فلانًا وفلانًا من أعز أصحابي.

الوكيل لا تكلف خاطرك بذلك فلا يليق الا ان أذهب اليهم بنفسي.

العمدة اذًا فكلنا نقوم معك اليهم ويأتينا الخادم بالشمبانيا عندهم.

الوكيل اذا أردت ذلك فلا بأس.

فيقومون فيجلسون مع أولئك الجماعة وتحضر الشمبانيا ويسألهم العمدة الشرب معه منها فيمتنعون فيشدد عليهم فيمتنعون فيحلف عليهم بالطلاق إلا شربوا الكأس معه ويقع على يد من بجانبه منهم يقبلها فيمتثلون ثم يتناول الكأس ويقوم متمايلا على الخليع يشرب معهم فلا يكاد يضع الكأس في فيه حتى تأخذه غصة فلا يملك نفسه فيتداركه الخليع والخادم فيدخلانه داخلا حتى يصلح أمره.

(*The ʿUmdah pays the waiter, and then asks the deputy Governor:*)

ʿUmdah (*to Deputy Governor*) What would you like to drink, Sir?

Deputy Governor A glass of cognac.

ʿUmdah Good heavens, no! You should only drink champagne just as his Highness the Prince did.

Playboy (*to the ʿUmdah*) Why haven't you introduced us to His Excellency in the proper way?

ʿUmdah Deputy Governor of our province, this gentleman (*pointing to the Playboy*) is one of Egypt's refined wits, and that gentleman (*pointing to the Merchant*) is an important merchant.

Playboy (*to the Deputy Governor*) How is the governor? He's one of my **29.13** friends, and I've often spent many enjoyable hours socializing with him.

ʿUmdah (*to the Deputy Governor*) I believe you've been working today on the Elections Committee.

Deputy Governor That's right. God willing, everything will turn out the way we want.

ʿUmdah (*to the Waiter*) Champagne!

Deputy Governor That's enough! I want to go inside to join my colleagues, judges and public attorneys, who are sitting over there. (*pointing*)

Playboy Don't move, Your Excellency. I'll invite them to join us. A and B are both good friends of mine.

Deputy Governor Don't bother yourselves. It would be more proper for me to go and join them.

ʿUmdah That being so, we'll all come with you, and the waiter can bring us a bottle of champagne.

Deputy Governor I've no objection to that, if you wish.

They all stood up and joined the other company. The waiter brought a bottle of champagne, and the ʿUmdah asked them to drink some. They declined and he insisted, but they still declined. Then he started swearing he would divorce his wife if they did not drink with him. He fell on his neighbor's hand and started kissing it. With that they all complied with his wishes. The ʿUmdah now grabbed a glass and stood up unsteadily alongside the Playboy in order to have a drink with them. But hardly had he put the glass in his mouth than he began to choke and could not stop himself. The Playboy, assisted by the waiter, hurriedly pulled him inside to put his sorry state to rights.

قال عيسى بن هشام: ولما صار أصحابنا في داخل المكان قال لي الباشا: ١٤،٢٩

الباشا واذ لم يبق امامنا ما يشغل الناظر والحاضر فتخبرني بالله عن أمركنت أحوم حول السؤال عليه في كل برهة فقل لي ما هذا البرنس؟

عيسى بن هشام البرنس هو لقب منتحل للامراء سبق لنا الكلام عنه وهذا الذي رأيته هو واحد منهم.

الباشا وكيف يدخل أمير في حان وما سمعنا من قبل أن هؤلاء الأمراء ينزلون إلى مخالطة الناس في مثل هذه الاماكن فهل نزل بهم الدهر فصاروا من القلة بحيث لا يقدرون على عقد مجالس اللعب واللهو في بيوتهم وسبحان الله لم يبق من عجائب الحدثان الا ان تطلع الشمس من المغرب.

عيسى بن هشام ليس ذلك منهم عن قلة ولا عوز ولكن ضاقت نفوسهم من سجن القصور ولم يبق لديهم من الجاه ما يدعو الناس للازدحام على أبوابهم والترامي على مجلسهم فهم يعيشون منفردين وبمعزل عن الناس الا ما احتاط بهم من الآفاقيين من الغربيين طلاب الرزق وبغاة الندى فيقيمون في معاشرتهم حتى تنفد الثروة وينضب المال بما يتفننون لهم فيه من الخداع والدهاء والمكر والرياء فترى فيهم من ينتبه الى هذه الحال ويعتبر بغيره فلا يرضى بالبقاء عليها وتطمح نفسه الى مخالطة الناس ومعاشرة الاهالي والتأدب بآداب المجالس والتروح بأحاديث المجتمعات ولما كان الغالب ان مجالس المصريين لا تكون إلا في هذه الحال فقد نزلوا هم أيضاً اليها فاختلطوا بالناس وتخلقوا بأخلاقهم ولعل من تراه منهم على هذه الحال هو أفضل أخلاقاً وأكمل آداباً وأرق طباعاً وأرضى أفعالاً ممن لا يزال مقتصراً على معاشرة أسافل الافرنج بعيداً عن الاختلاط بغيرهم من أهل بلده ووطنه. ١٥،٢٩

قال عيسى بن هشام: وما وصلنا الى هذا الحد من الكلام حتى رأينا العمدة قد أفاق من غشيته وخرج امامنا بين الخليع والتاجر يتهادى في مشيته وقمنا وراء النحيط بقية سيرته. ١٦،٢٩

ʿĪsā ibn Hishām said: Once our friends had gone inside, the Pāshā spoke to me: 29.14

PĀSHĀ At this point, if there's nothing left for us to see, then tell me about something that's been on my mind all this time. What is this "prince"?

ʿĪSĀ IBN HISHĀM "Prince" is a title conferred on royal children. We've talked about it before. The person you've seen here is one of them.

PĀSHĀ How can such a royal person enter a tavern? We've never heard before of such personages lowering themselves to mingle with common people in places like this. Has fate dealt badly with them? Are they so few that they can't hold soirées and parties in their own residences? God in heaven, the only thing more remarkable would be for the sun to rise in the West!

ʿĪSĀ IBN HISHĀM It's not a matter of either numbers or indigence. 29.15 They're bored with being imprisoned inside their own palaces. Not only that, but they no longer have the necessary prestige to bring people flocking to their doors in order to attend their councils. They lead lives that keep them apart from ordinary people; apart, that is, from Western travelers in quest of financial gain and generosity. As a result princes consort with foreigners who play a whole variety of tricks on them—falsehoods, cunning, deceit, and hypocrisy—until all the princes' wealth is exhausted and their funds have dried up. You can find some of them who have become aware of this situation and learned from others' mistakes. Not content to leave things as they are, such people are keen to mingle with ordinary people; they adopt the behavior common to such assemblies and enjoy the conversation in gatherings of this kind. Since the majority of meetings in Egypt are like that, princes have also descended to that level and adapted themselves to their moral standards. The prince whom you've seen here may actually be more ethical, cultured, amiable, and pleasant than other princes who only consort with the European riffraff and recoil from any contact with their own countrymen.

ʿĪsā ibn Hishām said: At this point in our conversation we saw that the ʿUmdah 29.16 had recovered from his drunken stupor. He staggered out between the Playboy and Merchant. We followed them to see what would happen next.

مصباح الشرق ٩٠، ٢٥ يناير ١٩٠٠

١،٣٠ قال عيسى بن هشام: وبعد أن خرجوا من ذلك المحل ونحن أتبع من الظل سمعنا العمدة يقول للخليع تالله لقد أجهدتنا فهلم الآن الى ما وعدتنا لنجلو أعيننا بالوجوه الصباح قبل ان يغير علينا الصباح فيبدي الخليع اهتمامه ويظهر اغتمامه ثم يقطع عليه كلامه ويدفع عن نفسه ملامه بأن طول الانتظار يذهب بحسن الاصطبار ولا يجمل بربات الجمال وصاحبات الدلال أن ينتظرن الرجال ويتحملن الضجر والملال فتلك لفرصة أضعناها لنزعة أطعناها فخاب ما كنا نرتجيه وفات ما كنا نبتغيه وقد جاءتني في غفوتك منها رسالة بأن قد غشيها ما غشيها من الملالة فندمت على جيئتها وذهبت لطيتها فيقول التاجر: اذن ما الذي اكتسبناه بعد الذي فقدناه وأين منا ما نجمع به شملنا ونبدد به ليلنا؟ فيقول له الخليع: لم يبق أمامنا في هذه الساعة الا ملاعب الرقص والخلاعة عسانا نجد فيها بديلا مما لم نجد اليه سبيلا فيخرج العمدة دراهمه من جيبه يعدها ثم يخشخش بها ويردها فيقول التاجر للعمدة: لا تهتم فدرهم الأنس ميسر وللخليع: تقدم فما من شيء عليك معسر

٢،٣٠ فيعطف بهما نحو مكان قريب من غير ما تراخ ولا تعقيب وقد دخلنا من ورائهم وجلسنا بأزائهم فرأينا المكان حومة وغي احتدم وطيسها وهيجاء حرب اصطدم خميسها ومعتركا عجاجته الدخان ومتاريسه الدنان ونباله أصمة القوارير وطبوله الدفوف والمزامير وصلصلة الحلي فيه بالحلي صليل المشرفي بالمشرفي وبريق الأكواب والاقداح بريق الآسنة والصفاح وقواده وأركانه قواده وغلمانه ومغافره العصائب وآزره اعلام الكتائب ودروعه الغلائل ومناديله حمام الرسائل ومنصة الرقص حصنه الحصين وصاحب الحان هو الكمين وحركات الردق والخصر هي حركات الكر والفر والجالسون هناك جيش محصور وجند مقهور والمغنون كماته وأقرانه والنساء حماته وفرسانه:

'Īsā ibn Hishām said: When they left the tavern, we followed behind, sticking closer to them than their own shadows. We heard the 'Umdah tell the Playboy that he had worn them out. "Let's go to the place you promised us," he said. "That way we can make use of comely faces to clear the dirt from our eyes before morning changes everything." The Playboy looked concerned and distressed. He interrupted the 'Umdah and palmed off his reproach by pointing out that, if someone has to wait too long, even the height of patience dissipates. Pampered maidens rapidly grow impatient if they have to wait for men and put up with aggravataion and sheer boredom. "We gave in to a whim," he told them, "and so we've lost an opportunity. Our hopes have been dashed and our goal has eluded us. While you were dozing, the girl sent me a message, complaining that she'd become utterly bored. She regretted ever coming and went on her way." "So then," the Merchant asked, "what can we get to compensate for what we've lost? Where can we sit together now and while away the night?" "At this time of night," the Playboy replied, "the only thing we can still do is head for one of those raunchy dance-halls. Perhaps we'll find some substitute there for what we've missed." 30.1

The 'Umdah now took out his cash, jingled the coins, then put them back in his pocket. "Don't worry," the Merchant told him. "Friendly company is readily available!" He turned to the Playboy. "Lead the way!" he said. "For you, nothing's a problem!"

So, without further delay, the Playboy took them to a place close by. We followed them inside and sat opposite them. We soon realized that the place was a veritable battlefield, its fiery furnace all aglow; in fact, a theater of war involving opposing armies. On this battlefield smoke was the dust cloud; wine casks served as ramparts, pitchers and glasses as armaments. Here flutes and oboes were substitutes for drums, and the clink of jewelry far surpassed the clang of Mashrafi swords.[30] Glasses and bottles gleamed as bright as lance-tips and spears. Here the generals and commanders were managers and waiters; headcloths replaced helmets, shawls replaced battle standards, mantillas replaced armor, and handkerchiefs replaced carrier pigeons. The dancing platform resembled an inaccessible fortress, and the hall's owner played the role of guard on watch. Swaying buttocks and waists were like attack and retreat. The people seated were beseiged, a vanquished army, while singers were its warriors and foes, and women its defenders and cavaliers: 30.2

ألات الظلم جئن بشر ظلم
وقـد واجهـنـا متظلمـات
فوارس فـتنة أعـلام غي
لقينك بالأساور معلمات

٣،٣٠ وترى فيه كل ذات ثدي بارز تنادي هل من منازل أو مبارز ثم تخطر وتجول وتختال وتصول فترمي كل طامع في وصالها بسهام اللحظات ونصالها فترشق بها الدنان فتسيل بدم العقار وتشق بها الجيوب فتسيل بدم النضار:

وقد أغمـدن في أزر ولكن
سيوف لحاظـهن مجردات
قد حن زناد شوق من زنود
بنار حـليها مـتوقدات

وترى في تلك المعركه من كل هلوك مهلكه تنساب في حلة رقصها كالحية في قيصها ثم تلقي بجرحاها في هاوية فترى القوم فيها صرعى كأنهم أعجاز نخل خاوية.

٤،٣٠ قال عيسى بن هشام: وقد رأينا اننا كلما طال جلوسنا ضاقت أنفاسنا وقصرت أعمارنا مما ينبعث من أركان المكان وينتشر من ارجائه ويتصاعد من أكنافه من روائح عكر الخمور وروائح عرق الابدان وروائح الغاز وروائح الأدخنة والحشيش وروائح أنفاس المخمورين وروائح تلك المراحيض التي لم تدخلها ماء وروائح الارض التي تسق باللاقذار وتنبت بالاوساخ فاذا امتزجت تلك الروائح ببعضها وانعقدت منها في سقف المكان سحابة سوداء تساقطت منها الادواء فاستنشقتها الأنوف وامتصتها الصدور ونفذت بها الابدان وتضاءلت منها ذبالات المصابيح كما تتضاءل في المناجم والكهوف فكدنا نختنق وكدنا نصاب بالغثيان فهم الباشا بالقيام فأمسكت به أقول له:

Agents of sweet oppression have wrought an evil tyranny,
turning to us in complaint.
Cavaliers of temptation, beacons of seduction,
they have met you bedecked in bangles.[31]

30.3 You observe every bare-breasted girl as she shouts, "Who's going to join us and compete?" Then she makes the rounds, prancing and strutting. Every man who desires to be in her company throws darting glances at her. She steers them all toward the wine casks, which proceed to gush forth with blood-red wine; she then splits open people's pockets which pour forth the blood of golden coins!

They have been sheathed in wrapping cloths,
but their sword-like glances are exposed.
They have used the flint of passion to kindle the flame,
gleaming with the fire of their jewelry.[32]

In the midst of this battlefield you could see a lewd tart in her dancing finery slithering around like a snake in its skin. She would toss her victims into an abyss, and you could watch people flattened like the stumps of desolate palm trees.

30.4 ʿĪsā ibn Hishām said: As we sat there for a while, we were aware that we could hardly breathe. Our lives seemed shortened because of the disgusting stench that wafted from all corners—the smell of wine dregs, body sweat, lamp oil, tobacco and hashish, coupled with drunken breath and lavatories unflushed by water. An equally foul stench rose from the floor which was littered with filth and dirt. When all these smells intermingled and clustered together like a black cloud from the ceiling, all kinds of pestilence rained down. People inhaled it and sucked it into their lungs; as a result their bodies became emaciated. It was enough to make light wicks go dim just as they do inside pits and caves. We almost choked and felt sick. The Pāshā got up to leave, but I grabbed him and said:

عيسى بن هشام مه، أيصير مثلي على هذا النحو ولما أشهد معركة ولم أحضر معمعة ثم لا تصبر أنت عليه وقد مارست الحروب وشاهدت الوقائع وشممت فيها روائح الرمم.

الباشا نعم شممت ارواح الرمم ولكن في الخلوات والفلوات ولم أشمها منحصرة انحصارها في هذا المكان ومع ذلك فاني اتجلد معك كيلا يفوتني شيء من بداية الامر الى نهايته في ما نحن بصدده.

٥،٣٠ قال عيسى بن هشام: وما أتم الباشا كلامه حتى رأيت صاحباً لي قد وقف بجانبي فسلم عليّ متبسماً متعجباً من وجودي في هذا المحل كتعجبي من وجوده فيه أيضاً فابتدرته السؤال.

عيسى بن هشام ما الذي جاء بك الى هنا؟

الصاحب اني أبحث على رجل احتال اليوم عليّ في امر وأعلم ان هذا المحل وأمثاله ممثوى لمثله من المحتالين فجئته على كره مني بعد أن كنت حرمت على نفسي دخوله منذ زمان ولكن حكم الضرورة مطاع وأنت فقل لي كيف دخلت في هذا العش عش الشيطان وهذا الوكر وكر الافاعي؟

عيسى بن هشام أدخلنا حب الاستكشاف وبنية الاستطلاع وأنت تعلم انني فيه غريب فهل لك أن تجلس معنا برهة تكشق لنا فيها ما يخفى علينا من غوامض ما يجري ههنا.

٦،٣٠ قال عيسى بن هشام: فيجلس الصاحب معهما وما يستقر مكانه ويأخذ يحدثنا من نوادر ما رآه أيام كان يكثر الترداد على هذه الاماكن ويخبرنا باصل نشأتها ومبدأ أمرها ورضا الحكومة بانتشارها الا يدخل رجل يتمايل سكرا فيخترق صفوف الجالسين وهو يقع بينهم ويقوم وهم سكوت منصتون لغناء احدى القيان المشهورات عندهم مشرئبة اليها أعناقهم شاخصة أبصارهم كأنما هم في سكوتهم تحت المنبر يستمعون

ʿĪsā Huh! If someone like me, a person who's never seen a battle in his life or witnessed the turmoils of war, can tolerate staying in a place like this, how is it that someone like you cannot stand it? You've been involved in wars, seen battles fought, and inhaled clouds of dust!

Pāshā True enough. I've inhaled clouds of dust, but that was in open and unconfined spaces. I've never had to inhale smells like the ones bottled up in this place. Even so, I'll grin and bear it like you. Then I won't miss anything and can carry through our intentions from beginning to end.

Hardly had the Pāshā finished talking before I noticed a friend of mine standing right beside me. He greeted me with a smile and expressed his surprise at finding me in such a place. I in turn expressed my surprise at finding him here as well. I immediately asked him: 30.5

ʿĪsā ibn Hishām What's brought you here?

Friend I'm looking for someone who's swindled me on a business matter. I'm well aware that places like this one are regular haunts for tricksters like him. So, even though I've been staying well clear of this place for some time, I've reluctantly come here again. When necessity calls, one must obey. Tell me, though, what's brought you to this den of Satan and nest of vipers?

ʿĪsā ibn Hishām We've come here to study and observe people's customs and morals. But, as you're aware, I'm a complete stranger here. Can you sit with us for a while and tell us about some of the covert and invisible things going on in this place?

ʿĪsā ibn Hishām said: My friend sat down with us both. After settling in his seat, he started telling us stories from the time when he used to frequent such haunts and giving us details about how they got started, how they were run, and how the government sanctioned their expansion. However, it was only a moment before a drunkard came in, staggering his way through the rows of seated customers. He stopped at a place between them and another group that was sitting there quietly, listening to a famous singer. They were all craning their necks and staring at her; it was as though they were sitting silently 30.6

حسن الحديث من وعظ الخطيب ولا يزال الرجل في عربدته حتى يصل الى منصة الرقص والغناء فيضرب عليها بعصا في يده مرارًا ويقول:

٧،٣٠ يكفي الغناء وعلينا بالرقص فيوافقه بعض الحاضرين ويقولون: نعم الرقص ارقص، فيغضب طالب دور الغناء ومن معه فيقولون مع بقية المستمعين: لا بل الغناء الغناء فيلتفت السكران يسبهم ويهزأ بذوقهم ويسفههم في سوء اختيارهم فيجاوبه سفيه منهم فيهجم عليه السكران بعصاه فيقفز صاحب المكان من محله ويهرول حتى يصل الى السكران فيمسك بتلابيبه يجره الى الخارج ويقوم طالب الغناء يشبعه شتمًا وضربا فيتعلق السكران بذيله وينادي البوليس البوليس فيجتمع غلمان المحل مع صاحبه يجرونه وهو قابض على ذيل ضاربه حتى يصلوا به الى الباب حيث يكون جندي البوليس قد حضر على صراخه فيريد القبض عليه وعلى رفيقه الضارب له فيمانعه صاحب المحل ويقول له: بل خذ هذا الرجل الذي جاءنا سكران من الخارج يعربد في محلنا فيأبى الجندي الا القبض على الاثنين فيغمزه صاحب المحل ليلين له فيقول أحد الغلمان: لا لزوم لما تعمل فان حضرة المعاون جالس عندنا في البار مع رفيقته فلانة.

صاحب الحانة (للجندي) لم يبق محل لتوجهك بهما الى القسم فتعالوا بنا ندخل الى حضرة المعاون في البار.

الجندي هذه حيلة أعرفها تريد بها تهريب صاحبك وكيف يكون حضرة المعاون هنا في البار وهو الليلة صاحب النوبة في القسم.

صاحب الحانة ما عليك الا أن تدخل وهما في قبضتك فتراه بعينيك.

٨،٣٠ الجندي يمتثل فيدخلون فيرون المعاون جالسًا بجانب رفيقته خالعًا رداءه على ظهرها وطربوشه على رأسها وهو يسقيها من كأسه وتعاطيه من كأسها.

beneath a pulpit during a preacher's sermon listening to the most flawless of discourse. The drunkard kept making a fuss till he reached the stage set up for singing and dancing. He banged on it with a cane he was carrying.

"That's enough singing," he yelled. "Let's have some dancing instead." 30.7
Some of the crowd agreed with him and yelled for dancing. The person who had originally asked for singing and those with him were furious. Along with everyone else, they kept yelling for more singing. The drunkard turned round and started cursing and mocking them, ridiculing their poor taste and stupid choice. Some fool answered back, whereupon the drunkard set about him with his stick. The proprietor got up from his seat, pounced on the drunkard, grabbed him by the collar, and dragged him toward the exit. The man who had wanted the song to continue swore at the drunkard and laid into him. The latter clung to his assailant's coattails, yelling "Police, police!" The waiters assisted the proprietor and dragged the drunkard towards the exit, but he kept clinging to his assailant's coat until they reached the exit. A policeman had responded to his cries and was waiting there. He was intending to arrest both men, but the proprietor stopped him taking in the drunkard's assailant. "Just take this man away," he told the policeman. "He got utterly drunk somewhere else first, then came to my place and started picking fights." But the policeman would only arrest both men. The proprietor made a gesture to the policeman as if to give way to him. Just then one of the waiters came rushing over. "You needn't do anything," he said. "The Police Adjutant's here; he's sitting at the bar with his girlfriend X."

PROPRIETOR (*to the Policeman*) Now you've no reason to take them both to the police station. Come along, we'll all go in and see the Adjutant at the bar.

POLICEMAN This is obviously a trick. I realize you're trying to rescue your friend. How can the Adjutant be in the bar? Tonight's his shift at the station.

PROPRIETOR Just bring these two men you've arrested inside and see for yourself.

The Policeman agreed, so they all went inside, only to find the Adjutant 30.8
sitting beside his girlfriend with his coat over her shoulders and his tarboosh on her head. He was giving her a drink from his glass while she did the same from hers.

صاحب الحانة (للمعاون) لقد تعطل يا حضرة الأفندي محلي وتعطيله لا يرضيك فان هذا الرجل قد دخل عندي وهو سكران من الخارج لم يشرب من هنا شيئاً فعربد في المكان واخل بنظامه ثم تعدى على هذا البك وهو من أكثر الناس ترددوا علينا والغريب أن جندي البوليس صمم على أخذهما معا الى القسم وحضرة البك من أبناء الكرام ولا يليق بكرامته أن يرافق السكران اليه ثم أن الجندي لم يسمع لي قولا عندما أوقفته على الحقيقة.

المعاون يلبس طربوشه ويستدعي الجندي فيدخل عليه رافعاً يده بسلام التعظيم.

المعاون (للجندي) اذا كان الرجل السكران يا فلان في سكر بين فخذه وحده الى القسم وما دام الآخر لم يحصل منه شيء بشهادة حضرة الخواجه فلا لزوم لأخذه والتسبب في تعطيل المحل ويكفي أن حضرة البك يعدنا بالحضور غداً لأخذ شهادته على هذا السكران.

عند ذلك يدفع صاحب الحان بالسكران الى الخارج فيتبعه الجندي.

الجندي (لصاحب الحان) اذا كنت في كل مرة تطاوع أجيرك في ما يشير به عليك فليس حضرة المعاون يكون عندك في كل ليلة والايام بيننا.

صاحب الحانة لا عليك فأرسله أنت الى الحبس ثم لا تفتكر.

قال عيسى بن هشام: وعدنا الى باب البار فرأينا البك خصم السكران وصاحب الحان ٩.٣٠
جالسين مع المعاون وسمعنا البك يطلب أدواراً من الكؤوس والزجاجات.

صاحب الحانة (للمعاون) لماذا أوعزت الى فلانة بالقيام من هذا المجلس؟

المعاون لم أوعز لها بشيء ولكنها قامت مغضبة.

صاحب الحانة ولأي سبب أغضبتها؟

المعاون لم أغضبها بل هي التي كدرتني وكدرت نفسها

PROPRIETOR (*to the Adjutant*) My dear Sir, business in my premises has been completely disrupted, and I'm sure that's not to your pleasing. This man arrived already drunk from somewhere else and didn't order anything in my place. He picked a quarrel, disturbed the atmosphere, and then proceeded to assault this gentleman who's one of my most regular customers. What's odd is that this Policeman has insisted on taking them both to the police station. This gentleman's someone of noble birth. It isn't appropriate for someone of his stature to be dragged off to court with this drunkard. The policeman refused to listen to me when I explained the story to him.

The Adjutant now put his tarboosh back on and called over the Policeman. The Policeman came over and gave a salute.

ADJUTANT (*to the Policeman*) Since this man's so obviously drunk, you need only take him to the station. As long as this gentleman did not instigate an assault, as the Proprietor tells us, there's no need to take him now and further disrupt things here. It'll be sufficient for the gentleman to promise us to come to the station tomorrow so we can take his deposition against the drunkard.

With that, the Proprietor pushed the drunkard towards the exit, accompanied by the Policeman.

POLICEMAN (*to the Proprietor*) It's all very clever for you to follow your waiter's cues. But then, the Adjutant isn't here every night; and there are always the days in between!

PROPRIETOR Never mind! Just put him in prison and don't think any more about it!

ʿĪsā ibn Hishām said: We went back inside and discovered the Proprietor and the gentleman who had been in the fight with the drunkard sitting with the Adjutant. The glasses were being passed to and fro. We listened as the gentleman was ordering glasses and bottles: 30.9

PROPRIETOR (*to the Adjutant*) Why did you tell your girlfriend to leave when we joined you?

ADJUTANT I didn't tell her to do anything. She went off in a rage.

PROPRIETOR Why was she in a rage?

ADJUTANT It wasn't my fault. She found a way to annoy me and herself as well.

صاحب الحانة أنا أدعوها لاصلح بينكما.

المعاون دعها فانه لا يمكن ان ترضى بالرجوع الآن فان غضبها مسبب عن منع الجندي من أخذ حضرة البك مع السكران الى القسم لان حضرته رفيق المغنية والمغنية من أعدائها.

صاحب الحانة لقد حرت في أمرها فان حماقتها لا تنتهي فهي تأتي كل ليلة بنوع من المشاكل يترتب عليه خسارتي ولولا خاطرك ما أبقيتها وما تكبدت اعطاءها مرتب مأمور مركز من الدرجة الأولى ولو رأيتها تنازع الناس وتخاصم صواحبها اعتمادا عليك ومباهاة باسمك لعلمت حماقَها.

المعاون ماذا أصنع في حماقَها؟ ولكنها على كل حال سليمة القلب خفيفة الروح وكم نبهت عليها بان تتجنب من أجلي الدخول في أسباب المنازعات والمشاجرات.

صاحب الحانة صدقت وهي مع ذلك تحبك كثيراً.

ويتتهي دور الغناء فتنزل المغنية الى البار فتجد ذلك البك قاعداً مع المعاون وصاحب الحان فتجلس معهم وتستفهم عن ما جرى للبيك بسببها فيسرها ما حصل. ١٠،٣٠

البك اني متشكر لحضرة المعاون غاية التشكر وأطلب منه السماح في أن أكون السبب في المصالحة بينه وبين فلانة حتى ينصرف غضبها وتصفو ليلتنا.

صاحب الحانة وأظن أن حضرة المعاون لا يأبى ذلك.

وبيناهم في هذا الكلام اذا بصاحبة المعاون قد دخلت عليهم وما وقع نظرها على المغنية جالسة معهم حتى انقلبت من الغضب جذوة نار أو لبوة هاجت لفقد أشبالها وشتمت وسبت ولعنت وقذفت وتفلت عليهم وهجمت على المرأة فأخذت ببرقعها فامالتها الى الارض توسعها ضربا ولكما وتتوعد المعاون بالشكاية فيه ثم تقسم أنها لا ترقص في ليلتها وانها لا تترك الجميع الا في القسم.

Proprietor I'll call her back at once so I can help settle your disagreement.

Adjutant No, let her be! She won't come back willingly at this point. She's angry because the Policeman didn't take this gentleman to the police station along with that drunkard. The gentleman here is a friend of the singer while she's one of her enemies.

Proprietor I've given up on this girl; there's no limit to her stupidity. Every night she causes me some new headache, and I suffer losses that I can't make good. If it weren't for you, Sir, I wouldn't keep her here and put up with paying her the monthly salary of a deputy governor first-grade. If you could just see her, she's always arguing with people and squabbling with her female colleagues. In all that, she's relying on you and boasting about her acquaintance with you. Then you'd realize how stupid she is!

Adjutant What can I do about her stupidity? Even so, she's good-hearted and lively. I've often warned her to stop getting into arguments and quarrels because of me.

Proprietor You're right. And beyond that she really loves you.

At this point, the singing came to an end. The singer came down to the 30.10
bar and found the gentleman sitting with the Adjutant and Proprietor. She sat down with them and asked what had happened to him because of her. He told her the entire story.

Gentleman I'm extremely grateful to the Adjutant for treating me justly, but I'm asking him to allow me to bring about a reconciliation between him and the other lady. Then her anger will disappear, and we can enjoy a pleasant evening again.

Proprietor I don't think the Adjutant will object to that idea.

While they were talking, the Adjutant's girlfriend came back in. No sooner did she spot the singer sitting with them than she flew into a fiery rage and started behaving like a lioness that has gone berserk because she has lost her cubs. She ranted, cursed, and swore, uttering obscenities and oaths, and then hissed and spat. She pounced on the singing girl, grabbed her veil and threw her to the floor where she punched and beat her. She threatened to file a complaint against the Adjutant and then vowed not to dance that night. She would make sure they all had to go to the police station.

فلا يسع صاحب الحان الا أن يتلافى الأمر فيجرها بالقوة جانباً فينسل المعاون هاربا ١١،٣٠
ويقول صاحب الحان لها: انظري فقد سبق المعاون الى القسم فان لم تعودي الى شغلك أرسلتك اليه مع المغنية وكل من في المحل يشهد أنك تعديت عليها بالضرب من غير سبب ولا تجدين احداً يشهد على المعاون أنه كان هنا وهو الذي يباشر التحقيق معك فينتقم لنفسه ولي منك فتقول له أفعلتها ولكن أناله والزمان طويل.

قال عيسى بن هشام: وعادت الى مرقصها وعدنا الى مجلسنا لنرى ما يحدث فيه من ١٢،٣٠
الغرائب وما يتجدد فيه من العجائب.

The only thing the Proprietor could do was to deal with the situation. He dragged her forcibly to one side, while the Adjutant slunk out as quickly as possible. The Proprietor then spoke to her in no uncertain terms, making it clear that the Adjutant had gone back to the station. If she didn't start dancing again, he intended to send her with the singer to the station. Everyone in the place could testify that she had assaulted the singer for no reason at all. She would not find anyone to testify that the Adjutant himself had been there. He would be the one conducting the inquiry, and he'd have his revenge on her on his own behalf and that of the Proprietor. In reply she told him that this time she'd do it, but in the future . . . 30.11

ʿĪsā ibn Hishām said: With that she went back to the stage, and we returned to our seats so we could watch what other amazing things would happen next. 30.12

مصباح الشرق ٩١، ٨ فبراير ١٩٠٠

١٫٣١ قال عيسى بن هشام: وما كاد يستقر بنا المقام ويأخذ صاحبنا في بسط الكلام بعد انتهاء ذلك الخصام حتى جاء دور الرقص فعلت الضوضاء من الامام واشتد النعيق والنعير واشتعلت الاكف بالتصفيق والافواه بالصفير واختلط العجيج بالعجيج واتصل الضجيج بالضجيج اذ قامت على المنصة هلوك ورهاء دميمة شوهاء فطساء فوهاء عمشاء مرهاء مزججة الحاجبين محمرة الخدين مبيضة الجبين مخضبة البنان بأنواع الطلاء والدهان قد أسدلت على وجهها من التزويق برقعاً ونقابا وأسبلت عليه من التمويه ستراً وحجابا من أصباغ شتى وألوان بين أبيض ناصع وأسود فاحم وأحمر قان فهي تتلون فيه تلون الحرباء في هجير البيداء ثم وارت ما تكشف من جسمها وتعرى من لحمها بالعقود والقلائد والأساور والمعاضد والمناطق والخلاخل والدمالج والجلاجل وانسابت في الجلان على توقيع الالحان وتلوت في الميلان تلوي الافعوان

٢٫٣١ وبجانبها خادم ما شككنا من سوء هيئته أنه ابليس في طلعته ركبت منه أشنع هامة على أقبح قامة بوجه قدّ من صخر وعينين كعيني الصقر وأنف كمنسر النسر وشفة مهدولة وعمامة مجدولة وفي يمينه ابريق يسقيها منه بكأس من حريق لا بكأس من رحيق ويعاطيها من غسلين وقطران ويجرعها من حميم آن وكلما أترع لها كأسا همست في أذنه همسا وهي تشير بطرف الكف الى بعض الجالسين في أول صف فيصيح صيحة الاسد من فريسته وقع بصره على فريسته فتأتي الزجاجات أزواجاً متعددة وأدواراً متجددة فيغض عنها الختام ويصففها عند مقعدها تحت الاقدام ولا يزال يملأ لها ويسكب وهي تشرب وتطلب لا تكتفي ولا تقنع مما لا يروي ولا ينقع كانما هو يمتح من قليب ويصب في واد جديب أو يملأ من ماء منبثق في دن منخرق فاذا دبت في عروقها نمال الخمر واشتعل منها جوفها اشتعال الجمر جدت في لعبها ودورانها واشتدت في قفزها وثورانها واحتدت في جمزها وجولانها وتلاعبت كالسلحفاة بعنقها وتثنت كالحية في طرقها

٣٫٣١ والخادم في صحبتها أتبع لها من ظلها وأطوع من نعلها ينازلها وتنازله ويغازلها

ʿĪsā ibn Hishām said: Once the row was over, we had hardly taken our seats again and our Friend had only just started telling us things before the dancing started. People were yelling and screaming; there was both applause and whistling. When a brazen tart took to the stage, a wholesale hubbub ensued. She was emaciated and ugly, flat-nosed and big-mouthed, bleary-eyed and nearsighted. With penciled eyebrows, she presented a riot of color—red cheeks, white forehead, and dyed fingers. Using greasepaint she had decorated her face with a veil of makeup and plastered on it a false, multicolored covering in a variety of hues—from gleaming white to pitch black and deep red. In fact she displayed as many different colors as the chameleon in the midday heat of the desert. The exposed parts of her body and naked flesh were covered with necklaces, bangles, bracelets, supports, armlets, bells, belts, and anklets. She started skipping and dancing to the beat of the music, twisting and turning like a snake. 31.1

Alongside her stood an assistant so repulsive that we had no doubt that he was the accursed Devil himself. He had an ugly head placed on top of a disgusting frame. His features seemed carved out of rock, with eyes like a hawk, a nose like a vulture's beak, drooping lips, and a tightly twisted turban. In his hand he held a pitcher from which he kept pouring glasses of sheer fire, not wine. He gave her pitch and tar, and made her swallow boiling hot water. Every time he filled a glass for her, she whispered in his ear and then pointed her finger at someone sitting in the front row. He would then roar like a lion once it has spied its prey. Bottles in multiple pairs and rounds one after another would appear, and he would uncork them and arrange them in rows at her feet. Her assistant kept pouring glasses for her, and she would quaff them and ask for more. She seemed never to be satisfied; her thirst was unquenchable. It was as if he were drawing water from a well and pouring it into an arid valley, or filling a cracked jug with water from a gushing stream. Once the wine had seeped like an insect through her veins and lit a red hot fire inside her, she started her twists and gyrations again. Her leaps and pirouettes became more violent and her jumps and turns intensified. She kept toying with her neck like a tortoise and twisting like a snake. 31.2

Her assistant stood beside her, closer than her own shadow, pliant as her own shoes. He kept making passes at her, flirting and dancing with her and 31.3

وتغازله ويراقصها وتراقصه ويقارصها وتقارصه وهي بين كل روحة وجيئة وبيئة وفيئة ترسل على الحاضرين الفاظاً بذيئة وأقوالا رديئة وتوسعهم فحشا وهجرا وتشبعهم هذيًا وهذرا فتغتر لها الثغور وتنشرح لها الصدور ليس فيهم الا كل مستحسن ومعجب ومستملح ومستعذب ومطنب ومستزيد ومحاك لحركاتها ومستعيد الى أن تخور قواها وتغور عيناها وتتقلص شفتاها ويهبط شدقاها وينضح العرق من أطرافها وتراقيها ويتعقد الزبد فوق خطمها وفيها فيغشي العرق بصرها ويملأ نحرها فتضطر الى مسحه وازالته وتحتاج الى نفضه وازاحته فتتناول المنديل تمسح به من وجهها وذراعها، فيتلون بأشكال الصبغة وأنواعها فكأن ما تصبب من اديمها ورشح مطر غدا به المنديل قوس قزح فانكشف التمويه والتلبيس ووضح التلفي والتدليس وظهر ما بطن وبرز ما كمن وانقلبت الى سعلاء تترآى في فلاه وغول تكلح وتصول ودب يهتز ويدب فحولنا وجوهنا استكراهاً واستنكارا ولوينا أعناقنا استقباحاً واستقذارا.

وقال الباشا: أعلى مثل هذه الافعى تحوم الافكار واليها تشخص الأبصار؟ ٤،٣١

الصاحب نعم وتتفتت القلوب وتنشق المرائر والجيوب فهذه التي تراها تهرب منها الوحوش ويتعوذ منها الشيطان هي عند هؤلاء المغرورين المدلهين دمية القصر وفريدة العصر ويتيمة الدهر كم ذهبت بأموال وأودت بأرواح وأضاعت شرفًا ومجدًا وأذلت رقابًا وأفسدت حكاما وكم فرقت بين المرء وزوجه وأوقعت العقوق بين الوالد وولده والعداوة والبغضاء بين الاخ وأخيه وكم خربت بيوتًا عامرة ودنست انسابًا طاهرة وكم ولدت للشر أسبابا وفتحت للمحاكم أبوابًا وكم تهتك عليها سري وشريف واحترق بجمرها سني وكريم وهؤلاء الذين تراهم جالسين في هذا المستنقع الوبيء والمرعى الوبيل يقضون فيه ليالي الشهر تباعًا وشهور العام ردافًا لا تظنهم لقبح المكان من أسافل الناس وأدنياء القوم بل انظر عن يمينك فان هذا الجالس بين اخوانه جلسة الكبرياء هو أحد أبناء الامراء مات أبوه وترك له أموالا جمة فالتف به قرناء السوء

exchanging suggestive pinches. Between her to-ings and fro-ings, she kept making lewd and disgusting comments to the audience, treating them to all manner of filth and lechery, and mouthing taunts and nonsense. Their mouths simply gaped, and their hearts were enthralled. Everyone was stunned and full of admiration; as they followed her every movement, they were all expressing their utmost pleasure. They kept asking for more and demanding an encore. Eventually her energy gave out; her eyes began to droop, her lips contracted, and her jawbone tensed. Sweat poured off her shoulders and sides, and foam thickened on her neck and mouth. Sweat blinded her and covered her chest, so she had to wipe it completely off. She took a handkerchief and used it to wipe her face and arms. It was stained with various types of makeup, as though all the sweat that came off her skin were a kind of rain that the handkerchief turned into a rainbow. As a result, the falseness of her appearance was exposed and the deception became clear; things that had been hidden were brought out into the open. She was transformed into the guise of a harpy appearing in a desert mirage, a ghoul grimacing and leaping around, or a bear quivering and crawling. We turned away in utter horror and disgust, so powerful was our sense of revulsion.

The Pāshā asked: "Do people's minds really focus on vipers like this and 31.4
stare longingly at them?"

FRIEND Yes, indeed they do! Hearts and souls have been riven and pockets shredded for her. This woman you're watching is so hideous that wild beasts would run away and Satan himself would take refuge from her. And yet the dupes in this audience regard her as a palace statue, a pearl of the era, the wonder of the age. She's taken piles of money from men and ruined their lives; for her sake honor and prestige have been lost. She's humiliated people and corrupted many governors. Many times she's broken up a man and his wife, and provoked disagreement between father and son and enmity between one brother and another. As she's worked her evil ways, she's managed to bring ruin to flourishing houses, to sully pure lineages, and to open the gates to litigation. Many's the distinguished and honorable man she's ruined; many's the noble and exalted person she's consumed in her flames. The people you see sitting in this plague-infested marsh spend night after night here every month, and month after month throughout the year. And please don't imagine that, because this place is so awful, they're from the lowest class of people. Quite

من أهل الفراغ والبطالة فبدأ في تبديد تلك الاموال باقتناء الخيول المطهمة والمركبات المعلمة وثنى بالاسراف الفاحش في مهرجان زواجه وانتهى بتسليم ما بقي لأيدي العواهر وأخصهن هذه اللخناء التي تراها وغاية ما بقي له منها أنه يتردد هنا كل ليلة ليتمتع منها بنظرة ويتملئ بلحظة فلا تنظر اليه ولا تسأل عنه.

٥،٣١ ثم انظر الى يمينك فان هذا الجالس يفتل في شاربيه ويحملق بعينيه ويغمز بحاجبيه من أبناء الكبراء أيضاً ماتت أمه فورثها ولم يمض على موتها بضعة أسابيع حتى أوقعه نحس طالعه في مخالب هذه الخداعة الغرارة فهو لا يصير منها ولا يقطع المجيء اليها كل ليلة وهي تسلبه كل ما تصل اليه يدها من خفيف وثقيل مما كان لأمه من حلي وجواهر وفرش ثمينة ومن ذهب منثور كل ليلة في أرض هذا المكان وانظر أمامك فهذا الذي تراه معظماً ومبجلاً بين جلسائه هو من كبار الموظفين بالارياف ما زال مغرماً صباً بهذه المرأة حتى كادت لفظاعة أعمالها معه تسلخه من شرفه وتنزعه من منصبه وهو مع ذلك لا يسلوها ولا يلهو عنها فاذا حضر الى القاهرة لم يكن له في كل أيامه بها الا بيتها مأوى والا مرقصها ملهى واذا عاد الى مقره عاد بغير لبه فلا يؤوب اليه حتى يتمحل الاسباب لاغراء العمد والاعيان في بلده باقامة الولائم تمهيدا لاستئجارها للرقص فيها وهذا الشيخ الجالس منفرداً الراشق يده بين صدغه وعمامته هو الرجل من أعيان الناس على ما بلغ من السن وما به من وقار الشيب قد انعكست أيامه عليه وانقلب دور الزمان فيه فتصابى في شيخوخته وأخذ يبدد ما جمعه في شبيبته ولوعاً بهذه البغي الفاجرة.

٦،٣١ <u>الباشا</u> علم الله انني لا أرى في هذه المرأة مزية ظاهرة توجب انكباب الناس عليها وانصبابهم اليها وأرى أن الامر على عكس ذلك فان الهروب منها أسلم من النظر اليها فهل تعلم من سبب آخر يحسن السكوت عليه.

the contrary, just look to your right. The man sitting there arrogantly among his comrades is an amir's son whose father died and bequeathed him piles of money. His evil companions, all of them idle loafers, have swarmed round him. Now he's started squandering the money by buying pedigree horses and sumptuous carriages. He spent an obscene amount on his wedding reception, and now he's ended up handing over what's left to whores and to this stinking tart in particular. But, when he comes here every night, the only thing he gets is to look at her while she neither looks at him nor even asks after him.

Now look to your left. Do you see that fellow over there twisting his moustache as he leers and makes lewd gestures with his eyebrows. He's the son of an important man too. When his mother died, she left him a substantial legacy. It was only a few weeks after her death that misfortune allowed him to fall into the clutches of this deceptive trickstress. He cannot stand not being with her; he comes here every night to see her while she proceeds to rob him of every single thing he's inherited from his mother—jewelery and costly furnishings, not to mention the gold that gets scattered on the floor of this place. Then look in front of you. The man who's being shown such deference and respect by his companions is an important provincial official; he's still totally besotted with this woman. The way she's treated him has been disgusting; she's robbed him of his honor and toppled him from his lofty position. And yet, in spite of all that, he still can't forget her or take his mind off her. Whenever he comes to Cairo, her house is the one place he heads for, and he always comes to the hall where she dances. When he goes back to his provincial seat, he's utterly distracted. The only way he can recover his senses is to devise ways of cajoling local ʿumdahs and notables into holding banquets, the sole purpose being to hire this dancer. Then look at that shaykh sitting by himself over there, with his hand wedged between his temple and turban. He's one of the leading men of the city, and yet, in spite of the sobriety and dignity of old age, things have redounded against him and the role of time has been reversed. Even in old age he's behaving like a youngster; he's crazy about this lewd temptress and is wasting everything that he'd kept for his latter years. 31.5

PĀSHĀ God knows, I can't see any obvious female qualities in this woman that would justify the way people seem so infatuated with her. As far as I can tell, it should be exactly the opposite: people should be running away from her rather than looking at her. Can you give me some other explanation which is better not mentioned? 31.6

الصاحب ليس في الامر الا المباهاة والمباراة والمسابقة والمفاخرة وحب الأثرة والاختصاص فان هذه البغي قد اشتهرت بالرقص وفاقت فيه وأنفس الجهلاء ولوعة بالشهرة الباطلة والصيت الكاذب يتشبثون به عمي النواظر عمه البصائر فهم يرون أن الاختصاص بمثل هذه الشهيرة على ما ترى من قبحها هو الفخر كل الفخر والفضل كل الفضل والسبق كل السبق وكلهم مجبولون على الحكاية والتقليد ولذلك نفذ فيهم سهمها وسرى في عروقهم سمها.

الباشا اذا كان الامر على ما ذكرت وقد فسد الناس الى هذه الدرجة وسفهت أحلامهم الى هذا الحد أليس لهم من واعظ يعظهم أو ناصح ينصحهم أو وازع يزعهم أو مانع يمنعهم أو حكومة تردعهم وتكف الاذى عنهم؟

الصاحب لا واعظ ولا ناصح ولا وازع ولا مانع فالناس مشتغلون ٧.٣١
بعضهم عن بعض وقل بيننا من يشتغل للناس في نفع الناس وان صادف بينهم ناصح لا يكون نصيبه الا الضحك منه والهزء به على ألسنة الفجار والفساق أما الحكومة وأسمع بها وأبصر فان هذه الامور تجري بعلمها وتصنع على عينها وهي تنظر اليها نظر الرضى وتتقبلها قبولا حسناً فهي التي تضع حدودها وتدير نظامها فتقرر له اللوائح وتصدر المنشورات فيشتغل بها الحكام ويتعب لها القضاة وان اضمحل بها حال الرعية وساء مصير الناس وماذا نقول في حكومة تعلم ان ثروتها من ثروة رعيتها وحياتها بحياتها ثم هي مع ذلك ترضى بانتشار هذه الموبقات المقوضة للثروة المتلفة للارواح والاجساد؟ او ماذا نقول في حكومة تجعل عاصمة بلادها عقداً واسطته بيوت الخمر وزوايا المقامرة ومكامن الفسوق محيطة بمحلة البغايا؟ ومما يقضي بالعجب ان اصغر حاكم في الارياف قادر بسلطته ان يكف عن بلده شر هذه الامور على أن مركز الحكم هذا والحكام ينظرون الى تفاقم الشر وتزايد البلاء ولا تسنح لهم سانحة في تخفيف وطأته على الاقل أو تلطيف شدته واعجب من ذلك واغرب ان هذه الحكومة لا تحتذي على مثال لحكومة إسلامية أو اجنبية فهي تعلم ان جميع عواصم اسلام خالية من اماكن معينة معلومة لبغايا المسلمات وان المنع فيها شديد لا يجسر

FRIEND The only reason is that people love to boast, compete, show off, and monopolize. This tart is famous for her perfect and matchless dancing. Ignorant people are passionately fond of phony prestige; they cling to it blindly and helplessly. In spite of this woman's obvious ugliness, people believe there's something distinctive about such a woman and regard it all as an object of pride, a primary virtue, and a stake worth pursuing. People tend naturally to imitate and copy each other. That explains why her arrows are so effective and her poison flows through their veins.

PĀSHĀ If things are as you say and people are that corrupt and their dreams so inane, is there no preacher to offer them guidance, no counselor to advise them, no restraint to stop them, or no government authority to impede them and keep them out of harm's way?

FRIEND There's neither preacher nor adviser, no authority or restrainer. 31.7
People are too busy with their own affairs; very few of them bother to help other people. If anyone does offer advice, all he gets by way of response is laughter and mockery from lechers and debauchees. For example, consider the government's attitude and listen to what it has to say! All these things take place with its full cognizance and before its very eyes. It regards them with approval and accepts them. It's the government that's supposed to lay down the laws and administer them. It formulates bills and publishes decrees that keep governors busy and wear out judges, even though people's lives are much worse and they are faced with a dire plight. What can you say about a government which realizes that its wealth comes from the people and that its life depends on theirs, and yet approves of the spread of these vile practices that result in the squandering of wealth and the destruction of body and soul; a government which has fashioned for its capital city's centerpiece, a necklace of taverns, gaming rooms, and brothels. It's incredible that in the provinces the most junior government official has the authority to rid his region of these evil practices, but here—where the center of authority actually subsists, people in government look at the way evil and misery are on the increase, and yet have no opportunity at the very least to soften the violence of its impact. What's even more incredible and peculiar is that this government does not follow the example of either Islamic or foreign governments. It's well aware that all Islamic capital cities are completely devoid of brothels where Muslim women prostitute themselves; any such thing is strictly forbidden, and no one dares to contravene it. It also knows that, in countries like England, no brothels exist

احد ان يتعداه وتعلم ان مثل بلاد الانكليز لا يوجد فيها بيت فاحشة تعرفه الحكومة وتعلم ان من شذ تلك الحكومات من هذا الحكم وأغضى عن أماكن البغاء فقد عين لها مواقع خاصة في أطراف البلاد بعيدة عن أماكن الناس ومساكنهم ومعتزلة عن نواديهم ومجامعهم ولكنها تخالف كل هذا فهي حكومة مسلمة وتصرح بفتح البيوت للفحشاء وتعطي بيدها الرخصة لأيدي الفاسقات المسلمات يفتحن بها بيوتهن في محلة تكتنفها أحياء الحرائر.

الباشا مازلت منذ دهر أرى العجيب وأسمع بالغريب وما زال التجول بي والتنقل يجمع لي بين النقائض ويزيدني معرفة بالنقائص حتى انتهى بي الحال من التعجب والتأثر الى التجلد لا بل الى التبلد.

٨،٣١ قال عيسى بن هشام: وكانت الراقصة بعد ان انتهت من رقصها ذهبت للتغيير ملابسها والاصلاح من حالها ثم جاءت تتهادى في مشيتها وقد جددت ألوانها بانواع أصباغها فتطاولت نحوها الاعناق وشخصت فيها الاحداق وتطلعت اليها النفوس وهلعت القلوب وزحزحت لها المجالس وحلت الحبى وجهز لها كل فريق كرسياً بجانبه فلم تعبأ بشيء من ذلك ولم تأبه له واستمرت في مشيها قاصدة مقر صاحب الحان فوقفت معه برهة في ملاعبة ومداعبة ومضاحكة وممازحة ثم شاهدنا ذاك الخادم جالساً في زمرة ذلك الحاكم المغرم يمزح ويمرح وينكت ويبكت فلما مرت به ولم تجلس همس الحاكم في أذن الخادم وغمزه في يده بشيء من الدراهم فوثب ولحق بها عند صاحب الحان وألقى في أذنها كلاماً فرأيناها تشير اشارة الرفض والنبذ فما زال ينفث فيها ويرقيها حتى لانت له فاسرع كانه يبشر الحاكم بحضورها ثم جاءت عقبه تجرر أذيالها فجلست بجانب الحاكم على الكرسي الذي أعده لها وجاء الغلام على أثرها وفي يده أربع زجاجات لشربها فض ختامها كلها مرة واحدة ففارت وفاضت على الارض والغلام صابر لها منتظر لسكونها حتى اذا لم يبق بها الا شفافة أو صبابة صبها في الكاسات فتلمس الفاجرة كل كأس لمسة بشفتيها ثم يعود الغلام

with the cognizance of the government; furthermore, that governments which are an exception to this rule and turn a blind eye to brothels put them in special places on the outskirts of towns far away from people's houses and well out of the way of clubs and meeting places. But this government (which is a Muslim government) has gone against all this and given Muslim prostitutes permission to open their houses in an area surrounded by quarters where respectable people live.

PĀSHĀ For some time now I've been seeing remarkable things and hearing strange information. My peregrinations have produced a series of contradictions while increasing my awareness of people's shortcomings. My perception and amazement has now reached a stage of resignation, or, perhaps even more, of apathy.

ʿĪsā ibn Hishām said: Once the dancer had finished her routine, she went to change her clothes and put herself in order. After putting on fresh makeup, she came out and started walking falteringly among the crowd. Necks and eyes strained in her direction, hearts and minds yearned for her, tables were adjusted to accommodate her, and gifts were readied. Each group put out a chair, but she paid no attention to any of this and kept walking till she reached the place where the Proprietor was standing. She stood beside him for a while, joking and laughing playfully. We then noticed her assistant sitting with the coterie of the infatuated provincial official; he was joking, jesting, and making merry with him. When the dancer walked right past him and didn't sit down, the official whispered something in the assistant's ear and slipped him some coins. With that, the assistant leapt up and went over to the dancer standing beside the Proprietor. He whispered something in her ear, and we watched as she rejected the idea. He persisted and kept on at her till she softened her stance. He rushed back to give the official the good news, and she reluctantly followed him over. She sat next to the official on a chair he had put out for her, and the waiter was soon back with four bottles of champagne. He opened all of them at once, and the bubbling liquid gushed all over the floor. The waiter bided his time and waited till the fizzing had stopped and there was barely anything left, barely a thimbleful to fill the glasses. The tart quickly touched all of them with her lips, and the waiter came back to collect the empty glasses. 31.8

ليأخذ فارغة فتأمره بإحضار غيرها فيفعل بها مثل فعله الاول ولا يزال الحال هكذا مرات أربعاً أو خمساً وقد قطع الناس كلهم حديثهم ولم يق لهم عمل سوى النظر الى حركاتها وسكناتها وما تأتيه من ضروب التقصف والتهتك كانما هم يرصدون كوكباً أو يرقبون هلالاً

٩،٣١ ثم رأينا الخادم وقد انقطع الطلب وقف بعيداً عنها على مرأى منها يشير اليها بحاجبيه تارة وطرف لسانه أخرى فتهم بالقيام فيبهت الحاكم فتصفعه صفعة مزاح على قفاه وتلعن لعن الضحك أباه كأنها تترضاه بذلك عن قيامها فيهش الجميع لها ويبشون وتنسل من حضرته الى حيث أشار اليها الخادم من موقفه فتأتي الى الفريق الذي عن يميننا وتخاطب ذلك الشاب الذي أفنى ماله وشرفه في حبها وتقول له: ماذا تريد مني ولأي شيء دعوتني ولم أقلقتني من مكاني؟ .فيتلعثم المسكين لا يدري بماذا يجيب ثم يجيبها متلطفاً منكسراً: ما دعوتك الا لأخبرك بما تم عليه الحال بيني وبين المحامي في قضيتك ووصولنا الى النتيجة المحمودة فيها فهلا تجلسين فأفصل لك الامر وأسكن منك البال فتقول له: لا بال ولا مال دعني أباشر مصلحتي وأقض حق ليلتي فان صاحب الخان ينظرني من بعيد وأنت تعلم ما نظرة صاحب الخان وأنا أعلم ما بك من القلة وأن ليس في يدك ما يرضيه فيأخذ يذكرها بالعهد القديم والحب الصميم وليالي الصفاء وأيام الوفاء وما جرى فيها من لطائف النوادر ومحاسن الآثار فتلطمه على وجهه لكمة المعلم المؤدب وتقول له: دع الذكر تلك الليالي والايام الخوالي فقد مرت بآثارها ولم يبق غير أخبارها وأنا أقص عليك عبرة من العبرة وحكمة من احكم , قصة الاضراس التي هي أساس عندنا في صناعتنا وقاعدة في فننا:

١٠،٣١ «زعموا ان شاباً كان يهوى غادة منا وتهواه فعاشا تحت جناح الهوى والحب زمناً سعيداً ثم طرأ على الشاب سفر يبعده عنها فجاء في يوم التوديع يسكب الدموع ويصعد الزفرات ولما انتهت من البكاء معه وحانت ساعة الفراق طلبت شيئاً منه تتذكره به مدة غيبته وتستنشق منه ريحه فقال لها: ما عندي شيء ألصق بجسمي وأعز على نفسي من ضرسي وعمد الى ضرسه فانتزعه واقتلعه غير مبال بشدة الألم ثم

She told him to bring some more, and the waiter did the same thing with them too. This continued for four or five more rounds. All conversation had ceased, and all they could do was stare at the way she moved and sat and the kind of mayhem and obscenity she was causing; it was as though they were looking at a star or waiting for a new moon.

When the requests came to an end, the assistant was standing at a distance where she could see him. He kept gesturing at her, sometimes with his eyebrows, at others with the tip of his tongue. She was about to get up, and that flummoxed the provincial offical. She gave him a playful slap on the neck and jokingly cursed his father to compensate for her departure. Everyone smiled at her as she slunk her way over to the place where her assistant had pointed. She joined a group to our right and spoke to the young man who had lost his money and forfeited his honor because of his passion for her. "What do you want with me?" she asked. "Why have you called me over and made me give up my seat?" The poor man had no idea what to say in reply. Feeling crushed, he tried to make amends by saying, "I just wanted to let you know how things stand between me and the lawyer regarding your case. We've reached a favorable conclusion to the matter. Won't you sit down for a moment and let me explain things to you and give you some peace of mind?" "Forget about money and peace of mind!" she told him. "Let me take care of my own interests and do what I have to do. The Proprietor's looking at me from over there, and you know what that means. I know how poor you are now; you don't have enough to satisfy him." He now began to remind her of their long acquaintance and their former love affair, the serene nights and earnest days they had spent together, and the beautiful memories and happy times they had shared. At that, she slapped his face like a school teacher. "Those days and nights of old are long past," she told him. "All that remains are the tales they tell. Instead let me tell you a cautionary tale with a message. It's the Tale of the Teeth, one that provides the basic framework in which women such as myself operate and the foundation of our craft: 31.9

"They tell the tale of a boy who loved a girl as much as she loved him. Under love's wing they spent a happy time together. Then the boy had to leave on an unexpected journey that carried him far away from her in quest of money. On the farewell day the boy arrived with tears and sobs. When she had stopped sharing his tears and it was time for him to depart, she asked him to leave her a memento to remind her of him during his absence and give her a hint of his 31.10

ناولها اياه وتزود بآخر زاد منها وسافر ومضت بعد ذلك الليالي والايام وآب الغائب من سفره وقد بلغها رقة حاله ونفاد ماله فلما طرق بابها تنكرت له وأنكرته فقال: أنا فلان فقالت: ومن فلان؟ قال: صاحب العشرة القديمة قالت: كل الناس عاشر وفارق فأيهم أنت؟ قال أنا صاحب الضرس قالت ألك عندي ضرس؟ قال: نعم قالت: فادخل فدخل فأخرجت له من صندوقها علبة فتحتها فاذا هي ملآى بالاضراس وقالت له: ان كنت تعرف ضرسك بين هذه الاضراس عرفتك هذه حالنا فاعلمنها وأسعد الله مصبحك وممساك.»

ثم تتركه وتذهب الى ذلك الشيخ فيقوم لها واقفاً ويبدي لها نواجذه في ابتسامة ١١،٣١
السرور بحضورها فتجلس معه ولغلام فوق رأسها فتقول له: دعنا الآن فليس صاحبنا بغريب فاذا ذهب قال الشيخ: لقد احضرت تلك الازرار التي طلبتها مني وهي ستة واستحسنت أن تكون من المجرات لا من الجنيهات لان عيار هذه أدنى من عيار تلك فتضحك في وجهه وتمد يدها تخرجها من جيبه ثم تقوم باسمة ويقيم الشيخ في ابتهاج وصفاء كأنما قعد منها تحت موعد اللقاء وتذهب لتنصب على سواه شباكها وترمي للصيد أشراكها.

scent. 'I have nothing that is part of my very body and more precious to me than my own tooth.' With that, he extracted one of his teeth without flinching at the intense pain and handed it to her. Taking his final leave of her, he departed. Days and nights went by, and then the absentee returned from his journey. The girl had heard that he was emaciated and had no money left. Thus, when he knocked on her door, she would not let him in and claimed not to know him. 'But I'm A!' he told her. 'And who is that?' she replied. 'I'm your old beloved,' he told her, to which she responded that everyone is a friend for a while, then leaves. 'Which one are you?' she asked. 'I'm the one with the tooth!' he told her. 'Do I have a tooth of yours?' she asked him. 'Yes, you do,' he replied. 'Then come in,' she said. He went in, and she produced a small case from her box and opened it. It was full of teeth. 'If you can recognize your tooth among that lot,' she told him, 'then I'll know who you are.' So that's the way we are. Learn the lesson, and may God bring you happiness morning and evening!"

With that, she left him and went over to the Shaykh. He stood up to greet **31.11**
her with a gleaming smile. As she sat down beside him, the hall waiter was standing right behind her. "Forget that for now," she told him. "This gentleman's no stranger." Once the waiter had left, the Shaykh told her he was bringing the buttons she had asked for. There were six of them; and fortunately they were of better weight than monetary pounds because the latter was less valuable than the former. She laughed at him and stretched out her hand to take them out of his pocket. She got up with a smile, and the Shaykh seemed serenely happy as though there was to be a rendezvous. She went away to work her wiles and cast her net over someone else.

مصباح الشرق ٩٢، ١٥ فبراير ١٩٠٠

قال عيسى بن هشام: وبقينا نتأمل في أفعال هذه البغي الفاجرة وأحوال تلك المحتالة الماكرة ونعجب كيف يقتدر مثلها على ختل الرجال ودفعهم الى مهاوي الغواية والضلال وان كانت عارية من لباس الجمال مجردة من محاسن الخصال مفرغة في قالب الوقاحة معجونة من حمأة الشناعة والقباحة وما زالت هكذا تتقلب بين الجالسين وتنتقل وتتردد بين الصفوف وتتحول وتروح الى صاحب الحان وتغدو وتختفي آونة ثم تبدو منطلقة اللسان بالسب والثلب منبسطة اليد بالنهب والسلب ممتدة الساعد باللطم والضرب مشتعلة الفكر بالخدع والخب مشتغلة الكف بالشرب والسكب دائبة العمل على الربح والكسب وهي في تنقلها بين طلابها تقطب تارة وتتجهم وترنو طوراً وتتبسم وتنحرف مرة وتزورّ وتهتف أخرى وتفتر وتنبسط حيناً وتنقبض وترضى ساعة ثم تمتعض فترسل من أفاعيلها الى كل واحد ما يناسبه ويلائمه وتعامله منها بما يوافقه ويوائمه فتتمكن من اختلابهم وتبرع في اجتلابهم وتأخذ بألبابهم وتمتلك رق رقابهم وأكبر آية عندهم على كمال انعطافها وميلها أن تصفع من يسعدها لحظ منهم بنعلها فيرى أنه الصفي المجدود والمحبوب الموعود ١،٣٢

فاذا أجادت ما شاءت في صفعه ولكمه فداها بأبيه وأمه واذا أضافت الى الضرب بالنعال شق القباء ونتف السبال استبشر ببلوغ الآمال وقرب ساعة الوصال ونظر الى لفيف خلانه وأخدانه وفريق أنداده وأقرانه نظرة المختال المباهي والمعجب الزاهي والمساجل المفاخر والزاري الساخر لا بل الظافر في معمعان الطعان والضراب الفائز بالغنائم والأسلاب القافل من حومة المنايا بالأسارى والسبايا فتراه غريقاً في الابتهاج والاستئناس تنبسط يده في الكيس وتنبسط يدها في الكأس والغلام واقف على رأسها بالآنية يصب لها زجاجة في كل ثانية كأن حلقها قناة وكأن الساقي ساقية أو سانية ٢،٣٢

'Īsā ibn Hishām said: We stayed where we were, observing the antics of this lecherous tart and the way she was tricking people. We were amazed that a woman like her could deceive men and hurl them into the abyss of sin and error. She had none of the trappings of beauty nor any redeeming features or qualities, but instead had been molded in a brazen form and kneaded from the sludge of all that was ugly and repulsive. She continued her rounds among the seated customers, meandering her way through the rows and going back and forth to the Proprietor; sometimes she would be lost to view, but then she would reappear. She kept freely mouthing obscenities and slander and reaching out to grab and steal. She often slapped and punched people with her outstretched hand, enflaming people's minds with her deceitful wiles and using her hand to grab and swallow glassfuls. Her every move was aimed at profit and gain. As she made her way amid her devotees, she would sometimes scowl and frown, and at others break into a smile. One moment she would turn aside, at another she would come back yelling and then sag. One minute she would look happy, then frown; be content, then aggravated. Each man received the treatment that suited him best, and she dealt with them all in the appropriate fashion. She had managed to attract their attention and excelled at keeping them in her clutches; she could play with their minds and had them all enslaved. For them, the clearest sign of her affection and inclinations came when she would use her shoes to give someone who pleased her a cuff; with that he would assume that he had struck lucky and his dearest hopes would be granted. 32.1

Once she had achieved her objective by cuffing and slapping him—along with insults to his father and mother, she would then go beyond mere slaps with shoes and tear his shirt and pluck his beard as well. He would now be sure that his hopes were achieved and the hour of union had finally arrived. He would give all his assembled friends and colleagues a boastful look, one filled with arrogant pride and scornful disdain—in fact, like a champion during the cut and thrust of conflict or a victor with the spoils of battle, escaping the jaws of death with prisoners and captives. Showing the utmost pleasure and sociability he would now extend his hand to his purse while she would stretch hers to the wineglass. The waiter would still be poised behind her, pitcher in hand, pouring her one glass after another, as though her throat were some kind of canal and he were a scoop or waterwheel. 32.2

٣،٣٢ هذا وصاحبها الوارث يتابعها في خطراتها بنظرته ويسايرها في خطواتها باشاراته لا تعبأ به ولا تنظر اليه ولا تنعطف نحوه ولا تعرج عليه وهو يتضجر ويتململ ثم يتوسل ويذلل ويتحف الخادم ويطرف الغلام ويدعو صاحب الحان معه لمعاقرة المدام ويظهر الخضوع والاستكانة للخادمة والقهرمانة فيجلسهما فوق صحبه واخوانه ويغدق عليهما من كرمه واحسانه ولا يزال يتملق ويخضع ويستشفع اليها ويضرع ويتأوه ويتوجع ويتوسل ويتخشع حتى يرق له قلب الخادمة فتستوي قائمة فتمضي الى مولاتها كأنها تتلطف في مرضاتها فتبقى بين أخذ وردّ واستعطاف وصد الى أن توفق الى القبول في سفارتها بحسن مهارتها بعد الالحاح واللجاجة على أن يفتح لصاحبته اثني عشرة زجاجة من أفخر المشروب وأشهاه وأثمنه وأغلاه فخضع لشرطها ونال رضاها بعد سخطها وقعدت بجانبه على حرف مغضية الطرف لا تتعلق بحرف وهو ينكسر في حديثه ويتأنث ويتقصف في حركاته ويتخنث استجلاباً لحبها واستجذاباً لقلبها فاذا أبانت سبب كدرها منه وانحرافها عنه قالت: لقد ساومت تلك التي تدعي أنها الجوهرة اليتيمة فاذا هي أحط من ذلك قدراً وأقل قيمة فعلمت أنك تسخر بي وتستهويني وتلعب بعقلي وتستغويني ولقد سألتك أن تعيرني مركبتك من قبل فلم تجبني بغير التسويف والمطل واعلم أنك اذا تماديت على هذه المعاملة وعدلت عن طريق المجاملة برئت من هواك واتخذت لي خلاً سواك فيقسم لها بشرفه وذمته ورأس أبيه وحرمته وتربة أمه وجدته والا تكون هذه الليلة آخرمدته أنه لا يعصي لها أمرا ولا يدخر عنها ذخرًا ولا يمنعها شيئاً من طارفه وتلاده اذا أجابته هذه الليلة الى مراده ثم ينتهي الامر بينهما الى الصفاء بعد زوال أسباب الجفاء.

٤،٣٢ وحانت منا النفاتة الى الخليع وصاحبيه واذا العمدة يشير بيديه ويغمز بحاجبيه

All this time her friend, the young inheritor, had been gazing at her and following her every move with his own gestures. But she completely ignored him and never looked in his direction or moved toward him. This made him angry, and he started muttering his complaints, asking people to intercede, and making a fool of himself. He gave her assistant something and caught the waiter's eye. He then called over the Proprietor and invited him to share some wine. He also showed all due modesty to the female steward and her assistant, invited them both to sit closer to him than all his friends and colleagues, and showered them with his generosity. He kept on cajoling and begging them, accompanied by abject sighs and pleas, until the assistant's heart softened. She stood up and went over to her mistress as though to acquiesce in what would please her. The dancer stayed where she was, undecided as to whether to accept or not, to be sympathetic or cruel. Eventually her assistant's mission was successful, but, using all her wiles after so much relentless pleading, the assistant insisted that twelve bottles of the very best vintage—the most expensive available—should be opened for her mistress. The man accepted her terms; she may have been annoyed with him, but now she seemed content. She sat down beside him on the edge of a seat, eyes closed and not saying a single word. He kept spluttering and fawning, twitching and swaying in an effeminate manner, all with the goal of gaining her affection and winning over her heart. Just then she told him bluntly exactly why she was so annoyed with him and kept avoiding him. "I've had that jewel assessed," she told him, "the one you said was so unique. It's much less valuable than the other one. I've come to realize that you're mocking and despising me, toying with my mind and doing your best to beguile me. I've asked you to let me use your carriage before, but your only response was procrastination and delay. I want you to know that, if you continue behaving like this and don't treat me properly, I'm going to throw you off and take another lover." The man now swore on his honor and dignity, on the revered head of his own father, on the grave of both his mother and grandmother—or else let this night see the end of it all—that if she accorded with his wishes this very night he would not refuse her anything, neither withholding his riches nor keeping his property, whether current or inherited, away from her. And so, now that the reasons for her refusal had been removed, everything ended on a serene note. 32.3

We happened to look round and saw the Playboy and his two companions. The ʿUmdah was leering and signaling with both eyebrows and hands. 32.4

ويقول للخليع وهو مرتبك مضطرب ووجهه مشتعل ملتهب:

العمدة لقد أسعدنا الجد وحسنت عاقبة الصبر ولئن فاتنا الأنس بالغائب فما أكمل أنسنا بالحاضر ولكن من لنا بهذه الغادة التي اجتمعت على محبتها القلوب وتزاحمت عليها النفوس وأحدقت بحسنها الاحداق وافتتنت بجمالها العقول:

الخليع

وانك ان أرسلت طرفك رائدًا
لقـلبك يومًا أتعبـتك المنـاظر
رأيت الذي لا كله أنت قـادر
عليه ولا عن بعضه أنت صـابر

هذه الفنانة المشهورة بكثرة العشاق والطلاب ولا عيب فيها غير المزاحمة عليها والمغالاة في التقرب اليها

التاجر هذه هي البضاعة الثمينة ربح من نالها وفاز من حازها ولوكانت الايام أيام رواج ورخاء لهلعت اليها النفس وصبا اليها القلب ولكن حسب المرء من هذه الايام شاغلا عن ذلك.

العمدة على كل حال لا يفوتنا منها الليلة أن تمتع بمجالستها ومغازلتها وتنشرح بقربها ومؤانستها ونروى الغليل بكلامها وتنزه الطرف بجمالها.

الخليع حبذا لو تيسر لنا منها الليلة ما تقول وفزنا منها بلحظة تجلس فيها معنا ولكنك ترى أن كثرة المزاحمة فيها والمنافسة في الغرام بها والغرم عليها مما يجعل المرام متعسرًا والمطلب متعذرًا

العمدة أما المنافسة في الغرم عليها فأمر مستدرك وأما كثرة المزاحمة فيها فانها لا تمنعنا من التمتع بها برهة من الزمن ما دام ذلك غير عسير على نباهتك ومهارتك.

التاجر لا شك في ذلك ولا ريب فان صاحبنا عنوان الانس ومثال اللطافة والظرف وعسى أن تنتهي ليلتنا بحسن الختام.

As he spoke to the Playboy, he seemed completely on fire with love and totally distracted:

'UMDAH We're in luck, and our patience has brought a happy conclusion! We may have missed out on the previous occasion, but now the present offers us a golden opportunity. But how can we get to this lovely woman whom everyone adores, their hearts and eyes unanimous in acknowledgment of her beauty and fascinated by her charms?

PLAYBOY

If you should happen to dispatch your gaze
as emissary for your heart, the sights would exhaust you.
You would espy that over all of which you had no control
nor indeed could you abide even a part.[33]

This woman is renowned for her numerous lovers and devotees. The only problem with her is the sheer number of people crowding around her and going to extravagant lengths to get to her.

MERCHANT She's certainly expensive goods! Whoever gets her is the winner! If it were still a time when commerce was good and there was plenty of trade, then people could fall for her and get infatuated, but, as it is these days, people have other things to think about.

'UMDAH Whatever the case, we shouldn't miss the chance to spend some enjoyable time sitting and flirting with her tonight. We can relax and have an intimate gathering, quenching our thirst with her words and soothing our eyes with her beauty.

PLAYBOY If only it were that easy to achieve what you're asking and get her to sit with us for a while tonight! But you can see for yourself how crowded the field is and how much competition there is in longing for her attention and paying the price. All that makes it difficult, if not impossible, to meet your request.

'UMDAH As far as the competition to pay her is concerned, everything's to hand. And, as long as we have your skill and renown at our disposal, the crowds all around her should not prevent us enjoying her company for a while.

MERCHANT In that case, there can be no doubt about it. Our friend here is the proverbial master of intimate gatherings, discretion, and good taste. Maybe our night will come to a pleasant conclusion.

الخليع ما عليّ الا أن أعمل جهدي وأبذل ما في وسعي ولي بها معرفة قديمة ربما سهلت عليّ الحيلة في اجتذابها وأنا أبدأ بالخادم أكلمه.

٥،٣٢ قال عيسى بن هشام: ويدعو الخليع الخادم ويهم باعطائه شيئاً من الدراهم فيسابقه التاجر فيمنعهما العمدة ويقوم مقامهما فيلقي الخليع على الخادم قولا ويطول الخطاب بينهما همساً فيذهب ولا يلبث أن يحضر بها من غير تمنع ولا تردد فتسلم عليهم جميعاً:

تحيي وجوه الشرب فعل مسالم
يضاحكه والكيد كيد محارب

وتحيي الخليع بابتسامة وتسأله عن ما جرى بعد انصرافها من ذلك المجلس بغتة وكيف كان وقعه بينهم فيقطع عليها الكلام بالقهقهة ويتلطف في عقد التعارف بينها وبين العمدة والتاجر ويشرح لها حالهما ويطنب في علوّ مركزهما فترحب بهما ويكرر العمدة رفع يده الى رأسه مراراً تحية لها فتلمح الخاتم يتألق فصه ويتوهج فتميل على عنقه تداعبه وتهوي الى يده توهمه أنها تقبلها وما قبلت في الحقيقة الا الحجر وما ينزع يده من يدها الا انزعاجه من صوت الأصمة عند نزعها من أفواه الزجاجات ولا يزال الغلام بعد ذلك يغدو عليهم ويروح والزجاجات ملء يديه وكلما تخوف التاجر من عاقبة هذا الغدو والرواح ومال على الخليع يساره سكن هذا من روعه ومسح على كتفه كأنه يطيب من خاطره فيميل عند ذلك الكأس يفرغها ويملأها والى المرأة يهازلها ويغازلها ويعاطيها ويناولها

٦،٣٢ والعمدة باهت شاخص متولع متوله والخليع منبسط مبتهج لا ينزل الكأس عن فيه الا وقد أتبعه بأخيه ، يلتفت بوجهه يمنة ويسرة كأنه يفاخر اقرانه بهجة مجلسه وانفراده بالأنس دونهم ثم يخرج العمدة ساعته من جيبه وتبقى في يده برهة وهو يتشاغل عن النظر اليها فتراها المرأة فتتناولهما منه وتنظر فيها وتقول لقد آن أوان الانصراف وحانت ساعة الرواح وتقوم مودعة فيتلهف العمدة ويسألها أن تتم جميلها باستمرار

Playboy I'll have to try my very best. I've known her for a while, and that may give me an edge when it comes to enticing her. I'll begin by talking to the waiter.

ʿĪsā ibn Hishām said: The Playboy now called the woman's assistant over. He was about to give him some dirhams, but the Merchant got there first. The ʿUmdah stopped them both and took their place. The Playboy had a word in the assistant's ear, and they spent a long time whispering. The assistant went away and came back almost immediately with his mistress; there was no resistance and no hesitation involved. She greeted them all: 32.5

She greets the drinkers with conciliatory banter,
yet the guile is that of a warrior.[34]

She greeted the Playboy with a smile and asked him what had happened after she had left the party so suddenly; she wondered how things had worked out between them all. He interrupted the banter with a hearty laugh and started introducing her to the ʿUmdah and Merchant, describing their influential position in exaggerated terms. She welcomed them both, and the ʿUmdah responded by raising his hand to his head several times in gratitude. She spotted the ring on his finger with its gleaming stone, playfully leaned over his neck, and bent down to his hand, a move that made him think she was going to kiss it whereas all she actually kissed was the stone itself. The only thing that made him pull his hand away was the sound of corks popping from bottles. The waiter now kept going to and fro, his hands full of yet more bottles. Whenever the Merchant felt worried about this continual process and leaned over to whisper to the Playboy, the latter calmed his fears and stroked his shoulder as a way of reassuring him. With that the Merchant turned to his glass, drank it down and refilled it, then turned to the woman and started handing her things and joking and flirting with her.

The ʿUmdah was in a complete daze, utterly infatuated, while the Playboy was preening himself and relaxed; one glass hardly left his mouth before another took its place. He looked to right and left as though to boast to his colleagues how he had managed to secure the woman exclusively for his gathering. The ʿUmdah took his pocket-watch out; he held it in his hand and was staring at it for a while. The woman saw it, took it from him, and looked at the time. "It's time to go," she said, "it's closing time." She got up to leave, but the 32.6

المجلس الى الصباح بعد انصرافها من هذا المكان فتضحك له ضحكة الرضا والقبول وتلطم الخليع على فمه بالمروحة وتذهب نحو صاحب الخان وتجلس معه ويأخذ الناس في الانصراف والخدم في رفع الكراسي واغلاق بعض الابواب حتى لا يبقى الا أولئك الموعودون المفتونون, ذلك الحاكم الرامق وذلك الشيخ المتصابي وذلك الغلام الوارث وهذا العمدة المغرور بتاجره وخليعه فاذا طال عليهم الوقت ويئس الجميع منها بعد أن يدعوها كل فريق ويراسلها يأخذون في الانصراف يصحبهم الهم ويرافقهم الكدر ويشتد بالعمدة السكران سكر الهوى وسكر الخمر:

سكران سكر هوى وسكر مدامة
ومتى يفيق فتى به سكران

٧،٣٢ ويقوم العمدة بتعثر في مشيته ويجرر وراءه في عباءته ويتخبط يميناً وشمالا حتى يصل الى مكان المرأة فيقف بين يديها يستنجزها الوعد فلا تلتفت اليه تستصغره وتفضل عليه سواه فيخرج من جيبه تلك الجنيهات التسعة فيبسط بها راحته نحوها فلا تزداد الا تباعداً منه وجفاء له فيشتد به الهيام فيترامى

عليها فتدفعه عنها برجلها فيقع على الارض فينتثر الذهب من يده فيقوم الخليع ليجمعه فيمنعه صاحب الخان فيلتقطه خادم المرأة فاذا تحامل العمدة وقام مد يده الى المرأة فأخذ بضفيرتيها فتلعنه وتسبه وتمسك بصاحب الخان ويشتد العمدة في جذب الضفيرتين فيقع على ظهره طريحاً والضفيرتان في يده والمرأة في مكانها تصيح فينتفض من أقصى المكان رجل رث الهيئة قبيح المنظر يرفع هراوة في يمينه وهو متابط صرة ثياب في شماله فيقع على العمدة يضربه فيدفعه عن نفسه ضرباً بالضفيرتين ويتوسط التاجر بينهما فيمنع الرجل ويقول له ما يعنيك فيسبه ويقول له انه زوجها وانه يدافع عن حريمه ولا يرجع عن غريمه فيقول الخليع للتاجر لا تتعرض له فان الرجل من أهل الحماية ولا محل لهذه الحمية والحزم في التوقي من مخاصمة من كان خارجاً عن حكم القانون فانه يجني ولا عقوبة عليه فما يسمع العمدة هذا القول حتى يستنجد بالخليع

'Umdah begged her to crown her kind gesture by extending their soirée somewhere else till morning. She accepted the offer with a laugh, then slapped the Playboy across the mouth with her fan, then went back to the Proprietor and sat by his side. People now started to leave; the waiters piled up the chairs and closed some of the doors. The only people left were the infatuated men who thought they had assignations: the Provincial Official, the enamored Shaykh, the Young Man with the inheritance, and the totally deluded 'Umdah along with the Merchant and Playboy. As time went on and everyone started to despair after inviting her again and sending her messages, they too started to leave, dogged by their anxieties and misery. The 'Umdah was twice besotted:

> Two kinds of drunkenness: love and wine;
> drunk with both, when will anyone recover?[35]

The 'Umdah stumbled to his feet, dragging his cloak behind him, and staggered over to the place where the woman was sitting. Standing right in front of her, he demanded that she keep her promise. She paid him no attention and scoffed at him, preferring someone else. He took nine pounds out of his pocket and thrust them at her. That only made her reject him even more strongly. Passion got the better of him, and he hurled himself at her, but she pushed him away with her foot. He fell to the floor, and all the gold he was holding scattered. The Playboy got up to collect it all, but the Proprietor stopped him. It was the woman's servant who picked it up. Once the 'Umdah had struggled to his feet, he stretched out his hand and grabbed hold of the woman's plaits. Cursing and swearing she held on to the Proprietor. The 'Umdah kept pulling on her hair till he fell flat on his face with the plaits in his hand. Meanwhile the woman kept shrieking from her seat. From a distant corner of the place a gruff-looking thug of a man sprang to his feet and came rushing over; he was brandishing a club in his right hand and bundle of clothes in his left. He set about the 'Umdah and started pounding him, while the 'Umdah used the plaits to ward off the blows. The Merchant now intervened between the two of them and stopped the man's assault. The Merchant asked the man what business it was of his. The man swore at him and said that he was the woman's husband; he was only defending his wife and was not to be turned away from his rival. With that the Playboy advised the Merchant not to object any further. This man, he told him, was a protected person; it was best not to antagonize anyone who was above the law. He could commit any crime he liked without incurring **32.7**

ينقذه من بلائه فيتقدم الخبيث فيكلم الزوج طوراً والحليلة تارة وصاحب الحان أخرى وينتهي النزاع بينهم على أن يترك العمدة ما اجتمع في يد الخادم من الذهب مرضاة للمرأة عن اهانتها وعوضاً لها من الضفيرتين فيقوم صاحب الحان وينادي غلامه وهو مشتغل باطفاء الانوار فيسأله عن حساب العمدة فيكونه له.

صاحب الحان (للعمدة) ادفع لنا قبل كل شيء ثلاثة عشر جنيهاً ثمن المشروب ٨،٣٢
وانظر ماذا تعطينا من العوض في تعطيل المحل بهذه الافعال الصبيانية.

العمدة ما هذه الحسبة وما هذا القول؟

صاحب الحان نعم انها أفعال لا تليق بمقامك ولكنها الخمر أم الشرور وما كان لك أن تتعلق بهذه المرأة المشهورة بشراسة الخلق وأمامك النساء غيرها متعددات في المحل وما اخالك تتوقف عن تسديد هذه الحسبة الصغيرة وأنا أعرفك رجلا شريف الاخلاق حسن الصيت ولا أرضى لك الاهانة ولا ترضى لنفسك الفضيحة وسامح هذه المسكينة على امتناعها منك فانها مضطرة الى ذلك بعيشها ومهنتها وان كان لا بد لك منها فأنا أتعهد لك بأن أصلح بينكما فتسترضيك عند تشريفك في الليلة الآتية.

العمدة (للتاجر) هل بقي معك ما يسدد عنا هذا المبلغ؟

التاجر لا وحقك وحق الصحبة ما بقي معي لا قليل ولا كثير.

العمدة (للخليع) دبرني في أمرى وانظر لي طريقة الخلاص.

الخليع يعزعليّ والله ما نحن فيه وعزت الحيلة عليّ الآن ولوكان صاحب الحان يقبل مني أن يرهن ساعتي هذه لرهنتها عنده ولكنه يستضعف بلا شك قيمتها عن قيمة المطلوب له ولوكان في الوقت سعة لتحصلت لك على مبلغ يسدعنا.

a penalty. As soon as the ʿUmdah heard that, he asked the Playboy to rescue him from his plight. With that the wretch now stepped forward and spoke in turn to the husband, the wife and the Proprietor. The disagreement was settled on the understanding that the ʿUmdah would relinquish the dirhams that the servant had picked up from the floor so as to mollify the woman after he had degraded her in such a fashion and to recompense her for the loss of her plaits.

The Proprietor now got up and called over the waiter who was busy putting out the lights. He asked him for the ʿUmdah's check, and the waiter duly made it out for him.

PROPRIETOR (*to the ʿUmdah*) Before anything else pay us thirteen 32.8
pounds for the drinks. Please make sure to add something extra to the total amount you're going to give us by way of compensation for all the business the establishment has lost tonight because of your childish behavior.

ʿUMDAH What's this check? What are you saying?

PROPRIETOR Yes indeed, your behavior tonight has certainly not been fitting for a person of your standing! Wine is the source of all evil. You had no business monopolizing this woman who's famous for her petulance, when there were plenty of other women in the place besides her. I only hope you won't hesitate to pay this paltry sum. I know that you're someone of fine morals and good reputation. I've no desire to insult you, and you certainly don't want to be involved in a scandal. Forgive this woman for rejecting you; her life and profession require her to do that. If you can't help falling for her, I'll try to make peace between the two of you, then she can be reconciled to you when you pay us the honor of another visit tomorrow night.

ʿUMDAH (*to the Merchant*) Do you still have enough money on you to settle this amount?

MERCHANT No, I don't. By your life and the sanctity of friendship, I've nothing left at all.

ʿUMDAH (*to the Playboy*) My friend, please settle this problem and find me a way out.

PLAYBOY I'm sorry we're in such a fix, but I can't think of a way out. If the Proprietor would accept this watch of mine as surety for the amount of the bill, I'd gladly leave it with him. But he may well say it's not worth the required amount. If only we had time to go and get the ready cash some way or other.

العمدة ان كان الامر ينقضي بالرهن فهذه ساعتي أثمن من ساعتك وهي عندي أعز من روحي لاني أخذتها هدية من دائرة البرنسيس يوم بعت لها أطيانها وعليها حروف منقوشة وقد قدرها صاحبي السيد فلان الجوهري بخمسين جنيهاً وأراد أن يشتريها مني فامتنعت ثم قدرها بعده الخواجه فلان بثمانين جنيهاً.

الخليع اذا كان الامر كذلك فلا يليق رهن هذه الساعة وان كان ولا بد فارهن الخاتم.

العمدة نعم هذا هو الاصوب وان كان الخاتم أغلى من الساعة ثمناً.

ويقدم العمدة الخاتم الى صاحب الخان فيأخذه يقلبه في يده ويقول له :

صاحب الخان هذا لا يكفي فاني لست آمن لهذه الفصوص اللماعة فقد غشوني فيها مراراً باحكام تقليدها وليس هنا من يكشف لي عن حقيقة هذا الفص الآن.

التاجر (بعد أن يتقدم ويمعن في الفص) كيف تقول ذلك وهو الماس قديم يساوي مائة جنيه وأنا أرهنه بخمسين فانتظروني ريثما أذهب الى الاوتيل وأعود بالمبلغ.

صاحب الخان (مكفهراً) ليس عندي وقت للانتظار فقد مضى ميعاد اقفال المحل وهذا البوليس واقف بجانبي ترونه يستعجلني في طاعة أوامر الحكومة.

البوليس نعم مضى الوقت ولا بد من الاقفال حالاً فانظروا معكم شيئاً آخر ترهنونه لفض هذا المشكل.

الخليع أعطه الساعة فلا حول ولا ، ولا تخف عليها وانتظرني غداً صباحاً في قهوة الموسكي لنسرع في استخلاصها من الرهن.

فيعطي العمدة الساعة لصاحب الخان فيتأملها ويقول :

صاحب الخان هذه لا تساوي المبلغ كله ولا بد من أخذ الخاتم مضافاً اليها.

العمدة هذا لا يصح فان المبلغ المطلوب لك مني هو ثلاثة عشر جنيهاً على فرض صحته.

ʿUMDAH If things can be settled by leaving something as surety, this watch of mine is more valuable than yours; it's worth more to me than my own soul. I got it as a gift from the Princess's office on the day I sold her her property. It has the letters of her name engraved on it. A jeweler valued it at fifty pounds for me. He wanted to buy it, but I refused. Then Mr. X valued it at eighty pounds.

PLAYBOY In that case, you shouldn't leave it as surety. You've a ring that you can leave as surety instead.

ʿUMDAH That's a better idea. The ring's worth more than the watch.

(*The ʿUmdah hands the ring to the Proprietor. He takes it and turns it over.*)

PROPRIETOR That's not enough. I've no confidence in gleaming stones like these. I've been taken in several times by perfect copies. There's nobody in the business here at the moment whom I can trust to assess the stone's real value.

MERCHANT (*after coming over and scrutinizing the stone*) How can you say such a thing? It's made from antique diamond; it's worth a hundred pounds. I'm prepared to provide surety for it with fifty pounds. Wait here. I'll go to the hotel and bring back the amount you want.

PROPRIETOR (*scowling*) I've no time to wait. It's time to lock up. The policeman standing here keeps telling me to hurry up and close so as to conform with government regulations.

POLICEMAN That's correct. It's time for the place to be locked up at once. Look for something else to leave as surety so that you can solve this problem quickly.

PLAYBOY (*to the ʿUmdah*) Give him the watch and heaven help . . . There's absolutely nothing to be worried about! We can redeem it tomorrow morning when you meet me in the Mūskī Café.

PROPRIETOR (*after appraising the watch*) The watch just by itself isn't equivalent to the required sum. Leave the ring as well.

ʿUMDAH That won't do at all! Assuming the check's correct, you're only asking for thirteen pounds.

الخليع ما دمنا على عزم فك الرهن غداً فسيان رهن قطعة أو قطعتين وأنا أرجو الخواجه ان يتجاوز عن مبلغ التعطيل.

صاحب الحان اني اتجاوز عنه لأجل خاطرك.

قال عيسى بن هشام: ويشدد اليولبس في طلب الاغلاق سريعاً فلا يسع العمدة الا التسليم في الساعة والخاتم. هذا والمرأة واقفة بين ذلك ترى وتسمع وتهزأ وتسخر وبينا الجميع يتأهبون للخروج اذ دخل رجل ثقيل الروح قبيح الخلقة جهم الوجه جاهظ العينين واسع المنخرين أهرت الشدقين فأخذ يجيل نظره في الحاضرين يميناً وشمالا ثم عمد الى المرأة في مكانهما وأخذ يسبها و يلعنها ويلكمها ويلطمها ويقول لها فات الوقت ومضى الميعاد وأغلقت الحانات وأنا قاعد في انتظارك وأنت هنا لم تنقضي بعد فأين هذا الصيد الذى ألهاك عني وأنساك أمري يا عاهرة فتقول له بذل وانكسار: اشتم بما شئت غير هذه اللفظة القبيحة وأنا وحق محبتك ما ألهاني شيء عنك ولا أنسانيك وانما وقعت لي حادثة مع أحد العمد أخرتني الى هذا الوقت فقد أهانني وضربني وقطع شعوري وتستشهد على ذلك بزوجها وخادمها فيشهدان فيقول لها وأين هو أرنيه ان لم تكوني كاذبة في دعواك فما تكاد تشير اليه حتى يكون العمدة عند باب المكان خارجاً مع أصحابه فيثب للحاق بهم فتقول لا تكدر علينا عيشنا وهلم الى البيت. ٩،٣٢

ولما خرجنا من ذلك المكان الفاسد أخذ الباشا يتحاور في طريقنا مع صاحبي في الذي رأى وسمع: ١٠،٣٢

الباشا الحمد لله الذى أخرجنا من الظلمات الى النور قدكدت والله يقضى عليّ الليلة من هول ما قاسيته ولقد ضاق بي النفس وقاربت روحى أن تزهق من فساد هذا الجو في هذا المكان ودونه في النتن وجار الضبع وعش الظربان والعجب لهؤلاء الناس كيف يعيشون فيه ليالي متتابعة ولا يدركهم الهلاك وما رائحة القبور علم الله الا كالعبير في جانب هذه الروائح.

PLAYBOY Look, as long as we've made up our minds to redeem the surety tomorrow, it doesn't matter whether it's in one part or two. I hope, Sir, you'll excuse us the sum you asked for to make up for loss of trade in the place tonight.

PROPRIETOR For your sake, Sir, I'll excuse you.

ʿĪsā ibn Hishām said: Now the policeman became even more emphatic, insisting that the place close immediately. The ʿUmdah was forced to hand over his watch and ring. The woman was standing there watching and listening; she kept scoffing and jeering. Just then, as everyone was getting ready to leave, an ugly, ill-tempered man came scowling his way in. With a thick neck, bulging eyes, flared nostrils and flabby lips, he was certainly not a pretty sight. Looking to right and left and scanning everyone present, he went over to the woman, started cursing and swearing at her, then gave her a slap. "The hours have gone slipping by," he yelled. "The time for our rendezvous has passed. Now all the taverns are closed. I've been sitting in the house waiting, and here I find you not finished yet. So, you tart, where's this great man who's kept you here and made you forget about me?" "You can curse me all you like," she replied meekly, "but don't call me that! By your love, I've not been distracted nor have I forgotten you. Instead I've had an unfortunate incident with an ʿUmdah which has kept me here till now. He's insulted and beaten me, and pulled off my hair." Her husband and the waiter both corroborated the details of her story. "So where's this man?" he asked. "If you're not lying, show me where he is." Hardly had she pointed at the ʿUmdah before he was hurrying toward the door with his two companions. The man was going to chase after them, but she begged him not to spoil their lives and to come home with her. 32.9

Once we had left that foul place, the Pāshā started talking to our Friend as we were walking. He was asking him about the things we had seen and heard: 32.10

PĀSHĀ Thanks be to God for taking us out of darkness into light! By God, tonight I've almost expired from the sheer horror of what I've been through. The foul atmosphere inside that place has made me feel short of breath; it's almost been the end of me. When it comes to filth, a hyena's den or a polecat's lair cannot be worse. What's amazing is how people can tolerate staying in that awful place night after night without being aware of the ruinous consequences. God knows, the stench of the grave itself is like a waft of perfume compared with the smells in that place.

الصاحب يعيش الناس فيه لترددهم عليه ولألف العادة وحكم الاستئناس وكأن أبدانهم تتسمم شيئاً فشيئاً فتحتمل السم وتذهل عن ألمه وأذاه كما يذهل المصاب عن الألم بشرب المرقد في عملية جراحية لبعض أعضائه أو كما يحكى عن بعض الهنود يترقى الهندي منهم في تعاطي الأفيون جزءا فجزءا حتى ينتهي به الامر الى تسمم الجسد فاذا لسعته عقرب أو لسبته حية لم يؤثر سمها في ذلك الجسم المتسمم من قبل.

الباشا ألا تحدثني أيها الخبير البعير عن ذلك الزوج وعن حمايته وعن هذا الداخل أخيراً ما شأنهما فاني عجبت لأمرهما.

الصاحب لك ذلك ، فأما الزوج فانه رجل من سفلة المغاربة من رعايا ١١،٣٢
دولة أجنبية تحميه من سلطة القوانين المصرية وقد اعتاد مثل أولاء العواهر أن تعمد احداهن الى مثل هذا الرجل فتتزوجه على أجر تقدمه اليه وعيش يعيش به فيكون حليلها اسماً وتكون هي خليلة جميع الناس فعلاً ويقوم بعد ذلك بخدمتها وحمايتها فان المرأة تلحق بزوجها في الحماية الاجنبية فاذا وقعت في ما يعاقبها عليه القانون حمتها منه نسبتها الى زوجها واذا همت الحكومة يوماً بمنعها عن الرقص والتظاهر بالفسق واعلان الفحش غيرة على الحشمة والمروءة لا تمتنع فاذا استعملت معها القوة طالبتها الماهرة بالعطل والضرر أمام المحاكم المختلطة لنسبتها الى ذلك الزوج وليس استعمال هذه الحيلة قاصراً على العواهر وحدهن فقد ألفه الناس وأنسوا به في غير ذلك واشترك فيه معهن بعض الجرائد يرحمنا الله ، والجرائد كما تعلم معدة لتعليم الناس وتهذيب الاخلاق فترى صاحب الجريدة ومحررها ينتحل اسم بائع نعال مغربي فيذيل به جريدته ويجعله صاحبها ثم يذكر فيها ما تسول له نفسه من طعن في الحكومة وأولياء الامر ووزراء الدول وعظماء الناس فاذا هم أحد بمحاكمته هرب من وجه المحاكمة وقال له ما سب الحكومة ولا طعن في الاشراف الا صاحب هذا الاسم فدونك فابحث عليه فاذا بحث عنه وجده يصفق بالنعال في الطريق ولم تكن له يد عليه في المحاكمة

Friend People can survive there because they frequent the place, make it a habit, and inure themselves to it. It's as if their bodies are being gradually poisoned, so they can tolerate its effects and ignore the harm and damage it causes. They resemble a sick person who can ignore pain by drinking an anaesthetic during a surgical operation on one of his limbs, or, according to stories told about Indians, resemble one who gradually increases his opium dose until his body eventually reaches the stage that, even if a scorpion stings him or a snake bites him, the poison has no effect on his body which has already been poisoned.

Pāshā I'd like you to explain to me, my august informant, about the woman's husband and his protection and also about the other man who came in later. What's the story with them both? I find it all amazing.

Friend With pleasure! The husband is one of the Maghribī riffraff **32.11**
attached to a foreign government, a status that makes him immune to the authority of Egyptian laws. Prostitutes like this woman have habitually chosen to rely on men like him; they marry such a man and pay him a fixed amount on which to live. So while he's her husband in name, in fact she can be everyone's girlfriend. In return he serves and protects her. The woman sticks with her so-to-say husband so as to get foreign protection. Thus, whenever she happens to get into a situation in which Egyptian law will seek to punish her, the fact that she's married to this man will serve to protect her from the law. Whenever, in the name of modesty and decency, the government attempts to stop her dancing, behaving in a lewd fashion, and blatently promoting sex, she can't be stopped. If the government forces her, the crafty woman can go to the Mixed Courts because of her relationship with her husband and claim damages for being forced out of work. This manipulation of the system is not confined to prostitutes alone. By now people are quite used to seeing it used in other contexts as well. Certain newspapers adopt the same procedure as prostitutes—God have mercy on us all! As you know, newspapers are available to educate the public and to inculcate morality. Even so, you'll find the owner of a newspaper and its editor adopting the name of some Maghribi sandal-seller. They put his name on a sidebar and make him the owner. They'll then put in the newspaper whatever takes their fancy by way of abuse directed at the government, ruling authorities, government ministers, and important people. If any one of these people should think of taking the newspaper to court, the actual owner gets away with it because he claims that the person who cursed

أمام محاكم البلاد التي يخضع لها الامير قبل الحقير بل يحاكمه أمام قنصله وبواب القنصلاتو لا ينصف المنتحي اليه ناهيك بالقنصل وأما هذا الداخل فهو عند تلك المرأة رفيق القلب وشقيق الروح دون أولئك المتفانين في حبها المتطلبين لرضاها المستعذبين لسخطها المفدين لها بأموالهم وأرواحهم يترضونها فلا ترضى ويلتمسونها فتأبي والنفس الدنيئة لا تألف الا من تقاسي منه أفعال الدناءة والاذاة ولا تحترم الا التسلط عليها بمثل أخلاقها فهي على ما تراها تفضل هذا الحيوان الضاري على جميع تلك الدواجن فيؤذيها ويضربها ويتمتع باموالها التي تجمعها بالطرق المختلفة وبعتقد بمكانه عن قلبها فينتظرها ويصبر عليها حتى تنتهي من شغلها في ليلتها ثم يأتيها آخر الليل فيأخذها بانواع الاذى من بين أولئك العابدين لها المتهالكين في طلب رضاها فتخضع له وتنقاد:

هلوك تهين المستهام بحبها
وتلقى الرجال المبغضين باجلال

الباشا تعالى الله ، لا شك ان هذا من حكمة الدهر في معاقبة مثل هذه البغي في بغيها وسلبها لأموال الناس وفتكها بارواحهم وقل لها مثل هذا العقاب وحده في الدنيا.

١٢،٣٢ الصاحب لا تظنن أيها الامير ان هذا هو العقاب الوحيد لها على ما تجنيه يداها فهي وامثالها كلهن في عيشة كلها هم وعذاب وألم وعقاب ومن تبصر في حقيقة احوالهن خفف من قسوته عليهن فان هذه الاسلاب التي يسلبنها والاموال التي يجمعنها يسهل عليهن انفاقها كما سهل عليهن تحصيلها فترى الواحدة منهن لا تنتهي حاجاتها من الزينة والحلي واللباس والانفاق على الرفيق والخليل فهي على الدوام غريقة في بحر من الديون وما تراه عليها من القلائد والأساور انما هي أغلال وقيود يسحبها الصائغ والجوهري منها الى أسره أما عيشتها فهي تمضي ليلها

the government and abused upright people was none other than the person with his name on the sidebar. And, if you should try to find that person, you'd find him peddling sandals on the street. There's no hope of bringing him to the kind of court with which princes have to conform just as readily as the lowly. To the contrary, the case is to be heard before the Maghribi's consul. Yet the consulate's doorman won't even give the sandal-seller the time of day, let alone the consul himself.

The man who came in later is the woman's actual beloved and soulmate, to the exclusion of all those other men who expire for love of her, beg for her affection, suffer agonies because of her anger, and sacrifice money and soul simply to please her. She is never satisfied; they long for her, and she turns them all down. The depraved soul will only feel comfortable with someone who treats it with equal depravity and cruelty; it will only respect a person whose evil morals are totally dominant. As you can see, this woman prefers this raging beast over all those other domestic animals. He hurts her, beats her, makes good use of all the money that she collects by various means. He retains his fixed place in her heart and waits patiently till she's finished her job each night. Then at night's end he comes here and beats her right in front of all these worshippers who have been falling over each other to please her. She then submits to him and is led away.

Perdition despises the one infatuated in his love for her,
and discards men whose glory has made them detested![36]

PĀSHĀ May God be exalted! This is undoubtedly fate's verdict in punishing this type of prostitute who robs people of their money and destroys their spirits. Rarely in such cases is such a penalty brought forward into this lower world.

FRIEND Noble amir, don't imagine that this is the only punishment for their crimes. She and others like her are all constantly prey to anxieties, suffering, and pain. Anyone observing their real situation will mitigate the bitter feelings he has toward them. The spoils that they plunder and the money they pilfer enable them to spend it just as easily as it is to get it in the first place. You'll notice that each one of them has never-ending needs when it comes to makeup, jewelry, and clothes, not to mention expenditures on their companions and male protectors. She is continually up to her neck in a sea of debt. The necklaces and bracelets you see her wearing are all chains and fetters 32.12

الى الصباح كما رأيتها في شرب السموم من الخمور وتقليب الاعضاء والاحشاء بتلك الحركات مع اشتغال فكرها بمراقبة الناس والتحيل عليهم وما يجره عليها ذلك من المخاصمات والمنازعات والمشاجرات فاذا ذهبت الى بيتها كانت منهوكة القوى مخدرة الاعصاب منحلة الاعضاء لا تشتهي طعاماً ولا تلتفت الى غذاء فترتمي من نومها وشدة سكرها في مكان أقذر هواء وأنتن رائحة من ذلك الحان ثم تقوم في نصف النهار أو بعده مصدعة مخمورة فاذا تماسكت قامت لزينها واشتغلت بمن يزورها في نهارها وتعود في المساء الى ماكانت عليه وهلم جرا تعيش في حلقة من الفساد لا منتهى لها فاذا افاقت لنفسها وعلمت بسوء حالها اسودت الدنيا في وجهها وتمنت الخلاص من حيلتها وحسدت من سواها من النساء وكان أقصى أمنية لها وأشهى كلمة تتردد على لسانها ان تتوب من مزاولة المعصية وان تصير في أدنى درجات الحرائر وفي أسوأ حالات المعيشة بينهن لا تزال هكذا حتى تدركها الشيخوخة بعيدة عن الاهل والاقارب الذين برئوا منها من مبدأ امرها الى منتهاه وهذا هو عذابها الاكبر وعقابها الاشد ولو علم هؤلاء البغايا سوء مصيرهن وعاقبة أمرهن لما خرجن من بين أهلهن مندفعات بسبب من الاسباب التي تخرجهن الى البغاء وهي الفقر والاغواء وسوء التربية وعدم الزاجر وكلها راجع الى عدم القيام بالتربية الدينية الاسلامية فلو تحسنت في النساء والرجال ووجدوا من الزجر والوزع ما ينبههم الى سوء المصير وتأدبوا بآداب الدين لما رأينا شيئاً من هذه المفاسد يجاهر به على رؤوس الاشهاد.

قال عيسى بن هشام: وهنا أخذت الديكة في الصباح تبشيراً بالصباح فتفرقنا للرواح ونحن نسأل رب الارض والسموات أن يغفر لنا السيئات ولجميع المسلمين من عباده والمسلمات. ١٣،٣٢

whereby goldsmiths and jewelers manage to keep her in a kind of imprisonment. Her entire life involves spending the night till early morning, as you've seen, drinking foul wine and contorting her limbs and muscles in a series of exhausting routines. She has to devote her attentions to being friendly with groups of people and finding ways of tricking them. That will often lead to nasty quarrels and arguments. Once she reaches home, she's utterly exhausted; her nerves are shattered and her body aches. She has no desire to eat and doesn't even look at food. Instead she throws herself on her bed, totally drunk, and in a place which may be even filthier than the hall itself and has a worse atmosphere. Next day she gets up at noon or later, with a terrible hangover. Once she's pulled herself together, she works on improving her appearance. Then she receives her daytime visitors. When evening comes, she starts the round all over again, and so on . . . The wretched woman thus goes round and round in a vortex of endless corruption. If she should happen to come to her senses and realize how bad her situation is, the whole world blackens in her eyes and she longs to be rid of all her tricks. She envies other women their lot in life; the thing she devoutly wishes for, the words most frequently on her lips are that she should repent of her disobedience, patiently endure the lowliest of social levels among honorable women, and live among such people in the worst possible conditions. This is the way she stays until old age catches up with her, still far removed from her family and relatives who have discarded her throughout her nefarious career. This is the worst agony of all and the harshest punishment. If only these prostitutes realized the wretched end to which they come, they would never leave their families, whatever the cause that pushes them into prostitution: poverty, seduction, poor upbringing, or lack of any moral restraining factor. It all boils down to a lack of initiative in Islamic religious education. If that worked effectively among men and women, if they encountered some moral force that would prevent them from following this evil course, if they were educated according to the precepts of the Islamic religion, then we would not see any of this corruption showing its face so blatantly.

'Īsā ibn Hishām said: At this point, the cock started to crow to announce the **32.13**
morning. We went on our way, begging the Lord of heaven and earth to forgive the sins of Muslims, men and women.

قال عيسى بن هشام: وقف بنا الحديث عن العمدة والخليع والتاجر بعد خلاصهم من ذلك الملعب ملعب كل فاجرة وفاجر وبعد أن نال العمدة من الهوان بما ناله وأضاع تحت أقدام الراقصات شرفه وماله وبعد أن رهن ما رهن من حلية ومتاع من غير ما هناء ولا استمتاع على أن تكون تلك القهوة موعداً للاجتماع ليتداركه الخليع بلطف تدبيره ويسعى بين يديه في إصلاح أمره وتيسيره ويستخلص له ما يستخلص به المرهون من حليته وغاب عنه أنه سيحيل عليه بجملته ويتمم بناء ما نصبه من عوامل حيلته ١٫٣٣

فلما ارتفع وجه النهار عدنا إلى ما نحن فيه من مزاولة الاختبار والتماس العظة والاعتبار فوجدنا الصاحب هنالك جالساً في الانتظار فقصدنا قصده وجلسنا عنده وأخذنا نتوسم وجوه القاعدين والقائمين فإذا العمدة وصاحباه عن ذات اليمين فحولنا نحوهم السمع والبصر نستقصي القصة ونستجلي الخبر فرأينا العمدة في هول هائل من أثر ليله اللائل شق مائل ولون حائل ولعاب سائل وطلعة مكفهرة وسحنة مغبرة وأنامل مصفرة وجفون محمرة وأحداق جامدة وأعضاء هامدة وأنفاس خامدة يفتح تارة فاه ويحك طوراً في قفاه فيخاله كل من يراه نضواً أضناه السرى وبراه أو عاملا بلغ في السخرة منتهى الشوط وقد أدمته العصا وألهبه السوط والتاجر بجانبه يقلب حدقتيه ويلعب بشفتيه ويتعسر في ابتلاع الريق ويصعد أنفاساً كالحريق كأنه ذئب يهم بالعيثان ويرهب صولة الرعيان أو صائد طاشت حيلته وأخفق كيده فطارت قنيصته وأفلت صيده ٢٫٣٣

ورأينا الخليع بستر ما في نفسه باطراق رأسه وينكت الأرض بعصاه ليصل من كيده إلى أقصاه ويتكلف إظهار كدره وكدمه ويغطي على ابتساماته بيده فهو يتلون بلونين ويظهر بوجهين كأنه الحرباء في اختلاف ألوانها وحركة لسانها أو الثعلب حول قفص الدجاج يحاول الاختلاس منه والاختلاج لا ينفك عن ترتيب الخدعة وتهيئة العدة ليوقعها على قلب التاجر ورأس العمدة ورأينا من دونهم نفرا لا يحولون ٣٫٣٣

Miṣbāḥ al-sharq 103, May 11, 1900[37]

ʿĪsā ibn Hishām said: The last episode finished with the ʿUmdah, Playboy, and Merchant managing to escape from the dance hall, that den of lechery and debauched behavior, but only after the ʿUmdah had been utterly humiliated and had lost both his honor and money at the feet of a female dancer. He had been forced to pawn his valuables and possessions without getting the least enjoyment in return. However, they had decided to meet in a specific café so that the Playboy could use his talents to make some amends and put things to right. That would involve redeeming the ʿUmdah's pawned possessions. The Playboy would then be able to proceed with the rest of his plans that had yet to be implemented in full. 33.1

When it was daylight, we continued our quest for information and morally useful lessons. We found our Friend sitting in the café waiting for us, so we went over and sat down with him. As we looked round at the people sitting and standing there, we spotted the ʿUmdah and his two companions to our right, so we turned in their direction in order to see and hear what had transpired and to catch up with their news. We could tell that the ʿUmdah was in terrible shape after the dreadful night he had just spent; he had, as they say, "a wilting side and pallid color, yet flowing saliva." His frowning features seemed layered in dust, and his fingertips had a yellowish hue; his eyelids looked red, but his pupils were dry. His limbs hung lifeless and his breaths were short. At one moment he was opening his mouth, at another rubbing his neck. Anyone setting eyes on him would have imagined he was a worn-out camel exhausted by night travel in the desert, or else a shift worker whose flesh had been beaten bloody with a cane or provoked with a whip. At his side, the Merchant kept rolling his eyes and licking his lips, finding it hard to swallow. His sighs sounded like fire, like a wolf about to strike and afraid of being attacked by shepherds, or a failed hunter whose traps have let him down so that his prey has got away. 33.2

Meanwhile the Playboy was keeping his thoughts to himself, head down. He kept scratching the ground as he tried to come up with a plan that would bring his wiles to a successful conclusion. He was faking a display of distress and disappointment while hiding his grins behind his hand. He was showing two separate faces and appearing in two different hues, like a chameleon flicking its tongue or a fox near a chicken coop trying to sneak in unnoticed. He kept on cooking up bits of trickery and preparing to inflict them on the 33.3

عنهم نظرا فعلمنا من الصاحب أنهم من تلك الفئة الرابحة الخاسرة فئة الوسطاء والسماسرة وكان الخليع يلحظهم من طرف خفي ثم يبتسم ابتسامة عالم بهم خفي ويميل على العمدة مهوناً عليه من أمره متكفلا له بتيسير عسره فكان يخاتله ويخامره ويقول له وهو يحاوره :

الخليع لا تهتم ولا تغتم فالأمر أيسر مما تظن. ٤،٣٣

التاجر لا أراهم يقرضونك شيئاً إلا برهن لزوال الثقة من بين الناس في هذا الزمن ، زمن المضاربات وإذا كان لا بد من الرهن فأنا أولى بخدمتك وأحرص على مصلحتك من الغير فأقرضك بفائدة أقل مما تقرض به عامة الناس الآن.

العمدة لا بأس بذلك لو كان في الوقت سعة وأنا في حاجة إلى النقود لا تسمح لي بالانتظار والتطويل وما يحتاجه الرهن من المعاينة والتحديد والتقويم والتقدير والكشف في الدفاتر والأوراق والتحرير والتسجيل.

الخليع ولا تنس ما وراء ذلك من الحطة والشنعة وسوء السمعة بين الناس وصدق الذي يقول «بيع الشيء خير من رهنه والرهن بيع وغبن» وأنت بحمد الله لك اسم وصيت وشهرة بالثروة والغنى وامضاؤك وحده يكفي لاكثر مما تطلب الآن ويغنيك عن كل رهن.

التاجر ما أحسن هذا إذا تم ولكن لا تنس أنت أيضاً أن الذي يقرضك على السمعة لا بد أن يأخذ فائدة شهر في جمعة ولا يخاطر بما له الا من يطمع في اغتنام الفوائد الجسيمة من وراء مخاطرته على أنني لا أظن أنه يوجد الآن من يقرض أمواله بغير رهن.

الخليع أنا الضمين بإتمام هذا الأمر في هذه الساعة بل في هذه القهوة ولا محل للخوف من جسامة الفائدة ما دام وقت الحصاد قريباً.

العمدة هذا هو التسهيل والتيسير المنتظر من صاحب مثلك وهكذا تكون الصحبة يا أبا الهمم.

Merchant and ʿUmdah. Next to them we noticed another group of people who kept their gaze riveted on our friends. When we asked my friend who they were, he replied that they were that cunning and ruthless mob of profiteers and scoundrels, middlemen and brokers. The Playboy kept giving them sneaking looks and then smiling to let them know that he had succeeded. He leaned over to the ʿUmdah, making light of the latter's plight and offering to help him solve his problem. Here's what he said as he continued his cheating ways:

PLAYBOY Don't worry, my dear fellow! Things aren't as bad as you think. 33.4

MERCHANT I don't think they'll make you a loan unless you pawn something else. These days people no longer trust each other in this age of speculation. If you have to pawn something, I think I'm the best person to offer you such a service, since I'll have your best interests at heart and can offer you a loan with less interest than what's generally on offer at the moment.

ʿUMDAH That would be satisfactory, provided there was enough time. I need money and cannot afford any wait or delay. Such procedures now involve supervision, definition of time limit, valuation, assessment, recording, registration, documentation, and so on.

PLAYBOY And don't forget the terrible opprobrium, disgrace, and loss of reputation you'll face with people. Whoever said "selling something is better than pawning it; pawning is selling and swindling at the same time" was certainly speaking the truth. Praise be to God, you're famous and respected for your considerable wealth. Your signature alone will be enough for more than what you need and will avoid the bother of pawning anything.

MERCHANT If that could be done, it would be fine. But at the same time don't forget another adage: "Someone who makes you a loan on the basis of reputation is bound to take a month's interest in a week." Nobody with money to lend is prepared to risk it without security unless he's guaranteed huge interest and considerable profit. Even so, I don't think anyone's willing to lend money these days without some kind of pawn.

PLAYBOY I can personally guarantee that we'll get the loan at this very moment, in this café. There's no need to worry about huge interest rates when harvest time is close at hand.

ʿUMDAH This is the kind of facilitation that one expects from real friends like you! That's true friendship, thou master of good intentions!

التاجر قد قلت ما عندي وما على الناصح من سبيل وكل إنسان حر في ماله.

الخليع (للعمدة) قل لي كم تريد أن يكون مبلغ القرض؟

العمدة يكفيني على ما أظن مائة جنيه.

الخليع وماذا ينفعك هذا المبلغ القليل وأمامك قبل كل شيء تسديد ما لصاحبنا التاجر في ذمتك ثم يتبعه تخليص الخاتم والساعة من ألحان وبعد ذلك تأجير البيت الذي ترغب سكناه في حلوان وابتياع ما يليق بك من أثاثه وأنواع زخرفته وما يلزم من النفقة لأوقات الأنس والطرب التي أنت محتاج إليها بعد هذا الكد والتعب لا سيما وأنت مضطر للإقامة هنا مدة في انتظار نجاز القضية التي علمت أنها تأخرت عن ميعادها المقدر لها فلا أرى لك بعد هذا إلا أن يكون مبلغ الاقتراض خمسمائة جنيه على الأقل لقصر المدة ولأن المرابين الذين أعرفهم لا يقرضون أقل من هذا المبلغ.

ويميء الخليع إلى جماعة السماسرة فيتقاطرون عليه فيهمس في أذن أحدهم كلاماً ثم يجهر لهم قائلا:

إن سعادة البك العمدة فلاناً من أعيان المزارعين الذين يمتلكون من الأطيان والعقار ما هو مشهور معلوم ولم يسبق له اقتراض قط وليس عليه دين مطلقاً وأملاكه وأطيانه خالصة له لا منازع ولا معارض ولا مشارك له فيها وقد صادفته في مصر ظروف استنفدت ما كان في يده للنفقة وبقي الآن في حاجة إلى اقتراض خمسمائة جنيه يدفعها في أوان الحصاد ولست أحب أن يقترض مثل هذا المبلغ الزهيد بالنسبة إليه من أحد البنوك الكبيرة لما في ذلك من التطويل وزيادة التحري لجهل أربابها بأعيان البلاد. ٥.٣٣

أحد السماسرة نعم نعم كلنا يعرف سعادة البك بما وصفته به من الشهرة وسعة المال زاده الله منه وكان لوالدي مع المرحوم والده معاملة قديمة وكنت أسمع منه وأنا صغير أنه لا يوجد في أعيان البلاد مثله في الصداقة والأمانة وكرم النفس ٦.٣٣

MERCHANT I was just expressing my opinion, but then a counselor may have no other resort. We are all free to use our money as we like.

PLAYBOY (*to the 'Umdah*) Tell me then, how much do you want to borrow?

'UMDAH As I see it, a hundred pounds should be enough.

PLAYBOY How can that small sum be enough? Before anything else, you have to settle up with your friend here for standing security for your debt. Then you need money to redeem the watch and ring from the dance hall. To which I would add the money you'll need to rent the house where you'll want to stay in Ḥulwān and to purchase furniture and decorations. Then there are expenses for your leisure time. After all this worry and exhaustion you'll certainly need some relaxation and fun, particularly because you'll have to stay here for some time while you wait for the successful conclusion of your court case which, as you know, has been postponed from its anticipated date. With all that in mind, I can't see you needing less than five hundred pounds at the very least in the short term. In any case, the moneylenders I know won't lend a smaller sum.

With that, the Playboy gestured to the group of brokers. They came rushing 33.5
over in a group, and he had a word in the ear of one of them. Then he spoke openly: "This Bey is 'Umdah X, an influential landlord, renowned for the lands and estates he owns. He's never borrowed before, has absolutely no debts, and is exclusive owner of his lands and possessions, with no rival claims or partnerships. Circumstances in Cairo have so turned out that he's used up all the money he's brought to spend. He needs to borrow five hundred pounds which he'll repay at harvest time. I don't want him to borrow a paltry sum like this from one of the big banks; they have to make lengthy inquiries and waste time. Their owners have no knowledge of key figures in the country."

ONE OF THE BROKERS Yes indeed, we're all well acquainted with the 33.6
Bey. We're well aware of the high repute and great wealth with which God has endowed him. In fact, my late father had dealings with his father in the past; when I was a small boy, I often heard my father say that, among the notables of the region, he knew of nobody who was so truthful and reliable, so noble-minded and generous as your late father. However you must realize that cash is hard to come by these days. Few people are willing to risk loaning such a sum

وسماحة الخلق ولكنك تعلم أن النقود عزيزة في هذه الأيام وقل من يخاطر منا بمثل هذا المبلغ على غير رهن يوازيه أضعافاً مضاعفة ولو كان الأمر قاصراً عليّ وحدي لما تأخرت عن إجابة هذا الطلب بلا صك ولا فائدة إكراماً للمعرفة القديمة وتجديداً للصحبة ولكن لي شريكا متفرنجاً من أبناء هذا الزمان لا يرضى بقرض المال إلا إذا كان جامعاً للشروط القانونية وعلى كل حال فإن في إمكاني أن أستجلب رضاه بضمانتي أولا وبتشريف الفائدة ثانياً فإن اتفقتم معي على أن الخمسمائة بسبعمائة إلى وقت الحصاد باشرت معه الأمر وقمت بالخدمة الواجبة عليّ لسعادة البك.

٧،٣٣ التاجر سلام قولا من رب رحيم خمسمائة بسبعمائة.. ما سمعنا بهذا في آبائنا الأولين.

أحد السماسرة (للتاجر) أظن أن سيدنا من المجاورين بالأزهر الشريف فإنه لا يستعظم مثل هذه الفائدة إلا من يعتقد تحريمها على أن الربا كما هو محرم عندكم فإنه أيضاً محرم عندنا ولكن أحوال المعائش تدعو إلى إباحة المحظورات.

العمدة لا ولكن حضرته من مشاهير التجار.

أحد السماسرة إذا كان الأمر كذلك فهو يكون أدرى بضيق الحال وقلة المال وأعلم بمقدار الفائدة عن قرض بغير رهن ثم هو لا يجهل معنى الشركات ولا المساهمات. (ويغمزه بطرفه)

التاجر ولكن مائتي جنيه فائدة على خمسمائة جنيه كثير على كل حال فلتكن بحكمي مائة وخمسين جنيهاً.

السمسار ما أصعب المعاملة مع التجار وما دمت حكمت بما حكمت فما علينا إلا القبول طاعة لك وإكراماً لسعادة البك فتفضلوا معي على بركة الله إلى البنك لإتمام الأمر مع شريكي،

الخليع لا حاجة بنا إلى قيامنا جميعاً فليذهب سعادة البك معك ونمكث نحن هنا في الانتظار.

without security equivalent to several times as much. If the decision were mine alone, I wouldn't hesitate for a moment. I would respond to your request without demanding any pledge of security or interest, all as a token of recognition of the former friendship between our two fathers and as a way of consolidating the friendship between us. But I have a European business partner who's a child of this age. He'll only agree to loan money when all the legal stipulations are properly met. Even so, I can satisfy him, firstly with my personal guarantee and secondly by letting him have the interest amount. So if you'll agree to the five hundred being valued at seven hundred till harvest time, I'll attend to the matter with him and serve the Bey here as I must.

MERCHANT Good grief! Seven hundred for five hundred! By the lives of 33.7
our forefathers, I've never heard of anything like it!

BROKER (*to the Merchant*) My dear Sir, I think you must be a student at the noble al-Azhar. Only someone who believes that interest is forbidden would consider it too much, using as his basis the fact that usury is forbidden to us just as much as it is to you. But then, as the proverb has it, "Life's circumstances legitimize what is otherwise forbidden."

'UMDAH The gentleman isn't a student at al-Azhar. He's a famous merchant.

BROKER If that's the case, then he's surely as aware as anybody of how tight the situation is and how short the supply of money actually is. He must realize what the interest rate is for loans with no collateral. Then he's surely not unaware of the meaning of partnerships and bargains.

(*With that he gives the Merchant a wink.*)

MERCHANT Even so, two hundred pounds interest on seven hundred is a lot. In my opinion, it needs to be one hundred and fifty.

BROKER Dealing with merchants is always tricky! But, as long as that's your view, we'll have to go along with it. Out of respect for the 'Umdah I'm prepared to accept what you say. So be so good as to accompany me to the bank with God's blessing so we can conclude matters with my partner.

PLAYBOY We needn't all go. The 'Umdah can go with you, and we'll wait for you here.

قال عيسى بن هشام: ويقوم ذلك السمسار ويأخذ معه العمدة ونشتغل بالحديث مع صاحبنا في أمور شتى نستفيدها من واسع علمه مقدار ساعة وإذا العمدة وحده قد عاد واضعاً يده على جيبه ينبسط وجهه تارة وينقبض أخرى فيستقبله الخليع والتاجر يستخبرانه الخبر فيقص عليهما: ٨،٣٣

العمدة لعن الله الاضطرار وماكان أغنانا عن هذا الخراب والدمار.

الخليع هل سرقت منك النقود؟

العمدة لا لم تسرق كلها ولكن سرق نصفها.

التاجر (شاهقاً والخليع محملقاً) وكيف كان ذلك؟

العمدة ركبت مع السمسار وذهبت إلى محل البنك فأجلسني هناك ناحية وكتب الصك وأمضيته ثم انفرد مع شريكه يكلمه وبعد برهة عاد إليّ السمسار وقال لي أن الأمر متعسر متعذر وأنه بذل ما في وسعه من طرق الرجاء والاستعطاف لشريكه فلم يتمكن من إقناعه لأعذار عرضها عليه وأنه يأسف كل الأسف لخيبة مسعاه ويعدني بالصبر أياماً حتى تنفرج الشدة فأريته ما بي من الحاجة الوقتية إلى النقود وعدم الصبر عليها وهممت بالرجوع إليكما لتنظرا لي في طريقة أخرى فدنا مني صاحب المحل وقال لي: يعز عليّ والله أن أرد طلبك ولكنك تعلم مقدار الضيق الذي لحق بهذا القطر في هذا العام وما نحن فيه من قلة النقود المتداولة وغلاء الأسعار التي لا تجهلها من حرب الترنسفال وانخفاض النيل وظهور الطاعون وكثرة المضاربات وانتشار الشركات فاعذرني ولا تعدّ امتناعي تقصيراً وأنا أقسم لك بشرفي وذمتي وأولادي وبما بيننا وبين بيتكم الكريم من الصحبة القديمة رحمة الله على والدكم أنني لا أمتلك من النقود في محلي هذا الآن سوى أربعمائة جنيه أمانة عندي ليتيم من أقاربنا نشتغل له في استثمارها وتنميتها وأنا أضن بها وأحرص عليها فوق حرصي على أموالي ومع ذلك فإني أضعها بين يديك إن أردت لتعرف درجة محبتك عندنا وحسن منزلتك لدينا ولتكون أول خدمة أقدمها لك.

ʿĪsā ibn Hishām said: The Broker got up and went off with the ʿUmdah. We spent an hour in conversation with my friend, during the course of which we learned a variety of things from his wide knowledge. Suddenly we spotted the ʿUmdah coming back alone, hand in pocket. Once in a while he smiled, but then he was scowling. The Playboy and Merchant welcomed him back and asked him how things had gone. The ʿUmdah told them: 33.8

ʿUMDAH God curse necessity! We could well have done without this ruin and desolation.

PLAYBOY Was the money stolen?

ʿUMDAH No, not all of it, but half of it was.

MERCHANT (*with a groan*) and PLAYBOY (*mouth agape*) How on earth did that happen?

ʿUMDAH I rode away with the Broker, and we went to the bank. He sat me down in a corner, wrote out the check, and I signed it. Then he went away arguing with his partner. After a while he came back and told me that matters were complicated and difficult. He'd done his utmost to convince his partner, begging and pleading, but he'd been unable to convince him to permit the offer. The Broker told me how much he regretted that his endeavors had failed. He suggested that I wait a few days till the crisis was over. I told him how desperately I needed dirhams at this moment and that I couldn't wait. I was about to come back so you could devise some other way of getting the money. At that point the owner of the place came up to me and said, "By God, I'm reluctant to reject your request, but you must be aware of the tight situation that is dogging the country's finances this year: the shortage of ready cash, the inflation caused by the war in the Transvaal, the low level of the Nile, the plague epidemic, the amount of speculation, and the spread of companies. So please forgive me and do not take my refusal as a sign of weakness. I swear to you, on my word of honor, on my own children and on the longstanding friendship that binds me to your honorable self through your father—God have mercy on him!—that at this moment the only cash I have in our place is four hundred pounds which represents a trust fund for an orphaned child related to us. We are investing it and letting it grow. I'm even more sparing and stingy about it than I am with my own money. Even so, I'm going to give it to you if you wish, so you can know the extent of my affection for you and the excellent opinion we have of you. Let this be the beginning of the service that I'm offering you."

فلم أر بدّا من قبولها فأحضر الخواجه صرة النقود ووزنها ثم وضعها أمامي فعددتها فوجدتها أربعمائة تماماً وبعد أن وضعتها في جيبي طلبت منه تغيير الصك لأن المبلغ المطلوب لي فيه خمسمائة لا أربعمائة فامتنع معتذراً بأن الفرق ما بين المبلغين باق عنده بعضه لربح اليتيم وبعضه لنفقات القضية من رسوم وأتعاب للمحامي إن وقع لا سمح الله توقف مني عن الدفع في الميعاد كما هي العادة المألوفة الآن ٩،٣٣

فعظم عليّ الأمر ورددت إليه صرة النقود وطلبت منه أن يرد لي الصك فاشتغل عني ببعض الوافدين وتركني على مثل الجمر وكلما أرت إليه شارة من بعيد لوى وجهه عني وتفقدت صاحبي السمسار فلم أجده في أنحاء المكان فاشتد بي الحال وتوقدت غيظاً فقمت إلى صاحب المحل فأمسكت به أطالبه بالصك فقال لي لا يمكنني أن أسلمه لك إلا بحضور شريكي الذي أتى بك إلى هنا فانتظر قليلا حتى يؤوب فلم أقبل وألحت في الطلب.

وبينما نحن على تلك الحال وإذا بفلان بك صهر مديرنا قد حضر ووقف بجانبنا فما بصرت به إلا وارتخت مفاصلي خجلا منه ثم سلم عليّ سلام انعطاف واحترام وسألني عن جلية الأمر فقصصت عليه قصتي منذ حضوري مع السمسار إلى ذلك المحل فقال لي: ليس ثم ما يوجب الشقاق والنزاع فإني أعرفك رجلا من عيون الأعيان في مديريتك مشهورا بكرم النفس وجميل السيرة وحضرة الخواجه رجل من أهل الثقة والأمانة وشهرته بحسن المعاملة لا يجهلها أحد فإن كان حجز منك مائة جنيه لنفقات القضية فلا شك أنه يردها إليك عند تسديدك مبلغ الصك في ميعاده وأنت من الثروة بحيث لا تلتجئ إلى التأخر في الدفع وإن لم يسبق لك معاملة مع حضرة الخواجه تؤيد لك حسن عهده وأمانته فأنا أكفل لك صدقه ووفاءه ١٠،٣٣

فلم يبق لي من وجه للتوقف عن استلام النقود وقلت لسعادة البك: والله لولا خاطرك واضطراري إلى هذا المبلغ لدفعه عربوناً في أطيان تورطت في اشترائها من أحد أولاد الذوات المحجوز عليهم لما رضيت بهذا الغبن فقال لي: بارك الله لك في

I could see no way of refusing the money. The foreigner brought a purse full of cash and weighed it. He put it in front of me, and I counted out four hundred pounds exactly. Once I'd put it in my pocket, I asked him to alter my check because the amount on it was five hundred, not four hundred. He refused, using as his excuse that he intended to hold on to the difference, some of it for the orphan's profit and some of it for court expenses and lawyers' fees in case, God forbid, I failed to pay the sum by the time stipulated, as was usually the case these days. At that I became alarmed. I gave him back the purse and asked him to give me back my check. He ignored me and turned to talk to some other people who had come to see him. Meanwhile he left me on tenterhooks. Every time I beckoned him from a distance, he turned away in disgust. I had completely lost track of my companion, the Broker; he was nowhere to be found. I became even more worried, and my anger got the better of me. I grabbed the owner of the place and demanded that he give me back my check. He told me that he could not return it unless his partner, who had brought me there, was present. He asked me to wait a while till his partner returned. 33.9

While we were thus involved, Y Bey, our governor's brother-in-law, came in and stood right beside us. As soon as I set eyes on him, my knees gave way in sheer embarrassment. He greeted me with sympathy and respect and asked me what the situation was. I told him what had been happening to me ever since I'd come to this place with the Broker. "There's no need for disagreement or argument," he told me. "I know that you're someone of high standing in the province where you live, renowned for your generosity and kindness. This foreign gentleman is completely reliable and trustworthy; he's renowned for his fair dealings with people, as anyone will readily admit. If he has retained a hundred pounds in case of court expenses, he'll certainly return them to you when the amount on the check is repaid at the stipulated time. With all the wealth that you have through God's grace, you won't need to postpone repayment. If you haven't done enough business with the esteemed foreign gentleman before to be able to confirm his reliability and trustworthiness, then I can vouch for his honesty and integrity." 33.10

At that point I had no alternative but to accept the cash. I bowed to the Bey. "By God, my dear Sir," I told the governor's brother-in-law, "if it weren't for your own initiative here and a pressing need that I have for this sum of money, something that I require as a down payment on lands that I've managed to purchase from some rich children whose property has been sequestered, then

البيع والشراء ثم حملني سلاماً لسعادة المدير وبعد أن عددت المبلغ ثانية وودعت البك والخواجه انصرفت وقد كتبت صكا بستمائة وخمسين جنيهاً لم يدخل جيبي منها إلا أربعمائة جنيه فهذا معنى سرقة نصف المبلغ مني.

قال عيسى بن هشام: وكنا نرى في أثناء هذا الحديث رجلا واقفاً على رأس العمدة ينتظر نهاية كلامه ويده ممدودة إليه تبين لنا من هيئته أنه سائق مركبة فسمعناه يقول له : ١١،٣٣

سائق المركبة خلصنا يا سيدي السيد فقد تعطلت وأنا واقف بين يديك.

العمدة أنا لا أعطيك زيادة عما دفعته إليك فإن فيه الكفاية.

سائق المركبة من يقول يا حضرة الشيخ أن ثلاثة تكفي أجرة المركبة طول هذه المسافة التي تنقلت فيها من مكان إلى مكان ثم ردتك ثانية إلى هذه القهوة ولكن الذنب عليّ فقد كنت عاهدت الله أن لا يركب معي أمثال هؤلاء المشايخ والعمد

الخليع دع عنك هذا الكلام الفارغ وهاك قرشاً رابعاً

سائق المركبة هذا شيء لا ينفع , أعطوني أجرتي على حسب التعريفة أو أنادي البوليس!

العمدة دونك نصف قرش آخر واتركنا وانصرف.

سائق المركبة كيف أقبل أربعة قروش ونصفاً في مثل هذه المسافة فهل تحسبها أجرة ركوبك من هنا مع الخواجه إلى البنك وطول انتظاري هناك أو أجرة ركوبك من البنك إلى دكان الكوارع وانتظارك مسافة الأكل أو أجرة رجوعك إلى هنا.

التاجر (للعمدة) دكان الكوارع... وهل هذا شرط الصحبة تفتكر نفسك وتنسى الأصحاب فتركتنا على الجوع منذ أمس وتنفرد دونا بالأكل.

العمدة ما ألجأني والله إلا الجوع المفرط فإني أحسست بالنور ظلاماً في عيني من شدته.

I wouldn't have been prepared to accept this swindle." "May God bless you in your commerce, both buying and selling," he replied and gave me a message of greetings to convey to the governor. I counted the amount again, then said my farewells to the Bey and the foreign gentleman. So, after I'd written a check for six hundred and fifty pounds, all I've got in my pocket is four hundred. That's what I meant when I said that half of it had been stolen.

ʿĪsā ibn Hishām said: While the ʿUmdah was talking, we had our eye on a man who was standing right in front of him waiting for him to finish. He kept stretching out his hand toward him. From his general appearance we gathered that he was the carriage driver. We heard him say: 33.11

Carriage Driver We've finished, my dear sir. While I've been waiting here, you've kept me from my work.

ʿUmdah I'm not going to use you any more. I've given you quite enough already.

Carriage Driver My dear Shaykh, whoever said that three piastres is payment for hiring a carriage for such a trip? I've taken you from one place to another, then brought you back to this café. But then, it's all my fault. I'd promised God that I'd never pick up these rustic shaykhs and ʿUmdahs any more.

Playboy Stop this stupid talk! Here's a fourth piastre.

Carriage Driver That's not enough. Either give me my fare according to the tariff, or else I'm calling the police!

ʿUmdah Here's another half-piastre. Now go away and leave us.

Carriage Driver How can I leave with just four and a half piastres for such a long ride? Have you included in the fare the ride from here to the bank, then the long wait, then another ride from the bank to the sheep trotters' shop where I waited while you ate, and finally the ride back here?

Merchant (*to the ʿUmdah*) Sheep trotters' shop? Is that your idea of friendship, thinking only of yourself and forgetting your friends? So you leave us here starving ever since yesterday and go off to eat without us!

ʿUmdah By God, it was only my incredible hunger that led me to do such a thing. I was so hungry that I thought light was darkness.

الخليع (للتاجر) لا تكن سيء الظن واعذره فما هي إلا بلغة تبلغ بها وسنتناول طعام الغداء معه سواء.

السائق أدركوني برحمتكم فهذا البوليس أخذ نمرة المركبة ليكتبها في المخالفات لاشتغالي عنها بأخذ الأجرة وهي في الطريق.

الخليع خذ قرشاً آخر وانصرف عنا وأنا أخلصك من البوليس فإني أعرفه وأخلصك من المخالفة.

١٢،٣٣ ويقوم الخليع إلى البوليس فيكلمه فلا يقبل منه فيصر السائق على رفض الأجرة ويطلب الزيادة أو توجه العمدة معه إلى مركز البوليس فيكتفي الخليع بإعطائه بطاقة عليها اسم العمدة ولقبه ومحل إقامته فيأخذها وينصرف عازماً على رفع شكواه إلى البوليس ويعود الخليع إلى مجلسه يكلم العمدة:

الخليع قد انتهينا والحمد لله من جميع العقبات فابدأ الآن بدفع مبلغ الصك المطلوب منك لصاحبنا ثم نقوم إلى صاحب الخان لتخليص الرهن.

يعد العمدة المبلغ المطلوب للتاجر ثلاث مرات ويضعه أمامه فيأخذه التاجر فيضمه في جيبه ثم يقول للعمدة:

التاجر تذكرت أن الصك ليس موجوداً معي الآن فالأولى أن تبقي المبلغ عندك حتى أحضره لك.

الخليع ما هذه المعاملة التجارية التي لا تذكر بين الأصحاب والأمانة من شعارهم ومعاذ الله أن يكون بينهم بعد ذلك صكوك أو عقود فإحضار الصك أو عدم إحضاره سيان ما دام المبلغ قد دخل في جيبك وهلم بنا إلى صاحب الخان.

الخليع (للتاجر) أنظر إلى حسن احتياله فلا يزال هواه يرمي إلى سكان تلك الديار.

العمدة أقول لكما الحق أن غيظي على تلك المرأة القاسية عظيم ولست أنسى مقدار تدلّلها في الامتناع عليّ ولا تلك النظرات التي كانت ترسلها نحوي عندما

Playboy (*to the Merchant*) Don't think badly of him! Forgive him! That's just the prelude; we'll get something else to eat with him later on.

Driver Please show me some mercy! This policeman's taking down the carriage number so he can write up a misdemeanor charge because I've left it unattended in the street while I was busy asking you for the fare.

Playboy Take another piastre and leave us. I'll get rid of the policeman for you. I know him and can get you off the charge.

The Playboy goes over and has a word with the policeman, but he refuses **33.12**
to agree. The Driver now insists on rejecting the payment and asks for more money. Otherwise the 'Umdah will have to go to the police station with him. The Playboy makes do by handing him a card with the 'Umdah's name, title, and place of residence on it. The Driver takes it and leaves, saying that he intends to take his complaint to the police. The Playboy returns to the café and talks to the 'Umdah:

Playboy Praise God, all our problems are at an end. First of all, pay our friend here the amount you owe him on the check, then you can go back to the dance hall Proprietor to get back your pawned goods.

The 'Umdah counts out the amount owed to the Merchant three times and puts it in front of him. The Merchant picks it up and puts it in his pocket. He then addresses the 'Umdah:

Merchant I've just remembered that I don't have your check with me now. It would be better for you to keep the money till I can bring it back for you.

Playboy What's all this commercial talk between trusted friends? Heaven forbid that there should be talk of checks and contracts! As long as the money's in your pocket, it's all the same whether you bring the check or not. Come on, let's go to see the dance-hall Proprietor.

Playboy (*to the Merchant*) Do you see the way his mind's working? His passion's still dragging him toward the denizens of those haunts!

'Umdah To tell you the truth, I'm still very angry with that nasty female. I haven't forgotten the flirtatious way she rejected my advances, nor the kind

سحبتها من ضفيرتيها وبودي لو أراها فأعنفها وأبكتها.

الخليع أنا فهمت غرضك وهو أنك تروم التلطيف بعد التعنيف والرضا بعد الغضب ولكن أقول لك قول مشفق نصوح أن هذه المرأة يعز الوصول إليها والتفرد بها في الليل أثناء شغلها ولكن عندي طريقة موافقة لغرضك وهي أننا نبحث بعد تناول الغداء عن خادمها ونعطيه شيئاً ونتفق معها على الغداء معنا غداً في الأهرام لتكون خالصة لنا من دون الناس.

فيوافق العمدة على هذا الرأي ويقومون جميعاً.

١٣،٣٣ قال عيسى بن هشام: وتركونا نتعجب من كيد الإنسان للإنسان بما لا يأتيه حيوان مع حيوان وعمدنا نحن أيضاً إلى القيام بعد أن اتفقنا على الذهاب غداً إلى الأهرام.

of looks she directed at me when I pulled her by her plaits. I'd like to see her again and give her a thorough scolding.

PLAYBOY I fully appreciate your intentions! What you're planning is for your scolding to be followed by a reconciliation; happiness after anger. But as a sympathetic counselor my advice to you is that, while that woman's at work at night, she's too difficult to get at and have to yourself. I've a plan to match your desires. After lunch we'll look for her assistant, give him some money, and come to an agreement whereby she'll eat lunch with us at the Pyramids. Then we'll have her all to ourselves.

(*The ʿUmdah agrees to the plan, and they all get up to leave.*)

ʿĪsā ibn Hishām said: They left us to marvel at mankind's treachery towards his fellow human beings, treachery such as no wild beast inflicts on other creatures. We too got up to leave, after agreeing to go to the Pyramids on the following day. 33.13

مصباح الشرق ١٠٤، ١٨ مايو ١٩٠٠

قال عيسى بن هشام: فلما صرنا عند الأهرام وقفنا موقف الإعجاب والإعظام قبالة ذلك العلم الذي يطاول الأعلام والهضبة التي تعلو الهضاب وتشرف الآكام والبنية التي تضارع بشممها رضوى وشمام وتبلي ببقائها جدة الأيام وتفني بدوامها أعمار الأعوام وتدفن تحت ظلالها أقواماً بعد أقوام شابت القرون ولم يلحق قرنها المشيب وبليت الدهور وهي في ثوبها القشيب فهي قائمة على كرور اللأعصار ومرور الأدهار تناطح النجوم وتسخر بالرجوم وتقيم الدليل والبرهان وتحدث حديث المشاهدة والعيان ما توالى الملوان وتعاقب الفتيان عن قدرة الإنسان على عجائب الأمكان وقوة هذا الضعيف الضئيل على هذا العمل العظيم الجليل وكيف بلغ بهذا القائي الباند أن يصدر عنه هذا الباقي الخالد فهي للدهر سبابة الشاهد على وحدانية الخالق الواحد وعظمة الواجد الماجد في تركيب هذا العارف الجاحد الصالح الفاسد الذليل القادر والمهين القاهر الذي كبر وصغر وعظم وحقر وعز وذل وكثر وقل وصعد وهبط وعلا وسقط وفني وبقي وسعد وشقي. فهو مجتمع الأضداد والأشكال ومختلف الأعمال والأفعال بينا تراه يصعد إلى السماء بسلم عرفانه ويزن كل جرم من أجرامها بميزانه ويجول بفكره في كواكبها ويمشي بعلمه في مناكبها إذ تراه يصعق لأقل حركة ويعقص بأدق حكة ويغص بريقه ويكبو بحصاة في طريقه ويطمع في شجرة الخلد فيهوي إلي مكامن الخلد. ١،٣٤

وأقام كل واحد منا برهة يتخيل ويتصور ويتأمل ويتفكر ثم انتقلنا من النجوى إلى المسامرة ومن السكوت إلى المحاضرة: ٢،٣٤

الباشا كنت أرى في عصري الأول الذي تلقيت فيه الأمور مسلمة ان هذه البنية لمصر تاجها الذي تفخر به على الأمصار وأعجوبتها التي تتيه بها على البلدان وشاهدها الذي يشهد لها بالتقدم في الصناعة والمدنية والعمران ولكنني أخذت الآن أنظرها بغير تلك العين لما استترت به من نور العرفان وما اهتديت به من دليل العقل

Miṣbāḥ al-sharq 104, May 18, 1900[38]

ʿĪsā ibn Hishām said: When we reached the Pyramids, we stood in awe and reverence before that landmark, one that bests all others, the mountain that overtops mountains and hills, that structure that in its pride rivals Raḍwā and Shamām. Their structure erodes the ongoing freshness of days, and their very permanence obliterates eras of time. They entomb people after people beneath their shadow, and centuries turn grey without affecting them in the slightest. Time's own clothing has become threadbare, and yet there they stand in fresh attire. Ages have been recycled and eras have passed, but they still remain, bumping stars and mocking meteors. As long as day and night follow each other in turn, they still provide an eyewitness account of man's talent for creating miracles of potential, of the ability of this weak and feeble creature to do amazing things, and to show how such a transitory and ephemeral creature can produce such an abiding and eternal structure. It is the index marker of the unity of the one and only God, the greatness of the glorious existent, in the construction of mankind who is both knower and denier, honest and corrupt, submissive and capable, scornful and powerful. He is great and small, mighty and lowly, glorious and contemptible, many and few, climbing and falling, high and low, ephemeral and permanent, happy and miserable—a veritable aggregation of opposites and types, of differing actions and deeds. You may see him ascending to the very heavens using the stairs of his own knowledge, getting his scale to weigh every single body and applying his learning to the stars and their byways. But then you can watch as he may be struck by the slightest movement, scratch a minor itch, swallow his own spittle, trip over a stone in his path. You can watch him aspire to the tree of eternity, yet tumble instead into a mole hole. 34.1

For a time we each spent a while using our imaginations, deep in thought and contemplation. We then progressed from private thoughts to conversation, from silence to discussion: 34.2

PĀSHĀ In olden times when I used to treat things as givens, I regarded this structure as the crown of Egypt, something with which to boast over other territories, a marvel to be proud of, and as evidence of advancement in industry, culture, and civilization. However, now that I've been enlightened by knowledge and have used reason to contemplate the inner nature of things, I've come to realize that it's not the way I thought; they're just a collection of

والتأمل في بواطن الأمور فبدا لي أنها ليست كما كنت أعتقد وما هي في عيني الآن إلا صخور مرصوفة وجنادل مصفوفة لا فائدة منها على ما أرى ولا عائدة سوى أنها تضاهي جبلا من الجبال أو تلا من التلال فهل تعلمون لها من سرخي عني كشفه؟

٣،٣٤ الصاحب ليس لها من سرخي ولا من فائدة حاضرة إلا أن بعض المتقدمين من جهلة الملوك وظلمتهم المنحطين في درجات الفكر كانوا يعتقدون بالرجعة في هذه الدنيا وأن أرواحهم تعود ثانية إلى أجسادهم بعد تنقلها مدة في أجسام أخرى فكان همهم في الحياة حفظ أجسادهم بعد الممات وكانوا يتخذون بيوتهم من لبن الطين ويمشون حفاة عراة ويأكلون الخشن من الطعام ثم هم يسخرون الأمة في نقل هذه الصخور ورفعها في مثل هذا البنيان ليكون لهم قبرًا بعد الممات يحفظون فيه أجسادهم إلى الرجعة (ولكن إلى المتحف، متحف الجيزة) فتسخير الأمة المصرية وتعطيل أعمالها وتمزيق أعضائها وإهراق دمائها وإزهاق أرواحها تحت هذه الصخور بفكرة ساقطة ورأي سخيف لفائدة موهومة لشخص واحد لا يكون فخرًا لمفتخر ولا عزًا لمعتز بل هو الظلم والغشم والاستبداد والاستعباد والجهل والوهم والضلال والبطل وما هذان الهرمان إلا شاهد عدل على ما ذكرنا من الجور والجهل. ولو كان ثم ما يشهد على مدنية أولئك الملوك في أزمانهم لرأينا هذه الصخور والأحجار مبنية بها القناطر والجسور والخزنات مما ينفع الناس وتالله ان باني القناطر الخيرية في نظر المتأمل الباحث لأحق بالاتصاف بالعظمة والمجد والشرف والفخر من أولئك الملوك عباد الأوهام ومستعبدي الأنام.

٤،٣٤ وما علمت لهذا الهرم من فائدة تذكر إلا أنه صار منبرًا يومًا من الأيام لجبار آخر صعد عليه فخدع جنوده وختلهم بكلمات ليصبروا على القتل في هواه وصار أيضًا مورد ارتزاق لهذه الجماعة من العربان التهوا به عن قطع الطريق ومما ذكره المؤرخون أن الملك الذي ابتناه كتب عليه متحديًا به عقب الفراغ منه قوله : «بنيته في ثلاثين عامًا فإذا جاء بعدي من يدعي القوة والعظمة فليهدمه في ثلثمائة عام» ولو علم المسكين

paved stones and neatly arranged rocks with no benefit that I can see and no return except that they're trying to emulate a mountain or hill. Do you two know of any hidden significance they have, something I haven't discovered?

FRIEND There's really no great secret behind them, nor have they any evident use. It's just that in olden times some ignorant and tyrannical rulers with their backward ideas believed that, after they died, they would return to this world; after spending some time in other bodies, their spirits would reenter their bodies. So their major concern in life was to preserve their bodies after death. They used to build their houses out of clay bricks, walk around naked and shoeless, and eat the coarsest of foods, and yet they enslaved the entire people in order to transport these rocks and erect them into this structure to serve as their grave after death, a place where their bodies would be preserved until they returned (whereas in fact they are kept in the Egyptian Museum in Giza). As a result, the entire population of Egypt was enslaved, all other work stopped, limbs were torn apart, blood was shed, and people's spirits were shattered beneath the weight of these rocks; all that because of the idiotic and fatuous beliefs of a single person, a ruler who imagined that he would get some benefit from it. No one can boast about it, and no mighty person can claim any kudos. It's just oppression, tyranny, enslavement, ignorance, delusion, falsehood, and futility. These two large Pyramids are simply a reliable witness to the injustice and ignorance we've been talking about. Were there to be the slightest evidence of the civilization of those monarchs in their own times, then these same rocks and stones would have been used to build viaducts, bridges, and storehouses for the benfit of the people. By God, to anyone who thinks about it, the builder of the Qanāṭir Khayriyya dam is far more worthy of praise, honor, and prestige than these ancient kings who were themselves both enslaved by delusion and enslavers of people. 34.3

The only other use for this first pyramid I know about is that it was once used as a platform by another tyrant who climbed up it, then duped his armies with ringing words so they would be prepared to kill at his whim.[39] Today it's become a source of income for a group of Bedouin who work here rather than robbing people on highways. Something else recorded by historians is that, once it was completed, the king inscribed this challenge on it: "I built this structure in thirty years. If anyone after me claims power and might, let him destroy it in three hundred years." If the poor fool had only realized that the age would come when anyone could blast this building to pieces in 34.4

أنه سيأتي زمن يمكن فيه لفرد من أفراد الناس أن يجعل هرمه هذا في لمحة واحدة كالعهن المنفوش أو الهباء المنثور بهذه المخترعات الكيماوية لما تحدى بشيء سلمه ليد الحدثان والحدثان لا أمان معه للإنسان اللّهم إن هذا كله عمل ضائع وجهل شائع لا ينبغي أن يراه المصري إلا بدمع منهمر وقلب منفطر لأنه شاهد أبد الدهر على ذل آبائه وكبرياء كبرائه.

٥،٣٤ قال عيسى بن هشام: وبينما نحن في هذا الكلام إذ بصرنا بالخليع والتاجر والعمدة والمرأة معهم قد انتظم مجلسهم تحت الهرم وإذا هم يضحكون ويلعبون في شربهم ونقلهم فخفنا أن يفوتنا ما نروح به أنفسنا مما يدور بينهم في مجلسهم فملنا إلى جوارهم وأصغينا إلى حديثهم فإذا العمدة يقول للتاجر:

العمدة أتعلم شيئاً عن أصل هذه الأهرام؟

التاجر وكيف لا أعلم وقد وقفت على قصتها في كتب قصص الأنبياء عند الكلام على سيدنا نوح عليه وعلى نبينا أفضل الصلات واتم السلام وهي:

«إن الملك سودون كان ملكا على مصر قبل الطوفان فرأى رؤيا أفزعته فاستدعى السحرة والكهنة والمنجمين وقص عليهم أنه رأى في منامه كأن النجوم تتناثر وكأن القمر قد سقط إلى الأرض فقالوا له أن هذه الرؤيا تدل على قرب وقوع طوفان عظيم يغمر الأرض ولا يبقي على شيء فيها فارتاع الملك واستشارهم ماذا يفعل للنجاة من هذا الحادث العظيم فأشاروا عليه ببناء هذه الأهرام فإذا جاء وقت الحادث نقل إليها كنوزه واستعصم بها هو ومن يعز عليه من أهله وحاشيته فحشد لذلك الألوف المؤلفة من الناس وأتم بناءها في مائتين وخمسين عاماً ولما انتهي منها كساها بالديباج وفرشها بالحرير ونقل إليها من نفائس الجواهر وذخائر الكنوز ما تعب الناس في نقله وحمله مدة شهور ثم جمع السحرة فحصنوها بالأرصاد والطلاسم فلما قرب زمن الطوفان انتقل إليها الملك وأهله وحاشيته وجاء الطوفان فلم ينج منه إلا أهل السفينة وعوج بن عنق.

a trice and use chemical components to turn it into powder like carded wool and scattered dust[40], he would not have used as a challenge a structure that he then committed to the hand of fate—and fate never offers any assurances. God knows, it's a wretched achievement, one that is based on prevalent ignorance. Egyptians should only look at it with flowing tears and broken hearts since it provides proof through the ages of the humiliation of their forefathers and the arrogance of their rulers.

ʿĪsā ibn Hishām said: While we were talking, we spotted the Playboy, Merchant, and ʿUmdah, and they had the woman with them. They had set up a place to sit by the Pyramid. They were laughing and having fun drinking and eating sweetmeats. We were afraid of missing the conversation between them that we had come to hear, so moved closer and listened to what they had to say. The ʿUmdah was saying to the Merchant: **34.5**

ʿUMDAH Do you know anything about the origin of these Pyramids?

MERCHANT How could I not, when I've learned their entire history in *The Stories of the Prophets*, where they talk about our Lord Noah (prayers and blessings on him and our Prophet), as follows[41]:

"Sodon was king of Egypt before the flood. One night he had an alarming dream and summoned the magicians, soothsayers, and astrologers. He recounted to them how he had seen the stars scattered and the moon falling to earth. They responded that this dream foretold a great flood which would shortly cover the earth and leave nothing on it. In great alarm the king asked them what he should do to protect against this great disaster. They told him to build these pyramids so that, when disaster struck, he could transfer his treasures there and take refuge himself along with his family and retinue. So the king gathered thousands and thousands of people and set them to work on the task. They completed the structure for him in two hundred and fifty years. When it was finished, he covered it in brocade, carpeted it with silk, and transferred to it so many precious jewels and priceless treasures that for many months he wore people out carrying them all. Then he gathered all the magicians together, and they fortified it with charms and magic chants. When the time for the flood's advent approached, the king took refuge in the Pyramid with his entire family and retinue. The flood inundated everything. The only people to survive were those in the ark, ʿŪj ibn ʿUnuq, and these Pyramids.

هذه الأهرام وعوج بن عنق هذا هو حفيد آدم عليه السلام ولد في زمنه وأدرك موسى عليه السلام. ٦٫٣٤

وذكروا أن الطوفان الذي علا الجبال وارتفع فوق الأهرام لم يبلغ ركبته وكان يمشي مع السفينة مستأنساً بها فكان إذا جاع أخذ السمكة من قاع الماء فشواها في عين الشمس ثم أكلها فلما انقضى الطوفان وعاد العمران إلى الدنيا أخذ يعيث في الأرض فساداً ولا زال على ذلك حتى بعث الله موسى فشكا الناس إليه ما يفعله عوج معهم فدعا الله أن يكفيهم شره وكان قد حمل صخرة على رأسه ليلقيها على أهل بلد غضب عليهم فأرسل الله تعالى طيراً منقاره من الفولاذ فلا زال ينقر الصخرة من وسطها حتى نقبها فنزلت إلى رقبته كالحلقة ومنعته الحركة فجاءه موسى بعصاه وكان طوله عليه السلام أربعين ذراعاً وطول العصا أربعين ذراعاً ووثب في الهواء أربعين ذراعاً فضربه فلم تتجاوز الضربة عقب قدمه ولكن قوة سيدنا موسى عليه السلام ألقته إلى الأرض لأنه من أولي العزم فوقع على نيل مصر فحسره عنها سنة كاملة وكانت الوحوش الضارية تأكل من رجليه فإذا مر أحد عند رأسه قال له: إذا وصلت بسلامة الله إلى قدمي فامنع عنهما ما يؤلمني من هذا الذباب فلما مات اتخذوا من أضلاعه قناطر للنيل واتخذت الوحوش من عينيه وأذنيه ومنخريه مغائر وأوكاراً وكفى الله الناس شره وفساده.»

العمدة سبحان الخلاق العظيم أرجوك بالله أن تستحضر لي نسخة من هذا الكتاب أحملها معي إلى البلد ليقرأها لنا إمام المسجد.

قال عيسى بن هشام: وكان الخليع مشتغلا في هذه الأثناء بمحادثة المرأة يشاربها وتشاربه ويضاحكها وتضاحكه فلما انتهى التاجر من قصته أقبل الخليع على العمدة يلاطفه ويؤانسه ويقول له فيما يقول: ٧٫٣٤

الخليع هل رأيت بالله عليك يوماً أعظم أنساً وأكثر سروراً وأجمع لأسباب الهناء والصفاء من هذا اليوم؟

"'Ūj ibn 'Unuq was Adam's grandson (blessings be upon him), who was born in his grandfather's lifetime and lived up to the time of Moses (God's prayers be upon him). It has been related that the flood (which overtopped mountains and the Pyramids) did not reach as far as his knee. He used to wade through the flood accompanying the ark. When he felt hungry, he would grab a fish from the sea bottom, roast it in the sun's eye, and eat it. Once the flood was over and civilization returned to the world, he wreaked havoc for a long time until God sent Moses. People complained to him about what 'Ūj ibn 'Unuq was doing to them. Moses asked God to deal with 'Ūj ibn 'Unuq's evil deeds. 'Ūj ibn 'Unuq had been carrying a stone on his head to hurl at the folk of any town with whom he was annoyed. So God Almighty sent a bird with a steel beak which kept on pecking at the center of the stone until it pierced it. The stone dropped down on 'Ūj ibn 'Unuq's neck like an iron collar that prevented him from moving around. Then Moses came up to him with his staff. He was forty cubits high—God's peace be upon him!—and so was his staff. He leapt forty cubits into the air, and struck 'Ūj ibn 'Unuq a blow that did not even get beyond his ankles. However, such was the strength of the blow that our Lord Moses dealt him that it threw him to the ground; for Moses was a man of great determination. 'Ūj ibn 'Unuq fell headlong into the Nile and removed it from Egyptian soil for a whole year. Wild beasts began to tear at his legs. Whenever someone passed by his head, he would say: 'When you get to my feet in God's safe keeping, please wave away those flies; they're bothering me.' When he died, they used his ribs as bridges for the Nile, and the beasts used his eyes, ears, and nostrils as caves and lairs to live in. Thus did God compensate the people for his evil deeds and corruption." 34.6

'UMDAH Praise be to God, the mighty Creator! Please get me a copy of this book that I can take back to my home town. Then the mosque imām can read it to us.

'Īsā ibn Hishām said: All this time, the Playboy had been busy chatting to the woman, drinking and laughing with her. When the Merchant had finished his story, the Playboy began an amiable banter with the 'Umdah, saying among other things: 34.7

PLAYBOY Have you ever witnessed a more pleasant and enjoyable day, one that offered more causes for happiness and laughter than this one?

العمدة (العمدة) نعم إنه يوم سعيد ولكن كنت أود أن يكون هذا المجلس في البيت لا في الخلاء وتحت السقف لا تحت السماء فأنت ترى كثرة السياح والعربان حولنا وفي ذلك من التضييق في الحرية وخشية الانتقاد ما لا يخفاك.

الخليع دعنا من الانتقاد والاعتراض واغتنم اللذات ولا تشغل نفسك بالخلق ولكن لا بأس إذا أردت أن نعمل عمل السياح برهة في الصعود إلى الأهرام.

التاجر اتركنا من هذا الاقتراح وما هي اللذة عندك من الصعود في الجبل وتحمل المشقة والتعب والتعرض للوقوع في الخطر؟

الخليع هذا أمر يأتيه كل من يزور الأهرام بلا تعب ولا خطر وانظر بعينك إلى هذه النساء الصاعدات النازلات في أيدي العربان هل تراها تخشى خطرًا أو ترهب تعبًا فهل نكون نحن معشر الرجال أقل منها جرأة وإقداما ولا بد لنا على أي حال من الصعود قليلا ليعلم من حولنا على الأقل أننا جئنا مثلهم لمشاهدة الآثار لا للهو دون سواه.

العمدة أنا أوافق على هذا الرأي ولا بأس من الصعود قليلا وعسى الله أن نعثر في صعودنا على فص من الفصوص العتيقة التي طالما عثرت عليها في التل الكفري بناحية بلدنا ولكن كيف نترك فلانة وحدها؟

التاجر أنا أنتظركما معها.

الخليع لا بل تصعد هي معنا أيضًا اقتداء بهذه السيدات.

قال عيسى بن هشام: ويقومون إلى الصعود ويتلكأ التاجر في أخرياتهم يحاول التخلف عنهم فيدفعه العمدة بكل قوة إلى الصعود يمازحه ويسخر منه لشدة تخوفه والخليع والمرأة يغريانه به ويضحكان لضحكه وما كادوا يبتدئون في الصعود حتى حانت من العمدة التفاتة إلى الأرض فهاله الفضاء فامتقع لونه وارتعدت فرائصه ومال على العربي يستغيث به أن ينزله ويعتذر لأصحابه بان الصفراء لعبت به فلا يقوى ٨،٣٤

ʿUMDAH Yes indeed, it's a delightfully happy day. But I'd have preferred our gathering to be indoors rather than out in the open; beneath a roof rather than the sky. You can see the hordes of tourists and Bedouin all around us. I'm sure you realize how it cramps our freedom for fear of being criticized.

PLAYBOY Don't worry about other people's criticisms and objections! Grab your pleasure with daring and resolution and don't bother yourself with other people. But if you'd like us to imitate the tourists for a while, there's no harm in climbing the Pyramids.

MERCHANT Forget that idea! What pleasure can you get from climbing mountains and putting up with the strain and exertion it involves, not to mention the risks you run?

PLAYBOY Everyone who visits the Pyramids does it; there's no danger or tiredness involved. Just look at those women on the way up, falling right into the Bedouins' clutches. Do you see them worrying about risks or bothering about the effort involved? Are we men less daring and audacious than them? At all events, we must go up at least a little way so that people around us will come to realize that, like them, we've come to visit the monuments and not just to enjoy ourselves.

ʿUMDAH I agree too. We can climb up a bit. Maybe on the way up we'll come across an ancient scarab like the ones I've often stumbled on at the Kufrī hill near my town. But how can we leave the lady by herself?

MERCHANT I'll stay with her and wait for you.

PLAYBOY No, no! She's coming up with us just like those other women!

ʿĪsā ibn Hishām said: They got up to start the climb. The Merchant kept dawdling and tried to lag behind, but the ʿUmdah kept pushing him as hard as he could; he was jeering and poking fun at him for being scared. The Playboy and woman were urging him on too and laughing scornfully. However, they had only gone up a little way when the ʿUmdah turned and looked downwards. When he saw the distance between himself and the ground, he panicked. Turning pale and trembling to his very veins, he leaned on the Bedouin guide and asked for help getting down. Claiming that his gall bladder gave him problems, he apologized to his companions that he could not climb any 34.8

على متابعة الصعود فيدركه الخليع فيسنده مع العربي محتضناً له ليستمر في الصعود فتخور قوى الرجل فيسقط بين أيديهما فيحمله الخليع على ظهر العربي لينزل به فما يبلغ به الأرض إلا ونسمع من المرأة صياحاً وعويلا تناديهم جميعاً من فوق رؤسهم أن يحضروا إليها ليبحثوا لها عن فص الخاتم الذي سقط منها فيلحق بها الخليع فيأخذ في البحث مع العربان فلا يجدون شيئاً فتنزل المرأة مع الخليع كالمغشي عليها من شدة التعب والحزن فيتلقاها العمدة بالتخفيض والتهوين ويغلب على ظن التاجر أن الفص ربما لم يقع حال الصعود في الأهرام ولكن وقع في الرمل مكان جلوسهم ويطلب من العربان أن يدركوه بغربال يغربل به الرمل عساه أن يعثر على الفص فيه هذا والمرأة لا يرقا لها دمع ولا ينخفض لها صوت ولا تنتهي لها شكوى والخليع يطيب من خاطرها تارة ويميل على العمدة طوراً يأسف معه لهذا الحادث والانقلاب لصفو بالكدر والأنس بالحزن وان هذه عادة الدنيا قلما تخلص فيها لذة إلا وتشاب بالأذى على أن المصاب هين إن كان في المال دون النفس ومن ذا الذي يدري بما هو مخبأ في الغيب؟

ولا يزال به حتى يتقدم إلى المرأة ويقسم لها أنها لا تبيت الليلة إلا ولديها فص أحسن من الفص الضائع وهي لا تنفك تتأسف وتتلهف وتقول: أنى لي بمثله وهو ياقوتة نادرة المثال؟ فيعيد لها القسم بأنه لا يأتي عليها الغد إلا وفي إصبعها فص بقيمته ثم يشد على يدها توثيقاً لوعده فيشكه موضع الفص المفقود من الخاتم فيتألم لذلك ويعز عليه خلو يدها من الفص فينتزع هذا الخاتم من يدها ويلبسها مكانه ذلك الخاتم الذي استخلصه من الرهن ثم يعودون إلى صفوهم في مجلسهم وحديثهم في أنسهم: ٩،٣٤

العمدة ما أحسن مجلسنا هذا وحبذا لو واصلنا فيه الليل بالنهار.

التاجر لعلك تريد أن تقضي ليلتنا كالليلة الماضية في ذلك الخان المنحوس؟

further. The Playboy came over and helped the Bedouin support him so that he could continue the climb, but the ʿUmdah's strength gave out and he collapsed between the two of them. The Playboy put him on the Bedouin's back and he was carried back down. He had barely reached ground level again when we heard the woman higher up the Pyramid let out a shriek. From higher up she yelled to them all to come up and help her look for the precious stone that had just fallen out of the ring on her finger. The Playboy dashed up to her, and he and the Bedouin started looking around, but they didn't find anything. The Playboy brought her down, almost fainting from exhaustion and sorrow, and the ʿUmdah did his best to make light of the whole thing. It occurred to the Merchant that the stone may not have fallen out while they were climbing, but might be somewhere in the sand where they had been sitting. He asked the Bedouin to bring a sieve in case they might find the stone. Meanwhile the woman made no attempt to dry her tears, lower her voice, or stop crying and complaining. At times the Playboy was trying to calm her down, at others he was leaning over to the ʿUmdah, regretting that this mishap had occurred to ruin their fun; now their gaiety had turned into sadness. This, he said, was the way of the world; it was rare for any pleasure to conclude without sorrow of some kind. However, he suggested, as long as money could provide compensation for the feelings of the heart, this particular disaster could be easily remedied. After all, who is to know what lies hidden in the world of the unknown?

The Playboy kept pestering the ʿUmdah till the latter went over to the woman and swore that, before the night was over, she would have another stone even better than the one she had lost. She was still unhappy and inconsolable. "How can I get another one like it?" she asked. "It was a rare sapphire." But the ʿUmdah repeated that the next day she would have on her finger a stone of equal value that he would be bringing her. He shook her hand to confirm his promise. He was so distressed to see a ring on her finger with no stone in it that he removed her own ring and replaced it with his own, the one he had just redeemed from the pawnbroker. With that, they returned happily to the spot where they had been sitting and resumed their amiable banter. 34.9

ʿUmdah What a delightful gathering this is! If only we could link our daytime with the night!

Merchant Could it be that you want us all to spend tonight in that awful tavern as we did last night!

الخليع وهل تظن أننا نحصل في الحال على مثل هذا الأنس والسرور والائتناس بفلانة خالصة لنا من دون الناس؟

التاجر وماذا العمل إذاً؟

الخليع إن كان ولا بد فأنا ألزمها بأن تتمارض هذه الليلة وترسل إلي صاحب الحان بالاعتذار عن الحضور.

١٠،٣٤ ويأخذ الخليع في استعطافها لهذا الغرض فتمتنع معتذرة بالشروط التي بينها وبين صاحب الحان ومن مقتضاها تقريضها عشرة جنيهات إذا تأخرت ليلة عن الحان فيلتفت الخليع إلى العمدة ينتظر رأيه فيجيبه العمدة بالإيجاب ويعده بدفع هذا التعويض ثم يدور الكلام بينهم على كيفية تمضية الليلة فيقول الخليع لا أرى أحسن من مشاهدة الرواية البديعة الجديدة التي تشخص هذا المساء في التياترو العربي وبعد انتهاء التشخيص نذهب إلى قهاوي الجزيرة فنقضي بها بقية الليلة فيهلل التاجر لذلك ويتفقون جميعاً عليه ويضع العمدة يده في جيبه لينظر في الساعة ويتبين الوقت فلا يجدها فيصيح بفقدها فتقع الضوضاء بينهم في البحث عليها فلا يجدونها فيقول الخليع هذه عادات هؤلاء العربان اللصوص ما سرق الفص إلا الذي كانت تستند عليه فلانة وما سرق الساعة إلا الذي كان يعتمد عليه سعادة البك ولا بد من رفع الشكوى إلى شيخ هؤلاء العربان وإلزامه بإحضار المسروق فهلم بنا إليه فيقومون جميعاً ويذهبون إلى ذلك الشيخ.

١١،٣٤ قال عيسى بن هشام: وعلى هذا انقضى مجلسهم وانتهى أنسهم، وكان الصاحب يلح علينا بالذهاب إلى متحف الجزيرة في رجوعنا قبل انقضاء النهار، فوافقناه على ما رأى، على أن نتوجه في المساء إلى ذلك الملهى، فنرى ماذا تمّ لهم من الشكوى، وماذا يكون من أمرهم في المنتهى.

PLAYBOY Do you imagine we'd be able to enjoy such a good time as this and have our lady companion to ourselves without other people?

MERCHANT So what's to be done then?

PLAYBOY If that's the way it has to be, then I'll tell her to say she's sick. I'll send someone to tell the Proprietor that she can't come tonight.

The Playboy now started cajoling the woman into agreeing to his plan. At first she declined on the grounds that, under her conditions of employment with the Proprietor, she had to pay him ten pounds compensation for every night she stayed away. The Playboy turned to the 'Umdah and waited for his opinion on that subject. The 'Umdah let him know that he was agreeable and undertook to pay such compensation. They now started discussing how to spend the night. The Playboy said that he could think of nothing better than watching the splendid new play being presented at the Arab Theatre. After that they could go and spend the rest of the time at the café on the Gezira island. The Merchant welcomed the suggestion, and they all agreed. The 'Umdah put his hand in his pocket to look at his watch and check on the time. He could not find it and let out a yell. They all made a big fuss searching for it, but without success. "That's the way it is with those Bedouin," the Playboy said, "They're all thieves. One of them stole the stone when she was leaning against him, and another stole the watch when the Bey was doing the same. We need to raise a complaint to the shaykh in charge of those Bedouin and compel him to recover the stolen goods. Let's go and see him now." They all stood up and went to see that shaykh. 34.10

'Īsā ibn Hishām said: So their cosy gathering came to an end. Meanwhile our Friend was insisting that we should visit the Giza Palace before the day was over. We accepted his idea, at the same time deciding that we would go to the theater in the evening to see what had happened about their complaint and what would happen thereafter. 34.11

مصباح الشرق ١٠٥، ٢٥ مايو ١٩٠٠

١،٣٥ قال عيسى بن هشام: فزايلنا الأهرام وخليناها، تندب من شادها وتنعي من بناها وملنا إلى دار التحف ومستودع الآثار لمشاهدة ما حفظته لنا من صنوف الطرف وعيون الأخبار، وما أخرجته الأيام من عالم الخفاء إلى عالم الظهور، بعد أن كان سرًا مكتومًا في خواطر العصور والدهور، وما صانته بطون القبور من الفناء والدثور، وحمته أحشاء الرموس من العفاء والدروس، وأجنته أرحام المعابد والهياكل من بقايا الماضين وخبايا الأوائل، وما انكشفت عنه سجوف الأحقاب، وديعة الأسلاف للأعقاب من مكنون الدفائن، ومكنوز الخزائن، وعجائب الفن الدقيق، وبدائع البدع الأنيق، وغرائب الصنع العتيق، بليت في اصطحابها بطون الأيام والليالي، وانحنت في احتضانها ظهور العصور الخوالي، وانقلبت البحار وهادا، وأصبحت الوهاد أطوادا، وغدت الأغوار أنجادا، وأضحى العمار خرابا، والخراب عمارا، والغمار سرابا، والسراب غمارا، وتمدنت بواد وتبدت مدائن، وبادت مواطن وقامت مواطن، ومضت دول بعد دول، وذهبت أول أثر أُول، وبدت أحوال وحالت، وظهرت أعمال وزالت، وهي هي كما تركها أهلها، مصون وضعها محفوظ شكلها، خبر صادق، ولسان ناطق، تخبر بالعبر، وتحدث عمّن غبر:

مضت غبرات العيش وهي غوابر
على الدهـر مكتوب عليها حبائس

٢،٣٥ فأخذنا نتنقل هناك بين الصور والتماثيل، والنقوش والتهاويل، ونجيل النظر في الحلي والزينة، ونتمعن في تلك الأحجار الثمينة، ونتنظر هذه الأجساد المنظورة، ونتأمل هاتيك الرفات المنشورة، ونتبصر هياكل تلك الرمم، كيف كانت ملوك الأمم، فأصبحت مع هذا الوجود في هذا العدم، وما زلنا نتبع المشاهدة والنظر بتتبع ماكتب في التواريخ والسير، من ذكر أحكامهم، وأخبار أيامهم والباشا ينظر في هذه الذخائر العالية القدر، الغالية المهر، الباقية على الدهر، شاهدة على ماكان لهم

Miṣbāḥ al-sharq 105, May 25, 1900[42]

ʿĪsā ibn Hishām said: We left the Pyramids behind, duly lamenting and reproaching the people who had built them, and made our way to the museum building, the repository of antiquities. There we would be able to look at the preserved artefacts and documents and view the things that time had brought out of darkness into light after being hidden for ages. These were objects that had been saved from oblivion and extinction by being enclosed in graves, protected from destruction and ruin by the interiors of tombs; relics of ancient peoples and secrets of our ancestors that had remained hidden inside temples and places of worship. The veils of centuries had been removed, to reveal them as deposits made by our forefathers for their successors—hidden troves and buried treasures renounced by the earth, miracles of delicate art, marvels of exquisite workmanship, and curios of ancient craft. Nights and days had been exhausted keeping company with them; past ages had bent their backs to embrace them. Seas had become lowlands and lowlands mountains; depressions were now plateaus, buildings ruins, and ruins buildings. Floods were mirages, and mirages floods; deserts citified, cities desertified. Countries had vanished, others had appeared. Dynasty after dynasty had vanished one after another. Things happened, then passed on; actions became evident, then fell into obscurity. Yet all these things were preserved in the form and shape in which people had left them. A sincere person speaking from experience once wisely declared about times past that: 35.1

Gone are life's traces, olden times that have vanished,
records inscribed on them, eternal for all time.[43]

We started wandering about among the figurines and statues and looking at the pictures, jewelry, and decoration. We examined the precious stones, viewing the bodies on display, contemplating the fact that these scattered bones and skeletons were once kings who ruled over peoples, but then came to exist in a state of nothingness. We continued to look at things and follow the sequence of histories and biographies about rulers and accounts of their reigns. The Pāshā kept observing these valuable treasures and priceless relics 35.2

من المجد والفخر، دون أن يأخذ العجب بلبه، أو يستولي الدهش على قلبه، فتحيرت في أمره، واستكشفت منه باطن سره، وكدت أعنفه في الخطاب، لذهوله عن الإكبار والإعجاب، فمال إلي الصاحب مستفسرًا مستفهما، فنظر الصاحب إليّ وقال متهكما:

الصاحب لمثلك أن يعجب ويفخر، ويعظم ويكبر، ويندهش ويتأثر، بعد أن صوّر فيكم الوهم هذه الباليات الأخلاق في صور نفائس الأعلاق، وبعد أن عدّها أولئك المتكلفون شواهد قاطبة، وبراهين شاهدة، على ما كان من حضارة القرون الأولى، وعلوّ قدمها في العلوم والمعارف والفنون والصناعات، ولكن ليس لك أن تلوم غيرك ممّن يأخذون الأمور على حقائقها، ويقدّرون الأشياء بمقاديرها، ولا يستفزهم الوهم، ولا يضلهم الخيال، ولا يغطي على بصرهم غطاء التقليد، وعلم الله أنها ليست في نظر كل خال من الوهم عار من التقليد بالنسبة للعصر الحاضر إلا ملاهي أطفال ولعب صبيان.

الباشا أصبت وأحسنت، فما هي في نظري الآن إلا كما قلت ووصفت، وما ٣،٣٥
وقع مشاهدتها في عيني بأعظم من وقع ما يشاهده الناس في أنحاء الأسواق من العروض المعروضة والسلع البائرة. وأمّا هذه الرمم البالية، والأجساد الفانية فإنها لا تزيد على أن تمثل أمامي قبورًا مقلوبة، ورموسًا معكوسة وأجداثًا منبوشة، فإن كان الغرض من عرضها العبرة والموعظة، فإنّ فيما هو أمام أعين الناس كل يوم من هبوط الملوك من ذهب العرش إلى خشب النعش، ومن وسائد الحبر إلى مساند الحجر، ومن ظهور الصافنات الجياد إلى بطون الزواحف وديدان الإلحاد ما فيه العبرة الحاضرة، والموعظة القائمة، وما هو أكبر سرعة في التأثير على الحس، وأعظم مزدجرًا للنفس.

الصاحب هذه هي الحقيقة بعينها، ولم تكن قيمة هذه الأشياء معتبرة عندهم أنها تعلو على كل قيمة إلا لتوغلها في القدم والبلى، وموضعها من التاريخ وما تحمله منقوشًا عليها من أساطير الأوّلين.

from the vestiges of the ages, witnesses to their glory and prestige, without showing any particular amazement or surprise. I was somewhat nonplussed and wanted to find out what he was thinking. I spoke to him harshly because he seemed so reluctant to appreciate what he was looking at. He turned toward our Friend to ask him for an explanation. The Friend looked at me and scoffed:

FRIEND It's all very well for people like you to admire and boast, praise and exalt, express amazement and emotion when your imagination recreates these decayed artefacts as emblems without price, and those would-be afficionados have characterized them as key evidence and proof of the high levels that the earliest stages of civilization achieved in sciences, learning, arts, and crafts. But you shouldn't blame other people who look at the realities of the situation and evaluate them according to their real worth. They're unimpressed by illusions and refuse to be misled by their imaginings. Their vision is not clouded by tradition. God knows, anyone who is unpolluted by fancy and free of tradition can only regard them as children's toys with reference to the present era.

PĀSHĀ You're absolutely right. Bravo! In my view the situation is exactly 35.3
as you've described it. What I've seen here is no more significant than the goods on display in various market stalls. For me at least, these faded relics and decaying bodies are no more than overturned tombs, upended graves, and exhumed corpses. If the purpose in putting them on display is to offer a warning for people to consider, then people surely have a very present illustration every day when they witness kings descending from golden thrones into wooden biers, from silken cushions to stone pillows, from the backs of neighing thoroughbreds to the stomachs of lice and worms in the grave. All that has a much swifter effect on the senses and is more fruitful for the soul.

FRIEND That's the truth. The only reason why they reckon things like this to be priceless is that they're profoundly interested in antiquity and things that decay, and also because of the place these antiquities have in history and the ancient writings inscribed on them.

عيسى بن هشام كيف لا تكون محل الإعجاب والإطناب، وموضع الدهشة والاستغراب وهي أثمن من كل ثمين، وأنفس من كل نفيس، بل هي أغلى قيمة من القناطير المقنطرة من الذهب والفضة، ولو لم تكن كذلك لما تغالى هؤلاء الغربيون في الاقتناء منها، وتنافسوا في شراء الحجر الصغير بالمال الكثير، ولما وفدوا من أقطارهم البعيدة وبلادهم الشاسعة للتمتع بالمشاهدة، والنظر واستشهاد الخبر على الخبر، ولا يظن ظان أنّ هؤلاء القوم مع توفر العقل والعلم عندهم ينفقون الأموال ويتكبدون في السفر الأهوال، لأجل المشاهدة فقط، والنظر البسيط دون أن يكون وراء ذلك من الفوائد والمنافع ما يربو في القيمة على ما ينفقونه من الأموال العظيمة، وما يركبونه من الأخطار الجسيمة.

الصاحب إذا كان وراء هذه الآثار وهذه الأشلاء من فائدة للغربيين كما تقول فإنما هي كما أبنته لك ممّا يتعلق بمباحثهم في أخبار الأوّلين، وعنايتهم بفلسفة التاريخ، وزد على ذلك حب الاقتناء والولع بالاختصاص بالنادر، ولذلك علت قيمتها عندهم وغلت أثمانها، وليس للمصريين منها أقل فائدة سوى أنّ عندهم متحفاً يفوق ما هو موجود من أمثاله في أوربا، ولو أمررت عليه أهل مصر بألوف ألوفهم لما استفادوا منه شيئاً ولا أفادوك منه شيئاً سوى النزر اليسير منهم، والعدد القليل ممّن يتعلم مع الغربيين، أو علم منهم شيئاً وخير للمصريين أن يخفف الله عنهم بثمنها ما على حكومتهم من أثقال الديون، وما عليهم من أثقال الضرائب والمكوس، وما هم فيه من العسر والضيق وإذا كان لا بدّ من بقائها لمجرد الفخفخة والمباهاة، ولم يكن سوى ذلك من منفعة فليتها لا تضرّ إذا كانت لا تنفع، وليت المصريين يكونون معها لا عليهم ولا لهم، ولكنها على كل حال لا يساوي نفعها الأدبي ضررها المادي، فهي تكلف الأمّة المصرية كل عام مبالغ معينة للاعتناء بها والتحفظ عليها والبحث عن دفائنها في خبايا الأرض، وناهيك بما أنفقته الحكومة على نقلها من أماكن العثور عليها وجمعها في متحف بولاق أوّلاً، وما أنفقته في نقلها إلى هذا المتحف ثانياً، وما ٤،٣٥

ʿĪsā ibn Hishām Why shouldn't these objects be admired and highly appreciated when they're so incredibly precious and valuable; they're worth more than countless ingots of gold and silver? Were that not so, then these Westeners would not be so keen to acquire them, spending large amounts of money to buy a tiny stone, coming here from far-off lands to enjoy looking at these things and confirming the information they've heard. No one should assume that people of such learning and intelligence are spending their money and putting up with the hardships of travel just to look at things. There have to be other advantages and benefits that accrue in value in recompense for the amounts of money they spend and the risks that they're prepared to take.

Friend If these relics and corpses do indeed possess any value for Westerners, as you say, then, as I've just explained to you, it's all linked to their research in archaeology and their interest in the philosophy of history; to which should be added their love of acquiring things and their specialized interest in rarities. So for them antiquities have risen in value, and their price has increased. However, Egyptians get no benefit at all, except that they have a museum whose contents surpass anything to be found in Europe. If I paraded Egyptians in their thousands of thousands through this museum, they wouldn't get anything out of it. Only a small group would be useful to you: the small percentage of Egyptians who've studied with Europeans and have learned from them. For Egyptians it would be much better if God used the price that these antiquities bring to lessen the heavy burden of debt on their government and the weight of taxation and levies which contribute to their difficulties and restrictions. If they had to be kept here for purposes of ostentation and pride and that was the only benefit, then how I wish they did no harm even if they do no good, and how I wish that Egyptians could have them with neither positives nor negatives. But, as things are, their benefits are nowhere close to the material damage they cause. Every year Egyptians are forced to pay fixed amounts of money in order to look after them, preserve them, and conduct archeological digs underground. And that's not even to mention what's spent on transferring them from the places where they're found and on their storage firstly in the museum in Bulaq, then their transfer again to this 35.4

ستنفقه ثالثًا على نقلها منه إلى المتحف الجديد الذي شادته لها في قصر النيل وبذلت عليه الألوف المؤلفة من الذهب النضار.

٥،٣٥ **عيسى بن هشام** أراك أيها الصاحب بعيد الغور في أحكامك، شديد التعمق في أبحاثك، لا تبالي بما يعلق بأذهان الناس من استعظام خرق العادة ولو كانت مضرة، واستكبار خروجهم من استعباد أوهامها، وإنك لترى في كل الممالك متاحف يحرص أهلها عليها ويضنون بها، ولا يرضون ببيعها وتبديدها ولو ساوموهم أغلى ثمن لها، فكيف ترى أنّ مصر تشذّ عن حكم هذه القاعدة ولآثارها القيمة العليا والقدر الأمثل؟

الصاحب نعم، يحرص أهل الممالك على ما في متاحفهم من الآثار لأنها من علامات التغلب والاستيلاء، ولأنهم في غير حاجة إلى أثمانها، ولأنّ بعضها من الهدايا التي لا يليق بيعها، أمّا الأمر عندنا فعلى العكس لأنّ هذه الآثار ما جاءتنا من طريق الفتوح والتغلب، بل من طريق الحفر والتنقيب، ثمّ إننا أكثر الناس احتياجاً إلى أثمانها، وزد على ذلك أنّ هذه الآثار تزيد عندنا يوماً بعد يوم، وقلما يمرّ عام إلا ويكتشف المستكشفون منها ما فيه الكفاية للفخفخة والمباهاة، فكيف لا يجوز بيعها وقد جاز لحكام مصر أن يهادوا بها ويغضوا الطرف عن سلبها، فترى منها في عواصم الممالك الأوربية والأمريكية ومتاحفها الشيء العظيم الجليل مأخوذاً بطريق السلب أو الغبن، أو من طريق الاستهداء والتلطف في الحيلة هذا هو نصيبنا في التحفظ على هذه الآثار وإنفاق المال عليها والضن بها.

٦،٣٥ وقد رأينا البلدان تباع بأهلها، فما بال الآثار لا تباع وهي على ما تراه فيها – ما لا يباع فإنه ينقسم – فالانتفاع بها كل الانتفاع عائد على الأجانب إمّا بمشاهدتهم لها في ديارنا، أو باستلابها إلى ديارهم ولو ألهم الله الحكومة القليل من الصواب لتصرفت في بعض هذه الآثار التي تنبتها لها الحفائر والكهوف في كل يوم، ولكانت لها مورد ثروة ورزق تنفق منه بعض الشيء في وجوه المنافع التي تنتفع بها الأمّة المصرية كنشر المعارف وبث الآداب بطبع هذه الكتب المخزونة للأرضة في الكتبخانة

museum, and finally to the brand new museum that's been built to house them in Qaṣr al-Nīl[44], costing thousands in pure gold.

ʿĪsā ibn Hishām Dear Friend, I realize that your verdicts are profound and your investigations on this topic have been thorough. But you don't seem to be taking into account the way in which people's minds attach great importance to the unusual, even though it be harmful, and relish the prospect of abandoning their slavish reliance on illusions. You'll see museums in every single country, institutions that they cherish and protect. Even if the highest prices were offered, they would not be willing to sell or disperse them. So how is it that you see Egypt as being an exception to this principle when its relics are so incredibly valuable and significant? 35.5

Friend Yes, people in other countries cherish antiquities in their museums because they are symbols of victory and conquest, and because they don't need the money they could get from selling them. Also some of them are gifts which should not be sold. But with Egypt it's exactly the opposite. These relics didn't come to us by way of conquests and victories; to the contrary, they came from excavations and digging. We're the people most in need of their value. Not only that, but there are more of them as day follows day. Rarely does a year go by without archaeologists discovering enough materials for ostentation and display. So why not sell some of them, particularly when Egyptian rulers have been allowed to give them away as presents and turn a blind eye to their plunder. You can see them in European and American countries, not to mention their museums where a sizeable portion of them has been taken either by plunder or fraud, or else by way of requests or sheer favoritism. This then is our share in the process of preserving these monuments, spending money on them, and jealously protecting them.

We've seen countries sold, so why not relics? At the moment they're not being sold, as you can see, but rather divided up. The benefits all redound to foreigners, either by coming here to look at them or else by taking them back to their own countries. If God were to give the Egyptian government a modicum of inspiration, it would be marketing some of these relics which our digs and caves produce on a daily basis. They could then be a source of income, some of which could be spent on things that would benefit the Egyptian people: the spread of education, stimulating culture by printing books 35.6

المصرية في تلك المطبعة الأميرية التي طالما باشرت طبع الكتب النافعة تحت رعاية الحكومة المصرية في الأزمان السالفة الموسومة بالجهل والغشم وخبّروني بالله أي نفع للأمّة المصرية الإسلامية في أن ينشر بين يديها وهم الفراعنة في الأنتكخانة وتحبس أرواح العلماء والحكماء والفقهاء والأدباء والشعراء في الكتبخانة وأيّ الأمرين أجحى بنا وأحرى وأنفع وأجدى أن يعرض على أنظارنا مثلا بهذه النفقات الطائلة من الأموال صورة أوزيريس أو إيزيس وتمثال أبيس وذراع رعمسيس ورجل أمينوفيس أو أن تتداول الأيدي مثلا جزء للرازي أو مقالة للفارابي أو فصلا للأسفرايني أو رسالة للجاحظ أو قصائد لابن الرومي؟ تالله ما تجري أمورنا إلا على التناقض وما تسير أحوالنا إلا على الاعوجاج.

٧،٣٥ قال عيسى بن هشام: فلما وصل صاحبنا إلى هذا الحد من الكلام إلا وقد آن أوان الانصراف من المتحف، فخرجنا مع من خرج من الزائرين، وبينا نحن نزاحم السياح في خروجنا إذ بصرنا من بينهم برجل من أرباب العمائم وبجانبه شاب من أرباب الأزياء الجديدة فاستخلصنا من كلامهما أنّ الرجل من أعيان البلاد، وأنّ الشاب ابنه ممّن تعلم العلوم الغربية، وإذا هو يقول لأبيه:

<u>الابن</u> أشهدت مشاهد عزنا ورأيت مجالي فخرنا ونظرت كيف كان مجدنا وإلى أي رتبة من المدنية بلغ أجدادنا، وعلمت ما كان عليه آباؤنا الأولون من الترقي في الفكر والإتقان في العمل، شهد الله أنه لو اجتمعت أبناء الأمم في يوم منافرة أو مفاخرة لكان المصري هو الفائز الأعلى، وصاحب القدح المعلى في ميدان هذا الرهان وهذه الآثار في يده يناضل بها وينافر وينشد:

تلك آثارنا تدل علينا (البيت)

<u>الأب</u> أمّا ما رأيته من هذه الصور والتماثيل والأحجار، فإنه لا يساوي في نظري إلا أنقاض قصر، أو بقايا طلول عفت ورسوم درست، وإن صح ما يقال

archived in the Egyptian National Library at the Amīriyyah Press (which has often helped people by printing useful books in the time of the previous government which was both ignorant and tyrannical).[45] Tell me, by God, what benefit can there be for an Islamic Egyptian people to put ancient Pharaohs on display in the Antiquities Museum and at the same time to keep the spirits of scholars, philosophers, jurists, literature scholars, and poets locked up in the National Library? If we're spending such huge sums of money, which of the two is more profitable and beneficial: putting on display a picture of Osiris or Isis, a statue of Ibis, the arm of Ramses and leg of Amenophis, or rather having at hand a work by al-Rāzī, a treatise by al-Fārābī, a chapter by al-Asfarayīnī, an essay by al-Jāḥiẓ, or poems by Ibn al-Rūmī? By God, in our country things only work in contradictions; they always operate contrary to what's in the public interest.

ʿĪsā ibn Hishām said: When our Friend reached this point, it was time for us 35.7
to leave the museum, and we did so with the other visitors. While we were on our way out along with the crowd of tourists, we spotted a turbaned gentleman accompanied by a younger man in modern dress. From their conversation we gathered that the man was an important person in the city while the young fellow was his son who had studied Western subjects. The son was saying to his father:

SON Have you noticed how our glory is mirrored in these shrines to our prestige? Do you appreciate the level of civilization that our ancestors achieved? Are you aware of the lofty ideas and artistic perfection that our earliest forebears developed? God is our witness that, if ancestors from different nations were gathered for a day of debate and argument, the Egyptian would emerge as clear winner; he would win the seventh arrow in the betting.[46] In so doing, he would be holding these relics in his hand as he competed, argued, and adjured:

These are our remains which point us out.[47]

FATHER I can see nothing in these pictures, statues, and stones to glorify. In my opinion they're just palace ruins, remains that have long since

عن هذه التماثيل أنها أشخاص قديمة نزل بها السخط والمسخ كان التعزز بها والتمجيد لها ممّا يغضب الخالق ولا يرضي الخلق، وأمّا قولهم بأنّ هذه الآثار من صنع أجدادنا، وأنّ أجدادنا هم هذه الرمم الفرعونية فإنه إثم ونكر ﴿ كَبُرَتْ كَلِمَةً تَخْرُجُ مِنْ أَفْوَاهِهِمْ ۚ إِن يَقُولُونَ إِلَّا كَذِبًا﴾ . ما كان آباؤنا وأجدادنا إلا هؤلاء العرب الكرام، لا نفاخر إلا بمفاخرهم، ولا ننتسب إلا إلى مجدهم وشرفهم، وأمّا إتقان الصنعة ففي صبيان الفلاحين العدد الكثير ممّن يشتغلون الآن بمثل هذه الأحجار والآثار، فتخرج من أيديهم وهم بين الروث والطين أتقن صنعاً من هذه المصانة في البلور المحجبة في القصور.

٨،٣٥ الابن (بصوت خفي) ﴿وَاغْفِرْ لِأَبِي إِنَّهُ كَانَ مِنَ الضَّالِّينَ﴾ (ثمّ يجهر له في القول) لو كان في لغتنا العربية الكتب المؤلفة في هذه الآثار مثل ما في اللغات الأجنبية من الكتب العديدة لوقفت على مزاياها الجمة وفوائدها العميمة على أنها مع ذلك لا تخفى على نظر المتأمل البصير، أفما رأيت ذلك التمثال، تمثال شيخ البلد ونظرت ما هو فيه من الدقة والإتقان وحسن إبراز الصورة على مثالها في خشب الجميز؟

الأب أنا أرى في كل يوم مائة شيخ من لحم ودم لا من خشب وحجر.

٩،٣٥ قال عيسى بن هشام: ووصلنا إلى الباب خارجاً، فركبنا والصاحب يقول لنا: أسمعتما هذه المجادلة في المفاضلة، وتحقق لكما صدق ما تقدّم من كلامي، وحسن إصابته في تلك المرامي، فيقول له الباشا: لقد صدقت فيما نطقت. ثمّ نأخذ في المسير إلى ملهى التمثيل والتشخيص، وملعب السير والأقاصيص.

been effaced, traces that have vanished. If what people say about these statues—that they represent ancient persons on whom wrath and transformation descended, then any glorification of their memory is something that will annoy the Creator and displease human beings. To claim that these monuments were made by our ancestors and that these Pharaonic corpses are our own ancestors is a foul sin. «A dreadful word comes out of their mouths. They speak nothing but lies.»[48] Our forebears and ancestors are those noble Arabs; it's through them that we have our pride and to their prestige and honor that we're connected. Talking about perfection of craft, there are many peasant children who labor making stones and relics like these. They may live in abject squalor, and yet their hands can craft objects far superior to the crystal objects stored in palaces.

SON (*silently*) «Forgive my father! For he is one of those who have gone astray.»[49] (*raising his voice*) If we had books written in our Arabic language like the many tomes in foreign languages, then you'd be aware of their many qualities and the public benefits that accrue because they're visible to the eye of the perceptive beholder. Just look at that statue of the village leader. Can't you tell how subtle, perfect, and accurate a portrait it is in sycamore wood? 35.8

FATHER I can see hundreds of shaykhs like him every day in flesh and blood. I don't need wood and stone.

ʿĪsā ibn Hishām said: We reached the exit. As we got into our carriage, the Friend said, "Did you hear that conversation about cultural superiority? It confirms for you everything that I've been saying and the correctness of my views on the topic." In reply the Pāshā said, "What you told us is obviously correct." With that we set off for the theater—the playhouse where lives and stories are presented on stage. 35.9

مصباح الشرق ١٠٦، ١ يونيو ١٩٠٠

١،٣٦ قال عيسى بن هشام: ولمّا مدّ الظلام حبالته ليقتنص من الأصيل غزالته، ونفرت منه إلى كناسها، وتصعد الشفق من أنفاسها، وذهبت نفسها شعاعا، واضمحل قرصها شعاعا، واختفت شقائق الشفق تحت أكمام الأفق، وطرأ من الليل شاربه، واخضر جانبه، واشتعلت مصابيح السماء في قباب الظلماء، حضرنا إلى دار التشخيص والتمثيل، وبيت التصوير والتخييل، فدخلنا مع الداخلين نساء ورجالا، أجناساً وأشكالاً، واخترنا لجلوسنا الكراسي دون الغرف لنبلغ المشاهدة من كل طرف، وقعدنا نحدد النظر في من حضر، وإذا نحن بين أخلاط اختلفت أزياؤهم، وعلت ضوضاؤهم، وارتفع صياحهم، وكثر مزاحهم سباً وشتماً، ولكزاً ولكماً، يضربون بأرجلهم وعصيهم الأرض، ويتمايل بعضهم على بعض، رجالا وغلمانا، شباناً وولداناً، مللا من الانتظار، وطلبا لرفع الستار. ثمّ رفعنا النظر إلى أصحاب الحجر، فرأيناهم أيضاً على مثل تلك الحال من التخلع والابتذال، ورأينا من بينها مقاصير عليها الستائر، تشف عن اللآلئ والجواهر، في نحور الحور من المحصنات الحرائر، بيضات الخدور، وبنات القصور، كما تتراءى زهر النجوم من خلل الغيوم، وتكشف عن طرر، تضيء بالغرر، ضوء الليل بالقمر:

وتنقبت بخفيف غيم أبيض
هي فيه بين تخفر وتبرج
كتنفس الحسناء في مرآتها
كملت محاسنها ولم تتزوج

٢،٣٦ والناس من تحتها يتشوقون ويتشوفون، ويتحرقون ويتلهفون، وكلهم على النظر إليها عاكفون، لا ينفكون عن عبادتها ولا يستنكفون، يوجهون أبصارهم وجهتها، ويولون وجوههم قبلتها، وهنّ يوالين الضحكات، ويتالين الحركات، ويتبادلن معهم الغمز، ويتبادلون معهن الرمز، والكل يشيرون بمناديل تغني عن الكلام، ويتراسلون بمراوح

ʿĪsā ibn Hishām said: When sunset extended its snare to snatch away the sun from late afternoon, the orb was forced to flee to its hide. Dusk then arose from its terminal breaths as sunbeams slowly vanished along with the disk.[51] Twilight's sisters disappeared beneath the horizon's sleeves, and night's darkness sprouted its mustache and its edges turned grey. Now evening lamps were lit in the domes of darkness. We had arrived at the theater where plays are performed and portraits and imaginings invoked. We joined other people at the entrance, women and men of all shapes and sizes. Choosing seats underneath the boxes so that we could look easily in all directions, we decided to sit down so that we could observe the people in the audience. We found ourselves in the middle of groups of people who were wearing a variety of fashions and raising a hue and cry. Their idea of fun seemed to consist of cursing and swearing, punching and kicking each other. They kept banging on the floor with their feet and canes, while some of them were leaning over each other—men and boys, young men and parents—all of them making it clear that they were tired of waiting; they wanted the curtain to be raised. Looking up at the boxes, we noticed that the same kind of vulgar and loose behavior prevailed. We could see curtained boxes that revealed pearls and gems on the necks of cloistered beauties, queens of the women's quarters in palatial mansions, looking like brilliant stars glimpsed through gaps in the clouds. Wisps of hair were now revealed on faces that glistened with highlights like the night beneath the moon: 36.1

She was veiled in a light white cloud,
  twixt concealment and display.
Like a maid's breath on her mirror
  her beauty was perfect, and she was not married.[52]

From below men looked up and stared on fire with passion. Their eyes never wavered, and they never turned away but continued their worship, gazing up at them with fixed attention. The girls kept laughing incessantly, gesturing and exchanging winks, while the men below kept making signs. Everyone was waving their handkerchief in ways that made words superfluous. Fans were employed to arouse passions and provoke longing. Fingers pulled back 36.2

تثير الهوى وتهيج الغرام، وقد خرقت الأصابع الأستار، لتنفذ منها رسل الأزهار، وتقابلت بينهم المناظير بالمناظير، تدني البعيد وتجسم الصغير، وكل شاب منهم يظن أنه المرمي بالنظرات، المعني بتلك الإشارات، فيتصنع التجمل والتظرف، ويتكلف التذلل والتلطف، وعند سقف المكان أقوام وأي أقوام، متزاحمين هناك أكواماً فوق أكوام، كأنهم في أسواق الأنعام، أو من وحوش الآكام، يجلبون ويضجون، ويلحون ويلجون، ثمّ إننا جلنا النظر في سائر غرف الملهى، فإذا العمدة وصاحباه في غرفة منها، والعاهرة وخادمها بجانبهم في غرفة أخرى، تشاغل العمدة بعينيها، وتقارصه بيديها، ثمّ يتباسطان الراح، لتناول أقداح الراح، من زجاجة عنده في يد الخليع المنادم، وزجاجة عندها في يد الخادم، والخليع في أثناء ذلك يروح ويغدو، ويختفي عن العمدة ثمّ يبدو، فتارة يكون في الحجرة عندها، وتارة في حجرة أخرى بعدها.

وبينما نحن على هذا الأمر إذ رنّ الجرس وانكشف الستر، وظهر أمامنا صف ٣،٣٦ من الممثلات والممثلين، ملحنين ومرتلين على طريقة يمجها السمع، وينفر منها الطبع، كأنهم حداة في مفازة، أو سعاة في جنازة، بكلام مبهم، وألفاظ لا تفهم، وهم في أزياء متعاكسة، وأشكال غير متجانسة، وملابس تعددت ألوانها، على أجسام اختلفت أوطانها، ثمّ نزل الستار ثمّ ارتفع، عن امرأة نصف وغلام يفع، يعانقها فتباكيه، وتعانقه وتشاكيه، يقول لها في أثناء الكلام، وشرح الوجد والهيام: «ما أعذب هذه الأقوال، هيا إذاً للوصال».

فتجيبه: «قد يكون ذلك أيها الوسيم، إذا ساعدتنا أمي نسيم، فدبر أنت ما عليك وها أنا ذاهبة لأرسلها إليك».

ويذهبان فيأتي بعدهما رجل وامرأة يتخاطبان تخاطب الزوجين، فيقول الرجل لها بعد تحايلها عليه «إنّ ذاك الشاب ألح من الذباب، وهو عندي أفسق من الشياطين، وأخبث من البراذين، لا يترك من النساء الدون، ولو كانت عجوزا حيزبون».

فتجيبه الأم: «لا تخف أيها الأفضل، فما كل الطيور تؤكل، وابنتنا العفيفة الحلوة،

curtains so that messengers with flowers could pass through. Opera glasses turned towards other opera glasses, bringing distant things close and magnifying small objects. Every young man assumed that he was the focus of these glances and gestures; he would put on dashing airs and pretend to be modest and suave. At the very top there were other people, and what a mob they were! They were boxed in, horde upon horde, like people at a sheep market or wild animals on hillocks, pestering and making a fuss. We looked around the theater for our companions and located them in one room and the tart and her assistant by her side in another. She was making eyes at the ʿUmdah and pinching him. Then they both stretched their hands and grabbed some glasses of wine; the ʿUmdah was getting his from a bottle that the Playboy was serving, while hers came from the hand of her assistant. All the while the Playboy kept coming and going, disappearing from the ʿUmdah's box and then reappearing; sometimes he would be in a box with her and then in another one.

While all this was going on, the bell was rung and the curtain went up. 36.3
A group of actresses and actors appeared, chanting and singing in an unbearable fashion, a spectacle against which human nature revolted. They were using obscure and unintelligible language and sounded like camel drivers in the waterless desert or people attending a funeral. They were wearing contrasting costumes: their shapes matched, but there were too many colors. Their bodies clearly hailed from different countries.

The curtain came down, and then rose again on a middle-aged woman and an adolescent boy. They were embracing each other and sharing their tears. As he spoke to her, he was detailing his passionate love. "What lovely words!" he was saying. "Come now, let's unite in love." "My handsome boy," she replied, "that might come to pass if my mother, Nasīm, would help us. Think of something because I'm going to send her to see you." As they left, a man and woman came on stage talking to each other like a married couple. She had been working on a strategy to deal with the boy. "That boy is more persistent than a fly," he was telling her. "As far as I'm concerned, he's more pernicious than a swarm of demons and more repulsive than a pack of old nags. He won't leave lowly women alone, even if they're old and ugly." "My dear good husband," his wife replied, "don't get alarmed. Not all little birds get eaten! Our daughter is

لا يخشى عليها معه في الاجتماع ولا في الخلوة»، ويذهبان ويدخل العاشقان، والمعشوقة تقول لمعشوقها:

«الحمد لله أيها الأنيق على التيسير والتوفيق، فقد سهّلت أمي لنا الطريق، ولم يبق إلا مرضاة الخادمة، لتكون لأسرارنا متكتمة، وإلا فتصبح حزينة نادمة».

فيقول العاشق: «نعم نعم يا بنت الكرام، وإن لم تطع أذقتها كأس الحمام، بحد هذا الصمصام، وإلا فهذا الكيس الذهب فيه كل الإرب».

فتقول له: «هيا بنا أيها الهمام، فإني أسمع صوت أقدام، حيث تطيب لنا الخلوة والجلوة، ونسبح في بحر النشوة بعد الصحوة».

فيقول لها: «حفظت يا مولاتي، ومنبع حياتي ومماتي، فالآن قد بزغت شموس سعودي، وعطر الأكوان عرف عودي، وبعد برهة نذهب للنزهة».

ثمّ ينتهي دورهما، ويحضر غيرهما، ويدور الكلام بينهم عن سرقة واحتيال، وخيانة واغتيال، وارتكاب واقتراف، واختلاس واختطاف، ثمّ ترتفع بينهم الضوضاء بصراخ يشبه الغناء، فيقابلهم الحضور بالصفير ورشق الأزهار، وعلى هذا ينتهي الفصل ويسدل الستار، ويقوم الناس متلاحمين متخالطين، متزاحمين متخابطين، فأهمّ أيضاً بالقيام في وسط ذلك الزحام، فيمسك الباشا بأذيالي ويأخذ عني سؤالي: ٤،٣٦

الباشا ألم تشبع عينيك من مثل هذه المراقص والملاعب؟ أو لم نسأم بعد من هذه المرائي والمناظر التي رأينا منها ما يكفي في باب الاعتبار والاختبار؟

عيسى بن هشام ليس هذا بمرقص ولا بملعب وإنما هو «التياترو» المعروف عند الغربيين بالتهذيب والتأديب، وتحسين الفضائل، وتقبيح الرذائل، وتمثيل سير الأوّلين لأنظار الآخرين ليتأدب بها من يتأدب، ويعتبر من يعتبر، وهو عندهم الموعظة الحسنة مجسمة للأبصار، لتفعل في النفوس ما لا تفعله الروايات والأخبار، فيشرح لك العمل القبيح ويريك عواقبه وسوء مغبته وقبح مصيره مهما ساعدت الأقدار صاحبه وصادفته العناية في بلوغ أمنيته، ونيل مآربه، وإدراك ٥،٣٦

intelligent and pretty. She has nothing to fear from him, either in company or in private."

They both left the stage, and the lover and his girlfriend reappeared.

"Praise be to God, my dear," she told him. "Things have been resolved, and my mother's worked things out. Now all we have to do is to keep the housekeeper happy. Then she'll keep our secrets to herself. If not, she's going to regret it."

"You're right, you lovely daughter of noble-minded parents!" the boy replied. "If she won't agree, I'll make her savor the cup of death at the point of this sword. This purse of gold should satisfy every wish."

"Come with me, my fine fellow!" she told him. "I hear footsteps. Let's go where we can be alone and bathe in passion's waters after waking!"

"May you be preserved, sweet lady!" he went on, "source of my life and death! Now the sun of my good fortunes has risen, and the aroma of musk has perfumed my existence! In a while we'll take a stroll."

Their dialogue now completed, other actors came on stage. They discussed 36.4
theft, fraud, betrayal, treachery, and murder at one moment, and then talked about committing various other crimes, such as embezzlement and kidnapping. They started making a colossal din and bellowing something that resembled a song. The audience greeted them with whistles and threw flowers at them. With that the curtain came down on the first act. The audience now resumed its pushing and shoving. I was about to get up in the middle of the crowd, but the Pāshā grabbed my coattails and started questioning me:

PĀSHĀ Haven't you had enough yet of these dance halls and nightclubs? Aren't we sufficiently bored with all these sights and scenarios. Surely by now we've seen enough to provide us with the experience and instruction we need.

ʿĪSĀ IBN HISHĀM This place isn't a dance hall or a nightclub. This is a 36.5
theater, something that Western peoples acknowledge as having educational and corrective qualities. It encourages virtues, exposes evil traits, and portrays the deeds of former generations so that people can be educated and learn lessons from them. In Europe theater is regarded as an excellent moral guide writ large so that it can achieve the same effects as narratives and stories. It portrays evil deeds for you and demonstrates the dire consequences of such actions however much help the person may get from fate and however hard he tries to reach his goals and achieve his wishes. By watching such things, the spectator

المرغوب، والظفر بالمطلوب، ليكون لك من المشاهدة زاجر ورادع، ومن العيان ناه ووازع، ويبسط لك الفعل الحميد ويرغبك فيه ويحثك عليه، ويكشف لك عن حسن ثمرته، وسلامة نتيجته مهما لقيت في سبيله من المتاعب والمصاعب، ولاقيت دونه من المكاره والمصائب، وجاز عليك في طريقه من الضنك والشدة، والعسر والضيق، ليكون لك من المعاينة والمناظرة ما يحضك ويحرضك على السعي وراء الخير، وسلوك سبل الرشاد والسداد في محاسن الأفعال والأعمال، ثمّ هو يوقفك على نكت التاريخ بأحسن أمثولة يخرجها من الغيبة إلى الشهود، فيغرس فيك أنواع الفضائل من كرم وشجاعة وأمانة، ووفاء وشهامة، وأباء وحزم، وإقدام وحلم، وأناة واستهانة بالآلاء، وصبر على المكاره والأحزان، وينزع منك ما يقابل ذلك من أنواع الرذائل وأصناف القبائح.

٦،٣٦ الباشا عجباً، كيف تزعم هذا وأنا لم أر فيما رأيته الآن في هذا المكان أثراً يدلّ على شيء ممّا ذكرت، بل الأمر عندي بالعكس، فإني لم أنظر فيه إلا ما نظرته في ذلك الحا, حان الرقص والعزف من معاقرة الراح، ومغازلة النساء، وتمثيل أحوال العشق بما يحض عليه، ويرغب فيه، ويسهل من طريقته، ويمهد من سبله، ويهيج من شهوته، ويشعل من سورته، فإذا كانت هذه المشاهد معدودة من فضائل التشخيص وآدابه فخير للإنسان أن يدخل مثل ذلك الحان وهو موقن أنه داخل على منكر لا يرضي الله ولا يرضي الناس، وأنّ ليس لديه في نفسه ما يعتذر به لها من أن يدخل هذا المحل على ما رأيناه فيه وهو موقن أنه دخل إلى بيت الفضائل كما تنعته، ومظهر الكمالات، ومنبعث الآداب ومكارم الأخلاق، فيدخله آثماً ويخرج منه آثماً، وله العذر في نفسه، والعذر أمام الناس بأنه لم يقصد إلا اكتساب الفضيلة، واجتناب الرذيلة، ولم يقدم إلا على ما يطهر الأخلاق من النقائص وينقيها من أدران القبائح.

٧،٣٦ عيسى بن هشام لا تأخذن ما تراه من هذا التقصير دليلا على أنّ هذا الفن غير مفيد للناس، فقد قدمت لك أنه فن غربي فلم يتقنه إلا الغربيون، وإني إنما وصفته لك على مقدار ما وصل إليه عندهم من درجة الارتقاء والإتقان، وهو لم يزل عندنا

is provided with a negative impression and a restraining force. Theater can also show you laudable deeds, which can encourage you to emulate them and lead you to do likewise. It can show you the happy outcomes that will ensue whatever troubles and difficulties are encountered on the way, whatever misfortunes you may suffer as a result, and whatever hardship, distress, and anxiety life may bring down on you. By watching such actions on stage you'll be encouraged to pursue what is good and behave in a proper and reasonable manner. Theater can also provide you with the best possible models culled from historical accounts which are brought out of obscurity for all to see. It thus endows you with examples of virtue such as generosity, courage, reliability, loyalty, gallantry, pride, resolution, audacity, prudence, and perseverance, along with a disregard for wealth and a tolerance of misfortune and sorrow. At the same time it separates you from the equivalent degree of evil deeds and qualities.

PĀSHĀ That's amazing! How can you be making such claims when what I've been watching here doesn't resemble in any way what you've just been describing? In fact, it's just the opposite. What I've seen here is just a repeat of what I've observed in the dance hall—drinking wine, flirting with women, portraying amorous situations in a highly suggestive manner, one that's designed solely to arouse people's passions, make such things more accessible and easy, and stir up lustful emotions. If these presentations are considered to be displays of virtuous and appropriate conduct, then it would be better for people to enter this theater with the firm conviction that they're coming to see something undesirable, something that pleases neither God nor people. Based on what I've just seen, there's absolutely no way that anyone can excuse himself for coming into this place on the pretext that it's a haven of virtue as you've just depicted it, a display of perfections, or a source of noble and refined qualities. Any such person is committing an error in coming here, and he will leave in the same state, even though he may try both to excuse himself and offer excuses to others by stating that he only came here in order to absorb virtuous deeds and avoid vice. His only reason for coming, he will claim, is to purge himself of faults and the pollution of evil. 36.6

ʿĪSĀ IBN HISHĀM Don't take the shortcomings you see here as evidence that this art has no value for people. I've already explained that it's a Western art form, and it's Westerners who have perfected it. I've described to you the degree of perfection it's achieved among Western people. Here it's still in its 36.7

الآن في أوّل نشأته ومبدأ خطواته، ولذلك وجب أن نغتفر له ما نراه فيه ممّا يؤخذ عليه لجهل الناس عندنا بحقيقته، وما وضع لأجله، لأنّ الكثير منهم يعدّه من الملاهي وأسباب اللهو والخلاعة، ومن وقف على ما يشخص فيه من الأقاصيص المترجمة عن أشهر الكتبة والعلماء من الغربيين، ووعى ما تضمنته من التهذيب والتأديب، علم مقدار الفائدة منه وأحس في نفسه بأثرها وتطلع إلى التزود منها ومثل هذا يرى أنّ التقصير كله واقع من الحكومة، لأنّ مثل هذا الفن المفيد في أوربا من المعارف التي لا يمكن انتشارها وترقيها إلا بعون من الحكومة أو عناية من الجمعيات، ولو كانت تنفق عليه مثلما تنفق على التياترو الأوربي فتتبرع له بالمكان والملابس والدراهم، لأصبح عندنا في أعلى درجات التقدم والنجاح، ولكن حكومتنا أهملته فهو على ما تراه، ولا يبعد أنها تلتفت إليه يوماً من الأيام فينتفع به أهل الشرق كما انتفع أهل الغرب.

الصاحب أظنك أيها الصديق تحكي فيما تقول حكاية الناس لا حكاية ٨،٣٦
الواقع، وإلا فكيف يتصوّر لك أنّ هذا الفن يترقى على هذه الحال بمساعدة الحكومة، وبذل المال في سبيله حتى يفيد الناس فائدة في التربية كالمزعومة منه عند الغربيين، فإننا لو سلمنا أنه مفيد للشرقيين لا فساد يخشى منه، ولا ضرر ينشأ عنه فأنى لنا سبل التقدم فيه وقد تقدّم كل شيء في مصر منذ نشأته إلى اليوم تقدماً محسوساً إلا هذا الفن؟ فإنه لم يطرأ عليه تحسين منذ أدخله في مصر بعض السوريين من نحو عشرين سنة، ولم يقبل عليه أحد يحسّن فيه، فلا شك أنه يبقى على مرور الزمن كما هو الآن من ترجمة الأقاصيص الغربية الغربية بمثل هذه الترجمة السقيمة والأسجاع السخيفة، فلا يتحمله إلا مثل هؤلاء المترددين عليه، الذين لا يرون فيه إلا محل تله، ومكان أنس، وحفلة سمر، ولا يقع في نفوسهم من معنى هذا الفن إلا ما يقع فيها من بقية الألاعيب التي يقوم بها جماعة المقلدين والحاكين والمشعوذين من أهل السيمياء، على أننا إذا نظرنا إلى هذا الفن على حقيقته عند الغربيين بنظر صحيح وجدناه لا يوافق الشرقيين، ولا ينطبق على عاداتهم وأخصهم المسلمون.

initial stages, the beginning of its emergence. For that reason we need to excuse the shortcomings that we can see here. People are unaware of its true essence and effects. Many of them regard it as some sort of farce, an excuse for frivolity and obscenity. Anyone who's acquainted with the plots translated from the most illustrious Western writers and intellectuals and who realizes the education and refinement that is offered will come to appreciate its benefits. Such people will find themselves affected and will strive to learn from it. Along the same lines, it can be said that these shortcomings are entirely due to the government. In Europe useful arts such as this are an aspect of knowledge that can only spread and develop with government support and the involvement of associations. If the same amount of money was being spent here as is the case with theater in Europe, then the government would be providing the location, costumes, and funding so that it could achieve the highest possible level of progress and success. However, our government has completely ignored it, and you can see the result for yourself. It's still not out of the question that one day the government will give it some attention, in which case people in the East will be able to gain some benefit from it as those in the West already do.

FRIEND My dear friend, I think you're simply repeating what people are **36.8** saying rather than reflecting the true situation. How can you imagine that in the current circumstances this art is going to improve with government support—which implies government funding—so that, according to European claims, people can be educated by it? Even if we were to admit that it was indeed beneficial for Eastern peoples and there was no worry about the corruption that it might cause, how are we to plot its forward progress when everything in Egypt—from its earliest days to the present—has made progress except for this particular art? Ever since some Syrians introduced it here some twenty years ago, there has been no sign of improvement. No one has stepped forward to give it approval. As time passes, it seems bound to remain just as it is now, namely translations of weird Western stories like the dreadful translated text and clashing rhymes that we have just witnessed. The only people who tolerate it are the kind of regular customers here who regard it as a place for amusement and socializing, a special kind of soirée. The impact that this art form has on them is no greater than that of all the other types of entertainment presented by phony imitators and magicians. If we take an honest look at this art form as it exists in the West, we discover that it does not suit Eastern people and does not accord with their customs—most especially Muslims.

٩،٣٦ وأنت تعلم أنه ينبغي للحكيم الباحث في مثل هذه الأمور المتعلقة بالتربية والأخلاق أن يراعي تأثير التربة والإقليم، وتركيب الغرائز والجبلات، فيرى أنّ ما يوافق في باريس مثلا لا يوافق في بكين، وما يستحسن في لوندرة لا يستحسن في الخرطوم، بل قد يكون الأمر أشد من ذلك، فما ينفع هناك يضرهنا، وما يكون عند الغربيين جدّاً قد يكون عند الشرقيين هزلا، وما يكون حقيقة في بلد قد يكون باطلاً في بلد آخر، وما يغيب عنك أنّ مدار التمثيل والتشخيص للأقاصيص هو العشق، وقلّ أن تخلو قصة من قصصهم إلا والعاشقان قائمان فيها مقام الفاتحة والخاتمة لها، وهذا وإن لم يكن عظيم الضرر عند أهل البلاد الغربية لكونه أمرًا مسموحاً به في عاداتهم يجهر به فتيانهم وفتياتهم لا يرون فيه نقصاً ولا عيباً، بل هو من أصول التزاوج بينهم، والأصل في ذلك حكم الإقليم بضعف التهيج في الخيال والاشتعال في التصور وفتور الشعور، إلا أنّ ضرره عظيم في البلاد الشرقية، ولذلك كان فيها سرًّا مكتوماً، وأمرًا محجوبًا، وجرى في بعضها مجرى العيب والعار حتى وصل الأمر عند العرب أنه إذا اشتهر بينهم عشق فتى لفتاة لا يزوّجونها منه، وربما توصلوا بأمر السلطان إلى هدر دمه بلا قود ولا دية، وعند الغربيين إن لم تعشق الفتاة فتاها فلا تتزوجه فهذا مثال واضح في تناقض العادات، وتنافر السجايا بين إقليم وآخر، وهذا العشق هو الركن الأوّل لهذا الفن، ولا بدّ أن يكون مهدوماً في الشرق، وإلا انتشر عنه الخلل والفساد، وخيف من ورائه ارتكاب القبائح واختلاط الأنساب لطبيعة الإقليم في حدة المزاج وسرعة اشتعال الخاطر، وتوقد الشعور، والتهاب الإحساس.

١٠،٣٦ ثمّ إنّ المقصود من هذا الفن التهذيب وتنقية الأخلاق، ولا يمكن الوصول إلى ذلك إلا باستعمال المألوف الذي تجري عليه النفوس في عاداتها فترجمة الأقاصيص الموضوعة على أخلاق أمّة خاصة بها لا تؤثر في أمّة أخرى كما تؤثر في تلك الأمّة، فلا بدّ لكل بلد أن يكون أصحاب هذا الفن من أهلها يمثلون أقاصيصهم بشرح

You're aware, of course, that when prudent researchers investigate matters connected with upbringing and moral education, they need to take into account local terrain and the construction of people's natural instincts and temperaments. They can tell, for example, that what works in Paris won't do in Beijing; what's approved in London won't be in Khartoum. Indeed it may be even worse than that. Something that's beneficial in one place may actually be harmful in another; what Westerners treat seriously may be regarded as a joke in the East, and what's true in one country may be false in another. The point that you're missing is that theater and acting involve plots that revolve around the topic of love. It's extremely rare for one of their narratives not to have two lovers as its beginning and end; and that's the way things are. It causes no great harm in Western societies because expressions of love are permitted by their customs, something that can be projected in public by their young men and women who see neither fault nor sin in it. Indeed it's one of the major bases for marriage. The basis for that custom lies in the judgment of that particular region that sentiments can remain fairly calm and that presentations such as these will not arouse and enflame the imagination to strong reactions. In Eastern countries by contrast the damage can be considerable. For that very reason love is kept secret, something to put under wraps. In certain quarters the mere notion of sin and disgrace has such a hold that, if a young man even proclaims his love for a girl, they will refuse to marry her to him. They may even raise the matter with the ruler who will order that he be put to death with no possibility of retaliation or blood payment. Among Westerners, if a girl does not love her boyfriend, then she doesn't marry him. That provides a clear example of the difference in customs and the contrast in traits between one region and another. Love of this kind is the primary focus of this particular art, and so it must inevitably be rejected in the East. Otherwise corruption and disorder will spread, all of which may lead to all sorts of evils being committed and a nasty intercultural mix in which crude emotions will be rapidly stirred and lewd sensations will be kindled. 36.9

The supposed purpose of this art is for education and moral purification. The only way of achieving that is by making use of what is familiar and in accord with people's habits. The translation of stories that have been composed with specific moral standards in mind cannot have the same effect on another people as they do on the one for which it was originally intended. The promoters of this art must inevitably be drawn from the same people so that their presentations 36.10

أحوالهم وعاداتهم، وليس في أخلاق الشرقيين هذا التشهير والتمثيل خصوصاً في معيشة الأهل والولد، وليس في آداب الدين الإسلامي أن يدخل النساء في هذا الفن لأنه ينهى النساء عن التبرج بالزينة فضلا عن الاختلاط، ويأمرهن بغض النظر فضلا عن طموحه، كما أنه ليس من أدب الإسلام أن نمثل تاريخه وتاريخ خلفائه وصلحائه، ونخترع عليهم المخترعات، ونفتري المفتريات، ونضعهم بين عاشق ومعشوق، وننطقهم بما لم ينطقوا به، وندخلهم فيما لم يدخلوا فيه كما يجترئ عليه في هذه الأيام كثير من غير أهل الدين الإسلامي بيننا، وماذا ترى في هارون الرشيد وهو يغني، وفي جعفر بن يحيى وهو يزمر، وفي الفضل بن الربيع وهو يرقص، لا جرم أنها مهانة للأسلاف وخرف في التاريخ.

١١،٣٦ هذا إذا كان الأصل في هذا الفن التهذيب والتأديب وطلب الكمالات، ولكن انظر معي نظرة إليه من حيث هو نافع هذا النفع عند الغربيين أنفسهم، فإنّ العقل والمشاهدة يخبرانا بأنّ ضرره إلى اليوم عندهم ظاهر ونفعه غير باد وبيان ذلك أنّ هذا الفن يكشف عن الفضيلة من طرق تمثيل الرذيلة، ويبين العفة بتصوير الشهوات، ولأجل بلوغ غرضه في ذلك لا بد له من الغلو والمبالغة في توضيح الرذائل وتبيين الشهوات وعرضها على الناس بحيلها ومكرها، وخداعها ومكائدها بما يخترعه خيال الشاعر من السبك والتنسيق، ولا يكون داعياً إلى كف صاحب الرذيلة عن ارتكابها، بل يستدرجه إلى التعمق فيها، والتوسع في أبوابها والتدرب عليها، فيعلم اللص حيل اللصوصية، والشقي سبل الجرائم والجنايا، والخبيث طرق المكر والخداع، والفاجر أبواب التحايل على الفسق والفجور، هذا فعله في صاحب الرذيلة وهو لا يغني صاحب الفضيلة بالطبع شيئاً فهو يزيد الشرير شرًا وربما جر إلى صاحب الفضيلة ضرًا.

١٢،٣٦ ومن تأمّل قليلا وجد أنّ الإسهاب والشرح والتفصيل في تبيان خفايا الرذائل وغوامض الشهوات مضر غير نافع، لأنه يجعل ما لا يجوز وقوعه ممّا يتوقع إمكانه،

will serve to elucidate their own conditions and customs. The morality of the peoples of the East does not include this kind of exposure and representation, especially in matters relating to family and children. The codes of the Islamic faith do not permit women to involve themselves in this art because it forbids them to display themselves in public, quite apart from mingling with others. Indeed it commands them to turn their gaze away rather than the opposite. Nor is it any part of Islamic practice that we should be portraying its history and that of its caliphs and holy men, devising various plots, making up stories, and placing them in amorous situations. By so doing, we make them say things they never uttered and put them in unreal situations. Even so, that is what many non-Muslims are daring to do these days in our country. What can you possibly say about the Caliph Hārūn al-Rashīd singing, his vizier Jaʿfar al-Barmakī playing the flute, and al-Faḍl ibn al-Rabīʿ dancing? Without the slightest doubt it's an insult to our ancestors and a distortion of history.

All this presupposes that the origin of the theatrical art is in education, 36.11
proper training, and a quest for perfection. However, if we take a closer look at it from the perspective of its benefits within the Western context, both intellect and observation make it clear that, even in their own cultural environment, the harm it does is clear enough while the benefits are nonexistent. The evidence of this lies in the fact that the art aims to reveal virtuous conduct by portraying evil and to illustrate chaste behavior through portraits of sheer lust. In order to achieve those aims, it has to exaggerate in its portrayal of illicit behavior and lewd desires and to portray them by using the tricks, falsehoods, and deceits that can be devised as a result of the plots and formats that the poetic imgination can devise. Not only does it not encourage the evil person to refrain from commiting such acts, but it also leads him to get even further involved in such activities and to expand and enhance his expertise in its various aspects. Thus the thief learns further arts of theft, the villain learns how to commit crimes, the swindler learns how to trick and deceive, and the lecher learns all kinds of debauchery and fornication. While these are the effects on wicked people, the virtuous gain no benefits. The wicked person becomes yet more evil, and the spectacle may even cause harm to the virtuous person.

It only requires a little thought to discover that the process of providing 36.12
detailed illustrations of the hidden aspects of evil and latent desire is actually harmful and unbeneficial. It turns what is not supposed to happen into something that actually might happen. That's why people say that the act of detailing

ولذلك قيل أنّ تفصيل الجرائم في القوانين ممّا ينبه إليها، وقد سئل الشارع الحكيم اليوناني عن إغفاله عقوبة القاتل لأبيه في شريعته فقال «ما أتصور أنّ يونانيا يقدم على قتل أبيه» فكان ذلك أنفى لوقوع هذه الجريمة من ذكر العقوبة عليها بأنواع شدتها هذا الشارع الحكيم تحاشى أن يذكر في شريعته ذكر من يقتل أباه، فما بالك بتمثيل ذلك ظاهرًا للعيان، وهذه روايات التشخيص مشحونة بذكر القاتل لأبيه، والمتزوج أمه أو أخته، والحاكم على الأب أن يشرب من دم ابنه إلى غير ذلك من مثل هذه الجرائم التي لولا تشخيصها في أقاصيص الغربيين لما صدّقنا بوقوعها بين الناس.

١٣،٣٦ نعم قد يتأثر الإنسان من وقوع مكروه على أحد إذا كان هذا المكروه صادرًا عن الغير، ولكن هذا التأثر لا يكفي لأن ينزع منه ارتكاب المكروه لأنّ الإنسان عادل ما دام الظلم يصدر عن غيره، فإذا شاهد منازعة لا دخل له فيها أخذ بجانب العدل والإنصاف وكل فصل من الشر تتألم له نفسه ما دام ليس له منفعة منه. كما أنّ الرجل ذو الوجه القبيح يستقبح الدمامة في وجه غيره ولا يستقبحها في وجهه أمّا إذا كانت له منه منفعة وله به علاقة فلا يطاوع نفسه في الكف، وحينئذ يميل إلى الشر الذي فيه نفعه ويحيد عن الخير الذي يأمر به العقل. وضح لنا إذًا أنّ تأثير التشخيص لاكتساب الفضيلة باطل في أصله أيضًا لأنّ إخماد الشهوات لا ينتج من إلهابها، وأنّ الاعتدال لا يأتي من جانب التهوّر وأمامنا مثل صغير وهو أنّ المرأة التي نقبت ستار الحجرة بإصبعها لمغازلة الرجال، لو كان التشخيص يكسبها العفة لعادت فخاطت الفتق بيدها، ولكن أنى يكون ذلك وهذه الخروق تتسع يومًا عن يوم، والفتوق تزداد حينًا بعد حين؟

١٤،٣٦ قال عيسى بن هشام: وعند هذا عاد الناس إلى مقاعدهم وأخذوا في الجلبة والصياح كما كانوا حتى ارتفع الستار، وإذا منظر غابة في فلاة وصوت مرتفع بصياح يشبه صياح المؤذن، فاستغرب الباشا وسأل هل يؤذنون أيضًا في التشخيص، ولم يكد يتم

particular crimes in law codes draws attention to them. A sage Greek lawgiver was once asked why he'd overlooked the provision of a punishment for parricide in his legal code. His reply was that he'd never imagined any Greek would ever dare to kill his father. That statement of his did more to prevent the occurrence of that crime than describing the various penalties for committing it. That lawgiver refused to mention parricide in his law code, so what can you say when the very same thing is acted before your very eyes. These theatrical plots are loaded down with depictions of father-killers and men marrying their mothers or sisters, decrees requiring that a father drink his son's blood, and other similar criminal acts that we would never believe actually occurred were it not for these Western plays.

It's true enough that human beings may be affected when someone suffers a mishap if that mishap is occasioned by someone else. However, that affect is not enough to prevent him from committing a reprehensible act because man will act justly as long as the wrong comes from somebody else. If, for example, he witnesses a disagreement in which he's in no way involved, he will adopt a posture of justice and fairness and will steer clear of any personally harmful evil action as long as he has no personal interest in it. That's why a man with an ugly face will loathe ugliness on someone else's face even though he doesn't do so with regard to his own face. But if he has some benefit to gain and is somehow connected with it, then he'll be unable to resist. At that point he will tend to commit the evil act that is to his advantage and will deviate from the right course that his mind has been dictating to him. All of which makes it clear that the notion of theater as being effective in the acquisition of laudable qualities is by definition false. Passions cannot be cooled by enflaming them in the first place; moderation does not emerge from recklessness. We have a minor illustration right in front of us. If the woman who draws back the curtains in her box to flirt with men actually learned about chaste behavior from the play, she would be using her hand to pull the curtains closed again. But how can we claim she has learned something when the gaps in the curtains grow ever wider? 36.13

ʿĪsā ibn Hishām said: At this point people returned to their seats, and the din resumed at its former level. The curtain now rose on a desolate woodland scene. A voice was raised imitating that of a muezzin. The Pāshā was perplexed and asked me if the call to prayer was performed in the theater as well. Hardly had he finished asking the question before the young man from the previous 36.14

السؤال حتى ظهر ذلك الشاب المغني يحمل شيئاً من المتاع وهو ينغنى بهذا الصوت ومن ورائه تلك المرأة النصف تتلفت وتتعثر كالهارب المتخوف يترقب المطاردة، ويخشى الدرك، فيتناشدان ويتغنيان ويتعالان بالنجاة والنجاح، ولا يلبثان على ذلك برهة حتى يظهر الرجل الذي رأيناه مع زوجته في الفصل الأول وهو مسرع في الجري ومن ورائه أولئك الجماعة الذين ختم الفصل بهم، فيدورون حول الشاب والمرأة ويقع بينهم وبينه كلام ثمّ خصام ثمّ مشاتمة ثمّ ملاكمة، فيخرج الشاب مسدساً فيطلقه على الرجل فيقع قتيلاً ثمّ يصوّبه على آخر فيقتله، فيولي البقية مدبرين، وتقع المرأة مغشياً عليها وينتهي الفصل.

١٥،٣٦ فنخرج مع الخارجين فننتهي إلى حان الشرب من التياترو فنراه مزدحماً بالناس، ونرى العمدة وصاحبته وصاحبيه جالسين جانباً على إحدى المناضد وأمامهم الراح والأقداح وقد أخذت منهم الخمر فنزوي ناحية، فما تمضي برهة إلا ونرى رجلا قد دنا منهم يقول للمرأة أتظنين أنّ الهروب من الميعاد يؤخرك عن دفع مبلغ الصك المأخوذ عليك، ولقد حملتني اليوم والليلة تعباً شديداً في البحث عنك في كل بقعة ومكان حتى عثرت بك هنا فأنا الآن لا أنفك عنك حتى تعطيني ما أستحقه أو تردّي إليّ هذه الحلي التي تزينين بها صدرك الآن أمام أخدانك وخلانك. ويمدّ يده لينتزع منها الحلي فيمنعه الخليع متوسطاً بينهما ويقول له ليس هذا وقته، فإن كان لك عندها شيء فطالبها به أمام المحاكم، فيأبى الرجل ويقول: أنا لا أطالب أمام المحاكم وأمامي مالي في صدرها ويمدّ يده ثانية فتميل على العمدة قابضة على الحلي بيدها صارخة مستغيثة به فتأخذه الحمية والنخوة فيدفع عنها الصائغ فيقول له: إن كان قد عزّ عليك مطالبتها فلا تدفعني بيدك بل ادفع لي من جيبك، فيسأله العمدة عن مقدار المطلوب فتقول له المرأة أنه أربعون جنيها فقط، فيتورط في دفعها ويأخذ الصك في يد والكأس في يد ويقدمهما إليها فتقبل الكأس شكرًا له، وينصرف الصائغ ضاحك السن.

act appeared carrying something and singing. Behind him was the middle-aged woman who kept looking behind her and stumbling as though she were running away and was afraid of being followed or chased by the police. Both of them were chanting, singing, and calling for help. It was only a moment or so before the man whom we'd seen in the previous act with his wife came rushing in, followed by the troupe who had closed the last act. They all surrounded the young man and his beloved. First there was an exchange of words, then argument, abuse, and fisticuffs. The young man now took out a revolver and fired it at the man who fell dead. He then fired it at another man, and he fell dead too. The rest of the men turned on their heels, while the woman fainted. With that the act came to an end.

We followed people out and headed for the theater bar. It was very crowded, but we spotted the ʿUmdah with his two companions and the tart sitting at a table with wine and full glasses in front of them. They had obviously drunk a lot. We moved to one side and had only been there for a few moments before we saw a man going up to them. He spoke to the woman: "Do you think that, by missing our appointment, you can put off paying the amount you owe me on the check? I'm exhausted having to search for you day and night in every possible spot. So now I've finally stumbled on you here! I'm not going to move till you give me what I'm owed; either that, or else you can give me back that necklace you're using to decorate your bosom in front of all your paramours and lovers!" With that he stretched out his hand to snatch the necklace from her bosom, but the Playboy stopped him by stepping between them. "This is not the right time," he said. "If she owes you something, then seek redress through the courts." But the man refused. "I'll not seek redress through the courts when my money's right there in front of me on her bosom." He stretched his hand out again, but the tart clutched her necklace. She leaned over in the ʿUmdah's direction and begged him to come to her aid. Anger and self-respect got the better of him, and he pushed the jeweler away from her. "If you don't like the way I'm demanding my due," the jeweler said, "don't push me away. Pay me yourself!" The ʿUmdah inquired how much was owed, to which the woman replied that it was a mere forty pounds. He paid the jeweler the amount and grabbed the check in one hand and a glass of wine in the other. He offered them both to the woman, and she kissed the rim to show her gratitude. The jeweler meanwhile left with a smile. 36.15

ويأخذون في شربهم ولهوهم برهة، ويقترح العمدة على أصحابه مفارقة هذا اللعب الذي لا يجب به إلا صبيان المكاتب، وأن يذهبوا إلى قهاوي الجزيرة ليجلسوا هناك بين خضرة الروض على شاطئ النيل تحت ضوء القمر، فيجبون جميعا بهذا الرأي، وما يكادون يهمّون بالقيام إلا وصاحب الخان الذي ترقص فيه المرأة واقف على رؤوسهم واضع يديه في خاصرتيه يهزّ رأسه مبكتا، ويقول لها: أهذا هو المرض الذي تعتذرين به عن الحضور إلى الشغل هذه الليلة، وهذا هو المستشفى الذي تستشفين فيه؟ وأظنّ أنّ حضرة العمدة من أكبر أطباء هذا العصر، ثمّ يأخذ بيدها لتذهب معه إلى الحانة فيمسكها العمدة من اليد الأخرى ويقول له: ما هذه الوقاحة وما هذا التهجم؟ تأخذ منها عشرة جنيهات نظير تأخيرها عن الحضور إلى الخان هذه الليلة وتروم الآن أن تذهب معك إليه، إنّ هذا لهو النصب والاحتيال بعينه، فيقول له صاحب الخان: إنما النصب والاحتيال منك ومنها، وإن كنت قد دفعت لها هذا المبلغ فهي حيلة منها وما أخذته إلا لنفسها، وإني أستغرب من وقاحتكم كيف تعطلون محلي وتغرونها على التأخير عن شغلها ليستنفع بها مثل هذا المحل. ١٦،٣٦

ولا يزال الخصام يزداد والشحناء تتسع بينهم حتى يفضي بهم الأمر أن تقوم إحدى المشخصات ممّن ليس عليهن الدور في هذه الليلة فتستصرخ البوليس لإخراجهم خشية التعطيل، فيأتي البوليس ويخرج بهم إلى القسم فنريد اتباعهم فيأبى الباشا قائلا أنا لا أتوجه إلى القسم لا شاكيًا ولا متفرجًا، فقد وقفت من أمره على ظاهره وخافيه، وجربت بنفسي ما يقع فيه.

قال عيسى بن هشام: ويشكو الباشا من التعب والملل فنقصد البيت على عجل. ١٧،٣٦

They started drinking and chatting again. The 'Umdah suggested to his companions that they leave the playhouse which only youngsters found enjoyable and go to the cafés on the Gezira. They could sit in the moonlight in the gardens alongside the River Nile. They all approved of the idea and were about to leave when the Proprietor of the dance hall where the woman regularly performed was standing right in front of them, hands on hips and shaking his head in annoyance. "So this is the illness that's kept you from coming to work tonight, is it? Is this the hospital where you're being treated? I assume that the 'Umdah is one of the era's most accomplished physicians!" With that he grabbed her hand to take her back to the dance hall with him. The 'Umdah grabbed hold of her other hand. "What do you mean by this impertinence?" he asked. "Why are you treating her so roughly? You've already taken ten pounds as compensation for her not coming to work in the tavern tonight. Now you want her to go with you. That's arrant deceit and fraud!" "You're the ones indulging in deceit and fraud," the Proprietor replied, "you and she both. If you paid her that amount, then she's tricked you and kept the money for herself. I'm surprised at your own impudence, bringing business in my place to a halt and tempting her into staying away from her job so you could bring her to a place like this." 36.16

The row got worse, and things became so heated that one of the actresses who had no role to play that night started yelling for the police to eject them all for fear the evening would be ruined. The police duly arrived and decided to take them all to the station. We were intending to follow them, but the Pāshā absolutely refused to go. "I'm not going to any police station," he said firmly, "whether it's to lodge a complaint or merely to observe. I've already had some experience of both the visible and hidden aspects of it all. I'm well aware of what goes on there."

'Īsā ibn Hishām said: Since the Pāshā was feeling both tired and bored, we headed for the house as quickly as possible. 36.17

مصباح الشرق ١٠٧، ٨ يونيو ١٩٠٠

قال عيسى بن هشام: ولمّا وصلنا إلى البيت عمد الباشا إلى غرفة نومه ليستريح من تعب يومه، فلحقه السهاد، وتجنبه الرقاد، فناداني لنحيي الليلة بالسمر، ونقتلها بالسهر، فأخذنا بأطراف الحديث، من قديم وحديث، والليلة في أخريات الشباب، أوشكت تستخف بالإزار وبالنقاب، ثمّ دبّ المشيب في فودها، وظهر الوضح في جلدها، فكبرت عن حمل الحلي والقلائد، وزهدت في اللآلئ منها والفرائد، فخلعت خواتيم الثريا من كفها، وألقت بالفرقدين من موضع شنفها، ورمت من نحرها بكل عقد منظوم، من جواهر الكواكب ودرر النجوم، فأصبحت وهي عجوز شمطاء، تدب على عصا الجوزاء، وانتقلت من دور التحجب والتدلل، إلى دور التبذل والتذلل، وهتكت من حجابها، وتكشفت عن جلبابها، فأشفق عليها الفجر كما يشفق على الأمهات الأبناء، فألقى عليها ملاءته الزرقاء، ثمّ ما لبثت أن أدركها حكم القضاء، بمحتوم الفناء، فدرجها الصبح في ملاءته البيضاء، ورمسها في جوف الفضاء ١،٣٧

٢،٣٧ ولمّا أن فتح الإشراق باب النهار، وخرج منه ساطع النور على الأقطار، دخل علينا «الصاحب» مع الشمس، لموعد كان بيننا من أمس، فيبدأ بالسؤال عن حالتنا، في تمضية ليلتنا، فنخبره بما كان من اتصال السهر إلى الآن، فيقول وعلام كانت تدور المذاكرة، وفيم كانت تجري المحاضرة؟ فأقول له: ما فتئ الباشا كلما تذكر ما يراه من عجيب المستحدثات، وما يسمعه من غريب الأقوال والمباحثات، وما يخبره في رحلته ممّا لم يكن له أثر في أيام دولته، يشكو من هذا الفساد والخلل، ويصبو إلى معرفة الأسباب والعلل، فأخبره بأنّ الأصل فيها راجع إلى تقليد الشرقيين مدنية الغربيين، فيعجب للأمم الغربية قياساً على ما يرى ويسمع، كيف تصرف أفكارها وتضيّع أعمارها في إحداث ما يضر ولا ينفع، وابتكار كل حادث جديد ممّا يفسد ولا يفيد، فأريه

Miṣbāḥ al-sharq 107, June 8, 1900[53]

ʿĪsā ibn Hishām said: When we reached the house, the Pāshā made for his bedroom to rest after the tiring day. However he could not fall asleep and was restless. He called out to me, wanting to while away the remainder of the night talking. We had a conversation about times old and new. Night was in the final stages of its youth and was about to dispense with both shawl and veil; old age crept into its temples, and traces of daylight appeared on its skin. Disdaining necklets and jewelry and stinting on pearls and precious gems, it took off the rings of the Pleiades from its hand and removed the twin stars of Ursa Minor—its earrings. From its neck it cast away clusters of lustrous pearly stars and emerged as a grey-haired old woman tottering along on the stick formed by the Gemini. A former veiled, coquettish posture was now turned into one of vulgar insignificance. Night was now stripped of her veil and revealed in her common gown. Dawn took pity on her as sons do their mothers and covered her with its blue sheet. Ere long the laws of closure imposed their inevitable decree. Morning wrapped her in its white sheet, then shrouded her in the belly of space. 37.1

As soon as sunrise opened the gates to daytime and radiant light shone forth over the world's regions, our Friend arrived along with the sun according to the plan we had arranged the day before. He began by asking how we were after the way we had spent the night. We told him that we had continued talking, to which he responded by asking what we had been discussing and what topics we had broached. I replied by telling him that, every time the Pāshā recalled the amazing modernities he had seen, the strange statements and discussions he had heard, and the things he had witnessed during his travels that were unfamiliar to him in the era of his own dynasty, he would complain about the corruption and imperfection that he kept seeing. He was keen to find out what the underlying causes for the situation were. The Friend replied that the root cause lay in the way Easterners were imitating Western civilization. When compared with what could be seen and heard, he found it amazing that Westerners' minds could be so preoccupied and their lives could be so squandered on the creation of things that did only harm, and no good, on the devising of new phenomena that only serve to corrupt rather than provide benefit. I showed him that, whereas Westerners only see advantages and gains in their civilization, the peoples of the East have chosen to imitate them without any 37.2

أنّ الغربيين يرون في مدنيتهم كل منفعة وفائدة، ولكن الشرقيين قلدوهم فيها على غير قاعدة، فجنوا الشوك من شجرها، وبلوا المر من ثمرها.

٣،٣٧ الصاحب صدقت وأصبت وبصرت، فقد دخلت هذه المدنية الغربية في أهل البلاد الشرقية على غير أساس وبغير ترتيب مع تغاير الأقاليم وتخالف الطباع وتنافر الأخلاق، فلم ينتقوا منها لأنفسهم الملائم من المباين، ولم ينتقدوا فيها الصحيح من الزائف، بل قابلوها بالتسليم والانقياد، واكتفوا منها بالظواهر الباطلة، والفضول التافهة، وتركوا لها ما كان فيهم من الأصول القويمة والدعائم المتينة، فوهى بنيانهم ووهنت أركانهم وتقطعت بهم الأسباب، فكان ضررها فيهم كما تراه بليغاً، وشرها مستطيراً، وأصبح هذا الطلاء من المدنية بيننا أحبولة يقتنصنا بها الغربي في غفلتنا، ومعولاً يهدم به بنياننا، ويقوّض جدراننا، ونخرب له بيوتنا بأيدينا.

الباشا لست أدري لأية علة أخذ الشرقيون بباطل المدنية دون حقيقتها، وبظاهرها دون باطنها، واقتصروا منها على القشور دون اللباب، وهم في التاريخ أعرق الأمم في المدنية وأسبقهم إلى الحضارة والعمران.

٤،٣٧ الصاحب ليس من سبب لذلك إلا ما يعقب العزة من البطر والأشر، وما يتولد عنهما من التواني والتواكل والتغافل والتكاسل، فيأخذون بما يخف حمله، وتهون كلفته، ولا يلجئهم إلى المشقة في التحصيل، والتعب في العمل، وانكبّ الغربيون في غفلتهم على ممارسة التكاليف الشاقة، والمواظبة على الجد والمداومة على الكد، فأحسنوا الصناعات، واخترعوا المخترعات، وانتشروا في عرض البلاد وطولها، فأورثهم بسطة في المال، وقوة في الحرب، وجذبت إليهم ثروة الشرق ودرت عليهم أخلافه، وباعوا أهله البهرج بالذهب، وانتفع الغربي بمدنيته فاستمر في صعوده، ولم ينتفع الشرقي بتقليده فيها فاستمر منحدراً في هبوطه.

firm basis for doing so. They have only picked the thorns off the fruit tree and tasted the bitter fruit.

FRIEND You're absolutely right! This Western civilization has reached the peoples of Eastern lands without any firm basis or acknowledgment of different regions, variant temperaments, and incompatible moral systems. People have failed to distinguish what suits them from what does not, and have not discriminated between the authentic from the phony. Quite the opposite, they have accepted it all willingly and have contented themselves with useless superficialities and utter trivialities. In so doing, they have abandoned all national norms and firmly rooted principles. As a result, structures and pillars have been weakened and links have been cut. You can see for yourself how severe is the resulting damage and how widespread the dire consequences. This patina of Western civilization has turned into a trap that Westerners can use to catch us unawares, a pickaxe to destroy our very foundations and undermine our walls. We're destroying our house with our own hands. 37.3

PĀSHĀ I can't understand why peoples of the East have chosen to adopt the useless aspects of civilization rather than its true essence, the surface rather than the core. They seem to confine their attention to the shell rather than the pith, whereas in earlier times they were of all peoples the most steeped in civilization and culture.

FRIEND The only reason is that the natural consequence of periods of glory is recklessness and hubris, and they in turn engender weakness, indifference, slackness, and neglect. They are only willing to bear light loads and minimal responsibilities, things that don't require any hardship to achieve or exhaustion in their execution. While Eastern peoples paid no attention, Westerners were willing to undertake difficult assignments and to persevere doggedly in burdensome activities. As a result they've developed industries, made inventions, and scattered across countries far and wide. That has bequeathed them wealth and military power. The riches of the East have attracted them and its resources have flowed for them in abundance. They've sold the peoples of the East utter trash for gold. Meanwhile Westerners have benefited from their own civilization and have continued ever upwards while the peoples of the East have gained nothing from imitating them, but have rather continued their downward trajectory. 37.4

الباشا يا حبذا مشاهدة هذه المدنية في مواطنها، ومعاينة خوافيها وبواطنها، والبحث فيها عن النافع والضار منها حتى يحكم الإنسان على النظر ويستدل بالعيان، ولكن بعدت الشقة وعز المطلوب.

عيسى بن هشام لا تستبعد بعيداً، ولا تستصعب مراماً، فأنا لا يزال يتردد في خاطري أن أصحبك يوماً من الأيام إلى رحلة نرحلها في أوربا لتقف معي على جلية هذه المدنية الغربية، ونتائج التقدم والترقي فيها بين أهلها، وترى من آثارها بعينك ما تسمعه عنها بأذنك.

الصاحب إن كانت هذه نيتك وتلك عزيمتك فليس أمامكما فرصة تفترص ٥،٣٧
ونهزة تنتهز أوفق لغرضكما وأبلغ لأربكما من السفر في هذه الأيام أيام المعرض العام في أم العواصم المتمدنة، هنالك تتجلى لكما المدنية في أجلى مظاهرها وتنبلج الحضارة في أبهى مناظرها وأسمى مفاخرها.

الباشا وما هو المعرض العام.

الصاحب هو سوق عظيم تقوم على إنشائه الحكومات الغربية في بعض السنين تدعو إليه حكومات العالم ليرحل إليه من يريد من أهاليها بصناعته وبضاعته، ويرسل إليه بما بلغه حد الإتقان من عمل الإنسان فتعرض فيه بضاعة العالم وصناعته على الخبيرين بها فيكافئون المتقن بعلامة من الشرف على إتقانه فيكون ذلك داعياً إلى تشويق الناس وتحريضهم على الإتقان في العمل والترقي في المعارف والفنون من جهة، وتربح منه الحكومة التي تقوم بإنشائه ربحاً طائلاً مع أهالي بلادها من جهة أخرى، لكثرة الوفود عليه الذين يعدّون بعشرات الملايين الداخلين فيه بأجر معلوم، ومما ينتجه من حركة التجارة، وكثرة البيع والشراء بين الأهالي والزائرين له من أقاصي المسكونة

وأوّل من أنشأ المعرض العام على هذه الصورة الدولة الانكليزية في سنة ١٨٥١ ٦،٣٧
ثمّ اقتفت أثرها الدولة الفرنسوية في سنة ١٨٥٥، وما زالت تقيمه هذه الدولة مرة بعد مرة على حسب ظروف الأحوال حتى تقرّر عندها أخيراً أن تقيمه في كل عشر سنوات

Pāshā How I wish I could see this Western civilization in its homelands! I'd be able to examine both its external and internal aspects and investigate what parts of it are useful and harmful. Then one could make judgments based on eyewitness experience. But that's a big challenge and would involve a lot of trouble.

'Īsā ibn Hishām The idea's not that remote; don't think it's so impossible! I'm still thinking of accompanying you one day on a trip to Europe so we can learn about the essence of this Western civilization and the benefits that progress has brought to its people. Then its effects will be as obvious to the eye as what you've been hearing with your ears.

Friend If that's your goal and intention, then no better occasion and opportunity exists for me to show you things than a trip at the present time to visit the *Exposition universelle* in Paris, mother of all Western capitals. You would be seeing civilization on display in its clearest form, culture shining forth in its brightest and most glorious guise. 37.5

Pāshā What is this "*Exposition universelle*"?

Friend It's a huge market that has been built by Western governments to last for a few years. They invite the governments of the world to send people with their crafts and products, things that demonstrate the perfection of man's work. The world's products and crafts are on display for experts to examine, and the best examples are awarded prizes for their perfect craftsmanship. In that way people are stimulated and encouraged to perform well in their own work, to aspire to higher goals in learning and arts on the one hand, while on the other the government that created the exhibition earns a large profit along with its own people because hordes of people who can be counted in millions enter the grounds for a fixed fee. And you can add to that the commercial transactions and the large amount of buying and selling that occurs between the native population and visitors who come from the remotest parts of the planet.

The first people to create an exhibition like this were the English in 1851; they were followed by the French in 1855. The French have followed the same pattern several times according to the circumstances of the period. Recently it's been decided to hold such an exhibition every ten years. The costs of 37.6

مرة، وقد بلغ مقدار ما أنفقته على إعداد هذا المعرض في المرة الأخيرة سنة ١٨٨٩ خمسين مليوناً من الفرنكات، وجاء ها بربح عشرة ملايين فوقها

وبالجملة فإنّ الإنسان يرى هناك فوق المدنية الغربية ما لا يتيسر له أن يراه في غير هذا المعرض إلا بإنفاق العمر في الأسفار، واحتمال المشاق في التجواب والتسيار، فإنك ترى فيه مجتمعاً ما تفرق في أنحاء العالم وأطراف المسكونة من أجناس البشر باديهم وحاضرهم، متوحشهم ومتمدنهم، ومن أنواع صناعاتهم وبضاعاتهم، وأسباب منافعهم ومرافقهم ما ليس يجتمع في مكان غير هوأي ميدان أوسع، وأي مجال أكبر لفكر الباحث في أحوال الأمم، وعاداتها وأخلاقها، وأسباب تقدمها وتأخرها، وعلل شقائها وسعادتها، من هذا المجتمع الذي هو سوق العالم أجمع، وعكاظ هذه العصور المتمدنة؟ وناهيك بما ورد في الأمر الصادر من رئيس الجمهورية الفرنسوية بإنشاء المعرض في هذا العام دليلاً على جلال هذا الأمر وفخامته حيث يقول: «إنّ هذا المعرض سيعرض على العالم ما أنتجته فكرة الإنسان وأوصله إليه اجتهاده في مسافة مائة عام من إتقان المعارف والفنون، ولا شك أنه سيكون لأهل العلم والمعرفة والحكمة والفلسفة مدخلاً جديداً إلى منهاج قويم يقود الأفكار إلى سبيل واضح تعلو فيه الحقيقة على التصوّر، ويكون هو المبتدع لطريقة الفلسفة التي يسير عليها هذا القرن».

قال عيسى بن هشام: فلحظت الباشا تلوح على وجهه علامات الميل والولع والتشوف إلى مشاهدة ما وصفه له الصاحب من أمر هذا المعرض العام، ثمّ التفت إليّ التفاتة المتطلب المتمني يقول: ٧.٣٧

الباشا تالله إنها لفرصة تشوّق الباحث المدقق، ولا ينبغي أن تفوت الطالب المحقق، وعسى الله أن يمكّننا من مشاهدة هذا المعرض قبل انقضائه، ويوفقنا إلى استقراء ما فيه واستقصائه.

putting on the most recent example in 1889 reached five million francs, and the profits were ten million.

In summary then, you get to see not only aspects of Western civilization but other things that it wouldn't be easy to locate unless you spent your entire life traveling and enduring all the hardships of travel. Things are brought together in Paris that are otherwise scattered across the globe among desert and urbanized societies—both primitive and advanced. The goods and products on display will never be collected in a single place such as this one or with broader scope for the inquiring mind that is interested in the states of the world's peoples, their customs, and their moral codes. One can investigate the causes of their progress and backwardness, and the factors influencing their happiness or misery. This collection of materials constitutes a market of the entire world, an 'Ukāẓ Fair for these periods of civilized society.[54] The significance of it all can be gauged from the decree issued by the French president, ordering the establishment of the exhibition this year. In it he says, "This exhibition will present to the entire world the products of the human mind; it will show how far mankind's initiatives have advanced in a hundred years of perfecting both knowledge and the arts. For scientists, intellectuals, philosophers, and sages it will undoubtedly offer a new gateway to sound strategies that will serve to guide mankind's ideas along a clear path through which truth will overtop fantasy. By so doing, the intellectual will be the inventor of a philosophical method to steer this century forward."

'Īsā ibn Hishām said: I noticed that the Pāshā's facial expression indicated a strong desire on his part to see the things at the exhibition that our Friend had been describing. The Pāshā looked at me, an obvious request evident in his expression: 37.7

PĀSHĀ By God, this is a huge opportunity for the inquiring scholar; no curious student should miss it! Maybe God will make it possible for us to see this "exposition" before it finishes, and we'll be able to examine what it has on offer.

عيسى بن هشام إن كنت على مثل هذا الاشتياق والتولع فما أستطيع لك ردًّا عن رغبتك، ولا أقصّر في إجابة طلبتك.

الصاحب فإن كان الأمر كذلك، فالمبادرة واجبة، وأنا معكما إن شئتما فلي عزم على ذلك من قبل ولست أجد مثلكما رفيقي سفر وأنيسي حضر يبحثان عن حقائق الأشياء، ويكشفان عن غوامض الأمور غطاء الأوهام، ويحسران عن أسرار النتائج ما تلبد عليها من تضليل الأفهام.

الباشا حبذا الصاحب ونعم الرفيق.

الصاحب فلنأخذ من الآن في أهبة السفر، وأرى أن تقوم في الحال لتدبر أمره، وتحصل على مكان لنا في إحدى السفن المسافرة في هذا الأسبوع، فقد بلغني أنه لا يوجد في السفن القائمة إلى أوربا مدى هذا الشهر مكان خال لتزاحم المسافرين على تأجير الأمكنة قبل السفر بالشهر أو الشهرين.

٨،٣٧ قال عيسى بن هشام: فما كان أسرع من أن نهض الباشا واستنهضنا معه للبحث عن مواضع لنا في أية سفينة كانت للتعجيل بالسفر، فلم نجد بعد شدة البحث والتنقيب وتتبع المظان سوى سفينة واحدة من سفن المحيط بها بضعة أماكن خالية، وهي ترسو على مدينة السويس، وتقصد في مسيرها ثغر مرسيليا من بلاد فرنسا، وها نحن نبارح القاهرة في يوم الأحد، ومن الله العون وعليه المعتمد.

'ĪSĀ IBN HISHĀM As long as you're that keen, I can't refuse or fail to respond to your request.

FRIEND If that's the case, we'll have to hurry. If you agree, I'll come with you. I've been thinking about it already. I can't imagine two more agreeable travel companions with whom to investigate the true nature of things, reveal those aspects that remain concealed behind a veil of fancy, and show the hidden consequences that emerge from mistaken ideas.

PĀSHĀ What a wonderful friend and fine companion!

FRIEND Let's make our preparations to travel. We'll need to start immediately by reserving places on a boat leaving this week. Many passengers booked their places a month or two in advance, and I've heard that there are no vacant spots on any boat leaving this month.

'Īsā ibn Hishām said: No one can have been quicker than the Pāshā to get to his 37.8
feet. We went with him to look for a place on any boat that was on the point of departing. After a good deal of checking and multiple visits we could only find a single boat with a few empty spaces. It was anchored at Port Suez from where it was heading for Marseille in France. So on Sunday we were to leave Cairo. It is from God that we request help, and upon Him that we rely.

مصباح الشرق ١١٦، ١٧ أغسطس ١٩٠٠

هذه هي الرسالة الأولى من حديث عيسى بن هشام عن زيارة معرض باريس بعث بها إلينا السيد محمد المويلحي بعد رسالته التي نشرناها في أحد أعدادنا الماضية عن زيارة سمو الجناب العالي الخديوي لجلالة ملكة الانجليز في بلادها. ١،٣٨

باريس

قال عيسى بن هشام: ومذ ألقينا بباريس العصا، واستقرت بنا النوى، قصدنا منها الطرقات الجامعة، والساحات الواسعة، فلا الخلق وهم يحشرون، ولا الموتى وهم ينشرون، ولا الأحياء تدعى وتهرع، ولا القبائل تحشد وتجمع، ولا الخميس في كبكبته تحت العجاج الأكدر، ولا الناس في فزعهم يوم الفزع الأكبر، يضاهي ما القوم فيه من اصطدام وازدحام، واقتحام والتحام، فتراهم يموج بعضهم في بعض، وتضيق بهم على رحبها رقعة الأرض، ويتدفقون في سيرهم تدفق السيل، تحت أضواء محت آية الليل فلا ليل يخشى فيها على الأبصار أن تعشو من شدة الأنوار، وتنخدع لها الديكة فتوالي الصياح، إيذاناً بانبلاج الصباح. ٢،٣٨

فإذا نظرت إلى الشارع من العلوّ، لم تبال بالغلوّ، إن قلت بحر مسجور، قام عليه شاطئان من نور، وإذا شاهدته عند أوّله من أسفله، قلت أسراب الدوّ تصعد في الجوّ، بين الكواكب الزهراء من كرات الكهرباء، وقد انعقدت فوقه من الأشجار قبة خضراء أغنت القوم عن قبة الخضراء، ثمّ ترى البيوت شاهقة باسقة، متآلفة متناسقة، كأنّ في اتساقها سطور الخط، وكأنّ ما تدلى من الأزهار على جدرانها شكل ونقط، تعلو بنيانها السحاب، وتحاول أن تعلق من السماء بأسباب، فأين منها ما بناه لفرعون هامان، وشاده جن سليمان لسليمان، ورفعه سنمار للنعمان، بل أين معارج الجبال من مدارج النمال، والبحر العباب من لامع السراب، لا بل أين شماريخ ثبير من سنام البعير، وأجرام الكواكب من بيوت العناكب.

Miṣbāḥ al-sharq 116, August 17, 1900[55]

This is the first episode of *Hadīth ʿĪsā ibn Hishām* concerning the visit to the Paris Exhibition. It has been sent to us by Muḥammad al-Muwayliḥī following his previous report on the visit of the Khedive of Egypt to Her Majesty the Queen of England. 38.1

Paris[56]

It was in Paris that we finally threw down our staff and reached our destination. We now started making our way along the network of streets and across broad squares. To tell the truth, no gathering on Judgment Day, no dead being raised, no living persons hastily summoned, no tribes gathering in assembly, no troops routed in the heat of battle, no people in the utmost panic—none of them could possibly rival the way people were crammed together, all shoving, pushing, clashing with, and jostling one another. They kept surging against one another so that even the broad expanse of earth was not spacious enough. They careened past us like a flood beneath lights that eliminated the dark. There was no night, and the lights were so bright that one would have to be worried about night blindness. Indeed the cock might have been deceived and started crowing to announce the arrival of morning. 38.2

If you surveyed the street from above, you would not consider it to be a hyperbole in stating that it was a veritable sea with crashing waves, with two shores of light on either side. Viewed from below, you would have said that they were desert flocks rising in the air amidst gleaming stars made up of electric lights. Over it all clustered trees, creating a green dome that replaced the heavenly dome itself. On either side there were lofty houses neatly arrayed; it was as though there was a kind of calligraphy in their harmony, with the flowers on their walls giving the letters shapes and dots. Their structures reached to the very clouds and tried to hang by ropes from the heavens. Compared with these, what can one say about Haman's construction for the Pharaoh, what Solomon's jinn erected for him, and what Sinmār built for Nuʿmān? And what, for that matter, concerning mountain slopes against anthills, the raging sea as compared to a gleaming mirage, the peaks of Mount Thabīr compared to mere camel humps, or celestial stars compared to a spider's web?

وتأمّلنا المارة في هذا الموقف المتزاحم، والمأزق المتلاحم، من كل شاب وكهل، وعجوز وطفل، وفتى وفتاة، يتسابقون ركبانًا ومشاة، وألوف العجل تخترق صفوف الناس، وتنفذ بينهم نفوذ السهام عن الأقواس، طائرة بالبخار أو بالكهرباء أو الأفراس:

ولما لم يسابقهن شيء
من الحيوان سابقن الظلالا

٣،٣٨ فترى كل سائر منهم في اضطراب العصفور، وتلفت القطا المذعور، إن خانته لفتته وافته موتته، وإن عثرت قدمه هريق دمه، وإن شمخ شامخ منهم بأنفه وقع في حتفه، فهم يلتمسون شاكلتي الطريق كما يلتمس الشاطئ الغريق، والحوانيت على الجانبين فيها ما شئت من بدائع البضائع، ونفائس الصنائع، تغوي الزاهد فيشتهيها، وتغري البخيل فيشتريها، والحانات بينها ممتلئة بالنفوس، مشحونة بالجلوس، أمام كل واحد منهم كأس الصهباء، وفي يده جريدة المساء، ونحن في هذا الموقف تكاد تطيش منا العقول، من شدة الدهش والذهول، وتطير منا الألباب من كثرة الاضطراب:

في ساحة لو أنّ لقمانًا بها
وهو الحكيم لكان غير حكيم

فمال بنا طلب الراحة، إلى حان في تلك الساحة، فلم نجد به مكانًا خاليًا من الزحام، فعكفنا واقفين على الأقدام، وكدنا نذهب عنه يائسين لولا أن قام بعض الجالسين فذهبوا لشأنهم، وجلسنا في مكانهم، وقعدنا في هذا المأمن نتصفح وجوه الحاضرين، وأشكال المارين، فإذا عدد ربات الحجال أربى من عدد الرجال، من كل ذات حسن وجمال، وتيه ودلال، وخد متورد، وقدّ متأود:

تختال في صفوف الألوان
من فاقع وناصع وقان

We watched as people hassled each other in such a close-packed situation, with everyone barging against everyone else—men both young and middle-aged, old folk and children, boys and girls—some of them riding, others on foot. Thousands of bicycles plunged through the crowd, clearing a path like arrows shot from a bow, seemingly flying as though powered by electricity, steam, or horses:

And, when no animal challenged them,
they chased their very shadows.[57]

They all seemed as frightened as sparrows, looking anxiously around like 38.3
scared sandgrouse in the desert. One false glance, and they would be dead; one slip of the foot, and blood would flow; a single disdainful stare, and perdition would soon ensue. They all stuck to the two sides of the street, like a drowning man clutching the shore. On either side the shops were loaded down with incredible wares, costly goods, things that would lead the most fervent ascetic astray and make him desire them, that would tempt the stingiest of misers into buying them. The bars alongside were all full of customers and crowds of people sitting down; everyone had a glass of wine in one hand and the evening newspaper in the other. In this kind of situation we were so shocked and befuddled that we almost lost our minds; such was the anxiety we felt that we hardly knew where to turn:

In a square where even Luqmān the wise,
were he there, would not be so wise.[58]

Needing some place to rest, we headed for a bar in the square, but, such was the crowd that we could find nowhere to sit down. After spending some time on our feet, we were on the point of departing in despair, but some people got up to leave and go their way, so we took their places and sat in a spot from which we could observe the expressions on people's faces and watch passersby. We immediately noticed that there were more women than men and that they were handsome, attractive, and flirtatious, with curvaceous figures and rosy cheeks:

In a kaleidoscope of color they swaggered,
Bright yellow gleaming and deep red.[59]

وهنّ يسرعن في المشي، ويرفلن في الوشي، ويتبارين في رفع الفضول من الأطراف والذيول:

ويبسمن عن درّ تقلّدن مثله
كأنّ التراقي وشّحت بالمباسم

وينتشر عنهن من النشر والطيب، ما لا ينتشر عن الزهر في الغصن الرطيب، ويضربن الأرض بأرجلهنّ، ويزحزحن ما استطعن من حللهن، ويرسلن سهام العيون، فيحركن ساكن الشجون:

إشارة أفواه وغمز حواجب
وتكسير أجفان وكف تسلم

وأصناف الباعة يكثرون بين ذلك من الغدو والرواح، ويبحون في النداء والصياح، بمثل العواء والنباح، ويبالغون في الإلحاف والإلحاح.

ولمّا أفقنا برهة أخذ الباشا كعادته في الاستفهام والسؤال، يستكشف مني جلية الحال، ويقول: ما أشك في أنّ هذا اليوم يوم عيد، عند أهل هذا العالم الجديد، أو هم سكان مهاجرون، أو جند ظافرون، قفلوا من حومة المنايا بالغنائم والسبايا، فأقول له: لا، بل هي كما يصفها الواصفون، ويعرفها العارفون، تلك «المدينة الفاضلة»، وأمّ المدنية الكاملة، وطن العمران والحضارة، ومظهر الزينة والنضارة، ومنبت العز والمجد، ومصدر النحس والسعد، بل هي تلك عندهم إرم ذات العماد التي لم يخلق مثلها في البلاد، لو رآها صاحب الإيوان كسرى أنوشروان، لم يفخر بإيوان ولا قصر، ولحكم بأنّ «المدائن» عندها سبسب قفر، ولو اطّلع عليها قيصر الرومان لرمى التاج عن جبينه، وقضيب الملك من يمينه، ولأقسم أنّ رومية وهي عاصمة الدنيا، قرية حقيرة لديها من الطبقة الدنيا، مثل التي ذكرها في كشفه عن طماعيته قبل ولايته، فقال أفضّل أن أكون الأوّل في أدنى قرية، ولا أكون الثاني في مدينة رومية، ولو ٤،٣٨

Strutting their finery and hurrying along, these ladies kept outdoing each other in showing off skirts and hems:

> As they smiled, they revealed pearly teeth,
> as though their very necks were bedecked in smiles.[60]

They exuded too the sweet fragrance of perfume, the like of which no flower ever exuded on a dewy branch. They kept tapping the ground with their feet and clinking their jewels as much as possible, shooting forth arrowed glances that stirred latent sorrows;

> Mouth gestures, the twitch of an eyebrow,
> eyelids aflutter, and the wave of a hand.[61]

Peddlers kept coming and going, yelling and shouting like so many howling hyenas and barking dogs as they proffered their wares with their usual insistence.

Once we had come to our senses, the Pāshā started asking questions, as was his wont. He wanted to know precisely what was happening. "I've no doubt," he said, "that this must be a festival day for the people of this new world; either that or they're immigrants or soldiers returning from combat; now that they're no longer facing death, they're bringing back spoils and captives." "No," I replied, "the situation was just as people had described and those in the know were fully aware: this is 'the virtuous city,'[62] the mother of perfect civilization, the very haven of cultured urbanity, site of refinement and grace, homeland of honor and glory, and source of both calamity and felicity. For these people it was Iram with its many pillars, something the like of which no other country could possibly create. Were Chosroes Anushirwan, the builder of the famous portico, to set his eyes on this city, he would no longer be able to boast of portico or palace; he would judge his famous Madā'in to be a desert wasteland. If the Roman Caesar were to lay his eyes on it, he would rip the crown off his brow and the royal staff from his hand, then swear that the city of Rome itself, the world's capital, was a pathetic little village, the kind that he described in this way before he came to power: 'I would rather be the first person in a lowly village than the second in a Roman city.' Were Plato, the philosopher of his 38.4

شاهدها أفلاطون حكيم الزمان، لم يقل فيما غبر من الأوان، أحمد الله على نعم ثلاث يعجز عن حمدها اللسان، ولا يقوم بحقها شكران، أن خلقني من نوع الإنسان لا من نوع الحيوان، ومن جنس الرجال لا من جنس النسوان، ثمّ جعل نسبتي دون البلاد إلى عاصمة اليونان، ولو نظر إليها هاروت وماروت، لم يماريا في أنّ بابل بجانبها فلاة سبروت:

لجنة الخلد تسرّ من رأى
فتزدري الخلد وسرّ من رأى.

٥،٣٨ هذه هي مدينة العلم والفضل، ودار السلام والعدل، ومهد الحرية والإنصاف، وحمى المساواة والائتلاف، والمدرسة التي يتلقى فيها الإنسان حقوق الإنسان، ويعرف منها وجوه الخير والإحسان، ولكل إنسان وطن، وهي وحدها وطن الأوطان، تشرق منها على العالم شمس الهدى والعرفان، فتنير العقول وتجلو البصائر، وتهدي في ظلمات الجهل كل ضال وحائر، لولاها لم يعرف الإنسان لنفسه من قدر، ولم يأمن في داره غائلة الاغتيال والغدر، فقدكفت عن الناس عاديات المظالم، وكفتهم بائقات المغارم، وعلمتهم كيف تؤتى المكارم، وتجتنب المحارم، وكيف يعيش البشر في دار البلاء والشقاء، عيشة الأخيار الأتقياء، والأطهار الأنقياء، تحت راية الحرية والمساواة والإخاء، إذا ناداها المظلوم من أي جنس وأي قوم، أجابته: لبيك مات الظلم فلا ظلم اليوم.

وهؤلاء أهلها كما تراهم يهجرون الرقاد، ويواصلون السهاد، ويصرفون الحياة في الجد والعمل، ولا ينتهي بهم أمل إلا إلى أمل فليس على هممهم شيء بمحال في كل حال، يذيبون بعزمهم الحديد، وتلين لإشارتهم صم الجلاميد، وينسجون الهواء، ويكتبون على الماء، ويفتلون الحبال من الرمال، ويزيلون راسيات الجبال برائشات النبال، وينضبون الدأماء بمتح الدلاء، ويصرعون ظلام الليل فلا يبلغ فيهم أمدا، ويجعلون النهار عليهم سرمدا:

age, to have seen it, he would never have declared in olden times: 'I praise God for three blessings that the human tongue cannot laud sufficiently nor offer due thanks, namely that I was created a man and not an animal; then that I was made a man and not a woman; and thirdly that I am a citizen of Athens and not of any other country.' If Hārūt and Mārūt had been aware of it, they would never have argued with the notion that, compared with Paris, Babylon was a wasteland:

Like paradise itself it pleases the viewer,
scoffing at the palaces of Khuld and Surra Man Ra'ā.

"Today this city is the home of learning and excellence, the haven of peace and justice, the cradle of liberty and fairness, and sanctuary of unity and concord. It is that school where humanity encounters the rights of man and learns the different aspects of charity and beneficence. All people have their own homeland, but this place is the homeland of homelands, the place from which the sun of guidance and knowledge radiates across the world. Minds are enlightened and insights are disclosed; anyone led astray and perplexed is guided out of the dark corners of ignorance. If it did not exist, mankind would not be aware of its own potential, nor would people feel safe from intrigue and assassination in their own homes. It wards off from people the ravages of injustice and compensates them against the calamities of debt. It educates them in the ways of generosity and the avoidance of burdens and taboos; how people living in hard times can still be content, devout, modest, and pure, all under the banner of 'liberté, égalité, fraternité.' Should any tyrant, no matter what gender or nation, proclaim that slogan, France will respond, We hear you! Death to injustice. There is to be no such thing today. 38.5

"As you can see, these are people who never sleep but are perpetually awake; they spend their entire lives on serious matters and work. One aspiration leads to another; where their ambition is concerned, nothing is impossible, no matter what the situation. Their resolution allows them to melt solid steel; a mere gesture on their part, and solid rocks disintegrate. They can melt air, write on water, plait ropes out of sand, level lofty peaks with feathered arrows, dry out entire seas with buckets, and defeat the darkness of night. For them it has no limit, and they can turn daytime into eternity.

أولئك النـاس إن عـدوا بأجمعـهم
ومن سواهـم فلغو غيـر معـدود
والفـرق بين الورى جمـعاً وبيـنهم
كالفـرق مـا بين معـدوم وموجود

أقول قولي هذا والباشا يسمع ويتأمّل، و«الصاحب» بجانبي يتضجر ويتململ، فالتفت إليه أستخبره الخبر، عن سبب الضجر، فما أتممت أحرف السؤال حتى انهال علينا في المقال، انهيال السيل من مشرف عال: ٦.٣٨

الصاحب قد شبعنا وسئمنا من سماع هذه المبالغة، وترداد هذا الغلو على آذاننا عن هذه الديار منذ سنين وأعوام، وأولى ما يوصف هذا الوصف للغائب عنها لا للحاضر فيها، وأنت رجل بحاث نباث من شأنك استنباط الغوامض، واستجلاء الدخائل، وألزم ما يكون لنا الآن أن نجعل فكرنا مجرداً عن هذه الأوصاف والأخبار التي شحنت خيالنا من قديم، والأجدر بنا أن نتناساها ولا نذكرها ليكون حكمنا على المشاهدة والعيان خالياً عن مقدمات سبقت لنا على الغيب، ورسخت في أذهاننا بالخبر.

وقد علمت أنّ ذهن الإنسان يغلب عليه الانقباض من الفحص والتمحيص، ولا يباشره غالباً إلا ملجأ إليه لما في التسليم المطلق والتصديق المعجل من راحة البال وقد يرتسم في خيال الإنسان أمر بالخبر فيستحسنه لأوّل وهلة، ثمّ يركن إليه فيرد كل ما يرد عليه من قبيله إلى صحيفة الاستحسان والقبول في نفسه، وإذا هو استقبح أمراً كان الأمر كذلك على هذا الترتيب ولذلك نرى العاشق يعجب بكل ما يصدر عن معشوقه ويعدّه جليلا نبيلا وإن كان في واقع الأمر معيبا مشيناً للميل الأوّل والاستحسان السابق، واستعداد لوحة الرضا والقبول لانتقاشه فيها، ومن هنا قولهم:

وعين الرضى عن كل عيب كليلة
كما أن اعين السخط تبدي المساويا.

Considered as a whole in comparison with others,
those people are a limitless riddle.
The difference between them and the rest of humanity
is like that between existence and nonexistence."[63]

As I was saying all this, the Pāshā sat there listening and thinking. Meanwhile the Friend was muttering and complaining. I turned to ask him what was on his mind, why was he so annoyed. Hardly had I posed my question before he burst into speech, regaling us like a flood from a lofty height: **38.6**

FRIEND We're tired and fed up listening to this type of exaggerated talk and the way it's been repeated about these places for years and years. It's all more appropriate for someone who has never been here rather than people who are actually in this country now. You're an astute observer of things, used to unraveling obscurities and looking beneath the surface of things. The key thing for us to do now is to separate our ideas from descriptions like this and the kind of information that has burdened our imaginations for such a long time. We need to forget it all and not refer to it, so that our judgments can be founded on actual observation and not on preliminary information that has become fixed in our minds.

You're already aware that mankind tends to avoid precise inquiry and investigation; for the most part people only get involved as a last resort because it's much more comforting simply to accept things as they are and acknowledge them without any fuss. When something gets implanted in a person's mind, he'll accept it at once, then rely on it and subsequently approve anything in that category. If he disapproves of something, the same principle applies. Thus we see a lover admiring everything about his beloved and considering it all to be sublime and noble, even though in fact it is reprehensible and wrong; and all because of the primary instinct, his former approval and his ingrained predilection to be content and happy with his decisions. This is why it's been said that:

The eye of pleasure is blind to all faults;
the resentful eye likewise evinces evil deeds.[64]

٧،٣٨ ولقد نرى الرجل الشاعر الأديب إذا أنشدته بيتاً من الشعر لم يكن يحفظه لأبي تمام أو لأبي الطيب ولم تسمّ له قائله ربما استهجنه ولم يستمله، فإذا سمّيته له عاد إلى الاستحسان وأخذ يتمحل وجوه التمحل لقائل البيت (وأبواب التمحل لا منتهى لحدها) إن كان في البيت ما يستهجن حقيقة وما ذلك إلا لما اطمأنت عليه نفسه وتعودته من القبول والاستحسان لشعر هذين الشاعرين.

ومن أجل هذا ترى كثيراً من الأمور التي يستحسنها الإنسان أو يستقبحها بالتسليم والتصديق دون الامتحان، لا بد أن يبقى منها أثر في النفس مهما حاول انتزاعها عند الفحص والتأمل واتضاح البرهان له جلياً على خطائه وفساد حكمه فيها، وربما أخذته العزة والأنفة أن يرجع إلى حكم البرهان في استقباح ما كان عنده حسناً، واستحسان ما كان لديه قبيحاً خيفة الاستشهار بالتناقض في الرأي والتقلب في الاختيار

ومن هذا كله يستخرج معنى البخت والحظ والإقبال الذي يصيب الإنسان في دنياه أن صادف عمله صحيفة الاستحسان في النفوس، ومعنى النحس والتعس والإدبار أن وافق ما يأتيه عند الناس لوحة الاستقباح:

إذا أقبل الإنسان في الدهر صدّقت
أحاديثه عن نفسه وهو كاذب.

٨،٣٨ وهؤلاء الغربيين عموماً والفرنسويين خصوصاً عهدناهم لا نتصفح لهم كتاباً، ولا نقرأ لهم سطراً، ولا نسمع لهم حديثاً إلا بتمجيد عظمة مدنيتهم، والافتخار على العالم طراً بنظام معيشتهم، وأنهم أرباب الخلق وسادة البشر، وأنّ الهدى هداهم، والضلال في من عداهم، وبفضلهم يخرج الناس من الظلمات إلى النور، ومن العمى إلى البصر، وذاعت فينا أقوالهم هذه عن أنفسهم، وأعانهم على ذلك منا من أعانهم، فاعتقدنا ما يقولون، وسلمنا لهم أنّ كل ما يأتونه منصرف إلى جانب الجميل، وفتحنا لهم صحيفة الاستحسان في النفس، يرتسم فيها كل ما يخيلونه لنا ويخبروننا عنه فلنطرح عنا إذاً

You may see, for example, an erudite poet listening as you recite a line of poetry by Abū Tammām or Abū l-Ṭayyib al-Mutanabbī that he hasn't memorized. When you don't name the poet, he may scoff at it and refuse to acknowledge its qualities. But once you tell him the name, he changes his tune and praises it to the skies. If there actually are some reasons for criticizing the line, he'll start wheedling his way around things (and there exists an infinite number of such ruses). The reason is that he has to reconcile himself to the fact that he habitually approves of any poetry by these two renowned poets. 38.7

That's why we can see that there exist numerous things to which humans either give their credulous approval or disapproval without close examinations that are bound to have a residual effect on them. Even when close investigation and evident proof make clear that their judgments are in error and based on false premises, they'll still find it hard to get rid of those preconceptions. People are frequently too proud and arrogant to change their opinions and disapprove of something that they previously regarded as good and vice versa, and all because they're afraid of earning a reputation for holding contradictory opinions and changing their minds.

From all this we can glean the extent of the good fortune and felicity that a person may acquire on this earth if his works manage to engender the approval of people, and, on the other hand, the degree of misery and revulsion that will result when the work meets with disapproval:

When a person ventures forth in his destiny, his depictions
of himself will be credited, though he be a liar.[65]

With regard to these Europeans in general and the French in particular, we've become inured to never leafing through a book, reading something they've written, or listening to a conversation of theirs without encountering encomiums concerning their civilization and boasts to the entire world about how well organized their life is. They're paragons of morality, lords of mankind. True guidance belongs to them, and anyone who opposes them is in error. Thanks to them people have emerged from darkness into light, from blindness to sight. Their statements about themselves have spread far and wide, duly assisted by those of us who have offered them help. We've believed what they've been telling us and granted them that everything they offer has to be good. For them we've opened a page stamped with approval on to which is imprinted everything they conceive for us and tell us about. So let's discard all 38.8

ما قالوا وما وصفوا، وما بالغوا فيه وتنالوا، ولننظر الآن هنا إلى الأمور في حقائقها، ونحكم عليها بحسب قيمتها في ذاتها لا على حسب ما رسمه فينا الوهم وسوله الخيال وهذا الباشا والحمد لله رجل يمتاز عنا بأنه كان بعيداً عن هذا الخلق، محتجباً عن دنيانا دهراً طويلا، فبقي خالي الذهن مماّ شحن رؤوسنا من حوادث هذه المدنية وأخبارها، فحكمه الآن على ما يشاهده العيان يكون أصح حكم، ونظره فيها أدق نظر فإذا نظرنا معه بمثل نظره متجردين عن الهوى أمكن لنا أن نقف خير وقوف على الحق والباطل، والخطأ والصواب في نظام هذه المدنية الغربية، فنكون منها على بيّنة نبيّنها لمن يريد أن يستبينها من قومنا وأهل بلادنا.

٩،٣٨ عيسى بن هشام كأنك تريد أن نفارق الإجماع، ونخالف السنّة، ونقابل الناس بما لم يتعوّدوه، ونواجههم بغير الذي ألفوه، وننتقد لهم ما هو خال عندهم من كل انتقاد، وننتقص ما هو لديهم بالغ حد الكمال بريء من العاب والذام، فيرمونا بغلظة الطبع وقلة الفهم وسخف الرأي وسوء الحكم ولا يفوتنك أنّ كثيراً من ذوي الرشد والسداد يقولون ليست كل حقيقة تقال، ولا كل صحيح يروى

أوليس من الصواب حينئذ أن نسير على أسلوب الذين زاروا هذه البلاد فنرجع على أهل الشرق باللائمة في انخفاضهم وارتفاع أهل الغرب فوقهم، ونصف لهم ما وصل إليه القوم من القوة والمنعة، والعزة والعظمة، والنعيم والسعة، والسعادة والترف، ونحن لا نزال راقدين رقادنا الطويل في كهوف الانكماش والخمول، وزوايا الخمود والخضوع، يقولون فنسمع ويأمرون فنمتثل، ويقتسمون أرزاقنا فنشكر، وينتقصون أرضنا فنحمد، ويحتلون ديارنا فنقبل؟ أفلا أقل من أن نسهب في بيان الأسباب التي ارتقت بهم إلى مرتبتهم في الوجود، ونطنب في شرح القواعد التي أسسوا عليها بنيانهم لنحذو حذوهم، ونعمل على شاكلتهم أو ليس الأليق بنا أن نحض قومنا أن ينفضوا عنهم غبار الكسل، ويخلعوا لباس الذل، ويهبوا إلى تقليد هؤلاء المجدّين المجتهدين في أنواع الكمالات، ويأخذوا فيما هم فيه آخذون، ويتبعوا ما هم له متبعون أو لست ترى من أبواب الحث والتحريض أن نعظم ونفخم ما استطعنا في وصف

the things they've said and described in such exaggerated terms. Instead let's now investigate things here as they really are. That way we'll be able to judge them according to their intrinsic merits rather than on the basis of whatever our fancies and imaginations have crafted for us. We have with us—thanks be to God!— the Pāshā, someone distinct from the rest of us in that he was far removed from such people and shielded from this world of ours by a considerable period of time. His mind is therefore uncluttered by the kind of information about this civilization that burdens our own minds. As a result his verdict now on the things he is observing will be more valid and his opinions more precise. If we can share such an untrammeled vision with him, ridding ourselves of other inclinations, we'll be able to point with complete accuracy to the elements of truth and falsehood, right and wrong, to be found within this system of Western civilization. That way we'll be better able to explain things to people in our country who ask about it.

'Īsā ibn Hishām You seem to want us to depart from consensus and 38.9
go against the norm; to present and confront people with the unusual and unfamiliar. We'll be criticizing things which in their minds are entirely free of criticism and finding fault with what they believe to be flawless and innocent of any notion of disapproval or disgrace. They'll accuse us of misguided and biased opinions and narrowmindedness. And don't forget that many insightful people say that not every truth needs to be pronounced and not every sound judgment should be told. So isn't it a good idea for us to follow the lead of people who've visited this country before by blaming Eastern peoples for their lower cultural status and the superiority of the West? Shouldn't we be describing the powerful position and symptoms of greatness that we see in the pleasant circumstances in which the peoples of the West are living, while we remain stuck in our profound slumber, happy to remain recumbent in the caves of lassitude and apathy? They do the talking, and we listen. They give the orders, and we obey. They apportion our livelihood for us, and we're duly grateful. They purloin our lands, and we give thanks. They occupy our territories, and we accept it all. Surely the least we can do is to research the reasons for their lofty position in the universe and go to great lengths to explore the bases upon which their civilization has been founded. In that way we'll be able to do likewise and follow their lead. Shouldn't we be encouraging our own people to throw off the dust of indolence and discard the garb of degradation so that they can start imitating these industrious Europeans who are assiduous

هذه المدنية، ونكبرها في أعينهم، ونعلي قدرها في صدورهم، ونبكتهم بأحاديثها، ونعيرهم بأخبارها، ونرفع من شأنها بقدر ما نحط من قدرنا، ليكون التعيير أشد، والاستنهاض أبلغ، والإثارة أعم وهذا الإنسان لم يتعلم في دنياه ما تعلم إلا بالمباراة والمنابذة، والمناضلة والمفاضلة في السباق واللحاق، ولو لم يقل الأستاذ للتلميذ إلا أجدت وأصبت ولم يعيره بسبق غيره له أكنت تراه يجد في الأخذ ويجتهد في التحصيل؟

١٠،٣٨ **الصاحب** ليس يخفى على فطنتك باديء الأمر أنّ جل الذين تحكي عن طريقتهم ومذهبهم ممّن زار هذه البلاد من قومنا ورجعوا إلى بلادهم فحدثوا عنها وكتبوا، ووصفوا وحكموا، ينقسمون إلى عدة أقسام:

القسم الأوّل قسم الطلبة الذين تلقوا في هذه البلاد دروسهم، وهؤلاء لما هم فيه من غلواء الشباب، ومن الاشتغال بالطلب، ولما هو أمامهم من وجوه الإباحة التي لم يتمتعوا بها في بلادهم يكتفون في ما يرونه بالظواهر، ولا يكادون يقدرون على البحث والفحص، ودقة التمييز بين الفضيلة والرذيلة في أهل هذه المدنية الغربية، بل هي تتصور لهم في صورة معظمة، ويأخذونها على الجملة زاهية زاهرة، فإذا انقلبوا إلى أهليهم رووا لنا عنها مثل حديث العاشق عن معشوقه في أوقات نشوته وإبان سكره، وأجهدوا أنفسهم أن يظهر عليهم أثر من علامات تلك المدنية المعظمة ممّا يخف عليهم حمله، وتهون تكاليفه ليلحقوا بأنفسهم شيئاً من تلك العظمة التي ارتسمت في خيالهم، وبهروا أعين الناس بوصفها ونعتها، ولسنا من هذا الصف.

١١،٣٨ القسم الثاني جماعة قصدوا هذه البلاد لمجرد النزهة والسياحة، وهم قلما يبحثون في ما ينظرون، فلا يلتفتون إلى هذه المدنية إلا من وجه تطبيق العيان على الخبر، ومن بحث منهم فانكشف له فيها عيب، أو بدا له نقص كره تغيير الرأي ونسخ ما تركب في الذهن، وعزت عليه خيبة المأمول فيعود إلينا يكمل من عنده ما نقص منها في نظره، واتخذ سبيل المغالاة سبيلا لاستعداد نفوس السامعين إلى تقبل ما يقال من هذا القبيل بالرضا وحسن القبول وأضف ما إلى ذلك ما في مخالفة المعهود من المشقة

in their pursuit of such perfection? Isn't it a good way of initiating such a process of encouragement to show this civilization in the best possible light and making them realize its great achievements? We can make our people aware of its enormous significance and use accounts of it to blame them for their own behavior. We'll be able to show how important this civilization is by making use of comparison in order to show how much lower our own is. The reproach will be all the stronger that way, the incentive to imitate will be more robust, and the stimulation will be more general. Mankind has only ever learned anything through competition, resistance, struggle, and the challenge to win. If a teacher only tells his student how well he's doing and never lets him know that he's not doing as well as others, do you imagine that he'll ever study hard or succeed in learning?

FRIEND To begin with, you're obviously well aware that all the people about whom you've been talking have visited this country and returned home again. They have talked about it all, written things, come to conclusions, and delivered their own verdict. They fall into specific categories: 38.10

The first group consists of students who have come here to study. They're all young and busy with their studies, and they encounter here a degree of license that they don't talk about in their own country. They content themselves with superficialities. They're hardly capable of any real research or of casting a discriminating eye on what is good and bad among the people in this Western civilization. Indeed it all emerges in a magnified light, and they paint the whole thing in glowing colors. When they get back to their families, they talk about it like a lover describing his beloved at the height of his passion. They try as hard as possible to show traces of this magnified culture so as to lessen the burdens it imposes and make light of its costs. They can then claim for themselves a bit of the aura of greatness that has been imprinted in their imaginations, an impression they use to impress other people as well. We don't belong to this particular group.

The second group consists of people who visit this country as tourists— 38.11
for pleasure, and that's all. Such people rarely investigate the things they're observing. The only way they look at this Western civilization is based solely on visual impressions. If anyone does go to the trouble of checking further and uncovers some of its flaws or if he comes to realize the problem of having to change his mind and cancel his previous impressions, then he finds his frustrated hopes hard to bear. He comes back to his own country ready to round

والكلفة، وما يكون في الاختصاص بمشاهدة المحاسن من المزية والفضل على من لم يشاهدها من السامعين، ولسنا من هذا الصنف.

١٢،٣٨ القسم الثالث فئة من أرباب المراتب والوظائف في الحكومة، يفرّون إلى هذه الديار من أسر الخدمة مسافة الشهر والشهرين فرار الأسير عند الإطلاق، وهؤلاء فيهم أولئك الذين تلقوا دروسهم فيها من أهل القسم الأوّل، وأمرهم كما تبيّن ظاهر، وحكمهم معلوم وفيهم من لم يتعلم مثلهم في أوروبا، فهم يبارونهم ويسابقونهم في ما جروا عليه ليلتحقوا بهم، ويحشروا في زمرتهم، ويرتفع عنهم امتيازهم عليهم فلا يرون إلا بمثل رأيهم، ولا ينظرون إلا بمثل نظرهم وعلى كل حال فأهل هذا القسم على العموم لا وقت عندهم للبحث والتأمل والتفكر والتدبر فيما يرونه، فإنّ كل واحد منهم لا ينفك مدة زيارته مشتغل الفكر، منقسم النظر بين أمرين: عين تنظر إلى ما بقي في صحيفة إجازته من الأيام، وعين ترمق ما بقي في كيس الدراهم من الدراهم، ولسنا من هذه المرتبة.

١٣،٣٨ وجميع هذه الأقسام كما ترى مكفوف عن البحث، مدفوع بالطبع إلى المبالغة في الوصف والغلو في الشرح، لأنّ الناس لا يرون لهم فضلا في الرواية والنقل منذ القديم إلا إذا أضافوا عليه من عندهم شيئاً، ولما في حكاية الغريب ورواية الجديد والاستماع له من اللذة والاستمتاع، وقلما استعصى فكر الإنسان عن الميل إلى التحدث بالغريب المعجب والجديد المطرب منذ خلق الله آدم إلى اليوم، ومنذ جرى حديث الأوّلين عن الجن والعفاريت، والأغوال والسعالي، إلى قصة ألف ليلة وليلة، وسيرة عنترة وعبلة.

١٤،٣٨ إلا أنّ عندنا قسماً رابعاً ربما بحث وفحص ووقف وعلم، ولكن له هوى خاصاً به يمنعه من كشف الحقائق، ويدفعه إلى المبالغة على القصد والغلو على العمد، فهو يروي لنا ما يرويه عن هذه المدنية بالتشييد والتمجيد باطلا كان أو حقاً لينصر مذهباً اعتمده، وغرضاً له عول عليه، فيدأب بيننا جاهداً في رفع الأجنبي، وإعلاء شأنه في مدنيته وحضارته ليرتفع معه بارتفاعه، ويعلو بيننا بعلوّه، ولينال بفضل جاهه وتمكين مكانته

off the faulty opinions he had in the first place and indulges in hyperbole as a way of preparing his listeners to accept such talk with pleasure and satisfaction. To which you can add the difficulties attached to going against the grain of the familiar and the fact that listeners will much prefer to concentrate on favorable impressions. We don't belong to this second category either.

The third category consists of holders of government offices who spend a 38.12 month or two escaping to France from the clutches of their jobs here—like prisoners loosed from their chains. Some of them have learned everything they know from representatives of my first category, so their attitude is obvious enough and their judgments are predictable. Unlike the first category, however, some of them have never studied in Europe, so they do their utmost to compete with them so they can join them, attach themselves to their coterie, and remove the distinction between the two categories. As a result, they copy their opinions and see everything through their eyes. At all events, people in this third category mostly have little spare time for research, contemplation, and evaluation regarding the things they are observing. So throughout the visit they all spend the entire time preoccupied and perplexed about two important matters: one eye looking at the amount of time left on his visa; and the other checking on how much money he has left in his purse. We don't belong to this group either.

As we've noticed, all these groups have their eyes closed to research and 38.13 naturally insist on exaggerating the things they describe. Since time immemorial people have only ascribed value to such accounts when things have been added. People obviously enjoy listening to stories about exotic and new phenomena. Rarely has mankind ever rejected a natural inclination to talk about strange and wonderful, fresh and exciting things from God's creation of Adam right up to the present day. Our forebears regularly talked about genies, demons, ghouls, and witches, all the way up to the tales of the *1001 Nights* and the Saga of ʿAntar and ʿAblah.

There may also be a fourth group, one that does do research, that investi- 38.14 gates, pauses, and learns. However, it has its own particular motivation that prevents it from uncovering truths and leads it to overemphasize its goals and intentions. This group only shares the things that it narrates about this civilization in order to bolster and extol the things that it describes, be they true or false, and all in order to support a designated idea or a predetermined goal. Such people are accustomed to doing their utmost to extol foreigners

فينا ما لم يكن ليناله بوسيلة سواه وفي هذا القسم من يرى أنّ في استيلاء المدنية الغربية على الشرق وتغييرها لقديم عاداته وأخلاقه، وانتصار أهلها عليه انتصاراً لدين بعينه، فهو في تشييدهم من أمر المدنية وتشيعهم لها وتبشيرهم بها كالمتشيعين لمذهب والمبشرين بدين، ولسنا من هذه الطبقة.

فقد تبيّن لك ممّا بيّنته أننا لسنا بمعدودين في قسم من هذه الأقسام، وأننا خرجنا من ديارنا، واضطجعنا في سفرنا على شريطة الفحص والتمحيص، والبحث والتنقيب، والانتقاد والاعتراض، والتحدث بما في هذه المدنية من ضار ونافع، ومعوج ومستقيم في منبت أرضها وتربة نشأتها، وأنا رجل مذهبي، إنّ كل حقيقة تقال وكل خبر صحيح يروى، فدعنا من التخيل في الوصف والمبالغة في الشرح، وخذ بنا في ما اشترطناه على أنفسنا، والباشا معنا ينظر إلى الأمور بعين الإنصاف، فلنسأله أولا عمّا وقع عليه من التأثير في نظرته الأولى إلى هذا العالم، وجملة ما حصل في نفسه منه.

الباشا ما أراني أميز شيئاً إلى الآن، فما رأيت سوى أني أرى خليطاً مزدحماً وحركة بين الناس لحركة الأسواق، ودوياً كدوي الخلايا، وأضواء ساطعة يتأذى منها البصر وجملة ما أنا فيه الدهشة والحيرة، ولعلّ هذا هو الذي يمنعني من التمييز، وكنت أودّ أن يقع اختيارنا على ناحية من المدينة تكون خالية من مثل هذه الحركة والزحام حتى نألف الديار وساكنيها. ١٥،٣٨

عيسى بن هشام ليس ما توده من هذا القبيل بميسور لأنّ الزحام منتشر في جميع أنحاء المدينة، وهذه الحركة لا تنتهي ليلاً ولا نهاراً، ولا غرو في ذلك فإنّ عدد سكانها بين المليونين والثلاثة، ولك أن تقول أنها بلاد متجمعة عدّت مدينة واحدة.

الصاحب وفي ذلك شيء من عظمة الملك لا يخفى على أحد.

الباشا إن كان الأمر كذلك فأرى أنه لا بدّ من هاد لنا يهدينا فيها من أهلها، ويرشدنا إلى جزئيات الأمور فيها وكلياتها.

and elevate the status of their civilization so that they too can gain in stature, lord it over us, and use the kind of prestige and power thus attained to achieve things that they could not otherwise do. People in this group believe that the process of imposing Western civilization on the East, the changes it brings to traditions and customs, and the triumph that it implies for a system of belief is what civilization comprises. Their support for and proselytization of civilization is exactly like that used by missionaries and advocates for a particular faith. We don't belong to this category either.

By now it should be clear to you that we don't belong to any of these groups. We've left our own homeland and have based our decision to travel on a desire to investigate things and subject them to analysis, criticism, and even opposition. We want to discuss every aspect of this civilization, its good and bad points, where things go astray and where they are appropriate, all by means of looking at things in the source culture—the land in which they've developed. I'm someone who's inclined to the view that everything true can be said, everything correct can be passed on. With that in mind, let's put aside all exaggeration and hyperbole and forget about fantasy when it comes to description. Let's now act on the terms we've imposed on ourselves. The Pāshā will be looking at things in a disinterested fashion. So let's ask him first what his impression is now that he's had his first glimpse of this world and what he's gleaned from it.

Pāshā I've not been able to make any distinctions on the basis of what 38.15
I've seen so far. What I've observed is just throngs of people and perpetual bustle, with the buzz of the markets sounding like beehives and the bright lights hurting the eyes. I find myself baffled and confused, and that may explain why I can't make any judgments. I'd have preferred for us to choose a district of the city without all these crowds and this bustle. Then we could really get to know the area and the people who live here.

ʿĪsā ibn Hishām That wish of yours is not easy to fulfill. Every district of the city is crowded like this. The bustle doesn't end, night and day, which is only to be expected since the number of people living in the city is estimated between two and three million. You might say that the entire country is counted in the inhabitants of a single city.

Friend Yes, and the richness of property is obvious to everyone!

Pāshā If that's the case, then we really need someone to advise us, a guide who can show us things in whole and in part.

الصاحب لست تجد في أهلها إلا كل مغال مفاخر بمدنيته، فإذا اهتدينا بواحد منهم كان همه أن يسرد علينا ما شاء من مجد قومه، وعز بلاده في كل دقيقة وجليلة فلا نستفيد منه إلا كثرة اللفظ وقلة المحصول.

١٦،٣٨ قال عيسى بن هشام: وجاء وقت الطعام فقمنا إلى المطعم فوجدنا الزحام فيه لا يقل عن زحام الطرق، ولمّا أخذنا مجالسنا، واخترنا من الألوان ما اخترنا التفتنا إلى من بجانبنا على المائدة فوجدناهم نفرًا ثلاثة، أحدهم شاب ضئيل الجسم متطرف في شكله متكلف في زيه محلوق اللحية والشارب معًا على النمط الجديد في الزينة والهيئة، وثانيهم رجل ضخم الجسم، منتفخ البطن، أحمر الوجه، وثالثهم رجل شيخ معتدل القامة، بسيط في لبسه، بعيد عن التكلف في هيئته وأصغينا لهم فسمعناهم يتجادلون بينهم أمر السياسة والحرب، ورأينا الشاب يضرب المائدة بيده والأرض برجله، ويقول في حدته:

١٧،٣٨ الشاب قد آن للمدنية أن تزيل الهمجية وتمحو الوحشية من هذا العالم، وأن تقوم بنشر الرسالة التي سخرنا أنفسنا لنشرها بين الناس لنصلح من شأن الإنسان في أي مكان كان، ونهديه إلى الرشد ونغرس فيه أصول المدنية التي تنتهي بالعالم إلى الراحة المستديمة، والسعادة المطلقة، وإلا فما مزية هذا الاجتهاد في الترقي والتقدم، وما فائدة هذه المخترعات والمبتدعات فإن كان المقصود من المدنية أن نضع هذه الآلات الحربية ونعدّ هذه القوى العسكرية ليقتل بعضنا بعضًا، ونخرب بيوتنا بأيدينا فبئست المدنية وبئست العلوم والمعارف التي تصل بنا إلى هذا الحد من التوحش، وبئس ما سخرنا له أنفسنا وأضعنا فيه أعمارنا ولقد كان الواجب على أهل الغرب أن يتحدوا مع بعضهم، وينصرفوا بكليتهم، ويندفعوا بقوتهم التي ولدتها لهم أفكار العلماء وذوي المعارف منا إلى تمدين بقية أهل هذا العالم المقيمين على الجهالة إلى اليوم، ليرفعوهم من حضيض الوحشية إلى معارج الرفعة الإنسانية، فيحق لكل واحد

FRIEND You'll rarely find any of the city's inhabitants who won't be extolling his civilization's values. If we do find someone, his primary concern will be to tell us about his wonderful people and marvelous country in every conceivable detail, boasting in ways that we certainly don't need. All we'll get out of it will be yet more verbiage and minimal value.

ʿĪsā ibn Hishām said: Mealtime arrived, so we got up to go to a restaurant. 38.16
We found it to be just as crowded as the streets. Once we had taken our seats at a table and chosen from the menu, we looked around and noticed three Parisians sitting at the next table. One of them was a thin young man, clearly very careful about the way he dressed, sporting a beard and mustache clipped in the latest fashion. The second was a portly man with a protruding stomach and ruddy complexion. The third was an older man of average height, simply dressed and unconcerned about his appearance. We listened to their conversation and discovered that they were arguing about politics and war. The young writer started banging on the table with his hand and tapping the ground with his feet. He was speaking angrily:

YOUNG MAN The time has come for civilization to put an end to savagery 38.17
and eradicate barbarous behavior from the world. We need to promulgate the message that we've engaged ourselves to bring to other people. We can then improve the lot of human beings wherever they may be, lead them on the right path, and inculcate in them the principles of civilization that will propel the world to a life of perpetual ease and absolute contentment. Failing that, what can be the virtue of our struggle to achieve the heights of advancement and progress; what are the benefits of these inventions and innovations? If civilization's purpose is to perfect the development of war machines and to keep armed forces at the ready in order to kill each other and tear down our houses with our own hands, then so much the worse for civilization, sciences, and learning, things that have brought us to this degree of barbarity. A curse on the goals to which we have dedicated ourselves, wasting our entire lives in the process! Western people should be uniting, acting collectively, and using the power that scientists and the intelligentsia have provided for them to civilize the peoples of the rest of the world who are still living in ignorance to this very day. They'll be able to bring them out of the depths of their primitive existence and place them on a loftier human plane. Once that is achieved, every one of

منا بعد ذلك أن يفتخر على الطبيعة بأنه أصلح فسادها، وسدّ نقصها وأقام اعوجاجها ولو كانت ممالك أوربا اهتدت إلى الصواب من أوّل الأمر لسارت مع جميع أهل آسيا وأفريقا سيرتها اليوم مع أهل الصين، فاتحدت عليهم، ونسيت ما بينها من الأحقاد والضغائن، واستجمعت قوّتها فمحت بها من الوجود هذه البقية فيه من أضاليل العصور الغابرة، وأباطيل الأجيال الخالية في طفولة الطبيعة، وإلا فسكوتها عن ذلك واشتغالها بعضها ببعض، وإهمالها في نشر المدنية على العالم عار عليها عظيم، وخطر عليها في المستقبل جسيم ولو كان في حكامنا بعض ما أظهره إمبراطور ألمانيا اليوم من النخوة والشهامة في المسألة الصينية ممّا خطب به عساكره عند سفرهم إلى تلك الأصقاع، وما وصّاهم به من أن لا يبقوا على أسير وأن يأتوا من الأعمال ما يجعل الصيني ترتعد منه الفرائص عند رؤية الألماني منذ اليوم إلى القرون الآتية لقامت فرنسا بالواجب عليها نحو المدنية، ولأدّت الرسالة التي انتدبت نفسها إليها، وتعهّدت للعالم بالقيام بها، ولحفظت ما هو مركوز لها في أفكار أهل الشرق جميعاً من الرفعة والجلال.

١٨،٣٨ القصير نعم، هكذا ينبغي، وإلا فكيف يتسنى لنا تصريف بضاعاتنا وصناعاتنا التي تضيق بها أرضنا، وتقوم عليها معائشنا إذا اجترأ أن يقوم في وجهنا مثل هؤلاء الضعاف الضئال ذوي الوجوه الصفراء من أهل الصين وكيف يليق بنا أن نشقى ونتعب ونبتدع ونخترع ونعصر الحجر فنستخرج منه الماء، ونصل في مراتب العلوم إلى أقصى غاياتها وفي العالم أقوام نيام على أرض من الذهب كالأرصاد على الكنوز لا ينتفعون بها ولا يتركون الانتفاع،فخيرات الطبيعة وطيباتها للذين استحقوها بكشف أسرارها، واهتدوا إلى استخدامها في مصالحهم، ثمّ نحن نبقي عليهم مع ضعفهم وعجزهم، ونتركهم يستهينون بني جنسنا، ويتعرضون لسد مآربنا، ويقفون في وجوه الرافعين لعلم المدنية القائمين بخدمة الإنسانية، ذلك ما لا يرضى به أحد ولا يقبله عقل.

us will be able to boast that he's helped correct whatever's corrupt in nature, put a stop to its shortcomings, and set it on a new course. If European nations had been doing the right thing from the outset, they'd have followed the same policy with the peoples of Asia and Africa as they've done with China today. Europeans united against them and forgot about older hatreds and disputes. By uniting their forces, they were able to eradicate the vestiges of delusions and falsehoods stretching back through the ages to nature's earliest stages. If Europeans didn't act but instead chose to bother themselves about each other's business and forget about the need to spread civilization throughout the world, it would be a huge mistake and an enormous threat in the future. If our government would only show the same level of honor and astuteness as the German Emperor is doing today with regard to the Chinese problem, dispatching his soldiers on the risky journey to those regions, instructing them to take no prisoners, and telling them to do things that will make the Chinese shudder in fright every time they set eyes on a German in future centuries, then France would be doing its part for civilization, fulfilling the mission it has set for itself, and pledging to the entire world to carry it through. It would then have preserved for itself that high standing and prestige that it possesses in the minds of Eastern peoples.

Short Man You're absolutely right. That has to be our policy. If not, 38.18
how are we supposed to make our goods available and find a market for our industry, the things for which our own country is too small and upon which our livelihood depends, if people like these weak, puny, yellow-faced Chinese dare to confront us? How can it be right for us to suffer and tire ourselves out devising and inventing things, crushing rocks to produce water and reaching the very heights of scientific achievement, when there exist in the world peoples who are content to sleep on top of piles of gold like guards over treasure without benefiting from them or letting anyone else benefit? The boons and delights of nature should by right accrue to the people who have discovered their secrets and pointed the way to their uses for the benefit of everyone. But, in spite of their weakness and impotence, we leave them alone and let them scoff at people of our race, stand in the way of our aspirations, and confront those people who are trying to serve humanity by hoisting the standard of civilization. No one should be satisfied with the situation and no intelligent person should accept it.

١٩،٣٨ شيخ إن كان كلامكما عن المدنية الصحيحة التي تقوم على الحرية والمساواة، والإخاء والإنصاف، والمعروف والإحسان ممّا يتعلق بسعادة الإنسان في حياته، وطلب الخير له في معيشته، ويوفر له أسباب الراحة والسكينة والدعة والرخاء والسلم والأمن، فبئست المدنية أن نصرف حياتنا ونقضي أوقاتنا في صنع الآلات المهلكات، وحشد الجنود وإعداد السلاح بما يجعلنا في احتياج وافتقار إلى ما في أيدي الغير، وتضيق علينا أرضنا بأرزاقها، فيرمي بنا الطمع والجشع على سوانا فنعمد إلى تلك المهلكات فنقتل بها النفوس، ونخرب الديار، ونسلب الأرزاق وليست المدنية أن نعتبر أنفسنا ملائكة الأرض وأرباب الخلق، ونحتقر جنس البشر ممّن عدانا، فلا نرضى منه إلا بأن يغير عاداته وأخلاقه، وما تلجئه إليه طبيعة أرضه وجو سمائه في لحظة من الزمن وبرهة من الوقت، وأن يسلمنا أمره، ويجعل بأيدينا تصريفه، ونقوم عليه كالقوام والأوصياء، نذله فيرضى، ونستعبده فيرضخ وليست المدنية أن نأتي الصيني وهو آمن مطمئن راض بعيشه بين أهله وولده في مقر داره، فنقول له: قم فقد جئناك بالحق، فهلمّ فكسّر أصنامك، واحرق كتابك، وغيّر ثيابك، وبدّل طعامك، واعدم مناسكك، وطلق زوجاتك، وارفع الحجاب عن بناتك، واترك صناعتك، وكن أوربياً في الصين القديمة، وغربياً في الشرق الأقصى.

٢٠،٣٨ فإذا قال لنا: يا قوم لست أدري ما تدعونني إليه، فإن كانت هذه هي المدنية بزعمكم فإنّ لي مدنية خاصة بي وضعتها فينا تجارب القرون الأولى، وقرّرها الأبناء في عقب الآباء، والآباء في عقب الجدود، ومن المعلوم أنّ مرور الزمن منخل استصفى به الغث، ويبقي الثمين، وما قدم شيء إلا وكان في بقائه وقدمه دليل على متانة أركانه وقوة بنائه، ولا يبقى على الزمن من الأخلاق والعادات إلا ما كان له أصل جيد، وجوهر نقي، وأنتم إن كنتم تؤرخون وجودكم في العالم بسبعة آلاف من السنين، فنحن نؤرخ وجودنا بمئات من الآلاف، وإن كانت مدنيتكم هذه بنت قرن واحد، فإنّ مدنيتنا تعدّ بعشرات من القرون استرحنا عليها، وطاب لنا العيش فيها ومن دلائل المدنية الصحيحة

Old Man If your conversation is about genuine civilization, one based on "liberté, égalité, fraternité," one that advocates both justice and charity as being traits on which depend the happiness of humanity in life, the quest for what is good in existence, and what provides people with the benefits of peace, serenity, security, welfare, and composure, then that same civilization is a complete failure in the conduct of our lives. We spend our time manufacturing lethal machinery, mustering troops, and preparing weapons, all of them activities that place us in need of things that are in the hands of other people and drain our country's resources. Greed and cupidity then propel us against other people; we embark upon destructive missions, kill human beings, lay waste to regions, and despoil them of their wealth. It's no part of civilization to consider ourselves as the world's angels and lords of the universe, to despise all those who oppose us—never satisfied unless such people alter their customs and morals, not to mention things that their natural habitat and climate dictate that they do at certain points in time. They're supposed to hand over their affairs to us and place all discretion in our hands. We can then serve as their regents and curators: we subdue them, and they're content; we enslave them, and they submit. It is no part of civilization for us to approach the Chinese people who are living with their families secure and content in their own homes, and to tell them, "We've brought you the true way. So come on! Destroy your statues, burn your books, change your clothing, eat different food, abolish your rituals, divorce your wives, remove the veil from your daughters' faces, and abandon your crafts. Instead be Europeans in old China, Westerners in the Far East." 38.19

A Chinese person might well reply, "You Westerners, I've no idea what it is you're inviting me to do. If this thing is civilization as you're claiming, then I've my own civilization too, one established among us by centuries of experience. Sons have inherited it from fathers, and fathers from their fathers. It's a well-known fact that the passage of time serves like a sieve, ridding culture of what is bad while preserving what is good. Nothing remains unless it's proven to have strong bases and firm structure. No ethics and customs can survive unless they are founded on fine principles and clear essentials. If you record your own existence on earth as dating back some seven thousand years, ours goes back hundreds of thousands. If your civilization is one hundred years old, then ours goes back dozens of centuries; thanks to it we have lived comfortably and enjoyed good lives. A primary characteristic of genuine civilization is that people should live in peace. No one should crave what does not belong 38.20

أن يعيش الناس فيها بسلم ولا يطمع أحد فيما ليس له، ولا يتعدّى على الغير، وقد علمتم أننا عشنا دهرنا الطويل لم نثر حرباً، ولم نفتح أرضاً، ومن دلائلها أن لا تصل بالإنسان إلى غايات الترف والنعومة، فيضمحل الجسم، ويضعف النسل، وقد علمتم أنّ أرضنا إلى اليوم أكثر الأرض عمراناً من النفوس، فنقول لهم ما أضلكم وأسخف عقولكم أن تعلموا بأنّ لا مدنية سوى مدنيتنا التي اهتدينا إليها بالعلوم والمعارف بما لم يصل إليها غيرنا من البشر، ولسنا نرضى للعالم أن يعيش بسواها، وقد وافقنا أنفسنا على دعوة الخلق إليها وهدايتهم بها ليكونوا جميعا في السعادة الدائمة والنعيم المقيم بهذا وصانا أئمتنا من غلادستون وغامبتا ولافيجري وهانوتو، فإن لم تقبلوا فدونكم ما يوصينا به حماة مدنيتنا من كروب ومكسيم ونوبيل وماوزر.

٢١،٣٨ إن كانت هذه هي المدنية الغربية التي نفاخر بها فلا جرم أن يعتقد فيها أهل الشرق أنها وسيلة من وسائل الفتوحات ونيل المطامع والمآرب، وأنها تدور على تغلب جنس على جنس، ومذهب على مذهب، ودين على دين، وحق لسلطان المسلمين أن يقول أنّ أوربا تحربنا حرباً صليبية في زي السلم نعم ليست هذه أعمال المدنية الصحيحة وما هي إلا الوحشية والهمجية والبربرية.

الشاب ما هذا الخليط والخلط وأنت تعلم أن لا دخل عندنا للدين في السياسة ونشر المدنية وهل ترى فينا الآن إلا كل منسلخ عن الدين، منخلع عن الاعتقاد واليقين، وأنّ أئمة الدين عندنا مضطهدون، والحكومة مع الأهالي عليه، وهذه انكلترا تحارب البوير وهم مسيحيون كما تحارب الصينيين وهم وثنيون، وإنما هي المصلحة السياسية في إعلاء كلمة المدنية؟ ولا بدّ من الإقناع بالفعل لمن لم يقنع بالقول، ولا محيص من استعمال القوة مع من لم يقبل الأمر بالإذعان.

٢٢،٣٨ الشيخ ما أنا بجاهل بشأن الدين عندنا ودرجة الاعتقاد فينا، ولكنه أمر لا يتعدانا في ديارنا ولا نعمل به إلا فيما بيننا، أمّا إذا كان الأمر خارجا عن بلادنا تعصبنا له وإن كنا لا نهتم بأئمة الدين هنا فإنّ سفراءنا ووكلاءنا في جميع الأقطار مكلفون

to him, nor should anyone launch hostile attacks against others. You're well aware that we've lived for many centuries without engaging in warfare or invading territory. As evidence I can note that our people have not aspired to the ultimate in luxury and fripperies which only weaken the body and diminish the procreation of future generations. Our territories, as you know, have the largest number of citizens." To all that we would respond, "How wrong you are, and how feeble is your intelligence! Surely you realize that there's no real civilization apart from ours, the one that we've been inspired to develop through science and learning, to reach heights not achieved by any other humans. We're not content to see the rest of the world living in some other way. We've committed ourselves to draw humanity to our way and to use it as a guiding principle so that they can all live in unending happiness and bliss. This is the charge we have received from our great leaders, Gladstone, Gambetta, Lavigerie, and Hanotaux. Should you not accept, then you should expect to encounter the charge that the guardians of our civilization, Krupp, Maxim, Nobel, and Mauser, have given us.

"If this is indeed the civilization that we're so proud of, then it's hardly sur- 38.21
prising that Eastern peoples have come to view it as simply another means of conquest so that we can grab what we want and achieve our goals. It involves one race, one sect, one religion overcoming another. The Ottoman Muslim Sultan is right when he states that Europe is engaged in another Crusade, albeit in the guise of peace. No indeed, these are not the deeds of genuine civilization, but of raw aggression, savagery, and barbarism."

Young Man What's all this nonsense and confusion? You know full well that religion has no part in politics in our society and in the spread of civilization. Now everything's completely divorced from religion and matters of faith and belief. In our society now religious leaders are being persecuted, and the government stands with the people against them. England itself is currently fighting the Berbers who are Christians and the Chinese as well who are pagans.[66] It's all a matter of political expediency as part of the process of proclaiming the concept of civilization. We have to convince people with actions if they cannot be convinced with words alone. Force has to be used when people otherwise refuse to submit.

Old Man I'm well aware of the place that religion and belief have in 38.22
our society. However, that's something that operates in our own country and should only apply in our midst. If on the other hand another foreign country is

بمعاونتهم ومساعدتهم والانتصار لهم في كل حال، ولا تنس كلمة غامبتا التي قالها عند اضطهاده لرؤساء الدين في أرضنا: «إنّ اضطهادنا للدين من البضائع التي لا تصدر إلى الخارج» وهذا إمبراطور ألمانيا يقول في بعض خطبه لعساكره وتحريضه لهم على مقاتلة الصينيين ونشر لواء المدنية وخدمة الإنسانية في العالم: «واعلموا أنّ كل مدنية لا يكون الدين المسيحي أساسها وعمادها فهي مدنية مقضي عليها بالزوال والانقراض.» وهذا للورد سلسبوري يقر بنفسه على منبر الخطابة اليوم بأنّ المبشرين في الصين تغالوا غلوّاً كبيراً حتى أحرجوا الصينيين فأخرجوهم، ولم يكتف المبشرون بالدعوة إلى الدين، بل عمدوا إلى طرق الإذلال والانتقام من دين الصينيين، وقد علم الناس كافة أنّ دين الصين يقوم أساسه وأصله على احترام الموتى وهو أكبر قواعد الدين عندهم، فإنهم يعتقدون أنّ الميت إذا لم يكن محترماً في قبره سخط على أهله وأهل ملته فسلّط عليهم المحن، وابتلاهم بالهلاك والقحط، فيعمد المبشرون إلى معاكستهم في أصل دينهم، ويأخذون أرض مدافنهم فينثرون منها عظام موتاهم، ويبتنون مكانها الكنائس والصوامع تعلو على قباب معابدهم وهياكلهم وتطل على قصر الملك نفسه فقل لي بالله هل كان يقدم أحد من المبشرين على مثل هذه الإهانة الكبرى لدين أمّة تتكون من أربعمائة مليون من النفوس لو لم يكن وراءه السفير يعينه ويأخذ بناصره، ومن وراء السفير البنادق والمدافع؟

المهم أنّ هذه كلها أمور ربما تأتي بما لا تحمد عقباه إن لم تتدارك أوربا نفسها ٢٣،٣٨
بالاعتدال وكف يد الطمع والعداء، وربما أظهرت الحوادث عند تكرار وقوعها مقدار قوة أوربا في حقيقتها، ويذهب ما على أعين الناس من غشاوات الوهم، وهذه حادثة الصين أرتنا كيف أنّ انقطاع سلك من أسلاك التلغراف الذي هو الاختراع الجليل لهذه المدنية أوقع أوربا في الحيرة والارتباك، وشمل أهلها بالهم والغم أياماً طوالا وكيف أنّ الدول أخذت تجهز وتعد وتعصر في نفسها حتى أمكن لها أن تستغني من قوتها التي تعدّ بالملايين من العساكر عن ثلاثين ألف مقاتل تهجم بهم على

involved that we are in league with, even though we are not concerned about religious leaders here at home, our ambassadors and agents in every region are charged with the obligation of offering those leaders assistance and support in every situation. Don't forget what Gambetta had to say when the religious leaders in our country were being suppressed: "The suppression of religious authorities in our own country is not to be exported abroad." Now here's the German Emperor addressing his troops and energizing them to fight the Chinese, raising the standard of civilization and service to humanity throughout the world. "You should know that the Christian religion is not the foundation and basis of every civilization. It is in fact a civilization in decline and on the path to extinction." Even Lord Salisbury from his rostrum today confirms that Christian missionaries in China have indulged in gross exaggerations in order to stir up the Chinese, and so they were duly expelled. Those missionaries were not content merely to call people to the faith, but went on to show contempt toward Chinese religion and show active hostility toward it. Everyone's aware, for instance, that the Chinese religion is founded on respect for the dead; that's the major principle of their faith system. They believe that if the dead person isn't shown respect in his grave he'll be angry with his family and community and will bring down all kinds of calamity on them—destruction and drought. The Christian missionaries deliberately targeted their religious principles; they grabbed cemetery land, scattered the bones of the dead, and constructed churches and monasteries on top of their shrines and temples, overtopping the royal palace itself. So please tell me, by God, would any of these missionaries dare to perpetrate this enormous insult against the religion of a people with over four hundred million souls if they didn't have an ambassador to support and assist them—he himself having guns and weaponry at his disposal?

What really matters is that all this may well lead to dire consequences if 38.23
Europe does not adopt a more balanced policy and put an end to this greed and violence. The frequency with which these events are happening may show the real extent of the power that Europe possesses and serve as a corrective to people's false ideas. What has happened in China shows us clearly that the severance of telegraph lines—itself a splendid invention of our own civilization—has thrust Europe into a very tense situation and caused everyone a good deal of grief and worry for a considerable period of time. Governments have started getting equipment ready in a rush so that, out of their total forces numbering in the millions, they can spare a mere thirty thousand soldiers, half of whom

الصين نصفهم من اليابان بعد أن أخذت تعنف بعضها بعضاً في بيع السلاح من معاملها إلى الصينيين من قبل.

قال عيسى بن هشام: وتأتي غادة هيفاء تتثنى وتخطر فتقصد الشاب فتضربه بعصا المظلة وتقول له مغاضبة معاتبة: أتتركني في انتظارك وتجلس هنا للجدال في السياسة؟ فينتفض قائماً مع الرجل القصير، ونسمع الشيخ يقول وهو يمضغ آخر لقمة من طعامه حزين النفس كاسف البال: ٢٤،٣٨

«هذه هي المدنية أن تعلن حكومتنا بين الأهالي أنها تدفع مائتي فرنك لكل من يرغب منهم في التوجه إلى قتال الصين فيلبيها العدد الجم ويبيعون حياتهم ويخلفون نساءهم أيامى، وأطفالهم يتامى بهذا القدر الذي تشتري به مثل هذه الفاجرة قميصاً واحداً تلبسه في ليلتها وتمزقه في صباحها».

ويلتفت إليّ الصاحب فيقول: ما أغرب أمر هذا الشيخ الفرنسوي وما أصلبه في قول الحق، وما أولانا بمصاحبة مثله، فالتفت إلى الشيخ فإذا هو يرمي بنظره إلينا، ويستمع لحديثنا بالعربية، ويظهر البشر لنا، ثمّ يوجه إلينا الكلام ويسألنا عن بلادنا فيرتبط معه الحديث، ونعلم أنه رجل من أساتذة الحكمة والفلسفة، درسها وانتفع بها، ونظر في الأمور على حقائقها، لا ينحرف به هوى، ولا يضله غرض، وأظهر لنا ولعه باستكشاف أخلاق الأمم ومعرفة أحوالها، فاتفقنا على مصاحبته نحكي له عن الشرق، ويحكي لنا على الغرب، فقابلنا على ذلك بالشكر والحمد وعزمنا على زيارة المعرض من الغد.

are Japanese, for the attack on China. And all that after the governments concerned have previously been competing with each other to sell weapons from their armament factories to the Chinese.

ʿĪsā ibn Hishām said: At this point a beautiful young woman came strutting over and headed straight for the young man. She hit him with her umbrella. "Are you leaving me waiting," she chided him angrily, "while you sit here arguing about politics?" He leapt to his feet along with the short man. We listened as the Old Man, sad faced and dejected, ate up the remainder of his meal. "This is the civilization," he said, "whose government has announced to its people that it will pay two hundred francs to anyone who wishes to go and fight in China. Many of them are doing so, selling their livelihoods and leaving their wives as widows and their children as orphans for a tiny amount of money that women like this prostitute can use to buy a single blouse—wearing it one night and ripping it apart the next morning." 38.24

The Friend now turned to me. "I'm surprised at this old Frenchman," he said. "He seems to be prepared to tell the truth. We really need someone like him to accompany us." I looked toward the old man; he was staring in our direction, listening to our conversation in Arabic and apparently welcoming us. He talked to us and asked us which country we were from. We now opened a conversation and gathered that he was a professor of philosophy, something that he had studied and profited from, investigating the reality of things and not allowing desires and aspirations to divert his attention. He told us how interested he was in researching the ethics of peoples and finding out about their conditions. We then agreed to keep his company; we would tell him about the Orient and he would do the same for the West. We accepted his offer with gratitude and agreed to visit the Exhibition the next day.

مصباح الشرق ١١٧، ٢٤ أغسطس ١٩٠٠

باريس

قال عيسى بن هشام: وانطلقنا نقصد عكاظ الممالك والأمم، وسوق الأقدار والهمم، ومشهد النفائس والعظائم، ومظهر القوى والعزائم، وحلبة الابتكار والابتداع، وميدان الإنشاء والاختراع، ومعرض التبصر والاهتداء في سبل التمثل والاقتداء ولهذا المعرض خمسون باباً، تختلف بينها ابتعاداً واقتراباً، فبلغناه من المدخل المقدم، والباب المعظم، فإذا الباب قبة تقوم على ثلاث قوائم، تلامس هيادب الغمائم كأنها البقاع في الارتفاع، أو تلعة من التلاع في الاتساع، يسلك في جوفها الجيش المتراكب، فلا تماس فيه المناكب، وعلى كلا الجانبين سارية تعارض غادية السحاب والسارية، يدور في رأس كل واحدة منهما نبراس وأي نبراس، إذا اشتعل أعاد فحمة الليل قبساً من الأقباس، فكلتاهما علم في رأسه نار، يستوي عندهما الليل والنهار، ومن لصخر الخنساء أن يأتمّ بهما وهو المؤتم به في دجنة البيداء: ١.٣٩

وإنّ صخراً لتأتمّ الهداة به
كأنه علم في رأسه نار

فهما عمودا فجر، لا عمودا صخر، يكتنفان تمثال غانية غيداء، واقفة في رأس تلك القبة الشماء، قد خلعت الإزار والوشاح، وتبدت في قميص الصباح، بارزة النهد، رشيقة القد، ممكورة لفتاء مجدولة عجزاء:

أبت الروادف والثدي لقمصها
من البطون وأن تمس ظهورا.

وكأنما النسيم هناك يجهد في رفع ذيلها وهتك سترها، فهي تضم ثوبها بيديها إلى خصرها، إذا عارض ضوء وجهها القمر، علا وجهه الكمد والكدر، ولان فيه النمش والكلف، فاحتجب بالغمام أو انخسف، وغارت منها الزهرة، غيرة الضرة من الضرة، ٢.٣٩

Miṣbāḥ al-sharq 117, August 34, 1900[67]

Paris

39.1 ʿĪsā ibn Hishām said: So we set off for the renowned ʿUkāẓ Fair of countries and peoples, the market for values and ambitions, the site of everything marvelous and amazing, the display of powers and resolves, the fulcrum of creativity and invention, the domain of formation and ingenuity, the exhibition of foresight and enlightenment in the appropriate use of tradition and imitation. This particular exhibition has fifty gateways, some close, others more distant. We ourselves entered through the principal gate, the main entrance, which consisted of a gate resting on three pillars high enough to touch the clouds, like some hill vast in both its height and breadth. Beneath it flowed a veritable army all crammed together; the tops were separated, and there was a column on either side. The pillars bordered the very clouds scudding back and forth. On the top of each pillar a lamp turned, and what a lamp it was! Once illuminated, darkest night became like a firebrand, each column a flag with a fire at its peak. Night and day became the same. And how could al-Khansāʾs brother, Ṣakhr, possibly have elegized them, since he himself was thus mourned in the desert darkness:

Ṣakhr is to be mourned by our chiefs,
like a standard with fire at its pinnacle.[68]

But these were columns of dawn, not of stone.[69] They framed the statue of a beautiful woman, placed at the very top of this lofty dome. She had removed dress and girdle and appeared in morning garb, bare-breasted, svelte, with shapely legs and ample backside.

Her buttocks and breast prevented her blouse
from touching her belly or her back.[70]

39.2 It was as though the breeze were doing its best to lift her garment and remove its covering. She was using her hands to clutch it to her waist. When the light of her face was placed next to the moon, the latter's expression showed anguish; it hid its freckled visage behind the clouds and went into eclipse. Venus herself would have been jealous, like a rival wife, and would have angrily disappeared

فغارت في الدجون، وغابت عن العيون، لو قام نابغة بني ذبيان من قبره، لشهد أنها الدمية التي وصف بها المتجردة في شعره:

أو درة صدفية غواصها
بهج متى يرها يهلّ ويسجد
أو دمية من مرمر مرفوعة
بنيت بآجر تشاد وقرمد
لو أنها عرضت لأشمط راهب
عبد الإله صرورة متعبد
لرنا لرؤيتها وحسن قوامها
ولخاله رشداً وإن لم يرشد

وعلمنا أنها عندهم نادرة النوادر في التصوير والتشكيل، وشاردة الشوارد في الرسم والتمثيل، وأنها تخيل نساء باريس في ترحيبهن بالزائرين والقاصدين، والواردين على المعرض والوافدين، والباب كله مرصع حقاق من البلور، إذا سطع فيها شعاع النور، قلت أذيال الطواويس في اختلاف ألوانها، وأنوار الأزهار على أغصانها، بل قلادة من الدر والجوهر، ونظم من اليواقيت، من أحمر وأزرق وأصفر، لا بل فصوص من الألماس، يتبين فيها طيف الشمس بالانعكاس، ولا غرو فالباب يعدّ عندهم غاية الإجادة والإحسان في جمال الصنعة والإتقان

٣،٣٩ ولمّا جاوزناه انتهينا إلى سهل رحيب، وواد عشيب، نبتت أرضه بالقصور المنيفة كما ينبت الروض بالأغصان الوريفة، تضل فيه الحداة، وتحار الهداة، فالمدينة في اتساعها قطر من الأقطار، وهذا المعرض في سرتها مصر من الأمصار، نرى فيه عوالي القباب، مموهة بالزرياب، فتخالها في شعل ولهب ممّا توقد عليها من الذهب، وما زلنا سائرين في أرض تعرض فيها أغراس الجنان والبساتين، وأعواد الأزهار والرياحين بين التماثيل من كل معنى متجسم، وخيال مرتسم، تكاد تبادرك بالخطاب، وترد إليك رجع الجواب.

from view. Were al-Nābighah al-Dhubyānī to rise from his grave, he would testify that she was the statue whose naked form he describes in his poem:

Or a pearly shell, whose diver
  is staggered and bows when he sees it gleam,
Or a marble statue,
  constructed in blocks and mortar.
Were she to be presented to a hoary monk,
  one who devotes himself unmarried to God,
He would delight in the sheer beauty of her image
  and consider it proper though it were not.[71]

We learned that people regarded the statue as a marvel of the plastic arts and an outstanding example of representation. She was envisioned as the women of Paris welcoming visitors, greeting all those coming to see the exhibition. The entire gate was inlaid with pieces of crystal. When rays of light shone on them, you imagined that they were multicolored peacocks' tails or flowers blossoming on their branches. Or rather you could say they were necklaces of pearls and jewels, clusters of emeralds, all of them in reds, blues, and yellows, bezels of diamond, with the reflected glow of the sun in them. No wonder then that people regarded this gate as the very acme of craftsmanship and a perfect example of fine art.

Once past the gateway we found ourselves in a huge open space, a grassy valley, its grounds planted with lofty pavilions just as bowers sprout leafy branches. It was large enough for camel drivers to get lost and guides to be baffled. And no wonder, because this virtual city was so extensive that it could be divided up into separate regions. The exhibition all told was in fact an entire city in itself. We could see lofty golden domes that seemed to flash and gleam with their gilding. We made our way around grounds that were bedecked in garden plants and orchards, scented bushes and flowers, all interspersed with statues representing everything that body and imagination could conceive, so much so that they almost seemed to be addressing you or responding to an implicit question. 39.3

ولمّا امتلأت عيني من هذه المحاسن الشائعة، ودهش لبي من هاتيك المرائي الرائعة، التفت إلى أصحابي أنظر ما يجري في خواطرهم، ويجول في ضمائرهم من أثر هذا المشهد الجليل، والمنظر الجميل، فرأيت الباشا ينظر ويحدق، ويمعن ثمّ يطرق، وإذا هو يقول في همسه، وحديثه لنفسه: لله أبوهم ما أبعد شأوهم في التشييد، وأجل شأنهم في التجديد، وما أسبقهم إلى الجد والاجتهاد في حب التوسع والازدياد، وما أشغلهم بما يكفل خير الإنسان أقله وأدونه، ويكفي لراحته أصغره وأهونه، ولو تيقن ابن آدم أنّ القبر غايته، لم تخفق على القصور رايته، ولقدّم اعتناءه بحفر القبر على اعتنائه بتشييد القصر، فبقاؤه هناك طويل، ومقامه هنا قليل، ولو علم أنّ هذه الأحجار المذهبة في شرفات المنازل لا تنشب أن تصير صفائح للمقابر وجنادل، لم يعمل عمل المخلدين، وهو بين أظفار المنايا رهين: ٤٫٣٩

تبني المنازل أعمار مهدمة
من الزمان بأنفاس وساعات.

وإذا «الصاحب» لا يزال في هذا الموقف على حالة لا تتغير، وهيئة لا تتأثر، ينظر إلى ما نستعظمه نظرة القروي إلى قريته، والبدوي إلى طلله ودمنته، لا يأبه لشيء ممّا يشاهد ويرى، وتفتتن به أعلام هذا الورى: ٥٫٣٩

لا معنيّ بكل شيء ولا كـ
ـل عجيب في عينه بعجيب

إلا أنه مع ذلك غير هادئ البال، ولا ساكن البلبال، كأنما هو يغوص على معنى يدق في الفهم، ويبحث في أمر يرتفع عن الوهم، ويستجمع لديه حواشي التفكير، ويلمّ أشتات التذكير، فاستخبرته عمّا يشغله، وسألته ماذا يذهله، فلم يسعف في الجواب ولم يسعد، غير أني سمعته يترنم وينشد:

Once my eye had had its fill of such stunning wonders and my heart had been sufficiently overwhelmed by such superb vistas, I turned to my colleagues in order to ask them for their impressions and find out what they were thinking about such amazing sights. I noticed that the Pāshā was staring in amazement, examining everything but remaining silent. I could hear him talking to himself: "My God, how far-reaching is their construction, how amazing their creative and innovative talents! Their initiative shows such seriousness of intent to expand and increase in every area. They seem preoccupied with the basic level of things that mankind needs, the least they may want in terms of a life of ease. If humans were sure that the grave was their goal in life, then standards would never flutter over palaces; they would be more concerned about digging graves than building palaces. After all, man spends a long period residing elsewhere after death and only a short time on this earth. If only he realized that these gilded stones on lofty balconies would soon be turned into tablets for dilapidated tombs, he wouldn't behave like some immortal when in fact he's a hostage hanging between fate's claws: 39.4

Eras long since demolished build
houses out of breaths and hours."[72]

Our Friend's attitude to all this had not changed; his expression was still the same. The things that we were admiring so much he was observing like a peasant in his village and a bedouin over his campfire. Nothing he was seeing impressed him, nor was he at all fascinated by these stellar examples of mankind's skill: 39.5

There is no meaning to anything; nothing
wonderful was wonderful for him.[73]

Even so, I could see that he was disconsolate and restless, searching anxiously for an idea to detail his thoughts, something beyond his conception, so that he could gather his impressions and scattered reactions. I asked him what was bothering him, but he did not reply directly. Instead I heard him recite these lines:

ما أقل اعتبارنا بالزمان ٦،٣٩
وأشد اغترارنا بالأماني
وقفات على غرور وأقدا
م على مزاق من الحدثان
التفاتا إلى القرون الخوالي
هل ترى اليوم غير قرن فان
أين رب السدير فالحيرة البي
ضاء أم أين صاحب الإيوان
والسيوف الحداد من آل بدر
والقنا الصم من بني الريان
والمواضي من آل جفنة أرسى
طنبا ملكهم على الجولان
يكرعون العقار في فلق الأب
ريز كرع الظمآء في الغدران
من أباة اللعن الذين يحيو
ن بها في معاقد التيجان
تتراءهم الوفود بعيدا
ضاربين الصدور للأذقان
في رياض من السماح حوال
وجبال من الحلوم رزان
وهم الماء لذ للعط
شان بردا والنار للحيران
ما ثنت عنهم المنون يد شو
كاء أطرافها من المران

How little we take note of time, 39.6
how much we are misled by desires!
Postures in banality, ventures down
misfortune's slippery slope.
Looking back on centuries past,
do we see today aught but a century wasted?
Where today is the Lord of Sadīr Castle and gleaming
Ḥīra, proud Chosroes with his famous portico;
Iron swords from the tribe of Badr,
mute lances from the Banū al-Rayyān?
Forebears from the family of Jafna,
their terrain firmly planted on the Golan.
They quaff dregs in cups of gold
like thirsty men at brooks.
Arrogant as they hurl curses as greetings
crowns intermesh.
You can see them in droves afar,
striking chests to chins
In decorous meads of tolerance
and mountains of dream serene.
For the thirsty they are water delicious
in its coolness; for those in despair they are fire.
No spiked hand, saber-edged, has
turned the fates away from them.

عطف الدهر فرعهم فرآه
بعد بعد الذرى قريب المجاني
وثلبتهم بعد الجماح المنايا
في عنان التسليم والإذعان
ليس يبقى على الزمان جريء
في أباء أو عاجز في هوان

وإذا بالشيخ الفرنسوي ينظر في عطفيه، ويهز كتفيه، ويقول في التفاتة إلينا، وانعطافه علينا: ما أشبه الأواخر بالأوائل في التفاخر والتطاول بالباطل، لا يظن ظان أن كل ما يراه من هذا المشهد الفخم، ولا بناء الضخم، بما أنفق عليه من الأموال الطائلة، وما اقتضاه من المشاق الهائلة، يبقى أعواماً على الدهر، بل هو يعدّ بقاؤه باليوم والشهر، وليس يمكث من كل هذا البناء والعمران، إلا هذان القصران، وأشار بيده إلى قصرين متقابلين، كأنهما هضبتا جبلين، وهنا أخذ الباشا يستفهم منه ويستعلم، وأخذت أنقل له وأترجم: ٧،٣٩

الباشا أترى هذا المعرض من عمل الحكومة أم من عمل الرعية.

الصاحب (لنفسه) إنه من عمل الشيطان.

الشيخ الفرنسوي هو من عملهم جميعاً.

الباشا وماكنه الأموال التي أنفقت في تشييده؟

الفرنسوي اشتركت الحكومة في الإنفاق عليه بمبلغ عشرين مليوناً من الفرنكات، وبلدية باريس بعشرين مليوناً أيضاً، وتألفت جمعية اشتركت فيه بستين مليوناً وضعت بها خمسة وستين مليوناً من التذاكر لأيدي الناس تحت ضمانة البنك العقاري.

الباشا وما الغرض منه؟

الفرنسوي الأصل فيه حب الغنى وطلب الربح، والغرض منه كما يزعمون

Destiny has lowered their branch, so that,
after much sifting, the fruits are at hand.
After their recalcitrance those fates have subdued
them with reins of submission and obedience.
For time there remains neither daredevil in pride
nor weakling in disgrace.[74]

The elderly Frenchman looked to either side and shrugged his shoulders. **39.7**
Looking in our direction, he said, "When it comes to boasts about things futile and ephemeral, how similar are the moderns to the ancients! No one bothers to pause and think that the amazing things he's seeing here, the huge buildings he's admiring, have cost enormous amounts of money and demanded incredible hardships and will last for years and years. However, the truth of the matter is that their existence can be counted in days and months; the only things that'll be left among all these constructions is those two palaces." He now pointed to two palaces opposite each other, each of them lofty enough to resemble mountain peaks.

The Pāshā now started asking him questions, while I served as his translator:

PĀSHĀ Do you think this exhibition is the work of the government or the people?

FRIEND (*talking to himself*) The work of the Devil!

FRENCHMAN All of the above.

PĀSHĀ How much money has been spent to put on this exhibition?

FRENCHMAN The French government has contributed twenty million francs and the municipality of Paris has put in another twenty million. An association was created that has contributed sixty million, added to which is sixty-five million from tickets which have been issued to people underwritten by the Agricultural Bank.

PĀSHĀ And what is the exhibition's purpose?

FRENCHMAN The primary purpose is a desire for profit and gain. But what they claim as the primary goal is to put things on display in order to

عرض الأعمال بما يشخص المسافة التي قطعتها الأمّة من وقت إلى آخر فتبيّن به للأنظار مقدار ما ترقت فيه الأمّة لتخرج منه متضاعفة الجسد والاجتهاد في متابعة تقدمها وسرعة سيرها في سبيل المدنية وتميم مأموريتها في الطبيعة.

الباشا وهل تظنه يأتي بربح عظيم؟

الفرنسوي كان المأمول منه كذلك، ولكن خاب الظن، فإنّ الشركة قدّرت ٨،٣٩
له عدد الداخلين بخمسة وستين مليونًا في مدة وجوده وهي مائتا يوم وأربعة أيام ولم يدخل فيه إلى الآن سوى عشرة ملايين، وقد مضى ما يزيد عن نصف المدة، ولا شك أنّ عدد الداخلين في النصف الأوّل يكون أكثر من عددهم في النصف الثاني، وأصبحت تذكرة الدخول التي تسمى قيمتها بفرنك يعني مائة سنتيم تباع اليوم في البورصة بخمسة عشر سنتيماً وقد بلغ عدد الشركات التي اشتهر إفلاسها فيه إلى اليوم ثماني وخمسين شركة، وآخر شركة منها شاهدتها بالأمس يبيعون معروضاتها وأثاثها في ناحية من نواحي المعرض بالمزاد بحكم المحكمة يقال لها شركة «شارع القاهرة» وكانت أقامت مكانًا فسيحًا جمعت فيه ما يكون في شوارع مدينتكم من لعب القرود، وتلوي الثعابين، ورقص الزنوج، وغناء العبيد، وتسريح الجمال وسوق الحمير فرأيت الجمال وهي ثلاثة بيعت كلها بمائتين وخمسين فرنكًا، وبيع الحمار بأربعين فرنكًا من التسعة والعشرين حمارًا، وكان من ينظر إلى هذه الدواب وهي تعرض للبيع بهذه الأثمان يتخيل من أعينها أنها تشكو نكد بختها وتندب نحس طالعها وبخس قيمتها في غربتها ولا تسل عن سوء الحالة التي كان عليها الرجال والنساء المجلوبون مع هذه الحيوانات من بلادهم، وقد تدارك حالهم مأمور التفليسة في آخر الأمر فخصص لهم قيمة ما ينفق عليهم لإعادتهم إلى وطنهم، وعلى الجملة فالخسارة في هذا المعرض عظيمة جليلة، وأرى أنهم أخطأوا كل الخطأ بالتوسع فيه والمبالغة في تكبيره، فإنك لا تكاد تبلغ الدورة فيه إلا بقطع مسافة لا تقل عن عشرة كيلومترات فوزّعوه وشتّتوه مع قلة الزائرين والواردين، ولو أنهم اختصروه لكان خيرا لهم.

showcase quite how far the French people have come from one point in time to another. People can clearly gauge how much physical exhaustion and sheer industry has been involved in achieving such continuous progress and how far they've come along the path of civilization and the process of taming nature completely to their demands.

PĀSHĀ Will there be an enormous profit?

FRENCHMAN People had hoped as much, but their hopes have been 39.8
dashed. The company originally made an estimate of the number of visitors who would visit the exhibition during the period that it's open, namely two hundred and four days, at sixty-five million, but up till now only ten million have come; and the period's over half over. Not only that, but the number of people who'll come during the first half is bound to be greater than during the second. The entry ticket which costs a franc—or a hundred centimes—is now being sold at the Bourse for fifteen centimes. Up to today some fifty-eight companies have declared bankruptcy. The most recent one was just yesterday. I watched as they were auctioning off its exhibits and furniture in one corner of the exhibition as the result of a court order. It was called "the Cairo Street Company." It had occupied a wide space in one section of the exhibition and brought together everything that you would be likely to see on Cairo streets: monkeys playing, snakes coiled, Africans dancing, slaves singing, camels wandering, and a donkey market. I saw the three camels sold off for two hundred and fifty francs, and each of the twenty-nine donkeys went for forty francs. Anyone watching those poor animals being sold off for such cheap prices might have imagined seeing in their eyes regret over their fate and intense sorrow at their misfortune and the measly price they were worth abroad. And please don't even ask me about the sorry state of the men and women who were accompanying the animals. The bankruptcy official has caught up with them and given each of them an amount of money to send them back to their homeland. All in all, the losses from this exhibition have been enormous. In my opinion they made a huge mistake in expanding the exhibition site and making exaggerated claims about it. To get round it even once demands a trek of no less than ten kilometers. But, even though only a few visitors were coming, they spread everything out and cut it all up into chunks. If only they had kept things modest, it would have been so much better for them.

الصاحب أهذه الشركة التي تذكرها لنا هي شركة المعرض المصري الذي نسمع به؟ ٩،٣٩

الفرنسوي لا، ولكنها شركة أخرى فرنسوية وليس من الضروري أن يكون أصحاب الشركة من أهل البلاد وإن كانوا في زعمهم يشخصونها.

الباشا ولماذا لم يقدروا في هذا المعرض حسابهم بما لهم في الأمور من البراعة وصحة النظر.

الفرنسوي كانوا يظنون أنّ أمم العالم ستهرع إليه من كل فج فقد دعوا من ممالك الدنيا إلى الاشتراك فيه ستا وخمسين مملكة فأجابهم إليها ثلاثون منها، وكانوا يعتقدون أنّ أكثر ملوكها يفدون على المعرض فينفقون فيه خزائن أموالهم ودفائن كنوزهم فلم يحضره من ملوك الغرب إلا ملك السويد ولم يزره من سلاطين الشرق إلا شاه العجم.

قال عيسى بن هشام: وكنا وصلنا في هذه الأثناء إلى باب أحد القصرين المذكورين المعدودين لعرض ما يسمّونه بالفنون النفيسة وهو المشهور بالقصر الصغير، وعوّلنا على الابتداء بزيارته فدخلناه فإذا هو في بنائه وتشييده وزينته وزخرفته ونقشه ورسمه يفوق كثيرًا من قصور الملوك والقياصرة، وناهيك أنهم أنفقوا عليه اثنى عشر مليونًا فرنكا، وقد عرضوا فيه نفائس المصنوعات ممّا حفظ عن الأوائل منذ العصر الروماني إلى القرن الثامن عشر من القطعة المعدن المضروبة إلى نقوش أبواب الكنائس، ومن أواني الفخار إلى الساعات والخواتيم، ومن النعل المطرزة إلى التاج المرصع، وهنا يعجز القلم عن الوصف والنعت، فالإحاطة بمثل هذه الأشياء لا تأتي من جهة الخبر والنقل، بل من جهة المشاهدة والعيان، ولا يمكن أن يكون أثرها في نفس القارئ مثل أثرها في نفس الرائي، هذا إذا أمكن الوصف لما لا يحد ولا يحصى من هذه الأشياء المعروضة في اختلافها ولمّا درنا في غرفات القصر دورة شاهدنا فيها ما شاهدناه استوقف «الصاحب» الباشا يسأله عمّا شاهده: ١٠،٣٩

FRIEND Is the company you've just mentioned the "Egyptian Exhibition Company" that we've heard about? 39.9

FRENCHMAN No, that's another French company. The company owners don't have to be from the country in question, even though they may claim to represent it.

PĀSHĀ Why couldn't they foresee what would happen with this exhibition since they are so sophisticated in such matters?

FRENCHMAN People assumed that the peoples of the world would flock to it from all over the place. They initially invited fifty-six countries to participate, but only thirty responded. They also assumed that the majority of the world's rulers would come and spend the wealth of their treasuries here. But among Western monarchs only the King of Sweden has come, while the Shah of Iran is the only one from Eastern countries.

ʿĪsā ibn Hishām said: By now we had reached the entrance to one of the two palaces noted above, built in order to display what they call "beaux arts," the building being known as the "Petit Palais." We decided to visit it first. When we entered, it was to find that its construction, ornamentation, decor, drawing, and painting were far superior to anything found in the palaces of monarchs or emperors. No wonder, when they had spent twelve million francs to build it. They were using it to display precious crafts preserved from as far back as the Roman era all the way up to the eighteenth century: beaten metal pieces from the doors of churches, pottery vessels, clocks and rings, embroidered sandals, and embossed ivory. Here the pen fails in any attempt to describe and detail such beauty. With such incredible *objets d'art*, the written word can never substitute for the act of seeing with one's own eyes; the effect on the reader can in no way rival what the observer experiences. And all this was predicated on the very possibility of describing the enormous variety of objects on display in all their profusion. When we had done a tour of the rooms in the palace and looked at its displays, the Friend stopped the Pāshā and asked him about the things he had just seen: 39.10

الباشا ما أرى إلا كثيرًا ممّا كان يوجد بعضه في الأسواق القديمة وبعضه في البيوت العظيمة، وما أرى هذا من المدنية الجديدة في شيء.

الفرنسوي اعلموا أنّ ما ترونه هو أنفس شيء وأعظمه قيمة لا يبلغ كنهها الظنون، واعلموا أنّ هذه الساعة التي بجانبنا التي لم تلتفتوا إليها في وقوفكم عندها، ولم تعتنوا بالإمعان فيها قد رغب في شرائها بعض الراغبين فساومها لصاحبها بثلاثة ملايين من الفرنكات فلم يقبل منه.

١١،٣٩ قال عيسى بن هشام: وعدنا إلى هذه الساعة نحقق فيها النظر فوجدناها شبه كرة يحملها ثلاث فتيات من الرخام وهي معروضة في دولاب من زجاج لا يجاوز طوله مترًا ولا يوازي عرضه نصفه، فدهشنا وعجبنا، واستدرك علينا «الصاحب» يقول:

الصاحب حقًّا إنّ التحفظ على الأشياء القديمة من حسنات أهل الغرب التي يغبطون عليها، فإنّ النظر إليها يورث إحساساً جليلاً في النفس، ويحدث احتراماً لتوقير أهل الأعصر الماضية، وتذكيرًا حميدًا بمجد الأمم الغابرة، ودرساً نافعًا لا يمكن أن يتصور في سطور التاريخ وبطون القصص، كما إنّ في ذلك من حفظ السلسلة في الصناعات ما يفيد الفكر ويساعد في العمل، وقد أهمل أهل الشرق هذا الباب وخصوصاً الأمّة الإسلامية إهمالاً يعار عليهم ويعاب، ولست ترى عند الشرقي أهون عليه من الشيء القديم لا ينظر إليه بنظر قيمة عالية، ولا يلتفت إليه التفاتة احترام وتوقير، بل هو عنده كله من المتاع الساقط حتى اندثرت المآثر، واندرست الصناعات بمرور الزمن عليها، ولم نعد نعلم من كيفيات المتقدمين في معائشهم إلا الأسماء، وغابت عنا المسميات، واتصل بنا الإهمال إلى حد أنهم لا يصفونها في كتبهم ارتكانًا على بقائها وهي تضيع بين أيديهم، فلم يبق لنا إلا الأسماء لا ندرك مسمّياتها ويعلم الله أنه لو كانت هذه الساعة في ميراث تركه أحد أصحاب البيوت الكبيرة عندنا لكان نصيبها من أهل البيت أن يعطوها لابن المرضعة، أو أخت الوكيل تلعب بها فينتهي أمرها إلى الحطم والكسر

PĀSHĀ I've just seen a lot of things, at least some of which were readily available in markets in the old days and also in the great mansions. I don't see any aspect of modern civilization in all this.

FRENCHMAN You should realize that what you're seeing here are the costliest and most precious examples of art in the entire world, something that people simply cannot fully appreciate. Take this clock for example, the one which we're standing beside but you haven't even noticed or looked at closely. Some people wanted to buy it and offered three million francs, but the owner refused.

ʿĪsā ibn Hishām said: With that we turned and took a closer look at the clock. 39.11
It was shaped like a ball supported by three girls made of marble. It was displayed in a glass case only a meter tall and half a meter wide. We were duly amazed. Our Friend now continued:

FRIEND True enough, the way Western people preserve ancient objects is to their credit. They take a good deal of pleasure in it. Looking at such things leaves a powerful sense in the heart; it engenders a respect for people from ages past, serves as a useful reminder of the glory of previous generations, and offers a useful lesson that cannot be replicated in history books and narratives of the past. Not only that, but it preserves the link for industries in a way that benefits creative thinking and leads to improvements in working conditions. By contrast, people in the East, and especially the Muslim community, have completely neglected this particular sphere in an unforgivable fashion. You'll not be able to find anything that a person of the East finds more despicable than an ancient object; it has no value whatsoever for him, and he pays it no reverence or respect. Quite the contrary in fact, he regards it as useless stuff. As a result, with the passage of time monuments have crumbled and crafts have vanished. All we know about the lifestyle of our forebears is a set of names with no meanings attached. With us neglect has reached such a stage that such things are never mentioned in any books, the hope being that they can survive somehow, although they are forever lost. All that's left are names with no significance. God knows that if this particular clock had been left as a legacy in one of our illustrious households its fate would be that the family would probably have given it to the wet-nurse's son or the agent's daughter to play with until it was eventually destroyed.

وقل لي بالله أي شيء يكون اليوم أجمل في العين منظراً، وأجل في القلب مقاماً ١٢،٣٩
لو حفظ لنا ما ضيعناه مثلا من درة عمر، وقميص عثمان، وصمصامة معدي كرب، وذي الفقار لعلي، وتاج الرشيد، وراية المعز، وثياب محمد علي في دخوله إلى مصر ولكنني أرى مع ذلك الغربيين تعالوا في تقدير هذه الأشياء القديمة وفي رفع قيمتها وفي التنافس في اقتنائها غلوًّا يلامون عليه، فإنّ ثمن هذه القطعة الذي يقدّر بثلاثة ملايين يشتريها الواحد منهم لينظر إليها الزائرون في إحدى الغرف يمكن أن يقتات به ثلاثة ملايين من النفوس من أهل هذا العالم يطوون ليلتهم على الطوى والجوع، ويصعد صراخهم التظلم من أعماق أفئدتهم إلى أنحاء الآفاق فيكاد ينزل بالعذاب من السماء، وهل يروق مالكها أن يحجز عن أمّة طعام يومها في قطعة من رخام إن كان ممّن يرحم ويعطف؟

الفرنسوي نعم، إنّ الغربيين تجاوزوا الحد في هذا التغالي لمجرد التفاخر الباطل للاقتناء، وقد صارت الأشياء القديمة في أعينهم إلى هذا المقام من الحرص على اقتنائها لندرتها، ولما ملوه من الأشياء الحديثة وكثرتها التي يسهل على السواد الأعظم اقتناؤها، ولذلك فقد عزت لديهم وغلت ورجعوا في زينتهم وأثاثهم إلى تقليد القديم حتى إنّ ثمن الخشب منه ليصل إلى ثمن الذهب من الحديث من مخترعات هذا العصر، عصر التقدّم في الصناعة والترقي في المدنية.

قال عيسى بن هشام: وهنا انقطع الكلام وخرجنا قبل أن يدركنا الظلام. ١٣،٣٩

Tell me, for heaven's sake, what would be more pleasing for the eye and more poignant for the heart than the kind of thing that our sheer negligence has forever lost for us: 'Umar's pearl, for example, 'Uthmān's shirt, 'Amr ibn Ma'dī Karib's sword, 'Alī's shield, Hārūn al-Rashīd's crown, al-Mu'izz's standard, and Muḥammad 'Alī's clothing when he entered Egypt. But, in spite of all that, I still think that Western nations have gone much too far in their regard for these ancient objects, by assigning them so much value and fighting each other to possess them in a way that is utterly reprehensible. The price of this piece of marble is three million francs, and someone will purchase it in order to show it to his visitors in one of the rooms in his house. That money could be used to feed three million of the world's population, people who spend their nights starving and raising their cries of hardship from the depths of their hearts to the very heavens—almost bringing down punishment from on high. Can it be right for the owner of this object to deprive people of food for a piece of marble, at least if he's endowed with a modicum of mercy and sympathy? 39.12

FRENCHMAN You're quite right. Westerners have gone to excessive lengths in silly boasting about their acquisitions. In their eyes ancient objects are so desirable because of their rarety and because they're bored with modern stuff that can be readily acquired by the majority of people. That's why these things have become so incredibly valuable. They've gone back to acquiring antique furniture and decorations for their homes, to such a degree that the price of wood has now become the equivalent of gold in this era of modern inventions, the so-called period of advancement in industrialization and progress in civilization.

'Īsā ibn Hishām said: Here the conversation came to an end, and we left before darkness fell. 39.13

مصباح الشرق ١١٨، ٣١ أغسطس ١٩٠٠

باريس

قال عيسى بن هشام: وزرنا القصر الكبير بعد القصر الصغير يعني المعجزة الكبرى بعد الآية الصغرى، في ما ابتدعوه من جمال الوضع، واخترعوه من حسن الصنع، وما احتواه البناءان من الكنوز التي لم تجتمع لأحد من قبل، ولم يظفر بمثلها في الدهر ملك ولا قيل، ما قرط مارية عندها إلا من خرز الإماء، ولا كنوز قارون إلا من حصى الدهناء، وما أسلاب الإسكندر لديها إلا من أطمار «المجاذيب الأولياء» ولا وشي دارا إلا من «فراوي» المشايخ الفقهاء، وما طوق عمرو إلا قلادة تمر، وما أقلام البلغاء إلا مغازل للنساء، إن هي حاولت في وصفها تسطيرا، ورامت لنعتها تحبيرا، وماذا تقول في خزائن المسكونة تسكن في دارين، وأفلاذ البسيطة مبسوطة بين جدارين، لو توزع بعض ما اخترناه على الخلق لم يجهد أحد بعدها في طلب الرزق، ولم يشك شاك من بؤس الزمان، وضيق الحرمان، ولأصبح الفقير في الورى بفضلها غنياً، وبات اسم الفقر في الدنيا نسياً منسياً، وخبرًا مطويًا، فلم يختلف بين الناس رتبة ولا قدر، ولم يسلكوا فيما بينهم طرق الختل والغدر، ولم يبق للنفوس مشتهى ولا مطلوب، ولم يطمع غالب في مغلوب، ولم يغر سالب على مسلوب، ولم ترتكب في العيش المآثم والذنوب، فهما قائمان لأصحابهما على الدهر، سيشهدان بأقصى المجد والفخر، ومنتهى الثراء والوفر. ١،٤٠

وسرنا في غرفات القصر نسرح الطرف ونمتع النظر في ما يعرضه من الطرف والغرر، وكلما تأملنا في التماثيل والصور، توقد فينا الوجد بحسنها واستمر، فكم هناك من صور جلاها الإتقان والإحكام، تمثل للعقول والأفهام ما لا يمثله تأليف الكلام، وتشخص لك حوادث التاريخ ومناظره، فتتوهم أنك كنت حاضره ومناظره، وتفصح لك بفصاحة سحبان، عن مكنون الأهواء والأشجان، بلفظ مبين من النقوش والألوان: ٢،٤٠

Miṣbāḥ al-sharq 118, August 31, 1900[75]

Paris

ʿĪsā ibn Hishām said: We followed our visit to the Petit Palais with one to the Grand Palais, by which I mean the even greater wonder after the minor miracle, a building beautifully situated and perfectly constructed. These two buildings contained treasures such as had never been brought together by anyone before; no king or chieftain had ever possessed the like. Māriyah's bangles would be mere beads and date pits, the treasures of Qārūn would be but dust and pebbles, Alexander's multiple spoils the rags worn by holy men and lunatics, Dārā's finery would be no better than the fur skins worn by jurists, and ʿAmr's necklace a mere garland of dates.[76] The pens of the eloquent would be no more than women's spindles, should they even try to describe all this on paper and find elegant ways of depicting what they had seen. How can you possibly talk about the treasures of the inhabited world all residing in two buildings, the *objets d'art* from across the globe spread out between two walls? If a small portion of what we've selected were to be distributed to people on earth, almost no one would ever have to seek his livelihood; no one would ever complain about hardships of time and the toils of deprivation. Thanks to such things, the indigent would be wealthy, the very word "poverty" would be a thing of the past. Everyone would have the same status and position, and there would no longer be any need for trickery and deceit. Desiring and desired would no longer exist; the conqueror would not impose on the defeated, and the despoiler would no longer attack the despoiled. Crimes and felonies would no longer be committed. These two palaces then have been erected by their builders in the face of fate, witnesses to the vast extent of their prestige, the very acme of wealth and plenty. 40.1

We started walking through the various rooms of the palace, looking at the wonderful objects on display. Every time we looked at statues and paintings, their beauty fired and bolstered our enthusiasm. There were so many pictures of such perfection and intelligence that no written word could possibly replicate the effect on mind and understanding. They presented for you historical events and scenes, so you could imagine that you were actually there witnessing it all. It invoked the eloquence of Saḥbān to reveal for you the concealed passions and sorrows, all clearly presented with color and brush: 40.2

أراك المنى فتمنيتها
وصاغ لك الطيف حتى انبرى

فما شئت فيها من أثر يجلو صدأ الحس، ويرفق حواشي النفس، فيتولاك جميل الاهتزاز لرؤيتها، ويتسلط عليك لطيف الانفعال من هيئتها، فتئن لصورة المقتول، وتعطف على المدنف المتبول، وتستغفر لقتيل الغرام كما تترحم على قتيل الحسام، وترى الفتاة العذراء، والفنانة الحسناء، فتكاد تصبو إلى محبتها، وتطمع في مودتها، وتكاد تخشى أعين الرقباء من أهلها، وهم ضاربون من حولها.

٣،٤٠ وترى هناك صورة غادة مشبعة الخلق، معرقة في نجار الجمال والعتق، جلت عن ابتذال الهوى والعشق، يتألق في وجهها نور العفاف والصيانة، وتبدو على سمتها خصال الرزانة والركانة وتتبين فيها قوة الشكيمة، وثبات العزيمة، قد وطئت تحت قدمها غولا من شر الأغوال، لها مائة رأس للنهش والاغتيال، بعد أن أنفذت رمحها في أحشائها، وأوردتها مورد فنائها، وعلى رأسها فوج من ملائكة النصر، يتوجونها بتاج الفوز والفخر- وتلك صورة «الفضيلة» في تغلبها على «الرذيلة»، وعن يمينها حرة بارعة الجمال، بادية العظمة والجلال، تتأملها باستبشار من ظفر حزبه، وانتهى إليه سؤله واربه- وهي «الحكمة» التي لا تنال الفضيلة إلا بها، ولا تبلغ السعادة إلا من بابها، وعن شمالها حرة أخرى تتلألأ في غرتها قوة الإدراك واليقين، وشدة الممارسة والتمكين، تحمل طفلا في سن الرضاع، وتمسكه بيده شبه القلم أو اليراع، وترمق «الفضيلة» بعين التوقير والتبجيل، ونظر التعظيم والتفضيل- وتلك صورة «العلم» وفضله، والطفل شبه الإنسان في جهله.

وترى امرأة وضعت على كل ثدي لها طفلا ترضعه وتضمه، وتقبله وتشمه، ومن حولها أطفال عراة تجذبهم إلى حجرها، وتسترهم بفضل إزارها، وتشرق على محياها علامات الغبطة والارتياح، وشارات الانبساط والانشراح، فينتشر فيها ما كادت تطويه يد الزمان من براعة الجمال والافتتان- وتلك صورة «الخير والإحسان».

I show you desires, you craved them.
For you a phantom was crafted, then broke away.[77]

Whatever impact the objects had on you, they burnished rusty feelings and softened the sharp edges of your soul. On seeing them you felt a shudder of sheer joy; their appearances breathed in you a waft of magic. You found yourself sighing over the dead cavalier, empathizing with the man stricken with grief, begging God's mercy as much for the victim of passion as you did for one slain by the thrust of a sword. You looked at the beautiful girl and buxom virgin, and you dearly wished to woo her and fall in love, and yet you felt almost scared of her eagle-eyed guardians standing all around her.

Over there you could see the portrait of a lovely girl, her image steeped 40.3
in beauty and antiquity, revealing love and passion in all their normality, her visage glowing with a chaste modesty. Her entire appearance suggested a staid dignity duly blended with a powerful disdain and determined resolution. Under her feet she had crushed an evil female ghoul who had a hundred mouths ready to mangle and kill; she had impaled the stomach with a spear and dispatched it to its death. Over the girl's head there hovered a cluster of victory angels awarding her the crown of glory and triumph. This picture was the portrait of "Virtue" in her conquest of "Depravity." To her right was another noble lady, also beautiful and august. To the viewer she showed the delight of someone proclaiming his party's success and relishing the achievement of his wishes and desires; this was "Wisdom," the only means of acquiring virtue and the only gate through which happiness could be obtained. To the left was another lady in whose appearance gleamed the power of knowledge and certainty, the sheer force of experience and potential. She was carrying a nursing child who was clasping a pen or reed in his hand as she clasped him. She was giving "Virtue" a gaze replete with awe and appreciation as a show of her reverence. This then was a portrait of "Knowledge" and its virtues, while the nursing child represented mankind in its ignorance.

Next you could see a woman of a certain age, clutching a nursing baby at each breast; as she held them, she kept kissing and smelling them. All around her were naked children whom she was inviting to sit on her lap and offering them shelter in her wrap. Her expression showed her joy, happiness and satisfaction, as though the very contents of time's own hand—outstanding beauty and craftsmanship— gleamed in her face. This was the portrait of "Charity and Beneficence."

وترى صورة وليدة من حسان الولائد، وخريدة من أبهى الخرائد، كأنها المهاة في ٤،٤٠
المخائل، والظبية في الشمائل، يطول شعرها بردها، ويقيها حرها وبردها:

بفرع يعيد الليـل والصبح نيّـر
ووجه يعيد الصبح والليـل مظلم

تبدت وسط غابة تنبت العود والند، وتزهر بالبنفسج والورد، فالأرض مفروشة من أزهار الأغصان، والسقف معروشة من مشتبكات الأفنان:

فهي تختل في زبرجدة خـضـ
ـراء تغـذي بلؤلؤ مـنثور
وغدت كل ربوة تشتهي الـرق
ـص بثوب من النبات قصير.

ترى الشمس في اليوم الشامس، تنثر على الأرض نثار العرائس، بدنانير تعيي يد ٥،٤٠
اللامس، كما عيي المتنبي بمثلها من قبلها وهو يخاطب بشعره الحصان في شعب بوان، وبودّه لوكانت دنانير نوال لا دنانير زوال، تسقط في جيبه لا في برده وثوبه، ولعله مات المسكين بحسرتها، وهو يردد في صفتها:

وألقى الشرق منها في ثيـابي
دنانيـرًا تفـرّ من البـنان

وكأنما الأطيار في نشيدها، والورق في تغريدها تجاوب الفتاة في تساؤلها عن خلها أين سار وذهب، وغاب عنها فلم يؤب- بأنّ لكل حمامة مثلها شوقًا ينازعها إلى ألف يضيعها، فيشتد بها الولع ويتملكها الجزع، فتهمل الراعية والسوام، وتشترك في الهديل مع الحمام، وتهم في الفضاء بالتهيام فيهمّ الناظر هناك بالسجود لجلال القدرة، في تزيين الطبيعة وإبداع الفطرة.

وترى هومير آدم الشعر اليوناني وهو أعمى البصر، متلفعًا بالوشي والحبر، تضيء ٦،٤٠

Then you could see a lovely young girl, a beautiful pearl, her features as gorgeous as a wild cow or gazelle, her hair reaching below her waist and shielding her against both heat and cold: 40.4

Tresses that bring the night in the full of day
and a face restoring day in darkest night.[78]

She appeared in the midst of a forest with branches of wood and musk amid fields of violets and roses. The floor was bedecked in scattered clusters of flowers while the ceiling consisted of tree bowers:

She sashayed her path amidst green emeralds
that gave forth scattered pearls.
Every hillock relished the dance,
clothed in a low covering of plants.[79]

Sunlight sprinkled golden dinar-beams on the ground as with brides, gold untouchable by human hands just as the poet al-Mutanabbī earlier described the same situation while riding through the Bawwān Pass, wishing that real coins might fall into his actual pocket, rather than empty favors on his clothing. And perhaps the poor poet died with such regrets as he repeated these words: 40.5

The eastern glow projected on my clothes
dinars that fled from my fingertips.[80]

It was as if all around her chirping birds and cooing doves were answering the maid who had asked about her beloved: Where had he gone, why had he left her and not returned?

They replied that like her, each dove among them had a love to rival the lover who was lost. All this made the girl yet more passionate, and she became alarmed, ignoring her flocks and herds. She was joining the doves in their cooing and expressing her desperate love in the open air. The observer would feel inclined to bow down in homage to nature's exquisite beauty and the superb skill shown in creation.

Next you would see Homer, the original Greek poet who was blind. Enveloped in a colorful wrap, his beard shone with the grey gleam of old age and 40.6

لحيته بالمشيب، وتمتلئ العين منه بمنظر مهيب، يجلس على سرير الملك ملك الأشعار لا ملك الأقطار، وسلطان الأوزان لا سلطان البلدان، والشعراء من الجن يكللونه بإكليل الانتصار، والشعراء من الإنس بين يديه في موقف الإعظام والإكبار، من «هيرنود» و«بسكيل» و«هوراس» و«فرجيل»، وعن يمينه فرسان الزمان، وأبطال الشجعان، في سمة الخضوع، وحيلة الخشوع من «أشيل» و«إسكندر» و«ايني» و«قيصر»، وعند رأسه كاعبان كأنهما اللؤلؤ والمرجان، متحدثان في جمال الوجه والجسم، وإن اختلف الشكل والرسم، هما فتاه اللذان سلكهما في الشعر من شيبة الدهر، والكل في وقوفهم يتأدبون بأدبهما، وينعمون بقربهما، والقيان من حولهما صفوف، بأيديهن المزاهر والدفوف، يوقعن النغم واللحن بذلك النظم والوزن ومن لي بهذا الشاعر وسواه من السابقين المقدمين شعراء الأوّلين والأقدمين، يصف لنا ما بين أيدينا من بدائع هذه الألواح والمهارق، فالتصوير شعر صامت والشعر تصوير ناطق.

٧،٤٠ ولمّا أفقنا من نشوة الإعجاب والازدهاء، واقتربت زيارتنا من الانتهاء إذا نحن برجل أمامنا رث الثياب، خلق الجلباب، غث المنظر، أشعث أغبر:

أخو سفر جواب أرض تقاذفت
به فلوات فهو أشعث أغبر

وقد اختلط شعر جبهته بشعر لحيته، فاختفت بينهما مقاطعه وملامحه، وغمضت أساريره ولوائحه، ونحل جسمه نحول الشاة بالأجادب، وطالت أظفاره فتقوست كالمخالب، واختزن فيها الوسخ فصارت كالمكاحل علقت بها المراود، أو كخطوط الحداد في صفحات الجرائد، يلحظ الناس بلحظة المزدري المحتقر، ويذهب بنفسه ذهاب المبتدع المبتكر، وهم يقابلونه بالاحترام، ويواجهونه بالإكرام، فالتفت الباشا إلى الشيخ الفرنسوي يستخبره ما هذه الكتلة من الدمامة، والكومة من القمامة، وكيف جاز لهم الجمع بين هذه المناظر الحسان، وبين مناظر هذا الشيطان، فاشتبك بينهما الخطاب، وأخذت أترجم لهما في السؤال والجواب:

filled your vision with an awesome spectacle. He was seated on a regal throne, but that of poetry rather than kingdoms, ruler of meters rather than countries. Other poet-djinn were crowning his head with victory garlands, while human poets stood before him in admiration and respect: Herodotus, Aeschylus, Horace, and Virgil, and to the poet's right, brave heroes and cavaliers of old, all humble and submissive, Achilles, Alexander, Aeneas, and Caesar. Above him were two buxom ladies, as beautiful as the purest pearl, similarly lovely in face and body but different in shape and size. They were his two muses, the ones whose path in poetry he had followed since the very beginnings of time. The other poets were standing there, being imbued with their twin culture and relishing their proximity. Circling them both were singing girls, playing on fifes and drums and performing their lays to the appropriate tune and rhythm. How can we talk adequately about this great poet and his colleagues, ancients and illustrious forebears, who manage to use their poetry to portray for us the images found in these paintings and parchments? For portraits are silent poetry, whereas poetry is a portrait that speaks.

When we had somewhat recovered from the sense of rapture and admira- 40.7
tion, and our visit was almost at its end, we saw in front of us a shabbily dressed man, scrawny and disheveled, his djellaba in tatters:

A traveler far and wide ejected by desert wastes
so he looked disheveled and dust-covered.[81]

His head-hair and beard blended together, concealing his face and features, so it was difficult to make out his expression. He looked as thin as a sheep in pastureless terrain. His nails were long and curved like talons; they harbored so much dirt that they looked like kohl-sticks with a nib attached or mourning columns on newspaper pages. This man kept giving people, those arriving and leaving, contemptuous looks and adopting the posture of a creative artist. Even so, people kept greeting him with respect and honoring him. The Pāshā turned toward our colleague, the aged Frenchman, and asked him about this accumulation of dirt and pile of rubbish. How could they possibly be showing a devilish figure like him such respect amid such a collection of beautiful objects and sights. The two men started to engage in conversation on the topic, and I served as their translator as they asked and answered questions:

الباشا أماكان ينبغي أن يحجبوا مثل هؤلاء العامة عن هذه الأماكن النفيسة ليحفظوا لها رونقها ولا يضيعوا بهجتها في نفوس الزائرين، وأن لا يؤذوا بهم أعين الناظرين، ويحطوا من مقدار هذه الزخارف والزين، ولكن لعلهم أرادوا بذلك صرف عين الكمال.

الشيخ الفرنسوي هذا الرجل وأمثاله من شكله من جماعة المصورين الذين اشتهروا بيننا بالنقش والتصوير، وهذا القصر الذي تراه قد أنفقوا عليه من مال الأمّة أربعة وعشرين مليونًا من الفرنكات، هو مقام لإظهار مجدهم والتنويه بذكرهم، وهذه النفائس التي تروقك هي من صنع أيديهم وبنات قرائحهم، ولا تعجب من تفاوت المنظرين، فالذهب يستخرج من التراب والألماس من الفحم. ٨،٤٠

الباشا ولماذا لم تنصفوهم وهذه أعمالهم فتدروا عليهم شيئًا من الأرزاق يصلح بها حالهم، وتحسن هيئتهم، وتنقذهم من هذه الرثاثة التي يرثى لها، وإن كانت هذه الصناعة كاسدة بينكم فلِمَ هذا التشييد لها والتزيين؟

الفرنسوي هؤلاء الذين تراهم وتأسو لحالهم هم بيننا أوسع الناس رزقًا، وأكثرنا بضاعة رائجة، وأقربنا إلى اجتناء الثروة واقتناء الغنى، فإنّ كثيرًا من هذه الألواح المعلقة لهم ممّا لا يعدّ ولا يحصى يساوي اللوح منها المئات من الألوف والآحاد من الملايين، وأقل واحد فيها يكفي ثمنه لأن يكون ذخرًا للمعيشة، وليست هيئتهم هذه عن حاجة ولا عوز، وإنما هي إهمال وذهول، ولا يخفاك أنّ الأشغال الدقيقة تحتاج إلى إعمال الفكرة وإجهاد القريحة، وازدياد الهم، فترى بعضهم من شدة ما أجهدوا الفكر، وحوّلوه إلى نقطة واحدة، اختلت فيهم بقية القوى، وذهلوا ذهولًا فاضحًا عن أمر معيشتهم في مطعمهم وملبسهم فيفسد حالهم، وتسوء أخلاقهم، ويصيرون من الشراسة والحماقة والطيش والخفة بحال لا تحسن معها المعاشرة، وقد جارى بعضهم بعضاً في هذا الباب، ومنهم من يتصنع له كما يتصنع بعض أهل الدين في الورع والنسك والتقى والزهد، وهم يطلقون على أهل هذا الفن لفظ (المتفنن) أو (الصناع) وربما لم يكن عند الكثير منهم من أدواته غير قبح المنظر وشناعة الرأي.

PĀSHĀ Shouldn't people like him be kept away from costly locations like this so as to preserve their splendor, not squander their attraction for the viewing public, and debase the value of their embellishment. But maybe they're trying to avoid the proverbial "evil eye?"

FRENCHMAN This man and others with the same appearance are part 40.8
of a group of painters who are renowned for their skill as artists and painters. The government has spent a total of twenty-four million francs to erect this palace you're now seeing; its purpose is to display their glorious achievements and extol their reputation. These precious works of art that have so impressed you are the products of their skillful hands and issues of their genius. But don't be shocked by the difference in the two images that you see before you; after all, gold is extracted from soil, and diamonds from coal.

PĀSHĀ But, if these are examples of their art, why don't you treat them properly? Why don't you give them enough to live decently, improve their appearance, and avoid looking so regrettably scruffy? If this artistic profession is so unprofitable in your country, then what's the point of constructing this building and all this decoration?

FRENCHMAN These people you're seeing and sympathizing with are among our wealthiest and most prosperous citizens. Of all our people they're most likely to gain a great deal of money. Of the countless number of works hanging here a single canvas may be worth hundreds of thousands or even millions of francs. The price of even a small one would be quite enough to provide a reserve for life. Their general appearance is not because of poverty or need; it's merely that they don't bother about such things and act distracted. You need to realize that such delicate artistry demands a lot of thought, inspiration, and application. Some of them will concentrate so intensely and focus on a single notion that all their other faculties dwindle; they become so distracted that they forget about feeding and clothing themselves. Their circumstances get worse, their moral posture deteriorates, and they become so mean, stupid, reckless, and fickle that it's difficult to spend time with them. They've even persuaded some of their colleagues to adopt the same pose. They've now started putting on the same kind of airs that are used by certain religious types—self-denial, displays of piety, devoutness, and abstinence. Such people are called "artistes." It may in fact be the case that, for many of them, the only tools they have are their scruffy garb and filthy appearance.

٩،٤٠ الصاحب إني لأعجب لقوم يعتمدون في أعمالهم على فكرتهم ثمّ يذهلون عن أنفسهم وأبدانهم هذا الذهول، والفكر النقي والقريحة السليمة لا تسكن إلا البدن الصحيح، وكيف يصح الجسد إذا لم تتعهده بحسن النظافة وطيب الغذاء وقضاء الفروض الطبيعية له وقد يعرض للإنسان المتفكر وهو في تجلي أفكاره أن يشمّ رائحة تعاف، أو ترى عينه منظراً يكره فيضيق حينئذ الصدر وينقبض الفكر، فكيف بمن يجد ذلك كل لحظة في نفسه، ويحس به في جسمه، كما أنّ الصانع المتفنن الذي يعشق الفنون النفيسة ويفتتن بها لذاتها لا بدّ أن يكون فيه من رقة الطبع ولطف الشعور ما يؤثر على أخلاقه بالليونة، وعلى شمائله بالحلاوة وعلى معاشرته بالإنس، وأن لا يشذ عن الناس في أطوارهم وأزيائهم، وما أدري فائدة العلم والمعرفة والبراعة فيها والإحسان إن لم يتولد عنه شيء من كرم الأخلاق وحسن الطباع يضمن سعادة الحياة التي يطلب من أجلها العلم، ويرغب في العرفان، وقد يخطئ من يظنّ أنّ بلوغ الشهرة بين الناس في باب من الأبواب (والشهرة أسرع شيء تقلباً) تكفي الإنسان في سعادة حياته، ورضا الله والناس، ورضا أهله ونفسه عنه وفينا جماعة ممّن يدّعون الولاية والكرامة والاتصال بحبل الله والتقرّب منه، تراهم أقذر الخلق هيئة وأبشعهم منظراً، ويُخدَع بهم الناس، ولا يستحيون من مبدع الكائنات بزينتها وفاطر الجمال في الخلقة، وكيف تنبت الزهرة في السبخة، ويسطع النور من مهجور القبور؟

الفرنسوي صدقت وأصبت، ومن نقص في تربية نفسه فلا يتعرض لتربية الخلق.

١٠،٤٠ الباشا قل لي بالله واين يذهب هذا الرزق الواسع وماذا يعملون بهذا الغنى ان لم يكونوا يختزنونه؟

الفرنسوي الغالب فيهم انهم لا يدخرون شيئاً وأن ثروتهم تضيع بسوؤ تدبيرهم وسفه تصرفهم وتشتت اهوائهم وما هم فيه من الذهول وهم بصناعتهم اقرب الناس للنساء ولرقة الصنعة وللشغف بالجمال فترى ثمن اللوح يخرج من كيس

FRIEND I'm constantly amazed at people who only use their heads as part of their work while neglecting their bodies to this extent. The traditional phrase, *mens sana in corpore sano* is well enough known, so how can anyone's body remain healthy if you don't keep it clean, properly nourished, well exercised, and generally well looked after? A thinker in the midst of his contemplations might smell something bad or witness something disgusting, in which case his entire being shrivels and his ideas dry up. How can it be for someone who can detect such things all the time in his own person and feel it on his own body? Any creative person who loves the fine arts and exerts his talents in that area has to possess an innate subtlety and gentleness so that their morals will be tolerant, their character will be pleasant, and their social traits will be friendly; and such a person should never behave or dress in a way different from other people. What can be the possible benefit of science, learning, intellectual talent, and expertise if they don't lead to the development of upright and good-natured behavior that can guarantee the kind of happy existence envisioned by the quest for knowledge and learning? It's totally wrong to imagine that the achievement of fame in a particular field (and fame is of all things the swiftest to be transformed) is enough to bring someone happiness in life, to please both God and mankind, and indeed to please his family and himself. We have among us a group of people who make all sorts of claims about being faithful, generous, and in the closest possible contact with God. Yet you'll find that they've the scruffiest appearance and present the ugliest of sights. People are deceived by them and have no qualms about artists who portray living creatures in all their beauty and paint nature in all its loveliness. But, that said, how are flowers supposed to grow in a swamp or the gleam of light to shine forth from a grave? 40.9

FRENCHMAN You're so right! Anyone who fails to monitor his own self cannot aspire to do so with other people.

PĀSHĀ But what do these artists do with all the money they earn if they haven't been hording it? 40.10

FRENCHMAN As a general rule they don't horde any of it. Their wealth gets squandered because of poor planning, stupid behavior, reckless desires, and general absentmindedness. Their art keeps them very close to women due to the delicacy of their craft and their passion for beauty. So you'll watch as the price for the canvas leaves the purse of the befuddled rich man to be placed first into the hands of its crazy creator, then into the pockets of a nasty harlot,

الغني المغفل الى يد الصانع المجنون الى جيب الفاجرة الهلوك الى حانوت البائع للزينة والحلي وفيهم من يتكلف بالانفاق على كثير من الامثلة.

الباشا وما هي «الامثلة»؟

الفرنسوي «المثال» هو المرأة التي يختارها المصور في حسنها ليملاء منها عينه ويصور على مثالها في حسن التركيب حتى لا تغيب عنه دقيقة في الجسم ما ظهر منه وما خفي فقلما تدخل في مصنع احدهم الا وترى امامه امراة مكشوفة البدن عارية الجسم لا يحتجب عنه عضو من أعضائها بحجاب ولا يستره ستر.

الباشا ما هذا العيب والفجور؟

١١،٤٠ **الفرنسوي** ليس هذا عندنا بعيب بل هو امر مقبول حتى صار بين النساء في مقام صنعة من الصناعات ومهنة من المهن وعندنا اليوم خلاف في هل يجوز للصانع ان يعمل هذا العمل وهو خارج عن مسالك السابلة فان احد المصورين عنّ له بالامس ان يصور بعثاً من القبور فقصد احدى المقابر في المدينة وقعد هناك بادواته ومن أدواته امرأتان اوقفهما أمامه عاريتا الجسد مكشوفتا العورة وأقام احداهما في هيئة السجود والاخرى في هيئة الانبطاح وهو يقيم الساعة والساعتين يمعن فيهما ويتأمل ويصور وينقش وبجانب المقبرة دار تبنى قام على حائطها البناؤون فاستحيوا من هذا المنظر وخجلوا من هذا التهتك والافتضاح فجاءوا الى المصور ينبهونه الى سوء ما يفعل وقبح ما يرون فاستجهلهم وسخر بهم ودام على عمله هذا اياماً لا يبالي بتعنيفهم وتعزيرهم فعمدوا آخر الامر الى الشرطة ثم الى المحكمة يطلبون كف هذا المنظر عن أعينهم ومنع هذا المجلس من الانعقاد أمامهم كل صباح ومساء والامر منظور الآن في المحكمة وقد اختلفت الجرائد فيما بينها هل يجوز المنع أم لا فبعضها يذهب الى انه يجوز لتطبيقه على نفس القانون الذي يعاقب على انتهاك حرمة الآداب العامة في الطرق وتمزيق ثوب الحياء والعفاف وبعضها يرى ان المنع انتهاك لحرية الأشخاص فكل انسان حر في صناعته لا يجوز منعه عن اسباب اتقانه في صنعه وما يحتاج اليه فيه.

and thereafter into the owner of a jewelry store. Some of them spend money on lots of models.

Pāshā What do you mean by "models"?

Frenchman A "model" is a woman chosen by the artist for her beauty. He can gaze at her and paint a likeness of her perfect proportions, the aim being that not for a single moment will the obvious and hidden aspects of the body be out of his vision. Whenever you enter an artist's studio, you will always find a woman in front of him, unclothed and naked, with every one of her limbs clearly exposed and totally uncovered.

Pāshā What is this disgusting debauchery?

Frenchman In our culture there's nothing shameful about it. It's completely acceptable, and for women it has become one of the respectable crafts and professions. In fact, there's a debate going on at the moment as to whether an artist needs to practice his profession away from public thoroughfares. Yesterday an artist decided that he wanted to portray resurrection from the grave, so he headed for one of the city's cemeteries and sat there with his paintbrushes and two models. He positioned them both, completely naked with their private parts exposed, with one bowed down and the other prostrate on the ground. He spent an hour or two gazing at the two women, contemplating, sketching, and then creating the painting. Right alongside the cemetery a house was under construction with builders standing on the wall. They were disgusted by what they were seeing and felt bashful about such a scandalous display. They went up to the painter and told him that what he was doing was wrong and they found the entire scene disgusting. But the painter not merely ignored their complaints and jeered at them but also carried on with his work for several days, still ignoring their complaints and disapproval. The construction workers raised the matter with the police and then took the matter to court in order to stop this scene from occurring before their very eyes and this lewd assembly from gathering every morning and afternoon. The entire matter is now before the courts, and newspapers have published different opinions on it: should such practices be prohibited or not. Some people say that the answer is "yes," basing their opinion on the law that punishes anyone for infringements of public morality on the streets and offending all guise of modesty and decency, but others claim that such prohibition is an infringement of personal liberty; everyone is free to practice his art and no one has the right to interfere in such a way as to impede his artistic creativity. 40.11

١٢،٤٠ قال عيسى بن هشام: ولما ألقيت في اذن الباشا هذا القول في ما أترجم له وجدت جبينه يندى بالعرق وكفه تستر وجهه خجلا وحياء وأخذ يستعيذ ويستجير وأومأ الينا بالمسير فسرنا نقصد الباب وكلما مررنا بحجرة دخلنا في حجرة حتى كدنا نضل في اتساع القصر وهو على هذا الاتساع غاص بالصور والتماثيل لا تجد فجوة خالية منها.

ولما تيسر لنا الخروج منه وصرنا في الطريق بين هذين القصرين اللذين هما تاج المعرض واكليل الصناعات عاد الباشا الى الفرنسوي يسأله:

الباشا وما عسى يكون شأن هذين القصرين بعد انتهاء ايام المعرض ومن يسكنهما؟

الفرنسوي لا يحلهما احد وانما يبقيان معدين لعرض بعض الصناعات وعرض الصور التي يصورها المصورون في كل عام.

الصاحب انني كلما نظرت الى هذه العناية الكبرى عندكم بالتصوير ورفعه الى هذه الدرجة العليا والمكانة القصوى والانقطاع له والتغالي فيه ثم نظرت الى انه لا يكاد يكون له اثر عندنا أخذني العجب وحرت في السبب فان كان ذلك ناشئاً عن الترقي في المدنية والسبق في الحضارة والتقدم في فضول الترف فاني اراه فيكم قديماً شائعاً والجاهلية شائعة فيكم وربما كان القديم في ذلك ابدع من الحديث فما هو السر في دوام هذه العناية بينكم وفقدها لدينا مع ان اهل الشرق منا على ما تخيلون اكثر مجالا في الخيال واوسع مداراً في التصور؟

١٣،٤٠ الفرنسوي أعلم ان كل ما تراه يدوم ويبقى في الامم من مثل هذه الامور وغيرها إما ان يكون لمنفعة مجربة فيه تدعو اليه الحاجة وتقضي به واما ان يكون لاعتقاد ثابت متوارث لعلة من العلل وقد علمت ان اهل الغرب كانوا قبل الدين المسيحي اهل دين يعبد الاصنام والاوثان فقضى الاعتقاد الديني بالتصوير والتمثيل لم يقدروا ان يتصوروا جلال الخالق فصوروه على ما ينطبق تصورهم عليه ولم يقدروا ان يرتفعوا

ʿĪsā ibn Hishām said: When I had translated all this for the Pāshā, I noticed that his brow was covered in sweat, and he was using his hand to cover his face in sheer embarrassment. Seeking refuge in God, he indicated that we should leave. We now did so, walking from one room into the next till we almost got lost due to the sheer size of the palace. There were so many rooms, all filled with paintings and sculptures, and no nook or cranny was left unfilled. After we had found the exit and left the palace, we walked along the road between the two buildings, they being the centerpiece of the exhibition as a whole, wonderfully constructed. The Pāshā now turned to the Philosopher and asked him: 40.12

PĀSHĀ So what's going to happen to these two buildings when the exhibition comes to an end? Who'll be living there?

FRENCHMAN Nobody will be living in them. They're going to stay the way they are, ready to hold exhibitions of crafts and paintings created by artists every year.

FRIEND Every time I consider the amount of attention that you pay to art in this culture—raising it to the very heights, giving it enormous prestige, devoting almost exclusive and even exaggerated attention to it, and, by contrast, the minimal concern that we show in the East, I find myself astonished and unable to come up with a reason. If it's the consequence of a superior level of culture and civilization and of increasing affluence, I find that your culture has possessed such qualities since ancient times and that the earliest historical periods are very much current among you. Indeed, what is ancient may be more skillfully rendered than what is modern. What's the reason for the interest that you people show whereas we do not? And we do not in spite of the fact that, in your conception, the peoples of the East have shown far greater imagination and potential in portraiture.

FRENCHMAN You should be aware that all the objects that you see here 40.13
that survive and persist among different peoples have either fulfilled some specific purpose or need or else responded to a fixed article of faith that has been inherited across generations for one reason or another. I've learned that, before the advent of the Christian faith, religious people in the West used to worship idols. Religious belief demanded the creation of paintings and statues. They were not capable of representing the majesty of the Creator, so they did their best to represent the concept according to their own limited thinking. However, they were unable to elevate their ideas to such an exalted plane,

بفكرهم الى سمو درجته فأنزلوه الى درجتهم وشبهوه على مثالهم وقد ترك لكم آباؤكم المصريون ما يبهر من التماثيل والتصاوير وقد انتشر هذا الامر في الدولة اليونانية والدولة الرومانية انتشاراً عظيما حتى تعدي الآلهة الى المخلوقات فاقاموا التماثيل لكبراء رجالهم وعظماء حكامهم ووصل الحال من التغالي فيه ايام الدولة اليونانية الى ان بلغ عدد ما اقيم من التماثيل لاحد الذين نالوا بينهم الشهرة الباطلة والصيت الكاذب ثلثمائة تمثال في شوارع مدينة اثينا لم تبق بعده ثلثمائة يوم والحكاية مشهورة ان احد الناس قال في كلامه لعظيم من عظمائهم جليل القدر جميل الفعال: اني لاعجب كيف اقيم لفلان ثلثمائة تمثال ولم يقيموا لك تمثالا واحداً وأنت الاجل المفضل فقال له: لأن يتعجب الناس كيف انهم لم يقيموا لي تمثالا خير من ان يعجبوا كيف أقيمت لي التماثيل هذا ولمّا دخل الدين المسيحي على هذه الحال لم يحظر التصوير ولم يمنع التمثيل فاستباح الناس فيه ما الفوه من قبل وتناولوه نفسه بهذا الفن وصوروا المسيح وأمه (عليهما السلام) في كثير من أطوار حياتهما وصوروا ما شاؤوا من حكايات التاريخ المقدس على ما تشاهده فبقيت العناية به وأظن ان سبب اهمال ذلك فيكم خاصة هو من حظر دينكم له في ما اعلم والا فهو منتشر في الشرق بين بقية الامم كالصينيين واليابانيين وأهل الهند والجدوى من التغالي في انتشار هذا الفن قليلة وهو لا يفيد عندنا الآن الا ان يجعل فئة بيننا من الناس في حالة المجانين لخدمة فئة تبذل فيه الاموال العظيمة من رزق المساكين.

قال عيسى بن هشام: وسرنا عن هذين القصرين نقصد غيرهما من المعاهد ونزور ما اشتهر من المشاهد. ١٤،٤٠

so instead they reduced the concept to their own level and made their images accordingly. Your own Egyptian ancestors left splendid portraits and statues. The trend spread widely during the Greek and Roman eras to such an extent that it went beyond the portrayal of gods to created beings. They put up statues to important men and great rulers. During the Greek era things reached such a pass that on the streets of Athens they put up three hundred statues for a single man who had acquired some fleeting fame and recognition among them. When he died, those statues did not even last three hundred days. One of the well-known stories in this connection tells how someone spoke to one of these worthy and noble citizens in these terms: "I'm amazed that the people of Athens have put up three hundred statues to this man, whereas they haven't put up a single one for you who are much more deserving and virtuous." The man replied that he would much rather have people wonder why he has no statue than have the same people equally surprised that he did have one. When the Christian faith developed, its adherents neither proscribed nor forbad this practice, so everyone continued the same way. In fact, the Christian community adopted the representational arts, portraying Jesus and his mother (peace be upon them both) at various stages in their lives and recording all kinds of stories from sacred history, as you can see here. Christians have remained interested in this field up to the present day, unlike the situation with regard to your own faith in particular, where, as far as I understand, such things are proscribed. Apart from that, it is widespread among other peoples—the Chinese, for example, the Japanese, and the Indians. Frankly, the widespread availability of such art does not bring great benefits to us now, that is, apart from the fact that it makes a small group of our people sufficiently crazy to satisfy the desires of a limited group who are prepared to spend enormous sums at the expense of the poor.

ʿĪsā ibn Hishām said: After leaving these twin palaces, we made our way to other institutions so we could get some impression of the famous sites. 40.14

مصباح الشرق ١٢١، ٢١ سبتمبر ١٩٠٠

باريس

قال عيسى بن هشام: ودخلنا معرض الاشجار وبستان الازهار في قصر لم يبن بناء القصور والديار ولم تشيد أركانه بالشيد والاحجار ولم ترتفع بالآجر حجره وغرفه او تتخذ من الخشب أبوابه وسقفه بل عقدت له القباب والابراج من ساقي البلور وسبيك الزجاج فهو صرح ممرد من قوارير كأنه لجة ماء او صفحة غدير لو دخلته اليوم صاحبة العرش في الايام الخالية لكشفت عن ساقيها مرة ثانية جمعوا فيه اشتات النبات الغض من كل بقعة من أطراف الارض مما ينبت من ثنيات الجليد وتنشق عنه صم الجلاميد وما اخضر في ربى الصحراء واورق في وهاد البيداء وأينع في الومد وأزهر في الجمد ومن حيث تجري الانهار والجداول الى حيث تعتصم الاراوي والاجادل ومن حيث تشدو الحمامة الورقاء تحت الظلال والافياء الى حيث تدور الحرباء حول الغزالة في كبد السماء ومن ادنى الشرق الى اقصى الغرب ومن طرف القطب الى طرف القطب فما شئت هناك من سائر الانواع في متفرق البقاع ما بين ملتف منه ومنتشب ومتشعب ومؤتشب يفتر بكل مصفر ومبيض ومذهب ومفضض ومشرق ومومض هناك تستبيك ألوان الأزاهر بما يزري بلمعان الجواهر وأين ابن الرومي يتأملها فيخلع عنه رداء الفخر والتيه ويقر بعجزه في الوصف والتشبيه ويحرق ديوانه بكبريته المذكور في تشبيهه المشهور: ١،٤١

ولازوردية تزهو بزرقتها
بين الرياض على حمر اليواقيت
كأنها وضعاف القطب تحملها
أوائل النار في أطراف كبريت.

فما الياقوت والزبرجد وما الفيروز والزمرد وما العقيق والجمان وما الدر والمرجان ٢،٤١

Miṣbāḥ al-sharq 121, September 21, 1900[82]

Paris

We entered the tree and flower pavilion. It was not constructed like other palaces and houses. The corners had no plaster over the stones, nor were bricks used to build its different rooms or wood for its doors and ceilings. Instead it consisted of domes and towers of polished crystal and glass. A construction like a polished bottle, it looked just like sea swell or the calm surface of a pond. If Bilqīs, the Sheban queen of old, had entered this building today, she would have uncovered her legs again.[83] In this building they had collected plants of every kind and from all corners of the globe, some of them poking out of ice, others growing on solid boulders; some plants that flourish in desert hills and some that grow in the lowlands of steppes, flowering amid snow and budding in extreme heat. Some emerge from places where streams and rivers flow, while others come from climes where goats and falcons are the denizens. Some come from regions where the mourning dove coos its melody in shady courts while others belong in places where the chameleon roams in the noonday heat—from nearest East to furthest East, and from one pole to the other. The flowers and plants were thus of every conceivable variety and from all the world's regions; some were coiled in a spiral while others climbed high and branched out. Yellow- and white-colored flowers opened up, as did others—silver and gold, bright and gleaming, all to enrapture you with their colors that flashed like jewels. What would the poet, Ibn al-Rūmī, have done as he contemplated their beauty? Relinquishing all pride and boast, he would have been forced to admit his failure to describe or compare them, and would even have been compelled to burn his poetry collection with its well-known simile: 41.1

How many a lapis lazuli in the meadows
  flaunts its blue color at the red ruby's expense,
As though both it and fragile stems were being
  supported by the initial flares on the tips of matches.[84]

Compared with flowers like these, what are rubies, emeralds, tortoiseshells, carnelians, pearls, and corals? How can stones be compared to trees 41.2

وكيف يقاس الحجر بالشجر وتستوي الحصباء اليابسة بأكمام الاغصان المائسة وكيف يتقدم الجامد الثابت على النامي النابت وأين الحركة من السكون والمنشور من المدفون وأين المنثور على ظهر الروضة الزهراء من الملحود في بطون الغبراء؟ ولئن انتظمت القلائد من هذه القرائد في لبات الخرائد وحلت من الحور في المعاصم والنحور فحل تلك الزهور بين الرئات والصدور وكم نثرت ميت النفوس والارواح بطيب الأنفاس والارواح؟

فوقفنا هناك نستنشق الاريج والنثر من أصناف الطيب والعطر حتى انتشينا من ٣،٤١
غير ما خمر وثملنا من غير ما وزر لوكان معنا ضرير المعرة رهن المحبسين لارتد مثلوج الصدر قرير العين فأنس من وحشته وذهل عن فقره وخلته ولعلم ان من المسكر ما هو حلال ولم يتلهف على شرب المعتقة حيث قال:

تمـنيت ان الخمـر حـلـت لنشوة
تجـهلني كيف اطمأنت بي الحـال
فأجـهل اني بالعـراق عـلى شفـا
رزي الاماني لا أنيس ولا مـال

وما زلنا في هذه الروضة الغناء والجنة الفيحاء نردد قول العبد الصالح الاواه: ﴿وَلَوْلَا إِذْ دَخَلْتَ جَنَّتَكَ قُلْتَ مَا شَاءَ اللَّهُ لَا قُوَّةَ إِلَّا بِاللَّهِ﴾ ونكرر النشيد لبيت التوحيد:

ففي كل شيء له آية
تدل على انه واحـد

حتى آن أوان الانصراف من بين هذه الالفاف فخرجنا منها خروج أبينا من دار الخلود والبقاء الى دار الهموم والشقاء ولما سرنا في نواحي المعرض ضؤل في أعيننا ما كان يروقنا ويزهينا وحقر في انفسنا ما كان يعجبنا ويشجينا وذبل ما كان من المناظر ناضرا وسفل ما كان عظيما نادرا وغلب ذلك المنظر على كل بديع رائع من مختلف

or dry gravel be measured against gently swaying boughs? How can what is fixed and immovable be preferred over what is ever growing and developing; movement over stasis, things spread over soil over those buried under ground; flora planted in a fertile meadow over what is interred in the dust? Were garlands like these to be strung for the necks of beauteous damsels and to deck the bosoms and throats of lovely ladies, then flowers like these should be found twixt breast and rib. How often have they refreshed body and soul with pleasant scents and lovely wafts.

We stood there, relishing the fragrant scent of different aromatic plants till 41.3
we felt intoxicated without wine and drunk without guilt. Had the blind poet of Maʿarrah, the ascetic Abū l-ʿAlāʾ, prison hostage, been in our company, he would have rejected his frigidity and blindness, emerging from his isolation and bewildered by his own poverty and lack. He would have realized that whatever is permitted can be just as intoxicating; he would have had no need to indulge in old vintages when he declared:

I wished for a wine that could engender an intoxication
  that could leave me ignorant as to why I feel so secure.
I am unaware of being on the edge in Iraq,
  all hopes lost and without companions or money.[85]

We stayed in this gorgeous garden, this splendid paradise, for a while, repeating the sighs of the devout worshipper: «Entering your own paradise, you must say: As God wills, there is no power unless it be through Him,»[86] and repeating the chant to the haven of Unity:

In every thing there is a sign of Him
  revealing that He is One.[87]

When it was time to leave, we made our way out of this luxurious garden, just like our forebear, Adam, as he made his way out of the haven of eternity into the world of cares and misery. As we headed for other parts of the exhibition, things that had been delighting us thus far diminished in our eyes; whatever had previously been of concern to us now seemed insignificant. Every view now seemed less glamorous, and all that was rare and imposing now

الفنون والصنائع و أين صنعة الانسان .من قدرة الرحمن وما تصوره يد البارئ الصانع مما تسويه آلات المصانع

٤،٤١ وكاد الباشا يهم بالرجوع من حيث أتينا ويقتصر في يومنا على ما رأينا لولا ان سمعنا الفرنسوي يقول للصاحب في عرض كلامه عن ترتيب المعرض ونظامه:

الفرنسوي نعم تنقسم أماكن المعرض الى قسمين, هذا القسم الذي نشاهد فيه ما نشاهده من معروضات الصناعة والطبيعة وهو مباح للداخلين بغير أجر وقسم آخر مقام لترويح النفس واستجلاب الانس بالمشاهدات الغريبة والمناظر العجيبة يدخله الداخل بأجر معين.

الصاحب لقد سمعت عن ذلك القسم ما يعجب ويدهش وقرأت ما تنشره الصحف كل يوم من المبالغة في وصفه والمغالاة في شرح ما يحتويه من المخترعات والمبتدعات وأشد ما تتولع نفسي لمشاهدته تلك النظارة الهائلة التي اخترعوها لمشاهدة كرة القمر على بعد متر واحد منا فنحيط بها العين كما يحيط الجالس في الغرفة بجدرانها فهلم بنا نقصد قصد ذلك المكان.

الفرنسوي ليس ذلك المكان ببعيد منا وهو القصر الذي يسمونه «قصر الاضواء والمرائي» وطالما ذكرت عنه الجرائد كما تقول ما يرغب في زيارته ولكنني لم أره بعد ولا بأس من زيارته الآن ان أردتم.

الباشا اسرعوا بنا اليه و والله لو كان ما يقولون عنه صحيحاً لكان ذلك من اكبر المعجزات ان لم يكن من اكبر اعمال السحر واني لأعجب لنا كيف نضيع الوقت في مشاهدة كثير من المعروضات التي كنا نراها بين أيدينا في بلادنا في اماكن التجارة والاسواق ولا نبدأ بزيارة هذا القصر العجيب الذي يدنو فيه القمر مثل هذا الدنو المدهش.

٥،٤١ قال عيسى بن هشام: فسرنا جميعاً نلتمس هذا المكان حتى وصلنا الى قصر مشيد يتباهى بمثله الامراء والملوك في فخامته وضخامته ووجدنا مكتوباً على بابه بين صور الكواكب والنجوم هذه العبارة باللاتينية «من هنا يصعد الانسان الى الكواكب

paled. The vistas we had seen were superior to all the various innovative and wonderful arts and crafts. For how can one compare human craft with that of the Creator? The products of factories can never rival the hand of the One Maker of all?

At this point the Pāshā was on the verge of going back the way we had come and confining his day's ration of visits to what he had already seen. But we heard the Frenchman talking to our Friend about the way this exhibition had been organized and arranged: 41.4

FRENCHMAN That's right. The exhibition space is divided into two sectors. The one devoted to exhibits culled from both industry and nature, is open to the public without charge. There's also another section that's been set up for entertainment and public appeal by putting weird and amazing things on display. Entry to the second section involves paying a special fee.

FRIEND The things that I've heard about this latter section have shocked and amazed me. What I've read in the newspapers every day contains exaggerated accounts of the various inventions that it includes. The one thing that I'm anxious to see is the amazing telescope they've invented that allows you to see the moon just a meter away, so close that it looks as though you were sitting there watching it in a walled room. So, come on, let's go there.

FRENCHMAN It's not far. They call it the palace of lights and mirrors. As you say, newspapers have been writing about it in terms that make you want to go there. I haven't been there myself as yet, so we can go there now if you like.

PĀSHĀ Yes, let's hurry. If what they say about it is true, it must be a real wonder, if not a piece of magic! For my own part, I'm surprised that we wasted so much time visiting exhibits that we've already seen right in front of us in our own country in commercial locations and markets. We could have started by visiting this amazing palace which can bring the moon so amazingly close.

ʿĪsā ibn Hishām said: So we set out for this other building and eventually arrived at another palace, one so splendid and huge that princes and kings would have proudly showed off the like. Over the door decked with stars and 41.5

ويتصل باللانهائية» ولما دخلناه رأيناه مزدحماً بالجموع فبدأنا معهم بالدخول في حجرة واسعة فرأيناها في اتساعها تبلغ خمسة عشر متراً في الطول وعشرة في العرض وهي مقسمة بالمثلثات والاضلاع من زجاج المرايا القائمة فيها يبلغ علو الواحدة منها مترين ونصفاً في عرض متر ونصف وقد تخللتها أضواء الكهربائية فاذا نظر الانسان فيها بين تلك الاضلاع والمثلثات رأى صورته فيها متعددة تعد أشكالها بالمئين واذا مشى فيها خطوات ضل الطريق ولم يهتد السبيل وتعذر عليه أن يهتدي السبيل وتعذر عليه أن يجد بابا للخروج وكلما ظن انه وجد منفذاً يخرج منه فيندفع اليه صدمه في وجهه زجاج المرآة فتعلو أصوات الضاحكين وهم بين حيرتهم وضلالهم ولا يزال كذلك مدة من الزمن حتى يهتدي الى نهج الطريق بالصدفة والاتفاق ولو كان معنا أحد الشعراء لاتسع له مجال الخيال في وصف اشكال النساء وانطباع الصورة الواحدة منها ألف مرة في صفحات المرايا كما تنطبع محبتها وهي واحدة على صفحات قلوب الالوف من الرجال

٦،٤١ ولما بصرنا بطريق الهداية للخروج من هذه الغرفة التي يضل فيها الزائر كما يضل الراكب الجاهل في الفيافي والمجاهل خرجنا نقصد غيره والفرنسوي يقول للصاحب في حديثه:

الفرنسوي ان الفكرة في اقامة الغرف والابنية على أوضاع وأشكال يضل فيها الداخل اليها قديمة في الوجود وقد علم أن قدماء المصريين هم اول من شيد بناء مخصوصاً للتيه ولا يزال في بلادكم اثر من ذلك الهيكل المقام على مثل هذا الشكل رآه هيرودوتس في زمانه ووصفه في تاريخه كان يحتوي على ثلاثة آلاف حجرة متداخلة في بعضها بكيفية ان من دخل في المعبد ولم يكن معه دليل ضل فيه حتى يهلك جوعاً واثره باق الى اليوم بقرب بحيرة موريس امام المدينة القديمة المسماة بمدينة التمساح وقد حذا القدماء من اليونانيين حذوهم فاقاموا معبداً يماثله في كريد ذكروا في خرافاتهم أن احد الغيلان كان يفسد في الارض ثم يلجأ اليه فلا يدركه احد فاراد احد الشجعان قتله فلم يتوصل الى ذلك الا بخيط مخصوص دلته عليه عشيقته علق

planets was inscribed the following text in Latin: "From here mankind ascends to the stars and links with infinity." Once we had gone inside, we found it crowded with people. We joined them all and made our way into a huge room fifteen meters long and ten meters wide, divided up by triangular-shaped glass mirrors, each of which was two and a half meters high and a meter and a half wide. They were all separated by electric lamps. If you looked at the triangular shapes, you could see your image reflected hundreds of times. By walking just a few paces, you could lose your way completely. It was impossible to find a way out. Every time you thought you had discovered a way out and headed towards it, your face would bang against the glass; everyone would start laughing because they were just as lost. This process would go on for quite a while until by a stroke of luck you eventually reached the right path. If we had had in our company a poet, he would have had a great deal of scope for his imagination to describe the shapes of the female visitors and the impression left a thousand times by their images in the mirrors—much as a single woman can leave an impression on the pages of men's hearts in the thousands as well.

Once we had made our way out of this room where the visitor can get as lost as any rider in desert wastes, we headed for other rooms. The Frenchman was talking to our Friend: **41.6**

Frenchman This idea of putting up places and buildings in maze-like patterns that will get people lost and not knowing the way out is an ancient one. We've learned that the ancient Egyptians were the first to construct buildings specifically so that people would get lost. Some traces of this type of temple that Herodotus saw and described in his history still exist. It contained three thousand interlocking rooms, constructed in such a way that anyone entering the temple without a guide would get so lost that he'd die of hunger; traces of it can still be seen by Lake Moeris next to the ancient city known as Crocodile City. The ancient Greeks copied the Egyptian model and erected a temple like it in Crete. One of their myths tells how a ghoul was causing all sorts of havoc on earth but then took refuge inside this labyrinth where no one could catch it. A Greek hero decided to go after it and kill it. To do so he had recourse to a piece of string that his beloved showed him. He tied one end to a door by the entrance before he went in, then entered the labyrinth, achieved

طرفه عند الباب قبل دخوله وسار به في طريقه حتى اهتدى في رجوعه به الى موضع خروجه والفرق ما بين صنع القدماء في السالف والمحدثين في الحاضر ان بناء اولائك من الاحجار وهؤلاء من الزجاج.

قال عيسى بن هشام: ودخلنا بعد ذلك في عدة غرف فيها اشكال متعددة من انعكاس الاضواء في المرايا فتخيل هنا بئرًا وهناك موجًا الى غير ذلك من وجوه التخيل ثم انهينا الى تلك الحجرة التي يرى فيها القمر على بعد متر فما جاوزنا بابها حتى أطفئت الانوار في وجوهنا وأقمنا في ظلام دامس ثم حرروا فيه أشعة الكهرباء على الحائط فأضاءت عليها خريطة للقمر مصنوعة بطريقة تتبين فيها مرتفعات كرة القمر ومنخفضاته فترى هذه بمقدار خروق الغربال وتلك بمقدار قلامة الظفر ووقف لنا رجل كالخطيب الشارح يبين لنا ما يبينه في هذا الرسم ويزعم انها صورة القمر بعينها على بعد سبعين كيلومترًا كما يرى في النظارة المعظمة التي قالوا عنها انها تريه على بعد متر واحد وأعلنوا عنها بالمقالات المهمة في الجرائد العلمية والسياسية في انحاء العالم مدة سنوات فخرجنا والصاحب يقلب كفًا على كف من شدة الدهش والعجب ويسأل الشيخ الفرنسوي عن هذا الغش والكذب: ٧،٤١

الفرنسوي لا تعجب ولا تدهش فان اكثر ما تراه من التفخيم والتعظيم لمثل هذه المسائل على صفحات الجرائد لا يعول عليه فانها تقصد ذلك قصدًا في مقابل أجر معلوم من الدراهم ولحبها النفع لابناء البلاد فتبالغ في الوصف لترغيب الناس واقبال الزائرين على زيارة هذه الاماكن بما يكون وراءه الربح العظيم للقائمين بأمرها وهي تستحل في ذلك الغش والكذب خدمة للمصلحة الخاصة والعامة على انك لو علمت ان الذي قام بهذا المشروع في انشاء هذا المحل هو الموسيو دلونكل صاحبكم الذي له عندكم ذكر وأثر لم تعجب ولم تدهش وأنتم أدرى بمشروعاته وليس هذا العمل بأول أعماله وان كان الكذب والغش فيه رسميًا على أعين الناس ورؤوس الاشهاد فانه بعد ان قام في مجلس النواب في سنة ٩٢ وطلب منه المصادقة على اقامة هذا المعرض العام ٨،٤١

his purpose, then made his way out. The major difference between what the ancients did long ago and modern people have been doing recently is that the ancients used stone whereas the moderns are using glass.

ʿĪsā ibn Hishām said: We now went into a number of smaller rooms; in each case, the pattern of reflected light in mirrors and the multiplicity of images was repeated. What you thought was a well turned out to be an entire sea, and so on. Finally we reached the room we were aiming for, the one where the moon could be viewed at a distance of a mere meter. No sooner had we made our way inside than the lights were all turned off, and we found ourselves in total darkness. They then projected rays of light on the wall, and a map of the moon's surface appeared in such a way as to show the moon's mountains and valleys; the former looked the size of a fingernail, while the latter were like the holes in a sieve. A man holding forth like a preacher was explaining to us the details of the image and asserting that it was a picture of the moon at a distance of seventy kilometers as seen through the telescope. This was the device that announcements had been claiming could show you the moon at a meter's distance, something that important articles in scientific and political journals had also been proclaiming to the world for years. As we left, the Friend was brushing his hands in surprise and amazement, as he asked the Frenchman to explain how such a piece of fraud and deceit was possible: 41.7

Frenchman Don't act so shocked! There can be no justification for the kind of hyperbole in discussing matters that you tend to read in newspapers. They do it quite deliberately for a fixed price and for their own benefit, with no advantage accruing to the French people. They exaggerate in this way because they're eager for visitors to come to these exhibits because huge profits are involved for the people who set them up. All that makes such fraudulent claims permissible in their eyes, since it's supposed to be a service to both private and public interests. If only you realized that the person who embarked on the project to set up this exhibition was none other than your good friend, Monsieur Deloncle who's well known in your part of the world, you shouldn't be surprised. You know about his projects; this isn't his first one, even though he's lied and tricked his way on a formal basis in front of everyone. After he had got up and made a speech in the assembly in 1892 in which he asked for 41.8

أعلن انه وجد عنقاء المعرض التي ستكون فيه المعجزة الكبرى من عمل الانسان بانشاء نظارة معظمة يرى الناظر فيها القمرعن بعد متر وما زال يحكي والجرائد تكتب حتى أنشأ في سنة ٩٦ شركة من بعض الفلكيين لعمل تلك النظارة التي يقولون اليوم انها تريه على بعد سبعين كيلومترًا وأنشأوا هذا القصر بمناظره لمشاهدة الزائرين لها واجتناء الربح من وراء زيارتهم وعلى هذا تدور أغلب أمور العالم من التهويل الباطل والغلو الكاذب بمقدار الفرق بين المتر الواحد والسبعين كيلو مترًا والربح فيه أعظم لمن كان أعظم مهارة في أنواع الغش والخداع وأبواب المكر والاحتيال.

٩،٤١ قال عيسى بن هشام: وانصرفنا ونحن نعجب من احتيال هذا السياسي الذي لم يكفه الاحتيال من طريق السياسة والاستعمار حتى ترقى فيها الى طريق الكواكب والاقمار.

an agreement to mount this Universal Exhibition, he proceeded to announce that he had discovered the exhibit's Phoenix, one that would be mankind's greatest ever miracle, a telescope through which you could see the moon just one meter away. He's kept on talking about it and newspapers have kept on repeating it till in 1896 he'd founded a company consisting of astronomers who would make the telescope which they now say can show the moon at a distance of seventy kilometers. They've built this structure—with all its vistas—in order to rake in the profits from the large number of visitors who would come to look at this amazing invention. This is the way things work with people in the world today, mouthing falsehoods and grossly exaggerating their accomplishments—to the extent of the difference between a single meter and seventy kilometers. The major profiteers in this process are the people who resort to deceit and trickery; the big winners habitually cheat and double-cross.

ʿĪsā ibn Hishām said: As we left, we were amazed to learn about this deputy 41.9
who was not content just to use trickery in his political life and colonial policy, but had to raise it as far as the stars and planets.

مصباح الشرق ١٢٣، ٥ أكتوبر ١٩٠٠

باريس

١،٤٢ قال عيسى بن هشام: وسرنا في قسم المرائي والمشاهد ندخل واحداً منها اثر واحد فلا نجد فيه عندما نوافيه ما سمعناه من وصف واصفيه بل ربما وجدنا ما يخالفه وينافيه الى ان وصلنا الى قصر مشرف منيف، يزهو على القصور بحسن الترصيص والترصيف أعدوه هناك لانواع الرقص والقصف والقفز والعزف يمثلون فيه كل شكل وصنف من ميلة قد وهزة عطف منذ عهد البداوة الغابرة الى عهد الحضارة الحاضرة ومن أيام عيش الخشونة والشظف الى عيش الليونة والترف ومن رقص الحماسة والشجاعة الى رقص الخلابة والخلاعة فترى رجال البداوة يرقصون بالسيوف في مواقف الحتوف وترى العذارى من حولهم يضربن بالدفوف ويصفقن بالكفوف تحريضاً لهم في ساعة الحرب وإلهابا وإثارة لهم على العدو واغضابا فتحلو لديهم مضاضة الاقدام كما تحلو لشاربها غضاضة المدام ويرتشفون كؤوس المنايا ارتشافهم رضاب الثنايا ثم ترى غيرهم يرقصون للنصر والظفر وفرحة الاوبة من السفر بين عذارى الحي وجواريه وأسارى القتال وموتوريه باشارات بالبنان تبين أيما بيان عن مكنون الغرام ومستتر الهيام في صدور ملؤها الغيرة والشمم وقلوب حشوها العفة والكرم ونفوس تفزع لصولتها الضراغم والاسود وتفرق من تنمرها النمور والفهود لكنها تخضع لذوات القدود والنهود فتتفرق لديها لماعا وتطير اوزاعا خشية لحظة من جفاء وصد او إيماءة من إباء ورد وهن يقابلن حركات التذلل والتزلف باشارات التدلل والتعفف ويجزين على التولع بالتمنع ويبدين التثني باشكال التجني ويغضضن من ابصارهن في إسفارهن ثم يسدلن من اثوابهن ويضربن بخمرهن على جيوبهن فيرتد طرف الولهان حسيرا وقلب الهائم كسيرا وماء الحياء في الوجه الجميل كماء الفرند في

Miṣbāḥ al-sharq 123, October 5, 1900[88]

Paris

ʿĪsā ibn Hishām said: We walked around the section of the exhibition called "sights and scenes" and went into one exhibit after another. Truth to tell, we did not find in any of them confirmation of the kind of things we had been hearing about; in fact, quite the opposite. But then we reached a lofty palace, beautifully constructed and laid out, which had been built for various types of dancing, revelry, gymnastics, and music—movements of every kind involving turns and pliés from way back in the distant past and up to the present day, from times of coarse and primitive living up to today's luxury and ornamentation. There were dances illustrating chivalry and heroism, and others that reflected aspects both charming and debauched. You could watch bedouin men dancing with swords in deathly postures, while young maidens behind them strummed on tambourines and clapped their hands, all to encourage the men to fight and stir them up and encourage them to confront their foes. With that the taste of fortitude would be as good as sipping wine, and they would be willing to quaff the cups of death just as eagerly as others did the sweet saliva of the beloved. Then you could watch the dances of people returning from a journey, as they relished their success and triumph amid the virgins and maids of the tribe and the prisoners and unassuaged enemy fighters. Their finger gestures spoke eloquently for themselves so as to reveal the love and yearnings that lay buried inside them, the zeal and defiance that filled hearts replete with honor and courage, spirits enough to make ravenous beasts cringe at the very sound of their voices and cause vicious lions and tigers to forget their own awesome repute. Even so they submitted to the svelte and buxom ladies and splintered off into separate groups, quavering in case a gesture of rejection or a suggestion of distaste should occur. Movements intended to fawn and flatter would be met with a chaste coquetry; a response to ardent love would be disdain and rejection. The most subtle of rebukes would be leveled through an exquisite plié. In their downcast eyes one could see the glow of purity. The women would spin, covering their exposed limbs as they did so, causing the infatuated observer to recoil and the admirer to admit defeat. How wonderful modesty looks on the cheek of the beautiful, like drops of water on a burnished 42.1

السيف الصقيل اذا قابل حياء الشجاعة في الدارع المغوار رد غربه عن ربة الحجل والسوار فكأن الشجاع منهم في يد الغاده ينشد قول أبي عباده:

نحن قوم تذيبنا الاعـين النجـ
ـل على اننا نـذيب الحديدا
طوع ايدي الغرام تقتادنا البيـ
ـض ونقتاد بالطعان الاسودا

٢،٤٢ ورأينا اشكالا من الرقص والخطران والتمايل والدوران مما يجري عند بعض أهل الاديان وسواهم من عبدة الاصنام والاوثان حتى يكاد يعتري المشاهد لحركة تلك الابدان ما يعتري المستنطق من الهيضة والغثيان وكأنهم يريدون انهاك القوى الجسدانية واماتة القوة الشهوانية

وشاهدنا بعد ذلك ما في رقص الحضارة من التهتك والفضاحة والخلاعة والوقاحة فترى اسراب النساء كاسراب الظباء لا يستر اجسامهن الا غلالة كالقشرة في لون البشرة منطبقة عليها انطباق الغرقيء بترائك الرئال والتصاق القميص باجسام الصلال فهن عاريات للناظر كاسيات في الخاطر فيأتين في رقصهن اشكالا تبين في الضياء مذاهب الاعصاب ومفاصل الاعضاء فتارة تنثني وتارة تنحني وطوراً تدور على اطراف أصابعها فلا تنتقل من مواضعها وترى احداهن ترفع ساقها فتلطم بالخلخال صفحة الخال والنظارة بين ذلك يستعذبون ويستجيدون ويصيحون ويستعيدون ثم عمدن الى نوع آخر من أحدث الانواع في ضروب الابتداع فتبدت كل واحدة منهن في ملاءة بيضاء متسعة الاطراف والانحاء اذا استدارت فيها الراقصة خلتها قطعة غمام أطل منها بدر التمام أو زفة حمائم بيضاء ترفرف حول الماء وفي قبالتهن عند سقف المكان مصباح من الكهرباء مختلف الالوان مدد الاشعة على تلك الاردية والاردان فتصير من اختلاف الالوان كأنها طاقة أزاهر او عقود جواهر او كأنها في سرعة تلونها على حركة اهتزازها رغاوة اللجة أهاجتها السفينة في اجتيازها

sword; set in opposition to the bravery of an intrepid cavalier, it would lose its grip to the lady-wearer of bangles and anklets. It is as though, in the clutches of gorgeous maidens, the hero keeps reciting the words of the poet Abū ʿIbādah:

We are a folk undone by lovely eyes,
even though we can melt very steel.
To the demands of love are we led by pale beauties,
while we ourselves are governed by gruesome thrusts.[89]

We now observed various types of dancing and varieties of twisting and twirling, the kinds of thing commonly practiced in various faiths and encountered with idol-worshippers. It seemed almost as though the observer of these movements were like someone worriedly asking questions about cholera and nausea. The general purpose seemed to be to exhaust the human body so as to dampen lustful desires. **42.2**

Following this spectacle we watched dancing of a more urban kind which seemed particularly indecent. There were bevies of women, like gazelle flocks, their bodies minimally covered in translucent, skin-colored garb which clung to their limbs like ostrich shell or snakeskin. To the observer they looked naked, just barely clothed. As they danced in the brilliant lighting they adopted poses that showed muscles and limbs, sometimes bending over, then straightening up again, performing pirouettes on point while staying in place. Some of them did high kicks so that their anklets clinked as they touched their very cheeks. Spectators kept showing their approval by applauding and demanding encores. They now introduced still another form of modern dance with its particular creativity, each dancer being dressed in a white gown with wide skirts; when each one did a turn, you imagined they were clouds in the sky with the full moon gleaming down or else an entire flock of doves hovering over a water pond. High above them from the ceiling, a stage light projected different shades and colors on their sleeves and dresses, all of which made the dancers look like bunches of flowers and clusters of jewels. So rapid was the change of color that the scene looked like sea foam stirred up by a passing ship, the shining sun reflected in its eddies with its seven different colors. Each dancer was carrying a staff that she waved in the air to reflect the electric light

فلمعت فيها الاشعة بالوانها السبعة وفي يد كل واحدة منهن عصا جرداء اذا حركتها في الهواء وقابلت بها شعاع الكهرباء اثمرت باثمار من البلور وأزهرت باشكال من النور فيخالها من يرى- كعنقود ملاحية حين نوّرا- لو رآها سحرة فرعون وهامان لأقروا بفضل العصا في كل مكان وزمان.

٣،٤٢ ولما توارت عنا هذه الادوار بسدل الستار خرجنا ونحن في دهش وذهول وأخذ الباشا يخاطب الفرنسوي ويقول:

الباشا أرى أن الرقص عندكم معشر الغربيين شأناً عظيما كانه لديكم من نفائس الفنون وجميل الصناعات وكانه لا عار بينكم من هذه المناظر والاشكال التي يأبى الادب انتشارها بهذه الكيفية واشتهارها على اعين بناتكم وحرائركم.

الفرنسوي ان شأنه عندكم لأعظم وأعظم وشكله بينكم افضح وافضح ولا يزال كتّابنا واهل النظر منا يعيرونكم ويستفظعون هذا الرقص المنتشر بينكم المعروف برقص البطن وهذا معرضكم كل من دخل فيه وشاهد النساء المصريات مكشوفات البطون يحركن سراتها ويلعبن بطياتها وأعكانها خرج يقطر وجهه خجلا وتجيش نفسه غثياناً وتنقلب امعاؤه تقززاً من قبح هذا المنظر في عينه وشناعته في نظره فيحكم عليكم بسقوط الآداب وقلة الاحتشام وفساد الاذواق وكل من قصد ملاهيكم منهم في بلادكم لم يجدها حافلة بسواه فاذا عرضتم في بلادنا من آثاركم شيئا كانت تلك الراقصات في اوائل معروضاتكم ومن أنفس بضائعكم وهم يعدون ذلك دليلا على نفاسة قدرها بينكم وعلو مكانها لديكم.

٤،٤٢ الصاحب ان الامر على غير ما يتوهمون فان هذا الرقص ليس مما هو منتشر بيننا في نسائنا وانما يشتغل به بضع نساء من العواهر في ما يأتونه من ابواب الفجور وأفانين الفحش في بيوتهن والذنب في انتشاره عندنا في الملاهي العامة لبعض الاجانب الذين يرون وجوه الربح متساوية لا حطة فيها ولا ضعة واهل الخاصة بيننا يشمئزون من هذه الحالة اشمئزازكم منها ويستقبحونها استقباحكم لها ولكنهم كلما حاولوا ايقاظ الحكومة الى ابطال هذا الرقص لم تقدر على اجابتهم اذ تقوم

and let the brilliant beams shine forth like crystal flowers duly ripened. Everyone watching would imagine them to be cluster of mature grapes. Were the Pharaoh and Haman to have seen them, they would definitely have vouched for the virtues of the staff in every place and time.

Once these dances were at an end, the curtain came down. We made our 42.3
way out, duly amazed at what we had seen. The Pāshā turned to the Frenchman and said:

Pāshā I can see that you Western people hold dancing in high regard; it seems to be one of the treasures of your culture and fine arts. I suppose you all feel no sense of shame in such performances and movements, even though they're obviously the kind of thing that all decency forbids being celebrated and disseminated for your daughters and young women to watch.

Frenchman But dancing in your culture is more highly regarded and even more debauched than it is here. Our writers and critics keep on blaming your society for putting on the style of dance known as "belly dancing." Everyone who's gone into the Egyptian pavilion here and watched Egyptian women with bellies exposed, twisting and gyrating, has left with sweating brow in sheer embarrassment and feeling almost sick after seeing such a lewd and disgusting display. Your own culture stands accused of cultural backwardness, immodesty, and a total lack of good taste. Anyone from here who goes to nightclubs in your country won't find them full of people like himself. Whenever you decide to display your heritage in our homeland, such dancers are the very first thing you offer as your most precious commodity, and that's because they're considered a valuable asset and are afforded such a prestigious status in your society.

Friend Things are not as you imagine. Such dances are not widely 42.4
known among women in our culture. It's only harlots who perform it. Such women practice all manner of fornication inside their own homes. The only reason why it can be seen in nightclubs is that foreigners who own such places can see no end of profit in encouraging such practices. The select public in my country are just as disgusted by it as you are here and totally disapprove of it. Every time people have tried to rouse the government into putting an end to it all, they've been unable to respond because the capitulations enjoyed

الامتيازات الأجنبية في وجهها حائلا دون مبتغاها وهو على العموم أمر منكر لا يشهده الا اهل البطالة والخلاعة ولا يعرفه من النساء الا الفواجر هذا غاية أمر الرقص عندنا وليس هو داخل في عاداتنا كما هو متأصل في عاداتكم يستوي في مشاهدته ومباشرته الرجال والنساء والغلمان والعذارى والازواج والحلائل ولا يكاد يتم لكم احتفال أو تقام لكم ولائم الا وهذا الشكل من الرقص في احتضان الرجل للحرة والفتى للعذراء وهي مكشوفة الذراع عارية الصدر من السوقة فصاعداً الى الملوك فنازلاً أكبر الاركان في الاحتفال وأعظم اساس في بهاء الاجتماع وقد بلغني أن في بعض البلاد الاوربية عادة أراها في ذلك من أغرب العادات وهي أن الراقص اذا أتم دوره مع الراقصة واعادها للجلوس في مكانها بين زوجها وأخيها أو أمها وبنيها تزود عدة قبل من فيها والرقص عندكم فن من الفنون النفيسة يتعلمه الرجال كما يتعلمون القراءة والكتابة والنساء كما يتعلمن التطريز والخياطة وليس الامر عندنا كذلك.

الفرنسوي ليس الرقص في أصله كما تتوهمونه من المنكرات ولا مما يهين ويشين وهو للانسان كالامر الطبيعي يدعو اليه تركيب الجسد لردّ حركة الاعصاب الى انتظامها عند انفعالها بما يلحقها من خفة الطرب وما يطرأ عليها من المؤثرات ولذلك تراه قديماً في الفطرة وكثيراً ما تراه عند بعض الطيور وقلما خلت أمة من وجوده فيها الى اليوم وهو ينقسم الى اربعة أقسام: قسم يستعمل في الحرب وقسم للصيد وقسم لحكاية الهوى من طريق الايماء وقسم للشعائر الدينية وقد اعتنى بأمره كثير من الامم الغابرة وبلغ عند قدماء اليونانيين مرتبة عالية بينهم وكان الكبراء والامراء فيهم مولعين به يرونه مزية من المزايا الفاضلة وفيهم من انقطع له واشتهر به ولقد كان السفير بين اهل اثينا وبين الملك فيليب والد الاسكندر رجلاً اسمه ارستوديم كان مشهورا بالبراعة في هذا الفن استاذاً فيه ثم ان هذا الملك نفسه تزوج براقصة مشهورة اسمها لاريسا وكان سقراط الحكيم المشهور يهوى الرقص ويميل له ولا يستنكره ولا يأنفه وكان ايامينونداس من اشهر الفلاسفة راقصا مبرزا في فن الرقص ٥،٤٢

by foreigners have stood in their way. In general the only people who go to watch belly dancing are idlers and debauchees and the only women involved are prostitutes. That's all there is to say about dance in our culture: it's certainly not part of our culture as is the case with you. In your cultural tradition, dance has deep roots, something that can be attended and practiced by men and women alike, boys and young girls, wives and spouses. There's hardly a single celebration or wedding here without this kind of dancing, with men clasping women around the waist, young men and virgin girls, while the women themselves are bare-armed and have their breasts exposed. This applies from the lowest levels of society all the way up to royalty and down again; it's a feature of every celebration and one of the hallmarks of a sparkling society. I've heard about a really strange custom in a European country, namely that, when the dance is over and the male dancer takes his partner back to her place between husband, brother, mother, and children, she is supposed to give him a number of kisses. In your culture dance is a valued art form which men study in the same way as they do reading and writing and which women learn as they do sewing and embroidery. But things are not like that in our culture.

Frenchman In its origins dance is not something to be disapproved of 42.5
or castigated as you seem to imply. For mankind it is something perfectly natural. It aims at bodily harmony, something to calm the nervous system and keep it in good order whenever someone finds himself excited or deeply affected. Its influence goes far back in nature, and we can even detect its effects in birds. From earliest times until today you will rarely encounter a people that has no form of dance. It can be subdivided into four types: dances used in war, in hunting, in love stories through mime and gesture, and a fourth, in religious liturgies. A number of ancient civilizations have focused on dance, and Greeks in particular achieved a very high level of perfection. Their grandees and rulers were devoted to it and regarded it as a primary virtue. Some of them even specialized in dance and became well-known. The ambassador who plied between Athens and King Philip of Macedon, Alexander's father, was someone named Aristodemus who was a famous dancer and dance teacher. Indeed, the very same king married a well-known dancer named Larissa. Even Socrates, the famous philosopher, enjoyed dance and never expressed any disapproval of it or disdain for it. Epaminondas, one of the most famous philosophers, was an accomplished dancer.

٦،٤٢ وكان الامر كذلك من جهة الرقص الديني في الدولة الرومانية منذ انشائها ثم انتشرت فيها بقية انواعه انتشاراً عاما الى ان جاء الدين المسيحي على الوثنية الرومانية فلم يستنكره في بادئ الامر باشكاله التي تفنن فيها الرومانيون بما هو معهود فيهم من التهالك على الملاذ الفاضحة في اواخر دولتهم فدخل في عادات الامم الغربية فتمسكت به ولم يصدها عنه بعد ذلك استنكار بعض رؤساء الدين له تارة بعد اخرى اذ كانت النفوس ألفته واعتادت على ان لا ترى فيه شيئاً او عيبا ورفع الحجاب عندنا عن النساء واختلاطهن بالرجال هو الذي جمله في اعينكم مشينا لاحتجاب النساء عن الرجال عندكم على انه لا يزال لديكم بين رجالكم ونسائكم نوعان من انواع الرقص لا يوازيهما في العيب والفضيحة والشناعة والفظاعة اسفل المراقص عندنا واني لاعجب لعقلائكم ونبهائكم الذين يستقبحون اشكال المراقص الاوربية كيف لا يلتفتون الى استقباح ما لديهم.

٧،٤٢ قال عيسى بن هشام: ووصل بنا الحديث في طريقنا الى مكان وجدنا عليه ازدحاما عظيما فسألنا عنه فقيل لنا انه ذلك المحل المشهور الذي أقاموا فيه سفينة عظيمة تسير بمن يركبها من الداخلين في مياه البحر المتوسط فتمر به على كثير من الثغور العظيمة فيرى بنيان بيوتها ويشاهد حركة سكانها وكنا قبل ذلك قرأنا في الجرائد العالية الفرنسوية مثل الديبا والفيجارو فصولا متعددة في الكلام عن هذا المنظر والتمدح به والاسهاب في وصفه فبادرنا الى دفع الاجرة وبعد ان صعدنا السلالم انتهينا الى هيئة سفينة كبيرة فدخلناها فاذا هي تميل الى جانب بعد جانب كما تميل كفتا الميزان بحركة ممثل حركة السفينة عند اضطراب الامواج ويحف بها من كلا الجانبين حائط من قماش فيه رسم امواج البحر وبعض الثغور الكبيرة مثل نابولي وفينيسيا وغيرهما وهو متصل بآلة السفينة تديره بسرعة عظيمة والمركب واقفة في مقرها على اهتزازها فيتخيل للناظر عند ذلك انها تسير به في عرض تلك الامواج المرسومة في القماش وتقف به عند الثغور المنقوشة فيه فلا يبقى للزائر ادنى استغراب من هذا المنظر والاعجاب به الا ريثما يلتفت الى الآلة التي تسحب القماش وتحرك السفينة حركة الارجوحة

The same was true for religious dance in the Roman Empire from its earliest phases. Various categories of dance spread until the Christian religion was superimposed on Roman paganism. Even so, they didn't initially condemn the varieties of dance perfected by the Romans, despite all the debauched aspects that were characteristic of the latter days of their empire. Dance became part of the customs of Western nations, and they kept it going, undaunted by the resistance of religious authorities on numerous occasions. People had grown used to it and could see nothing sinful or shameless about it. The fact that women in our culture are unveiled and mingle freely with men is the factor that makes dance seem so sinful in your eyes. Women in your cultural tradition are kept veiled from men's eyes, even though among your men and women there still exist two types of dance which in their sheer debauchery and lechery outperform the shoddiest dance halls in our culture. I'm truly amazed at the way your intellectuals and aristocrats who express their disapproval of European dance halls utterly fail to condemn the situation in their own culture. **42.6**

ʿĪsā ibn Hishām said: Our conversation was interrupted when, as we were walking around, we noticed a place crammed with people. We found out that it was one of the most famous exhibits, one where they had built a huge boat that would take its passengers on a Mediterranean cruise, visiting large ports where they could see the buildings and inhabitants going about their daily work. We had already read a number of articles describing and extolling this exhibit in the major French newspapers like *Le Débat* and *Figaro*. After paying the price of admission we climbed a walkway and found ourselves inside a replica of a large boat. Once we were "on board," it started swaying like the two sides of a weighing scale, rocking just like a boat in a stormy sea. On both sides was a cloth wall with images of sea waves and ports like Naples and Venice—among others. The boat machine kept things moving at a fast pace, while the vessel stayed where it was, swaying from side to side. It all gave visitors the impression that they were actually at sea, being buffeted by the waves on the cloth and stopping at the various ports of call shown there. All in all, there seemed nothing particularly remarkable about the whole thing, that is, until the visitor looked at the machine pulling the cloth along and moving the vessel like a seesaw. **42.7**

وخرجنا منه والصاحب يعجب من شدة المبالغات عما في قسم المرائي والمناظر من ٨،٤٢
عجائب المدهشات اذ تبين لنا انها كلها مصنوعة بالتمويه الذي لا ينطلي الا على صبيان المكاتب في نظره ولا يعجب بها الا من يعجب بكل ما يصدر عن الغربيين من الاعمال في هزلهم وجدهم ولما رأى صاحبنا الفرنسوي ما عليه الصاحب من عدم الاكتراث بهذه المناظر وعلم رأيه فيها اشار علينا بان نزور من قسم المرائي والمناظر ما اعجبه من هيئة القرية التي اقامها بعض أهل السويسرا في المعرض يمثلون بها جبالهم وانهارهم ومعيشة أهل قرية منهم على حال تزينها الفطرة الطبيعية لا الزخرفة الصناعية ولما دخلناها ودرنا في نواحيها أخذنا جميعا الطرب والانشراح من حسن تلك الهيئة ومنظر تلك الجبال الشامخة التي اشتغل في اقامتها ونقل احجارها ثلثمائة عامل في مدى ثلاث سنوات تسيل من قممها السيول الى قرارة الوادي فتتشعب منها جداول وأنهار تقر عين الناظر وتسر الخاطر وهناك بيوت بين الماء والخضرة باشكال بسيطة وحولها حوانيت يباع فيها ما لذ وطاب من فواكه تلك البلاد واثمارها وطيب مآكلها وحسن غذائها وشاهدنا البقر هناك على مذاودها تحتلب البانها لمن يريدها من الزائرين بأيدي ولائد وجواري تتألق فيها نضرة الشباب ويتجلى على اجسامها حسن الصحة والسلامة وكذلك كل من شهدناه هناك رجالا ونساء يملؤن العين من حسن المنظر ويشرحون النفس بجمال الهيئة فاقمنا هناك زمانا نتكلم في فضل المعيشة الطبيعية على معيشة المدنية الصناعية.

As we left this exhibit, we were amazed at the excessive nature of the allegedly amazing wonders to be witnessed at the Sights and Scenes section of the exhibition. It was clear to us that they were utterly phony, the kind of things that would only appeal to schoolboys; the only people impressed by it all would be people who were prepared to admire anything coming from Western societies, whether serious or frivolous. Once the Frenchman realized how little our Friend was bothering with the exhibits and learned what we really thought about them, he suggested that we visit the single exhibit in Sights and Scenes that had given him any satisfaction. It was a model village set up by some people from Switzerland, which showed their mountains, rivers, and village life, with its natural beauty and complete lack of artificial frippery. When we entered the exhibit and made the rounds, we were delighted by the wonderful spectacle with views of lofty mountain peaks; transferring the stonework had required some three hundred workers over a period of three years. Streams flowed downhill from mountain peaks to valleys below, with brooks and rivers branching off, enough to delight the eye and warm the heart. Interspersed between the water and greenery were simply built houses, surrounded by stores where various kinds of fruit, food dishes, and delicious meals were on sale. We could watch the famous cattle of the region at their feeding troughs, and young boys and girls whose features were bursting with the freshness of youth and the sheer beauty of country life would milk them by hand for any visitors who wanted some. We were delighted by the entire exhibit, with both men and women filling the eye with lovely scenes and soothing the soul with the sheer beauty of the surroundings. We spent a good deal of time talking about the virtues of a simple country life as opposed to urban industrialized existence. **42.8**

مصباح الشرق ١٢٦، ٢٦ أكتوبر ١٩٠٠

باريس

١،٤٣ قال عيسى بن هشام: وفيما نحن ندور بين اقسام المعرض ونجول اذ سمعنا صوت زمور وطبول هاج منا الشجن وذكرنا بالوطن ذكرى العاشق للمعشوق والشائق للمشوق واهتياج انضاء النوق بلامعات البروق تنبعث من افق ديارها وتنازعها الاشواق في انجادها واغوادها فمالت اليه الاعناق وشخصت نحوه الاحداق وانحدرنا نقصد تلك الجهة بقلوب متولعه متولهة عسانا نرى من آثار البلاد ما نباهي به الاقران والانداد ونبصر من آيات الفخر والمجد ما يلهي عن الحنين ويسلي عن الوجد ونشهد ما يذكر في التقدم لمصر وبنيها وما يدل على فضل الديار وساكنيها

٢،٤٣ ولما وصلنا الى مكان تلك المزامير وجدنا عليه اخلاط الزمر والجماهير ورأينا في وسطهم رجلاً كظاً غليظاً في هيئته فظاً ثقيلا في طلعته بوجه تثور منه السماجة ثور العجاجة ولا غرو لحوافر الخيل في وقعها تظلم الجو بمثار نقعها وكأنما هو جلمود صخر او كتلة جليد لو استزاد من الغلاظة لم يجد له من مزيد وعلى رأسه طربوش تجمد عليه من دهن الوسخ والعرق ما لو أصابه شعاع من الشمس لاشتعل واحترق وهو يصيح بصوت من أنكر الاصوات ويعج مثل عجيج الابل في الفلوات وفي يده مروحة يتروح بها لاتصال النفس كلما ضاق عليه واحتبس وتراه يذهب في الحلقة يميناً وشمالا ويتمايل عجباً واختيالا وينادي في الجمع بألفاظ يمجها السمع فسمعناه يكرر في نباحه عليهم ويقول:

٣،٤٣ «هلموا ايها الناس الى الدخول لتروا من أسباب الانس ما تستمتع به الحواس الخمس ويجلي صدأ الكروب من النفس ومن انواعها السرور ما يزيل بلابل الصدور ويقي نكبات الدهور ومن لطف الصنع وحسن الشكل ما يبعد الحزن وينفي الثكل هلموا لا تحرموا انفسكم من منظر ليس له نظير ومشهد يفوق ببهجته كلّ تخمين وتقدير ويعلو برونقه على كل تخييل وتصوير هلموا فانظروا كيف بذت مصر في المجد

Miṣbāḥ al-sharq 126, October 26, 1900[90]

Paris

43.1 ʿĪsā ibn Hishām said: As we were wandering around the various exhibits, we suddenly heard the sound of flute and drums, which aroused in us many memories and a sense of nostalgia. It made us feel a longing for our homeland, as a lover does with his beloved and a craver does with the object of his craving. We were like travel-weary camels amid lightning flashes that crash on the far horizon while conflicting urges are leading them to desert hollows and steppes. The exotic sounds made people turn around to glance in that direction. We too headed for its source, our hearts on fire with expectation, hoping perhaps to discover some traces of our country, something to show off to our peers and look on as samples of our prestige and glory; something to distract us from our nostalgia and console us from our pangs of emotion. We would be able to see how far Egypt and Egyptians had advanced and the ways in which the country and its inhabitants showed particular qualities of excellence.

43.2 When we reached the place where the flutes were being played, we discovered a crowd of people. Right in the middle was a coarse specimen of a man, grossly overweight. His face was a tissue of ugliness, so ugly that it seemed to roar like a herd of camels, and no wonder! It hit you like the clop of horses' hooves that stir up muck and blacken the air. He looked like a rock boulder or a chunk of ice. Had he been any more boorish, it would have been impossible to find the excess. He was wearing a tarboosh on his head that was caked in sweat and filth. Were the sun's rays to alight on it, it would have caught fire and burned. He kept on yelling in a foul voice and snorting like a desert camel. He was holding a fan with which he kept fanning himself whenever he ran out of breath. You could watch as he circled to right and left and swayed proudly from side to side. He kept shouting at people. We listened as he barked out his message:

43.3 "Come inside, folks! You'll have lots of fun and see enough to satisfy all five senses, things to wipe corrosive cares from the soul and replace them with joy sufficient to banish all anxiety and guard against fate's calamities. Delicately crafted, beautifully shaped, there are things to banish sorrow and annul grief. Come on now, don't deprive yourselves of a sight unparalleled, a spectacle so

سائر الامم وحلت من الفخر بحيث ترتقع الذرى والقمم ولا غرو فهي لا تزال منذ القدم عالية الكعب بينها سابقة القدم هلموا فهذه خلسة من الدهر تختلس وفرصة لا بد ان تلتمس من لم يبادر اليها فقد اساء الاختيار وأوقع نفسه في الخسار وضيع النفيسين من وقته وماله ولم يقف من المعرض على موضع حسنه وجماله هلموا فمن لم يبشهد صنعة زهرة ومعتوقه لم يعرف سابقه ومسبوقه ولم يحصل الا على الخيبة في السفر والاوبة.»

٤،٤٣ فدخلنا نكتشف الاثر وننظر ما الخبر فتلقانا بالباب رجل وسيط القامه نظيف الثوب والعمامة.

ذئب تراه مصليًا
فاذا مررت به ركع
يدعو وجل دعائه
ما الفريسة لا تقع

فرحب بنا وهنأ بالسلامة ثم تبعنا وسرنا امامه فكاد يقضى علينا في دخولنا من الدهشة والعجب اذ تبينا اننا في مكان من امكنة اللهو واللعب ومنزل من منازل العزف والطرب وانكشف لأعيننا الستر عن بضع نساء من ذوات الفجور والعهر واخذن في الرقص بتلك الاشكال القبيحة والتفنن في اساليب التهتك والفضيحة فحسبنا اننا عدنا الى اطوار تلك المدة في مصاحبة الخليع والعمدة ثم سارعنا نحو الباب وقد تبللت منا الخدود والثياب بعرق الخجل ودموع الاكتئاب وخرجنا نستر وجوهنا بأيدينا واكامنا ونجتهد في اخفاء نسبتنا الى بلادنا واقوامنا لنخلص من وصمة هذا العار والشنار وما يجره علينا من سوء الازدراء والاحتقار وسرنا نهرول الابتعاد عن هذا المنظر الشنيع والتفادي من رؤية ذلك المرأى الفظيع مقسمين على ان لا نمر من هذه الناحية مرة ثانية لولا ان استوقفنا صاحبنا الفرنسوي يخاطبنا ويقول لنا وهو يعاتبنا:

٥،٤٣ <u>الفرنسوي</u> لم هذا التعجل منكم والتسرع اما شاهدتم المعرض ينقسم الى قسمين

amazing as to defy surmise or estimation, so dazzling as to surpass all imagination and conception. Come and witness how Egypt has bested all other nations in glory, so steeped in prestige as to overtop mountain peaks. And no wonder, for ever since time immemorial, Egypt has played a distinguished role among peoples and held a prominent position. So come now, here's a golden opportunity to be seized, a moment in time to be snatched. Anybody who fails to rush in is making a bad choice and condemning himself to be a loser and wasting two valuable commodities, time and money, by not seeing the beauties of this exhibit in its best light. Anyone who fails to see the skills of Zuhrah and Maʿtūqah will never in their life fully realize who wins and who loses; his only return will be disappointment both coming and going."

We made our way inside to see what things were like. At the door we met an average-sized man wearing a clean djellaba and turban: 43.4

A wolf whom you see praying,
 when you pass by, he makes a prostration.
He prays and prays,
 but only as long as there's no prey.[91]

He greeted us and congratulated us on our safe arrival. We walked ahead, with him following us. When we got inside, we almost died of shock: we were obviously inside a gaming room, a place for music and entertainment. The curtain was drawn back to reveal a troupe of lewd women who started belly dancing, using all kinds of disgusting gestures and movements. For a moment we thought we had gone back in time and were still in the company of the Playboy and ʿUmdah.[92] We rushed for the door, our faces moist with tears of remorse and sheer embarrassment. As we hurried out, we were covering our faces with hands and sleeves, doing our utmost to conceal our association with our homeland and people and to rid ourselves of the stain of such an utterly vile display, one that only served to make other people look down on us with contempt. We rushed to put as much distance as possible between ourselves and this awful spectacle and to reject such a dreadful sight. We swore an oath not to pass by this sector of the exhibition again. However the Frenchman stopped to talk to us and upbraided us:

FRENCHMAN Why are you in such a hurry? Don't you remember that this exhibition is divided into two separate parts: one for crafts and antiquities, 43.5

قسم المصنوعات والآلات وقسم المرائي والمشاهد؟ وليس من الرأي ان تقتصروا من المعرض المصري على زيارة هذا القسم وحده الذي ساءتكم رؤيته واحزنتكم مشاهدته وهو قسم الهزل دون زيارة القسم الثاني وهو قسم الجد ولعلنا نجد فيه من محاسن اعمالكم وصنع ايديكم ما يصرف عنكم الذي انتم فيه من الهم والكدر.

الباشا ما اظن هذا القسم الا عنوان القسم الآخر ومن اساء الاختيار في قسم المشاهدات لجدير ان يسيء في قسم المصنوعات ومن بلغ به الانحطاط الى انه لا ينتخب من مشاهد بلاده ومرائيها الا عرض بطون النساء وثدي الفتيات للغادين والرائحين في هذا المعرض من اطراف المسكونة وانحاء المعمورة فلا يرتقي الى حسن الانتخاب في ما يجمل عرضه ويحسن نشره من آثار البلاد وصناعات اهلها.

٦،٤٣ الصاحب ما أرى الا ان الطمع في الربح هو الذي اغمض جفونهم عن قبح هذا المشهد وغرهم اقبال السفهاء عليه في مصر وحدوا اصحاب الحانات فيها وضياع اموال الوارثين في مهاويها ولم يقدروا على مباشرة هذه الحرفة في مصر فاقدموا على افتتاح امثالها في بلاد الغربة وظنوا الغربيين يقبلون عليها مثل ذلك الاقبال في بلادهم فيتحصلون على مثل ذلك الربح الطائل ويتخلصون من التعيير والتنديد بهم في وطنهم فان فيهم من اذا ذكرت له في مصر لفظة الرقص غطى وجهه بجبته ولوى عنقه يستعيذ ويستغفر ويستفظع ويستقبح ويرى حضور مجالس الرقص من المنكرات المحرمات التي ينهاه عنها دينه ولكن جاء الامر على خلاف ما يقدرون فان أدب المتمدن والمتوحش من زوار المعرض ينهاه عن حضور هذه الفضائح ويبعد به عن مشاهدة هذه القبائح ولذلك فاننا نرى المكان خالياً من الزائرين خاوياً من القاصدين واني لأعجب من هؤلاء القائمين بالمعرض المصري الذين يأنفون في بلادهم من اقامة مثل هذا المرقص خشية العار بين ابناء جنسهم ولا يخجلون من العار الذي يلحق ببلادهم وسكانها واقطارهم وأهلها ولا يلتفتون الى تعيير الامم لنا وسخريتهم منا واستهزائهم بنا ولكن طلب الربح يعمي ويصم.

and the other for sights and scenes? You shouldn't base your opinion of the Egyptian pavilion on a single visit to this part that has caused you so much distress and sorrow. This is the frivolous section of the exhibit. You need to visit the second section which is more serious. Maybe we'll be able to find there some nice examples of beautiful objects crafted by your hands to dispel the sorrow and aggravation you're feeling.

Pāshā I can only envisage this second section as being a prelude to the other. The person who's made such an appalling selection for the scenes section will undoubtedly do just as badly on the other section devoted to crafts. Anyone who stoops so low as to decide to display women's bellies and girls' breasts to all comers at this exhibition can hardly be expected to make a better selection for display and exhibition when it comes to relics and crafts.

Friend As I see it, it's the profit motive that has blinded these people to 43.6
the sheer vileness of these presentations; they've been duped by the way stupid people flock to see them in Egypt, and that has aroused the jealousy of bar owners, not to mention the way that young heirs of families have squandered family resources in such nefarious haunts. They've not managed to control the profession in Egypt itself, so instead they've grabbed this opportunity to do it in a Western country. They imagine that people will flock to it as they do at home; that way they'll be able not only to make a huge profit but also avoid the opprobrium that they face in their own country. If you even mentioned the word "dance" to people in Egypt itself, they would cover their face and turn away, seeking God's help and expressing their outrage and condemnation, believing that dance halls are objectionable and forbidden by their faith. However, things have turned out exactly the opposite of what they had been expecting. Visitors to the exhibition, in all their variety, have enough taste to shun such disgusting displays and avoid watching such debauchery. So, as we can see, the entire place is empty; nobody's come to visit the exhibit. I'm astonished that the people who set up the Egyptian pavilion here, yet who would definitely refuse to establish such a dance hall as this for fear of their countrymen's condemnation, have felt no qualms about the blame that'll attach to their country and its citizens because of this exhibit. They simply don't care about the way other nations are condemning and poking fun at them. All they're bothered about is profit, and that has both blinded and deafened them.

قال عيسى بن هشام: وطاوعنا صاحبنا الفرنسوي فعدنا الى زيارة القسم الثاني من ٧،٤٣
هذا المعرض ولما جاوزنا باب الملهى قليلا وجدنا بجانبه بناء مشيداً على هيئة أبنية الجوامع ورأينا عند مدخله حانة للخمر تقوم عليها امرأة من عجائز باريس وحولها بعض بناتها ورأينا على باب المسجد رجلاً تنطبق القبعة على سحنته اكثر مما تنطبق العمامة التي يلبسها على خلقته وأمامه درج فيه دواة وقرطاس ومن حوله جماعة من أجناس الناس يتقدم الواحد منهم اليه فيسأله صاحب العمامة عن اسمه بعد ان يأخذ منه دريهمات معلومة فيكتبه له بالعربية في ورقة مع بعض الدعوات الصالحات وسمعنا بعض الواقفين عليه يقول لامرأة معه: «هلم الى شيخ المسلمين هذا يكتب لنا شيئاً من قرآن محمد» ولما انفض الجمع عن ذلك الشيخ قليلا تقدمنا اليه وعرفناه بانفسنا وسألناه عن امره فلم يستطع ان ينكر علينا انه من غير دين الاسلام وان طلب القوت يضطره الى التزيي بغير زيه ليصيد بهذه الحبالة ما يتعيش به من الدراهم فكدت أعذره بعد الذي رأيته في زيارتي الى لوندره اذ وجدت في المنتزه المسمى «اكزيبيشن» رجلا ذا عمامة قاعداً في حلقة من الصبيان يمثل بهم هيئة الفقيه في الكتاب ويقرئهم فاتحة الكتاب وآياته ويعلمهم كيفية الاهتزاز عند القراءة والنظارة من رجال الانكليز ونسائهم حوله يعجبون ويضحكون ويستهزئون ويسخرون ومنهم من يقعد له فيتلقن منه شيئاً من القراءة ثم يعيدها بين الواقفين ضاحكا مقهقهاً ولما سألت صاحب العمامة عن اسمه قال لي ان اسمه الشيخ حسن فعذلته لسوء عمله فقال ان التعيش أحوجه الى ذلك وان الضرورات تبيح المحظورات

ثم تركنا الشيخ السوري يكتب ويرقم ودخلنا الى فسحة البناء فوجدنا سوقاً شبيها ٨،٤٣
باسواق الموالد وحوانيتها فعن اليمين بائعة لب وحمص وعن الشمال بائع عرقسوس وفي هذا الجانب بائع حرائر شامية وفي قبالته بائع حلوى ومن دونه بائع احذية ولما سألناهم أهذه كلها آثار مصر وصناعاتها قالوا نعم ويزيد عليها معروضات المصنوعات والمزروعات داخل هذا المكان فقصدناه فاذا هو مكان متسع على

ʿĪsā ibn Hishām said: Once outside, we followed the advice of our French friend and returned to the pavilion to visit the other part of the Egyptian exhibit. Once past the dance-hall structure, we found alongside it another building in the form of a mosque, with a wineshop to its right overseen by an elderly Parisian woman surrounded by her children. By the mosque door was a man whose appearance was such that a skullcap would have been more suitable attire than the turban he was wearing. In front of him was a table with an inkwell and paper on it. Around him were all kinds of people who came up to him one by one; after they had paid him a few dirhams, he would ask each one for his name and then write it out for him on the yellowing paper, along with a few pious prayers. We heard one of the visitors say to a woman who was with him, "Come on, let's get the shaykh to write us something from Muhammad's Qur'an." Once the crowd around the shaykh had gone away, we went over to talk to him, introduced ourselves, and asked him about himself. He was unable to hide from us the fact that he was not even a Muslim; it was the sheer need to earn a living that had forced him to change his usual dress in order to earn some money by setting this trap for visitors. I almost found it possible to forgive him, as I recalled a visit to a park in London called Kensington where I'd watched a man in a turban sitting with a circle of children; he was playing the part of a traditional teacher in a Qur'an school, reciting verses from the Opening Surah of the Qur'an, and teaching them how to sway in rhythm to the reading. English spectators, men and women, were standing around, utterly amazed at what they were seeing and poking fun at the whole thing. Some of them even sat down and learned how to recite, only to go back to the other spectators laughing at the whole thing. When I'd asked this turbaned shaykh what his name was, he replied "Shaykh Hasan." When I upbraided him for what he was doing, he replied that it was the need to earn a living that forced him do this, duly quoting the proverb, "Necessity legitimizes the forbidden." 43.7

We now left this Syrian to his writing and scripting and went inside the building. There we discovered a market just like the ones for festival days along with their various booths and stores. To the right there was a vendor of *libb* seeds and humus, while to the left licorice juice was on sale. In one corner someone was selling Syrian silks, in another halva, and still another shoes. When we asked whether all these things were authentic Egyptian products, we were assured that they were, and there were still more things on display along with industrial and agricultural products further inside. So we went 43.8

شكل المعابد المصرية وعلى هيئة حانوت العطار الذي انتقل منه صاحبه الى غيره فانك ترى في زواياه صرة فيها بذر قطن وصرة فيها حبوب ذره وصرة فيها بذور حلبة وفي صدر المكان صورة مطرزة بالذهب داخل دولاب من زجاج مما يلبسه العداؤون (القمشجيه) الذين يعدون امام العجلات والخيول ورأينا منشوراً هنا وهناك كثيراً من تلك الصرر تحتوي على أمثال تلك الحبوب وعلى أصناف من أنواع البخور والعطور

٩،٤٣ فانقلبنا خارجين من قسم الآلات والمصنوعات على حالٍ من الغم والحزن أشد وادهى من الحال التي خرجنا عليها من قسم المرائي والمشاهد وكان خجلنا عليها من هذه الآثار والمصنوعات قدر خجلنا من مناظر هاتيك الراقصات وفزعنا الى الهروب من هذا المعرض وسيئاته فلحقنا واحد منهم يقول لنا قد فاتكم النظر الى ما لم تحوه خريدة العجائب وجريدة الغرائب وجرنا الى حجرة مظلمة فارانا هناك فتاة من فتيات سوريا مقطوعة اليدين تغزل برجليها وتكاد تدخل بهما الخيط في الابرة وتفعل بهما افعالا شتى فكان العجيب لدينا اعجابهم بمثل هذا في وسط عجائب المعرض العام وغرائبه وخرجنا لا نلتفت وراءنا وقد حان وقت الغروب حتى انتهينا من هذا المعرض المصري وماكدنا نجاوز ساحته حتى صدمنا قطيع من النساء في أيدي بعضهن الشموع وفي أيدى بعضهن الدفوف وفي وسطهن امرأة عليها زينة العرائس وهن يضربن على رأسها بالدفوف وينشدن أناشيد الاعراس في زفاف المصريات فرأينا كأنهن يردن ان يشن المصريين بفضيحة مجسمة فانزوينا ناحية لنعلم معنى خروجهن من قسمهن الى الجولان في شوارع المعرض وبينا نحن كذلك اذ بصر «الصاحب» بصديق له من المصريين الوافدين لزيارة المعرض فاستوقفه يسأله هل زار المعرض المصري.

١٠،٤٣ الصديق نعم زرته وشاهدت فيه ما شاهدتموه من المنديات المخزيات وانا واقف الآن اشاهد هذاا الزفاف الذي يدور امامكم في انحاء المعرض.

further in and found ourselves in a wide space along the lines of ancient Egyptian temples, with produce from a typical perfumer's store brought over by its owner. In one corner was a bag full of cotton seeds, others with maize and hulba seeds, while further inside was a glass case with a gold-framed picture showing the uniform worn by "runners," the people who run in front of horses and vehicles in Egypt. All around we could see a number of pictures like this one showing types of cereals and various kinds of scents and perfumes.

As we turned to make our way out of this industrial and agricultural products section of the pavilion, we felt even more aggravated and distressed than when we had left the sights and scenes section. Our sense of shame at the sight of these relics and products was just as great as we had felt seeing the belly dancers. Anxious to get as far away as possible from this dreadful Egyptian exhibit, we were stopped by one of its regular clientele who told us that we should not miss seeing the wonder of wonders that it contained. Following his advice, we entered a curtained room where a screen revealed to us a Syrian girl with no arms using her feet to weave (and she could almost thread a needle with them) and perform a number of other functions. What we found so astonishing was that they could regard this as somehow miraculous in the context of the exhibition as a whole. 43.9

By now it was late afternoon, and so we left the Egyptian pavilion without glancing behind us. But we had hardly crossed the square in front before we were accosted by a group of women, some of them holding candles while others were shaking tambourines. In their midst was a girl wearing bridal costume; they were hitting her on the head with their tambourines and chanting the kind of wedding songs used at Egyptian nuptials. To us it seemed as if their goal was to bring a further, even more tangible, scandal down on the Egyptian people. We moved to one side in order to find out why they had left their section inside the exhibit and come outside to wander around the exhibition's streets. While we were watching our Friend noticed an Egyptian colleague of his who had come to see the exhibition. He stopped him and asked him if he had visited the Egyptian pavilion:

Egyptian Colleague Yes, I've visited it and seen the various disgraceful and shameful exhibits inside. Now here I am standing with you, watching this would-be wedding right in the midst of the exhibition. 43.10

الصاحب قل لي بالله ما الغرض من تفنن اصحاب هذا المعرض المصري في وجوه الافتضاح وهل لم يكفهم من ذلك ما هو داخل معرضهم حتى ترقوا الى تسيير هذه المناظر امام أعين الوافدين في طرقات المعرض العام وما الذي يدعوهم الى هذا التشنيع؟

الصديق ليس غرضهم في ذلك التشنيع وانما دعاهم اليه كساد الحال وقلة الزائرين لتلك الراقصات والمغنيات وهن في ملاعبهن فهم يخرجوهن في انحاء المعرض مرارًا متوالية في الليلة يعرضوهن على انظار الناس على هذا الشكل لتنبيههم الى زيارة المعرض المصري وذلك بمثابة الاعلان عندهم.

الصاحب اراك تتكلم عن المعرض المصري وما يؤلمنا منه كلام الغريب عن المصرية ومن لا يبالي بالخجل من هذه المناظر وعهدي بك في المصريين من صميمهم.

الصديق ان وقوفي على حقيقة أمر هذا المعرض المصري خفف عني ما اشتد بكم من امره وهون علي خشية ما يلحقنا من العار به فان هذا المعرض وان اطلقوا عليه لفظة المصري الا انه في الواقع بعيد عن هذه النسبة لان سائر أقسام المعارض في المعرض قد اشتركت حكوماتها فيه رسميا الا الحكومة المصرية فانها امتنعت عن ذلك وامتناعها منصوص عليه في الجرائد وفي منشورات المعرض الرسمية واذا تأملت قليلا في نساء المعرض المصري ورجاله لم تجد فيه من المصرية الا ذلك البك الذي اشتهر منذ زمان باعتياده على المتاجرة في المعارض وغير الراقصتين المشهورتين فيه والا فجميعهم من غير المصريين وهاته النساء التي تسير امامك كانها قطيع الغنم اخرجهن من أرض سورية الاحتياج والعوز وليس الامر قاصرا في ذلك على المعرض المصري وحده بل الحال كذلك في كثير من أقسام المعارض الشرقية كما شاهدته في المعرض التركي ومعرض الجزائر وغيرهما ولهم العذر في ذلك لاحتياجهم الى أسباب المعاش ولشهرة النسبة الى غيرهم.

الصاحب وهل تظن ان المعرض المصري يأتي بالربح للقائمين به بما يكافئ ١١،٤٣
هذا التعب وذلك الخروج عن الحد.

FRIEND But tell me for heaven's sake, what's the purpose of the owners of this exhibit in putting on such a variety of scandalous spectacles? Isn't it enough for them to put such things on display inside the pavilion? Why have they decided now to bring such spectacles outside on to the public street for everyone to see? What on earth is making them do such a disgraceful thing?

EGYPTIAN COLLEAGUE That's not the issue here. The primary motivating factor here is the poor returns they're getting and the fact that very few people are visiting the dancers and singers in the dance-hall exhibit inside. So every night they come outside several times and display themselves in public like this. The aim is to get people to notice the Egyptian pavilion; for them it's a kind of advertisement.

FRIEND I notice that you keep talking about "the Egyptian exhibit." What distresses us so much is what foreigners will say about Egyptian women. It completely ignores the damage that such a spectacle will cause. My experience with you suggests that you are a true Egyptian.

EGYPTIAN COLLEAGUE In fact, I've investigated the truth about this Egyptian pavilion. What I've learned has lessened the sense of outrage that you've been feeling and may indeed calm the fears you have of the opprobrium that may be aimed at us. Even though the label "Egyptian" has been applied to the exhibit, Egypt itself is actually far removed from any involvement. Whereas every other exhibit here is the result of the official response of the government concerned, Egypt is an exception. The Egyptian government declined the invitation, which has been duly noted in newspapers and the official publications of the Exhibition. If you take a quick look at the women and men involved in the Egyptian exhibit, the only Egyptians are the Bey who is well known for speculating on exhibitions and two famous Egyptian female dancers. Apart from them everyone else is non-Egyptian. The women you see here acting like a flock of sheep are Syrians brought here by poverty and the need to earn a living. Incidentally this situation does not apply only to the Egyptian exhibit; it's the same with many of the exhibits from eastern countries, as you've probably noticed with the Turkish, Algerian, and other Middle East pavilions as well. These people have an excuse, in that they all need to earn a living while the reputation belongs elsewhere.

FRIEND Do you think the Egyptian pavilion will make a large profit for 43.11
its sponsors to compensate for all the hardships and disgrace involved?

الصديق أرى ان الشركة التي قامت بانشاء هذا المعرض لا تخسر ان لم تربح وانما الخسارة على الذين تهافتوا على شراء اسهمها وهم يقدرون الخسارة الآن بثمانين ألف جنيه وعسى الله ان ما يصيبهم من الخسارة في هذه المرة يعتبرون به فلا يقدمون مرة أخرى على هذه المشروعات التي لا يسلمون فيها من الخسارة ولا يسلم المصري فيها من المعرة.

قال عيسى بن هشام: ثم تركنا هذا الصديق وانصرف بعد ما هون قليلا من كربنا ١٢،٤٣
وخفف

EGYPTIAN COLLEAGUE I don't think the company that set up the exhibit is going to lose anything or make any profit. The people who'll be losing are the shareholders. Current estimates put the losses to date at eighty thousand pounds. Maybe this time God will inflict sufficient losses on them that it'll serve as an object lesson. They won't be trying again to embark on projects like this which run the risk of not only their own loss but also the denigration of Egyptians.

ʿĪsā ibn Hishām said: With that we said our farewells to this Egyptian colleague, and he left. He had managed to lessen our pained feelings somewhat. 43.12

مصباح الشرق ١٣٠، ٢٣ نوفمبر ١٩٠٠

باريس

قال عيسى بن هشام: واتهينا في زيارتنا الى اقسام الدول فرأينا فيها من مفاخر الأواخر ومآثر الاول ما استوقفتنا معاهده واستهمتنا مشاهده فانهن قد تبارين في مضمار المناضلة والمصاولة وتسامين في درجات المفاضلة والمطاولة فكانت الدولة الالمانية من بينهن أعلاهن مكانا وأعزهن شانا كأنها لم تقنع ان تسبق صواحبها في ميادين الطعان فارادت ان تسبقهن ايضاً في ميادين العرفان وأن تبذهن في الحالتين حالة الحرب وحالة السلم بشدة البأس وقوة العلم يشهد بذلك ما يراه الداخل من الرسم في مدخل ذلك القسم فانه يرى غادتين كالأختين في زي اهل الولايتين يستطلع من وضعهما معنى الانتصار ومغزى الاقتدار ويستكشف هناك من منظر اؤلئك الذين خرجت الولايتان من أيديهم الى قبضة أعاديهم كيف يكون السكون والاصطبار على احتمال الهوان والعار فلا يخليهم من خلتين ولا يبريهم من احدى الخطتين اما للشره والطمع واما للذلة والطبع ومن العجب العجاب في سرعة التقلب والانقلاب ان الذين أقاموا خمسة وعشرين حولا يتزيدون ما استطاعوا قوة وحولا وينادون في كل يوم يا للغارات لأخذ الثارات. - والذين كانوا اذا اراد احدهم أن يهيج بينهم ساكن الاحقاد والادغال ويقدح زناد الاضغان والاذحال ألبس وليدته ذلك اللباس لباس الالزاس فترى صدوراً جاشت وعقولا طاشت حتى كأن كل واحد منهم في شدة هيجانه. وحدة ثورانه ثور أسعر لوّحت له بثوب أحمر أو ثوب قيصر في بني الاصفر وان جاز التشبيه قلت قميص عثمان رآه بنو مروان قد أصبحوا اليوم يرون ذلك العدو الظافر والمتغلب القاهر يعرّض لهم بذلك في معرضهم ويسخر بأولائك الاسود في مربضهم فسبحان مالك الملك يعطي الملك من يشاء وينزع الملك ممن يشاء ويعز من يشاء ويذل من يشاء. ١٠٤٤

Miṣbāḥ al-sharq 130, November 23, 1900[93]

Paris

ʿĪsā ibn Hishām said: Our tour of the exhibition now took us to the pavilions of other nations. There we saw such wonderful things, both ancient and modern, that we stopped to admire their provenances and savor what they offered the eye. They vied with each other in fierce competition and tried to outrival the others in sheer excellence. Among them all, the German pavilion had the loftiest status and the greatest impact. It was as though the Germans were not content merely to show their superiority in warfare, but had also decided to outpace everyone else in learning, the goal being to beat everyone else in both spheres, war and peace. Evidence of this was the painting that the visitor saw at the entrance to the pavilion. It showed two girls like sisters dressed in the costumes of the two states, France and Germany. From the picture one could glean the idea of victory and potential, and assess the fate of those people in countries no longer under their suzerainty and now in the clutches of their enemies—forced to endure humiliation and shame. There were only two choices before them: greed and avarice, or contempt and instinct. What was most remarkable of all about the speed with which things change was that people who had spent twenty-five years enhancing their strength and power, every single day calling for raids of revenge—the kind of people who, whenever any one of them decided to stir up latent hatreds and jealousies, would stoke the flames of revenge. These people would dress their own daughter this way, namely in Alsatian costume. Then you would see hearts astir and minds on fire; it would be as if every single one of them was so enraged and belligerent that he turned into a fierce bull, flourishing his red uniform or, if you prefer, Caesar's own garb amid the Greeks.[94] If the comparison is valid, I would compare it to ʿUthmān's shirt seen by the Marwanids.[95] Today, however, these people are accustomed to seeing this all-powerful nation putting on such a display at this exhibit and scoffing at those so-called lions in their lairs. So all praise be to the Lord of Lords, the one who assigns monarchy to whomsoever He wills and similarly snatches it away when He so decides, raising up the one and humiliating the other. 44.1

ولما وصلنا الحديث مع صاحبنا «الفرنسوي» في ذلك الامر قال لنا في كلامه وهو يتقلب على مثل الجمر: ٢،٤٤

الفرنسوي ما تركت لنا هذه المدنية بفضولها وزوائد حاجاتها وتعدد الرغبات والتغالي في حب التنعم والترفه بين الخاصة والعامة اثرًا في النفوس لاحساس شريف وخلة حميدة وسجية فاضلة ومبدأ قويم وأصبح فيها شأن الامم كشأن التجار في تهالكهم على سبل الكسب وتراميهم على ابواب الربح وقد اشتد بهم العوز وتملكهم الاحتياج وكالذئب اذا سغب لا يدري أي سبيل سلك ولا على أية جيفة وقع واخالنا قد وصلنا اليوم في مدنيتنا الى مثل ما انتهت اليه مدنية الرومانيين حيث بلغ الامر في ارتكاب الدنايا اى حد سقوط العار عنها وزوال العاب فيما بينهم منها او صار لصحة الرذائل والنقائص مثل الحجج القاطعة والبراهين الفاصلة على صحة الكمالات والفضائل بلغ الامبراطور الروماني في أواخر دولتهم ان احد الحكماء المتأدبين انتقد عليه الدناءة التي ارتكبها في وضع المكوس على مباول الطرقات فاستدعاه اليه وحادثه مليًا لما همّ بالانصراف أخرج هذا الملك العظيم والامبراطور الكبير دينارًا من جيبه ووضعه على أنف المنتقد وقال له: «سألتك بالله هل تجد لهذا من رائحة» فلما شمه مرارًا قال: «لا أجد رائحة» قال له: «فالآن فاذهب فقد بطل انتقادك وارتفع اعتراضك وليس يهتم العاقل في الحصول على الدراهم الا بالبحث عن كشف مواردها لا بالبحث عن فساد مصادرها».

وكذلك حال الامة الفرنسوية اليوم ألهاها حب الكسب من المعرض وشدة حاجتها اليه عما اختلط بدمائها وتغلغل في احشائها من حب الأخذ بالثار وكشف العار واسترداد المسلوب واسترجاع المنهوب وذهلت عما اجنته صدورها من التحرق والتحدم على العدو المتغلب والتغيظ والتضرم على السالب الظافر وسهل على النفوس ان يطير صيته وترتفع شهرته بينهم وهم يساعدونه على اغراضه ويمهدون له السبل فلا تكل ألسنتهم وأقلامهم في انطلاقها مدحًا له وتقريظًا وهو لا يرعى لهم مع ذلك جانبًا ولا يحترم لهم رأيًا فيذكرهم بما يذكرهم ويضع في صدر معرضه ذلك ٣،٤٤

Once the conversation reached this point, our French friend addressed us with a fiery passion: 44.2

FRENCHMAN This modern civilization has its virtues, but it also has increased needs, multiplied desires, and instigated an excessive craving for luxury and comfort among both the elite and common people. It has left no vestige in the human heart for noble sentiments, laudable instincts, and sound principles. The fate of whole nations now resembles nothing so much as commerce where merchants are falling over each other in quest of gain and the means of profit making. Need and lack have now overwhelmed them, just like a starving wolf that has no idea which path to take or which corpse it has stumbled on. As I see it, this civilization of ours has now reached the same point as the Roman Empire did, when salacious acts reached such a stage that they were no longer considered sinful or blameworthy. All sorts of vile action and shortcomings came to have validity and legitimacy to the detriment of all virtues and laudable qualities. As their empire was drawing to a close, an erudite philosopher criticized the Roman emperor for imposing a tax on public toilets. The Emperor summoned him. After a brief conversation the philosopher was about to leave, but the Emperor, that mighty ruler, took a dinar out of his pocket and put it on the nose of his critic. "Let me ask you, by God," he asked the philosopher, "can you smell anything?" After sniffing several times, the philosopher replied that he could not smell anything. "In which case," the Emperor told him, "go away. Your criticism is baseless, so stop criticizing me. The intelligent person in quest of money should only be concerned about its true worth, not about the corrupt sources it may come from."

This then is the situation in which France finds itself today. The country's yearning and great need for profit from this exhibition has managed to divert all their attention away from their gut instinct, one that is blended with their very blood, to seek revenge, reveal dishonor, and retrieve what has been either lost or stolen. The French have entirely forgotten about the fire and destruction they intended to inflict on their victorious enemy and the raging anger they showed against the nation that has snatched away their land.[96] People have apparently thought nothing about raising Germany's prestige here in their own midst, helping it achieve its goals, and opening avenues for it. Tongues and pens are constantly heaping praise on Germans and extolling their virtues even though the Germans themselves basically ignore them and 44.3

الرسم بعد أن بذل جهده في ان يكون جميع ما يعرضه من كل فن وصناعة من جنس ما اشتهر الفرنسويون بعمله واختصوا بصنعه ليكون السبق عليهم أظهر والتقدم له بينهم أوضح.

٤،٤٤ الصاحب وليس ذلك وحده ما لحقكم في هذا المعرض فقد وجدنا حكومتكم لغواً غير معدود في مضمار السياسة الاوربية منذ عشر سنوات حذراً منها ان يحدث من الارتباك السياسي ما يشوش عليها في نجاح المعرض ويسبب له ما يسببه من الفشل وناهيك بما خسرته من النفوذ السياسي امام العالم اجمع في مسألة فشوده التي لا يعوضه على اهلها أي ربح مادي من المعرض مهما عظم شأنه وتضاعف قدره الى غيرها من المسائل التي امتثلت فيها واطاعت بما كانت تأباه كل الاباء حتى انتهى الامر ان قبل القواد الفرنسويون الدخول بعساكرهم في حرب الصين تحت امرة القائد الالماني وأضحى الذين يحدثون انفسهم بهزيمة الجيوش الالمانية مع قوادها يوماً في يد قائدهم الاكبر يرسل بهم الى اين شاء من مواقع الحرب ويقذف بهم كيف يريد في افواه المنايا.

الفرنسوي فهذا يدلك على ما انتهت اليه الحال في المدنية من ارتكاب الدنية وامتطاء السفالة وسلوك سبل التخوف والتحذر والركون الى اسباب التوقي والتحرس وان عاقبة امرها والقوة متنقلة فيها غير ثابتة لا بد ان يجر أصحابها الى الضعف والخذلان والذل والهوان.

٥،٤٤ قال عيسى بن هشام: وبينا نحن في هذا الحديث اذ سمعنا ضجة اهتزت لها ارجاء المعرض ورأينا الناس يتقاذفون على بعضهم كالموج في البحر اللجيّ قد ركبوا رؤوسهم من شدة الفزع وطارت عقولهم من كثرة الهلع وعلا منهم الصراخ والصياح واحتد فيهم العويل والنواح ولما تمكنا من انفسنا في وسط هذا الهول سألنا عن الخبر فقيل لنا ان القنطرة قد هوت بمن فوقها وسقطت على من تحتها فتوجهنا ناحيتها ولما وصلنا من بين الزحام الى مشاهدة هذا المنظر الشنيع انقبضت منا النفوس وسالت العيون

pay their opinions not the slightest respect. The Germans choose what they wish to emphasize, and that explains why they've put up this picture right at the front of their pavilion. Not only that, but they've made sure that every art and craft on display is precisely the kind of thing for which the French are renowned specialists, all with the explicit purpose of showing how superior their own products are and how much more advanced their culture is.

FRIEND Nor is that the only result of this exhibit. In the context of European politics we've noticed that your government has committed any number of blunders over the last decade, all out of concern that it might have a negative political impact on the exhibition and lead to its failure. And that's not even to mention the effect it's had on its political effectiveness on a world scale, particularly regarding the problem of Fashoda.[97] This exhibition may be a major and prestigious event, but it can never be a substitute for what the French people have lost in dealing with this problem and any number of other issues where France previously played a major role. France has now accepted to do something that it has previously refused to consider; it's reached such a point that French generals have agreed to send their soldiers to fight in the China War under the command of the German general. People who were telling themselves about the defeat of German armed forces and their commanders now find themselves controlled by their supreme commander who can send French troops wherever he wishes and throw them to the fates as he sees fit. 44.4

FRENCHMAN All of which shows you the kind of ignominy and shame that modern civilization has brought us, all based on a policy of caution and reliance on prevention. The consequences are dire. Control can be easily manipulated, leading policymakers inevitably to positions of weakness, humiliation, and contempt.

ʿĪsā ibn Hishām said: While we were conversing, we were suddenly aware of a loud noise that made the entire exhibition grounds shake. We watched as people fell on top of each other like roaring waves on a dark night. Everyone was in a complete panic; people were going crazy, yelling and screaming everywhere accompanied by wails and sobs of grief. Once we had calmed down amid so much chaos, we asked what had happened. They told us that the bridge at the entrance to the exhibition had collapsed, piling people on it on top of the people underneath. When we went over to the place in question, we were greeted by a horrendous, heart-rending sight, enough to evoke tears and 44.5

وذابت القلوب اذ رأينا ما يتجاوز الاربعين عدداً من زوار المعرض يئنون تحت الردم ما بين قتيل وجريح ودام وكسير وفيهم الرضيع والفطيم والفتاة والغلام والعذراء والشاب والشيخ والعجوز والدماء تسيل كالجداول من بين الحلي والحلل والوشي والديباج ورأينا الوالد يجمع من اعضاء ولده المقطعة وشلوه في يده والأم تجمع من اشلاء بنتها المتمزقة وجرحها يسيل والناس يترامون على الارض ليتعرف كل منهم بمن عساه ان يكون بينهم من آبائهم وابنائهم واصهارهم وانسبائهم واهليهم واقربائهم واصحابهم وخلانهم فكلهم يتوجس وقوع المصيبة ويتحسس سقوط النائبة ويترقب نزول النازلة ويتربص حلول الداهية فالبكاء شامل والأنين عام والاطباء يضمدون ورجال الصحة يحملون واشتد علينا الكرب باشتداد الزحام فضاق علينا النفس كما ضاقت النفس عن احتمال هذا المشهد المؤلم والمنظر المحزن فجذبني الباشا اليه يطلب الابتعاد بنا عنه فأسرعنا الى مطاوعته للخلاص من هذا الموقف الكريه وسار بنا وهو يقول:

الباشا تالله ما يفي كل ما رأيناه في هذا المعرض من بهاء ورواء وبهجة وسناء ٦،٤٤
وما احتواه من جملة الطرف ومجموع التحف في صفاء النفس مقدار ما اعترانا من الكدر من هذا المشهد الفظيع وتالله لقد حسبتني انني واقف بلا سلاح في يوم للكريهة وواقعة للحرب انجلت عن قتلاها وجرحاها وانكشفت عن اسرائها وسباياها.

الصاحب صدقت وفوق ذلك فان الوقائع الحربية اهون من مثل هذه الحادثة في النفوس وقعاً وأقل منها بلاء لان للحرب رجالا استعدوا لها واستأنسوا بها ونشأوا فيها ومرنوا عليها دميت فيها اجسادهم وغلظت لها اكبادهم لا اهل ولا اقارب حولهم ولا اطفال ولا صبيان بجانبهم ولا بنات ولا نساء بين ايديهم رقق النعيم اديمهن ورفه الرغد حواسهن يهبن منظر الابرة ويفرقن من مس الريشة ويصرخن من نقيق الضفادع من مثل اولائك اللواتي تركناهم وراءنا في أنين وعويل تحت الردم وبين الانقاض هذه فظائع المدنية في سلمها لا تنقص عن فظاعة وقائعها في حربها.

rend the very heart. Over forty visitors to the exhibition were groaning under the pile of wreckage, some of them dead, others wounded, covered in blood, and with broken bones. There were all sorts of people—nursing mothers and weaned babies, young girls and boys, nubile girls and youths, and old men and women. Blood was flowing in torrents amid the jewelry, bangles, finery, and brocade. We watched as a father collected the broken limbs of his son, and a mother gathered her daughter's shattered limbs, blood pouring from them. People were throwing themselves to the ground, anxious to find out if any of their relatives—fathers, daughters, in-laws, kinsfolk, family, relatives, friends, or colleagues—were among the dead or wounded. Each one of them was assuming the very worst, expecting to face a disaster and prepared to confront a dreadful truth. Everyone was crying and moaning while doctors kept doing their best to bandage wounds and health workers carried people away. As the crowd grew larger and the situation went from bad to worse, we found it increasingly difficult to watch such a disastrous occurrence and horrendous sight. The Pāshā grabbed hold of me and urged us to get away. We hurriedly accepted his suggestion that we leave this terrible situation. As we were walking, he said:

PĀSHĀ By God, all the wondrous and delightful spectacles we have seen 44.6
at this exhibition and all the beautiful objects and relics designed to soothe the heart cannot in any way compensate for the anxiety and grief we've been feeling as we've watched this dreadful event. By God, I had the feeling that I was standing there unarmed on a battle day during a war when inevitably both dead and wounded and prisoners would be taken.

FRIEND You're right. Not only that, but the horrors of war have a lesser effect on people and cause less distress because war involves soldiers who have been trained and are used to it; they have been brought up in its midst and performed drills for it that have bloodied their bodies and given them a steely resolve. They are not surrounded by family and relatives, and no babies and children stand alongside them. No girls or women are to be seen in front of them, people whose bodies are used to the comforts of life and whose feelings are accustomed to a life of ease. The sight of a needle scares them, they hate being brushed by a feather, and scream when a frog croaks. It's not the same for the women we've just left behind us, groaning underneath the rubble and in the bridge's wreckage. This is a disaster involving civilized society at peace, and it's no less terrible than battles during wartime.

الباشا هلم بنا الى الباب على ان لا نعود الى هذا المعرض في زيارة أخرى أفما آن لنا ان ننتهي منه ونخلص الى غيره في رحلتنا فقد سئمناه ومللناه وطفناه طولا وعرضا ودرنا فيه يميناً وشمالا فلم نجد فيه الى الآن من عجائبه عجيبة لم نرها ولا من نوادره نادرة لم نسمع بها.

الفرنسوي ان كنتم عزمتم على الانتهاء من زيارة المعرض بعد اليوم فلا بأس من ان تنتهوا بزيارة العجيبة التي هي في الحقيقة مصدر العجائب والمنبع الذي تسيل منه تلك الطرائف والغرائب والاصل الذي تتفرع عنه فروع الفنون والصنائع والمطلع الذي تشرق منه شمس الحضارة والعمران.

٧،٤٤ قال عيسى بن هشام: فشوقنا الى رؤيته بكلامه واتبعناه وسار أمامنا حتى وصلنا الى بناء عظيم ولما دخلنا فيه انتهينا منه الى فوهة هاوية دعانا الى النزول فيها فوجدنا على شفيرها آلة للهبوط كأعظم ما يكون من الدلاء فوضعونا فيها فما نشعر الا ونحن في قاع بئر عميق فوقع عليّ من الذهول ما أنساني كل شيء في ذاكرتي مما يحفظه اهل الارض الا ثلاثة ابيات أبقاها عليَّ ما انا فيه من هذا الهويّ في الليل الدجوجيّ:

فلما استوت رجلاي في الارض نادتا
أحيّ يرجى أم قتيل نحاذره
فقلت ارفعا الاسباب لا يشعروا بنا
ووليت في اعجاز ليل أبادره
هما دلتاني من ثمانين قامة
كما انقض باز أقتم الريش كاسره

٨،٤٤ ولولا ان طول الخلطة والعشرة مكن الثقة في انفسنا بصاحبنا الفرنسوي لتيقنا انه كاد لنا وأوقعنا في مكمن لاغتيالنا فيه او أراد ان يفعل بنا ما فعله ابناء يعقوب بيوسف اخيهم ولما افقنا من هذه الدهشة سألناه أين نحن فعلمنا اننا في مكان صنعوه تحت الارض يمثلون به معدن الفحم الحجري وكيف يستخرجونه ولما أمعنا في تلك الظلمات

PĀSHĀ Let's head for the exit. There's no need to come back. Isn't it time now to have done with it all and to use our journey here for something else? We've gone back and forth, hither and yon, and now we're bored and tired. Up till now we've seen nothing among its marvels and wonders that we didn't know about already, nor are there any rarities that we haven't heard about.

FRENCHMAN As long as you've decided to end your visits to the exhibition as of today, you should certainly make your last inspection be to the miracle that is the masterpiece of all these remarkable exhibits, the source from which flow all the signs of civilization and shines the sun of refinement and culture.

ʿĪsā ibn Hishām said: We were attracted by what he was saying and followed behind him till we reached a splendid edifice. Once we had gone inside, we ended up by a deep hole in the ground. He invited us to go down. At the edge we found a machine that went up and down like a gigantic bucket. They put us in the bucket, and, before we knew what was happening, we were inside a very deep well. The experience made me forget everything human beings remember except for three verses that stayed with me while I descended into darkest night: 44.7

Once my feet had touched the ground, they demanded,
Hopefully alive or dead and a risk?
"Remove the ropes," I said, "they will not detect us."
I then took off into the night without delay.
My feet directed me from a massive height, like a
a rapacious, black-feathered falcon swooping down.[98]

But for our long acquaintance with the Frenchman and the confidence that we had in him, we would have said that he was trying to do away with us or else playing the same trick on us as the one used by Jacob's sons on their brother, Joseph.[99] Once we had recovered from our shock, we asked him where exactly we were. He informed us that we were in a place underground that was modeled on the concept of a coal mine; the aim was to show how miners extracted coal. When we stared into the darkness, we managed to make out in front of us some men acting as workers who could only see what was right in front 44.8

شاهدنا امامنا رجالاً يمثلون العملة لا يبصرون ما بين ايديهم في عملهم الا بضوء سراج كهربائي معقود برؤسهم فكنا نراهم كالحباحب حول الاشجار في حندس الليل وأنى لهذه السرج ان تشق عباب هذا الظلام المتكاثف الذي يكاد يمسك باليد ويقبض بالراحة؟ وكأنهم لم يجعلوها هناك لانارة الظلام واضاءته وانما جعلوها لبيانه واراءته ثم خطونا قليلا فرأينا من المنعطفات والسراديب والكهوف والفجوات ما تضل الصلال فيها لكثرة التوائها وقلة اهتدائها ورأينا في كل فجوة أشباحاً على مئين من الهيئات المختلفة التي يمكن لجسم الانسان ان يتشكل بها لضرورة العمل في تلك الفجوات وفي أيديهم ما ثقل من آلات القطع والحفر وأخشاب الاسناد يسندون بها ما يريد أن ينقض من جدران الفجوات اثناء الأخذ منها فمنهم الواقف في عمله على أصابعه والمضطجع على جنبه والمتربع والقاعد القرفصاء والجاثي على ركبتيه والمنكب على وجهه والمياه تسيل عليهم من جدران الكهوف.

٩،٤٤ هذا بعض ما على الجسم من المتاعب وما يدريك بما في القلوب من توقع الهلكات وترقب الاخطار بالاختناق والاحتراق والانبثاق والغرق وانهيال الاحجار وأصغر فتحة في احد تلك المصابيح المعلقة برؤوسهم تدكدك عليهم تلك الفجوات لالتهاب الغاز وتراهم في ثلاث ظلمات فالفحم ظلام جامد والظلام فحم سائل وبختهم بين ذلك أسود حالك فسبحان من اقام الناس في ما اقام ثم وصلنا من معدن الفحم الحجري الى معدن الذهب فلم نجد عماله أسعد حالا ولا متاعبه اهون احتمالا ولما كادت الرطوبة تعقد دماءنا في مجاريها اسرعنا الى محل الصعود فخرجنا من بطن الارض نقول الخلاص الخلاص وبقينا على وجهها برهة نعالج تحمل الضياء ثم خرجنا من ذلك المكان نتمتع بالنظر الى الجو يميناً وشمالا لا نحير خطاباً ولا ننطق حرفاً.

١٠،٤٤ واذا بصاحبنا الفرنسوي من بيننا يشير باصبعه الى ناحية فيه يرينا اسطوانة ذلك المدفع الهائل المطل من مسبك المدافع المشهور بعظمته وضخامته وهو يقول لنا:

الفرنسوي وهذا هو الثالث من امهات المدنية واقانيم الحضارة فقد رأيتم الاقنوم الاول وهو الفحم الاقنوم الثاني وهو الذهب وهذا الاقنوم الثالث وهو الحديد

of them by the light of an electric lamp tied to their heads. They looked to us just like fireflies glowing in trees on a dark night. Heaven only knows how the electric lamps were supposed to pierce such utter darkness, so thick that it could almost grab hold of your hand. It was as though the lights were not there to illuminate the darkness but rather to demonstrate quite how dark it actually was. We made our way slowly forward and saw enough chambers, caves, and trenches to make even an adder get lost and coil up in despair. In every nook and cranny we spotted specters of human beings whose postures in their hundreds provided examples of the need to work in such mine shafts. In their hands they carried heavy and light pickaxes and spades, along with wooden planks that they put in place to stop the shaft walls from crumbling while they were being mined. Some of them were standing on tiptoe, others were lying on their side, others on their knees, and a few of them flat on their faces. Water poured over them from cracks and crevices in the rock face.

These are just some of the aches and pains to which the human body was 44.9
being exposed, and God alone knows what expectations and worries the men had in their hearts and minds because of any number of threats they might face from lack of oxygen, and possibility of fire, inundation, drowning, and rockfalls. The tiniest crack in the lamps attached to their heads could ignite gas explosions. They were in three types of darkness: coal being hard and dark; darkness itself a liquid form of coal black; and the pitch-black livelihood of these men. So all praise be to the One who has set up mankind as He has. From the coal mine we now moved on to the gold mine, but the workers there were no better off or less burdened than the others had been. When the humidity began to clog the very blood inside our veins, we hurried toward the way up and emerged from the belly of the earth. Relieved to be above ground at last, we stayed where we were for a while adjusting our eyes to the light. We then left the place and started strolling in the fresh air, looking to left and right but not saying a word or even trying to speak.

All of a sudden our French Philosopher friend directed our attention to 44.10
a spot where he showed us the barrel of the enormous gun overlooking the famous gun foundry renowned for its size and girth. Here's what he told us:

FRENCHMAN So this is the third of the major wonders of the exhibition and constituents of civilization. The first, as you have seen, is coal; the second

يستخرجون الذهب فيشترون به الفحم ليصنعوا به الحديد فتصنع منه آلات السلاح وآلات الصناعات ويتفننون بها في ابداع ما تشاهدونه من عجائب المخترعات وغرائب المبتدعات وكل ما ترونه مما يبهر الانظار ويأخذ بمجامع القلوب وكل ما يهولكم من قوة ويستوقفكم من فخامة أصله ذلك الفحم الاسود الذي هو اليوم خبز المدنية وادام الحضارة في نعيمها ورفاهيتها وبأسها وقوتها .تبًا للانسان فما اقبح صنعه وأعق عمله يهوي بنفسه الى اسفل درجات الارض فيمزق أحشاءها ويخرب بطونها ليستخرج منه ما يخرب بها وجهها ويزعم انه يسعى وراء الحظ في العيش والسعادة في الدنيا وهو يقضي عمره في مثل هذا الشقاء وهذه التعاسة حتى يوافيه حمامه فيخرج منها بعد ان لبث فيها برهة كان اضل حالا فيها من حال الحيوانات وهو أفضلها.

الباشا قل لي بالله وكم يكون أجر العامل في باطن الارض على الحال التي رأيناه عليها وكم يكون له من المكافأة؟

١١،٤٤ الفرنسي يشتغل في معادن الفحم الحجري بالبلاد الفرنسوية ١٠٠ الف عامل ويستخرجون ٢٧ مليونًا طنًا من الفحم تباع بمائتين وستين مليونًا من الفرنكات في العام ويعمل العامل منهم في بطن الارض على عمق المئات من الامتار والاقدام والمتوسط في عدد حوادث الخطر بينهم في العام ١٥٠٠ حادثة يقتل فيها من يقتل ويجرح فيها من يجرح وتعتريهم الاسقام الصدرية والامراض الرئوية من استنشاق الكربون وفاسد الهواء ومنهم من يشتغل بالليل ومنهم من يشتغل بالنهار ومعهم اولادهم ونساؤهم ويصيب العامل في كل هذا البلاء اجرة تختلف من اثنين الى خمسة من الفرنكات.

الباشا وأين تذهب هذه المئين من الملايين من ثمن ذلك الفحم الذي هو ثمرة كدهم ونتيجة تعبهم؟

الفرنسوي يذهب الى صناديق فئة قليلة من أرباب الشركات والامتيازات فينفقونه في وجوه الشهوات وزوائد المدنية الباطلة بعد ان حرموه هؤلاء المساكين الذين تفضلهم الحشرات والدواب في معيشتهم ولا تظنن ان هذه الفرنكات التي يأخذها العامل أجرًا له في اليوم يصل الى يده منها شيء فان أكثر الشركات تبتني المحال

is gold; and the third is this one, iron. They extract gold so they can buy coal and weld it into iron and steel. They use it to make weapons and all kinds of industrial instruments, not to mention the marvelous inventions and strange creations that you've seen here. All these dazzling and amazing objects with their incredible power and sophistication originate in that black coal which today constitutes civilization's bread and is the source of mankind's luxury and refinement, not to mention civilization's power and vigor. But a pox on mankind! How utterly evil is everything it makes and how disdainful everything it does! It sends people to the lowest levels of the earth to rip out its guts and destroy its inside, all in order to extract something that will wreak as much havoc on its surface as well. The claim is that they're striving for a decent way of life and contentment on earth, whereas mankind spends its life in such misery and suffering. Eventually death arrives to take them away, and all that after spending a short while on earth even more lost than animals—of which they are supposed to be the most superior.

PĀSHĀ Tell me, by God, what's the wage for coal miners who have to work in the conditions that we've just seen. What other rewards are there?

FRENCHMAN In France there are a hundred thousand miners working **44.11** in coal mines. They extract twenty-seven million tons of coal which is sold for two hundred and sixty million francs per year. Miners work underground at a depth of hundreds of meters and feet and in dangerous conditions. Each year there are on average fifteen hundred mining accidents which cause a large number of deaths and injuries. Then there are the chest and lung diseases from inhaling carbon and breathing foul air. Some work by day, others by night, and they're joined by sons and wives as well. For all this hardship the miner receives a wage of two to five francs.

PĀSHĀ So what happens to all the hundreds of millions earned from the coal that they extract at the cost of so much effort and exhaustion?

FRENCHMAN They go into the coffers of a select minority of company and concession owners. They spend the money on their own desires and the fripperies of civilized life, having deprived these poor, wretched laborers whose lives are no better than insects or pack animals. But don't even think that the few francs that a miner earns as a daily wage ever actually reach his own hand. The majority of companies construct housing and stores, so the

والاماكن فيسكن العامل في دار الشركة ويشتري مؤنته وملابسه من سوق الشركة والشركة تخصم عليه من اجرته فاذا خرج آخر الشهر لا عليه ولا له كان من اسعد السعداء وانعم المتنعمين.

الصاحب من هنا نشأت المذاهب اشتراكية والفوضوية ومن يصبر على مثل هذه الحياة واحسن منها حياة لواحس الترب ونواهس الارض ومن يبصر هذا الفرق العظيم في تفاوت المعائش بين أهل البلاد الى درجة ان يقضي الانسان حياته دفيناً يعمل في بطن الارض لمعتوه يقعد من مراتب النعيم في اعلى عليين ويرقد على بساط الراحة والهناء بين مقصورات القصور التي تستلم السحاب بعلوها وتحاكي ابراج السماء في زينتها.

١٢،٤٤ قال عيسى بن هشام: ووصلنا في مسيرنا الى البرج الشهير فاسندنا ظهورنا الى بعض جوانبه واخذنا نتفكر في غريب اعمال الانسان وما ياتيه من فنون الجنون في كل زمان وان زعم انه الفاضل الكامل والمتبصر العاقل.

miner lives in a company house, buys his food and clothing from a company store, in return for which the company deducts a certain amount from his salary. If a miner finishes the month with neither credit nor debt, he considers himself the happiest and luckiest of mortals.

FRIEND It's this situation that's given rise to socialist and anarchist movements. How is anyone supposed to live such a life, working like insects underground or crawling reptiles. How can anyone regard this enormous gap in lifestyle between the people in the country? And to such a degree that there are some who spend their lives buried underground, slaving away for some idiot living in the utmost luxury and lounging on plush cushions in the boudoirs of a mighty mansion lofty enough to reach the clouds and rival the very towers of heaven in their decoration?

ʿĪsā ibn Hishām said: We now reached the famous Eiffel Tower. We leaned **44.12**
our backs against one of its columns and started contemplating the strange achievements of mankind and varieties of insanity that have been perpetrated in every age, claiming all the while that man is the perfect creature and wise observer.

مصباح الشرق ١٣٣، ١٤ ديسمبر ١٩٠٠

باريس

١،٤٥ قال عيسى بن هشام: ووقفنا برهة عند ذلك البناء البديع والعماد الرفيع والبرج المنيع فهالتنا رفعته وأدهشتنا صنعته وتأملناه فوجدناه في المشاهد الفريدة العصماء والغرة الشهباء والهضبة العلياء والقلة الشماء فهو أعجوبة الصنائع احسانًا واتقانًا وبكر هذا المعرض وان كان فيه عوانا تنحني أمامه الآطام والآكام وتخرّ له الربى والأعلام فأين من بنائه الهرمان ومن ارتفاعه صرح هامان لو رآه فرعون لهدم ما شاد وأعلى ولم يقل أنا ربكم الأعلى ولطرح هامانه فجلده ألفا وعلقه بعد ذلك في الجذع شنقا وأين برج بابل من برج يشافه بروج السماء ويشارف برأسه الشعرى الغميصاء اذا حوّم عليه نسر الجو صار ثالث النسرين واتخذ وكره في منازل القمرين وأنى للمتخيل أن يعلو علوّه وللمشبه أن يسمو سموّه فيحيط بنعته ووصفه ويلم بشرح نسقه ورصفه لا جرم اذا ضاق على الوصاف نطاق التشبيه شبهوا الأكبر بالاصغر ومثلوا الاعظم بالأحقر كما شبهوا شمس النهار بكأس العقار والبدر التمام بعين مفجورة في بركة مسجورة وشبهوا الثريا بعنقود والجوزاء بعصا أو عود وكما شبهوا كواكب الافلاك بالودع المنظوم في الاسلاك وكما شبهوا الليل الدجوجيّ بأسود زنجيّ والأشفاق بدم مهراق وعلى هذا فلنا أن نشبه ذلك البرج بألف الهجاء في كتاب التقدم والارتقاء مدتها راية تخفق في صحيفة الأفق أو أول العدد المرقوم في جريدة الفنون والعلوم أو الابرة التي توضع علامة على موضع المدنية من خريطة الكرة الارضية أو هو القلم يخط في أديم البدر ما بلغته هذه الامة من فخامة القدر او هو في زعم البعض قرن الثور نفذ من بطن الارض.

Miṣbāḥ al-sharq 133, December 14, 1900[100]

Paris

ʿĪsā ibn Hishām said: We stopped for a while to take a look at this imposing tower, a lofty structure whose sheer height amazed us and whose construction was astonishing. In the category of wondrous sights, amazing rarities, prized entities, lofty peaks, and highest summits, this was certainly a remarkable feat of design and engineering—obviously the precious maiden of the entire exhibit, albeit of a certain age. Castles and hills would bow down before it, mountains and flags would be prostrate. In comparison what could one say about the height of the pyramids or Haman's lofty tower? If the Pharaoh had seen it, he would have demolished everything he had built and erected. Nor would he have stated, "I am your lord most high." He would have turned on his builder, Haman, and flayed him a thousand times, then hung him from a tree. And how could you compare the fabled Tower of Babel with this Parisian tower that addresses the very constellations in the heavens and whose top looks down on twinkling Sirius itself? Were a vulture to alight on it, it would immediately become the third of the Two Vultures, building its nest in the twin stars of Ursa Minor. How could an imaginative person conceive of overtopping its lofty heights or a crafter of similes rise so far upwards as to find the appropriate epithets to depict it and detail the modes of its construction? Needless to say, words would fail him. For, in a context where comparison becomes impossible, people liken the biggest to the smallest and the greatest to the lowliest, just as they have compared the daytime sun with a cup of wine, the full moon with a spring gushing into a swollen lake. The Pleiades have been compared to a cluster of grapes, the Gemini to a stick or piece of wood, stars in the heavens to strings of seashells, darkest night to black slaves, and dawn to spilt blood. On that basis we would say that we are depicting this tower as the letter *alif* in the alphabet of progress and development, while its vowel sign is the flag fluttering at the top against the distant horizon. Either that, or it comes first in the list of crafts and sciences; the needle that marks the spot of civilization on the map of the globe; the pen that draws on the new moon's surface to indicate the level of sophistication that this nation has achieved; or, as some people would claim, the bull's horn poking out of the earth's surface. 45.1

هذا ولما انتهينا من الطواف حوله مرارا وامتلأت له نفوسنا اعظاماً واكبارا ٢،٤٥
وخرست الألسنة عنده وتاهت العقول مال علينا الصاحب يحدثنا ويقول:

الصاحب هذه سنة الدهر منذ القدم وطريقة الزمن كلما ترقت أمة من الامم في معارج المدنية والحضارة شيدت لها اثرًا من بديع الصنعة يشهد لها بين الورى بعلو المرتبة و رفعة الدرجة في سماء المجد والعز وأفق العظمة والقدرة فيبقى على مرور الدهر حيناً من الأحيان يذكر أهل الاجيال اللاحقة بأهل القرون السابقة. . وقد اشتهر لكل مدينة أثر عجيب يذكر لها في باب المحامد والمفاخر ويشير الى سبقها في مضمار العلوم والفنون ويعلم الله أن مدنية أهل الغرب أتت في تشييد هذا البناء بالآية الكبرى والمعجزة العظمى وجاءت بالاثر الذي تسجد لعظمته الآثار وبالعجيبة التي تبتلع العجائب السبع وان كانت تخلب الابصار بحسنها وتحير الافكار في صنعها في ما يحدثون عنه من أعمال الامم الغابرة ومدنية القرون الخالية.

الباشا وماهي تلك العجائب المعدودة؟ ٣،٤٥

الصاحب هي اهرام مصر والحدائق المعلقة للملكة سميراميس وسور بابل وتمثال المشتري من عمل فدياس و صنم رودس وهيكل ديان في ايفيس ومدفن الملك موصل في هاليكارناس.

الباشا وهل هي باقية الى اليوم؟

الصاحب لم يبق منها اليوم غير تلك الاهرام التي علمتها وشاهدتها وقد لعبت أيدي البلى بالبواقي منها ولا نعرف عنها اليوم شيئاً الا من طريق الاحاديث والذكر والى هذا ينتهي عمل الانسان مهما كان عظيما فلا يلبث الا بضع ثوان من ساعة الدهر.

الباشا وهل تعرف من احاديثها خبرًا تخبرنيه فان نفسي تتوق الى التحدث بالقديم ومعرفة الآثار العتيقة.

الصاحب اما الاهرام فمعلوم امرها مشهود. ٤،٤٥

We all walked around it several times and duly admired it; it was awesome enough to silence all talk and baffle the mind. Our Friend turned to us and said: 45.2

FRIEND This is the way things have been since ancient times, the manner in which time behaves. Whenever one nation achieves superiority in civilization, it builds a monument that testifies to all mankind about the elevated status that has accrued to it in the realms of glory and prestige. It survives for a while to remind the present generation of people about previous centuries. Every single city was famous for a remarkable monument that was duly memorialized on the pages of prestige and glory and indicated its superiority in arts and sciences at the time. God alone knows that, by constructing this tower, Western civilization has presented the world with an incredible marvel, a monument to which others bow down in admiration, an amazing construction that can even surpass the seven wonders of the world, monuments that were also beautiful to observe and equally amazing to the mind according to what people have to say about the achievements of ancient peoples and the civilization of earlier centuries.

PĀSHĀ What are those seven wonders? 45.3

FRIEND The Pyramids in Egypt, the Hanging Gardens of Queen Semiramis, the Wall of Babylon, Pheidias's Statue of Zeus, the Colossus of Rhodes, the Temple of Diana at Ephesus, and the Tomb of Mausulos at Halicarnassus.

PĀSHĀ Do they still exist today?

FRIEND Only the Pyramids still exist today. You know them well and have seen them. The hands of decay have done their work on the rest of the wonders. All we know about them today comes from anecdotes and mentions in texts. That is what happens to mankind's works, however great they may have been. On the scale of time they don't last longer than seconds.

PĀSHĀ Do you know things about the wonders you can share with us? I find myself eager to talk about olden times and to learn about ancient monuments.

FRIEND The Pyramids are well known. 45.4

واما تلك الحدائق فكانت مغروسة فوق الربوة التي تعرف الآن بربوة عمران ابن علي وهي في اتساع اربعين فدانًا وكان الفرات يجري من تحتها وقد خطط مختصر الحدائق على ارتفاع سطحها باشكال صناعية تشبه اشكال الجبال والسبب في وضعها ان احدى نسائه كانت تحن الى اعلام ديارها وربى بلادها فانشأ لها بالصناعة ما يماثل الطبيعة ليعوضها عن منظر اوطانها وينسيها الحنين الى مشاهدتها وكان المتنزه فيها يسير تحت قباب معقودة فوقها الاشجار والازهار محمولة على عمد واساطين مفرغة ملاؤها بالطين وغرسوا فيها الاشجار العظيمة تورق في رؤوسها وتنساق فيها جذورها وفي القباب درج يصعد منه الصاعد الى السطح حيث تزهر الازهار وتعشب الاعشاب وتثمر الثمار وتدور الدواليب لرفع الماء من مجرى الفرات الى اعلى القباب.

٥،٤٥ واما سور بابل فهو عدة اسوار متداخلة في بعضها محيطها ٩٣ كيلو مترًا مربعًا يعني انه يسع في داخله سبع مدائن مثل مدينة باريس هذه وارتفاع السور ٤٨ مترًا وعرضه ٢٧ مترًا ومن حوله خندق عظيم وكان عليه ابراج متعددة في علو ١٠٨ مترًا ولهذا السور على ما رواه جماعة المؤرخين مائة باب من الحديد.

وأما تمثال المشتري الآله الاكبر بين الآلهة عند اليونانيين فقد صنعه لهم فدياس الشهير وكانت قامته ١٤ مترًا راعى المصور فيه دقة التناسب وهو جالس على العرش مكلل باكليل من ورق الزيتون وفي يمناه تمثال «اله النصر» من الذهب وسن الفيل وفي يسراه صولجان منضد بجميع انواع المعادن وعلى رأس الصولجان نسر وكان طيلسانه وحذاؤه من الذهب الخالص وكذلك التخت من الذهب الخالص وكذلك التخت من الذهب وسن الفيل ومن الرخام والآبنوس وكان موطيء قدميه من التخت اسدين من الذهب وما كان يوجد عند القدماء شيء انفس من هذا التمثال واتقن فقد كان كل يوناني في العالم يعد نفسه شقيًا ان مات قبل ان يحج اليه ويراه.

٦،٤٥ واما صنم رودس فهو تمثال للآله ابولاون اقاموه في مواجهة مدخل المرفأ في رودس وكان ارتفاعه ٣٢ مترا وهو أعظم ارتفاع كان في تماثيل القدماء من اليونانيين والرومانيين فاسقطه زلزال وبقي الى القرن السابع ونقلت العرب كثيرًا من بقاياه

The Hanging Gardens were constructed on a hill that is now known by the name ʿUmrān ibn ʿAlī. The area is forty feddans wide, and the River Euphrates used to flow past at the bottom. Artificial shapes like mountains were used to trace miniature versions of the gardens on the top. The reason was that one of the king's wives felt nostalgic for the hilly features in her homeland, so he had a replica of nature built that would compensate for what she was missing and make her forget her nostalgia. Underneath was a park with interlocking domes over which were suspended trees and clusters of flowers on pillars and empty cylinders that would be filled with soil. Large flowering trees planted in the cylinders would spread their roots. The domes were equipped with staircases by which you could ascend to the rooftop where flowers and plants were growing, fruits were ripening, and waterwheels kept turning to raise the water from the Euphrates below to the top of the structure.

The Wall of Babylon was actually a number of interlinked walls enclosing ninety-three square kilometers—in other words, large enough to contain seven cities the size of Paris. The wall was forty-eight meters high and twenty-seven meters wide, surrounded by an enormous trench, and with a number of towers one hundred and eight meters high. According to a number of historical accounts, the wall had a hundred gates made of iron. 45.5

The Statue of Zeus in Greece, he being the chief of the Greek gods, was the work of the famous sculptor Pheidias. It was fourteen meters high. The artist took great pains to make its proportions exact. The deity sat on a throne, crowned with olive garlands and holding a gold statue of the god of victory and an elephant's tooth in his right hand; in his left, was a scepter studded with all kinds of metals, and at its tip sat an eagle. The god's shawl and shoes were both made of pure gold, as were the throne itself and the elephant's tooth, which used ebony and marble as well. His two feet were placed on top of two lions, also made of gold. For the ancients this statue was the most valuable thing in the world, and every Greek considered himself unlucky if he died before being able to make a pilgrimage to see it.

The Colossus of Rhodes was an enormous statue of the god Apollo erected opposite the entrance to Rhodes Harbor. It was thirty-seven meters high, making it the tallest statue known to the Greeks and Romans. It fell in an earthquake, but bits of it remained until the seventh century when Arabs removed most of what remained of it. 45.6

وأما هيكل ديان في ايفيس فهو المعبد الذي لم يكن له مثيل في البناء والزخرفة والنقوش والصور بين معابد القدماء على الاطلاق ومن نوادر التاريخ ان احد اصحاب الافكار السيئة من اليونانيين دبر في نفسه ان يأتي عملا يذكر به بين الامم على مدى الادهار فسولت له نفسه ان اكبر عمل يشتهر به اسمه في الوجود ان يحرق هذا المعبد فاحتال حتى احرقه وكان احراقه في الليلة التي ولد فيها الاسكندر الاكبر وقد اعلن الجاني بنفسه للحكومة انه هو المحرق له ففهم مجلس الحكومة قصده وهو تخليد الذكر فحكم عليه بالتعذيب حتى يموت وأمر بان من يذكر اسمه يلحق به فكان ذلك من موجبات تخليد ذلك الذكر بين الناس الى اليوم وقد اراد الاسكندر بعد ذلك ان يعيد لهم بناءه من ماله على ان يكتب اسمه على احد جدرانه فأبوا عليه ذلك حتى لا يكون لاجنبي عليهم فضل على معبدهم واخذوا يبنون فيه ويعيدون له رونقه وزخرفته حتى تم على مرور الاجيال في ظرف مائتين وعشرين عاماً وما زال على ذلك حتى جاء نيرون احد قياصرة الرومانيين فنهب ما فيه من الذخائر والكنوز ونقل من ارضه الفسيفساء فوضعها في أرض قصوره بروميه ثم انتهى الامر بان خربه الجرمانيون في حروبهم.

وأما مدفن الملك موصل فهو مدفن مشهور أقامته له امرأته وكانت أخته بعد موته جمعت له مهرة الصناع من انحاء الارض وخصت كل طائفة منهم بجانب من العمل فكان ارتفاعه ٤٢ متراً وكانت أساطينه من المرمر النقي عليها صور الوقائع والحوادث التاريخية وكانت تماثيله من أبدع التماثيل اتقاناً وكان غطاء القبر صخرة من المرمر صورت عليها وقائعه الحربية وبقي هذا المدفن موجوداً سليما الى القرن الرابع ثم اندثر أثره في القرون الوسطى ونقل جانب من أجزائه لبناء قلعة بُدرون في القرن السادس عشر وبقي الرخام المنقوش لاصقاً بالارض الى أواسط هذا القرن حتى اشترت انكلترا قطعه ووضعتها في متحفها بلونده وكان لهذا المدفن شهرة عظيمة حتى دخل ذكره في محاورة جرت بين هذا الملك وديووجين الحكيم بعد موتهما يتبين فيها قدر ذلك المدفن وانه كان عند الملك اكبر مفاخره على كثرتها. ٧،٤٥

The Temple of Diana at Ephesus was one whose structure, decoration, paintings, and detail knew no rival among all ancient temples of its type. An interesting historical anecdote tells how an evil Greek intellectual decided that he wanted to do something for which he would be remembered for all time; the thing he chose to do was to burn down this temple. He did indeed contrive to set it on fire, on the very same night that Alexander the Great was born. When the perpetrator of the crime informed the government that he was the one who had started the blaze, they realized that he was in quest of fame. The government ordered that he be tortured to death and that anyone who even mentioned the man's name would suffer the same fate. This requirement for rendering this episode eternal has remained in place. After that, Alexander wanted to rebuild the temple using his own money, a condition being that he put his own name on one of the walls; but the people refused since they did not want any foreigner to lord over them in their own temple. They themselves undertook the task of rebuilding and redecorating it, a project that lasted two hundred and twenty years. That is the way things stayed until Nero, the Roman Emperor, came and robbed the temple of all its treasures and transferred the mosaics to his own palaces in Rome. The whole thing came to an end when the Germans destroyed it during their wars.

The Tomb of King Mausolus is very famous. His wife had it built. After 45.7
his death, his sister gathered together all the skilled craftsmen in the known world and assigned each group a separate part of the project. It was forty-two meters high, with marble columns on which were portrayed major battles and other events. The statuary was the finest of its kind, and the tomb itself was covered with a piece of marble on which were carved images of important battles. The tomb survived intact until the fourth century, but gradually it fell into ruin, and parts of it were taken away to build the fortress of Bodrum in the sixteenth century. Pieces of its decorated marble remained on the site until earlier this century, when England purchased them and transferred them to the British Museum in London. The tomb was very famous; it is even mentioned as part of the dialogue between the King and the philosopher Diogenes. Once both of them were dead, the worth of the tomb became evident, as was the fact that the king regarded it as his greatest monument, even though there were many others.

الباشا أحسنت أيها الصاحب وأجدت بما فصلت لي من هذه العجائب التي انزوت عني في بطون التواريخ ولكن بقي لي ان أسألك عما جاء في كلامك من أمر التحاور بين الاموات. ٨،٤٥

الصاحب جرت عادة بعض الفلاسفة ان يضموا ما يبثونه من الحقائق في ضمن المحاورات تارة بين الاحياء وتارة بين الاموات ليعتبر بها من يعتبر ويهتدي بها من يهتدي ومم يدل على ان هذا الاسلوب أعلق بالنفس وأثبت أثرًا في الذهن انه لا يزال يتردد على فكري أشياء من موعظة تلك المحاورة على كثرة المناظر والمشاغل.

الباشا ما أراك تبخل عليّ بمثل تلك العظة.

الصاحب اجتمع ديوجين بالملك موصل فتحاورا بينهما في عالم القبور:

«ديوجين ما لي أراك أيها الاسيوي تائهاً متكبراً كأنك تريد أن تنزل هنا ايضاً منزلة أشرف من منزلتنا؟ ٩،٤٥

«الملك لا بدع في ذلك فاني أستحق التمييز بما حزته من عظم الملك واتساع السلطان وما افتتحته من الممالك و فوق ذلك ما أوتيته من الجمال والبهاء و البسطة في الجسم والشجاعة في النفس ولك ان تدع كل هذا فلي مزية فوق المزايا كلها و رتبة فوق كل الرتب وهي ذلك المدفن الذي لم يكن لاحد من الملوك مثله في فخامة بنائه وحسن اتقانه وهو وحده يكفي لسلسلة من الملوك أن تفتخر به مدى الادهار فهل ترى بعد ذلك ان ليس من حقي ان أترفع و أتكبر؟

«ديوجين ولكن يا أيها الملك الجميل أراك لم يبق عندك من ذلك الجمال ولا من تلك القوة شيء وأرى اننا اذا تحاكمنا الى منصف لم يفرق بين عظام جمجمتي وعظام جمجمتك فكلتاهما مثقوبتا العينين مفغورتا الانف بارزتا الاسنان وأما ذلك المدفن الكبير وتلك الصخور المزخرفة فلا فائدة لك منها وانما فائدتها للاحياء من أهل بلدك يتباهون بمنظرها في أعين الوافدين عليها ويجتنون منها ما يجتنونه من الاعتبار ولكني لا أعلم ما هي الثمرة التي تعود عليك الآن من تشييد ذلك البناء الا كونك أسوأ منا حالا هنا بما فوق رأسك من تلك الصخور والاحجار.

PĀSHĀ That is all wonderful, my friend! You have given me plentiful detail about wonders that existed far in the past. But I still have to ask you about the issue of dialogue among the dead. 45.8

FRIEND Certain philosophers made a habit of putting some of the theses they were advocating in the form of dialogues—some of them involved living people, others the dead—as object lessons and guides for people. As proof of the way that such dialogues remain fixed in the mind, I can tell you that pieces of wise counsel from those dialogues keep occurring to me personally in a number of different situations.

PĀSHĀ I assume you won't stint in sharing such counsel.

FRIEND Diogenes had a meeting with King Mausolus in which they discussed the world of tombs:

"DIOGENES How is it, Asian monarch, that I see you here strutting arro- 45.9
gantly around, as though you expected to occupy a loftier position than ours?

"KING There's nothing surprising about that. I merit such a status by virtue of being a king with wide powers and also due to the fact that I have conquered so many countries; and not merely those things, but also because of my own beauty and elegance and the courage I've displayed. And, if all that isn't enough, then I can claim a distinction and rank above all others, thanks to my tomb which is superior to any other tomb in its perfect construction and craftsmanship. It alone is sufficient for a whole series of monarchs to be celebrated through the ages. With all that in mind, do you still think that I've no right to boast?

"DIOGENES But, o thou handsome king, I notice that none of that former beauty and power is now left. If we were to adjudicate matters fairly, then your cranium and mine are the same size. Neither of them have eyes, our noses are cracked, and our teeth exposed. And, when it comes to that temple and all its fancy decoration, it brings you no benefit; that only accrues to the people still alive in your country who can boast about it to visitors and glean whatever kudos they wish from its existence. But I can't see anything accruing to you from the construction of that building. I can only see you as being in a worse situation here than all the rest of us because you have all those stones and rocks over your head.

«الملك: ما هذا الكلام أيكون كل ما أتيته عبثاً لا مزية لي منه واكون مساوياً لديوجين؟

«ديوجين: لا تقل انك مساو لي فانك لا تنفك تتألم على فقد ماكنت تملكه على ظهر الارض وتعده السعادة العظمى وغاية الأمر انه لم يبق لك الا ان يمر المار بمدفنك فيقول ما أجمل هذا المنظر وأما ديوجين فانه لا يبالي ان كانوا دفنوه في نمش أو ألقوه في العراء ولكنه قد ترك في قلوب اهل الفضائل والكمالات ذكراً حسناً لا يذكر بجانبه عظم ملكك وجمال مدفنك يا أيها العبد الذليل.»

قال عيسى بن هشام: ولما انتهى صاحبنا من حديثه اشار علينا الشيخ الفرنسوي بالصعود الى البرج فدخلنا من من احد جوانبه في غرفة فارتفعت بنا فما هي الا برهة كلمح البصرحتى ارتفعنا من وجه الى عنان السحاب فنزلنا في الدور الثاني منه واذا هو سوق كبير فيه حوانيت الباعة لاصناف البضائع وفي وسطه مطعم كبير وحوله عدة حانات فاخذنا مجلسنا عند حافة الدور وسرحنا الطرف نحو الارض فوجدنا الناس كالنحل ووجدنا تلك القصور الشامخة والدور الفسيحة مثل قرى النمل وبدأ الباشا يسأل عن تفصيل امرذلك البرج فيجيبه الفرنسوي عما يسأله عنه فمما قال له ان ارتفاع البرج ٣٠٠ متر وزنته ٩ ملايين كيلوجراماً وعدد قطعه ١٢ الفاً من المعدن وعدد الخطاطيف مليونان ونصف وبلغت جملة ما انفق عليه من المال٧ ملايين فرنكا تقريبا و بلغ دخله في المعرض الماضي ٨ ملايين فرنكا واتم حديثه بان صاحب هذا العمل العظيم والبناء الذي فاق في الاتقان الاولين والآخرين انتهى أمره الى المحاكمة للاختلاس وحكم علية بالحبس في القضية المشهورة بقضية بناما. ١٠،٤٥

الباشا أيصل العلم بكم الى هذا الحد من التقدم والارتقاء في الاعمال الصناعية ولا يهذب منكم الطباع وينقي الاخلاق؟ أو ليس من عجيب الأمر ان هذا المتفنن الماهر يعمل إلى اختراع ما يدهش العالم في المعرفة والعلم و يأتي له بالثروة الواسعة ١١،٤٥

"KING What's this I'm hearing? Is then everything I've ever done completely wasted? Am I to merit no distinction because of it, and to be the equal of Diogenes?

"DIOGENES Don't claim to be my equal. Here you are, still suffering for the loss of what you had when you were alive and what you reckoned to be supreme happiness. What it all adds up to is that all you're left with is to have people walk past your tomb and say that it is indeed very beautiful. Diogenes on the other hand isn't bothered by the fact that they've buried him in a grave or tossed him out in the desert somewhere. But in the minds of virtuous and goodly people he's left behind a fine memory, compared with which your mighty kingdom and your beautiful tomb are worth nothing, you deluded servant!"

'Īsā ibn Hishām said: Once our Friend had finished talking, the Frenchman suggested that we should go up the tower. With that we entered an elevator at one side of the tower, and it took us from the ground level into the heavens in the blinking of an eye. It let us off at the second floor, where we found a large market with stalls and merchants selling a variety of goods. In the middle was a superb restaurant and a number of bars. We took seats close to the edge of the floor. When we looked down below us, people looked like ants, and all the lofty palaces and expansive mansions resembled mere anthills. The Pāshā now started asking for further details about the tower. The Frenchman responded by noting that the Eiffel Tower rises three hundred meters from the ground. It weighs nine million kilograms. It is made up of twelve thousand separate pieces, and there are two-and-a-half million rivets. The total amount spent on it comes to almost seven million francs, and the revenues from it during the exhibition are eight million francs. To complete his account the Frenchman told us that the person who designed this amazing structure, one that surpasses anything built by ancients or moderns, has landed up in bankruptcy court and has been sentenced to a prison term because of the infamous Panama crisis.[101] 45.10

PĀSHĀ How is it that science can rise to such heights of industrial production among you, and yet it fails to train people to behave appropriately and keep their ethics in check? Isn't it amazing that this clever engineer can 45.11

ثم تسفل به أخلاقه الى السرقة والاختلاس؟ واذا كان هذا عمل الكبراء و أرباب الرفعة فيكم فماذا تقوله في أولئك الذين رأيناهم يعيشون معيشة الحشرات في جوف الارض بين ظلمات المناجم؟

الصاحب لا تعجب فان هذه المدنية الغربية ان كانت هذبت من الصناعة تهذيباً لم يبلغه أحد من قبل فلم تأت بتهذيب الطباع والاخلاق على ما كان ينتظر من نتيجة الترقي والتقدم في المعارف والعلوم ولا تحسبين الذين تراهم أمامنا الآن يخطرون في أحاسن الازياء وأجمل الزخرف أحسن أخلاقاً من المصبوغين بصبغة الفحم في أسفل المناجم:

بنو آدم يطلبون الثراء
عند الثريا وعند الثرى
هو الشر قد عم في العالمين
أهل الوهود وأهل الذرى.

قال عيسى بن هشام :والتفت الشيخ الفرنسوي عندما هممنا بالقيام للانصراف من المعرض يقول لنا في آخر كلامه: ١٢،٤٥

الفرنسوي والآن فقد احطتم بمشاهد المدنية ومناظرها وصنائعها وآلاتها وأدواتها من بطن الارض الى سطح البرج فرأيتم فيها ما يدهش ويعجب ولكن هناك ما هو أعجب وأغرب عند الحكيم العاقل وهو الاطلاع على أحوال الجمعية في معايشها ومعاملاتها وأخلاقها وعاداتها فان أردتم ان لا تخرجوا من المعرض الى بلادكم بوصف هذه المناظر المموهة وحدها فما عليكم الا ان تقيموا في باريس معي اياما لتقفوا فيها على بواطن الاخلاق والعادات ما يستحسن منها وما يستقبح والعاقل لا يغتر بزخرف الظاهر بل يزيحه لينظر ما وراءه وكما أنه يرى الناس متساويين في الصف امام بصره من فوق البرج كذلك ينبغي ان ينظر اليهم بعين بصيرته مجردين عما يغش ويخدع من التستر والتكلف.

devise something to amaze the entire world for its science and knowledge and bring in abundant revenues, but then he gets involved in shady deals and bankruptcy. If this is the way that grandees and people of substance behave in your country, what are we supposed to say about those poor wretches whom we observed living like insects underground in dark mines?

FRIEND Don't be so surprised. This Western civilization may have achieved a level of education in technology unachieved by any culture before, but, when it comes to ethical training, it's certainly not achieved the kind of progress in science and knowledge that might have been anticipated. Above all, don't regard the people whom you see strutting around here in all their finery as being in any case morally superior to the coal-stained miners you saw.

Humans search for wealth
  in every conceivable place,
Evil is rampant in both worlds,
  lowland and mountain.[102]

'Īsā ibn Hishām said: As we were about to get up and leave the exhibition, the Frenchman finished by telling us: 45.12

FRENCHMAN Now you've seen our civilization—its various sights and the variety of exhibits of tools and machines that you've looked at both below ground and up the tower, all of them wonderful and amazing. But for the intelligent person there's something even more wonderful and curious, namely to learn about the way society lives and to study its transactions, morals, and customs. If after leaving the exhibition you don't want to go straight back to your country with some surface descriptions of what you've seen, then you should spend a few more days with me in Paris so that you can get a better idea of peoples' manner and customs, both good and bad. The intelligent person is never fooled by superficial frippery, but rather avoids it in order to see what really lies behind it all. Just as everyone seems to be of equal status when you look down from the Eiffel Tower, so such a person needs to use his insight to consider people once they've been stripped of all pretense and deprived of different kinds of cover and affectation.

قال عيسى بن هشام: فقابلنا رأيه بحسن الموافقة واشترطنا عليه المصاحبة والمرافقة ١٣،٤٥
وبهذا انتهينا من زيارة معرض النفائس والأعلاق لنبدأ في النظر في معرض الاطوار والاخلاق.

ʿĪsā ibn Hishām said: We gladly accepted his offer, on condition that he stay with us and accompany us. And that's how we came to leave the grounds of this exhibition of precious objects for the realms of customs and ethics. 45.13

مصباح الشرق ١٩٢، ١٤ فبرايير ١٩٠٢

باريس

قال عيسى بن هشام: وقف بنا الحديث في زيارتنا ام العواصم الغربية واقامتنا في مدينة الحضارة والمدنية إلى الانتهاء من وصف ذلك المعرض العام وما اجتمع فيه من مختلف الانام وغرائب الليالي والايام وما احتواه من انواع النفاسة والبداعة في كل فن وصناعة وما انتشر فيه من كل جانب من ضروب الملاهي والملاعب وما تألق فيه من منظر مونق وانطوى تحته من مخبر موبق وخرجنا منه انا والباشا والصاحب ما بين مادح وناقد وثالب ومعنا ذلك الفرنسوي الحكيم والشيخ الذي ابيضت مفارقته في التثقيف والتعليم نهتدي في غربتنا بهديه ونستصبح في ما يشكل علينا بنور رأيه نتبعه اتباع الابل لحاديها والسيارة لهاديها ونحمد القدر الذي ساقه لمرافقتنا وأنزله على موافقتنا وسرنا على ما رسمه لنا لنأمن الانتقال من معرض النفائس والاعلاق الى معرض الاطوار والاخلاق ١،٤٦

فقضينا معه شهور العام وكأنها حلم من الاحلام ينتقل بنا في النوادي الحافلة والمجالس الآهلة ويدور بنا في اختبار الطباع والصفات بين جميع أهل الطبقات فنرتفع معه تارة الى اعلى مراتب الخاصة والحلمة وننزل معه أخرى الى أدنى منازل السوقة والعامة فنكون يوماً في مجالس الامراء والكبراء ويوماً بين الصناع والاجراء وطوراً نحضر محاضر الحكم والسياسة وآناً نقعد بين أهل التكهن والفراسة وننتهي من زيارة القصور العالية الى الاطلال البالية ومن منابر الوعظ والخطابة الى مجامع أهل الدعارة والدعابة ومن جمعيات العلوم والمعارف الى مغاني الاغاني والمعازف ومن نوادي الادباء والفضلاء الى مكامن الاشقياء والجهلاء حتى لم يبق مجتمع تخبر فيه الفضائل والرذائل وتسبر فيه الاخلاق بين الاعالي والاسافل الا و لدينا طرف من خبره وعلم من أثره وصاحبنا الشيخ يسلك بنا في كل ذلك طريق الاطناب والاسهاب في تبيين العلل وشرح الاسباب ويخرج لنا من كل مبحث حكمة معدودة وضالة ٢،٤٦

Miṣbāḥ al-sharq 192, February 14, 1902[103]

Paris

'Īsā ibn Hishām said: Our coverage of the visit we paid to the mother of all European capitals and our stay in the hub of civilization finished with a description of the Great Exhibition: the different people we met there, the strange happenings day and night, the variety of exotic items, the precious and creative objects of every conceivable kind of craft that were on display, the nightclubs and music halls scattered across the grounds, the splendid views it afforded visitors, and the undesirable subtext out of sight. The Pāshā, our Friend, and I had emerged from it with a mixture of feelings: praise, criticism, and outright condemnation. We were still in the company of the sage Frenchman, his temples whitened by his willingness to share with us his culture and learning. We had used him as our guide through the unfamiliar terrain and had gladly accepted his enlightened views in explaining complicated issues for us. We followed him as camels do with their cameleer and a caravan does with its guide, praising the good fortune that had led him to accompany us and enabled him to meet our needs. We adopted his plan so as to be sure to make the transfer from the exhibition of precious objects to the realms of customs and ethics. 46.1

We spent months of the year as though in a dream, with our French colleague taking us round packed clubs and crowded meetings as we selected different moods and qualities from among the different classes of society in the city. Thus at one moment we would be ascending to the highest levels of exclusivity among the elite, then at another we would descend to the most plebeian of venues. One day we would be at a meeting with men of influence and prestige, and then it would be with artisans and laborers. Some meetings that we attended would involve power and politics; others would be concerned with prediction and observation. From visits to lofty palaces we would move to dilapidated ruins, from pulpits for homilies and speeches to gatherings of the debauched and facetious; from learned societies to music halls with songs, from literary salons to havens of the wretched and ignorant. Eventually there was not a single assembly where you could experience both virtues and vices and probe morality at its highest and lowest points that we 46.2

منشودة في حسن الاعتبار ولطف الازدجار وجميل التحذير والانذار وهدى وذكرى لأولي الابصار فنأخذ من ذلك الرأي السديد بكل ما ينفع ويفيد

وها نحن نعود الى ذلك الحديث المتتابع فنروي للقراء ما شاهدته الاعين ووعته ٣،٤٦
المسامع وأول ما جرى به لسان الباشا في السؤال والاستفهام ذكر الحكام والاحكام.

الباشا واذا انتهينا من رؤية تلك المعالم والمشاهد وامتلأت العين من هذه المرائي والمناظر فلننظر هنا نظرة من الجد ولنبحث في أصول هذه المدنية وقواعدها ونظام هذه الأمم في أحكامها وسيرة رؤسائها وحكامها وكيف حال ملك هذه البلاد وما هي سيرته وما اسمه؟

الشيخ الفرنسوي ليس للملك عندنا اسم ولا جسم.

الباشا فأنتم حينئذ في حال من الفوضى كالسوام المهمل وكالابل بلا راع وكيف ينتظم على ذلك شملكم ويستقيم جمعكم؟

الشيخ الفرنسوي أستغفر الله بل لنا ملك وليس بملك يقيم على عرش المملكة الفرنسوية ويسمى رئيس الجمهورية.

الباشا وما هي هذه الجمهورية في اصطلاح مخترعاتكم فانني لم أسمع بهذا الاسم من قبل وكانكم أبيتم معاشر الغربيين الا ان تحدثوا لكل أمر قديم بدعة جديدة وما اسم هذا الرئيس ومن أي سلالة هو ولأي سلسلة ينتمي أصله ونسبه ومتى ورث الرئاسة والامارة عن أبيه؟

الشيخ الفرنسوي أما اسم الرئيس فالمسيو «اميل لوبيه».

الباشا أراك أيها الشيخ الفاضل تسلك بنا اليوم في حديثك مسلك المفاكهة والممازحة وكيف تدعو سفلائكم ورئيسكم بالمسيو وهو لفظ طالما سمعته ينادى به عامة الناس بعضهم بعضاً.

الشيخ الفرنسوي ما مزحت وما قلت الا الصدق وستعلم بعد وقوفك على ٤،٤٦
ترتيب نظامنا في حكومتنا انه لا عيب عندنا في اطلاق هذا اللفظ على رئيس الحكومة في دست حكومته وعلى مثل الحجام في حانوته والخمار في حانته لاعلان المساواة بين

had not experienced and learned from in some way. In everything that we did, our French colleague went to enormous lengths to provide reasons for what we saw and explain rationales. From every single issue he managed to provide us with a notable piece of wisdom and a much-needed axiom. His demeanor throughout was one of careful consideration, restraint, caution, and admonition, all of which provided sound guidance for any perspicacious person. We took it all in as sound common sense and useful counsel.

So here we are now going back to the previous conversations. We will relate 46.3
for readers what we saw and heard. We can begin with the Pāshā's questions and inquiries regarding rulers and laws:

PĀSHĀ Now that we've finished observing all those sights and monuments and have filled our eyes with its vistas, let's now take a serious look at the bases and principles of this civilization: how nations establish their laws, and how their presidents and governments conduct themselves. What is the status of the king of this country and what does he do? What's his name, for example?

FRENCHMAN For us in France, kingship has no name and no human form.

PĀSHĀ So then you must be in a chaotic situation, like stray livestock or camels with no shepherd. How can you organize the work you do and keep society in order?

FRENCHMAN Heaven forfend! We have a ruler, but he is not a king who sits on the throne. He is called the President of the Republic.

PĀSHĀ What is this thing called "republic" that you seem to have devised? I've never heard the word before. It seems as though you Western people have decided to create some new-fangled entity to replace everything that's old. What's the name of this "president," and what's his ancestry and lineage? When did he inherit the position from his father?

FRENCHMAN The president's name is Monsieur Emile Loubet.

PĀSHĀ (*cackling*) My dear friend, I can see that you're poking fun at us today. How can your ruler possibly be called "Monsieur"? That's the term I've heard people using on the street to address each other.

FRENCHMAN I wasn't joking; what I've said is the absolute truth. Once 46.4
you have learned about the form of government that we have, you'll see that there's no harm in referring to the president of the country in that way. He is no different from the cupper in his shop or the wine-seller in his bar. The purpose

الرضيع والرفيع والصغير والكبير وتلك قاعدة الحكم عندنا واما نسبه فهو رجل من اهل الفلاحة والحراثة وغاية ما انتهى اليه امره في مسقط رأسه بين أهل بلاده انه كان شيخاً للقرية التي ولد فيها وامه لا تزال على حالتها الاولى في تلك القرية مقيمة في ذلك المسكن ولم يرث الرئاسة عن اب أوجد وانما توصل اليها بعد وفاة سلفه فيها وكان رجلاً دباغاً يدبغ الجلود قبيل ارتقائه الى الرئاسة.

الباشا ان لم يكن حديثك هذا غير صحيح فانا اقسم بكل يمين انكم بلغتم من الانحطاط درجة تذهب برونق ما تبهرون بها نظار العالم من الزخرف والزينة والاحسان والابداع في أبواب الصناعات وضروب المستحدثات وكيف يدخل في حكم العقل تطبيق ما نراه من الابهة والجلال والعظمة واسباب الفخار على رئاسة فلاح او دباغ فوق الامة الكبيرة والمملكة العظيمة؟ وما اظنكم تستقيم لكم امور في حكومتكم على هذه الحال زمناً طويلا ولا اخالكم الا في شغب دائم وفتنة متصلة ستؤول بكم عاقبتها الى التفرق والتوزع ثم الخراب والدمار.

الشيخ الفرنسوي هون عليك فانك ان علمت ما معنى الجمهورية لم تركب ٥،٤٦
في حكمك متن الشطط وانا ابادر بتعريفك اياها وكيفية تأليفها اليك فالجمهورية على التعريف العام هي حكومة لاهالي بعضهم بعضاً بانتداب جماعة منهم يقومون بينهم بالحكم والفصل عل قوانين يضعونها ويعملون بها كالشريعة المقدسة وينتدبون فريقاً منهم لتنفيذ احكامها والمحافظة على بقائها ورئيس هذا الفريق هو رئيس الجمهورية الفرنسوية وانتخاب هذا الرئيس يكون باجتماع اعضاء المجلسين مجلس الشيوخ ومجلس النواب, في يوم مشهود كلما خلت الرئاسة ومدة رئاسته سبع سنوات وهو عندنا كالملك في رئاسة الممالك الاخرى ويكون انتخابه بالأغلبية المطلقة ومن وظيفته انه يشترك مع اعضاء المجلسين في وضع الشرائع والقوانين فيصدر بها الاوامر بعد تقريرها فيهما ويراقب تنفيذها والمحافظة عليها وله حق العفو والتصرف في القوة العسكرية وتعيين الحكام والمأمورين في الوظائف الملكية والعسكرية وله الرئاسة على جميع الاحتفالات الرسمية والاعياد الاهلية وهوصاحب العلاقة مع سفراء الدول

is to proclaim the principle of equality between the elite and lowly, old and young. For us, that's a primary principle of the way we're governed. The president's actually of peasant agricultural origins. The highest post he occupied in his local area was as mayor of the town where he was born. His mother still lives in the same house, just as she's always done. The presidency isn't inherited from either father or grandfather. It comes to someone following the death of his predecessor. Before becoming president he worked as a tanner.

PĀSHĀ If what you're telling us is in fact the case, then I can only assert in the strongest terms that you've reached a level of decadence that negates all the finery, creativity, and splendor with which you've previously been dazzling the world in the realms of industry and innovation. How could anyone conceive of consigning all the glory, pride, and splendor that we witness to a president who's just a peasant or tanner and who's supposed to rule this wonderful people and great nation? I can't imagine your system of government remaining stable for a long time. Instead, I can only envisage a continuous state of chaos and intrigue, the end result of which can only be division and discord followed by devastation and ruin.

FRENCHMAN Steady on now! If you knew what the word "republic" 46.5
meant, you would not be going to such extremes in your opinions. I'm now going to give you a definition of the term and the way in which it functions in our country. In general terms "republic" implies the government of the people by the people by delegating a select group of them to serve as government and arbiters of the laws, which they compose and under which they operate as a law code just like the holy Shariah with you. They duly elect a group of people who will implement those laws and make sure that they're maintained. The head of such a group is the president of the French Republic, and he's elected by a voting majority of the two legislative houses, the Senate and the Chamber of Deputies, on a designated day whenever the presidency becomes vacant. The president's term is for seven years; for us he's just like a king in other countries. He's selected on the basis of an absolute majority. His duties include joining the members of the two houses in creating laws and regulations, then issuing orders for their implementation after they've been ratified by both houses; he also will oversee their implementation and the people's adherence to them. He has the right to issue pardons, to use discretion regarding military force, and to appoint governors and officials to both military and civilian positions. He presides at all official ceremonies and public festivals,

ومندوبي الحكومات ولا بد لكل أمر يصدر منه في أي شأن كان ان يكون موقعاً عليه بتوقيع أحد الوزراء.

٦،٤٦ وهو الذي ينتخب أعضاء مجلس استشارة الدولة باتحاده مع الوزراء وله ان يفض مجلس النواب قبل انتهاء مدته بالاتفاق مع مجلس الشيوخ ولا مسؤولية عليه البتة في ما عدا ارتكابه لخيانة مصالح الأمة وهو الذي يبدأ بالمخابرة في عقد المعاهدات والموافقة عليها الا انه يتحتم عليه عرضها على المجلسين اذا لم يكن في افشائها ما يمس مصلحة المملكة الا المعاهدات التي تختص بعقد السلم وبالتجارة وبالامور المالية وما يختص منها بأشخاص الفرنسويين وأملاكهم في الخارج لا يمكنه الموافقة عليه ولا يتم تنفيذه الا بعد عرضه وتقريره في المجلس كما انه لا يمكنه التنازل عن شيء من الاراضي الفرنسوية أو المبادلة بها الا بقرار منهما أيضاً ولا يجوز له اعلان الحرب الا بعد أخذ رأي المجلسين أولاً أما صلب محاكمته عند ارتكابه لخيانة مصالح الأمة فلا يكون الا من مجلس النواب وحده ولا يجوز محاكمته الا أمام مجلس الشيوخ وهو الذي ينتخب رئيس الوزارة من بين أعضاء مجلس النواب ويكلفه باختيار أعضاء الوزارة ثم يوافقه على اختياره ويكونون من اعضاء مجلس النواب ما عدا ناظر الحربية وناظر البحرية في بعض الاحيان ورئيس الوزارة هو المسؤول عن جميع اعمال الحكومة امام مجلس النواب فاذا لم تنل الوزارة ثقة المجلس تعين عليها تقديم الاستعفاء لرئيس الجمهورية ليعين أخرى مكانها وبالجملة فان حقوق رئيس الجمهورية تماثل حقوق بقية الملوك في الممالك المقيدة بالمجالس النيابية الا ان خلوه من المسؤولية قد جعل الامر كله في يد الوزراء لوقوع المسؤولية عليهم في جميع أعمال المملكة امام مجلس النواب وانحصر كل نفوذه في اختيار رئيس الوزارة وأما بقية اعماله فهي قاصرة على المظاهر الرسمية.

٧،٤٦ الباشا يتضح لي من هذا التفصيل في أمر رئيس الجمهورية انه ملك بالاسم وان الملك والحكم كله في يد المجلسين وما كان أغناكم عن هذا الرئيس لولا أنكم ترون

and is the point of contact for ambassadors and delegates from foreign governments. Every document emerging from the president's office has to carry the signature of one of his ministers.

He's the one who nominates the consultative Council of State in conjunction with the ministers. By agreement with members of the Senate he can dissolve the Chamber of Deputies before the conclusion of its term in office, its sole responsibility in that case being connected to some breach of the nation's best interests involving the president. The president is also the person who initiates negotiations on treaties and agreements pertaining to them, although he's required to present them to the two chambers provided that disclosing them does not involve disclosing what are known as "state interests." However, he's not allowed to agree to any treaties involving peace, commerce, and financial matters, along with other things involving French citizens and their property outside the country. He can only conclude such agreements after they have been presented to the Chamber and approved by it. In the same way, he's not allowed to relinquish or exchange any French territories unless he has prior agreement from the Chamber. He may not declare war without first consulting both chambers. If he should commit some act of treason against the people's best interests, then he may only be charged by the Chamber of Deputies, and his trial may only take place in the Senate. He also nominates the Prime Minister from among members of the Chamber of Deputies, and charges him with the selection of the cabinet of ministers and approves of his choices. They are all members of the Chamber of Deputies, except for the Minister of War and Marine, on some occasions. The prime minister is responsible to the Chamber of Deputies for all actions taken by the government. If it happens that the ministry loses the confidence of the Chamber of Deputies, then a petition demanding its resignation is submitted to the president of the republic in order that another ministry can be elected in its place. All in all, the rights of the president of the French Republic resemble those of other monarchs where such matters are tied to a parliamentary system. Where there's an absence of such responsibilities, the entire burden falls on the ministers regarding all matters pertaining to the country, and they are responsible to the Chamber of Deputies. The president's influence is basically limited to the appointment of the prime minister and other official functions. 46.6

Pāshā From all this detail, it's now clear to me that the president is in fact a monarch in all but name, and that executive authority lies entirely with 46.7

من الضروري في حكم الامم ان يكون فوقها ملك ولما رأيتم ان تحكموا أنفسكم بأنفسكم لم تقدروا على ذلك الا بتخييل صورة الملك عندكم في شخص هذا الرئيس والا فأي ضرورة ترونها في هذا التكلف في تعيين رجل تقلدونه من ناحية مقالد الملك في سعة السلطة ثم تقيدونه من ناحية أخرى بالقيود التي تعفي آثار تلك السلطة ولماذا لا يكون الامر في يد رئيس مجلس النواب ومجلس الشيوخ ما دام الحكم كله راجعاً الى رأي المجلسين؟

الشيخ الفرنسوي أعلم ان سلطة الحكومة عندنا تنقسم الى قسمين, قسم رئاسة الجمهورية والوزارة وهو المعروف عندنا بالسلطة التنفيذية وسلطة مجلس النواب ومجلس الشيوخ وتعرف بالسلطة التشريعية, وان كان الحكم كله في الواقع للسلطة التشريعية الا انها لا بد لها من أن تنتدب جماعة يقومون بتنفيذ ما تضعه من الاحكام ويكونون مسؤولين أمامنا عن حسن القيام بتنفيذها.

٨،٤٦ الباشا الان علمت ان اعضاء مجلس النواب ومجلس الشيوخ اصحاب الامر والنهي وان كل واحد منهم ملك في ذاته لا مسؤولية عليه ولا قيد يقيده فكأنكم استبدلتم ملكاً واحداً يدبر أموركم ويجري احكامكم ويسأل عن حكمه فيكم امام الله والناس بعدة ملوك ليس فيهم سجايا الملوك ولا هم السلاطين ولا حسن التجارب في ادارة الأمور التي تكون عند سائر الرؤساء والامراء وأي ضمان للدولة عندكم اذا كان امرها شائعاً في ايدي جماعة من الرعية وأي نظام للامور يمكن الاعتماد عليه في مثل هذه الحال؟

الشيخ الفرنسوي ان لدينا في هذا الباب عدة روابط وقيود تضمن نظام الامور واستقامة الأحكام فان اعضاء المجلسين مسؤولون امام بقية الرعية ولا بد لوقوفك على ذلك من بيان يقتضيه انتخابهم وشروط تأليف المجلسين وطريقة سريان الاعمال فيهما

the two chambers. You might not even feel the need for such a president were it not for the fact that, in matters of governance, you find it necessary to have a kind of monarchical figure over you. But you also want to govern yourselves, and you can only achieve that by creating an image of such a figure along the lines designed for this presidency. Otherwise what's the point of spending so much effort appointing a man whom you grant all the broad trappings and authority of monarchy, but then proceed to tie him down with procedures that impede the exercise of power? As long as executive authority reverts to the Chamber of Deputies and the Senate, why doesn't the whole thing rest in the hands of the heads of the two chambers?

Frenchman You should realize that in our country governmental authority is divided into two parts: the presidency and the ministry, which we term "executive authority," and the Chamber of Deputies and the Senate, termed "legislative authority." Governance may indeed be in the hands of the legislative branch, but they have to elect another group who will undertake to implement the laws as written and supervise their proper implementation.

Pāshā Now I see that the members of the two chambers are the ones 46.8
with the real authority; each of them is a king in his own right, with no responsibility or ties restraining his actions. It's as though you've replaced a single monarch—someone who's supposed to control affairs, implement your rules, and question his suzerainty over you before God and people—with a number of monarchs who have no regal characteristics: they're not sultans, and they have neither the kind of experience in administration such as other presidents and rulers. How can they feel any notion of liability towards your state if discretion in such matters is shared with a group of people from the populace? In such circumstances how can there be any sort of organization that can be relied on?

Frenchman In that particular context we possess a number of linkages and restraints which guarantee that matters will be properly run and regulations will be observed. The members of both chambers are responsible to the populace at large. In order to understand that fully, you need to learn what the requirements are for nomination, how the two chambers are set up, and how affairs are conducted in them.

مصباح الشرق ١٩٣، ٢١ فبراير ١٩٠٢

باريس

١،٤٧ قال عيسى بن هشام: ولما قعد الشيخ للباشا يشرح له ويحكي عن نظام مجلس النواب وكيفية تركيبته وترتيبه وانعقاد الحكم به في أمور المملكة عارضه «الصاحب» بقوله:

الصاحب (للشيخ الفرنسوي) أريد منك أيها الجليل والباحث الحكيم أن تذكر لي شياء عن رأيك في هذه المجالس النيابية وادارتها لامور الممالك بينكم داخلاً وخارجاً قبل ان تدخل في تفصيل نظامها للباشا فاني أحيط من الفروع بقدر غير يسير يؤهلني للتأمل في الاصول وأحب ان اكون حاضر الحكم في أثناء شرحك وتفصيلك فاستمد منه ما يرجح جانبه او يخفف وزنه ويكون لي من رأيك الثاقب ما أستعد به وأطبق ما نقصه فيها على وفقه.

٢،٤٧ الشيخ الفرنسوي لست أرى في ما أريكم اياه وأطلعكم عليه وأكشف لكم من خوافيه أن أبادركم بالرأي فيه والحكم عليه فليس هذا طريقي معكم وانما طريقي الذي أريد ان أتوخاه في مصاحبتكم هو ان أجلي عليكم الامور وأوضح الاحوال لأنظر ما يكون من وقعها فيكم ومن كيفية تأثيرها عليكم واختلاف أحكامكم فيها فانتفع بذلك في حكمي السابق عليها اثباتاً له وتأييداً او نفياً وتفنيدا. والانسان مهما كان جليل الرأي سديد

الحكم لا ينبغي ان يثق بنفسه الا اذا نظر في أمره بمرآة غيره ولذلك ترى كثيرًا من أولي الرأي والتدبير في أمور الناس يفضون المشاكل ويحلون المعضلات فاذا أرادوا جانب الصواب من الرأي لانفسهم في بعض ما يقع لهم من الامور الخاصة لا يخليهم هوى النفس في نجاح الرأي من ارتباك الفكر والتشويش عليهم في صحة القياس وصحة الاستنتاج وهذا تراه واضحاً جلياً في اصغر الامور واكبرها وادناها واعلاها حتى بين المشتغلين بالالعاب التي تضيع الوقت وتفني العمر سدى كالشطرنج والنرد ونحوها فتجد اللاعب المجيد يرتكب الخطأ تلو الخطأ وبجانبه من هو أقل منه

Miṣbāḥ al-sharq 193, February 21, 1902[104]

Paris

'Īsā ibn Hishām said: While the French philosopher was sitting with the Pāshā and explaining to him the French Chamber of Deputies, the way it is organized, and the methods by which it conducts the affairs of state, the Friend interrupted him: 47.1

FRIEND (*to the Frenchman*) My dear learned colleague, I'd like to know what you yourself think of these parliamentary chambers and the way they administer your country's affairs at home and abroad. Before you go into even more detail with the Pāshā, I find myself having a good deal of information about incidentals, but too little about essentials. While you're explaining things in even greater detail, I'd like to have some principles for judgment at my disposal, something that will make it that much easier to form an opinion on things and to be more discriminating in reacting to your account.

FRENCHMAN I don't think it is necessary for me to express a personal opinion or pass indiviual judgment while I'm giving you information about various less obvious aspects of the system. That's not the way I've been dealing with you. My preferred method is to lay things out clearly for you and discuss current conditions so that I can assess the impact that my commentary has on you and hear the different judgments that you may make about them. In that way I myself can benefit from my own previous verdicts on things, whether it is to support or oppose them. However intelligent and clear-sighted someone may be, he should only have self-confidence to the extent that he views himself in the mirror of other people. That's the way you'll observe many people of discretion and sound judgment in public affairs settling problems and resolving knotty issues. They may well be eager to have the correct opinion about things that happen in their private lives, but the very fact that at heart they want their opinion to be the one that wins cannot spare them a good deal of confused thinking and indeed of fudging when it comes to making fair comparisons and coming to sound conclusions. You can see the principle in operation quite clearly in matters both large and small, both exalted and lowly, even among people who play time-wasting games like chess, backgammon, and other similar pastimes. An expert player will be making one mistake after another 47.2

اجادة يدرك دونه صواب ما أخطأ فيه. ومما يجري مجرى لامثال بينهم في هذا الباب قولهم: «يرى المشاهد ما لا يرى اللاعب». وأنتم لخلوكم عن الهوى في أمورنا وبعدكم عن غمارها محل لان يستفاد برأيكم فيها ويستعان بحكمكم عليها كما انني أرجو أن تستفيدوا بي كذلك في ما تشرحونه مما أجهله من أحوالكم ويغيب عني من أموركم واعلموا ان أخذكم برأيي ومذهبي في أحوالنا يعطل عليكم حرية الانتقاد ويميل بكم الى جانب دون جانب وذلك ما لا أرضاه لا تُنفع باستقلالكم في وجوه الرأي والحكم.

٣،٤٧ الصاحب ان بخلت عليّ برأيك فلا أقل من ان تجود عليّ برأي سواك فانني أريد أن اعلم هل هذا الشكل من الحكومات واقع عندكم موقع الكمال ونهاية الاحسان في حكومة الناس وسيرة الامم وان كان هذا هو غاية ما وصل اليه علم البشر في استقامة الحكم بين الناس واستظلالهم بظلال العدل والانصاف؟

الشيخ الفرنسوي سيظهر لك ذلك كله ويتضح من نفسه بما فيك من شدة النقد وقوة البحث اذا رأيت بعينك ما اشرحه الآن على سمعك وقارنت بين تطبيق القول على العمل ووقفت على ما عساه يوجد من الفرق بين حسن الوضع وقبح الأخذ عندما انتقل بكم من الرواية بالخبر الى المشاهدة بالعيان. وان كان لا مناص لك البتة من الوقوف على شيء في هذا الباب فدونك حكماً كلأحكم لست أخشى عليك من تأثيره ولا أخاف على طريقتي معكم من افشائه لكم.

٤،٤٧ قال الفيلسوف الكبير والعالم الشهير سبنسر الانكليزي نابغة أوروبا اليوم في البحث والتدقيق لمعرفة اخلاق الناس وأطوار الامم وكيفيات تكوين الجمعية البشرية عند كلامه على المجالس النيابية التي تجري الامم الغربية على شريعتها في هذه العصور:

انما مثل المجالس النبيابية كمثل الآلة المتركبة من قطع متعددة غير متحدة الأطراف ولا محكمة الاتصال ولا مؤتلفة الاوضاع فلا انتظام لحركة سيرها الا بكثرة التعديل والتصليح ودوام التغيير والتبديل وان كان ذلك كله لا يضمن دوام انتظامها فان هناك عيبا أصلياً وخللا مستديماً وهو أن كل دولاب من تلك الآلة لا يستمر مستقيما في حركته الا اذا أخل بحركة ما يجاوره بما يخل سير الآلة بتمامها. الا أن مضارها

while right next to him someone who is much less proficient will be benefitting from his errors. On such matters there's a proverb which says, "He can see the squares, but he can't see the player." All of you are spared any desire to get involved in French affairs and far removed from the ups and downs involved. As a result there's an opportunity for us to benefit from your opinions and make use of your judgments. In the same way, I hope that you'll let me benefit from your explanations of your own situation and your elucidation of things that I don't know about your own culture. You should be aware that simply going along with my own opinions about my own society will deprive you of the ability to criticize things freely and present you with a biased viewpoint. That's precisely what I wish to avoid so that your views and opinions can be totally independent.

FRIEND While you may not want to share your own opinion with me, you can at least let us know what others have to say. What I'd like to know is whether this system of government that you have is the most complete and perfect way of governing people and directing the affairs of nations. Is this then the ultimate stage achieved by mankind regarding the way in which human society is to be organized and governed justly and fairly? 47.3

FRENCHMAN Your own critical abilities and lively interest are quite enough to make everything clear to you. You've already observed the kinds of thing that I'm explaining to you now; you've been able to compare what I say with what is actually happening, and have realized the differences that may exist between something good in theory but bad in application, all resulting from seeing the things I've told you about in their actual context. It seems inevitable to me that you'll come to realize a good deal concerning this topic on your own, but I'm completely untroubled by the effect it may have on you or the way in which I'm explaining everything to you.

Here is what the renowned English philosopher and sage, [Herbert] Spencer, a paragon of contemporary European thinking about ethics, national traits, and the modes of creating human societies, has to say about parliamentary chambers under whose regulations Western nations function in this era: 47.4

"Parliamentary chambers are like complex machinery, with many working parts that are neither unified, connected, or harmonious. Their course is only moderated through frequent adjustment and correction and a continuous process of change and alteration. But even that does not guarantee continuing

على كل حال أقل من مضار حكومة الاستبداد وشكلها أهون من بقية الاشكال لمطلقة في الحكومات. ولهذه المجالس النيابية فائدة كبرى وهي انها تكفل أن يأخذ كل فرد من الافراد بنصيبه من العدل والانصاف في الحقوق من جهة المعاملات في ما بينهم. ولم يدع الى انشاء هذه المجالس النيابية الا حاجة الاهالي الى ما يدفع عنهم ظلم المستبدين من الحكام وقد دلت التجارب على ان هذه المجالس انما تصلح لوضع الشرائع وسن القوانين وانه لا بد للانتفاع بها من وقوفها عند هذا الحد لا تتعداه ولا تتجاوزه فانها ان تعدته صارت من أعظم المضار على البلاد فتركت وظيفة التشريع الى الاشتغال والارتباك في مضائق الادارة والسياسة كما هو حالها اليوم في جميع الدول الغربية.

٥،٤٧ الباشا دعنا من هذا الآن وخذ بنا في طريقنا الاول واخبرني ما هو مجلس النواب واشرح لي كيفية تركيبه وسيرة اشغاله فاني احب استيعاب الشرح قبل التعجيل بالحكم.

الشيخ الفرنسوي يتألف مجلس النواب من ستمائة عضو أو يزيدون مجتمعون تحت رئيس ينتخبونه لهم مع أربعة من الوكلاء وأربعة من المساعدين ثم يؤلفون في ما بينهم عدة أقلام وعدة لجن تشتغل بالنظر في ما يقدم اليها من الاعمال. وتنقسم هذه الاعمال الى قسمين, قسم يتقدم لها من جانب الحكومة وهو يعرف بمشروعات للوائح والقوانين, وقسم يقدم لها من تلقاء اعضاء المجلس ويطلق عليه اسم المطلب. وتشتغل كل لجنة في ما يتعلق بها من هذه الامور ثم تقدم عنه تقريرًا الى جلسة الاعضاء العامة للمناقشة والمجادلة فيه وتعديله بالزيادة والنقصان وتقريره او رفضه بأغلبية الاصوات ويبلغ عدد تلك الاقلام واللجان احدى عشرة دائرة وتجدد بين اعضاء المجلس في كل شهر مرة وأهمها اللجان الكبرى المؤلفة من ثلاثة وثلاثين عضوًا وهي لجنة الميزانية ولجنة الادارة ولجنة العسكرية ولجنة السكك الحديدية ولجنة المعارف ولجنة البحرية ولجنة المستعمرات ولجنة التجارة والصناعة ولجنة التشريع الجنائي ولجنة التشريع العقاري ولجنة الاقتصاد في ادارة الحكومة.

order. For there exists a basic and ongoing flaw, namely that every single gear will only keep functioning as long as its motion does not impair the functioning of the machine as a whole. Even so, its flaws are far less than those of autocratic rule and much easier to tolerate than other absolute forms of government. Parliaments have one overriding advantage, namely that they ensure that every single individual has his fair share of justice and equality of rights in dealing with other people. The only thing that leads people to create such parliamentary chambers is a need to make sure that tyranny and autocratic rule are kept at bay. Experience has shown that this type of parliament is useful primarily for promulgating laws and regulations, and that the jurisdiction needs to be restricted to that and nothing beyond. If it so happens that they do go beyond those bounds, the negative effects on the country are considerable. The legislative function gets lost and distracted in a maze of administrative politics, which is currently the case with all Western governments."

PĀSHĀ Let's put that aside for now and start on our inquiry. Tell me 47.5
about the Chamber of Deputies, how it's made up and how it functions. I'd like to be able to respond to your description before I make too hasty a judgment.

FRENCHMAN The Chamber of Deputies is made up of six hundred or more members who meet under the leadership of a chamber president whom they elect along with four vice presidents and four aides. They are then constituted into a number of departments and committees that focus on particular matters brought to their attention. Such matters are subdivided into two categories: one dealing with things forwarded from the government itself, known as the "statutes and laws" division; and the second that receives business from the Chamber deputies themselves, known as the "requests" division. Each of these committees handles the business relevant to their charge and then forwards a report to the Chamber session where it is debated and discussed, as a result of which there may be amendments, additions, and omissions, following which the measure will be either accepted or rejected by majority vote. There are a total of eleven such committees, and in each case membership is renewed every month. The most significant of the major committees consists of thirty-three members, namely those dealing with budget, administration, army, railways, education, navy, colonial affairs, commerce and industry, criminal law, property law, and government economics.

ولكل من هذه اللجان رئيس تجتمع تحته ومندوب يقوم بقراءة تقريرها امام الجلسة العامة ويجتمع اعضاء المجلس في هذه اللجان يومين في كل أسبوع. وكيفية تقديم المشروعات لديها من الحكومة ان أحد الوزراء الذي يختص به المشروع يقدمه باسم الحكومة الى الدائرة المعنية لذلك من المجلس فتسرع في الحال بطبعه ونشره على جميع الاعضاء ثم يرسل رئيس المجلس بنسخ منه الى اللجنة المختصة بالنظر فيه. وأما ما يأتي من المطالب التي تتقدم من جانب النواب فينبغي أن تكون على شكل قانوني منقسم الى بنود ومواد ومقدمة تبين أسباب الطلب وضرورة الحال اليه فيرسله الرئيس الى لجنة معدة لقبول هذه الطلبات والنظر في ضرورتها ومناسبتها فان اتضح لاعضائها وجوب قبوله واحالته على اللجنة المختصة بالنظر فيه والا فانها ترفضه. ٦،٤٧

أما التقرير الذي تقدمه كل لجنة عنة اعمالها لعرضه على مجلس النواب في جلسته العامة فينبغي ان يكون وافياً بالغرض مستكملا للبحث في جميع القضية مع اطرافها مع مراعات النظر من جهة تطبيق ما فيه على القوانين واللوائح الماضية ومناسبته لاحوال الزمان الحاضرة وكيفية تأثيره في بابه على المستقبل مع بيان ما اختلف فيه اعضاء اللجنة من الرأي وتوضيح أدلة كل فريق وحجبه توضيحاً تاماً حتى اذا اطلع اعضاء المجلس عليه في الجلسة العامة لم يعوزهم الرجوع الى كثرة المناقشة والجدال في ما حرر لاجله. ويتوزع على كل عضو نسخة من قبل عرضه على الجلسة باربع وعشرين ساعة. ويفتتح الرئيس الجلسة العامة بقراءة محضر الجلسة الماضية وبالتنبيه على ما تجري عليه المناقشة على حسب ترتيب التقارير المقدمة من اللجان في الجدول المختص بقيدها فيوضع التقرير موضع المناقشة ويتقدم من الأعضاء من يتقدم منهم الى موضع الخطابة للموافقة على المشروع الذي احتوى عليه التقرير او لمخالفته فاذا لم يبق احد من الراغبين في الكلام عليه عرضه الرئيس على هيئة المجلس للاقتراع على المناقشة في مواده وأبوابه باباً باباً فان نال في ذلك الاغلبية ابتدأت المناقشة فيه حتى تنتهي ابوابه ثم تعاد قراءته على الهيئة كذلك بعد خمسة ايام فاذا نال الاغلبية مرة أخرى صار ٧،٤٧

Each committee has its own president under whose authority it meets, and a person delegated to read its reports to the general meetings of the Chamber. Each of these committees meets two days a week. The means by which the government forwards projects to them is that the minister in whose jurisdiction the project lies forwards the proposal in the government's name to the administrative committee charged by the Chamber with the receipt of such documents. It is quickly printed and circulated to all the members of the Chamber. The chamber's president then forwards it to the committee that is charged to look into the matter. Requests received from chamber members themselves have to be submitted in the proper legal form, with clauses and materials, all preceded by an introduction that explains the reason for the request and the need for its submission. The chamber president sends all such requests to a committee that is prepared to receive them and considers their necessity and appropriateness. Should it become clear to the members of this committee that the request should be accepted, then they will duly forward it to the committee that deals with such matters. If not, the request is rejected. 47.6

Any report submitted by the relevant committees for consideration by the Chamber of Deputies in general session is required to conform exactly with the stated purpose of the proposal in question and to reflect a comprehensive investigation of the issue in all its aspects. It should also conform to all clauses to be found in legal precedents, be in line with contemporary circumstances, and take into account future impacts of the measure in question. It needs to reflect debating points raised by members of the Chamber and to provide necessary clarification of arguments put forward by members of the Chamber, so that when the full chamber considers the issue, they do not need to go back and argue the points all over again. Every member receives a copy of the motion twenty-four hours before the session. The president opens the session by reading the minutes of the previous session and then detailing the items that are to be discussed in accordance with the agenda promulgated by the various committees. Every motion is thus identified, and the members are then at liberty to make speeches in which they either advocate for its approval or argue against it. Once no one else wishes to speak on the subject, the president then presents the measure to the Chamber to be discussed clause by clause. Assuming that the majority of members approve of the measure in general, they go through every clause. If there is general agreement, the measure is resubmitted five days later. If it is once again approved, then it becomes effective, actionable 47.7

حكماً نافذاً وقانوناً معمولاً به بعد نشره في الجريدة الرسمية وموافقة مجلس الشيوخ عليه واذا لم تتفق الاغلبية على المناقشة في ابوابه كان المشروع والتقرير لاغيين.

ولكل واحد من عضاء مجلس النواب الحق في الاستفهام والاستجواب عن كل حادث يروم توضيحه على الملأ فله أن يسأل الحكومة عن سياستها العامة ويسأل كل وزير عن اعمال وزارته الخاصة وعلى كل وزير منهم ان يجيب عن السؤال بما لديه من الشرح والتفصيل حتى تقتنع الاغلبية برأيه وتقترع على قبول ما جاء به من الاقوال او تظهر في اقتراعها عدم الثقة فيتحتم الاستعفاء على الوزارة أو انها تملي على الحكومة غرضها في الخطة التي ينبغي ان تسير عليها في الحادثة ويقدم صاحب السؤال طلبه الى الرئيس فيخبر الوزير به ويطلب اثناء الجلسة تعيين اليوم له ولا يجو اغفاله اكثر من شهر فيما يختص بالسياسة الداخلية. ٨،٤٧

اما طرق الاقتراع فمتعددة, منها القيام والقعود في الجلسة لمعرفة عدد الموافقين من المخالفين ومنها رفع اليد وعدم رفعها ومنها وضع كل عضو اسمه بالموافقة أو المخالفة في اناء مخصوص لذلك ومنها وضع قطع بيض أو سود. على كل حال لا تكون الأغلبية للمشروع الا اذا زادت الاصوات عن نصف اصوات المقترعين ولو بصوت عضو واحد فاذا تقرر المشروع في مجلس النواب ارسل الى مجلس الشيوخ. ٩،٤٧

الباشا وما مجلس الشيوخ؟

الشيخ الفرنسوي لا يختلف مجلس الشيوخ في ترتيبه ونظامه عن مجلس النواب الا من جهة الانتخاب. ووظيفته ان ينظر في المشروعات التي يقرعليها مجلس النواب وهو يتكون من ثلثمائة عضو وله ان يضع من المشروعات ما يشاء ويرسلها الى مجلس النواب للموافقة عليها ايضاً كما انه يوافق على مشروعات مجلس النواب ويرسلها الى رئيس الجمهورية ليمضيها بواسطة الوزير الذي يختص به المشروع.

الباشا تكرر في كلامك ذكر الانتخاب في هذين المجلسين فارجوك ان تخبرني عن شكله وطريقته وكيف ينتخب الاهالي بعضهم بعضاً وما هي شروطهم التي تضمن للاهالي استقامة الذين انتخبوه عنهم في اجراء الاحكام عليهم. ١٠،٤٧

law; that is, once it has been published in the official gazette and approved by the Senate. If on the other hand the majority does not approve of the measure, then the proposal and the report on it are both null and void.

Every member of the Chamber of Deputies has the right to ask questions regarding any event or matter on which he requires clarification, and without any restraints. He can question the government about its general policies and ask any minister about the workings of his particular ministry. Every minister is obliged to respond to such inquiries in a satisfactory fashion so as either to convince the majority of members of the Chamber so that they will vote in favor, or else the majority will not be convinced, in which case the government is forced to resign; either that, or else it has to dictate to the government the precise fashion in which it intends to proceed on that particular matter. In that case the person who raises the question in the first place submits his request to the president, and he in turn informs the relevant minister and requests discussion during the course of the session on a particular day. Any internal matter cannot be ignored for a period longer than one month. 47.8

There are several ways of casting votes. One involves standing and sitting in the Chamber itself in order to count the number of votes in favor and against. Others include raising hands or keeping them lowered, casting positive and negative ballots in an urn for that purpose, and using black and white pieces of paper. At any rate, there can be no majority without over half the members voting in favor, even if the majority is just one. Once a motion is passed in the Chamber of Deputies, it is forwarded to the Senate. 47.9

PĀSHĀ And what exactly is the Senate?

FRENCHMAN In its organization it is no different from the Chamber of Deputies, except in matters of election. Its function is to examine projects passed by the Chamber of Deputies. It consists of three hundred members. It can propose projects on its own and send them to the Chamber of Deputies for approval, just as is the case with the Chamber of Deputies sending proposals to the Senate. They are then forwarded to the president of the republic for his signature, all by means of the minister in whose sphere the project falls.

PĀSHĀ In discussing both these chambers, you have kept talking about "elections." Please explain to me how that works. How do people elect each other, and what are the requirements that can guarantee that the people whom they elect will perform their duties in a proper fashion? 47.10

الشيخ الفرنسوي نعم لك ذلك فاني بدأت لك في ترتيب الحكومة من الاعلى الى الاسفل دفعاً للتشويش عليك فبدأت برئيس الجمهورية وها انا انتهي بك الى باب الانتخاب بين الاهالي الذي تبتدئ منه سلة الحكم وتنتهي اليه.

FRENCHMAN   I'll explain it all to you. I've started my explanation with the organization of the government from top to bottom so as not to confuse you. So I've talked about the president of the republic and the government itself. Now I'll explain the electoral process which marks the beginning and end of all governmental authority.

باريس

١،٤٨ قال عيشى بن هشام: واستمر الشيخ الفرنسوي يسرد على الباشا شرح ما يرغب الوقوف عليه من كيفية الانتخاب لمجلس النواب الذي ينتهي اليه كل امر ونهي في أمور الامة الفرنسوية على نحو ما ترى:

الشيخ الفرنسوي يتألف في كل قسم من كل لجنة من شيخ القسم ومن مندوب ينتدبه المدير ومن مندوب ينتدبه المجلس البلدي ثم يباشرون تحرير صحيفة الانتخاب المتضمنة لاسماء الذين يحق له الانتخاب على ترتيب حروف الهجاء. والشروط التي تعطي الحق في الانتخاب هي أن يكون الرجل فرنسويا يتجاو سنه العشرين سنة وان يكون له مسكن في البلدة قد أقام به على الأقل ستة أشهر. أما من كان موظفاً في الحكومة او قائماً بخدمة الدين فلا يشترط عليه الاقامة لمدة معينة في البلدة. وأما أهل الجند فلا حق لهم في الانتخاب ما داموا تحت السلاح تطبيقاً على القاعدة التي تقضي بانعزال الجند عن التداخل في الأمور السياسية أو التحي للاحزاب.

٢،٤٨ وأما الموانع التي تمنع من حق الانتخاب فهي:

أولا - كل العقوبات البدنية والعقوبات التي تشين السيرة وتحرم من الحقوق المدنية والسياسية

ثانياً - احكام المحاكم التأديبية بالحرمان من حق الانتخاب

ثالثاً - العقوبة بالحبس عند استعماله الرأفة

رابعاً - العقوبة بالحبس مدة ثلاثة اشهر بسبب ارتكاب الغش في البضائع

خامساً - العقوبة على السرقة والاحتيال والخيانة والاختلاس وانتهاك حرمة الاداب

سادساً - العقوبة على الاخلال بالآداب العامة والاعمال الدينية والطعن في أصول التملك والحقوق الاجتماعية

Miṣbāḥ al-sharq 196, March 14, 1902

Paris

ʿĪsā ibn Hishām said: The Frenchman continued with his explanation to the Pāshā about the electoral process for the Chamber of Deputies, the beginning and end of everything for the French people. Here is what he had to say: 48.1

FRENCHMAN In every subdivision of every town and city in France there's a committee made up of the local chief, a delegate selected by the mayor, and another delegate selected by the town council. They're responsible for putting together the electoral roll containing the names of people who have the right to vote listed in alphabetical order. The requirements for such a right are that the man must be French, must be over twenty years old, and must have had a domicile in the town and lived there for at least six months. Civil servants and religious personnel do not have to meet the six months' residency requirement in the town. Military people are not permitted to vote while they are in service in accordance with the principle that requires the army to stay out of politics and not to involve itself in party differences.

Among factors that will prevent anyone having the right to vote are: 48.2

1) all bodily impairments, and other impairments that compromise walking and deprive citizens of their civil and political rights;
2) court verdicts that interdict the right of participation in elections;
3) prison terms imposed on compassionate grounds;
4) three-month prison terms on grounds of commercial fraud;
5) court verdicts for theft, perfidy, treason, embezzlement, and breach of public morality;
6) offences involving breaches of public decency, matters of religion, and assaults on ownership principles and social rights;

سابعاً - العقوبة بالحبس لمدة ثلاثة اشهر لارتكابه الغش في المسائل الانتخابية وسوء التعرض لاوراق الانتخاب في صناديقها

ثامناً - الاحكام التي تصدر بعزل من يستحق ذلك من وكلاء الاشغال وكتبة المحاكم ورجال الادارة

تاسعاً - الاحكام التي تصدر على المتشردين والمتسولين

عاشراً - العقوبة بالحبس ثلاثة أشهر على من يرتكب تمزيق الدفاتر والسجل وتدمير موارد الصناعة وتخريب المزروعات واقتلاع الاشجار وتسميم الخيول والمواشي والاسماك

حادي عشر - الاحكام التي تصدر في شأن من يتلف عضواً من اعضائه للتخلص من الخدمة العسكرية

ثاني عشر - الاحكام الصادرة بالحجر

ثالث عشر - الاحكام الصادرة بالتفليس.

٣،٤٨ وتجتمع هذه اللجنة التي تقدم ذكرها في آخر شهر مارس من كل عام فتضع في صحيفة الانتخاب اسم من لم سكن مذكوراً في العام الذي قبله وتحذف أسماء من طرأ عليهم مانع من تلك الموانع ثم تنشرها على الاهالي وتعلقها على جدرها مشيخة القسم فاذا آن أوان الانتخاب وصدر أمر رئيس الجمهورية اجتمع الاهالي في الاقسام وتعينت لجنة منهم للمراقبة فينتخبون من يرضونه من المرشحين أنفسهم للانتخاب بالاقتراع السري فاذا نال أحدهم أغلبية الاصوات أصبح عضواً في المجلس. وأول ما يشتغل به هؤلاء النواب في اجتماعهم انهم ينظرون في المطاعن التي تقدم في من وقع الغش أو الفساد في انتخابه فيقترعون على كل واحد من المطعون فيهم بصحة انتخابهم أو بفساده وتجديد من يخلفه.

الباشا وهل هؤلاء المرشحون لانفسهم ليكونوا أعضاء في مجلس النواب هم من طبقة معينة من ذوي الرأي والتدبير وأهل المعرفة والتجارب وغير ذلك مما يؤهلهم لاجراء الاحكام وتدبير السياسة في هذه الامة العظيمة التي ملأ الآفاق صيتها؟

7) three-month prison terms for committing fraud on matters relating to elections and ballot rigging;
8) decisions made concerning the justifiable dismissal of public works officials, court clerks, and administrators;
9) regulations applying to beggars and vagrants;
10) a three-month sentence for anyone convicted of destroying public records, agricultural machinery, uprooting trees, or poisoning horses, cattle, or fish;
11) verdicts issued against anyone who kills a member of the Chamber as a means of avoiding military service;
12) decisions made regarding legal competence;
13) decisions made regarding bankruptcy.

The above-mentioned committee meets at the end of March every year. 48.3
It then places on the electoral list anyone whose name has not come up in the previous year and omits the names of any people who are prevented because of one of the above-mentioned conditions. The list is then published and posted on the wall of the local town hall. When the time comes for the election itself, the president of the republic issues instructions for the people to participate in the election, and a committee is appointed to supervise the process. The people then vote for their favored candidates by secret ballot, and the person who wins the majority of votes becomes a member of the Chamber of Deputies. The first item of business those newly elected members have to undertake is to consider protests against anyone accused of fraud or corruption during the electoral process. A vote is taken on every case, resulting either in the validation of his election or its annulment, in which case someone has to be selected to replace him.

Pāshā Do the self-nominated candidates for election in this fashion come from any particular class of intellectuals and *penseurs*, people who have had experience in matters of administration and the like, things that will qualify them to pass laws and conduct policy for this great nation whose repute is so widespread?

الشيخ الفرنسوي لا عبرة عندنا بالطبقات ولا يمتا منا فريق دون فريق بالمعرفة والتدبير في امور الحكومة بل كلنا أهل رأي وتدبير وكلنا أهل لان ندير امور الحكومة ونسوس هذه الملايين من الامة الفرنسوية. سواء لدينا ان كان من ينتخبه الاهالي سيداً شريفاً أو وضيعاً دنيئاً بل ربما غلب عدد أهل الصنعة وعامة السوقة على أهل الرفعة والسدود في مجلس النواب فترى بينهم جانباً عظيماً من أهل الصناعات المنحطة كالحلاق والاسكافي والعطار وهلم جرا. ٤،٤٨

الباشا اخبرني اذن عن وجوه المزايا التي يمتا بها الناس ليقع انتخاب الاهالي عليهم وما هي القاعدة في تفضيل بعضهم على بعض؟

الشيخ الفرنسوي جرت السنة عندنا على ان يتحزب كل فريق منا لحزب يدير اموره بعض اهل الاطماع ومن تطمع انظارهم للشهرة والصيت او للكسب والربح من وراء الاشتغال بسياسة الامور العامة ولكل حزب عدة جرائد وجملة خطباء يروجون على الناس اهواءهم واغراضهم ويعقدون الحفلات لجمع الدراهم لينفقوها في وجوه شتى أيام الانتخاب ويستميلوا بها الاهالي لاختيار من يرشحونه منهم. فمنها ما ينفقونه على المطبوعات المختلفة التي يوزعونها على الاهالي ويستجلبون بها قلوبهم ومنها ما ينفقونه في رشوة بعض أهل النفوذ من بين الاهالي ليجمعوهم على رأيهم ومنها ما يتحفون به الاهالي أنفسهم اثماناً للخمور التي يتناولونها في حفلاتهم ومجتمعاتهم. وكل مرشح يعمد الى تحرير وثيقة عليه ينشر بها على الاهالي ٥،٤٨

ما هو عازم على اجرائه وتنفيذه في مصلحتهم ان هم انتخبوه نائباً عنهم فاذا كان أهل القرية في حاجة الى فتح ترعة أو تنزيل ضريبة أو تخفيف خدمة أقسم لهم في وثيقة انه لا يرجع من المجلس الا ظافراً ببغيتهم قاضياً لحاجتهم.

وكثر ما تنصرف همة المترشحين الى الطعن والقدح في بعضهم بعضاً على حسب اختلافهم في مشاربهم وانتمائهم الى آراء احزابهم. فتجد المترشح الذي ينتمي لحزب الراغبين في اعادة الملكية في فرنسا بدل الجمهورية يملأ الحيطان والجدران في انحاء المدينة بالطعن واللعن في من يرشحه حزب الراغبين في اعادة الامبراطورية بجانبه. ٦،٤٨

FRENCHMAN When it comes to administering government affairs, we make no such class distinction, nor do we favor one sector over another. When it concerns the conduct of government business, we all have our own opinions and ways of doing things. We're all qualified to direct government affairs and exert authority over the millions of French citizens. It doesn't matter whether the person elected by the people is a nobleman or someone from the lower classes. In fact, a number of members of the Chamber of Deputies will often come from industry and the commercial classes rather than from the aristocracy. Many of them come from the more plebeian trades: hairdressers, shoe repairers, perfumiers, and the like. 48.4

PĀSHĀ Well then, tell me the kind of qualities for which members are elected. How do people choose one such person over another?

FRENCHMAN In France it's the custom for each group to form a political party that is directed by ambitious men who aspire to either fame or wealth by working in the political arena. Each party has a number of newspapers behind it, along with a cluster of public speakers who regale the populace with talk of their goals and ambitions, hold lavish receptions to get funds that they can spend in a variety of ways at election time and persuade voters to cast their ballots in favor of their candidates. For instance, they will distribute various kinds of pamphlets to people in an attempt to win them over. They also give bribes to influential people in order to bring them over to their point of view, and will spend money on the populace in general for the costs of wine that is served at their receptions and gatherings. Every candidate prepares a statement in which he outlines the agenda that he intends to follow in serving the people if they elect him to serve as their representative. If people need to have a new canal built, for example, to have their taxes lowered, or to have some particular service performed, the candidate will swear in his statement only to return to them from the Chamber of Deputies with their desires fulfilled and their needs answered. 48.5

Members spend the majority of their time and energy attacking each other according to their different viewpoints and as part of this party affiliation. For example, you'll see someone who belongs to a party that advocates the return of the monarchy to France plastering walls all over the place with scurrilous attacks on any members nominated by another party that wants to bring back the Empire. A member who supports the Republican Party will attack both those other members—indeed the Republican Party is subdivided into 48.6

وترى المترشح للاحزاب الجمهورية يطعن ويلعن في هذين الاثنين وترى حزب الجمهورية نفسه مقسماً الى عدة أحزاب يلعن بعضهم بعضاً. ولا تقتصر هذه المطاعن على الامور العامة بل تكون في الامور الخاصة وتتناول أسرار المعيشة وخفايا الاحوال في البيوت فتصبح البلاد الفرنسوية أيام الانتخاب ميداناً للخصم والنزاع والطعن والضرب ومجالاً لذكر الفضائح واعلان المساوئ وتغدو الامة كلها في صياح وصراخ ويتحكم الطيش والنزق في رأس الكبير قبل الصغير منهم الى درجة يضل فيها لب الحكيم ويزول فيها حكم القياس. هذا والقابضون على أعنة الاحكام في اوقات الانتخاب من الوزير الى الخفير يتعاونون ويتساعدون في استمالة الاهالي تارة بالترغيب وأخرى بالترهيب لينتخبوا من المترشحين من يتقدم اليهم من المتحزبين لحزب الحكومة والحاملين لرايتها. وبقية الاحزاب يجتمعون على تسويد صحيفة الحكومة وتقبيح اعمال القائمين بادارتها ونشر معايبهم ونقائصهم بما لا يقل عما يتقارضون بينهم من المشاتم والمساب والمطاعن والمذام.

٧،٤٨ الباشا اني لأعجب من نظام اموركم وقيام حكومتكم على هذا الاسلوب الغريب من رئاسة العامة على الخاصة. وكيف يصل النواب الى انجا ما يمدون الاهالي به ويمنونهم اياه مع اختلاف الاحزاب وتباين الآراء والمقاصد واستحكام الشقاق والنزاع في ما بين المترشحين للنيابة.

الشيخ الفرنسوي ان المترشح اذا تم انتخابه بالغ في خلف الوعد ونقض العهد بمقدار ما كان يبالغ في تأكيد الانجا وتوكيد الاقسام في تنفيذ ما يرغب به الاهالي ويدعوهم الى انحيازهم نحوه ويكون احتقاره لمطالبهم واهماله لمصالحهم وهو فوق كرسي النيابة بمقدار تزلفه لهم وتضرعه اليهم ايام الانتخاب. وهو في كل أيام نيابته لا يلتفت الا الى التداخل مع ارباب الحكومة بالتوسط والرجاء ببركة نفوذه عليهم لقضاء بعض المصالح التي يكون له من ورائها كسب وربح هذا اذا لم يقنع بالسكوت والاكتفاء بما يجري عليه من المرتب في كل عام.

الباشا وما هو مقدار مرتب النائب في كل عام؟

a number of different groups, each of which attacks the other. These attacks are not concerned purely with public affairs, but involve private ones as well—people's personal lifestyles and households secrets. At election time, France turns into a battlefield for slanderous attacks and even fights. All sorts of scandal and misconduct are described, and everyone starts yelling and screaming. The whole thing now becomes totally chaotic and reckless, to such a degree that even the most sage of people lose their sense of perspective, and all notion of proportion is lost. Not only that, but during election season everyone in public positions, from ministers to local policemen, get together and help each other put pressure on voters—whether by incitement or threats—to vote for those candidates who represent the governing party and fly its flag. The other parties also get together and start blackening the government's reputation, denigrating the actions of the people who work there, and broadcasting their various faults and peccadilloes, not to mention the equally substantial number of taunts and slanders that they hurl at each other.

Pāshā I am astonished by this weird form of government that you 48.7
describe, one that gives the general populace authority over the aristocracy. How can these members of the Chamber of Deputies manage to effectuate all the things that they promise people, when there are all these different parties, ideas, and goals, and there is so much dissension and strife among the elected members?

Frenchman Once the candidate has been elected, he goes to great lengths to break his promises and annul the virtual contract he made with the people, to the same extent in fact as he initially made exaggerated promises to do what the people wanted and on the basis of which they voted for him. Now that he is sitting on his member's chair in the Chamber of Deputies, he can treat their desires and interests with as much contempt as was demanded by the toadying behavior he adopted in order to win their votes in the first place. As long as he occupies his position, his only interest and concern is to intercede with his governmental bosses and plead for some influence with them in return for a few favors that may earn him some reward and profit. That is, of course, to assume that he doesn't instead say absolutely nothing and make do with collecting his yearly salary.

Pāshā How much does a member of the Chamber of Deputies earn each year?

٨،٤٨ الشيخ الفرنسوي تدفع الامة الفرنسوية لكل نائب من مجلس النواب في العام تسعة آلاف فرنك ومرتب الرئيس ٧٢ الف فرنك وهو يسكن بأهله في قصر المجلس. وفيهم من اهل الصناعات الوضيعة من لا يصل بعمله طول العام الى ربع هذا الدخل.

الباشا ما أرى هذا المجلس بنوابه على ما اتخيل الا تكية من التكايا او مصنعاً من المصانع, لا مجلساً للحكم ولا بيتاً للسلطان ما دام الوصول الى الدخول فيه يجري على هذه الطرق المنافرة للصيانة والعفاف والمخلة بمحاسن الاخلاق ومكارم الطباع وما دام التغلب فيه لأهل السوقة ورجال العامة.

الشيخ الفرنسوي واما كيفية الانتخاب في مجلس الشيوخ فلا تختلف عن مجلس النواب الا بان اهل الحق في الانتخاب هم طبقة معينة اذ يجتمع في كل مقاطعة اعضاؤها في مجلس النواب واعضاء المجالس البلدية لينتخبوا من بينهم العضو المطلوب لمجلس الشيوخ.

وإذ انتهى بنا الكلام عن كيفية الانتخاب في المجلسين، واستأنست بترتيب إدارة الأمور في الحكومة عندنا، فقد آن أن ترى بالمشاهدة ما سمعته بالحكاية، وتقف بالعيان على ما اتصل إليك بالخبر، وأنا على عزيمة أن أذهب بكم غداً إلى مجلس النواب لتحضروا جلسة من جلساته، وتقفوا على طرفيه من البحث والجدال.

٩،٤٨ قال عيسى بن هشام: فوافقناه كلنا على رأيه، وشكرناه على سعيه.

FRENCHMAN The French people pay each member of the Chamber of Deputies nine thousand francs a year. The president of the republic gets seventy-two thousand, and he lives with his family in the Council Palace. There are people in the lowly professions who work all year but don't make even a quarter of that amount. 48.8

PĀSHĀ As far as I can see, this chamber and its members are a cross between an asylum and a factory. It can certainly not be a place for lawmaking or a seat of authority as long as the process of earning a living by it involves means that are so contradictory to probity and decent behavior, and clearly in breach of all notions of ethics and nobility of character. And that's not even to mention that the majority in it belong to the merchant class and the general populace.

FRENCHMAN The electoral process for the Senate only differs from that of the Chamber of Deputies in that people eligible for election come from a particular class. In each *département* of the country, the members of the Chamber of Deputies get together with the local council and select the person to serve in the Senate.

Now that I have finished explaining to you the way people are elected to the two houses and how our government functions, I think the time has now come to show you what you've heard about and let you see it for yourselves. Tomorrow I propose to take you all to the Chamber of Deputies to attend one of its sessions. Then you will be able to observe precisely how its two sides, investigation and debate, function.

'Īsā ibn Hishām said: We all agreed to his plan and thanked him for all his efforts.[105] 48.9

Notes

1 This point marks the beginning of a new chapter in *Ḥadīth ʿĪsā ibn Hishām*: the title "Al-ʿUmdah fī l-ḥadīqah" ("The ʿUmdah in the Gardens") was added to the text of the third edition of the book (1923).

2 A typically gnomic line of poetry by al-Mutanabbī, *Dīwān*, 197 (with *tatabayyanu*).

3 The book edition of *Ḥadīth ʿĪsā ibn Hishām* identifies the poet as Ḥabīb ibn ʿAws, i.e. Abū Tammām. See his *Dīwān Abī Tammām*, 198. The text there has *bikr* instead of *arḍ*. The Cairo 1951–65 edition has *ruʿā'* instead of *arḍ*.

4 The first hemistich is by al-Mutanabbī (*Dīwān*, 771), where it is the second hemistich of a line beginning *fa-bātat fawqahunna bilā ṣiḥābin*.

5 This is a near-verbatim quotation from Q Raḥmān 55:27.

6 No source for this line of poetry has been identified.

7 *ʿUmdah*: a provincial village headman.

8 Q Āl ʿImrān 3:173.

9 This point marks the beginning of a new chapter in *Ḥadīth ʿĪsā ibn Hishām*: the title "Al-ʿUmdah fī al-mujtamaʿ" ("The ʿUmdah in the Meeting Hall") was added to the text of the third edition of the book (1923).

10 The image of the sandgrouse (*qaṭā*) is frequently encountered in the depictions of the desert contexts of pre-Islamic poetry.

11 A line of poetry by Shihāb al-dīn Aḥmad al-Fayyūmī (d. 917/1511), in al-Shihāb al-Khafājī, *Rayḥānat al-alibbā'*. The first hemistich is also found anonymously in Ibn Dāwūd's *Zahrah*, ed. al-Sāmarrā'ī, 717.

12 The reference here is to the original Cairo Opera House, constructed during the reign of the Khedive Ismāʿīl and dedicated in November 1869. Verdi had been commissioned to compose *Aida* for the occasion but it was not finished; *Rigoletto* was performed instead. The building was destroyed by fire in 1971.

13 Al-Buḥturī, *Dīwān*, 2:1160 (from his famous *qaṣīdah* on Īwān Kisrā).

14 The topic of the Stock Market (Bourse) was a sensitive one for the al-Muwayliḥī family, in that Muḥammad's father, Ibrāhīm, lost the entire family fortune in speculation and was only rescued through the generosity of the Khedive Ismāʿīl. It is probably for that reason that Ibrāhīm al-Muwayliḥī makes the risks of the Stock Exchange a major theme

of his companion piece to *Fatrah min al-Zaman*, *Mir'āt al-'Ālam* (later known as *Ḥadīth Mūsā ibn 'Iṣām* as an echo of the title of his son's work in book form).

15 Al-Arrajānī, *Dīwān*, ed. Muḥammad Qāsim Muṣṭafā, 1:32.

16 This point marks the beginning of a new chapter in *Ḥadīth 'Īsā ibn Hishām*: the title "Al-'Umdah fī l-maṭ'am" ("The 'Umdah in the Restaurant") was added to the text of the third edition of the book (1923).

17 Al-Ma'arrī, *al-Luzūmiyyāt*, 1:105.

18 Q Baqarah 2:30.

19 Al-Ma'arrī, *Saqṭ al-zand* (1869), 2:7; (1948), 3:1012.

20 Q Qalam 68:10–13.

21 Al-Ma'arrī, *al-Luzūmiyyāt*, 63.

22 The name of the street running from 'Atabah Square to al-Azhar Mosque.

23 This point marks the beginning of a new chapter in *Ḥadīth 'Īsā ibn Hishām*: the title "Al-'Umdah fī l-ḥān" ("The 'Umdah in the Tavern") was added to the text of the third edition of the book (1923).

24 Middle Eastern tradition includes a number of narratives related to King Solomon and the jinn. The relationship is cited in the text of the Qur'an, Q Naml 27:17 and Saba' 34:4. The tale "Madīnat al-nuḥās" ("The City of Brass") in *A Thousand and One Nights* is an elaborate morality tale centered around a quest for the bottles in which Solomon is alleged to have imprisoned the jinn.

25 In *Ḥadīth 'Īsā ibn Hishām*, the name "Euclas" is replaced by "someone erecting hovels in a village."

26 Q A'rāf 7:116.

27 The joke involves using both of the sibilant "s" sounds in Arabic: with "ṣ" the meaning is "to accompany"; with "s," "to drag."

28 A feddan is a measure of area commonly used in Egypt, slightly larger than an acre.

29 This point marks the beginning of a new chapter in *Ḥadīth 'Īsā ibn Hishām*: the title "Al-'Umdah fī l-marqaṣ" ("The 'Umdah in the Dance Hall") was added to the text of the third edition of the book (1923). This chapter consists of three episodes from al-Muwayliḥī's *Fatrah min al-zaman*, *Miṣbāḥ al-sharq* 90, 91, and 92.

30 In pre-modern Arabic poetry, the epithet "Mashrafī" by itself was sufficient to refer to the very finest of swords.

31 Al-Ma'arrī, *al-Luzūmiyyāt*, 1:188.

32 Ibid., 1:165–166.

33 Lines of poetry cited anonymously (*qāla ākhar*) in Abū Tammām's *Ḥamāsah*; see al-Marzūqī, *Sharḥ Dīwān al-Ḥamāsah*, 1238 (beginning *wa-kunta matā arsalta*). Also attributed to a girl (*jāriyah*) in Ibn Qutaybah, *'Uyūn al-akhbār*, 4:22.

34 Al-Maʿarrī, *al-Luzūmiyyāt*, 1:117.

35 A line of poetry by al-Khalīʿ al-Shāmī Abū ʿAbd Allāh Muḥammad ibn Abī l-Ghamr Aḥmad, in al-Thaʿālibī's *Yatīmah*, 1:271.

36 Al-Maʿarrī, *Saqṭ al-Zand* (1957), 286.

37 This point marks the beginning of a new chapter in *Ḥadīth ʿĪsā ibn Hishām*: the title "Al-ʿUmdah fī l-rahn" ("The ʿUmdah's Property in Pawn") was added to the text of the third edition of the book (1923). Since this episode follows the previous one after a gap of some three months, it begins with a summary of the previous "Dance Hall" episodes.

38 This point marks the beginning of a new chapter in *Ḥadīth ʿĪsā ibn Hishām*: the title "Al-ʿUmdah fī l-ahrām" ("The ʿUmdah at the Pyramids") was added to the text of the third edition of the book (1923).

39 The reference is to Napoleon (whose name is included in the book versions of the text). The reference is to the Battle of the Pyramids fought in July, 1798.

40 An allusion to Q Qāriʿah 101:5, in which the Day of Judgment is depicted: «The mountains will be like carded wool»; also to Furqān 25:23, in which God will turn wrongdoers into «scattered dust.»

41 Parts of this account are to be found in al-Kisāʾī's *Qiṣaṣ al-Anbiyāʾ*, 233ff., and in al-Thaʿālibī's *Kitāb Qiṣaṣ al-anbiyāʾ*, 151ff.

42 This point marks the beginning of a new chapter in *Ḥadīth ʿĪsā ibn Hishām*: the title "Qaṣr al-gīzah wa-l-matḥaf" ("The Giza Palace and the Museum") was added to the text of the third edition of the book (1923). In the book edition, the Father/Son discussion appears first, followed by the dialogue between Pāshā and Friend.

43 Al-Maʿarrī, *Saqṭ al-zand* (1869), 2:198; (1948), 1987.

44 "Qaṣr al-Nīl" refers to the current Egyptian Museum on Taḥrīr Square in central Cairo.

45 Not coincidentally, the Amīriyyah Press was to be the publisher of the first edition of *Ḥadīth ʿĪsā ibn Hishām*.

46 A reference to *maysir*, the traditional game of chance in which arrows were used as lots.

47 The first book edition of *Ḥadīth ʿĪsā ibn Hishām* also includes the second half of this line: "Once we are gone, look to these relics."

48 Q Kahf 18:5.

49 Q Shuʿarāʾ 26:86.

50 This point marks the beginning of a new chapter in *Ḥadīth ʿĪsā ibn Hishām*: the title "Al-ʿUmdah fī l-malhā" ("The ʿUmdah at the Theater") was added to the text of the third edition of the book (1923).

51 The author is punning here on the dual meaning of the Arabic word *ghazālah*, both "a gazelle" and "the sun's disk."

52 Lines of poetry by Abū Bakr Muḥammad al-Khālidī (d. ca. 380/990) in al-Thaʿālibī's *Yatīmah*, 2:190.

53 This point marks the beginning of a new chapter in *Ḥadīth ʿĪsā ibn Hishām*: the title "Al-Madaniyyah al-gharbiyyah" ("Western Civilization") was added to the text of the third edition of the book (1923). This original version is considerably longer than the one now found in the book versions, no doubt because the author found it necessary to describe the Exposition Universelle in Paris for his Egyptian newspaper readers.

54 ʿUkāẓ, a town a short distance from Mecca, was the site of an annual fair in pre-Islamic times, famous, among other things, for its competitions in poetry.

55 This point marks the beginning of *al-Riḥlah al-thāniyah* (*The Second Journey*), referring to the trip that took the author to France following "The First Journey" around Cairo and Egypt. Chapter titles were added when these episodes were included in the text of *Ḥadīth ʿĪsā ibn Hishām* for the first time (in the fourth edition, 1927). This episode is entitled "Bārīs" ("Paris").

56 This title occurs in the original newspaper article.

57 Al-Maʿarrī, *Saqṭ al-zand*, 48.

58 Abū Tammām, *Dīwān Abī Tammām*, 3:266 (where the text reads *fī sāʿatin*).

59 A line of poetry attributed to Abū Tammām, see Muḥsīn al-ʿĀmilī, *Aʿyān al-shīʿah*, 4:531.

60 Al-Mutanabbī, *Dīwān*, 316.

61 This line is one of three sung by a girl to the Caliph al-Ma'mūn. See Ibn ʿAbd Rabbih, *al-ʿIqd al-Farīd*, 6:210; and al-Masʿūdī, *Murūj al-dhahab*, 4:307. Quoted by (and composed by?) Abū l-Faḍl Aḥmad ibn Abī Ṭāhir or al-Faḍl ibn Abī Ṭāhir in Ibn Dāwūd's *Zahrah*, 153.

62 In addition to the Western model of the ideal society offered by Plato, *al-Madīnah al-fāḍilah* is one of the principal works of the philosopher al-Fārābī (d. 339/950).

63 Ibn Hāni' al-Andalusī, *Dīwān*, 95 (where *fa-laghwun* is used in the first line).

64 A line of poetry by ʿAbd Allāh ibn Muʿāwiyah al-Jaʿfarī (d. 130/747). See al-Jāḥiẓ, *Ḥayawān*, 3:488 and many later sources, most of which have *wa-lākinna ʿayna*; some have *kamā ʿaynu* (e.g., al-Ibshīhī, *Mustaṭraf*, 1:213). *Kamā anna aʿyuna* is unmetrical.

65 Al-Maʿarrī, *al-Luzūmiyyāt*, 1:74.

66 Needless to say, neither of these statements is correct.

67 This point marks the beginning of a new episode of *al-Riḥlah al-thāniyah*: the chapter title "Al-Maʿraḍ" ("The Exhibition") was added to the text of the fourth edition of *Ḥadīth ʿĪsā ibn Hishām* (1927).

68 Al-Khansā', *Dīwān*, [1986], 305; [1988], 386.

69 The name of the poet al-Khansā''s brother, Ṣakhr, killed in pre-Islamic tribal warfare, means "stone, rock."

70 A line of poetry cited anonymously in many sources, e.g. *Ḥamāsat Abī Tāmmām* (see al-Marzūqī, *Sharḥ*, 1284); Ibn ʿAbd Rabbih, *al-ʿIqd al-farīd*, 3:462 and 6:108; and al-Qālī, *Amālī*, 1:23.

71 Al-Nābighah al-Dhubyānī, *The Divans*, ed. Wilhelm Ahlwardt, 10–11 (vss. 15–16, 26–27). In the last line, other sources read *la-ranā* in place of *innā*.

72 Al-Maʿarrī, *al-Luzūmiyyāt*, 1:174.

73 A line of poetry by Abū Tammām, see ʿĀmilī, *Aʿyān al-shīʿah*, 4:480.

74 These lines are by al-Sharīf al-Raḍī, *Dīwān*, 2:877–80.

75 This point marks the beginning of a new episode of *al-Riḥlah al-thāniyah*: the chapter title "Al-Qaṣr al-kabīr" ("The Grand Palais") was added to the text of the fourth edition of *Ḥadīth ʿĪsā ibn Hishām* (1927).

76 While the names Alexander and Qārūn can be traced to particular figures (see the Glossary of Names and Places), the names Māriyah, Dārah, and ʿAmr may refer to multiple historical or mythical persons.

77 Al-Maʿarrī, *al-Luzūmiyyāt*, 1:66.

78 Al-Mutanabbī, *Dīwān*, 178.

79 Lines of poetry quoted anonymously (and in reversed order) in al-Muḥibbī, *Nafḥat al-rayḥānah*, and al-Shihāb al-Khafājī, *Rayḥānat al-alibbāʾ*. In the first line, the alternative reading is *takhtālu*.

80 Al-Mutanabbī, *Dīwān*, 767 (in his "Shiʿb Bawwān" *qaṣīdah* for ʿAḍud al-Dawlah).

81 A line of poetry by ʿUmar ibn Abī Rabīʿah, from his famous *rāʾiyyah*. See, among many other sources, al-Iṣfahānī, *Aghānī*, 1:80, 82.

82 This point marks the beginning of a new episode of *al-Riḥlah al-thāniyah*: the chapter title "Al-Ashjār wa-l-azhār" ("Trees and Flowers") was added to the text of the fourth edition of *Ḥadīth ʿĪsā ibn Hishām* (1927). It is interesting to note that Muḥammad al-Muwayliḥī seems to have taken longer than usual in sending this episode back to Cairo for publication. In the interim, number 119 of *Miṣbāḥ al-sharq* (September 7, 1900) includes an episode of Ibrāhīm al-Muwayliḥī's parallel narrative, entitled *Mirʾāt al-ʿĀlam*. For that text, see Ibrāhīm al-Muwayliḥī, *al-Muʾallafāt al-Kāmilah*, 161–202. My translation of this work into English is published in *Middle Eastern Literatures*, 15, no. 3 (December 2012): 318–36; and 16, no. 3 (December 2013): 1–17.

83 In the Qur'an's account of the meeting of King Solomon and the Queen of Sheba, (Q Naml 27:44), the queen is shown an image of her throne. Since it shimmers like water, she bares her legs to avoid getting them wet.

84 These lines of poetry may be by Ibn al-Rūmī; see his *Dīwān*, 1:394, but they are also attributed to others. See the apparatus by Helmut Ritter in his edition of ʿAbd al-Qāhir

al-Jurjānī, *Asrār al-balāghah*, 117. Also in Ibn al-Muʿtazz's *Dīwān*, 2:168; and the *Dīwān* by Abū l-Qāsim al-Zāhī, 72.

85 Al-Maʿarrī, *Saqṭ al-zand*, 232 (where *fa-adhhalu* is found instead of *fa-ajhalu*).

86 Q Kahf 18:39.

87 Abū l-ʿAtāhiyah, *Dīwān*, 104; al-Iṣfahānī, *Aghānī*, 4:35.

88 This point marks the beginning of a new episode of *al-Riḥlah al-thāniyah*: the chapter title "Al-Marāʾī wa-l-mashāhid" ("Sights and Scenes") was added to the text of the fourth edition of *Ḥadīth ʿĪsā ibn Hishām* (1927).

89 Lines of poetry attributed to ʿAbd Allāh ibn Ṭāhir ibn al-Ḥusayn Dhū l-Yamīnayn in Ibn Khallikān, *Wafayāt*, 3:85–86. The first line is attributed to Abū Dulaf in Ibn Wakīʿ, *al-Munṣif*, ed. al-Dāyah, 411.

90 This point marks the beginning of a new episode of *al-Riḥlah al-thāniyah*: the chapter title "Al-Iftirāʾ ʿalā al-waṭan" ("Slandering the Homeland") was added to the text of the fourth edition of *Ḥadīth ʿĪsā ibn Hishām* (1927).

91 Lines of poetry cited anonymously in al-Ṭurṭūshī, *Sirāj al-mulūk*, 167, 330–31; Yāqūt, *Muʿjam al-buldān* (Dār Ṣādir), 2:311. These sources read *mā li-l-farīsati* instead of *mā l-farīsatu*.

92 This is a reference to the previous episodes of *Fatrah min al-zaman* set in Cairo.

93 This point marks the beginning of a new episode of *al-Riḥlah al-thāniyah*: the chapter title "Khubz al-madaniyyah" ("Bread of Civilization") was added to the text of the fourth edition of *Ḥadīth ʿĪsā ibn Hishām* (1927).

94 Edward Lane's dictionary (s.v. *aṣfar*) explains that this use of "sons of yellow" refers to an early Greek king named al-Aṣfar ("son of Room, son of Eysoon" [Esau]).

95 A reference to the shirt worn by the third caliph ʿUthmān when he was assassinated. The bloody shirt was later publicly displayed in Damascus by its governor, Muʿawiyah, in order to provoke popular anger and public demands to avenge his kinsman's murder.

96 This, and the specific reference to the portrait of the girl wearing Alsatian costume, is a reference to the Franco-Prussian War (1870–1) which brought about a crushing defeat for the French army and the cession of much of Alsace to Germany.

97 The so-called "Fashoda incident" occurred in Sudan in 1898. French forces seeking to control the upper reaches of the River Nile and thus cause problems for the British in Egypt were confronted by a British force. As a result of vigorous diplomacy, the French were eventually forced to withdraw their claims. This incident was widely reported in the al-Muwayliḥī newspaper, *Miṣbāḥ al-sharq*, but references to the incident in the original episodes of *Fatrah min al-Zaman* were omitted from the book version of *Ḥadīth ʿĪsā ibn Hishām*.

98 In the editions of *Ḥadīth ʿĪsā ibn Hishām* the author notes that these lines are by al-Farazdaq, *Dīwān*, 1:212.

99 The Joseph narrative is to be found in the Qur'an, Surah 12 Yūsuf.

100 This point marks the beginning of a new episode of *al-Riḥlah al-thāniyah*: the chapter title, "al-Muʿjizah al-thāminah" ("The Eighth Wonder"), was added to the text of the fourth edition of *Ḥadīth ʿĪsā ibn Hishām* (1927).

101 The so-called Panama Scandals (1892) involved large-scale corruption in the construction of the Panama Canal. Gustave Eiffel was among those involved, but his jail sentence was later revoked.

102 Al-Maʿarrī, *al-Luzūmiyyāt*, 1:63–64.

103 This is the first of three episodes of *Fatrah min al-zaman* which were published after a gap of more than two years, and long after the author's return from Paris to Cairo (*Miṣbāḥ al-sharq* nos. 192, 193, 196). When the author prepared the episodes of *Fatrah min al-zaman* for publication in book form (1907), he added a new final chapter to the "Second Journey" entitled "Min al-Gharb ilā l-Sharq" ("From West to East") which was not part of the original episodes in *Miṣbāḥ al-sharq*. These three episodes were never included in any edition of *Ḥadīth ʿĪsā ibn Hishām* in its book form.

104 This is the second of the three episodes of *Fatrah min al-zaman* that were published after an interval of over two years. While the previous episode begins with a characteristic piece of virtuoso language in the traditional style of *sajʿ* (rhyming and cadenced prose), this episode and the one that follows it do not begin in that way but merely continue the Frenchman's description of the French governmental system.

105 Even though this episode of *Fatrah min al-zaman* ends, like all its predecessors, with the phrase "to be continued" (*wa-l-ḥadīth yutbaʿ*), no more episodes appeared.

Glossary of Names and Terms

'Abbās the First (1812–54) grandson of Muḥammad 'Alī and, from 1849–54, his successor as *walī* of Egypt (nominally under Ottoman suzerainty).

'Abbāsiyyah suburb of Cairo which, in al-Muwayliḥī's time, was on the outer edge of the city.

'Abdallāh ibn Ja'far (d. between 81/700 and 85/704) nephew of 'Alī ibn Abī Ṭālib, who tried to prevent 'Alī's son, al-Ḥusayn, from going to al-Kūfah to be proclaimed Caliph.

Abū l-'Abbās Aḥmad Al-Rifā'ī (512–78/1118–82) founder of the Rifā'iyyah order of Sufis, which originated in Iraq with rapid spreading to Syria and Egypt during the course of the seventh/thirteenth century.

Abū l-'Alā' al-Ma'arrī (363–449/973–1058) famous blind Syrian poet, whom al-Muwayliḥī admired greatly and who is quoted throughout this work. A picture of the poet used to hang in the hall of al-Muwayliḥī's house.

Abū Ḥanīfah (80–150/699–767) founder of the Sunnī Ḥanafī school of Islamic jurisprudence.

Abū Tammām (172–231/788–845) Ḥabīb ibn Aws al-Ṭā'ī, a renowned Arab poet, famous (and also much criticized) for the complexity of his imagery.

Abū l-Ṭayyib al-Mutanabbī (303–54/915–65) premodern Arab poet widely regarded as one of the greatest. He composed a large number of ringing odes—both praising (*madḥ*) and lampooning (*hijā'*) the most prominent rulers of his time as to have become proverbial in the centuries since his death.

Alexander (356–323 BC) "the Great," King of Macedon, who launched a number of military campaigns and defeated the forces of the Persian Empire. He founded a number of cities named after himself, including Iskenderun and Alexandria.

'Alī ibn Abī Ṭālib (d. 40/661) cousin and son-in-law of the Prophet Muḥammad, and the fourth Caliph. In his name, the Shi'ah (originally *shī'at 'Alī*, "'Alī's Party") was established.

'Amr ibn Ma'dī Karib renowned Yemeni warrior-poet from the pre-Islamic era who lived on into the Islamic era and is alleged to have witnessed the Battle of Qādisiyyah in 15/636.

'Antar and 'Ablah renowned pre-Islamic poet 'Antarah who is the subject of one of Arabic's most famous popular sagas, *Sīrat 'Antar*. 'Ablah is the name of his beloved, to win whose hand he undertakes a large number of difficult tasks.

al-'Aqīq valley in central Arabia.

al-Asfarayīnī (Esfarayeni), Abū Bakr Khurasani physician and author of *Zubdat al-bayān fī 'ilm al-abdān* (*The Best Explanation in the Science of Bodies*), a work on the human body.

al-'Aynī, Badr al-dīn (762–856/1360–1453) full name al-'Ayntabī, Ḥanafī jurist who also served as *muḥtasib* (inspector of public morality) of Cairo during the Mamluk era.

Bāb al-Lūq district in central Cairo.

Baudry-Lacantinerie, G. (1837–1913) main compiler (with other collaborators) of *Traité de droit civile*, first published in 1895.

Bawwān Pass probably a reference to Shi'b Bawwān, a well-forested area in Fars, Iran.

Baybars, Sulṭān al-Ẓāhir (620–76/1223–77) fourth Mamlūk Sultan of Egypt and a redoubtable warrior who defeated the forces of the Seventh Crusade under Louis IX of France and later those of the Mongol Hūlāgū Khān at the famous battle of 'Ayn Jālūt (Goliath's Spring) in 658/1260. His exploits are celebrated in one of Arabic's best-known popular sagas, *Sīrat al-Ẓāhir Baybars*.

Bilqīs, Queen of Sheba renowned queen, whose encounter with King Solomon is mentioned in both the Hebrew Bible and the Qur'an. The latter account occurs in Surahs 27 Naml ("The Ants") and 34 Sabā ("Sheba").

Bonchamps, Marquis Christian de (1860–1919) famous nineteenth-century French explorer of the African continent. In 1897 he was dispatched by the French government from Ethiopia to the Sudan to secure the region around Fashoda (see below).

Buṭrus Ghālī (1846–1910) prominent Egyptian politician and minister (later to be prime minister) who was assassinated in 1910. He interceded on al-Muwayliḥī's behalf when the latter was condemned to death for distributing nationalist literature in 1882 and obtained a commutation of sentence to one of exile.

Chosroes Anushirwan (r. AD 531–79) Sasanian emperor who built the city of Ctesiphon, the famous portico of which is celebrated in a poem by the poet al-Buḥturī (d. 284/897). The site is at al-Madā'in to the south of Baghdad.

Cromer, Lord (1841–1917) Evelyn Baring, major British diplomat and statesman. He was appointed Controller General of Egypt in 1879 (following the exile of the Khedive Ismā'īl). After the quelling of the 'Urābī Revolt of 1882, he became consul general (and virtual ruler) of Egypt until his resignation from the post in 1907 as the result of furious reactions to a notorious incident in the Egyptian village of Dinshaway, in which—whilst Cromer was on leave—several villagers were hung for challenging British officers engaged in a pigeon shoot. His two-volume study *Modern Egypt* (1908) presents his own view of the events of Egypt's recent history.

Dalloz, Victor (1795–1869) member of a prominent French legal family and author of *Jurisprudence générale.*

al-Dawlah, Sayf (303–56/915–67) the Ḥamdānid ruler, attracted to his court at Ḥalab (Aleppo) many famous writers, including the poet al-Mutanabbī and the philosopher al-Fārābī.

Day of Resurrection/Reckoning (*Yawm al-Qiyāmah*) in Islamic eschatology, the day when all believers will be called to account.

Deloncle, François (1856–1922) French politician and member of the French Chamber of Deputies who held a number of cabinet posts in the second half of the nineteenth century.

al-Dhubyānī, Al-Nābighah (ca. AD 535–604) prominent pre-Islamic poet, closely associated with the Lakhmid court at al-Ḥīrah.

Al-Durr al-Mukhtār work on Ḥanbalī jurisprudence by the Damascus scholar 'Alā' al-dīn al-Ḥaṣkafī (d. 1088/1677) consisting of a commentary on an earlier work, *Tanwīr al-Abṣār,* composed by Muḥammad ibn 'Abd Allāh al-Tamartāshī.

Euripides (ca. 490–406 BC) one of the three famous writers of Greek tragedy (along with Aeschylus and Sophocles). Among his most famous works are *Medea, Women of Troy,* and *The Bacchae.*

Ezbekiyyah Quarter district of Cairo named after Amir Ezbek al-Tutush, a general in the reign of the Mamluk Qā'it Bāy. It contained a large park that separated the old city of Cairo from the modern (Ismā'īliyyah) section constructed in the nineteenth century. In the late 1890s, the gardens were filled with trees and plants, and there was an ornamental lake in the middle of the area.

al-Faḍl ibn al-Rabīʿ (138–207/755–822) chamberlain and chief minister to two Abbasid Caliphs, Hārūn al-Rashīd and al-Amīn.

Fakhrī Pāshā, Ḥusayn (1843–1910) Egyptian cabinet minister and, for only three days in January 1893, Prime Minister of Egypt. On the orders of the Khedive Tawfīq, Fakhrī had replaced Muṣṭafā Fahmī who was considered too pro-British, but the order was rapidly rescinded.

al-Fārābī (ca. 295–338/908–50) renowned philosopher who wrote commentaries on the works of Aristotle, a study on the ideal society, *al-Madīnah al-fāḍilah* (*The Virtuous City*) modeled on the earlier work of Plato, and a series of treatises on music, of which the most famous and complex is *Kitāb al-mūsīqā al-kabīr* (*The Great Book on Music*).

Fashoda site in Sudan of a famous late nineteenth-century confrontation between British and French forces. The Marquis de Bonchamps was sent from Ethiopia and Major Jean-Baptiste Marchand from Brazzaville in the Congo to secure the region around Fashoda in the Sudan as French territory. When the British sent a flotilla down the River Nile, the confrontation led to an ignominious French withdrawal.

Gambetta, Léon (1838–82) French statesman and prime minister who came to prominence in the period during and after the Franco-Prussian War (1870–71).

Garraud, René (1849–1930) author of *Traité théorique et pratique du droit pénal français*.

Ghumdān a famous palace in Sanaa in the Yemen, which was legendary for its beauty.

Gladstone, William Ewart (1809–98) British Liberal politician who served as prime minister for four separate periods during the nineteenth century.

Gordon, Charles George (1833–85) British major-general, often known as "Gordon of Khartoum." He entered service for the Egyptian government in 1873 and was appointed commander-in-chief of the Sudanese army. He confronted a revolt by Muḥammad Aḥmad who declared himself the "Mahdī"; after evacuating a number of British troops from the Sudanese capital, Gordon decided to stay behind with a small force. When the British government did not intervene in time, the city fell and he was killed.

Griffith, George Richard (1857–1920) veterinary officer in the British army who was sent to the Sudan in 1884, took part in several campaigns there, and later served as general in charge of veterinary medicine for the Egyptian army between 1905 and 1907.

Haman mentioned in the Qur'an as being a minister of the Pharaoh at the time of Moses.

Hanotaux, Gabriel (1853–1944) French diplomat and statesman who, from 1894 to 1898, served as Minister of Foreign Affairs. Among his tasks as minister was to negotiate the colonization of Africa with the British, thus including the "Fashoda incident." (See above and below under *Fashoda, Bonchamps*, and *Marchand.*).

Hārūt and Mārūt two angels mentioned in the Qur'an, Q Baqarah 2:96. They taught men sorcery (*siḥr*) and, for their sins, they were punished by being imprisoned in Babel.

Hélie, Faustin (1799–1884) author of *Analyse et commentaire du code du procédure pénal.*

Homer name traditionally assigned to the "author" of two famous Greek epic poems *The Iliad* and the *The Odyssey*. Since both poems are the products of a lengthy process of oral transmission and performance, we have to assume that they constitute the result of multiple contributors.

Horace (65–8 BC) Quintus Horatius Flaccus, famous Roman lyric poet, best known for his set of *Odes*.

Ḥulwān town to the south of Cairo, the location of the al-Muwayliḥī family home.

Hunter, Archibald (1857–1939) British general in the Egyptian army who served in the Sudan from 1884 to 1899. He later moved on, first to India and then to South Africa.

Ibn ʿĀbidīn, Muḥammad Amīn (1198–1258/1784–1842) author of a legal textbook known as *Majmūʿat rasāʾil Ibn ʿĀbidīn* (*Collected Letters of Ibn ʿAbdīn*).

Ibn al-ʿArabī, Muḥyī al-dīn (560–638/1165–1240) Sufi author. one of the most famous figures in the history of Sufism, he has remained an inspirational and often controversial figure in the history of Islamic doctrine. Among his most famous works are *Fuṣūṣ al-Ḥikam* (*Bezels of Wisdom*) and *al-Futūḥāt al-Makkiyyah* (*The Meccan Illuminations*).

Ibn Malak (d. ca. 797/1395) also known as Ibn Firishteh, teacher of Islamic sciences under the Ottoman Sulṭān Bāyezīd (r. 792–805/1389–1402) in the town of Tīre in southwest Anatolia. A Ḥanafī jurist, he commented on the *Majmaʿ al-Baḥrayn* (see below) and other famous Ḥanafī law books.

Ibn al-Rūmī (221–83/836–96) Arabic poet of Byzantine descent who was born in Baghdad. While his poetic gifts were quickly recognized, his lampoons earned him enemies, in particular Al-Qāsim ibn ʿUbaydallāh, who is alleged to have had the poet poisoned.

Ibrāhīm (Abraham) patriarch in both the Hebrew Bible and the Qurʾan. In the latter he earned the title "Khalīl Allāh" (friend of God) after enduring great hardship in his wars against King Namrūd. See Q Anbiyāʾ 21:51–72.

Ibrāhīm ibn al-Mahdī (162–224/779–839) son of the Abbasid Caliph al-Mahdī, and brother of Hārūn al-Rashīd. His prowess as a singer is discussed in detail in the famous work of Abū l-Faraj al-Isfahānī (283–356/897–967), *Kitāb al-Aghānī* (*Book of Songs*).

Ibrāhīm Pāshā (1789–1848) son of Muḥammad ʿAlī who led the Egyptian army in victorious campaigns against the Wahhābīs in Arabia and the Ottoman army in Syria. When his father became mentally ill, he took over as regent, but died before his father in 1848. A statue of him riding a horse was a prominent feature of Opera Square in Cairo.

Imām ibn al-Wardī (691–749/1292–1349) author of a work entitled *Kharīdat al-ʿAjāʾib wa-Farīdat al-Gharāʾib* (*Pearl of Wonders and Gem of Marvels*).

Imām Shāfiʿī Cemetery cemetery which surrounded the mausoleum of Imām Shāfiʿī (150–204/767–820) and lay outside the city walls of Cairo at that time. One of al-Muwayliḥī's ancestors was buried there.

Ismāʿīl Bāy al-Kabīr (d. 1205/1791) Mamluk of Ibrāhīm Katkhudā (who was an influential figure in Egypt during the years 1156–67/1743–54). Ismāʿīl Bāy joined himself to Muḥammad Bāy Abū Dhahab, who eventually overthrew ʿAlī Bāy and, on his return to Egypt, became very powerful despite attempts by Murād Bāy to have him killed.

Ismāʿīliyyah quarter the modern section of Cairo, constructed during the reign of the Egyptian Khedive Ismāʿīl (r. 1863–79) along the lines of Haussmann's Paris.

al-ʿIzz ibn ʿAbd al-Salām (Al-Sulamī) (578–660/1182–1261) famous Sufi and theologian of the Shāfiʿī School, known as "Sultan of the Religious Scholars."

Jabal Qāf proverbially distant mountain in early Arabic cosmology.

Jaʿfar al-Barmakī (150–87/767–803) vizier of Caliph Hārūn al-Rashīd, in both fact and fiction. He was a major patron of the arts and also a supporter of the translation movements during Hārūn's reign. His own downfall and that of his family is alleged to have resulted from his affair with the caliph's sister, ʿAbbāsah.

al-Jāḥiẓ (160–256/776–869) ʿAmr ibn Baḥr, the most illustrious composer of works in Arabic prose in the pre-modern era, given the nickname "goggle-eyed" by which he is known. A genuine polymath, he composed an enormous repertoire of works on a wide variety of topics.

Jayḥūn river known in Persian as the Amū Daryā and in European languages as the Oxus.

al-Jīlānī, ʿAbd al-Qādir (470–561/1078–1166) Ḥanbalī theologian who gave his name to the Qādiriyyah order of Sūfis.

Kaʿb al-Aḥbār (d. 32/652–53) Yemeni Jewish rabbi in the pre-Islamic era who converted to Islam. The epithet "Aḥbār" is an acknowledgment of his proverbial wisdom.

Kawthar traditionally a river in Paradise; some commentators discussing the Qur'an, Q 108 Kawthar, relate this word to the verbal root *K-Th-R* (with the meaning of "abundance").

Khān al-Khalīlī famous bazaar of Cairo in the Fatimid section of the city (also known to tourists as the "Muski").

al-Khansāʾ (first/seventh century) Tumāḍir bint ʿAmr ibn al-Ḥarth, one of Arabic literature's most famous elegaic poets. Many of her mosts famous elegies were in memory of her brother, Ṣakhr.

al-Khawarnak fortress near the town of Najaf in Iraq. It was originally constructed by al-Nuʿmān, the Lakhmid ruler of al-Ḥīrah.

al-Khiḍr mysterious figure who appears most prominently in the Qur'an in the Surah of the Cave (Q 18 Kahf), where he tests Moses in a series of complex situations. Al-Khiḍr is also a major reference-point in Sufi literature.

Khuld palace built by the Abbasid Caliph al-Manṣūr on the banks of the River Tigris.

kiswah black brocaded cloth used to cover the Kaaba in Mecca.

Kitchener, Horatio Herbert (1850–1916) British Field-Marshal and major figure in British colonial administration. Sent to the Sudan, he secured the country in 1898 and was appointed Chief-of-Staff (*Sirdār*) of the Anglo-Egyptian armed forces there. He later participated in the Boer War in South

Africa and was subsequently sent to India. In 1914 he was appointed as Secretary of State for War in England.

Kordofan province in the central regions of the Sudan. It was the site of vicious fighting between the forces of the Mahdī Muḥammad Aḥmad and the British army, but by 1898 it had become part of Sudan as a whole.

Krupp family from Essen who founded the renowned German steel producing company, which was thus heavily involved in the manufacture of ammunition and weapons.

Lavigerie, Cardinal Charles (1825–92) French priest and later cardinal, he was Primate of Africa (based in Tunisia and Algeria) and campaigned against slavery on the continent.

Lāẓoghly, Muḥammad Bey "katkhudā" to the ruler of Egypt, also known as Muḥammad Aghā. He played a major role in organizing the massacre of the Mamluks in the Cairo Citadel in 1811.

al-Maʿarrī See Abū l-ʿAlāʾ al-Maʿarrī.

al-Mahdī, al-ʿAbbāsī (1827–97) grand mufti of Egypt and author of *al-Fatāwā al-Mahdiyyah.*

Al-Majmaʿ *Majmaʿ al-baḥrayn wa-multaqā al-nayyirayn* (*Meeting-place of the Two Seas and Rendezvous of Sun and Moon*), a Ḥanafī law book by Muẓaffar al-dīn Aḥmad ibn ʿAbdallāh ibn Thaʿlab Ibn al-Sāʿātī (d. ca. 694/1295).

Mamlūk (lit. "owned," "a slave") dynasty of rulers in Egypt between 648/1250 and 922/1517. Drawn primarily from Turkic tribes in the Caucasus region, all those who assumed the position of "Sulṭān" were required to be manumitted slaves. Even after the Ottoman invasion of Egypt in 1516–17, the Mamlūks remained the primary authority in Egypt until Muḥammad ʿAlī organized their corporate massacre in the Cairo Citadel in 1811..

al-Mānastirlī, Ḥasan Pāshā prominent political figure during the reign of Muḥammad ʿAlī. He is best remembered for the elaborate palace (*sarāy*) that he had constructed at the southern tip of Roda Island in Cairo (completed in 1851).

al-Manīkalī, Aḥmad Pāshā Minister of War during the reign of Muḥammad ʿAlī. See ʿAbd al-Rahmān al-Rāfiʿī, *ʿAṣr Muḥammad ʿAlī* (Cairo, Maktabat al-Nahḍah al-Miṣriyyah, 1951), 191 and 308.

maqāmah, pl. maqāmāt picaresque narrative genre originated in the tenth century by Badīʿ al-Zamān al-Hamadhānī (358–98/969–1007), which became a widely used literary form in the ensuing centuries and which is invoked, along with al-Hamadhānī's narrator, ʿĪsā ibn Hishām, in this work of al-Muwayliḥī.

Marchand, Jean Baptiste (1863–1934) French explorer in Africa who was sent in 1897 to help secure the region around Fashoda in the Sudan. Once there, he and the French forces were confronted by British forces under Lord Kitchener and were eventually forced to withdraw.

Marwān, Marwānids name of several prominent members of the Umayyad dynasty, including two Caliphs.

Mauser German arms manufacturer, founded in the 1870s, that specialized in the production of bolt-action rifles and automatic pistols.

Maxim first recoil-operated machine gun, named after Hiram Stevens Maxim who invented it in 1884.

Maẓlūm Pāshā (1858–1928) Egyptian Minister of Justice in the 1890s who frequently clashed with the British occupation authorities on matters of law and its implementation.

Miles, Nelson A. (1839–1925) American Civil War general who was appointed Commanding General of the United States Army in 1895 and was thus involved in the invasions of both Cuba and Puerto Rico during the Spanish-American War.

Muʿallim Ghālī (1190–1237/1776–1822) Minister of Finance and Foreign Affairs in Egypt during the reign of Muḥammad ʿAlī.

Muḥammad ʿAlī (1183–1265/1769–1849) Ottoman soldier of Macedonian origins and later ruler of Egypt. He was originally sent to fight against the Napoleonic invasion of Egypt in 1798. Filling the vacuum left following the French army's withdrawal and following the massacre of the Mamluks at the Cairo Citadel in 1811, he became the ruler of Egypt and founder of what was to become its royal dynasty—lasting until the July Revolution of 1952. He was the initiator of a large number of reforms that turned Egypt into a major military power and also the fulcrum of a good deal of innovation and reform in the financial, social, educational, and cultural sectors of Egypt.

Muḥammad the Conqueror (Mehmet Fātiḥ) (835–86/1432–81) Ottoman sultan who conquered Constantinople in 1453, bringing the Byzantine Empire to a close.

al-Muʿizz (319–65/932–75) Faṭimid caliph who gave his name to a large section of the post-fourth/tenth-century city of Cairo.

Muskī area of Cairo lying between al-ʿAtabah al-Khaḍrāʾ Square and the mosque of al-Ḥusayn, still renowned for its artifacts of metal and leather. The term may perhaps be an arabization of the French word *mosquée* (mosque).

Muslim Ibn al-Walīd (ca. 130–208/748–823) celebrated early Abbasid love-poet in the tradition of pre-modern Arabic poetry, known as *ṣarīʿ al-ghawānī* ("victim of beautiful maidens").

al-Mutanabbī see Abū l-Ṭayyib al-Mutanabbī.

al-Muʿtaṣim (178–227/795–842) Abbasid Caliph, son of Hārūn al-Rashīd. Noted for his campaigns against the Byzantine forces in Anatolia, he also established a new caliphal city in Samarrāʾ.

Nobel, Alfred (1833–96) Swedish chemist and arms manufacturer who invented dynamite and was also the owner of the Bofors arms manufacturing company. His will established the set of prestigious prizes that are awarded annually in October.

Nuʿmān of al-Ḥīrah (r. ca. AD 580–602) last king of the Lakhmid house of al-Ḥīrah (in present-day Iraq), also known as Abū Qābūs.

Parquet (*Al-Niyābah*) agency within the system of French law (the Code Napoléon) that is responsible for the prosecution of crimes.

Qāʾim maqām Ottoman term used to describe the governor of a province.

Qanāṭir Khayriyyah barrage which spans the two branches of the River Nile some fifteen miles north of Cairo. The project was begun in 1843, but only finished in 1910.

qanṭar unit of weight.

Qārūn figure of legendary wealth described in the Qurʾan (Q Qaṣaṣ 28:76–82) as "of the people of Moses."

Qaṣbat Ruḍwān formerly a palace near the Ezbekiyyah gardens, although Stanley Lane-Poole reports in the late nineteenth century that it was "no more to be seen."

Questioning angels Munkar and Nakīr in Islamic eschatology, the two angels who question the dead concerning their deeds during their lifetime.

Raḍwā mountain in Saudi Arabia to the west of Medina.

Rāghib Pāshā (1819–84) official in various departments during the reigns of Muḥammad ʿAlī and Ismāʿīl. It is interesting to note that Ibrāhīm al-Muwayliḥī worked for him when he was Minister of Finance.

al-Rashīd, Hārūn (145–93/763?-809) most famous of the Abbasid Caliphs (a status further enhanced by his frequent presence in tales from *A Thousand and One Nights*), whose reign was marked by an efflorescence in scientific and cultural learning. He established the famous library Bayt al-Ḥikmah in Baghdad, which was to become the depository of a large number of works translated from Greek and Syriac.

al-Rāzī, Muḥammad ibn Zakariyā (250–313/864–925) renowned physician, chemist, and philosopher who wrote numerous works on medicine and other sciences.

Rhodes, Cecil (1853–1902) major figure in British imperial policy in Africa, and especially southern Africa where an entire country, Rhodesia (now Zimbabwe), was named after him.

Riḍwān the Angel of Paradise in Islam.

Mr. Rollo like the Suarez and Circurel families, the Rollos were prominent members of the Jewish business community in Egypt, with a lengthy history of involvement in the public affairs of the country.

al-Sadīr proverbially impressive fortress usually associated with the castle of Ukhayḍir in the Iraqi desert near Al-Karbalāʾ.

Saḥbān famous orator from the pre-Islamic era whose eloquence led to the coining of the phrase "more eloquent than Saḥbān."

Saʿīd Pāshā (1822–63) one of the sons of Muḥammad ʿAlī, the founder of the ruling dynasty in Egypt, Saʿīd, educated in France. He succeeded his murdered nephew, ʿAbbās, as viceroy (*walī*) of Egypt (nominally under Ottoman suzerainty) in 1854.

Sāmī Pāshā Muḥammad ʿAlī's private secretary.

San Stefano One of the most opulent districts of Alexandria, on the Mediterranean coast.

Sayf al-dīn prince of the Egyptian royal family. The case of his involvement in a shooting incident at a Cairo club was heavily covered in the al-Muwayliḥī newspaper. Attempts to have him declared legally incompetent failed, and he was sentenced to seven years in prison, later reduced to five. In December 1899 he was declared insane and sent to England for treatment.

Sayḥūn river known in Persian as Sir Daryā and in European languages as the Jaxartes.

Shamām presumably, like Raḍwā (see above), a proverbially high mountain peak.

al-Sīrah al-Ḥalabiyyah biography of the Prophet Muḥammad written by ʿAlī ibn Burhān al-dīn al-Ḥalabī (974–1044/1567–1635) and based on previous works by Ibn Sayyid al-Nās and Shams al-dīn al-Shāmī.

Solomon and the Jinn the Qur'an contains a number of references to King Solomon and the jinn (e.g. Q Naml 27:17 and Q Saba' 34:14). The tale in *A Thousand and One Nights* entitled "The City of Brass" (*Madīnat al-Nuḥās*) includes a quest for the bottles in which, according to legend, Solomon imprisoned the jinn.

Suarez famous Jewish family in Egypt, members of which were prominent participants in the foundation of the National Bank of Egypt in 1898.

Surra Man Ra'ā literally "the viewer's delight," the city of Samarrā', which was constructed by the Abbasid caliph, al-Muʿtaṣim, as a new capital to the north of Baghdad, beginning in 255/869.

al-Taʿāyishī (ca. 1846–99) "Khalīfa," or "successor" to the Mahdī Muḥammad Aḥmad, who took over leadership of the revolt in the Sudan in the 1890s.

Thabīr "a famous mountain," as al-Muwayliḥī puts it in a footnote, frequently mentioned in pre-Islamic poetry.

Tombs of the Caliphs name commonly given to the Eastern Cemetery in Cairo, although the people buried there are not actually "caliphs," but rather Mamluk Sultans from the eighth/fourteenth to tenth/sixteenth centuries.

ʿŪj ibn ʿUnuq mythical figure, concerning whom stories are to be found in the records of *Qiṣāṣ al-Anbiyā'* (*Stories of the Prophets*) by al-Kisā'ī and al-Thaʿālibī.

ʿUmar ibn al-Khaṭṭāb (d. 23/644) Companion of the Prophet Muḥammad and second caliph of Islam. He succeeded Abū Bakr in 13/634 and was assassinated in 23/644.

ʿUmar al-Khayyām (439–526/1048–1131) prominent Persian-born polymath, algebraist, philosopher, and poet. His collection of poetry, the *Rubāʿiyyāt* (*Quatrains*), was made famous through the rendering of at least part of their meaning into English by Edward Fitzgerald (1809–83).

ʿUthmān ibn ʿAffān (d. 35/656) Companion of the Prophet Muḥammad and third caliph of Islam (23–35/644–56).

Virgil (Publius Virgilius Maro) (70–19 BC) renowned Roman poet and composer of both the *Aeneid* and *Georgics*.

Wingate, Francis Reginald (1861–1953) British Army general. After service in India and Aden, he joined the Egyptian Army. He was involved in the operation to relieve Khartoum in 1885 and was later involved in campaigns in the Sudan, notably against the forces of the "Mahdī," Muḥammad Aḥmad.

Ziyād ibn Abīhi (d. 53/673) governor of Basra during the caliphate of Muʿawiyah.

al-Zubayr, Raḥmah Manṣūr (1830–1913) Sudanese slave-trader and nemesis of General Gordon who, following his imprisonment in Egypt, was eventually returned to his native country as its governor. In 1887 he returned to Cairo, but, after the successful conclusion of the Sudanese campaign in 1899, he was allowed to return to his homeland.

Bibliography

1. Works by the al-Muwayliḥīs

Ibrāhīm al-Muwayliḥī

"Al-Inshā' wa-l-'Aṣr." In *Mukhtārāt al-Manfalūṭī*, edited by Muṣṭafā Luṭfī al-Manfalūṭī, 181 ff. Cairo: Maṭba'a al-Sa'ādah, n.d.

Mā Hunālik. Cairo: Maṭba'at al-Muqaṭṭam, 1896.

"Mir'āt al-'Ālam." *Miṣbāḥ al-sharq* nos. 60, 61, 62, 109, 110, 111, 115, 119 (June-July 1899, June-September 1900); reprinted in *Kawkab al-sharq* (March-April 1930).

Al-Mu'allafāt al-Kāmilah. Cairo: Al-Majlis al-A'lā li-l-Thaqāfah, 2007.

"Der Spiegel der Welt." *Die Welt des Islams*, translated by Gottfried Widmer, N.s. 3 (1954): 58–126.

Hamzah, 'Abd al-Latīf. *Adab al-Maqālah al-Ṣaḥafiyyah fī Miṣr.* Cairo: Dār al-Fikr, 1965, 3: 83: 166 ff.

Ḥusayn, Ṭāhā, ed. *Al-Muntakhab min Adab al-'Arab.* Cairo: Wizārat al-Ma'ārif al-'Umūmiyyah, n.d. 1: 268 ff.; 2: 554 ff.

Zaydān, Jurjī. *Bunāt al-Nahḍah al-'Arabiyyah*, Kitāb al-Hilāl series no 72. Cairo: Dār al-Hilāl, 1957: 155 ff.

Muḥammad al-Muwayliḥī

"Ayyuhā al-Maḥzūn." In *Mukhtārāt al-Manfalūṭī*, edited by Muṣṭafā Luṭfī al-Manfalūṭī, 249 ff. Cairo: Maṭba'at al-Sa'ādah, n.d.

Ḥadīth 'Īsā ibn Hishām. 1st ed. Cairo: Maṭba'at al-Ma'ārif, 1907.

———. 2nd ed. Cairo: Al-Maktabah al-Azhariyyah, 1912.

———. 3rd ed. Cairo: Maṭba'at al-Sa'ādah, 1923.

———. 4th ed. Cairo: Maṭba'at Miṣr, 1927.

———. 5th ed. Cairo: Maṭba'at Miṣr, 1935.

———. 6th ed. Cairo: Maṭba'at al-Ma'ārif, 1943.

———. 7th ed. Cairo: Maṭba'at al-Ma'ārif, 1947.

———. 8th ed. 2 vols. Cairo: Dār al-Hilāl, 1959.

———. 9th ed. Cairo: Dār al-Qawmiyyah, 1964.

"Iktisāb Malakat al-Inshā' bi Ḥifẓ al-Ash'ār." *Al-Muqaṭṭam*, 18 August 1893.

'Ilāj al-Nafs. Cairo: Al-Maṭba'ah al-Amīriyyah, 1932; Dār al-Qawmiyyah, 1962.

"Jawhar al-Shi'r." In *Mukhtārāt al-Manfalūṭī*, edited by Muṣṭafā Luṭfī al-Manfalūṭī, 196 ff. Cairo: Maṭba'at al-Sa'ādah, n.d.

"Kalima Mafrūḍa." *Al-Mu'ayyad*, 9 February 1908.

"Naqd Dīwān Shawqī." In *Mukhtārāt al-Manfalūṭī*, edited by Muṣṭafā Luṭfī al-Manfalūṭī, 139 ff. Cairo: Maṭba'at al-Sa'ādah, n.d.

"Ṣawt min al-'Uzlah." *Al-Ahrām*, 30 December 1921.

2. References in Arabic

'Abbūd, Mārūn. *Badī' al-Zamān al-Hamadhānī.* Cairo: Dār al-Ma'ārif, 1963.

'Abd al-Laṭīf, Muḥammad Fahmī. "Ibrāhīm al-Muwayliḥī." *Al-Thaqāfah*, no. 711 (1952): 7.

'Abduh, Ibrāhīm. *'Alām al-ṣiḥāfah al-'arabiyyah.* Cairo: Maktabat al-'Arab, 1944.

———. *Taṭawwur al-ṣiḥāfah al-miṣriyyah.* Cairo, 1945.

Abū l-'Atāhiyah. *Dīwān*, ed. Shukrī Fayṣal. Damascus: Maṭba'at Jāmi'at Dimashq, 1965.

Abū Rīḥ, Maḥmūd. *Jamāl al-dīn al-Afghānī.* Cairo: Dār al-Ma'ārif, 1961.

Abū Tammām [Ḥabīb ibn Aws]. *Dīwān Abī Tammām.* Beirut: n.p., 1905.

Afghānī, Jamāl al-dīn, and Muḥammad 'Abduh al-. *Al-'Urwah al-wuthqā.* Cairo: Dār al-'Arab, 1957.

Aḥmad, 'Abd al-Ilāh 'Abd al-Muṭṭalib. *Al-Muwayliḥī al-ṣaghīr.* Cairo: Al-Hay'ah al-Miṣriyyah al-'Āmmah li-l-Kitāb, 1985.

'Alam, Muḥammad Mahdī. "Ṣafaḥāt min al-adab al-'arabī: Ḥadīth 'Īsā ibn Hishām." *Al-Siyāsah al-Usbū'iyyah*, 13 November 1943, 22 January 1944.

'Āmilī, Muḥsīn al-Ḥusaynī al-. *A'yān al-shī'ah*, 10 vols. Beirut: Dār al-Ta'āruf, 1983.

Amīn, Aḥmad. *Zu'amā' al-iṣlāḥ fī l-'aṣr al-ḥadīth.* Cairo: Maktabat al-Nahḍah al-Miṣriyyah, 1948.

Amīn, Qāsim. *Taḥrīr al-mar'ah.* Cairo: Maṭba'at 'Ayn Shams, 1899.

———. *Al-Mar'ah al-jadīdah.* Cairo: Maktabat Muḥammad Zakī al-dīn, 1901.

'Aqqād, 'Abbās Maḥmūd al-. *Murāja'āt fī l-adab wa-l-funūn.* Cairo: Al-Maṭba'ah al-'Aṣriyyah, 1926.

———. *Rijāl 'araftuhum*, Kitāb al-Hilāl no. 151. Cairo: Dār al-Hilāl, 1963.

Badawī, Aḥmad. *Rifā'ah al-Ṭahṭāwī Bey.* Cairo: Lajnat al-Bayān al-'Arabī, 1950.

Badr, 'Abd al-Muḥsin Ṭāhā. *Taṭawwur al-riwāyah al-'arabiyyah al-ḥadīthah fī miṣr.* Cairo: Dār al-Ma'ārif, 1963.

Bishrī, 'Abd al-'Azīz al-. "Muḥammad al-Muwayliḥī." *Al-Risālah*, nos. 72, 73, 74 (1934): 1886, 1927, 1966.

———. *Al-Mukhtār.* 2 vols. Cairo: Dār al-Ma'ārif, 1959.

Buhturī, Al-Walīd ibn ʿUbayd al-. *Dīwān*. Cairo: Maṭbaʿah Hindiyyah, 1911.

Ḍayf, Aḥmad. "Al-Adab al-miṣrī fī l-qarn al-tāsiʿ ʿashar." *Al-Muqtaṭaf*, May 1926: 543.

Ḍayf, Shawqī. *Al-Adab al-ʿarabī al-muʿaṣir fī miṣr*. Cairo: Dār al-Maʿārif, 1957.

———. *Al-Fakāhah fī miṣr*, Kitāb al-Hilāl series no. 83. Cairo: Dār al-Hilāl, 1958.

———. *Al-Maqāmah*. Cairo: Dār al-Maʿārif, 1954.

Dhihnī, Ṣalāḥ al-dīn al-. *Miṣr bayna l-iḥtilāl wa-l-thawrah*. Cairo: Maktabat al-Sharq al-Islāmiyyah, 1939.

Disūqī, ʿUmar al-. *Fī l-adab al-ḥadīth*. 2 vols. Cairo: Dār al-Fikr, 1966.

Farazdaq, al-. *Dīwān al-Farazdaq*, 2 vols. Beirut: Dār Ṣādir, 1966.

Fikrī, Amīn. *Al-Āthār al-fikriyyah*. Cairo: Al-Maṭbaʿah al-Amīriyyah, 1897.

———. *Irshād al-alibbāʾ ilā maḥāsin urūbbā*. Cairo: Maṭbaʿat al-Muqtaṭaf, 1892.

Ḥakīm, Tawfīq al-. *ʿAwdat al-rūḥ*. Cairo: Maktabat al-Ādāb, n.d.

———. *Yawmiyyāt nāʾib fī l-aryāf*. Cairo: Maktabat al-Ādāb, n.d.

Hamadhānī, Badīʿ al-Zamān al-. *Maqāmāt*. Edited by Muḥammad ʿAbduh. Beirut: Al-Maṭbaʿah al-Kathūlikiyyah, 1958.

Hamza, ʿAbd al-Latīf. *Adab al-maqālah al-ṣaḥafiyyah fī miṣr*. Cairo: Dār al-Fikr, 1964.

———. *Mustaqbal al-ṣiḥāfah fī miṣr*. Cairo: Dār al-Fikr, 1961.

Ḥaqqī, Yaḥyā. *Fajr al-qiṣṣah al-miṣriyyah*. Cairo: Dār al-Qalam, 1960.

Ḥarīrī, Abū l-Qāsim al-. *Maqāmāt*. Beirut: Dār Ṣādir, 1958.

Hawārī, Aḥmad Ibrāhīm al-. *Naqd al-mujtamaʿ fī Ḥadīth ʿĪsā ibn Hishām li-l-Muwayliḥī*. Cairo: Dār al-Maʿārif, 1981.

Ḥusayn, Ṭāhā. *Al-Ayyām*. 2 vols. Cairo: Maṭbaʿat al-Maʿārif, 1939–44.

Ibn ʿAbd Rabbihi. *Al-ʿIqd al-farīd*. Cairo: Lajnat al-Taʾlīf wa-l-Tarjamah wa-l-Nashr, 1946.

Ibn Dāwūd. *Zahrah*, 2 vols., ed. Ibrāhīm al-Sāmarrāʾī. Al-Zarqāʾ, Jordan: Maktabat al-Manār, 1985.

Ibn al-Muʿtazz. *Dīwān Ibn al-Muʿtazz*, ed. Muḥammad Badīʿ Sharīf. Cairo: Dār al-Maʿārif, 1977–78.

Ibn Qutaybah, ʿAbd Allāh ibn Muslim. *Kitāb al-Shiʿr wa-l-shuʿarāʾ*. Edited by de Goeje. Leiden: E. J. Brill, 1902.

———. *ʿUyūn al-akhbār.*, 4 vols. Cairo: Dār al-Kutub al-Miṣriyyah, 1925–1930.

Ibn al-Rūmī. *Dīwān Ibn al-Rūmī*, 6 vols., ed. Ḥusayn Naṣṣār. Cairo: Maṭbaʿat Dār al-Kutub, 1973.

Ibrāhīm, Aḥmad Abū Bakr. "Ḥadīth ʿĪsā ibn Hishām." *Al-Risālah*, 10 (1942): 1080.

Ibrāhīm, Ḥāfiẓ. *Dīwān*. Cairo: Maṭbaʿat Dār al-Kutub, 1937.

———. *Layālī saṭīḥ*. Cairo: Dār al-Qawmiyyah, 1964.

Ibshīhī, Muḥammad ibn Aḥmad al-. *al-Mustaṭraf fī kull fann mustaẓraf.* Cairo: Sharikat Matba'at wa-Maktabat Muṣṭafā al-Bābī al-Ḥalabī, 1952.

Iṣfahānī, Abū l-Faraj al-. *Kitāb al-Aghānī.* Cairo: Dār al-Kutub, 1927–61.

Jabartī, 'Abd al-Raḥmān al-. *'Ajā'ib al-āthār fī l-tarājim wa-l-akhbār.* Cairo: Dār al-Fikr, 1965–.

Jāhiẓ, 'Amr ibn Baḥr al-. *Kitāb al-Ḥayawān.* Cairo: Muṣṭafā al-Bābī al-Ḥalabī, 1938.

Jurjānī, 'Abd al-Qāhir al-. *Asrār al-balāghah*, ed. Helmut Ritter. Istanbul: Govt. Press, 1954; Wiesbaden: F. Steiner, 1959.

Khafājī, Shihāb al-dīn Aḥmad ibn Muḥammad ibn 'Umar al-. *Rayḥānat al-alibbā' wa-zahrat al-ḥayāt al-dunyā*, 2 vols., ed. 'Abd al-Fattāḥ Muḥammad al-Ḥulw. Cairo: 'Isā al-Bābī al-Ḥalabī, 1967.

Khansā', al-. *Dīwān al-Khansā'*, ed. Ibrāhīm 'Awḍayn. Cairo: Maṭba'at al-Sa'ādah, 1986.

———. *Dīwān al-Khansā'*, ed. Anwar Abū Suwaylim. Amman: Dār 'Ammār, 1988.

Khiḍr, 'Abbās. *Al-Qiṣṣah al-qaṣīrah fī miṣr.* Cairo: Dār al-Qawmiyyah, 1966.

Kisā'ī, Muḥammad ibn 'Abd Allāh al-. *Kitāb Qiṣaṣ al-anbiyā'.* Edited by Eisenberg. Leiden: E. J. Brill, 1922.

Labīd ibn Rabī'ah. *Der Dīwān des Labīd.* Vienna: C. Gerolds Sohn, 1880.

Ma'arrī, Abū l-'Alā' al-. *Al-Luzūmiyyāt.* Cairo: Maṭba'at al-Maḥrūsa, 1891.

———. *Siqṭ al-zand.* Cairo: Būlāq, 1869; Cairo: n.p., 1948–.

Marzūqī, Aḥmad ibn Muḥammad al-. *Sharḥ Dīwān al-Ḥamāsah*, ed. Aḥmad Amīn and 'Abd al-Salām Hārūn. Cairo: Lajnat al-Ta'līf wa-l-Tarjamah wa-l-Nashr, 1951–53.

Malṭī-Douglas, Fadwā. "Layālī Saṭīh." *Fuṣūl*, 3, no. 2 (Jan.-Mar. 1983): 109–117.

Manfalūṭī, Muṣṭafā Luṭfī al-. *Mukhtārāt al-Manfalūṭī.* Cairo: Maṭba'at al-Sa'ādah, n.d.

———. *Al-Naẓarāt.* Al-Maktabah al-Tijāriyyah al-Kubrā, n.d.

Maqrīzī, Taqī al-dīn al-. *Al-Mawā'idh wa-l-i'tibār fī dhikr al-khiṭaṭ wa-l-āthār.* Cairo: Institut français d'archéologie orientale du Caire, 1911–13.

Mas'ūdī, al-. *Murūj al-dhahab*, 7 vols., ed. Charles Pellat. Beirut: al-Jāmi'ah al-Lubnāniyyah, 1965–79.

Mubārak, 'Alī. *'Alam al-dīn.* Alexandria: Maṭba'at Jarīdat al-Maḥrūsah, 1882.

———. *Al-Khiṭaṭ al-tawfīqiyyah al-jadīdah.* Cairo: Al-Maṭba'ah al-Amīriyyah, 1887–88.

Mubārak, Zakī. "Ḥadīth 'Īsā ibn Hishām." *Al-Risālah*, 10 (1942): 995, 1016, 1035.

Mutanabbī, Abū l-Ṭayyib al-. *Dīwān*, with commentary by al-Wāḥidī, ed. Friedrich Dieterici. 1861. Reprint, Baghdad: Maktabat al-Muthannā, 1964.

———. *al-'Arf al-ṭayyib fī sharḥ dīwān Abī al-Ṭayyib*, 2 vols., ed. Nāṣīf al-Yāzijī. 1882–88. Reprint, Beirut: Dār Ṣādir, 1964.

Muwayliḥī, Ibrāhīm al-. "Hadīth 'Īsā ibn Hishām." *Al-Risālah*, 10 (1942): 1042.

———. "Ibrāhīm al-Muwayliḥī." *Al-Risālah*, 6 (1939): 617, 658.

———. "Tarjamat al-Sayyid Muḥammad al-Muwayliḥī." Introduction to the 6th and 7th editions of *Ḥadīth ʿĪsā ibn Hishām*. Cairo: Dār al-Maʿārif, 1943, 1947.

Qālī, Abū ʿAlī Ismāʿīl ibn al-Qāsim al-. *Kitāb al-Amālī*. [need biblio info.]

Raḍī, al-Sharīf al-. *Dīwān al-Sharīf al-Raḍī*. Beirut: al-Maṭbaʿah al-Adabiyyah, 1890–92.

Rāfiʿī, ʿAbd al-Raḥmān al-. *ʿAṣr Ismāʿīl*. Cairo: Maktabat al-Nahḍah al-Miṣriyyah, 1948.

———. *ʿAṣr Muḥammad ʿAlī*. Cairo: Maktabat al-Nahḍah al-Miṣriyyah, 1951.

Rāʿī, ʿAlī al-. *Dirāsāt fī l-riwāyah al-miṣriyyah*. Cairo: Al-Muʾassasah al-Miṣriyyah al-ʿĀmmah li-l-Taʾlīf wa-l-Tarjamah wa-l-Ṭibāʿah wa-l-Nashr, n.d.

———. "Ḥadīth ʿĪsā ibn Hishām." *Kitābāt Miṣriyyah*, 2 (1956): 54.

Ramadī, Jamāl al-dīn al-. "Muḥammad al-Muwayliḥī." *Ṣawt al-Sharq*, November 1960.

Ramitch, Aḥmad Yūsuf. *Usrat al-Muwayliḥī*. Cairo: Dār al-Maʿārif, 1980.

Rikābī, Jawda al-. *Fī l-adab al-andalūsī*. Cairo: Dār al-Maʿārif, 1960.

Ṣābā, ʿĪsā Mīkhaʾil. *Nāṣīf al-Yāzijī*. Cairo: Dār al-Maʿārif, 1965.

Ṣabrī, Ismāʿīl. *Dīwān*. Cairo: Maṭbaʿat Lajnat al-Taʾlīf wa-l-Tarjamah wa-l-Ṭibāʿah wa-l-Nashr, 1938.

Ṣalāḥ, Bhoury. "Al-Maqāmah." *Bulletin des études arabes*, September-October 1948: 149–53.

Sarkīs, Yūsuf. *Muʿjam al-maṭbūʿāt al-ʿarabiyyah wa-l-muʿarrabah*. Cairo: Maṭbaʿat Sarkīs, 1928.

Sharqāwī, ʿAbd al-Raḥmān al-. *Al-Arḍ*. Cairo: Dār al-Kātib al-ʿArabī li-l-Ṭibāʿah wa-l-Nashr, 1968.

Shawkat, Maḥmūd. *Al-Fann al-qaṣaṣī fī l-adab al-miṣrī al-ḥadīth*. Cairo: Dār al-Fikr, 1963.

Shaykhū, Lūwīs. *Al-Ādāb al-ʿarabiyyah fī l-qarn al-tāsiʿ ʿashar*. Beirut: Al-Maṭbaʿah al-Kathūlikiyyah, 1908.

———. *Taʾrīkh al-ādāb al-ʿarabiyyah fī l-rubʿ al-awwal min al-qarn al-ʿishrīn*. Beirut: Maṭbaʿat al-Ābāʾ al-Yasūʿiyyīn, 1926.

Shayyāl, Jamāl al-dīn al-. *Rifāʿah al-Ṭahṭāwī*. Cairo: Dār al-Maʿārif, 1958.

Shidyāq, Aḥmad Fāris al-. *Al-Sāq ʿalā l-sāq fī mā huwa al-fāriyāq*. Paris: n.p., 1865.

Ṭāhir (anonymous). "Muḥammad al-Muwayliḥī." *Kull shayʾ wa-l-ʿālam*, 22 March 1930: 20, 40.

Ṭahṭāwī, Rifāʿah Rāfiʿ al-. *Takhlīṣ al-ibrīz fī talkhīṣ Bārīz*. Cairo: Dār al-Taqaddum, 1905.

Tarrāzī, Fīlīb dī. *Taʾrīkh al-Ṣiḥāfah al-ʿarabiyyah*. Cairo: Al-Maṭbaʿah al-Adabiyyah, Al-Maṭbaʿah al-Amrikiyyah, 1913–33.

Taymūr, Aḥmad. *Al-Amthāl al-ʿāmmiyyah*. Cairo: Dār al-Kutub, 1956; Maṭābiʿ al-Ahrām al-Tijāriyyah, 1970.

———. *Fann al-qiṣaṣ: dirāsāt fī l-qiṣṣah wa-l-masraḥ*. Cairo: Maktabat al-Ādāb, n.d.

———. *Nashr al-qiṣṣah wa-tatawwuruhā*. Cairo: Al-Maṭbaʿah al-Salafiyyah, 1936.

———. *Al-Qaṣaṣ fī adab al-ʿarab*. Cairo: Al-Maṭbaʿah al-Kamaliyyah, 1958.

———. *Shaykh Sayyid al-ʿabīt wa-aqāṣīṣ ukhrā*. Cairo: Al-Maṭbaʿah al-Salafiyyah, 1926.

Thaʿālibī, Aḥmad ibn Muḥammad al-. *Kitāb Qiṣaṣ al-anbiyāʾ*. Cairo: n.p., 1906.

———. *Yatīmah al-dahr fī maḥāsin ahl al-ʿaṣr*, 4 vols. Beirut: Dār al-Kutub al-ʿIlmiyyah, 1979.

Ṭurṭūshī, Muḥammad ibn al-Walīd al-. *Sirāj al-mulūk*, ed. Jaʿfar al-Bayātī. London: Riad el-Rayyes, 1990.

ʿUmar, Muḥammad. *Ḥāḍir al-miṣriyyīn aw sirr taʾakhkhurihim*. Cairo: Maṭbaʿat al-Muqtaṭaf, 1902.

Yāqūt ibn ʿAbd Allāh al-Ḥamawī. *Muʿjam al-buldān*. Beirut: Dār Ṣādir, 1955–57.

Yāzijī, Nāṣīf al-. *Majmaʿ al-baḥrayn*. Beirut: Dār Ṣādir, 1966.

Zaghlūl, Aḥmad Fathī. *Sirr taqaddum al-inklīz al-saksūniyyīn*. Cairo: Al-Maṭbaʿah al-Raḥmāniyyah, 1899.

Zāhī, Abū l-Qāsim al-. *A Poet of the Abbasid Period: Abū l-Qāsim al-Zāhī (ʿAlī b. Isḥāq b. Khalaf al-Zāhī) 313–352 AH/925–963 CE: his life and poetry, annotated, edited and with an introduction by Khalid Sindawi*. Wiesbaden: Harrassowitz Verlag, 2010.

Zakī, Aḥmad. *Al-Safar ilā l-muʾtamar*. Cairo: Al-Maṭbaʿah al-Amīriyyah, 1894.

Zaydān, Jurjī. *Bunāt al-nahḍah al-ʿarabiyyah*, Kitāb al-Hilāl no. 72. Cairo: Dār al-Hilāl, 1957.

———. *Tarājim mashāhir al-sharq fī l-qarn al-tāsiʿ ʿashar*. 2 vols. Cairo: Dār al-Hilāl, 1910–11.

———. *Taʾrīkh Ādāb al-lughah al-ʿarabiyyah*. 4 vols. Cairo: Dār al-Hilāl, 1937.

Ziriklī, Khayr al-dīn al-. *Al-Aʿlām*. Cairo: Maṭbaʿat Kustatsumas, 1954.

3. References in European Languages

Abdel-Meguid, Abdel Aziz. *The Modern Arabic Short Story*. Cairo: Dạr al-Maʿārif, 1955.

Abou-Saif, L. "Najīb al-Rīḥānī: From Buffoonery to Social Comedy." *Journal of Arabic Literature*, 4 (1973): 1–17.

About, Edmond. *Le fellah: Souvenirs d'Egypte*. Paris: Hachette, 1869.

———. *The Fellah*. Translated by Sir Randal Roberts. London: Chapman and Hall, 1870.

———. *L'homme à l'oreille cassée*. Paris: Hachette, 1935.

Abu Lughod, Ibrahim. *The Arab Rediscovery of Europe*. Princeton: Princeton University Press, 1963.

Adams, Charles. *Islam and Modernism in Egypt*. London: Oxford University Press, 1933.

Ahlwardt, Wilhelm, ed. *The Diwans of the Six Ancient Arabic Poets Ennabiga ʿAntara, Tharafa, Zuhair, ʿAlqama and Imruulqais*. London: Trübner, 1870.

Bibliography

Ahmed, Jamal. *The Intellectual Origins of Egyptian Nationalism*. London: Oxford University Press, 1960.

Allen, Roger. "The Early Arabic Novel." In *Cambridge History of Arabic Literature*, Vol. IV. Cambridge: Cambridge University Press, [forthcoming].

———. "Ḥadīth 'Īsā ibn Hishām: The Excluded Passages." *Die Welt des Islams*, N. S. 12 (1969): 74–89, 163–81.

———. "Ḥadīth 'Īsā ibn Hishām: A Reconsideration." *Journal of Arabic Literature*, 1 (1970): 88–108.

———. "Ibrāhīm al-Muwayliḥī." In *The Encyclopedia of Islam*, 2nd ed., 1954–[forthcoming].

———. "Ibrāhīm Al-Muwaylihī's *Mir'āt al-'Ālam*: Introduction and Translation." *Middle Eastern Literatures*, 15, no. 3 (December 2012): 318–36.

———. "Ibrāhīm Al-Muwaylihī's *Mir'āt al-'Ālam*: Introduction and Translation." *Middle Eastern Literatures*, 16, no. 3 (December 2013): 334–50.

———. "Muḥammad al-Muwayliḥī." In *The Encyclopedia of Islam*, 2nd ed., 1954–[forthcoming].

———. "Some New Al-Muwayliḥī Materials, or the Unpublished Ḥadīth of 'Īsā ibn Hishām." *Humaniora Islamica*, 2 (1974): 139–80.

———. "Writings of Members of the Naẓlī Circle." *Journal of the American Research Center in Egypt*, 8 (1971): 79–84.

Ammar, Hamed. *Growing Up in an Egyptian Village*. London: Routledge and Kegan Paul, 1954.

Anderson, J. N. D. "Law Reform in Egypt, 1850–1950." In *Political and Social Change in Modern Egypt*, edited by P. M. Holt. Oxford: Oxford University Press, 1968.

Artin Bey, Ya'qub. *L'instruction publique en Egypte*. Paris: E. Leroux, 1890.

Ayrout, Henri Habib. *The Egyptian Peasant*. Translated by J. Alden Williams. Boston: Beacon Press, 1963.

Baedecker, Karl. *Egypt, Handbook for Travellers*. Leipzig: Karl Baedecker, 1902, 1908.

Baer, Gabriel. *A History of Landownership in Modern Egypt 1800–1950*. London: Oxford University Press, 1952.

———. *Population and Society in the Arab East*. Translated by Hanna Szöke. London: Routledge & Kegan Paul, 1964.

———. "Social Change in Egypt, 1800–1914." In *Political and Social Change in Modern Egypt*, edited by P. M. Holt. London: Oxford University Press, 1968.

———. *Studies in the Social History of Modern Egypt*. Chicago: University of Chicago Press, 1969.

———. "Urbanization in Egypt, 1820–1907." In *Beginnings of Modernization in the Middle East*, edited by William Polk and Richard Chambers. Chicago: University of Chicago Press, 1968.

Baudry-Lacantinerie, G. et al. *Traité de droit civile*. Paris: L. Larose et L. Tenin, 1905–9.

Bencheneb, Saadeddine. "Edmond About et Al-Muwailiḥī." *Revue africaine*, 88 (1944): 270–73.

———. "Etudes de littérature arabe moderne: I. Muḥammad al-Muwailiḥī." *Revue africaine*, 83 (1939): 358–82; 84 (1940): 77–92.

Berger, Morroe. *Bureaucracy and Society in Modern Egypt*. Princeton: Princeton University Press, 1957.

Berque, Jacques. *Histoire sociale du village égyptien au XXième siècle*. Paris: Mouton, 1957.

———. *L' Egypte: Impérialisme et révolution*. Paris: Gallimard, 1967.

———. *Egypt: Imperialism and Revolution*. Translated by Jean Stewart. London: Faber and Faber, 1972.

———. "The Establishment of the Colonial Economy." In *Beginnings of Modernization in the Middle East*, edited by William Polk and Richard Chambers. Chicago: University of Chicago Press, 1968.

Blachère, Régis, and Pierre Masnou. *Al-Hamadhānī: Choix de maqāmāt*. Paris: Klincksieck, 1957.

Blunt, Wilfrid Scawen. *Gordon at Khartoum*. London: S. Swift and Co., 1911.

———. *My Diaries*. 2 vols. London: M. Seeker, 1919.

———. *Secret History of the Occupation of Egypt*. 2 vols. London: Unwin, 1907.

Bosworth, C. Edmund. *The Medieval Islamic Underworld*. Leiden: E.J. Brill, 1976.

Brinton, Jasper. *The Mixed Courts of Egypt*. New Haven: Yale University Press, 1930.

Brockelmann, Karl. *Geschichte der arabischen Literatur*. 3 Supplement-banden. Leiden: E.J. Brill, 1937–42.

Burckhardt, J.L. *Travels in Arabia, Comprehending an Account of Those Territories in Hedjaz Which the Mohammedans Regard as Sacred*. London: Henry Colburn, 1829.

Burton, Sir Richard. *Personal Narrative of a Pilgrimage to El-Medinah and Meccah*. London: Longman and Sons, 1855, 1857; W. Mullan and Son, 1879; G. Bell and Sons, 1898, 1906.

Chirol, Sir Valentine. *The Egyptian Problem*. London: MacMillan and Co., 1921.

Civil Code of Egypt-Native Tribunals. Cairo: Ministry of Justice, 1901.

Clerget, Marcel. *Le Caire: étude de géographic urbaine et d'histoire économique*. Cairo: Imprimerie E. et R. Schindler, 1934.

Code of Civil and Commercial Procedure. Cairo: Ministry of Justice, 1904–11.

Colvin, Sir Auckland. *The Making of Modern Egypt*. London: Seeley and Co., 1906.

Coulson, Noel. *Islamic Law*. Islamic Surveys, no. 2. Edinburgh: Edinburgh University Press, 1964.

Crecelius, Daniel. "The Organization of Waqf Documents in Cairo." *International Journal of Middle East Studies*, 2, no. 3 (July, 1971): 266–77.

Creswell, K. A. G. *The Muslim Architecture of Egypt*. 2 vols. Oxford: Oxford University Press, 1952.

Cromer, Lord. *Abbas II*. London: Macmillan and Co., 1915.

———. *Modern Egypt*. 2 vols. London: Macmillan and Co., 1908.

Dalloz, Victor. *Codes d'audience*. Paris: Dalloz, 1926.

———. *Jurisprudence générale*. Paris: Bureau de la jurisprudence générale, 1896.

David, René, and Henry de Vries. *The French Legal System*. New York: Columbia University Press, 1954.

Demolins, Edmond. *A quoi tient la superiorité des anglo-saxons?* Paris: Firmin-Didot et al, 1897.

Deny, Jean. *Sommaire des archives turques du Caire*. Cairo: Royal Geographical Society of Egypt, 1930.

Dodwell, H. *The Founder of Modern Egypt*. Cambridge: Cambridge University Press, 1931.

Elgood, P. *Bonaparte's Adventure in Egypt*. London: Oxford University Press, 1931.

———. *Egypt and the Army*. London: Oxford University Press, 1924.

Encyclopedia of Islam. 4 vols. Leiden: E. J. Brill, 1913–36; 2nd edition, 1954– [in process].

Ende, Werner. "Europabild und kulturelles Selbstbewusstsein bei den Muslimen am Ende des 19. Jahrhunderts, dargestellt an den Schriften der beiden ägyptischen Schriftsteller Ibrāhīm und Muḥammad al-Muwailiḥī." D. Phil. dissertation. Hamburg: Hamburg Universität, 1965.

Forster, E. M. *Aspects of the Novel*. London: Penguin Books, 1962.

Freytag, Gustav. *Arabum Proverbia*. Bonn: A. Marcus, 1838–43.

Garillot, J. Aristide. *La réforme judiciaire en Egypte*. Alexandria: n.p., 1893.

Garraud, René. *Traité théorique et pratique de droit pénale français*. Paris: L. Larose et L. Tenin, 1913–35.

Gendzier, Irene. *The Practical Vision of Yaʿqūb Sanūʿ*. Cambridge: Harvard University Press, 1966.

Gibb, Sir Hamilton A. R. *Modern Trends in Islam*. Chicago: University of Chicago Press, 1947.

———. *Studies on the Civilization of Islam*. Edited by Stanford Shaw. London: Routledge and Kegan Paul, 1962.

Gibb, Sir Hamilton A. R., and H. Bowen. *Islamic Society and the West.* 2 vols. London: Oxford University Press, 1950, 1957.

Goadby, Frederic. *Commentary on Egyptian Criminal Law and the Related Criminal Law of Palestine, Cyprus and Iraq.* Cairo: Government Press, 1924.

Gran, Peter. *The Islamic Roots of Capitalism: Egypt 1760–1840.* Austin: University of Texas Press, 1979.

von Grunebaum, Gustave. E. *Medieval Islam.* Chicago: University of Chicago Press, 1962.

———. *Modern Islam.* Berkeley: University of California Press, 1962.

———. "The Spirit of Islam as Shown in its Literature." *Studia Islamica*, 1 (1953): 101–19.

Hakim, Tawfiq al-. *The Maze of Justice.* Translated by Aubrey Eban. London: Harvill Press, 1947; Austin: University of Texas Press, 1989.

Halton, H. W. *An Elementary Treatise of the Egyptian Civil Codes.* Cairo: National Printing Department, 1904.

Ḥarīrī, Abū l-Qāsim al-. *The Assemblies of Al-Harīrī.* Translated by C. Chenery and F. Steingass. London: n.p., 1870; London: Gregg Reprint, 1970.

Hartmann, Martin. *The Arabic Press of Egypt.* London: Luzac and Co., 1899.

Hélie, Faustin Adolphe. *Analyse et commentaire du code de procédure pénal.* Paris: Librairies techniques, 1959.

Heyd, Uriel, ed. *Studies in Islamic Institutions and Civilization.* Jerusalem: Hebrew University Press, 1961.

Heyworth-Dunne, J. *Introduction to the History of Education in Modern Egypt.* London: Luzac and Co., 1938.

———. "Society and Politics in Modern Egyptian Literature." *Middle East Journal*, 2 (July 1948): 306–18.

Holt, P. M., ed. *Political and Social Change in Modern Egypt.* London: Oxford University Press, 1968.

Hourani, Albert. *Arabic Thought in the Liberal Age.* London: Oxford University Press, 1962.

Hussein, Taha. *A Stream of Days.* Translated by Hilary Wayment. Cairo: Dār al-Maʿārif, 1943.

de la Jonquière, Taffanel. *Journal de l'expedition de l'Egypte.* 5 vols. Paris: Henri Charles-Lavauzelle, 1904.

Keddie, Nikki. *Sayyid Jamāl ad-Dīn 'al-Afghani': a Political Biography.* Berkeley: University of California Press, 1972.

Khadduri, Majid, and H. J. Liebesny. *Law in the Middle East.* Washington: Middle East Institute, 1955.

Kirk, George. *Lord Cromer in Egypt: a Retrospect.* Cambridge: Harvard University Press, 1958.

Kurd ʿAlī, Muḥammad. *Memoirs.* Translated by Khalil Totah. American Council of Learned Societies Near Eastern Translation Program, No. 6. Washington: American Council of Learned Societies, 1954.

Lamplough, A., and R. Francis. *Cairo and Environs.* London: Sir Joseph Causton and Sons, 1909.

Landau, Jacob M. "Abu Naḍḍārah, an Egyptian Jewish Nationalist." *Journal of Jewish Studies,* 3 (1952): 30–44.

———. "An Insider's View of Istanbul: Ibrāhīm al-Muwayliḥī's *Mā Hunālika.*" *Die Welt des Islams,* XXVII (1987): 70–81.

———. *Parliaments and Parties in Egypt.* Tel Aviv: Israel Publishing House, 1953.

———. "Prolegomena to a Study of Secret Societies in Modern Egypt." *Middle Eastern Studies,* 1, no. 2 (1965): 35–86.

Landes, David. "Bankers and Pashas." In *Men in Business: Essays in the History of Entrepreneurship,* edited by William Miller. Cambridge: Harvard University Press, 1952.

Lane, Edward. *The Manners and Customs of the Modern Egyptians.* London: Everyman ed., 1954.

Lane-Poole, Stanley. *Cairo Fifty Years Ago.* London: J. Murray, 1896.

———. *Cairo: Sketches of its History, Monuments, and Social Life.* London: J. S. Virtue and Co., 1898.

———. *The Story of Cairo.* London: J. M. Dent, 1902.

Lewis, Bernard. *The Middle East and the West.* Bloomington: Indiana University Press, 1964.

Liddell, R. *A Treatise on the Novel.* London: Jonathan Cape, 1947.

Little, Tom. *Egypt.* London: Ernest Benn, 1958.

Lubbock, Percy. *The Craft of Fiction.* London: Jonathan Cape, 1963.

Lutfi as-Sayyid, Afaf. *Egypt and Cromer: A Study in Anglo-Egyptian Relations.* London: John Murray, 1968.

———. *Egypt in the Reign of Muḥammad ʿAlī.* Cambridge: Cambridge University Press, 1984.

Malortie, Baron Carl von. *Egypt: Native Rulers and Foreign Interference.* London: W. Ridgeway, 1882.

Marcel, Jean-Jacques. *Les contes du Cheykh el-Mohdy.* Paris: Henri Dupuy, 1835.

Margoliouth, D. S. *Cairo, Jerusalem, and Damascus: Three Chief Cities of the Egyptian Sultans.* London: Chatto and Windus, 1907.

Marlowe, John. *Cromer in Egypt.* London: Elek, 1970.

———. *A History of Modern Egypt and Anglo-Egyptian Relations.* London: Cresset Press, 1954.

Marshall, J. E. *The Egyptian Enigma 1890–1928*. London: John Murray, 1928.

McCoan, J. *Egypt As It Is*. London: Cassell, Petter and Galpin, 1877, 1898.

———. *Egypt Under Ismail, A Romance of History*. London: Chapman and Hall, 1899.

Milner, Lord. *England in Egypt*. London: Edward Arnold, 1899.

Monroe, James. *The Art of Badīʿ al-Zamān al-Hamadhānī as Picaresque Narrative*. Beirut: American University in Beirut, 1983.

Moosa, Matti. *The Origins of Modern Arabic Fiction*. Washington: Three Continents Press, 1983.

Mūsā, Salāmah. *The Education of Salāmah Mūsā*. Translated by L. O. Schuman. Leiden: E. J. Brill, 1961.

Muwailihi, Ibrahim al-. "Ibrahim al-Muwailihi." *Cahiers d'histoire égyptienne*, 2 (1949): 313–28.

———. "Muḥammad al-Muwailihi." *Cahiers d'histoire égyptienne*, 6 (1954): 168 ff.

Nicholson, R. A. *A Literary History of the Arabs*. Cambridge: Cambridge University Press, 1907.

Penfield, F. *Present Day Egypt*. New York: The Century Co., 1899.

Pérès, Henri. "Editions successives de Hadīth ʿĪsā ibn Hishām." In *Mélanges Louis Massignon*, 3 (1957): 233–58.

———. "Les premières manifestations de la renaissance littéraire arabe en Orient au XIXième siècle: Nāṣīf al-Yāzijī et Fāris al-Shidyāk." *Annales de l'institut des études orientales*, 1 (1934–35): 232–56.

———. "Origines d'un roman célèbre de la littérature arabe moderne: Ḥadīth ʿĪsā ibn Hishām." *Bulletin des études orientales*, 10 (1944): 101–18.

Polk, William, and Richard Chambers, eds. *Beginnings of Modernization in the Middle East*. Chicago: University of Chicago Press, 1968.

La réforme judiciaire en Egypte et les capitulations. Alexandria: n.p., 1874.

Report on Egypt. London: Intelligence Department War Office, 1882.

Safran, Nadav. *Egypt in Search of Political Identity*. Cambridge: Harvard University Press, 1962.

Sawa, George Dimitri. *Music Performance Practice in the Early ʿAbbāsid Era 132–320 AH/750–932 AD*. Toronto: Pontifical Institute of Medieval Studies, 1989.

Scott, J. H. *The Law Affecting Foreigners in Egypt*. Edinburgh: William Green & Sons, 1907.

Senior, Nassau William. *Conversations and Journals in Egypt and Malta*. London: Sampson Low and Co., 1882.

Sharqāwī, ʿAbd al-Raḥmān al-. *Egyptian Earth*. Translated by Desmond Stewart. London: Heinemann, 1962; Delhi: Hind Pocket Books, 1972.

Shaw, Stanford. *Ottoman Egypt in the Age of the French Revolution*. Cambridge: Cambridge University Press, 1964.

———. *The Financial and Administrative Organization and Development of Ottoman Egypt, 1517–1798*. Princeton: Princeton University Press, 1958.

Index

About the NYU Abu Dhabi Institute

NYU
ABU DHABI
INSTITUTE

The Library of Arabic Literature is supported by a grant from the NYU Abu Dhabi Institute, a major hub of intellectual and creative activity and advanced research. The Institute hosts academic conferences, workshops, lectures, film series, performances, and other public programs directed both to audiences within the UAE and to the worldwide academic and research community. It is a center of the scholarly community for Abu Dhabi, bringing together faculty and researchers from institutions of higher learning throughout the region.

NYU Abu Dhabi, through the NYU Abu Dhabi Institute, is a world-class center of cutting-edge research, scholarship, and cultural activity. The Institute creates singular opportunities for leading researchers from across the arts, humanities, social sciences, sciences, engineering, and the professions to carry out creative scholarship and conduct research on issues of major disciplinary, multidisciplinary, and global significance.

About the Typefaces

The Arabic body text is set in DecoType Naskh, designed by Thomas Milo and Mirjam Somers, based on an analysis of five centuries of Ottoman manuscript practice. The exceptionally legible result is the first and only typeface in a style that fully implements the principles of script grammar (*qawāʿid al-khaṭṭ*).

The Arabic footnote text is set in DecoType Emiri, drawn by Mirjam Somers, based on the metal typeface in the naskh style that was cut for the 1924 Cairo edition of the Qur'an.

Both Arabic typefaces in this series are controlled by a dedicated font layout engine. ACE, the Arabic Calligraphic Engine, invented by Peter Somers, Thomas Milo, and Mirjam Somers of DecoType, first operational in 1985, pioneered the principle followed by later smart font layout technologies such as OpenType, which is used for all other typefaces in this series.

The Arabic text was set with WinSoft Tasmeem, a sophisticated user interface for DecoType ACE inside Adobe InDesign. Tasmeem was conceived and created by Thomas Milo (DecoType) and Pascal Rubini (WinSoft) in 2005.

The English text is set in Adobe Text, a new and versatile text typeface family designed by Robert Slimbach for Western (Latin, Greek, Cyrillic) typesetting. Its workhorse qualities make it perfect for a wide variety of applications, especially for longer passages of text where legibility and economy are important. Adobe Text bridges the gap between calligraphic Renaissance types of the 15th and 16th centuries and high-contrast Modern styles of the 18th century, taking many of its design cues from early post-Renaissance Baroque transitional types cut by designers such as Christoffel van Dijck, Nicolaus Kis, and William Caslon. While grounded in classical form, Adobe Text is also a statement of contemporary utilitarian design, well suited to a wide variety of print and on-screen applications.

Titles Published by the Library of Arabic Literature

Classical Arabic Literature
Selected and translated by Geert Jan Van Gelder

A Treasury of Virtues, by al-Qāḍī al-Quḍāʿī
Edited and translated by Tahera Qutbuddin

The Epistle on Legal Theory, by al-Shāfiʿī
Edited and translated by Joseph E. Lowry

Leg Over Leg, by Aḥmad Fāris al-Shidyāq
Edited and translated by Humphrey Davies

Virtues of the Imām Aḥmad ibn Ḥanbal, by Ibn al-Jawzī
Edited and translated by Michael Cooperson

The Epistle of Forgiveness, by Abū l-ʿAlāʾ al-Maʿarrī
Edited and translated by Geert Jan Van Gelder and Gregor Schoeler

The Principles of Sufism, by ʿĀʾishah al-Bāʿūnīyah
Edited and translated by Th. Emil Homerin

The Expeditions, by Maʿmar ibn Rāshid
Edited and translated by Sean W. Anthony

Two Arabic Travel Books

- **Accounts of China and India**, by Abū Zayd al-Sīrāfī
  Edited and translated by Tim Mackintosh-Smith
- **Mission to the Volga**, by Ahmad Ibn Faḍlān
  Edited and translated by James Montgomery

Disagreements of the Jurists, by al-Qāḍī al-Nuʿmān
Edited and translated by Devin Stewart

Consorts of the Caliphs, by Ibn al-Sāʿī
Edited by Shawkat M. Toorawa and translated by the Editors of the Library of Arabic Literature

What ʿĪsā ibn Hishām Told Us, by Muḥammad al-Muwayliḥī
Edited and translated by Roger Allen

The Life and Times of Abū Tammām, by Abū Bakr Muḥammad ibn Yaḥyā al-Ṣūlī
Edited and translated by Beatrice Gruendler

About the Editor–Translator

Roger Allen retired in 2011 from his position as the Sascha Jane Patterson Harvie Professor at the University of Pennsylvania, where he served for forty-three years as Professor of Arabic and Comparative Literature. He is the author and translator of numerous publications on Arabic literature, modern fiction and drama, and language pedagogy. Among his studies devoted to the Arabic literary tradition are: *The Arabic Novel* (1995) and *The Arabic Literary Heritage* (1998; abridged version, *Introduction to Arabic Literature*, 2000).

CPSIA information can be obtained
at www.ICGtesting.com
Printed in the USA
LVHW040836110523
746502LV00041B/69/J

9 781479 862252